THIRTY YEARS IN TIME

PETER FRANCE

Published in Australia by Sid Harta Books & Print Pty Ltd,
ABN: 34632585293
23 Stirling Crescent, Glen Waverley, Victoria 3150 Australia
Telephone: +61 3 9560 9920, Facsimile: +61 3 9545 1742
E-mail: author@sidharta.com.au

First published in Australia 2023
This edition published 2023
Copyright © Peter France 2023
Cover design, typesetting: WorkingType (www.workingtype.com.au)

France, Peter
Thirty Years in Timee
ISBN: 978-1-922958-17-4
pp620

After leaving school, Peter France wanted to become a builder and took on an apprenticeship, unfortunately though, the firm went broke, and he was out on the street. He applied for a job with a firm selling clothing, hosiery and furnishings and spent some two years with them. Then he was called up with the army, did a cadre course with the Special Air Service and became a member of B-Troop, eventually serving with them in Vietnam. He was about to re-enlist and rang his parents in Tasmania, only to be bluntly told that the farm may not be there when he got out, so he told his father that he would purchase the farm as if it was Joe Blow off the street; thus, with his military career ended, he became a dairy farmer and is still on the farm today.

DEDICATION/ACKNOWLEDGEMENTS

These books are dedicated to my late wife Sandra; a trained nurse whose quick response to me having a stroke – immediately recognising the problem and getting me to good medical care most likely saved my life.

She later suggested that I should use words and writing to slow down any further mental deterioration, so all of these fictitious stories are thanks to Sandra. *Thirty Years in Time* is the first of six science fiction novels that I've written, which are outlined in the Author's Note.

Having spent four years in the army, three and a half of those in the Special Air Service, with one in Vietnam and, knowing the type of work the Unit does, gave me the incentive to loosely use them as a foundation of my stories. Sitting at the centre of all the theatres of war, I'm proud to say that this Australian Unit has excelled in all of these aforementioned conflicts, distinguishing across two tours of Vietnam, Timor, Afghanistan and finally Iraq.

Outlined below are other works involving the life and times of our hero – Peter Jackson.

Thirty Years In Time, my first book, was written utilising my experiences in the army along with a blend of science fiction; I hope to have constructed an interesting story for you all.

The second in the series introduces my heroine – Sandra Ashfield – an American dairy farmer's daughter who while tidying up his office, stumbles upon her father's background, who appears to have been a Nazi scientist gone to ground. She learns of his past and decides to follow in his footsteps and finish building his time machine that had been his life's work.

The third story is a 'holiday in time' where Jackson and his army friends Mick and Terry and a few others decide to have a holiday: with some outstanding results and happenings to each of these adventures.

The fourth story begins just before they come home when alien invaders come down to Earth with the intention of mining our minerals while conveniently using cave people as slave labour and naturally, they receive a sharp rebuff when they run into Jackson and his mates.

Retirement plans of the friends are brought to the fore when in the fifth in the series, one of their American friends in the CIA becomes involved with drug Barons and desperately calls on his time-travelling friends for help getting him out of a very sticky situation in Columbia.

Fast-track back to around thirty-five thousand years ago where Jackson and his friends finish off the tales as told by bringing the Martin miners all back to our time, which benefits Earth today, effectively saving the day once again.

Peter France

This book is meant to interest readers by introducing the possibility of time travel …

One minute falling off a rope below a helicopter in a hot extraction, our man Peter Jackson wakes up in a glass case in a museum in Hanoi some thirty years into the future.

Having inexplicably lost such a large chunk of time, Peter has also been unlucky in love – firstly robbed of his fiancé by being held suspended in time and displayed as a museum 'attraction' in Hanoi, then once again when he meets a beautiful young woman in Timor who falls in love with him but is confused with his strange dreams. Trying to make sense of the dreams, she tapes them to show her superior, but is unfortunately killed later in a riot in Dilli before anything is resolved.

Lastly, will anything come out of the meeting with the Danish female back packers that Sergeant Peter Jackson and his team of skilled soldiers rescue in Iraq?

The five ropes dropped by the rescue helicopter have finally reached us through the trees canopy right on top of us, so we quickly hook the Karabiners onto them and ready ourselves for this rope extraction. *'All hooked on—ready to go!'* I yell into the Urc10 as I get thumbs up from all. 'Now for *Christ's* sake get us out of here *fast* because there are Charlies in the scrub *everywhere* around us.'

The ropes instantly go taut as the helicopter rises further into the sky above the trees, and we're pulled rapidly into the air at a fast rate; suddenly we start breaking through the tree's canopy. The next moment, all five of us are clear of the trees and are hurtling along above the jungle at what appears to be breakneck speed. I suddenly see green tracer starting to come through the tree's thick foliage from the ground towards us with some zipping past us. We desperately try to crowd together at the ends of our ropes to make ourselves smaller targets to hit.

'We're just about out of it, fellas, is everyone okay, nobody hit?' I get a thumbs up from all of them and the odd strained smile.

'Good; hold tight—bunch together if you can—we'll soon be out of this shit!'

All of a sudden, I feel the rope snap about three feet above my head, and as if in slow motion, I watch Clicker desperately trying to grab hold of me, but his snatches are into thin air as I slip past him. My fall for some reason seems gentle at first as I leave my companions and career down towards the trees. The last thing I remember is hitting the foliage then nothing, nothing at all, just blackness …

CHAPTER 1

THE AMBUSH

We've been in Vietnam close to six months now; just over our halfway mark of the tour, doing exactly what we'd practised training in the bush south of Perth and later on in the unrelenting jungles of New Guinea. Today, I find myself lying under a large leafy bush next to the track in the left-hand cut-off position for the ambush we've set up to find out who is operating in this section of Phuoc Toi Province. The track on which we set the ambush three days previously is small and insignificant, not much bigger than a footpath and far too small to take any vehicle bigger than a motorbike.

I'm in a normal SAS ambush patrol, some forty kilometres north-west of the Australian Taskforce base at Nui Dat. The taskforce hierarchy, in their never-ending wisdom, have sent the patrol out to gather enemy unit identification in this area because, since the battle of Long Tan on August eighteen the previous year, the command has been very windy of any large enemy movements in the proximity of the taskforce. They continually want intel showing what units are in each region and the simplest way for us to do that is to collect fresh data from ambushing tracks north of the taskforce. There had been numerous reports from both ARVN and civilian sources about North Vietnamese troops being seen operating in the area for quite some time. The ambush is not just to verify North Vietnamese troops being here, but in the event that they are, we're to send a very strong message to the North that they can't expect to come into the Australian area of responsibility and operate with immunity.

The night is not far off. We've probably two hours to go before once again, the claymore mines will be laboriously lifted, and the patrol will pull back fifty or so metres away from the track. We'll then crawl into some thick bush located well behind the ambush site and spend another long night lying close together while being eaten by every insect known to man and beast. Most of us think the repellents only encourage them to come out for a free feed and, unfortunately for us, repeatedly bite any uncovered skin for most of the night.

Like most ambush patrols I've been on, it's terribly boring if nothing comes along and it's hard to lie there trying to be positive and keeping one's mind attentive to any sound foreign to the jungle. This day has been a little different, for the local squirrels had put on a floorshow for me. The last three hours I'd watched as they scampered up and down the trees across the track gathering food. Their little button eyes are almost popping out of their small, sleek heads. My pondering about these small creatures continues as I watch the track, hoping something of significance will come along and break this eternal boredom. Thankfully, there's not much more of the day left.

Scurrying in the trees next to this small insignificant track, the small creatures suddenly stop. Standing on their hind legs with ears pricked up, they listen attentively to something large approaching our mutual position and, as if by magic, they disappear ...

Crunch, crunch, crunch!

Instantly alert, I immediately forget about the squirrels, looking down the track towards these human sounds that are now quite clearly coming towards the ambush site. I quietly slip the safety off my rifle and ready the weapon, tensing muscles that a few seconds ago felt cramped and tired but now are free and in expectation of the approach of enemy soldiers. Adrenalin is racing as I ready my rifle and wait in anticipation of something sharp and violent to occur in front of me on this tiny track to nowhere.

The first man who enters the killing ground has his green pith helmet strapped squarely on his head almost at eye level and has his AK-47 at the ready, moving the weapon from side to side along with his gaze, as if he too anticipates something springing out at him. His speed is quite fast for a forward scout – possibly too fast for him to pick up anything alongside the track unless it was blatantly obvious. Behind him by no more than a metre is another man and then another. I count fifteen, all heavily armed as if they're expecting trouble at any time. The last one is opposite me, almost passing, then there is nothing, just a few seconds silence, while my anticipation goes into overdrive.

Boom!

The edge of the track erupts as Johnno has ignited the claymore mines. Black smoke and a huge gust of warm air surge past me carrying small sticks, leaves and other debris. I lift myself up off the ground and move quickly forward onto the track. It's chaotic – their bodies are strewn haphazardly. Some are still writhing, desperately clasping onto their last seconds of life. They look as if they are trying, in vain, to get up. Others are lying in contorted positions where they've been dumped by the blast, their last gasp of life extinguished.

I reach the track and peel off from the others in the killing ground – a procedure we've practised a thousand times before – and move swiftly ten metres to the right. I stop, going to ground, aiming my rifle down the track.

Rifles crackle behind me, sharply breaking the still air as the two in the killing ground finish off anyone who is badly wounded. We do not have the ability to take wounded with us. Quickly the fallen NVA soldiers are searched for documents or items of intelligence value. A minute passes, then two, three minutes, when I hear Johnno's voice above the now-silent jungle.

'Pull back everyone, *pull back!*' is his sharp command. 'Let's put some distance between this place and us.' I rise automatically just as another North Vietnamese soldier charges madly around the corner.

Crack!

The SLR spits death while the nogs following hit the ground with a thud. Then, all hell breaks loose as more Vietnamese, totally unconcerned about their safety, come at break-neck pace around the corner. The big rifle jumps once more, this time on full automatic, with two more falling. The others drop on either side of the track as they return a large volume of automatic fire into the ambush position. An M79 belches from somewhere behind. A rush of air whistles past me and explodes amongst the Vietnamese crouching on the track, allowing me time to pull back to the other three. Our four weapons now plaster the track with automatic fire and M79 grenades, turning that section of the jungle into a soldier's nightmare. A couple of white phosphorous grenades are hastily thrown down the track to cover our withdrawal and, by skilful use of fire and movement, our men pull out, breaking the contact. Swiftly, with as little noise as possible in the damp conditions, we move back, disappearing into the folds of the jungle.

The nearest clearing that can be used for a Landing Zone is close to an hour away, so there is ten minutes of hurried activity clearing the contact area and getting well away from the track before the pace is slowed down to adopt a regular, almost normal, patrol speed. The jungle is damp from rain the night before, facilitating quick movements in our tactical withdrawal. After half an hour, the patrol stops and listens. There are no sounds of the NV following us, but there is the occasional screech of birds and a troop of monkeys moving noisily high up in the trees well above us. We've come to expect these and other barely discernible sounds from the jungle around us.

Each member of the patrol carries two or more of the enemy's weapons, either awkwardly pushing through their webbing or slung over their shoulders in makeshift slings. Clicker is carrying the enemy patrol commander's pack – a prize, as we need some idea of what the NV military objectives are in the Phouc Toi Province. Due to their close proximity to the Australian taskforce and to our troops when doing operations, intel acquired before they staged a full-blown attack on one of the nearby hamlets, or worse – the taskforce itself, would be gold. We all feel the weight of the pack but know it will have to wait for a while before its value is uncovered.

'The nearest Landing Zone is now some half an hour away if we keep this speed up,' Johnno whispers to the patrol's 2IC after looking at the maps. 'How's everyone coping with the extra weight? Tell me, do we need to make any further weight adjustments before we move off again?' Each man nods in response.

After seeing that no one had anything to add, Johnno says in his usual jovial way, 'Good. We'll move out again.' Like most of us, he didn't like large numbers of well-armed enemy troops chasing us through the jungle, especially if the jungle is wet and we are so far out from the taskforce with little chance of much immediate help. 'I want to get to this LZ here well before it's dark; there's a couple of cold beers waiting for me back at Nui Dat. I can almost feel them now, going down my throat.'

The jungle begins to thicken up, so the speed slows as the patrol encounters prickly bamboo – a nocuous plant that grows around most of the province's clearings that, conveniently, indicates our close proximity to the proposed Landing Zone.

'The LZ must be just up ahead of us,' comes the whispered signal back from our forward scout, which is followed by silence for a while as we move on a little further into the bamboo. We are quite wary now as, where there is bamboo, there is very little understorey for coverage. 'The zone is in front of us, about the size of four tennis courts. It should be big enough for the choppers to come in to get us out.'

Johnno signals Clicker to move to the other end of the zone, a good precautionary procedure in a situation when we may have been followed. 'We'll put the LZ between us and any pursuit that may come from the track,' he tells us quietly. 'They may have some idea of our evacuation procedures and they could be checking any zones within proximity of that track.'

So, keeping clear of the edge of our potential Landing Zone, we cautiously move around to the other side of the clearing, putting a large clear space between us and any possible follow-up from behind.

'Run the aerial out,' Johnno quietly orders one of the nearest diggers to the sig as he fumbles in his pack for the aerial. 'While you do that, I'll get the message encrypted, but for *Christ's* sake be on the ball fellas, as I've got a very bad feeling about this one – way too many well-armed nogs potentially on our tail.'

'Patrol 23 to Base. Ambush successful. Could be followed up. Require X-fill urgent.'

The message is hastily encrypted into the one-way code book, and the request for our immediate extraction is tapped through on the sixty-four set.

'The choppers are in the air,' our sig tells us with a sigh of relief, as he receives a return signal almost immediately and quickly deciphers the incoming message. 'They'll be here within half an hour; they're leaving Nui Dat as I speak.'

We wait for almost half an hour, lying low but fully alert with our small defensive perimeter just out of sight on one side of this small inhospitable clearing, each of us listening for any noise of the VC or North Vietnamese who've followed us. It's gratifying to eventually hear the welcome throb of the incoming helicopters in the distance – a distinct noise that no patrol member will ever forget.

'It won't be long now,' says Clicker, looking down the Landing Zone. 'We'll soon be in a chopper and back at Nui Dat and having that beer that you've been talking about buying us, Johnno. *Shit!* I wish you'd shut up about them.' With a grin, he turns to look at some of the other men. 'After this though, I could do with something a bit stronger, particularly as you said it's your shout.'

Johnno ignores the banter.

'This is Patrol 23; we're at the southern point of the Landing Zone.' A short staticky hiss comes from the URC-10. *'Do you read me? Over.'*

'I hear you loud and clear 23. Throw your smoke boys, and we'll come in. Over.' The broad Australian voice brings a brief flutter of expectation that the patrol is almost over.

'This is Patrol 23; we have thrown blue smoke,' says Johnno, as Clicker hurls a smoke grenade onto the Landing Zone directly in front of our position; we watch as the thick blue smoke starts to waft up into the still air.

'I can see your blue smoke 23,' crackles the voice through the still air. *'Wait. There is red smoke at the other end of the LZ. I'll send in the gunships first. The Yanks'll come through low and soften things up for us first so keep your heads down, boys; it seems like the shooting is just about ready to start.'*

The two *Iroquois* gunships fly in flat out just above the tops of the trees. They seem to be halfway down the Landing Zone when they open up and start firing both their rockets and miniguns in and around the red smoke. The bamboo is mown back as if it's been cut with a scythe, falling into the clearing and creating a mangled heap of debris on the end of the zone.

The racket of exploding ordinance is horrific and the patrol watches as the gunships home in on their targets with both rockets and machine guns. We see the enemy's ominous green tracer starting to zip towards the incoming gunships. There are more explosions as salvo after salvo of rockets hit their targets.

The slick comes in fast just behind the gunships, causing smaller arms fire to erupt from near the red smoke. Suddenly there's additional fire coming from another place further up the Landing Zone on the other side of the clearing. Johnno goes down in a heap, hitting the ground in a flail of arms and legs, obviously hit.

'Get Johnno to the chopper fast!' I yell and go to ground firing towards the bush where I can see the green tracer coming from.

'Get him into the slick fast while I cover you. Now, bloody get moving before we're all hit!'

Two of the other patrol members pick Johnno up by the shoulders and carry him quickly towards the helicopter. I see Clicker weaving his way from the other direction and know that he's almost there. He clambers into the chopper and turns, firing his M16 over my head to give me support. Now I can see people in the bamboo just behind us, so I continue to fire at them. The chopper, however, is now taking heavy fire and the door gunner slumps over his M60. I see Clicker roughly pull him aside, taking his place and immediately spraying the bamboo in my direction with this weapon, forcing the Viet Cong down.

I'm about to rush to the chopper but, in the confusion of the other three scrambling onboard, to my horror, the helicopter takes off.

'Shit!' I scream out loud, realising I've been left behind and have no option but to head for the bamboo again.

I finally make it there and quickly move further away from the Landing Zone for fear of being hit by streams of tracer that seem to be coming indiscriminately from gunships towards me. Whether they are covering me or not, I don't know, but they are certainly keeping Charlie's head down.

I bolt further away as the fire from the helicopters is now getting heavier and I certainly don't want to be captured by the NVA, who would be surrounding the Landing Zone by now. A hail of forty-millimetre M79 rounds comes slicing through the jungle towards me, randomly exploding as they hit the bamboo and trees above. I dive headfirst behind a log just away from the bamboo. More projectiles pass directly over my head, hissing, followed by explosion after explosion as they detonate in the thick undergrowth nearby.

Abruptly, limbs from a large tree above crash down, covering me with debris. It's a very close escape and if it hadn't been for the log, I'd have been in deep trouble.

It's raining buckets now; the heavens seemed to have opened up once more, drenching everything as if it'd also been hit by helicopter fire. *Thank God for that*, I think to myself. I lie still under this debris for the next ten minutes, which seem like ten hours, listening until the gunships are finally finished.

I get up and ease myself out of the foliage that's hidden me and head away from the clearing to the east as fast as I can run. Noise means nothing now in this heavy downpour, I'm just another shadowy figure in the scrub. I now have to put as much distance as I can between the NV and myself, hoping the rain will deaden any sounds I make in my frenzied getaway.

Pushing my way through the dense undergrowth for the first few hundred metres, I stop and stand attentively for a moment, breathing hard, listening for any sounds of a follow up. Fortunately, there's nothing, certainly no human sounds. As it pelts down on me in torrents, I'm completely saturated and move on once more, a little faster than patrol speed, covering much distance.

I don't want to fall into their hands, especially after the killings we inflicted on them back at the track and the casualties they would have suffered at the hands of the gunships. They'd be well and truly pissed off with us and would want to scalp anyone they could get their hands on.

Thank heavens it's getting dark and I'm now well clear of the Landing Zone. There's been no firing for quite some time, so I stop and listen once again for any sounds of pursuit. Thankfully, I find only the incessant drumming of the rain coming down in torrents, as if the sky is falling in.

I stop moving, as I'm making far too much noise in the dark and it's time for me to lay up for the night. I should be far enough away from the Landing Zone to be safe from anyone who's out there looking for me. I hope that in the mêlée I had gone unnoticed.

I find a patch of extremely thick scrub and crawl in, checking my ammo and find I still have three twenty-round magazines left for the SLR. I also have the two captured AK-47s that Johnno had thrust on me as we left the ambush site, along with a set of Noggy webbing that's pulled down over mine, which I also check. The webbing is holding four of the curved AK-47 magazines, some one hundred and twenty rounds of ammunition and I also have a thirty-round magazine on each of the AK-47s. I strip one of the captured weapons down and then scatter the parts around the area. I won't need two of them now, it's only extra weight that I don't need to carry.

Suddenly feeling pangs of hunger, I immediately think of my dehydrated rations. I need a feed badly to help me think, but am I too close to the Viet Cong? *Fuck 'em!* I desperately need something warm to eat, so I open up a pack of chilli con carne and huddle over the small flame of the hexamine tablet. It's low to the ground behind the buttress of a large tree, so I pull my poncho around me, trying to hold the flame in as close to the ground as I can to prevent its flickering being seen. Shivering, I need to sort through the best options I have for getting back to Nui Dat and out of this bloody mess I find myself in.

Even though the LZ was first place they'll check, so too, enemy eyes would be searching like hawks for any movement. It would be far too risky to return and, even if I could, I'd be seen. The nearest alternative Landing Zone was some two thousand metres away, almost to the Phouc Toi provincial border and I don't have an URC-10, so I have no way of contacting any helicopters or planes. This time I'm afraid I'm on my own and will have to fend for myself and use my initiative to get back to the unit at Nui Dat.

I wake early in the morning, still a little damp from last night's heavy downpour, but otherwise, the hoochie cover has done a good job and kept me warm. The sun is almost up, so I have a quick cold breakfast. I have to get away as fast as I can just in case the NV expand their search of the undergrowth. With breakfast over, I break out my picto map to study the area I'm in. I have two choices open to me – either south-east to Highway Two (a bloody long way and the obvious way they'd expect me to take), or west to Highway Fifteen, away from Nui Dat. I choose the latter because the jungle appears to be thicker and will give me more cover while I'm travelling, and it is also quite a bit shorter to get to that highway. I look through my pack and estimate I have four days' worth of dehydrated rations left – six to eight days if I'm prudent and conserve what I can. It should be plenty for me to reach the highway and flag down a friendly vehicle. Water for the dehydrated rations wouldn't be a problem this time of year, for there are plenty of streams running on the way to the west, and it rains damn near every night.

My sun-tanned face is dirty and has five days' growth, so a white face isn't going to be a problem. I strap the AK ammo over mine and then make a sling for the SLR and slip that over my shoulders as back up. I'll use the AK-47 as my first option, for there is plenty of ammo and that will keep mine in reserve. I confidently slide my pack on over all this webbing, finding it a little tight, but with this done I'm ready to go.

The jungle is as expected – dripping wet in the morning after heavy rain, then stinking hot through the day. Then after four in the afternoon, the rain would hit sporadically, sometimes quite savagely. Although the sun has dried my clothes stiff, I know I couldn't afford to be saturated to the bone. 'I'll have to make damn sure that I'm well and truly holed up by four this time so I can sleep dry,' I say to myself, desperately trying to keep my concentration levels up. 'Somewhere nice and dry or at least get my hoochie up in time to ward off the blasted rain so I can get a good dry night's sleep.'

I move through the jungle, heading due west at almost double normal patrol speed. Although it's faster, I'm still extremely careful because I don't want to walk into any VC and have to blast my way out on my own. I stop for park time, brew up and eat one of my dehydrated rations, before moving on once again. I'm lucky it's still all primary jungle. Large trees cover the jungle floor making the understory lighter and much easier to move through.

At close to four it becomes overcast once again, and I'm sure the rain won't be long in coming, as the signs are quite bleak. Unfortunately, the jungle here is very thin because of the large trees suppressing the undergrowth. I keep pushing on, clutching at my compass at times, hoping for a thicker spot to spread out my sleeping gear. Another hour passes and at almost five, I know I'm now on borrowed time. I look to the heavens once again and find the sky is ominously black. Suddenly, just in front of me is a wide, well-worn track running almost north-south. I pause inquisitively at this unexpected find and kneel down to inspect the track's surface to see if there's been any recent use.

There are tyre marks that look like a tractor, so it's being used regularly by the look of the wheeled vehicle tracks and plenty of footprints. '*Shit*! It's big, much bigger and very much wider than most tracks that we normally come across,' I whisper, trying to keep myself alert. What the hell could it be that they are driving? I wonder as I note two different types of wheel marks. One set is big, wide and definitely look like a tractor, others look as if the wheel has a steel rim such as the ox carts I'd seen the Vietnamese using.

We'd been finding tracks on most patrols I'd been on, and they were like the one we'd hit the day before – no more than footpaths and really easy to ambush. On this one, however, it was so wide in places you could almost pass cars, and it was still well hidden under the canopy of enormous trees so no aircraft flying over would ever see it. I pull out my map and check once more to see if it is a gazetted road, but it's not there. There's nothing there, just jungle, so I mark this thoroughfare on to the map for future reference.

'I'll have to remember this one,' I mutter as I look up and down this bush thoroughfare, still wondering who's using it and feeling a bit fatigued and mumbly. 'This is certainly a good one for future reference for one of our ambush patrols; the Nogs could move munitions extremely quickly along this track for a big attack in Phuoc Toi Province … certainly would be worth watching and putting a good ambush on this in the future … this would have to be a major resupply route to their troops in Nui Tie V—.'

I'm just about to cross the track when there's a faint noise from the north. I prop and listen to something heavy coming my way. I quickly move back into the shade of the undergrowth and wait, my curiosity now is as strong as ever. What would it be? Who or what would use a track of this size? I don't have long to wait to answer that question. It's an ox cart, with a man and young woman sitting on the seat idly chatting to each other in their high-pitched voices as the cart rumbles slowly along towards me.

The woman has an ancient rifle across her knee as if she's the guard on a stagecoach in some old western. Noticing how attractive she is, I thought she'd be better placed in one of the Vung Tau bars, but more pressing – what is she guarding? I see two other VC nonchalantly following the cart some twenty metres behind, as slack as ever with their rifles slung over their shoulders, talking to each other, their prattle disturbing the quiet of the forest. Their look of total boredom indicates that they aren't expecting anyone to be here and have switched off. Then I noticed another person stumbling along close behind the cart, to which he's tied. By the look of his uniform – a tiger suit or what's left of it – he looks like one of ours. Peering closely, I see that he's a black American, and with the ox cart now fully abreast of me, I have no option but to help this man. I can't leave this poor bugger with them; he may be a Yank but he's still one of our men and in a dire situation.

Quickly looking at the options, I try to sum up the situation. There are four of them, I reason. I can't let the ox cart bolt, but there may be others following behind on this track. I'll have to be fast; the cart will be first.

I have the AK-47 in my hands and put one well-directed shot into the ox's head. I yell my lungs out, hoping to scare the shit out of them. Charging forward, I send a short burst into the two on the seat, which pitches them over backwards with the weight of the slugs in their chests. Screaming still, I race past the cart to the second two. Their eyes are like saucers staring at me as I charge towards them. They stand there desperately fumbling, trying to pull their rifles off their shoulders but to no avail; I'm far too quick. I can almost taste their fear as I move forward towards them. It's written over their faces, as if they know what will happen. I give them three short bursts and watch as they're flung unceremoniously to the ground. My whole ambush is over in less than half a minute. I turn my attention to the American who, like any good soldier, had instinctively dropped to the ground.

'Good afternoon, my friend. How are you today?' The American appears to be in a state of shock. He gingerly pulls himself up off the ground, staring at me, clearly wondering who I am. 'I think we'd better get what we want from the cart and get the hell out of here before the cavalry comes. What do you reckon?'

I quickly cut his hands free with my K-bar. He's a big man, well over six feet. The leather straps he'd been bound with have cut into his wrists, but other than that, he seems to be okay.

'Who the hell are you, man?' he finally splutters, as he shakes his wrists, trying to get the circulation back into them. He shoots me a few curious looks. 'Where the hell did you come from?'

'I'm Pete,' I say, ignoring his other question for the moment. 'We'd better get what we want off the cart and destroy the rest before any more of these pricks come along. If they're close, they would've heard the shooting and would be coming our way by now at top speed.'

He grabs an SKS off the ground near one of the bodies and pulls the webbing from one of the blokes at the rear, while I check the back of the ox cart for anything that may be of use. I'm surprised it's full of food and ammo; it must be some sort of resupply they run from the north to their bases in the Nui Tie Vies.

'Grab a bag and fill it with food. I'm a bit short of that myself,' I tell him as I pull a grenade out of my webbing. 'I'll set a time pencil on one of my grenades for five minutes and put it in amongst some of their ammo. That should give us plenty of time to make a quick getaway.'

'Okay, Pete,' he said, still a little rattled, grabbing a sack and stuffing it full of food while I fiddled with the time pencil and the grenade, crimping the end and carefully shoving it in the back amongst the mortar rounds.

'They're coming, from the sound of things,' I say, as I hear the shrill sounds of Vietnamese voices not too far down the track and from the north, the same direction as the cart. 'Grab anything you want and let's get off this track.'

We quickly move off into the jungle to the west before going to ground and we wait, rifles at the ready, as the chattering increases. There are around twenty of them with rifles, peering in all directions at the scrub around them. Lucky for us, most appear to be collecting around the cart looking at the two bodies on the seat and at the dead ox.

'They are asking themselves what has happened,' the American explains quietly as we listen to their conversation. That he knows their language so well surprises me and makes me extremely envious of him. 'They think it was an *Uc Dai Loi Ma Rung* ambush,' he smiles across at me, a little amused at hearing this. 'You guys have certainly got them running scared; they are seeing men behind every tree.'

Boom!

My grenade is quickly followed by large secondary explosions as the mortar rounds also start exploding. There is a rapid cascading effect as the cart suddenly goes up, causing the small arms ammunition that was boxed to catch on and start exploding.

'With a bit of luck some of the Charlies were on the bloody cart or very close to it when it blew,' I whisper. 'We'd better get clear before they start looking for us; or ... maybe not, after what just happened.'

Just as I speak, the heavens open up and the rain comes belting down on us and in no time at all we're both soaked to the skin. The rain effectively drowns out any noise that we make in our rapid escape.

Travelling westward again, we can't stop now as we're far too close to the track, with too many angry Vietnamese now looking for us.

'I think they'll certainly want vengeance,' I tell the American, who's following me. 'The only good thing for us is the rain will cover our tracks and the pricks back at the ox cart won't hear anything.'

He looks at me and says nothing.

We've moved probably five to six hundred metres and thankfully the bush has finally begun to thicken somewhat, giving us a good place to lay up. No one would be mad enough to try to follow us in such a heavy storm especially now that night is not far off.

'This should do,' I tell him. We crawl in under a wet thicket with large broad leaves. We're both completely drenched by this time, but so what, we're still alive; that's the main thing.

'Peter Jackson. One Squadron, Special Air Service of the Australian Army.' Once both settled under the leaves, I extend my hand to my new companion. 'Sorry about the weather but unfortunately I've no control over that.'

'Abraham King. Fifth United States Special Forces. Boy, am I glad to see you.' Abraham shakes his head in disbelief while vigorously pumping my hand. 'Who the *hell* are you, and how come you're out here by yourself? Where's the rest of your guys and where's your backup?'

I explain my misfortune to him while I make us both something to eat. He listens intently and is quite surprised as I briefly go over the events of the last few days, brushing over our ambush but explaining how I was left behind by the helicopters at our LZ and the continuous firefight we had with the NVA when desperately trying to get aboard the choppers.

'So here I am, heading for Highway Fifteen and just about to lay up when you and your lot come along. I couldn't leave you with them. The worst thing of all – I was getting sick of talking to myself.' I pause briefly, passing him a cup of coffee and one of my dehydrated packs and he passes over some of the fruit he'd taken from the cart. 'Mate, all we have to do to get out of here is to stop one of your bloody trucks when we get to Highway Fifteen and then go south towards Baria. What do you think?'

'That sounds nice and easy, Pete; a good ploy,' he tells me, smiling. Then his expression changes quite dramatically. 'They'll be quite surprised to see me when I turn up after what happened at Nang Tie.' Disappointment and sadness play across his face before he starts to unload his own sorry story of how he was captured some two weeks before.

'We had a small outpost at a place called Nang Tie, quite a bit north of here where we were training Popular Forces soldiers. There were three of us – a major and two sergeants. We'd been there close to two months, and I thought that we were just starting to make a difference with their soldiers, you know – getting them knocked into shape and being able to use the weapons we had for them proficiently; teaching them a few of our tactics so we could do good ambushes like yours. Around six nights ago, the NV made a full-blown attack on the outpost. We had virtually no warning that it was going to happen, that an attack was imminent. The attack had been synchronised extremely well as they'd crept up and pushed Bangalore torpedoes under the wire. They went up at the same time as their mortars came in on the buildings and pounded the shit out of us. I was organising a group of our men to get ready to repel them when a mortar round exploded not far away from where I was. Unfortunately, that's the last thing I can remember. I regained consciousness and found I was a prisoner and had my feet and hands tied up like a Christmas turkey, and NV were running all over the place shooting at anything that moved. Unfortunately for us, it was a complete rout.'

'What happened to the other two?' I ask, interested that such a large and well-coordinated attack had happened in the next province up from Nui Dat, very close to the taskforce area. 'Did they get away during the attack?'

'The other two? Well, unfortunately, their bodies were there. I think they were killed along with a big part of the garrison, with a few lucky ones getting through the wire on the other side and fleeing. Anyway, after the shooting finished, the NV ransacked the place and removed everything they wanted, even taking the goddamned corrugated iron from off the buildings. They set fire to what little was left. I was supposed to be taken down to the Nui Tie Vies, to be held there for a while as they were going to use me somehow in some form of propaganda they have going on down there. What it was, I don't know. I'm guessing after the propaganda I'd be taken north again to some prison camp they have in the jungle somewhere towards the Cambodian border.' He pauses for a while, as if reflecting on what might have been. 'I was taught how to speak their language back in the States before coming over here with the forces, and boy, am I pleased about that because as a prisoner I didn't let on and was able to know what they had in store for me. I just played dumb and only spoke to them in English, so the gooks had no idea I understood what they were saying.'

'I'm afraid I don't speak their language. It's something I should consider before coming over here next time.' I snort out a short laugh. 'Even if it only gives me the ability to chat up the bar girls when on leave in Vungers, I'm sure it'll be an asset.'

'The gooks passed me on to these local bandits to ship me south – the ones with the ox cart. I've been tied to the back of that cart for three days now. They would feed me but wouldn't untie me. The girl you shot was a real doozy; one minute she'd be as nice as pie making up to me as if we were good friends, but the next minute she'd be spitting at me as if I was some sort of low life.'

We pull out our ponchos and roll them around us like large plastic blankets. Abraham was lucky and had grabbed one when he was getting the food off the ox cart. The rain is still as heavy as ever, belting down continuously, but fortunately for both of us we're dog-tired and soon fall asleep.

Morning comes quickly enough. Still damp, we sit listening for ten minutes before we have our breakfast. After we've eaten, we continue our journey towards the west, putting as much distance as we can between us, the bush track and what's left of the ox cart. The day is thankfully uneventful, and we take it in turns leading until about four, when once again we can see the ominous rain clouds slowly building up in the west, and it soon becomes very overcast. We're lucky in this instance as we have a little time on our side to find a thick spot to harbour up for the night.

'Let's put our hoochies up this time,' I say to Abraham, sick of sleeping wet for the last two nights. 'We're due for at least one dry night while we're out here. The scrub is thick enough to hide any glare the hexamine will make.'

'Good idea, I'm with you on that, Pete. Let's put the goddamn things up, there's no gooks out here and yeah, I'm sick of it too.'

So, we put up our little tents and crawl into them to get a dry, peaceful night's sleep – a little luxury we are sure we can afford as we hadn't seen or heard anything of the enemy throughout the day.

By midday the next day we finally strike Highway Fifteen, a very welcome sight. It's only a matter of time now – waiting for some Allied Forces to come our way, so we conceal ourselves by the side of the road. We sit there in our commanding position overlooking the long, sealed road, nicely out of sight of the many prying eyes we imagine that may be looking for us. We wait.

It's close to one o'clock, past the time for the Nogs to take a spell and have their siesta, when an old ox cart comes rumbling slowly along the highway, south towards the town of Ba Ria. Two civilians are on the driver's seat of the cart – an elderly man and woman – as it clip-clops slowly along the highway. With not a care in the world, the old people chat in high-pitched voices, probably scaring everything within earshot of their ancient vehicle. Suddenly, without any warning, out of the scrub no more than forty metres away from us, come four scruffy-looking people; one is armed with a very old rifle and another with what looks like a machete. They race down the bank to the highway, the one with the rifle going around the front of the ox cart and menacingly pointing his ancient weapon towards the elderly couple, while the one with the machete leaps onto the cart and threatens them. It's too far for us to hear the conversation, but their aggressive actions speak for themselves.

'It looks like we're watching a highway hold-up scene from one of your old Hollywood Westerns,' I say, immediately lifting up the SLR into a firing position. 'You take the one with the machete, as he's on your side, and I'll take the one with the rifle. Fire on the count of three. Ready?'

Both weapons explode almost simultaneously, spitting out death to the armed bandits, the force throwing them to the ground. The other two would-be robbers are left hesitating, perhaps thinking of running, but they are well out in the open with no cover, and instead they instinctively raise their hands high above their heads.

'*Don't shoot, don't shoot. We unarmed!*' is the plaintive cry from one of them in Vietnamese.

'Do you want to cover me?' Abraham's face lights up as he gives me a big broad smile. 'I'll go down and sort things out with the elderly couple.'

He moves forward, his rifle at the ready, and is soon at the vehicle. I watch as he ties up the hands of the two thieves to the back of the cart. He then yabbers something in Vietnamese to the old couple who grin and wave towards me and then continue on their way with the hapless two walking along behind the cart. Abraham watches for a moment as the cart slowly plods down the road. With a bit of a skip in his step, he briskly walks back to the ridge.

'I told them that we had a company up here doing an ambush and that the only thing that saved them was they didn't have any weapons,' Abe says to me when he's back on the rise. 'I told the old couple that they could take them into Ba Ria and turn them over to the White Mice, and if there's any reward for them, he and his wife could claim it, if they wished, as compensation for the grief these two caused them.'

We sit high on this sharp little hill talking to each other, learning the other's background and enjoying the day's heat on our bodies. We haven't got long to wait. To our delight we see an American convoy coming slowly along the highway towards us. We get up, quite excited, thinking this saga is finally coming to an end, and walk down onto the road towards them. Everyone aboard the trucks is in a flak jacket with rifles poking out in every direction. We walk towards them waving our arms with our rifles slung on our backs.

As soon as they see us approaching in our camouflage clothing, there're rightly suspicious, and the fact that we're both carrying firearms doesn't help. Clearly, the Yank troops are quite apprehensive about two armed strangers dressed in dirty camouflage approaching, and soon every rifle in the trucks is pointed our way, making me feel quite uneasy. I'm putting my trust in a bunch of foreign blokes who're armed to the teeth, knowing that their track record for indiscriminately shooting people isn't very good. They've got me lined up. Tension cruises through my body. It would only take one idiot to get nervous, lose his cool and pull his trigger and I'm dead. Abraham on the other hand is elated to meet so many of his countrymen, and with hands in the air and rifle slung around his neck, he strolls towards them as if it's a Sunday outing – and far too quickly for my liking.

He's game, I think, as we both walk forward towards them.

'Hey! I'm an *American,* you guys! I'm an *American!*' he shouts as we walk forward towards the trucks.

They hear his accent and I'm relieved to see most of their weapons lower or are lifted away from us.

'We've waited a couple of goddamn *hours* for you guys to turn up,' he tells them with a big smile on his face, pointing back the way we'd come. 'Where have you been on such a lovely day?

Hell, man, we could have gone to sleep up there and missed you guys coming.'

A soldier gets out of the leading truck and comes across to meet us and before he gets too close, introduces himself. 'Major Nichols.' He eyes us both off suspiciously before looking directly at Abraham. 'Where the *hell* did you two guys come from? There aren't supposed to be any of our troops out here.'

'Sergeant Abraham King, Fifth Special Forces, and this is Private Peter Jackson of One Squadron Special Air Service, Australian Army. It's a long story, Sir,' says Abraham, a broad smile plastered on his face. 'I'll tell you all about it as we go to Ba Ria. We could both use a ride, that is, if you can fit us in.'

We pack in with the Yanks and are soon on our way south towards Ba Ria. I'm separated from Abraham and have a chit-chat with another officer who seems amazed at my accent and doesn't know anything about Australia, except that it's big and down in the South Seas somewhere and we have kangaroos everywhere. He has no idea that we even have troops in Vietnam and is amazed when I tell him there are over five thousand of us at Nui Dat, which is not far from here. I feel sorry for him being so ignorant, because if he meets some of the boys in Vung Tau after they've had a few too many beers and are wanting a brawl, he'd be in trouble. After a while, he's all talked out and thankfully clams up, which I don't mind as this almost allows me to nod off to sleep.

We have gone some miles when well before Ba Ria we pass the ox cart, and the two survivors of our ambush are still walking along behind like lost sheep. They do nothing as we pass them and don't even look up as the convoy moves slowly by.

By the time we come to the outskirts of Ba Ria, I'm wide awake and thankfully find there's a Land Rover waiting just as we enter the town. They must've called the taskforce and let them know I was with them. I see some of our fellas that I know – Hills from the Q-store is behind the wheel and Van, one of my mates from B-troop, is waiting in the Rover with him. The convoy stops, allowing me to get out. Abraham approaches me and gives me a massive hug with big bear arms before stepping back onboard.

'I'll be in touch, Pete,' he says with a lot of emotion in his voice. 'I owe my life to you, buddy. Thank you for stepping in when you did and the way you did.'

The trip back to the taskforce is hurried and it's not long before we're going through the gates and going past the ASCO store. We turn off up towards the hill and are soon going by Oka's Opry House. I'm relieved and thankful to be home in one piece after being away by myself for so long.

'Johnno's okay,' I'm told, 'the wound was superficial. He's at the hospital at Vung Tau and they may send him home early.'

'What about the Nine Squadron bloke? How's he doing? I saw him slump over the M60, then Clicker took over.'

'The Nine Squadron blokes say their gunner is okay as well but will be sent home to recuperate. He took three bullets in the body and was evidently a very lucky man, but they feel he needs a good doctor to look after him and plenty of well-earned rest.'

The Land Rover has pulled in at the officers' mess where we normally form up when patrols go out. Here I'm met by what seems to be half of the squadron, all there to see if I'm okay and to get firsthand details of what had happened after the choppers left me in the scrub, as I'd been missing for four days. They hadn't expected to see me in one piece after the shooting at the LZ. I'm no sooner on the ground than the operations officer whisks me away to be debriefed by him and the officer in charge.

I give a detailed debrief to them both, for they had been frantic but couldn't re-enter the LZ because there were enemy troops everywhere and the RAAF was worried about losing a chopper. All they could do was hope that I'd gotten away and would head for one of the highways. However, they all thought I'd go south and head for the nearest LZ towards Highway Two and hadn't thought of me going west to Highway Fifteen, even though it was a shorter route but further from Nui Dat.

'It's lucky I did go that way, Sir. I was able to release a captured American Special Forces Sergeant from an ox cart that was coming down a track towards the Nui Tie Vies. Evidently there's a large camp somewhere in those hills where they were taking him to. He speaks Vietnamese extremely well but kept that to himself and was able to listen in to what they were talking about and knew what they had in store for him.'

After a long, tiring afternoon, I'm glad when the debrief is finally finished and I can go back to my lines, have a shower, clean up and then head straight to the boozer. Boy, after this I need a beer badly …

CHAPTER 2

THE US OF A

South Vietnam

Our tour of Vietnam is almost over, and we've been joined by the advance party from Two Squadron who have been with us now for a few weeks. So that we can quickly and effectively introduce them to the art of reconnaissance patrolling that we've established, some of their patrol commanders have been included in many of our patrols. Although we had to learn and refine many small practical skills the hard way, we readily pass on our claymore ambush methods that we frequently use against the Viet Cong, as none had prior experience in using the lethal anti-personnel mines.

There is a wealth of experience in the combined One and Two Squadrons, many having already completed tours of Borneo before the conflict escalated into a fully blown guerrilla war. We were almost set to go home, when very experienced members of Two were seconded to us. My last patrol contains two members of the new squadron, bringing our number up to six. As we have only a short time together before we go home, the new members' objectives are to adopt vital skills and utilise them. These skills are particularly crucial during each run through the scrub, when we head through the wire via chopper on an operation.

We land the helicopter and move quickly from the Landing Zone into the jungle. I have been given the job of scouting this time – a job I relish compared to being down the back of a patrol as the medic, aka 'tail-end Charlie' or 2IC. We have an hour before dark to make some distance from the LZ. We establish our lay-up point in an area of thick protective jungle in case anyone heard the chopper land and is searching for us.

'This will do us nicely,' says Johnno, who is now almost fully recovered from his gunshot wound. He didn't go home as we all thought he would but insisted on finishing the tour. 'The scrub is nice and thick here,' he tells the newcomers. 'Charlie won't get anywhere near us with all this thick shit around, well, not without making a damn lot of noise.'

Our objective this time is a well-used track that was found and documented by another patrol some months before while they were doing a routine reconnaissance of the area. The track should be within a half-day of our present position, and when we reach our destination, Johnno will take his time showing the new blokes the art of setting up the claymore ambush so that there are minimal errors. As old hands having done in excess of thirty patrols, this routine is achieved by hand signals and is virtually automatic and mostly wordless.

Some four hundred metres from the LZ in a good thick patch of primary jungle, we lay up and listen for just over ten minutes, sitting silently on our packs looking outwards. Fortunately, there are no signs of the enemy, so we have our evening meal of dehydrated rations before quietly rolling out our ground sheets and going to sleep in this familiar small, tight circle.

The next day on patrol, it's after some three hours of walking when we finally reach the track. It's barely big enough for two people to walk on together and, by the looks of its surface, the Nogs are using this one frequently. I quickly turn and signal to Johnno that we're here and look along the track while he carefully approaches to have a look for himself.

'It looks like we have a good section of track that's straight. I'll get you two to help,' Johnno whispers to the two new patrol commanders, then he carefully leads them onto the small track while two of us take either end to watch for the enemy. 'I'll show you how we set the claymores up again so that you can get in much closer behind them than the book says,' continued Johnno, further explaining the reasons behind this essential step. 'In establishing the ambush this way, the patrol misses most of the shit that comes back at you when the claymores are initiated; you miss most of the backblast and you're able to get onto the track really quickly after initiation. We finish the search in three to four minutes at the most, just in case there are other groups following them up.'

The new guys are both good operators, each with a wealth of jungle experience in Borneo. The mines are laid with little fuss, with the lines running back to Johnno's position. They are camouflaged, making them virtually invisible to anyone moving along the track. We begin the wait.

It's about an hour after park time when I hear the familiar crunch of many feet rapidly approaching our position. I ready myself and look through the undergrowth and count to seven. Village guerrillas, judging by the type of arms they carry. At first glance, they look like old WWII rifles, possibly taken from the Japanese when they occupied their country and reused against the French when they returned in the fifties. However, at a second glance these weapons appear longer than I first expected, and I suddenly recognise the triangular folding bayonet on the second guerrilla's rifle as being of Russian origin, from either the First or Second World War. I snigger to myself as the second-to-last man has no rifle at all – just a dead monkey tied to a stick and slung over his shoulder. *Shit! They must be short of meat*, I think.

They are well into the killing ground now and I'm waiting in anticipation for the claymores to explode. The claymores go off as one, followed by the usual blast of hot air, falling leaves and dirt flinging in all directions. I rise and move forward quickly into the killing zone before immediately turning some ten metres to the left, taking my position down the track. My eyes are peeled for any movement further down the track, but there's none. So, this group is on its own, probably moving back to their village somewhere close by.

'Pull back,' Johnno calls as soon as the bodies have been searched and the rifles and any other documents or things of value have been scavenged and put in someone's pack for safekeeping.

Rifles and other items of weight are distributed between the whole patrol, evening up the extra weight. We're soon clear of the track and continue moving towards the designated LZ, which is still some two hours away.

It's close to nightfall when finally, we strike the open area we intend to use to evacuate. There is no mucking around with Johnno; he soon has the message encrypted and our sig sends this back to Nui Dat on the sixty-four set, calling for the choppers to be sent in for an immediate extraction.

Half an hour passes before they finally come. Initially we hear the droning throb of their rotors and see the familiar black blobs in the sky growing bigger as they approach. Choppers are always a welcome sight to a patrol, but to us it's special this time as we're so close to going home. The slick eventually lands, and we scramble aboard, hearing the rush of the gunships as they pass just overhead. Soon we are whisked up to safety, the pilot tacking on behind them. Being a creature of habit now, all I want is a shower and a cold beer and that will finish the day off nicely.

After five days without a shower, I allow the water to run over my body, invigorating me. There are no more patrols. I'll just pack up in the morning and go. But then I suddenly think of what I'll do when I get home with this adventure now over – retraining for the next one I expect. I quickly dress and move out of the tent to join a group of friends out the back, where we begin yoffling about our last patrols, waiting for our dose of Paludrine – the twice-daily antimalarials – and the last mail of this tour. Then we'll ready ourselves for our final session at the boozer.

'There's only a few letters for you pricks today; some came in on yesterday's mail for you blokes who were out.' Snowy, our orderly room clerk, holds up one with what looks like foreign stamps. 'This one looks like it's from the American Embassy or something like that.' Snowy is as interested as I am, but a damn sight less patient than me. 'Come on you slack prick, Jackson, open the bloody thing so we can see what it's about. I'm losin' booze time as well as you bastards. Stop frigging around and open it up for Christ's sake!'

'Well, let's see what those buggers want,' I say, snatching the letter out of his hand. 'It looks a bit official to me. I have a strange feeling you bastards are playing some sort of game on me. Come on, which one of you pricks thought this up?' I'm suspicious that one of them had concocted this, whatever it is.

'*Open the bloody thing!*' chorus some of my friends.

Finally, the letter is opened, and I'm staggered when I read what it's about. It is from the Americans alright. I can see from the stamps and from the badges on the envelope that it appears to be from the military in Washington DC. All the faces around me are trying to second guess the contents.

'The letter says that I'm invited to Washington at the end of next month to be presented with the Silver Star by the President of the United States, for outstanding duties in saving the life of an American serviceman. What do you think about that? Are you pricks sure you had nothing to do with this? I hope it's not a set-up or some stupid shit.'

'Let's have a look at it,' says my friend Van, who snatches the letter, waving it in the air like a trophy before he starts reading the contents out loud.

Thankfully, it's treated as a curiosity for a few moments, but it is soon overlooked in favour of some hard drinking on our last night in Vietnam. It's likely to be the last we'll see of some, as a number of the fellas will leave the squadron when we get home and either transfer to another unit, or get out of the army altogether and disappear somewhere into Civvy Street. One guy's next comment brings us back to reality.

'Let's get some of the good stuff into us now fellas, because we've got one night to go on this cheap grog. Let's make the most of it.' He starts up the track towards the boozer and as he is known for watching his dollars carefully, surprises us with his next statement. 'The first one is on me, then Jacko can buy the first when we get home.'

The whole lot of us tear up the hill behind him to make the most of his offer. Most of the squadron is there for the last night's fling, which turns out to be quite a session. Most let go of the tension that has built up over the time we've been here. It's just after midnight when we stagger back to the lines as full as farts, arm in arm, singing some stupid yippee song from Clicker's past.

'Just be bloody careful that we don't end up in the prickly bamboo and do damage,' Clicker says with a laugh, breaking off the song and almost tripping the lot of us into the bamboo. 'We're well insulated now fellas, but in the morning it's gonna be a different story when the effect of the grog is gone.'

The morning comes around too soon. My head is thick from the beer but I'm still able to jump out of bed and pack my gear as no one wants to be late. The squadron is lining up outside the officers' mess, kitbags at feet, ready to go and only waiting for the trucks to arrive to ferry us to the plane at Nui Dat's Luscombe Airfield.

Four flights later and after a short car trip from Launceston, I'm walking in the front door of my parents' home in Tasmania, less than twenty-four hours after leaving my tent in Vietnam. My parents had been at the airport to meet me because I'd rung them when I reached Melbourne to let them know I was on my way. They were pleased to see me, and we exchanged hugs and kisses as we retrieved my kitbag from the luggage and headed for Dad's old car.

* * *

'Dad, Mum, I'll only be home for a little over a month because

I've been asked to go to America. They have some sort of award they're going to give me for services rendered, I suppose I'd call it.'

'What's this all about, Son?' my father asks, staring at me curiously. 'You never said anything about this in your letters.'

'I only knew the day before we came home. Look, I helped one of their soldiers get away from the Viet Cong not long before we left. It was nothing much really. You know what the Yanks are like, don't you? They throw gongs at anyone for nothing really. It's just a storm in a teacup, I think. They're paying the airfare, so I'd be mad not to go over, especially when they've asked me. Then after that, the bloke I was involved with is going to show me around the place. Look, Mum, Dad, I'll never get a chance like this again, so I've got to make the most of it and I'm taking up the offer.'

They both seem happy with this type of vague explanation. I never tell them much about my work as I don't want to worry them. No one really knows much about the Special Air Service except what is rumoured, so I keep much to myself and remain silent and numb about what we did.

This homecoming is a real treat. Surrounded by the security of my bedroom, I find myself sleeping in for the first time in twelve months, knowing that the bad fellas are thousands of miles away. I show them my slides one night to give the family and friends some idea of what Vietnam was like. These slides are all of camp scenes, across from the gun emplacement on top of Nui Dat, and Nui Tie Vies can be seen in the distance. Some were taken from the back of the unit Land Rovers or one of the trucks while going on R and C. Vung Tau was popular, as were Singapore and Hong Kong where I had been. These are all happy scenes with shots of the blokes in the unit enjoying themselves, or of the tents in the camp. There are vehicles rushing around, helicopters on kangaroo pads and of course plenty of bar girls mixing with the fellas on leave.

Over the next few weeks, I meet up with the friends that I'd had before joining the army. I also take a former girlfriend out a few times, but I find that she and my friends have different interests from me now and that we have very little in common. The time home is going quickly when, to my surprise, I receive a phone call.

'Hi, this is Abraham,' comes the distinct American voice. 'I hope you've got your ticket booked for DC, buddy, and that you're right to go. It's all ready for you this end when you get over here. I've made sure of that and we're looking forward to you getting here so we can show you 'round our little piece of the world, and then you can tell me if it's anything like Australia.'

Although quite surprised to receive his call, I tell him, 'It's all booked. I'm counting down the days 'til I fly out of Launceston. Now, you'll have to remember that when I get over there, I'll be a stranger in a strange land, so you'll have to keep an eye on me.' I decide to have a bit of fun and lay it on. ''Cause you know, I'll have trouble finding out the differences between a bar, a saloon and a hotel, and I'm *sure* you won't want me going into the wrong one or getting lost.'

'No worries, buddy. We'll do a bit of that too while you're over here,' he says with a laugh. 'As soon as the presentation is over, y'all 'll be comin' down home to Alabama with me to meet the family. They's lookin' forward to meetin' you as you'll be the first Australian they done *ever* met, and we'll even do a bit of shootin' up in them there hills if you like, just to keep your eye in for your next tour so you don't get rusty with yo' rifle. What y'all think about that?' I can hear Abraham barely stifling another laugh.

'That sounds great, Abe. I'm looking forward to having a look at Alabama.' I think of my ignorance. 'I'd like that because the only thing I know about your neck of the woods is what I was taught at school and that was about a long time ago when you had your civil war.'

We chat for another five or so minutes before we say our goodbyes.

Washington DC

I have accumulated just over two months' leave, so I intend to use the last month of it having a good look around the US with Abraham and his family. I soon find myself on a plane bound for the United States, half a world away. I have a stopover in LA for a half day. I'm cleared by customs there and spend the rest of the time waiting for my next flight. I look around the airport newsagencies, trying to find a book on Alabama but to no avail. The airport is massive compared to anything we have in Australia, and I'm pleased to finally be on another flight bound for Washington DC. I've arranged to meet Abraham and I hope he's there to greet me, if the size of Washington's airport is anything like LAX. I have nothing to worry about; he's there waiting as I come through the terminal doors, as big as ever, a broad smile on his rugged face. From now on everything to do with this adventure of mine will be out of my hands.

'It's good to see you again, Pete,' he says as we give each other a big hug. 'Did you have a good flight coming over?'

'It was okay, Abe, but I'm glad I'm not your height; I'm afraid I was a little cramped on the plane,' I tell him as we move away towards the pick-up point to get my luggage. 'I can't get over how enormous your airports are over here compared with what we have at home – Sydney and Melbourne. Here, you'd get lost in any one of them without a good compass to get from point A to point B.'

He laughs at my country-hick comments, then goes on to explain what's ahead of us as we get into the taxi. 'I've booked us into a good hotel not too far from the White House, so we'll have plenty of time to get to the function, which is at twelve o'clock tomorrow. Today we'll be able to have a good look around DC, so you don't get lost and have to pull out that goddamn compass of yours,' he says with a little laugh, perhaps remembering the instrument dangling around my neck as we made our way to Highway Fifteen. 'You should find Washington very modern and a little different from what I'm told you have in Australia. There's a hell of a lot to see in our capital city.'

We drive past the White House on our way to the hotel. I find it almost unreal, and it makes me feel a little uncomfortable, as if I'm in one of the movies I used to watch as a boy. The city is staggering and much bigger than I'm used to – the farm boy from Tasmania is really here!

'We have nothing like this in Australia,' I tell him as I look out the taxi window at the monuments that seem to be everywhere, some with large, pillared entrances. 'The suburbs look big, and the streets are so wide. I'm sorry to be like this, Abraham, but I'm a little overwhelmed to be actually here seeing all this firsthand. You'll have to be patient with me and keep me out of trouble.'

'That's alright, Pete, I was a bit the same as you when I first saw this place, but after the first trip you know what to expect and you'll find you soon settle down when you get used to see'n what's been built here.'

I still pinch myself to see if I'm awake and not dreaming. I'm pleased to hear Abe's commentary and when we arrive at our hotel, I find I've begun to settle down somewhat.

The pub is nothing flash but I'm sure we'll be comfortable. I grab my case and follow Abraham up the stairs and to our rooms. I look out the window of mine, feeling a little tired, but then decide to check out Abraham's room.

'We'll head out for a stroll as soon as you clean up,' he says as I enter the room. 'We can have a good look around the city and then go and have a few of those "nerve tighteners", as you like to call 'em, so we'll be ready for the big day tomorrow. What do you think?'

'That sounds like a great idea,' I tell him. 'We can have a few drinks and tell each other a few tall stories. Yes, I'd like that, Abe.'

My room is not big but comfortable. Abraham has done a good job finding this place and it's exactly what I need for the short time that I'll be in Washington – somewhere to put my head down and get a good night's sleep, as I didn't get much on the plane. The shower refreshes me, and I feel I could stay under the water forever. I quickly iron some of my clothes and suddenly wish I'd brought more. I look at myself in the mirror, a little disappointed with what I see. I feel quite shabby, but then I'll be in uniform for the presentation so that should take care of that.

The walk around Washington is interesting. Each memorial and building is huge in its own right, symbolising events, people and conflicts the Americans have been involved with over some three hundred-odd years since gaining their independence from England. I think that we have a long way to go to catch up with the Yanks. Washington is so well presented, showing their pride, not only to visitors like me, but to their own people who visit.

It's getting towards dusk, so to finish the day off, we drop into a bar just down the road from our hotel to have that 'nerve tightener' before the important events of tomorrow. I haven't thought much about the ceremony until today, and now I'm getting a little nervous as Abraham starts talking about the events that brought us irreversibly together.

'It's a lot of bullshit that they're going on with,' I tell Abraham, my feet getting colder as each beer takes hold. 'It just happened. There was nothing out of the ordinary with what we did. Look, you would have done the same thing for me if the positions had been reversed.'

We laugh and talk about how things get blown out of proportion when the bureaucracy gets hold of events.

'I just put in a report exactly as it happened when they debriefed me; I told them everything from start to finish – the attack on the hamlet, my capture, how you came along by yourself in the jungle and how we made our escape together.' He laughs a bit before he continues with his story. 'And the last little bit with those four trying their roadside robbery just in front of us. Believe it or not, according to our intelligence who did a thorough check on us and what happened, the elderly couple, you know; they put those two into the White Mice when they eventually reached Ba Ria later that afternoon.'

'Good heavens, it would have taken that old cart the whole day to reach Ba Ria at the speed they were travelling!' I say, laughing at the way he describes it, before picking up our glasses to get another beer.

'I'll have another two of the same please.' I smile at the barmaid, a shapely blonde girl with big boobs, and ask her where the restrooms are. 'I'll pick them up when I get back.' Flat out, she gives me a hurried smile and nods me in the direction of the restrooms. It's a good five minutes before I return.

'You'd better get over to your friend quickly,' the barmaid

tells me, looking in the direction of our table. 'He's having some trouble with those people who've just come in. They're hassling him. I don't like the look of them, there's trouble written all over them.'

There are three scruffy young white blokes who are standing around Abe looking very menacing. Thanking the barmaid for her help, I reach our table just in time to hear one of them say, 'You're sitting in our seat, *Nigger*. I won't tell you again, now move your fuckin' ass, right now or you'll be sorry!'

The effects of the alcohol suddenly gone; I offer my help. 'Is there a problem, fellas? Can I help you?' I move in close behind them, forcing them to turn towards me.

They spin around at the sound of my voice and stare at me, sizing me up; I'm slightly smaller at just over five foot nine.

'You can fuck off too, you Limey asshole, this is between us and the Nigger!' the first says, looking at me as if I'm some sort of amoeba that he's just brushed off his food-stained coat. 'Now *beat* it or you'll wish you hadn't interfered.'

I hate being mistaken for a Pom, so I need no further introduction. I kick him straight in the nuts, then, as his head drops, I hit him again with all my power, catching him in the face with my fist and feeling his nose squash satisfyingly against my knuckles. He goes down like a log, hitting the floor, bounces a little then doesn't move. I can tell that the advantage is mine by the surprised looks on their faces, which are quickly replaced by anger. With lips set in a thin grimace, the next one moves slowly towards me. Although threatening at first, he hesitates as if unsure of himself. Abe's big fist cuts him off in his tracks, *bang–bang*, and Lips crashes to the floor, out cold.

This distracts the third as he catches Abe's movement. For a fraction of a second, he doesn't know what to do with his raised and meaty fist, so I help him decide by bashing him hard in the face. His feet seem to leave the ground for a few seconds as Abe's large fist smashes his stomach, then he crumples and gracefully slides to the floor. Abe and I are admiring our handiwork when a great cheer comes up from the rest of the bar as everyone stands and claps. We do our best to act humble though, and enjoy the moment, particularly when the barmaid, who introduces herself as Sandra, roughly plonks two beers and almost her chest on the table, saying, 'The drinks are on the house for you two. Now tell me, where are you boys from?'

'Thanks, Ma'am. I'm from Alabama,' says Abraham, who knocks the froth off his beer before finishing his sentence, 'but my good friend here is from Down Under, from Tasmania, Australia.'

Sandra looks at me as if I'm a man from Mars, but she's interrupted by the arrival of the police who look at the three unconscious thugs on the floor and then at us. The barmaid butts in and explains what happened, having noticed the unspoken query written all over their faces.

'Those three people have been causing trouble for these two gentlemen, Officer, and got exactly what they deserve.'

Off for a night in the cells, the three, who are starting to come around, are unceremoniously removed.

'We fought in 'Nam together.' Abe says, resuming his conversation with the barmaid as if nothing has happened. He is getting up a little steam from the beers. 'He saved my life over there and will be gettin' a medal tomorrow from the President for what he did.'

We are once again inundated with drinks as people come up and congratulate us. Word spreads that I'm Australian. Many people want to know about kangaroos, so immediately I become an expert, telling them stories about the creatures and how they live in the wild. I'm very pleased when we are finally able to leave the bar and stagger arm in arm the short distance back to our hotel.

I'm up early with a slight hangover. I shower, put on my winter uniform then pin my two medals onto the left side. When finished, I knock on Abraham's door. I see him with almost two rows of medals. I suddenly value my two even more.

'Are you ready to go and get it over with?' I ask Abraham, who I'm pleased to see seems a little nervous, like me, with this important event now being so close and neither of us knowing how it will pan out.

'You bet, I'll be with you in a sec, Pete,' he says, ruffling his uniform and pulling some imaginary creases out. 'There, that's it; we're set to go.'

We grab a taxi and go directly to the White House. It's only a short trip but by the time we get through the red tape to where the ceremony will be held, my nerves have begun to play up big time and I'm having reservations about the whole affair. The worst part is I'm a stranger in a strange land and the only thing stopping me from bolting is the big man sitting next to me, who's probably as nervous as I am.

When we arrive there's quite a large crowd gathering on the lawn, talking in groups or sitting on seats arranged for the recipients. As we walk past, looking for our position, some turn and stare for a brief moment at my strange uniform with a sandy-coloured beret. In front of us are rows of seats with names stuck to the back, which have been set up for the presentation. We walk towards them, looking for ours, when we're stopped by a representative of the Australian Embassy – a strange-looking little man in his mid-thirties who for some reason appears a little flushed and is quite out of breath.

'Private Jackson, congratulations! Well done! We're so very proud of you,' he says, and hardly catching his breath, he continues, 'Unfortunately, the Ambassador is unable to be here today for your presentation – very pressing business you have to understand. I tried to ring you early last night, but you were evidently out, so if there is anything at all you need don't hesitate to let me know. Anything at all, you understand?'

'I have everything I need thank you.' I say, hoping he'll give us a little space to let my nerves settle down properly.

I am pleased when the little man moves on and we are shown to our seats. There are about twenty people representing all four US services, making me the only foreigner.

After more fanfare, the President arrives to the delight of the crowd and gives a good speech before he begins the task of presenting the gongs. First are the Medals of Honour, their equivalent to the Australian Victoria Cross. I look at the winners and think how worthy they are and how brave these men must be to receive such an award and I realise how in awe I am of the occasion and the dignitaries present. The Presidential Citations are next, and we watch as recipients collect their awards. Then they move to Abraham and me.

'Sergeant Abraham King, Fifth Special Forces, United States Army, and Private Peter Jackson, One Special Air Service Squadron of the Australian Army. For conspicuous bravery and services rendered to both the United States of America and Australia.'

We both get up and move forward to the President who looks at us both briefly – Abraham in his green beret and me with my sandy beret – before pinning our medals on.

Although we receive different medals, I am proud to have received any, and a little overwhelmed by the pomp and pageantry. Although I hear every word of the President's congratulatory words to us, it is all a blur and over with before I know it and I quickly respond, as does Abraham.

'Thank you, Sir,' we both say, saluting the President together before stiffly turning and moving back to our seats.

The presentations go on until all the medals are given out. Once over, the ceremony is thrown open to a feed and drinks, and then again unfortunately I'm subjected to the bloke from the embassy who'd hung around before the ceremony. I'm quite relieved when Abraham comes over and rescues me, having interpreted my silent plea for help.

'I've got a surprise for you, Pete. Come over and meet my family. They've come all the way from Alabama just for this day. They're standing over here. Damn it!' He says this last part to himself, more out of frustration than anything else. 'They got in last night on a late plane. If we'd known, we could have met them and taken them out for dinner.'

We move through the crowds of servicemen and their supporters until we're sure the man is out of eyesight and change tack for a cool drink. Jostling again, we stop very close to an older couple and a young, very attractive girl, obviously Abraham's sister.

'This is my Australian friend, Peter Jackson, that I told you about.' He turns to me, smiling. 'Pete, this is my father – Andrew, my mother – Silvo, and this is my sister – Alicia.'

Looking around the same age as my parents, his father is a fairly large man in his fifties and looks as if he wouldn't take nonsense from anyone. His mother, on the other hand, is quite thin, and not what I expected. Alicia is just into her twenties if she's lucky – and boy is she beautiful!

'I'm very pleased to meet you,' I say, shaking each of their hands. 'Abraham has told me a lot about you and your part of America; I'm looking forward to getting to know you better and seeing some of your country while I'm over here.'

'Abe has told us that you saved his life in Vietnam,' his dad states. 'From what I see on television and hear on the radio, things aren't very good over there are they?'

'That's not an appropriate thing to ask,' Abraham says sharply.

I quickly cut in to avoid embarrassment. 'It has been trying times, Mr King, but you have to understand, I was on the run from the Viet Cong myself when I came upon them. I only did something that anyone would have done. You have a great son, Sir, and you can be proud of him. Heavens, he survived Nang Tie just before I met him, and I wouldn't have liked to have been there with all that trouble going on and being tied down training a heap of ARVN recruits. He's extremely lucky to still be alive after surviving that assault.'

My outburst must have been unexpected because there is silence for some time as they re-evaluate the situation. I am a white man and although I don't know him that well yet, I know I can trust Abraham as a good friend. After last night, I know I can rely on him without question if things get tight.

There's a stony silence from everyone before finally Silvo speaks out, quickly breaking the deadlock. 'Does your Momma worry about you being away so much of the time in strange foreign places?' She looks at me before breaking out an agitated smile. 'I'll bet she worries a lot about you – her boy being away from home so much.'

'We are country people, Mrs King. I live in a small country town of about two hundred people. We've been on our farm since nineteen thirty-two, not long by your standards in America.' I smile at her, trying to put her at ease. 'I tell Mum a lot of poppycock – sons do that you know, just so their mothers can sleep easier at night and not have to worry about where their children are or what they're doing. I expect you are the same, Mrs King?'

'My boy, you'll have to come down and spend some time with us and have some good old-fashioned southern hospitality.' Silvo smiles broadly, obviously happy with the answer from this strange white man with a funny accent. 'Now that son of mine will be able to show you around our little neck of the woods and you'll be able to do a good comparison with your part of the world, for I expect it's quite different to what we have in Alabama.'

We stay at the function talking happily together for probably another half hour before we are able to finally sneak off and make our way back to the hotel. Abraham's family are staying at another hotel not very far away, so we'll be going out to dinner tonight, and it is sealed with Silvo's parting words: 'An' kick our heels up just for you boys.'

The small restaurant chosen is conveniently situated between both hotels, so we saunter down the street to meet them. I ask about his parents.

'My folks have lived in Alabama all their lives. They've battled hard to get me and then Alicia through college and I have to say it's Alicia who is the bright one; she's halfway through university doin' medicine and is well on her way to becoming a doctor of medicine. The way she's going she'll be qualified in just under two years, which will make us all extremely proud of her. By the way, call me Abe.'

'Your parents sound just like mine – great people who go without a lot just to give us kids a good chance with an education.

Once achieved, then it's up to us what we do with it; you know what I mean, Abraham–uh–Abe, what we do after we leave school with our lives?'

Our conversation is cut short when we reach the restaurant and find his family sitting at a table huddled together talking quietly, and it's easy to know what the subject is.

'I hope you three aren't talking about us,' says Abe, giving me a wink and smiling profusely at them as we walk in. 'You know, Mamma, I could feel my ears burning all the way down the street and, by lookin' at Pete, so could he.'

'Now don't be like that, my boy,' his mother says, probably a little too quickly, as obviously he'd been right. 'We're just biding our time wait'n' for you two boys to come along but just tryin' to work both of you out, 'cause in some ways you're *so* different but in others you're both the same, very unpredictable in what you do. Anyway, come and sit down and make yourselves at home and then you can tell us all about Vietnam, what you did over there and how you met.'

'Thanks, Mamma, we will,' says Abe, before giving her a little kiss. He then shakes his father's hand and as they shuffle around the table, Abe fakes a stern look and says, 'You're in Washington now so you behave yourself, do you hear?'

I'm sitting between Alicia and Abe, looking across the table at his parents and I'm drawn into their conversation right from the start. The four of them ask me about Australia and particularly about Tasmania, which they'd never heard of, so I give them a run-down on the people, the climate – everything.

'Now it's my turn,' I tell them, much to their surprise and they seem a little taken aback. 'You've learnt about me and where I come from; now you can have a go. What about your history? I only know what I've learnt about Alabama at school and I'm afraid that's not very much. Unfortunately, the only thing I know about you is the briefing that this bloke gave me one night. We were sitting together extremely wet and cold. It was miles from anywhere and we were as wet as shags on rocks, trying to keep dry and get out of the rain, which was impossible with what we had and particularly where we were.'

They look at each other for a few seconds before they burst out laughing. I begin to know and like these people, and the evening turns out to be really nice. Even nicer is how beautiful the girl sitting next to me is.

We'd gotten up early in the morning and all taken the same plane down to Alabama. We have entered what I've heard some Americans graciously call the 'deep south', which to my thinking, is not a great deal different to outback Queensland or New South Wales.

We piled into Abe's parents' car that they'd left at the airport, and as we drive further into town, I begin to see Negro people both sitting and standing in groups in the streets. I must have shown my interest, as while I'm in deep thought, Abe cuts in and starts to explain the situation.

'We have very little work for our people down here. That's why when I finished college, I joined the army to get away from all this, but it still annoys me when I come home on leave and see the situation they're in.' He pauses for a short time, and I see he carefully thinks through what he's about to tell me. 'Good people mostly, wanting to work but with very few jobs available, most just hangin' about waiting for an opportunity or something to happen, and when it does, it's mostly bad and some find they're in trouble with the law. For them, it's tough to find a way out; unfortunately, a big percentage don't.'

'I'm sorry to hear that; we have nothing like this at home. We have very few people of Aboriginal descent in Tasmania. They were the original inhabitants, and the remaining are only part Aboriginal. There were a few in the army and most of them that I met were good blokes and the army treated them on their merits and not the colour of their skin. I expect your army would be like ours?' I venture.

'I have a trash business that I've built up over the years. You'll have to come out with me and see how it's done.' Abe's father, Andrew, had been rather quiet, listening to what we were saying as he drove. He speaks with pride in his voice of what he's been able to achieve and establish with his business. 'I started the business with an old pick-up and increased our loads and now we run three trucks and are lookin' at buying a fourth. We're flat out collecting the stuff and work from daylight to dusk just movin' it to the dump. You'll find what we do very interesting 'cause people throw out a heap of good stuff. You know we just about equipped our house from the tip.' He catches my eye as he briefly turns his head, and I lean forward to reply, but Silvo cuts in.

'Now you just hold on there, you know that ain't right! We built the new kitchen and didn't take anything from the tip, and upstairs is all new and we bought *everything*, down to the flannel that you wash your face with. How *dare* you say something like that to our guest – you're deliberately given' him the wrong slant on the whole family!'

He'd hit a soft spot obviously. I retreat back in my seat, mouth shut. She wasn't going to let him get away with it, so, we spend the rest of the trip just listening to their dad getting it in the neck. When I look at Andrew's profile, I see he's fixated on the road in front of him. Abe and Alicia are grinning at each other over their parents' performance, and I'm reminded of home – Mum when

Dad puts his foot in something. Noticing me looking at them, I'm met with smiles from both. *God, she's beautiful*, I suddenly think and immediately drop my eyes away from Alicia.

Abe's mum finally stops her tirade when Andrew pulls into their driveway, stops, gets out quickly and disappears into the garage.

Their home is quite a large brick house on a tree-lined street, which tells me they are relatively well-off. The house is quite old, likely from the turn of the century, but what stands out is the large second storey that appears to be new, with large modern windows looking out over the street.

'Abe, you show our guest where he's sleepin' while he's with us,' Silvo directs her son. It appears we've just moved into her domain, as she now takes over the situation after Andrew's rapid strategic exit. 'You take your friend to our guest room upstairs and make sure he's comfortable and knows exactly where everything is. You hear me, Son?'

Feeling a little like a kid, carrying my meagre possessions, I follow Abraham to a very large, cosy room upstairs. He turns, smiling at me before pointing to the room opposite to mine, echoing my thoughts.

'That's the bathroom across there. Dad and Mum have an ensuite to their bedroom so we kids have this one to ourselves.' With a little laugh, he continues, 'For some reason they still prefer to sleep downstairs, leaving all the good rooms up here to Alicia and me when I'm home. I hope you'll be comfortable in the guest bedroom, Pete. It hardly ever gets used these days. With me being away most of the time, that leaves only Alicia sleepin' up here by herself. Go in, freshen up a bit if you want and I'll meet you downstairs, have a good coffee, then we'll slip out and I'll show you around our little neck of the woods.'

'You know, Abe, there are only two two-storey places in my hometown. One is my grandfather's, and he still sleeps downstairs. Most including ours are single storey, so it's a novelty for me being upstairs, honest.'

'Put your things away and I'll meet you downstairs for that coffee and a bite, then I'll show you how we live down here in the South. Unfortunately, as you've already seen as we came in, some of it isn't very pretty.'

I only have my small case with a few clothes, so I hang them and slip across to the bathroom for a quick shower. Afterwards, I go downstairs to find Alicia alone in the kitchen, getting drinks ready. I've hardly said a word to her since we'd met and I've had trouble controlling my eyes ever since. I know she goes to university and is in her early twenties, so I think I'd better break the ice and get to know this beautiful young woman a little better.

'Abe told me you are going to university and studying to be a doctor. I did an army med course myself and learnt how to patch up wounds. I expect your study would be extremely tiring and quite complicated having to learn all about the human body in detail and its functions and how to fix something that's wrong?' I could feel myself rambling, so I stopped.

She looks at me for a long time, taking me in before she smiles and answers the question. 'I'm well over halfway now. I have not quite two years to go before I'm finally finished.'

'I admire anyone who takes on an occupation such as yours, Alicia. Do you find learning all this hard?'

'I'll be honest, it hasn't been easy, Peter, but I'm passing my subjects okay now. Here, let me make you a coffee while the others are still changing.' She smiles at me a little coyly. 'It will take Abe quite some time to get ready as I expect he'll want to go and catch up with Ophelia.' Alicia explains that Ophelia is

Abe's steady girlfriend since college.

'Thank you, Alicia, that'll be nice. I'll just have a straight black with no sugar. Well, I guess I might meet Ophelia today. So – not quite two years to go; where do you hope to practise after you have qualified?'

She moves over to a pot, fills it with hot water and switches it on but doesn't answer my question. Instead, she asks one of her own.

'What do you think of the United States now that you've seen some of the good and bad parts of our lives?' I realise she's also noticed my interest, and I must look surprised, as she explains, 'Abe was telling me you both had a little scuffle at a bar the other night when you were having a drink. He told me the three guys confronted him because he's black. Unfortunately, I'm afraid that wasn't a very good introduction to our country.'

'That was just a storm in a teacup really. People like that are nothing new to me; we have those sorts of yobbos at our pubs as well, don't worry. They try to pick a fight because their footy team lost or some other excuse. But the country I've seen so far seems nice enough. You have to realise I've only seen the inside of an LAX and then had two nights in Washington – and I might add one of those nights was spent with you and your family. Not really much to judge your country on.' Alicia looks into my eyes, and I give a little nervous laugh. 'The worst person I've met so far on my trip was the bloke from our embassy when we were presented with our gongs.' As her eyebrows arch in query, I elaborate on my terminology and continue. 'You've got to realise, Alicia, the American people I've met so far have been very nice on the whole and I look forward to meeting a lot more of you before I finally have to go home.' Thinking exactly how much more I'd like to meet of her, Abe, who is dressed to impress, interrupts my thoughts.

'It's good to see both of you getting along so well. Hope you've got the coffee going, Sis, because I need one *badly*. We'll have a quick bite before we have a look around town and see how it's changed since I was here last. I'll pick Ophelia up at her home on the way so we can have a night out on the town. Do you want to come with us, Sis?'

'I think I'd better, otherwise Peter may get the wrong impression of us, because that girl of yours can certainly talk,' she says with a smile. Abe and Alicia exchange knowing looks, which sparks my curiosity. 'Now, tell me, are you picking anyone else up while we're out?'

'No, only Ophelia,' he says with a sly look on his face before explaining a little about his girlfriend. 'I've written to her a number of times while I was in 'Nam but haven't seen her for well over twelve months. She'll want to come and meet you as well, Pete.'

We drink our coffees and have some sandwiches that Silvo made before we head out towards town to pick up Ophelia.

She comes out of her house. She's quite tall, very busty and loud. Boy is she loud! It doesn't take me long to understand Alicia's remarks as she starts talking while getting into the car, monopolising the conversation and giving none of us a chance.

We drive around, having a good look at the city, with my three hosts taking turns, when they can, to explain each area we're driving through. Surprisingly, for a small city, Kirkdale has a number of industries. Towards late afternoon, we stop at a bar for a drink. We end up having a number of drinks, with the conversation still being dominated by Ophelia.

'Do you mind if we go and do a bit of shopping before closing time?' asks Alicia. 'I have a few items I need for college tomorrow; Peter could come with me and give me a hand if he'd like to.' She turns her eyes to me.

'Certainly, it would be my great pleasure,' I respond awkwardly, feeling that perhaps Abe would like some time alone with his girl. I can't get away quick enough from the talkfest, so with Alicia taking my arm and steering, we head towards the shopping centre.

We amble slowly down the street, looking at shop windows and taking our time. I find the goods in the windows fade away, as all I can focus on is her and her reflection. As we walk, I can feel her presence beside me, and I walk as close as I can to her. Being by ourselves is intoxicating and we begin to enjoy each other's company. Alicia subtly questions me about Australia and particularly where I come from.

'So, you're from Tasmania, Abe tells us? I'd never heard of this place until he told me about meeting an Australian in Vietnam. I looked it up in the atlas, but it didn't give me much information. It just showed an island at the bottom of Australia, with only two cities marked, one at the north end of the island and one at the south but nothing else about the island or the people who live there.'

'The two largest cities are the second and third oldest colonies in Australia behind Sydney,' I tell her with a lot of pride in my voice, then with a bit of a laugh I expand on the reasons. 'The English established settlements on both ends of the island just after eighteen hundred. Hobart, the capital in the south, and Launceston in the north, were settled to stop the French from establishing colonies there. The English were at war with France at the time and there were a number of French explorers nosing around our coast and the English didn't want them establishing settlements on the island. Unfortunately, once those settlements were made, it became convenient for them to establish penal settlements on the island for convicts as there was great poverty in England at the time. You didn't have to do much to be transported; some copped it for stealing bread. So, you see, our little island unfortunately has quite a long and chequered history in its short hundred and sixty-odd years of settlement. The Dutch first discovered the place in sixteen forty-two and initially called our island Van Diemen's Land, after the Governor of Batavia, but later the British changed that to Tasmania, after Tasman, the captain of the Dutch ship who first discovered the island almost a hundred and fifty years before Cook.'

'Have you any convict ancestors?' she says with a wicked little grin that she tries to hide from me. 'Come on, there must be something a little devious back there that you're trying to hide from everyone.'

'A lot of my friends have convicts in their backgrounds,' I say, laughing at her gentle digging at my past and then tell her, 'but as far as I know, there are no convicts hidden in my family tree.'

We continue to stroll, making small talk, stopping from time to time to look into a shop window at nothing in particular. She's interested in Australia and is amazed when I tell her that it's almost the size of America if you don't count Alaska, but that our population is miniscule compared to that of the United States.

'Yes, I understand it's almost the size of America,' she says, looking at me, her big brown eyes sending me completely to water – a situation I hope she doesn't recognise. 'But I can't get over how few people you have compared to us!'

After a wonderful, entertaining afternoon we arrive back at the bar, parcels in hand, and join the other two who are still in deep conversation and don't seem to have missed us at all.

'It's been a wonderful afternoon guys so let's have another

drink before we call it a day and head home,' Abe says with a smile as he looks across at the flush on his sister's face. 'You'd like another beer, Pete? What about you, Sis, another Bacardi?'

'Thanks, that will be lovely, Abe, but not too much Coke please.'

'A beer will be fine,' I tell him, taking a seat next to Alicia. She puts her hand in mine. 'We had a good look at your city's shopping centre; I found it quite a bit larger than the one at home. Alicia was an extremely good guide, but I find there was quite a large difference. I expect this would be caused by your larger diversity in cultures?'

'Could be, Pete,' Ophelia says, breaking her conversation with Abe and looking across at me. 'Abe was telling me there are no Negroes in Tasmania.' She turns back to her conversation with Abe and continues without missing a beat. I think perhaps she must be making up for the year Abe has been away.

We finish our drinks and Abe slowly drives us back to the house for dinner and I am surprised that like at home it's a casual affair in front of the TV watching a favourite show. After a while, Silvo and Andrew leave for bed, and I don't last much longer because I'm tired from travelling. I also make my excuses and head upstairs to my room. It's probably the amount of beer I've drunk over the last three days or more likely jet lag I think I'm suffering from; it's been a long three days and to be quite honest, I'm stuffed.

An hour later, I'm woken by the faint rustling sound of someone entering my room. I'm instantly wide awake as old habits die extremely hard. I hadn't drawn the curtains and, in the moonlight, I see to my surprise the intruder is Alicia.

'Do you mind if I join you, Peter? I don't normally do this sort of thing with our guests, but I enjoyed this afternoon immensely, just talking to you and being in your company. Are all Australians like you? I hope you don't mind me doing this, but I don't want to waste this wonderful day we've had and have it end prematurely.'

I move over in the bed allowing her to slide in next to me. I can only see the outline of her body covered in a long, white, floral nightie. I feel her as she moves in, pulling the covers right up to her chin as if she's hiding something before turning slowly towards me.

'I'm afraid I couldn't stop thinking about you all afternoon,' I tell her as I take her in my arms and lightly kiss her on the lips. 'Do you realise, Alicia, you're the most beautiful person I've ever met?'

'Strange isn't it, but that's the way I feel in your company as well. I feel there is something beautiful and quite different about you that I can't place; it's there but I don't know what it is.'

We hold each other tightly, tenderly kissing each other, our noses touching as we look at the other in the soft light, almost afraid to move. Then she gently pulls away. Momentarily I'm disappointed, but then she sits up and slowly takes off her nightgown. I feel her nakedness slowly move against mine for the first time and the feeling almost overpowers me, as if there's something spiritual about her. Her hand moves over me, tracing delicious curves over my skin as she gently strokes me, tenderly touching me in a way I've never been touched before by anyone. I cup one of her large firm breasts and gently roll her nipple in my mouth, tantalising her a little before I reach down and caress the softness of her womanhood, gently arousing her until everything is hard and open and we can't stand this tantalisation any longer. We roll together as one and tenderly love.

We lie there, inseparable, quite exhausted, holding on to

each other and not wanting to let go, both afraid if we do move the other may disappear. Perhaps we'd wake to find this was only a beautiful dream and a wonderful figment of our wild imaginations. We continue to lie in bed holding each other, unsure of the situation, hoping this moment will go on forever.

I feel her leave me in the early dawn, quietly slipping out of my bed, pulling the long night gown over her head before she turns towards me.

'Thank you for being so gentle; it was such a beautiful night,' she says softly, bending over and lightly kissing me on the lips before quietly moving out the door and disappearing.

I rise when the sun comes peeping through the window and quickly dress before moving downstairs to the kitchen where I can hear the soft banging of a frypan against the stove.

'Good morning, Silvo.' I feel like giving her a giant hug but find she's prancing around the kitchen like a real pro, getting enough breakfast ready for a battalion.

'I wasn't expecting you for at least another half an hour, young man,' she says, looking up at my clothes, clearly surprised to see me up so early and dressed in shorts and singlet. 'You'll be full of that jet lag from your plane trip and useful to no one if you go out like that. You'll have to catch up on your sleep or you'll fade away to nothing and I don't want to send you home looking as tired as you do. Heavens, I'd never live it down if people saw you like that.'

'Most mornings I go for a bit of a run before breakfast so I can keep my fitness up to par, Silvo. After that, I'll be back to eat all the eggs and bacon you can cook.' I still feel like giving her a big hug, so I catch hold of her and give her one, much to her surprise. I quickly head out the door and down the street and away from the astonished woman before she can say anything. I'm away three-quarters of an hour before I'm back from sweating out the beer of the last three nights and feel the residues of this running down my back and chest, wetting my singlet as if I've been caught in some spring rain.

Andrew is sitting at the table and Silvo is just putting his eggs into the pan. I race upstairs and catch Alicia heading for the shower. I grab her firm young body, giving her a whirl around before planting a big kiss on her lips.

'Stop that, you'll wake everyone,' she whispers to me before returning the kiss. 'You've got to be quiet, or you'll wake Abraham and Ophelia. I think they've had a long night. Unfortunately, I've got to get to classes today otherwise you'd be in trouble, Mister. Some of us have to study, you know.'

I follow her into the bathroom and watch as the most beautiful creature I've ever seen takes a shower. It's too much for me. I can't help myself and quickly get out of my shorts and singlet and join her.

'Come here, don't be shy, let me wash your back because you can't reach there,' I say, grabbing her slight figure and pulling her towards me. I then soap my hands and gently roll this over one of her breasts before taking the nipple in my mouth, kissing it until it's very hard and standing erect.

'You'd better get out now before someone comes,' she whispers, holding me by my very erect member and stroking me forcefully. 'This is just to keep you interested in me until tonight, Mr Jackson, until I finish my classes. Now get out so I can finish my shower and get ready.'

With her help, I wash the soap off then reluctantly step out of the shower and leave her under the water. I quickly dry off and change, spruce myself up and return just as Alicia steps out of the shower. So, I grab a towel and help dry her off.

'I'll see you at breakfast,' I whisper, kissing her once again before heading down to the kitchen.

'I normally drop Alicia off at the university on the way to work,' says Andrew, munching through his eggs as I enter the room. 'But for some reason she's a little late this morning. I'll have to have a word with that girl because her classes are full-on you know and she has to be right on the ball with everything she does, otherwise if she's not careful, she'll find she's falling behind the others and, from what I've been told once that happens, it's very hard for a student to catch up again.'

'Can I give you a hand this morning, Andrew? I'd like to see what you do. I think Abe will be a little late this morning after last night. It's his first day home on leave for a while and I expect it'll take him a few days to make that adjustment of being able to sleep in of a morning.'

'Why thank you, Pete; that's very kind of you, I'd like that,' he says, looking up at me and a little surprised but then he sees his daughter as she gracefully comes into the kitchen. 'Ah, here she is now! I was starting to get a little worried about you. Come on girly; hurry up or you're gonna be late for your class and that just won't do; you can't afford to miss anything or you'll drop behind the others and from what I hear it's hard to catch up once that happens.'

'Come on, Dad; everything will be fine,' she says, sitting down as Silvo pushes a plate in front of her. 'You know we have a spare period first thing this morning that's set aside to do study. So, don't worry — I can assure you it won't be wasted.' Alicia risks a quick smile at me.

With breakfast over, we drive quickly through the streets in the heavy dump truck and eventually reach the university campus. Andrew pulls over a little before the entrance, as if not wanting anyone to see her coming to class this way, leaving her a short walk to reach the main campus buildings. I jump down and help Alicia out. She literary falls into my arms just out of sight of her dad, giving me a quick peck on the lips.

'I'll see you tonight, handsome,' she whispers, before spinning around and looking up into the truck's cab and yelling out, 'Bye, Dad. Have a good day. I'll catch you both tonight for dinner.' She turns quickly and walks towards the university buildings, her hips swinging in her brisk confident walk, seemingly without a care in the world.

The job entails lifting bins and dumping them in the back of the truck while it slowly travels up the road from house to house. It would have been a long, hard day if you had to stop the truck each time you wanted to put rubbish in as Andrew had been doing. It is no harder than picking up bales of hay at home, a job I had to do most summers, but this is much more interesting, for the variety of stuff we find in the bins is staggering. It instantly makes me think of the fun we had as kids at the local tip just east of the farm – the things my brother and I found going through the throw-a-ways that regularly used to accumulate.

I think we find a bit of everything – a part of a lounge suite, children's toys – and now I fully understand why Silvo was very sensitive to the comments Andrew made in the car on the way home, and why he made them.

The truck is finally loaded, and we head for the rubbish tip, which turns out to be another experience, with Andrew backing in and tipping the refuse out. We both carefully go through everything and pick out what he wants to sell later. The floor of the truck is covered with interesting items we've retrieved from our load.

'I have a big shed not far from here,' he tells me with a confident grin while not giving much of his operation away. 'I park the trucks there; do any mechanics that needs to be done and sort things out. I give some things a bit of a clean-up, so they look better when I on-sell them to the dealer man who comes 'round once a month. The other drivers I hire drop things back to my shed for me, and I give them a percentage for bringing them back. We'll have another load this afternoon and that's it for the day.' He gives me some credit for the speed of this first load we've picked up. Andrew then emits a gut-wrenching laugh and looks at me shaking his head, a little surprised at what we've achieved. 'You know for a white boy you did a damn good job with those cans, rushing around and throwing them on the truck the way you did. It made me laugh this morning though as I watched you in the rear-view mirror; a white dude throwing up all that rubbish to a black man who's just sittin' on his ass in the cab just driving the truck to the next pickup point. Hell, boy! My friends won't believe a word I say when I tell 'em what you just did for me today.'

'You have to realise, Andrew, that all the blokes that do this job at home are white people,' I tell him much to his surprise. 'It's good training for me, though. After a while, with you driving, I'll be as fit as a bally bull and twice as dangerous.'

He bursts into another laugh that almost breaks his sides at the strange comments I make. The truck pulls up outside his home and we go in for our lunch. Abe has just managed to get himself up; he's fairly shaky from the drinks he had last night but there is no sign of Ophelia. I expect she had work to do. It's a quick feed. However, Abe doesn't have much to eat and prefers to stay at home and, using his own words, 'I gotta recuperate before another session tonight, 'cause I only have a month here. I'll be ready to go when you get back this afternoon. So don't be too late, I don't want to have to come out on the street looking for you.'

I change into boots, shorts and singlet, much to Andrew's surprise. After lunch, it's back to the truck to do the last load of the day, a load that goes quickly with not too many articles for the shed. Loading is good exercise for me – running out, grabbing the bin, throwing the contents into the back, then on to the next one while the truck slowly moves down the street.

'You know, we've saved over three hours today with you doin' the trash an' me just drivin' slowly up the street. I owe you a couple of beers for all your effort today so we'll go over to a bar, and you can meet two of my good friends.'

'That'll be good, Andrew, but make sure the froth is on the top so it's easy to drink.'

After a couple of beers with him and some of his old cronies, I borrow Andrew's car and go to the university to pick up Alicia.

Pondering over finding such a wonderful person, I wait for some twenty minutes before she finally appears with a few friends. She seems quite surprised to see her father's car waiting for her and not the dump truck but, on seeing me sitting behind the wheel, she comes over very quickly. Her friends inquisitively tag along just behind her, curious to see who is driving her dad's car and who is taking their friend out. I wonder if Alicia said something to them about me staying with her parents.

'We finished collecting the rubbish much earlier than normal,' I tell her, getting out of the car and coming around to meet her. 'I thought I'd surprise you and come and give you a lift home.'

'Why thank you, gallant sir,' she says, giving a little curtsy, but suddenly realises that her two friends are just standing behind her and are eager to know who I am. 'This is Peter Jackson, an army friend of Abe's who's staying with us for a while. Pete, these are two good friends of mine – Wendy and Felicity.'

'How do you do? My word, you have a lovely spot here at

this campus. I've been really privileged at having Alicia acting as my guide yesterday and showing me around this beautiful city of yours.'

Maybe it's my accent or what I said, but the girls' mouths are open and for a while there's no sound, so I shake the first one's hand.

'Very nice to meet you.' Her voice is followed by a fit of giggling as they realise I'm not American.

'We've got to go now, girls. Bye,' says Alicia, gripping me by the arm and grinning as she steers me back towards the car, almost pulling me away from her friends as if protecting me. 'I'll see you both tomorrow about those papers I was given, so don't be late.'

Not being used to the left-hand drive vehicle, I drive back to her home very slowly and carefully but more so as not to miss one moment with her. I look across at her smiling face and find it's lit up with excitement as if she's studying me, making me think it's me that's giving her this excited look.

'Did you see the looks on their faces as soon as you opened your mouth? They didn't know what to do. When they first saw you, they must have thought I was going out with a white boy from around here, then *bang*! You opened your mouth and asked how they were and *bang* you destroyed them again.

'Oh, Peter, I love you so much and I've only just met you. I really, really love you. I've never had a feeling like this before about anyone; you're just so different to anyone I've ever met, black or white.'

'I love you too, Alicia. Each time I look at you I see this beautiful young woman standing there and have to pinch myself just wondering how the hell it's *me* who you're interested in. It was just sheer chance I ran into your brother in the jungles of

Vietnam and made friends with him and that brief incident has led to our meeting.'

We stop the car a couple of blocks from their house and Alicia slides over the seat towards me. We look at each other for a brief moment, drinking each other in as if there's no one else in the world. We kiss gently, then pausing, we look into each other's eyes and let the world go by. We hold each other tightly, not wanting to lose even a second. Without words we both feel the stab of our parting, both knowing that in a few weeks I'll be leaving, moving back to my uncertain world in the military. I desperately don't want to move, wishing we could stay here together. After a while of holding each other tightly, we kiss then I start the car and drive the last two agonising blocks to her home.

Abe has fully recovered from last night and wants to have another night out with Ophelia.

'Don't worry about us; you go out with her by yourself tonight, Abe. Alicia can't come because of her studies and you two need a little time to be by yourselves. You must have a heap of things you wish to talk to her about. We'll be here watching TV with your folks after we've finished Alicia's homework.' Abe shoots me a funny look and I fumble when I explain. 'Ah, I'm going to try and help if I can.'

'You sure you won't come? Hell man, you won't be in the way if you do, you should know that. You won't be playing gooseberry or anything stupid like that you know. We'll only be going out for a few drinks and a chat.'

He finally takes off, leaving Alicia and me around the kitchen table delving into her homework. I try but it's far too sophisticated for me to understand. I may have done four months at the Royal Perth Hospital's casualty ward doing sutures, but this is something else much more detailed, so I eat humble pie and reluctantly retire to the lounge to watch the soapies with Andrew and Silvo.

'I tried to help her as well when she first started her course at college,' says Andrew without his eyes leaving the television screen. 'It's far too complicated for me. I think I had her confused with some of the big words I used so I just had to leave her alone and let her do her own thing and work it all out herself.'

With their soapies over, Andrew and Silvo finally say their goodnights and head for bed, leaving me in charge of the TV. I whip the dial around and find something I don't mind – a good Western where the goodies are all nice clean-cut people and take no nonsense from the baddies who always look as evil as they are supposed to be with a week's growth of beard on their faces. *Oh, if only life was really as uncomplicated as they make these movies!* I think as the movie continues. It's close to ten-thirty before finally a very tired Alicia comes into the lounge room and pushes herself down onto the couch next to me and snuggles under my arm, looking up at me with her beautiful big brown eyes. I melt.

'I've had my work up to *here* but not my wonderful Australian man,' she says, lifting her hand to show how much. Looking up at me, she kisses me gently, gets up and turns the TV off, then takes me by the hand leading me slowly upstairs.

We make love gently and going to sleep in each other's arms is the last thing I remember.

Morning comes slowly through the window, waking us up. We look at each other long and hard then quietly make love once again before finally I watch as Alicia slips out of bed and makes her way to her room and the shower. To me, another beautiful day has arrived, making me even look forward to the dump truck.

I'm at the breakfast table when Alicia comes down ready for her studies. She looks the ideal student, dressed very smartly but with a cheeky smile on her lips, ready for anything, anytime. I can't wait for the weekend when she'll be home for two days. I just hope they don't load her up with too much homework because I intend to spend as much time as I can with her over the next two days …

My time with the family goes far too quickly. I have the weekends with Alicia and at night we catch up with Abe and Ophelia at some restaurant or nightclub and late each night we have each other.

With a week to go, Abe and I go bush to do some deer and pig hunting in the hills. We're doing it rough, not showering and sleeping in our clothes like we do in the military. After all, it's only two days and both of us have spent much longer periods of time in the scrub in much worse conditions than this. At night we lie back in our sleeping bags just looking up at the stars shining brightly high above us and talking of the future.

'I'll be back in 'Nam in probably a year and a half,' Abe tells me one night as we gaze at the heavens after a successful day looking for the elusive stag. 'All indications are that this time I'll be sent into the mountains somewhere either in the One or the Two Corps areas.' He pauses again, thinking deeply about his future. 'You know, Pete, I might just get out of the army when my time is up and marry my Ophelia. She's a terrific girl really. Talks a bit too much but a really nice girl.'

'Oh, and what will you do when you get out, Abe?' I say, looking across at him as he looks up staring at the stars in the night sky. 'Will you go back to school and study something because I hear they have a good re-education system here for young veterans when you leave the services?'

'Well, I might just go into politics,' he says, surprising me. 'There is a lot to do as far as civil rights are concerned for my people and it's gaining momentum quickly. Our people have had enough of playing second fiddle in this country. Things have got to change in the United States so there is equality for all people no matter what colour, class or creed they may be. It's so wrong at the moment, particularly here in some of the southern states.'

'Are you looking forward to another tour?' I ask, looking across at my friend and trying to suss this out. 'I could be back in Vietnam in just over twelve months myself, but it will be as we do – as one unit.' Then I explain the way our military do our replacements. 'We change units as a whole, battalion for battalion, squadron for squadron. It's quite different to what you blokes do – just changing personnel and leaving the unit there intact.'

We chat for quite some time about our coming commitments over the next couple of years when he suddenly turns and asks me about Alicia. 'What are you going to do about my sister now that you're going back to Australia? She's hooked on you; you know that don't you?'

'I intend to marry her if she'll have me after my next tour is over. I told everyone I was going for a run the other day, but really I had visited a local jewellery store and bought a ring I think she'll like. It was all I could think about. Would you like to see it and give me your opinion if it's suitable? I brought it with me.' I roll over and fossick in my pack and bring out the small box. 'I brought it with me, I was going to show this to you and seek your approval first.' I pass the small box over to him and he flicks it open. 'Would I have your permission to ask Alicia to marry me?'

'Come on man, you don't need my permission,' he says, looking at the ring before giving it back, a little surprised at my asking. 'I'm just so happy for you both and I hope she accepts you, Pete; at least you know what you're going to do. Goddamn it man, you're putting pressure on me now, I hope you realise that! What will Ophelia's reaction be when she finds out about you proposing to Alicia? Hell man, I'll *have* to ask her now!'

'Ours will be an extremely quiet relationship until my service is finished with our army,' I tell him, hoping to relax his raw nerves that have come to the fore. 'I wouldn't want to leave her as a widow because who knows what can happen in Vietnam. Everything over there is so unpredictable once you get into the scrub.'

We chat on a little more until finally we're overtaken with sleep. It's been a long but extremely successful day, and tomorrow we'll both be back with our catch to hopefully impress our girls.

Each Saturday night we've taken the girls out to a restaurant and then to some show, coming back home in the wee hours of the morning with our girls under our arms. It's quite obvious to both Andrew and Silvo that Alicia and I are together. I don't know if they approve, but fortunately for me, they say nothing and are very kind, making no comment about our blossoming relationship. Alicia has moved in with me and has stopped the charade of the other bedroom across the hall. I don't think we were fooling anyone anyway. I try to help her with her homework as much as possible, although I keep asking myself – who is teaching who? With what I've learned in these homework sessions, I'll probably be the most qualified patrol medic that our army has, I reckon. I quickly find out that it's a long way from being a patrol medic to being a doctor. It becomes a routine, as does Andrew and I doing the daily rubbish run and having a beer after with his friends, before I pick Alicia up from college or the hospital. I see Alicia's two friends daily and find they're nice people and have gotten over my accent. They chat about Australia at every opportunity and even talk about Tasmanian devils after one of the girls saw a fierce-looking animal in a *Looney Tunes* show. The show portrays a Tasmanian devil but this thing they've concocted doesn't resemble the real animal at all.

It's my last night in America with Alicia; we're snuggled up after having spent the night out at a club. We'd gone with Abe, who is a member, and we'd danced close together most of the night. Sometimes we'd let Abe and Ophelia do their thing and we'd watch from the table, happy to be by ourselves, sitting there holding hands, not speaking much. Simply being together is the most important thing of our romance. Unfortunately, we know that by this time tomorrow I'll be gone. We wonder how our love will cope with the huge distance between us, as we'll be half a world away. Later on, in bed, we're doing the same again – lying there together thinking about us and the future and how we will cope with being so far apart. We're both wide awake, holding onto the other tightly. It's me who breaks the silence.

'In two days, I'll be back in Western Australia, half a world away from you and a year off going to Vietnam once again. I'll ring you when I get there and I'll write and … oh that reminds me, I bought something for you the other day, so you won't forget me.' I reach under my pillow, pull out the small box and pass it to her. She's quite surprised by this, and lifting herself up and resting on an elbow, she opens it and finds the ring with a diamond and two black sapphires on either side.

'Alicia, will you marry me?'

She carefully fits the ring on her finger with tears welling in her eyes. She looks at me with those great big brown eyes of hers and grabs me with both arms, pulling me to her, kissing me so hard on the lips.

'Yes, Peter. Yes, I will, but I have nothing for you, nothing,' she sobs. 'I should be buying something for you, so you never forget me.'

'You don't have to buy anything, you have yourself,' I tell her, not ever wanting to let her go. 'Just promise me one thing please – study hard and pass your exams, become a doctor and make your parents and me proud of you.'

She says nothing and folds up into my arms, holding me tightly, and after a while we both fall asleep.

After breakfast I say my goodbyes to Andrew and Silvo. They are emotional as well, Silvo almost suffocating me with her hug.

'Now you come back as soon as you can, do ya hear?' She gives me another enormous hug. 'We want you around this place, do ya understand? We want ya here with us and not over there in Vietnam with people shooting at you.'

Abe and Alicia drive me to the airport. Alicia and I hold each other very tightly, not wanting to leave.

'I'll write every day,' she says, bursting into tears once again. I kiss her long and hard, not wanting to go; it's a horrible tearful farewell.

'Look after her for me please, Abe, she means a lot to me.' I turn and give Abe a hug and then finally board the plane for home.

CHAPTER 3

REGROUPING

Perth

Leave is well and truly over, and I find time moves on so fast when you're young and enthusiastic, especially if you're like me and enjoy what you're doing. We're in the process of squadron rebuilding, so everything, including Alicia, has to take second place behind our training. Many of the old hands I did the first tour with have left, either going to a more placid unit with a substantial lift in rank, or out of the army completely to try their hand on civvy street, one tour of Vietnam being enough for them. We're totally reliant on our cadre courses to forward these replacements to get the squadron back up to full strength for our next tour of duty. These gruelling courses are run every few months to test the young soldiers over a ten-week period to assess their suitability for our type of unit. The aspiring soldiers mostly come from the battalions but, after this gruelling course concludes, only around thirty percent of these men meet the stringent requirements to make the grade as SAS soldiers. So, with these new people in our ranks and the possibility of other soldiers who'll hopefully cross from the Two Squadron when they return, our squadron will be almost full.

I've been promoted to a full corporal and I'm now Johnno's patrol 2IC, while Clicker has gained his first hook but remains as our scout. Our main aim is to get a coherent patrol functioning as a single unit, and this can only be done by hard work and many long hours in the scrub learning how each of the new members works and passing on important skills we've acquired from our first tour. This will enable us to see what these new people are made of and what skills, such as signals and the basics of a med aid course, they'll be required to learn during this hectic time of squadron rebuilding. We place these new soldiers out in different patrol positions, initially trying to determine if they are compatible with the type of work we'll be doing when our next deployment to Vietnam occurs. They can then slot into one of the vacant positions within the patrol. The majority of these new recruits are good, energetic young men, but they still need to learn the basic skills required to work as a team in a small, isolated patrol. They need to get used to working in a four- to five-man patrol, which is quite different to how a section of a battalion's company works. We've been back doing this exhausting training for some three months now, when to my surprise I'm called into squadron headquarters by the new officer in charge of our unit.

'Well done, Corporal! It gives me great pleasure to tell you that you have been awarded the Military Medal for your services in Vietnam when covering your patrol's extraction and for using your initiative in getting back to your unit when you were separated from your patrol on that Landing Zone. They're also very pleased with the way you handled yourself in the contacts you initiated with the Viet Cong you came across. You'll be pleased to know that Two Squadron has set some very successful ambushes on that road, disrupting an important resupply line the Viet Cong had in that area. This award is also for saving that American sergeant in October last year. We'll be presenting this award to you in a special parade to mark the occasion. Again, well done, Corporal. The unit is proud of your achievements and the commitment you have to the men of your unit.'

'Thank you, Sir, I'm quite surprised,' I tell him, my mind on reforming the squadron and our own patrol. 'I'd forgotten the incident entirely after my trip to the US. It seems such a long time ago now. We've moved on quite some way getting the squadron refitted and active for the next tour of Vietnam.'

The officer in charge is new to the squadron – a very experienced officer who has spent time in the training team in One Corps with the hill tribesmen called Montagnards, who evidently hate the Vietnamese with a vengeance. He's like all our officers – new to the ways of the unit, so he's got a lot of learning to do before we deploy. He's also got a lot to learn about us, so it's good to get to know this man better; after all, we'll be in his hands totally on our next tour. We make small talk for quite some time, as he learns as much as he can about the key people in the squadron who he'll be working with. My mind has been too full of Alicia and my patrol. One seems to take over from the other, leaving very little room for me to think of anything else. Boy! I can't wait to see her again – to hold her and look into those lovely big brown eyes. I find it quite hard waiting to get back there to her again, even if it's only for a short time.

The squadron is formed up into three ranks on the parade ground while I wait for my call. Our troop sergeant marches me forward to the officer in charge some twenty metres to the front of the ranks where I salute him.

'Corporal, for services far above the call of duty, it gives me great pleasure to award you with this medal for valour. Wear it with pride.' He pins the medal on next to the others, steps back and we salute each other again. The medal fills me with more pride than the Silver Star I received from the Yanks a few months before. I about turn quickly and move back to the ranks with a feeling of pride running through me at being recognised by my own country for doing my job well.

It's winter so I'm expected to wear the appropriate clothes. Our new winter uniforms make us all look like officers and make me wish I'd had something as modern as this when I was presented with my medal in the US instead of the old battle dress that was a leftover from WWII and was quite old-fashioned. Unfortunately, we're the only squadron at home, with Two Squadron still on leave and Three operational in Vietnam, so there are fewer people about to do the duties around camp. We're plagued with these additional duties between training courses. Time refitting the unit moves quickly with duties, courses and training in the bush. I put my name down for most courses available and I'm lucky a number of them come my way over this training period. A shallow water diving course and then a demolition of blinds course, both run locally in the west and, towards the new year, a Vietnamese language course, which is run in South Australia. I gain a lot when I remember how easy it was for Abe to listen to what was said after he was released, and having listened, quite fascinated, while he translated their conversations to me as we lay low, watching them crawl over the ox cart. I was fascinated at how easily he was able to talk to them at the roadside. This gives me much more incentive to learn this skill and I just hope I'm able to learn this intriguing language as well as he'd done, for this will add another extremely important arrow to my quiver on the coming deployment.

It's been almost a year now since I saw Alicia last, with me sending at least two to three letters a week and receiving just as many back. I lie on my bed reading, running over every word she writes, thinking of her, visualising her happy face, almost hearing her voice as I go through her letters time and time again and drooling over whatever she writes.

Towards the end of the year, the squadron spends two months in the rugged hills of New Guinea doing acclimatisation and our final jungle training in these hot, harsh conditions. Unfortunately, this hard training on these steep slopes sorts out many of the new recruits, including some new officers, and their suitability is found wanting. Some techniques are things that patrols are expected to do instinctively, things that could save or cost lives in the thick jungles of Vietnam. Our lives depend on doing the right thing and learning to live in this harsh, unforgiving environment and we are continually assessed. It establishes the order in which members of the patrols will work and in many cases the conditions we'll be in. We spend most of these two months in the scrub getting to know how the other soldiers in the patrol operate and helping each other climb the large, rugged features. It's hard work carrying these heavy packs but it's good for us, getting us extremely fit for the coming tour, so by the end of our training, everyone in our patrol knows exactly what to expect from the other.

When this vigorous jungle work is over, we find ourselves back in Perth where I'm pleased to take my annual leave.

I have two weeks at home for Christmas. Mum and Dad have accepted that I have other interests and the army is now my life, but they still worry about me going back to Vietnam as the media keep showing graphic pictures almost every night on television. They are curious at me going to the United States again for I've told them nothing about my relationship with Alicia. I want to bring her home after my tour and surprise them when it's over, and boy, what a surprise that'll be!

The annual harvest is in full swing, so I help my married brother cart in the hay to the barn as he's running the farm now. I'm pleased that my father has eased into almost semi-retirement but he still keeps a finger on the pulse. My brother is pleased to see me for we're quite close and I get into the habit of having quite a few beers of an evening after the hay and milking; but I still keep Alicia quietly to myself, leaving him to be surprised along with my parents.

I can't wait to get back to the United States and see my Alicia. She's well into her final year of training. I can't believe that in less than twelve months she'll be a doctor. I think about this a lot on the way over. She'll be a doctor and I'm a what? What have I got to offer her now except myself?

The United States

The plane has finally landed and there is my wonderful girl waiting at the terminal for me; she's as beautiful as ever. We rush together and hold each other tightly for a long period of time, soaking each other up. God, I've missed her. I hold her, hoping that time will stand still and I'll be with her forever.

'I wear this all the time now. It doesn't come off at all,' she says, putting her hand up so that I can see the ring I'd given her. 'I put it on the day you left. Ma and Pa were a little surprised and initially quite upset when I showed them – not because of who you are but mostly because you're white. But as I told them, you aren't an American, you're Australian, and fortunately that made them feel a little better.' She snuggles into me, looking up with a worried expression on her face. 'Abe is in Vietnam again, somewhere up north in One Corps training in the hills with people he calls Montagnards.' I can tell she worries about him being in a war zone with strange people she doesn't know. 'He's trying to turn them into soldiers because they will need to be able to cope with what he says is a large North Vietnamese appearance and, from what he's heard, they seem to be all over the country now putting pressure on our forces everywhere.'

'I know, he wrote to me just before I left Perth.' I try to settle her down a little. 'He's doing a great job training those people with not a lot of support. You can be proud of Abe, sweetheart.'

'Training to be a doctor is hard now,' she tells me, trying to steer the conversation off the war and onto her work. 'I'm working in the hospitals at nights at the moment. Unfortunately, I start at six in the evening and don't finish until six in the morning. It's a long shift.' Next, she gives me a sad little laugh as if trying to emphasise the stupidity involved. 'It's quite frantic when the bars and drive-ins close and people are either drunk or drive home too quickly; I just wish they'd slow down or let someone who is sober drive the car. If they did that, I'm sure there wouldn't be these terrible car accidents we seem to be getting at the moment.' She suddenly steps back and looks at me, a troubled look on her face. 'Darling, unfortunately I'll only see you for a bit through the day for most of your time here, but just think of it, in less than a year I'll be a doctor and then I'll be coming over to Australia to meet your family; so, you'd better get back from Vietnam in one piece so I can look after you.'

'I'll keep out of trouble, I promise,' I say, holding her tightly for I'd found that it's the best way to get around where I'll be going. 'From all accounts things have quietened down in Phuoc Tuy Province and much more emphasis is now being placed on reconnaissance – more than ever before.'

Andrew and Silvo are waiting at home to meet us. They're lovely; they haven't changed at all, and I'm welcomed into their family as though I'm one of them. Nothing else has changed as Silvo is still bashing around the kitchen and Andrew is flat out collecting his rubbish.

'I took a leaf outa' your book,' he tells me with a lot of pride in his voice. 'I've got an assistant now. Thanks to you, I've got this young fit fella, who runs alongside the truck and assists me with the pick-ups like you did last year.' I laugh as Andrew tells me about the new assistant he's put on, visualising him frantically running alongside the truck as I'd done. 'Yes, he runs alongside the truck and grabs the bins and throws all the trash in.' He pauses for a few seconds before continuing proudly, 'I've also replaced my old truck and bought an extra one that brings my fleet up to four. I now do three runs a day instead of the two like we were doin' last year. We move just about all the trash for the city now.' He puts his hand over his mouth and speaks softly so Silvo can't hear him. 'And boy; do we find some good stuff in the trash now, stuff that, once it's been cleaned, I quietly slip into the house when the good woman is otherwise occupied.'

The civil rights movement has gained a lot of support in the last twelve months from both black and white factions, and it appears to be coming to a head. After the 1968 death of a black minister of religion, Martin Luther King Jr, the push for equal rights escalated with many public figures now calling for equality for both black and white Americans. In the southern states like Alabama there's been a large backlash about this from the establishment. People of both colours are very careful what they say and do and especially to whom they speak. I get the feeling that it's like sitting on a powder keg that's getting ready to blow.

I collect Alicia at six each morning when she finishes at the hospital and bring her home so we can have breakfast together. She's normally worn out so I get her to bed as quickly as I possibly can to have a good sleep; unfortunately, it's without me.

I go on the truck with Andrew doing his runs, collecting the trash. He's happy having his men do the extra run and gets three done easily in the day. I don't notice the dark skins of my working companions and they appear after a while to treat me as just another worker and not as a white man who is honing in on their job. Each evening I still have my few beers with Andrew and his old mates after the second run is finished in the afternoon, but then I quickly skip home and spend as much quality time as I can with Alicia before I have to take her to the hospital at six.

I've been following this routine now for just over a week and have just about finished my beer this day; it's almost time to go and wake Alicia up and spend some time with her before taking her to the hospital, when four young white men come in. They stand by the bar watching us for a while before two of them arrogantly walk over to where I'm sitting with Andrew and his friends.

'Hey, you white boy. What you think you're doin' sittin' with them Niggers?' one says with cold, hard eyes staring directly at me. 'Don't you know you should be drinkin' with your own kind and not with this old black trash?'

I continue my conversation with Andrew and his mates, ignoring them, hoping that by this action they will leave us alone.

'Hey, I'm fuckin' talking to you, snowdrop! What you think you're doin' here boy, drinkin' with these old Niggers?' Then, with a laugh he continues, 'You tryin' to turn black or somethin'?'

I turn and look the young punk up and down. He's an arsehole, the type of person I don't like mixing with at the best of times.

'I'll drink with whom I like, arsehole, now piss off.'

Even though he's had a fair amount to drink himself, he notices my accent, and this spurs him on. I think he sees me now as a foreign white person mixing with Negroes and helping the black man become his equal.

'This motherfucker is a Limey, a Nigger-lovin' fuckin' Limey,' says the second one to his mates, putting on a false laugh, annoying me more. Unfortunately, by the sound of this idiot, they've had more than their share of booze.

I stand, quickly turning towards them just in time to see the first one pulling a large hunting knife from his belt. 'I'd put that away if I was you and go back to your friends before you get hurt.'

He's on a bit of a roll, so ignores me. 'I'm gunna cut you inta real little pieces and feed y'all a piece at a time to these coons you was drinkin' with, snowflake,' he says, and makes a drunken move towards me with the knife. 'See how you like a piece of good steel like this being shoved right up into your guts, you asshole.'

I don't wait for more and move in quickly, grabbing his arm as it comes towards me, pushing the knife up, then with all my might, I knee him in the balls. He gasps in surprised agony and goes down like a sack of potatoes, hitting the floor, gasping in pain. He groans before pulling his knees up into his chest and thankfully doesn't move after that. Shock shows all over the other bloke's face at seeing his mate go down so easily. Unfortunately, however, this is only temporary, and I watch as he turns, sneering nastily at me before rushing in with his arms flailing like some ancient harvesting machine.

'You fuckin' *asshole*, I'm gunna *kill* you for what ya'll just done to Jethro!' He rushes in at me, screaming.

I step aside, coolly anticipating his moves. Just as he gets to me, I duck under the haymaker, put my foot out and trip him as he passes. I bash both hands straight down on the back of his neck. He hits the floor close to his friend and also doesn't move. The two at the bar back off a little; then the bigger of the two slowly draws a large pistol from under his coat and starts to aim it at me. I see the knife that's lying on the floor where his friend had dropped it and dive sideways and grab it just as the revolver explodes. I roll across the floor with the blade firmly in my hand, sensing the gun is swinging around, following each of my movements. I quickly stand up and with all my might I let the knife go just as the gun explodes again. I watch as this large weapon flies towards the thug and instantly feel a sharp thump on my side followed by a severe burning sensation as the bullet passes just under my arm, tearing through the muscle. In pain, I look over towards the thug and thankfully see my aim has been good and the knife has struck him deep in the shoulder of his gun hand. He screams out pitifully, dropping the gun on the bar, staggering backwards against some of the other drinkers who'd been too slow to get out of his way. He staggers into them, crying out, desperately grabbing at the knife in a frantic effort to pull it out. In a quick hand movement, the weapon is instantly taken by the trigger guard by one of the bar staff who pulls the weapon out of range.

The other roughneck steps back. Initially, from the look on his face, he thinks of doing a runner, but then he looks around and sees they haven't got a lot of sympathy in this bar. The gutless prick gives a strange smile and slowly puts his hands up in a manner of submission, perhaps hoping he won't be done over in the same way as his friends. I'm just as thankful that this whole damn, unnecessary mess is over without any deaths.

'Call the police and an ambulance,' I tell the barman. 'This shooting has got to be put in the right perspective while everyone who saw what happened is here. You! Sit down over there and don't move!' I tell the other thug firmly before he has second thoughts and tries to get out, then turning to the bar staff I yell, '*Ring the police!*'

The police come quickly. I hear their sirens and the noise of the vehicles as they pull up outside the bar and hear the commotion as they come streaming into the bar with guns drawn and, by the look of them, ready for anything that may happen.

'Okay, okay, settle down. Now tell me, what went on here?' says a big policeman. The officers look around at the still-prone bodies groaning on the floor and then at the bar and the patrons who have gathered around, watching as this saga unfolds in front of them. Unfortunately, this cop does nothing to fill me with any confidence whatsoever in him enforcing the law. He has a big fat gut and can hardly move from one side of the bar to the other without losing his breath. 'Calm down y'all. Now, who caused all this goddamn ruckus that we have in here? Come on, speak up goddamn you; we need all the facts. Now who caused this fight to start?'

'I was sitting here having a beer with these gentlemen when these four came in and started the trouble,' I tell Fat Guts, who turns and looks at me, trying to sum me up. 'That one just regaining consciousness there on the floor pulled a knife, so unfortunately I had to defend myself and things from that point on began to get out of hand and seriously snowballed into what we have on the floor.'

'That's right, Officer,' confirms a thin white bloke over near the bar. 'He was sitting there drinking a beer when these four came in and two of 'em started abusing him for drinking with those Negroes.' He points down at the two men on the floor now groggily trying to get up. 'The next thing we know, that one over there pulls a knife and goes for him. Boy I've never seen a guy drop another one so quickly. Then the other one came in and he put him down just as quick; neither of these guys knew what hit 'em.'

'What about young Jones? Yes, you over there,' says the fat cop, obviously in charge. 'How did you get that there knife stuck in your shoulder, boy?'

'He pulled this gun,' says the white barman before the youth can answer, and everyone turns as he speaks, and watches, almost captivated, as he pulls up the revolver carefully by the barrel. 'He had two shots at the young guy but must have missed with both. The young guy just dived across there, picked up the knife that the first guy dropped when he went at him and just pelted it at this Jones guy – you can see what happened – hitting him right in the shoulder, and then, Officer, that finished the fight.' He points at the fourth man with a sound of contempt in his voice. 'This other guy there didn't have the guts to do anything.' He laughs at the circumstances that have arisen so quickly in the room. 'Then again I don't suppose I'd do anything either after seeing him throw that goddamn big knife.'

The police, who are all white, aren't what you'd call greatly sympathetic towards me or what I've done and it's quite obvious that they don't want black people as their equals in this state and the fact that I'm a foreigner doesn't help my cause at all.

'Where you from, boy?' Fat Guts says, turning towards me. The fact that I was drinking with three black men is something I can see he doesn't like either, so I feel I should be very careful.

'Australia,' I tell him, saying as little as possible. 'I'm over here on holiday having a look around your state.'

'What you doin' in here then, boy, drinkin' with them Niggers?' he says, as if I was a troublemaker. 'You shouldn't be in places like this during the day. It ain't healthy drinkin' here, particularly if you are new to town an' don't know how the rules work around here.'

'Excuse me, Officer,' says another man who has come from across the room. 'My name is Frank Calhoun; I'm a lawyer for the United States Army. This man was acting as he told you, in self-defence. I suggest that you, Sir, take some statements as to what actually happened here so it can be cleaned up quickly. We don't want it said that you were harassing people here, do we? Especially foreign tourists who by their presence are helping our economy. I will also remind you, Sheriff, if you don't already know, it was this very gentleman that was assaulted who asked for you people to be rung in the first place. You see, you would have no difficulty getting the correct facts of what happened from the people who are here in this bar who actually saw this cowardly altercation from start to finish.'

Fat Guts looks at this man as if he's some form of strange parasite that's just crawled out from under a rock but immediately backs off, muttering to himself. Thankfully, he goes about the room with the other officers getting statements from people. Fortunately, there are plenty of people, both black and white, who saw what happened and are more than willing to testify and corroborate the statements I've already made to these police officers – that is, that I'd done nothing wrong and was acting in self-defence.

Andrew is just near me and knows I've been shot, and as soon as the police leave he takes me to the hospital to have my wound seen to, and before long a very tearful Alicia bursts into the casualty ward and rushes over to me. Obviously, Andrew or one of his offsiders has somehow told her I wouldn't be coming home.

'What have you been doing?' she says, her eyes full of tears. 'I let you out of my sight and you end up getting shot!'

She stands with the doctor as he looks at the wound across my ribs. They are tender to touch but I have been very lucky, and the wound is only a superficial graze caused by the bullet tearing a little meat out. It hasn't damaged my ribs; it looks much worse than it really is.

'You can dress his wound, Alicia; it'll be good practice for you,' the other doctor tells her, smiling to himself as he notes her concern for me. 'You appear to have an interest in the young man, so you go ahead.'

'Look, Alicia, I was only having a beer with your dad like I do every day,' I tell her, trying to explain my actions. 'These four rough-heads came into the bar and started abusing me for having a beer with your father, and the fight, if you could call it that, was all over in just a few minutes.'

'I don't care, Peter, this isn't Australia. You have to be aware of people like them because they're everywhere in the south and they don't need any excuses to get into a fight,' she tells me with a patronising voice. It's the first time I've seen her mad. She is Silvo all over again but in a lovelier, younger form. 'You should have just got up and left when they started talking to you because they were drunk and stupid and didn't know what they were doing. If you had got up and left when these people first came in, this horrible thing would *never* have happened!' she hisses at me.

'But it did happen, sweetheart, and so quickly. One minute your dad and I were having a beer and the next thing I'm in a fight with knives and guns. I couldn't afford to let your father be involved in anything like this Alicia. He has to live and work here with these people and it wouldn't do him any good to be part of something as stupid as this.' I suddenly start to get annoyed with her for her obstinate stance. 'These people were after a fight no matter what and may have picked on them instead of me. Your dad and his mates could have been very easily hurt if the fight had gone that way.'

'You have a week to go,' she says, simmering down somewhat and looking down at me with those lovely big brown eyes and thankfully pulling back from her aggressive stance. 'I'm going to take a week off. They owe me some time and we can go somewhere different, somewhere we are not known. I've wanted to do it anyway so we can spend your last week in the States together – somewhere away from home where people don't care what race or colour you are.'

The next morning, we take a plane to Florida and move into a holiday apartment with a stunning view right on the coast overlooking the sea. It's wonderful, lazing about with the most beautiful woman I have ever met. It's a great place, away from anyone who knows Alicia. Down here, we have hardly a care in the world and it's as if we're on a different planet, a planet that seems to be devoid of reality, and it's amazing to see all races – Hispanic, black and white – appear to mingle freely together. At night we go out to dinner and come home to make love desperately, knowing full well that time is running out so quickly for us. The climate is wonderful, with warm nights that allow us to sleep with virtually nothing on, and hot through the day without the burning sun like we have at home. We lie naked in each other's arms lingering in the love we have for each other, sometimes looking out along the beach or just falling asleep holding each other tightly. There is no mention whatsoever of going back to Australia, or Vietnam for that matter, until the last night, but I can tell that it has been bothering Alicia, by what she *didn't* say.

'Promise you'll write as soon as you get back to Perth,' she says to me as we lie close together on this last night. 'Please don't take any unnecessary risks while you're over there. I want you back to me as soon as you can finish your time in the army. Promise me, Pete, that you'll do that for me.'

'I'll write as soon as I get to Western Australia,' I assure her. 'But I can't make any promises about Vietnam because that's out of my control, but I'll be careful, I promise you that. You don't have to worry about things in Vietnam. There are always a number of us together.'

We are too scared to make any vain promises in a situation that is changing rapidly day by day, and out of our control like some strange kaleidoscope.

The next day we hold each other very tightly while I wait for the plane. It's too soon in coming and I have to tear myself away from her to leave. 'I'll write as soon as I get back to Perth,' I promise her again. 'You'll see, sweetheart, the next twelve months will go very quickly, and I'll be back here annoying the life out of you before you realise I've even gone.' We hug each other and kiss, trying to savour those last few fleeting moments together, but I have to go. I break away from her and quickly walk out to the plane, too scared to even look back for fear of not getting on board.

Perth

I arrive back at the unit with a month to spare before the unit does its next tour of Vietnam. Most of this time is being put aside for our last chance to practise rappelling from the *Iroquois* helicopters. We've done a lot of this in the last twelve months, for in our case it will replace the need to find a Landing Zone if the Viet Cong are pushing a patrol and we have to get out fast.

At one of the training areas, which happens to be the unit football oval, the officer in charge barks, 'This could be your lifeline! You may *think* you know what you are doing but I want these skills to be second nature to all patrols because this, gentleman, will be your last chance to practise this drill before you find you're doing it for real; so, make sure you know each procedure off by heart. We can't have you looping the rope through the wrong part and dropping off your karabiner.'

Our patrol moves from the rappelling tower to the football ground where we climb on board the helicopter as if we're leaving to go on patrol, and in a few minutes the aircraft rises vertically some one hundred feet above the oval and hovers there as we look out at Swanbourne camp and east towards the city of Perth.

'Make sure your ropes are properly attached,' Johnno tells us as we start preparing for our exit. He and I, as his 2IC, check each person's ropes before we check each other's. 'We can't afford to lose any of you bums because the patrol hasn't started, and you've cost the Australian Government a fortune doing this bloody training on the chopper. Are all you blokes right now? Ropes secure? Good; drop your ropes.'

The ropes cascade down to the ground, so we hook on our karabiners that we've attached to ropes around our waist then confidently move out onto the helicopter's skids and wait for Johnno's command.

'Go!' he yells at the top of his voice.

Each member of our patrol kicks out together into nothing, exiting the helicopter and sliding down our ropes using our right arm as a brake and slowing our body down until we reach the ground.

'Well done fellas; now unhook. Good; now reattach the rope to your karabiner so we can do a fast extraction, as if Charlie's after you and breathing down your neck.' He sees the disgruntled looks on some of the patrol members' faces and a few moans erupt from us, spurring him along. 'Yes, I know – you think it's unnecessary; I know that but it's good bloody practice. You all know only too well that this is your lifeline – do it strictly as the book says so we can get out of here for that beer you all promised to buy me.'

Once we're hooked back on again, he signals the door gunner that we're ready for the extraction and we're whisked up into the air and taken away, dangling below the chopper like expensive bait on a fishing line. The helicopter does a large loop over the nearest suburbs, simulating a quick extraction with us clasping onto each other before the aircraft turns back towards the oval.

'You know,' says Clicker in his dry way as we near the oval, 'Sarge, these air force blokes could make a bloody fortune doing a spin like this at the Royal Perth Show, giving civvies a ride around like this over a few suburbs. They could drop the altitude over the river and get the bastards wet.'

'Yeah! Clicker's right, Sarge,' Jerry tells us. 'Once they see us at the ends of these ropes, they'll all want to have a go at this.'

He ignores their taunts and we're soon over the oval once more. The helicopter hovers while we detach from the ropes and then it's the next patrol's turn at their final roping drill. I feel it's a day well spent because I know full well, when we get back to Vietnam, we'll be using this type of extraction much sooner than a lot of the patrol members think.

We have one day to go, and people are madly packing their gear. It's almost a charade now, taking some stuff and leaving the remainder to go into storage at the Q-store where it will be kept until we return home from our next tour of Vietnam.

My month has gone too quickly as I post my final letter to Alicia from Australia, on the way to the airport.

CHAPTER 4

VIETNAM AGAIN

South Vietnam

The next thing we know, we're flying into Nui Dat on one of the ever-reliable old Australian Air Force *Hercules* transport planes. We're unsure of what the next twelve months will bring as the situation we're flying into is continually changing with new hotspots emerging throughout the province. I still write to Alicia every day; however, our phone calls have stopped and very soon the letters do too as we're out in the scrub.

Initially they're short excursions, getting the new hands used to the environment and not seeing a Charlie behind every bush. I'm Johnno's patrol second in command and last in the patrol formation. Tail End Charlie is my job; covering the rear is a thing we've continually practised. I still use the SLR because I'm used to the big rifle; it's reliable and if I pull the trigger, it fires. I've carried this weapon every time we've been overseas and swear by it now, for if anything is hit, it stays hit.

Three months fly past, and the patrol has been doing reconnaissance in and around Phuoc Toi and the bottom end of Long Khan Province as the taskforce has extended its area of influence further north. It's very slow, selective work, taking hours to move only a few hundred metres or so, marking every track and stream for the reference of future patrols to hone in on. On one such occasion, we find a small track. It's a well-worn one, obviously being used, so I get the finger from Johnno to come up from the back to take a look with him.

'Pete, we've got just over a day to go,' he whispers to me when I reach him. 'We've covered our area, so to me we should watch this track for the rest of the day and see if there is any movement of the VC along it. What do you reckon?'

'That's a good idea, Johnno,' I tell him, looking along the track both ways. I can see it's been used regularly. 'We've just about done our four grid squares, and this will enable us to see if there is anyone moving about in this area. It's been very tame so far this time. Who knows what may come along on our last two days.'

'I'll get Jerry to radio base and let them know our exact position and what we're proposing to do.' He appears a little unsure of what we should do in this situation, but I also note he's a little pissed off at not seeing anything of Charlie. Next, I see a big smirk appearing on his face. 'Ya know, if anything happens to the patrol, Base'll know about it, and we'll have some back-up real quick. I like to hedge my bets in situations like this, particularly if things turn ape-shit and the baddies come along in large numbers.'

The sixty-four set is opened, and his message is tapped through to headquarters, letting them know what our position is and what we're intending to do for the rest of the day. With one member of the patrol staying with Jerry and the sig set,

Clicker, Johnno and I spread out along the track a little closer together and back quite a bit further than we'd do in an actual ambush. We've positioned ourselves so we have a good view of the track and will be able to back each other up if for some reason we're seen, and the proverbial 'shit hits the fan'. The other two position themselves well to our rear, with the radio set up, so they only have to tap through a contact signal if we're spotted, which gives us all-round protection in case we're seen moving into this track and they try to come around behind us. The tall undergrowth virtually makes us invisible to anyone moving along this small thoroughfare in front. So we lay low and quietly wait, watching to see what this surveillance action will bring so we can establish who's using this track and if they are main force units that we can easily identify.

We aren't lying there very long, probably no more than thirty minutes, when there are sharp sounds of movement to our front left. Safeties are off in a flash, and we wait with bated breath to see what type of enemy we have this time. They are North Vietnamese, not in a hurry, moving along at intervals and looking from left to right as if they expect to be hit at any moment. My count is now in the eighties as I watch the pith-helmeted men pass by no more than five metres in front of me, their green uniforms blending in well with the forest. They move as if they are an integral part of the ground cover in this part of the jungle environment. The armament they're carrying surprises me – ranging from normal side-arms, the ever-reliable AK-47s to what looks like a team with the heavy tri-podded machine guns, which are split up with different members jointly carrying their components. Also, strategically among these troops are others. I reckon they're grenadiers as they're carrying RPGs over their shoulders, loaded as if expecting trouble at any time and positioned so that firing position could be immediately adopted in the worst-case scenario. One hundred and twenty-three have passed before what I believe to be the final man walks through. We wait half an hour before we pull back and Johnno has the information compiled for the radio and taps through this message, alerting the taskforce of this large number of well-armed enemy soldiers on their way, the direction they are heading and, most importantly, the type of weapons they're carrying.

'*Shit!* I'm glad it wasn't an ambush patrol,' Johnno says. 'We'd have fired the claymores, knocked over probably the first ten or so then we'd have the rest of their troops to contend with coming around the back behind us trying to cut off our escape routes.'

'I'll never forget that other patrol last trip, Pete,' Clicker says, looking at Johnno's and my dirty faces. 'I don't want to have to go through something like that again, Johnno, because you've put on some weight while you've been home, and we'd have trouble carrying ya this time.'

'Nor do I. I hope I don't have to do anything like that either because I hate being by myself in this damn jungle,' I reply with a happy smile, remembering the gun battle at the Landing Zone and later, Abe tied behind the ox cart. I also recall what these important events had led to. The smile on my face is for Alicia, for if these strange events hadn't occurred, I'd never have been invited to the United States, which resulted in the sheer good luck of meeting her.

We continue our route south-east, carefully crossing the track, moving slowly on for another hour before it's time to stop for the night. Things are more tactical than usual, with everyone on high alert after seeing so many well-armed enemy soldiers moving in this area and so darn close to us that we could have almost touched them as they moved past our position.

The final day is spent carefully moving through this thick primary jungle to the south-east of our four allotted grid squares. With the exception of one well-used track, the area seems totally unoccupied, so the helicopters are called in for a rope extraction as the nearest Landing Zone is some kilometres away and would take a day to reach. The noise of the choppers is immense as they approach our position, and the slick begins hovering just above the trees where the smoke had been thrown.

'Lower the ropes,' Johnno commands through the URC-10 as finally the chopper is in the right position high above us with the skids almost level with the treetops.

The ropes tumble down through the tree canopy and I quickly grab one, wasting no time to hook it on with my karabiner. I look across at the others to see if they are ready to be pulled out.

'Everyone right?' Johnno gets the thumbs up from each of us. '*All hooked and ready to go!*' he barks through the URC-10, and the helicopter immediately starts to lift us up through the canopy of trees.

We've just reached the top of the trees when all hell breaks loose below us. We're surrounded by lots of green tracer that can be seen ripping through the undergrowth and coming straight towards us and the choppers. I can hear the crackle of many weapons below and I wonder where the nogs have come from because we'd neither seen nor heard anything since we left the track yesterday. We're now at our most vulnerable position – clasped together, only just clearing the trees. The helicopter has just gone into overdrive with both door gunners firing at the mass of incoming rounds, causing the hot, spent shells to cascade out of the chopper down amongst us.

'*Shit!* I'm *hit!*' yells Johnno. '*Arr, damn!*' He then passes out.

I grab my URC-10 from my belt and click the voice button up. '*We're taking fire; Johnno's hit!*' I yell into the receiver. '*He's passed out. We'll have to land soon and patch him up or we could lose him.*'

'*Roger 23. We'll head for the nearest LZ, so you'll have to hold onto things 'til we get there. It could be a little bumpy.*'

The chopper is heading flat chat for a large clearing a few kilometres away and puts us down in the middle of a grassed area. As soon as the ropes are off, we're onto Johnno. His trouser leg is saturated with blood and is quickly ripped open. There is a bullet hole straight through his upper thigh, bleeding profusely.

'We've got to stop the bleeding,' I tell the others, my medical background coming forward. Clicker quickly applies a tourniquet above the wounded area, and we soon have two shell dressings strapped on either side of the gunshot wound. 'Now crack open one of those blood bottles and we'll give him a drip, because he's lost a shit-load of blood,' I tell the medic who pulls out one of the containers of plasma from his pack. He quickly breaks the tin open, removing the plastic bag with lines and needles. I grab the line and insert the needle into a vein in Johnno's arm while Clicker holds the bag well above him, allowing gravity to do the rest.

By this time the chopper has ditched the ropes and landed, so we carry Johnno under the rotors to the aircraft. With Clicker still holding the bag above him, we reach the body of the helicopter, and I can't help but see the volume of fire that must have come up. Luckily it missed us but it hit the back end of the chopper, filling this section with holes. Fortunately, nothing important has been hit.

'Don't worry about Nui Dat; just get us to the hospital at

Vungers,' I tell the pilot as we enter the aircraft. 'He's been shot through the thigh, higher than before. He's still unconscious but we've been able to stop the bleeding temporarily, so tell the hospital he has a drip and that we're on our way, and for *God's* sake boys, put your damn foot down because he's important to us and we don't want to lose him.'

The gunships are now circling us as we take off and head for Vung Tau. They've dropped a lot of their rockets and ammo into the area when they picked us up. I'd hate to be one of the Charlies firing at the helicopters while they're plastering the area with both mini-guns and rockets, because we'd be able to follow the route of each Charlie's tracer straight back down to him. It would be like going straight through the doors of hell with such a huge volume of fire falling in on top of you from the gunship's large arsenal of weapons.

Johnno is stirring and starts to throw himself around, so we take turns holding onto him, talking to him and reassuring him of his safety. Although barely conscious, he has to know he's in safe hands. I think we're all pleased to see the outskirts of Vung Tau coming up quickly below us. John, our medic, is holding him and thankfully his touch appears to calm Johnno down. As we approach, I can see the medical staff waiting patiently on the LZ as we come in. As soon as the skids touch the landing pad, the orderlies rush out to the helicopter, and we help place Johnno onto their stretcher. We watch as the orderlies quickly take charge of him and swiftly carry him out of sight into the hospital buildings.

'He's now in the hands of God,' John says sadly as the stretcher disappears through the door. '*Hell!* It looked like there were hundreds of 'em all firing at us. We were certainly lucky to get out of this alive, what with all that shit coming up at us from the

Nogs. It makes you wonder if they were the same as yesterday – no RPGs were fired because they would have made a mess of the choppers if the aircraft was hit with one of those.'

'I don't know, John, but I do need a good drink of something very strong. I know that,' I tell the others as we move back to the helicopter. 'You know, with all that shit coming up at us, I didn't fire a shot.' The others laugh nervously, as they were all in the same situation. We were all too busy fussing after Johnno to think about looking for someone to shoot at.

I undo my pack and take out what's left of our rum ration and hand the bottle across to the others, as I'm sure they need a drink as badly as me. It's at this stage that I see the bullet holes puncturing the bottom of my pack and, by the look of this, the only thing that wasn't perforated from their fire was the rum bottle and me.

'Look at this,' I say to them, holding the pack up. 'Those bloody piss pots must have been aiming for the damn rum bottle and not us.'

They look at my pack and laugh, a very dry laugh that completely lacks mirth, likely because they think, as I do, how lucky we've just been to get out of this with only one of us wounded.

The trip back to Nui Dat is a very sombre affair with the only thing moving between us being the water bottle holding the rum, passed from one to the other until it's empty. Very little is being said by anyone. We sit apart, staring into nothing. Poor old Johnno! It's the second time he's been shot in the leg, and I hope he goes home after this because he's done his fair share.

The debriefing by the officer in charge and the intelligence officer takes about half an hour. I've filled in the patrol report in Johnno's absence, and I'm sitting there listening as we individually give an account of what happened at the pick-up point. After the debriefing is over, the whole patrol head for the boozer to still our raw nerves. A good drink is the only way to unwind after such a close encounter.

Two days later, I'm summoned to the officer in charge's tent to be told about Johnno and how he's recovering.

'Your swift, decisive action in ordering the helicopter to land at the first Landing Zone, Corporal, means you probably saved Johnno's life. It was a very courageous thing to do, while being under such intense fire, to put down no less than a kilometre from that position. According to doctors, if you'd gone to here or Vung Tau, he would have died. Well done! Oh, and by the way Corporal, I have the great pleasure of promoting you to sergeant. Congratulations, Pete.' He gets up from where he's sitting, smiles at me and shakes my hand. 'I'm sure you're going to make an excellent patrol commander.'

'Thank you, Sir, I'll do my best.' I salute, before briskly turning and leaving his tent.

I am elated with my promotion, it's something I've always wanted, but it has come at a high price and much quicker than I'd anticipated. I expected to be made up when we got home after this tour was over, but not in this manner with a good friend being shot.

I go back to my tent to write to Alicia to tell her the good news, but say nothing of our lucky escape, of Johnno being wounded or the extensive damage to the rear of the helicopter by the ground fire on our extraction.

My next patrol is to do a recce of the area north-east of Binh Ba, a relatively safe area just out of the rubber plantation, with the prime aim of establishing if the enemy is in that region, who they are and what numbers they're in. We will be dropped off by the armoured personnel carrier at a designated spot in this overgrown rubber plantation. We huddle together in this steel monster's belly with our packs between our feet, waiting in anticipation for the signal to come through.

'We're approaching your drop-off point,' advises the vehicle's commander.

'Packs on, boys,' I say unnecessarily as we ready our equipment. Then the back grinds down and we rush out of this armoured dreadnought and quickly go to ground, watching as this monster grinds quickly away before we move out of the plantation into the forest. We have been given six days to cover the four grid squares that we've been assigned to recce. It's slow, tedious work, carefully moving our way through this primary jungle that's just to one side of a degraded rubber plantation.

On day five we find a track going diagonally across the top grid square, so we watch this for half a day as it's the only man-made obstacle we've seen so far; but on close inspection, we see nothing to indicate that the enemy is in the vicinity, so the patrol moves on. The reconnaissance finishes late the next day; unfortunately, it's a complete non-event. I give a sigh of relief, very pleased that my first patrol as leader was an anticlimax, having seen no signs of enemy movement in this area at all.

On getting back, a number of the patrol go to Vung Tau to see Johnno. We roll in and find him sitting up in bed, a smile on his weather-beaten face, welcoming us in, but I quickly notice the frame set up to keep the bedclothes from touching his wounded leg.

'Nice to see you, fellas,' he says, putting on a brave face. 'How's the patrolling going? I reckon you've been out again since. Is there anything happening that I should know about?'

'Not a great deal,' I tell him, a bit reluctantly, hoping he'll be pleased because it's his patrol I've taken over, but he seems happy. 'They've given me the patrol, so I promise you that I'll look after all these bloody reprobates for you.'

'Where was it this time?' he asks, smiling at us, ignoring my answer as if he knows I would.

'We just swanned around for six days on a recce up to the east of Binh Ba. We saw a few monkeys and they were the closest thing to a Viet Cong we saw, and you know, Johnno, Clicker thought some of them were better dressed than Charlie.'

We fill him in, making light comments about any narrow squeaks some of the other patrols had. Then he tells us the news that he'll be flown back to Australia in the next few days, making me pleased it's over for him and we've seen him before he goes.

'You know, Johnno, those bloody nogs are damn alcoholics,' says Clicker out of the blue, making Johnno stare at him, wondering what is coming next. 'As you know, Pete here had the bloody rum bottle. Well, the bastards shot the shit out of his pack trying to get the bottle to drop out, but you'll be pleased to know the bottle hung on in the pack and the best news we can give is we didn't lose a single bloody drop of rum. So we said, "Bugger you Charlie", and we finished the bottle off going home in the chopper after we dropped you off. So you'll be pleased, none of it was wasted.'

We have a good laugh, including Johnno. Our laughter must have been heard, and a nurse who comes in with a stern look on her face ushers us out of the ward.

'Sergeant Johnson has a long day ahead of him, gentlemen, so I'll have to ask you to leave so he can get some well-earned rest.'

Just as we're leaving, Johnno grabs my hand and holds me back from following the others out of the ward.

'That's two I owe you. They tell me if you hadn't ordered the chopper down and got that drip in me as quick as you did, I'd be history,' he whispers, squeezing my hand tightly as if not wanting me to go. 'You take care, Pete; and take care of the boys for me because they're a good bunch of blokes and they'd go through hell for you.'

'I'll take care of them, Johnno, I promise you that.' I take his hand in mine and rub the back of it roughly. We are both a bit embarrassed. 'You've taught me everything I know and showed me how to become a good soldier. You've been a wonderful role model for me, and I owe you a lot. Thanks, mate.'

Over the next two months I do another five patrols, mostly recce in areas north and west of Binh Ba towards the border of Long Kahn Province. It's the wet season again and while our movements are concealed by the rain and wet conditions, so are the enemy's. Sleeping in wet clothes takes a toll on my patrol members. They've had recurring colds and have missed some of the patrols. We have another out with bronchitis and each time we go out there is a different patrol member out sick. The new fellas are good but there are little things that each patrol has that are different, so it takes a day or so for them to get the gist of what we do.

'I want you to do a reconnaissance of this area here,' the officer in charge tells me at a patrol commander's briefing, pointing to the large map on the operations room wall. 'The patrol you'll lead will be required to do a detailed reconnaissance of this area here, so after four days you can set up an ambush on any reasonable track you find within the area, allowing you two days at the ambush site. Now, are there any questions you may have concerning this patrol, Sergeant Jackson?'

'I know that the area is primary jungle, Sir, but are there any reports of enemy movement in this section that we should know about?' I ask, hoping that he may have some more information from other sources. 'I note that it's quite a while since any patrols have been in that area, so have the ARVN, or for that matter the Americans, got any of the latest information dealing with that section that we could use?'

'Unfortunately, not that I know of, Sergeant. They may have had troops in that area, but we have no record of any enemy troop movements recently – by that I mean the last three months; that's what you'll have to find out. I'm afraid you'll be on your own as far as this patrol is concerned as we have no up-to-date information that could be of help. We'd need to know what forces have moved into that area or what type of infrastructure they may have established since any contact has been made.'

Our helicopter and the escorting gunships drop down to treetop height at a position they call 'the gate' and then fly blind, guided in by the chopper called 'albatross leader', who is still flying two thousand feet above us. We're now flying at breakneck speed across the jungle, lifting over any high trees and dropping down again, listening to the commands coming in from this lone helicopter that seems so high above us that we don't even see or think of him except for his sharp commands coming through the radio into the cockpit.

'*Right turn, then left turn,*' I hear coming from the cockpit. '*You're almost there, now left turn and you'll see the Landing Zone dead ahead.*'

There it is – the small Landing Zone coming up fast, so we brace ourselves, ready to leave the chopper as soon as the skids hit the ground. The helicopter finally touches the tops of the long grass and by this time the rain is pelting down once again, so we're out and almost immediately wet as shags on a rock and straight into the water up to our knees. The helicopter's downdraft has flattened the long grass, making it almost impossible to move as this tangled mass is kept in the water and doesn't rise until the aircraft lifts up and is gone. With Clicker leading, we crash awkwardly through both the long grass and water to the welcoming jungle, and thankfully, once into the trees the ground is almost dry. Clicker has moved into the jungle some twenty metres before he goes to ground facing away from the Landing Zone. We join him, forming our small tight perimeter and wait, listening for any man-made sounds for some ten minutes before I signal Clicker to move out. Thankfully, there's only the sound of the rain pelting down on the foliage above us.

Clicker moves out towards the south as I direct him to an area that from the air looked like heavier jungle that I'd seen while doing the aerial recce of the area. We're all totally saturated and are moving at a slightly quicker pace than we'd normally do when clearing the Landing Zone. It's raining heavily now and the noise on the foliage is horrendous, making travelling even worse as we won't hear the sounds of the enemy, although it's also killing any sound we are making ourselves. I think of Charlie, hoping he has his head down in some bunker complex or hut somewhere far, far away from us and hopefully he's crouching around a fire talking and out of the rain and hasn't heard the choppers as we came in. It's quite frustrating as we've travelled now for over an hour, and the bush is still far too open to lay up in, even though our noise is shielded by the heavy rain. We need much thicker scrub than this to conceal the light from the small hexamine stoves that we'll be using to brew up and heat the water for our dehydrated rations.

The rain has eased somewhat now so we keep moving on our course due south in the jungle that is finally becoming thicker. Suddenly Clicker stops, raises his hand with the thumb going down, indicating the enemy and then he cautiously beckons me forward to him. I carefully move up to his position, expecting the worst.

'There's some sort of structure just through the trees in front, Pete. I can just see its shape through the bush,' he whispers, pointing to his front with his M16. I follow the direction of his rifle barrel and can just see something through the scrub to the right, then immediately, smell the aroma of food cooking.

There are a number of buildings situated neatly under these large trees, so they are completely invisible from the air. The rain has eased off considerably now and the next thing we see is people moving around between the huts and we can hear them talking in their shrill, high-pitched voices. They are sheltering from the drizzle in one of these buildings, which could be a primitive mess, as a number of the figures can be seen to be eating. Occasionally they scurry out of the drizzle from this building to the next with food in their hands. For a few moments, we watch these interesting domestic scenes unfold in front of us, trying to assess who the hell they are. They are plainly Viet Cong as we can tell by their black pyjamas, but then I see a man dressed in a green uniform looking out into the rain from under his green pith helmet. He's plainly a North Vietnamese. On seeing this, I indicate to Clicker and the others to pull back slowly, so we gradually make our way back some two hundred metres until well out of sight of the huts. Once out of range of the VC, I stop the patrol and signal them to take up defensive positions.

'Set up comms and we'll patch through what we've just found so we can give them an accurate position of this camp,' I tell the sig, a new man to the patrol, who quickly opens the sixty-four set and taps through the accurate location of this camp. 'Now, fellas, let's get the hell out of here before one of them sees us.'

I take a bearing and we start moving to the east, but unfortunately, we've gone no more than fifty metres when Barnsy, my second in command, opens fire. It's just a short burst but the noise is shattering and scares the shit out of us.

'*Three just to our left, one got away!*' he yells out. '*He took off towards the left back towards the camp.*'

'Let's put some distance between them and us,' I tell the patrol, knowing that our cover has been well and truly blown and that it won't be long before the screaming hordes come looking for us. 'Don't even bother to search them; we haven't the time. Just leave them where they fell, we'll get out of here before the rest arrive.'

We make another two hundred metres before Barnsy again sends word forward and stops me. I quickly move back to him.

'Pete, I'm sure we're being followed up,' he tells me, looking back over his shoulder. 'I keep hearing noises from behind me from time to time – not a lot but there are occasionally different sounds as if people are there and coming after us, probably tracking us.' We stand quietly, listening for a moment trying to hear any sounds of movement when there's a sharp crack as if someone has trodden on a stick, breaking it. 'There, you would have heard that? They are definitely coming towards us.'

'Form a line across there and cover Barnsy and me,' I whisper to the remainder of the patrol, indicating with hand signals what

I want done. 'We'll put out two of our claymores against those trees. Don't worry about covering the wires because it's dull enough not to see them now. Move back fifteen metres and wait. If some of them are following us up they'll get more than they expect because the claymores will certainly slow them down and may even give us just enough time to get further away.'

Two claymores are quickly pulled out of our packs and placed in position, their curved backs fitting snugly onto the base of trees. We run the cords out as the patrol moves back to a safer position and goes to ground. We haven't got long to wait as Barnsy had been right, there are about fifteen of them coming towards us close together in an extended line. We can plainly see them emerging straight out of the gloom directly towards us with their AK-47s at the ready, their green uniforms and pith helmets telling me exactly who they are. Every so often one in the centre of the group goes to the ground as if he's following our tracks then points in the direction we've come from.

'*Come on you bastards,*' I mutter to myself through clenched teeth, a little annoyed at this man's unique ability to track us in these conditions but also waiting impatiently as they come straight towards us, with their rifles to the front. '*A few more metres you bastards; come on, you're nearly there,*' I whisper to myself, confident in the ambush, particularly if we can get their tracker.

They are now within the claymore's killing ground, so I hit both the switches, detonating the mines.

Boom!

The claymores explode together, cutting everything down in front like a scythe, covering all of us and spraying everyone with black smoke, hot air and debris. As soon as the explosion is over, we get up and pull out, firing a few shots, heading south again away from the scene as fast as we can go. We move away at this rapid pace until it's quite dark and we begin to make far too much noise. We stop for the night and lay up in a small circle, so close together that we can touch each other. If everyone's nerves are like mine, they're tight. The strain on all of us is tremendous and the look of being chased can be seen on each of our blackened faces.

It's about three in the morning when I hear a plane fly over our position. The URC-10 has had its aerial up all night sending out our distress signal, so I push the voice switch on to communicate with this aircraft.

'This is Patrol 23, come in. This is SAS Patrol 23, come in, over.'

There is nothing, no response and the plane keeps flying as if we aren't there. It's a great disappointment as I watch the navigation lights cross high above us and finally, they are lost in the night sky.

It's a long night, dragging on slowly, all of us feeling this extreme pressure and I have the welfare of the other four to think about. Suddenly the night is punctuated by random mortaring of the area, which initially makes me think that they know our position. Unfortunately, the second salvo of three rounds is closer and lands within fifty metres of us, so close in fact that we're showered with debris from one of the exploding shells.

'I have a horrible feeling they know where we are,' I whisper to the patrol. 'So, we'll get ready to move our position.'

Just as we're about to move, we hear the pops made by the bombs being dropped down the mortar tubes, so we wait with bated breath for the shells to land even closer this time. However, I'm extremely relieved when the next three shots are quite a way off, so we stay still, not wanting to give our position away. The next moment we could also hear the movement of people running through the jungle with the occasional sharp but brief conversation as if some officer is giving orders to his men, but thanks to the Vietnamese language course I did, I determine they have no idea where we are and are evidently quite confused at where we could be.

'They are putting out listening posts on the off chance they have spooked us with their mortar fire and these soldiers will be in a position to hear any movement we make changing our position. We'll run a piquet tonight, fellas,' I whisper to them, so the men know what's going on. 'They are quite some distance from us, so this is just in case they realise where we are. We'll each take an hour.'

The piquet is run with each person doing an hour. It's the first one I've ever been on in the bush and I hear each man wake the next person up for his shift. I think everyone in the patrol is in the same position.

The morning slowly arrives, and in the distance I hear the noise of a helicopter in our vicinity, a welcome sound as he must have heard the automatic beeping coming from the URC-10. So once again I switch it on to voice.

'*Helicopter, do you read me? Over. Helicopter, do you read me? Over. This is SAS Patrol 23; Do you read me? Over.*'
    '*Coming through loud and clear helicopter 23. Over.*'
    '*Where the hell are you guys?*'
    '*I haven't found your bird yet. Over.*'
    '*This is SAS Patrol 23. We're in the shit and need your help urgently. Over.*'

'Helicopter 23, we'll get you out buddy, okay? Just stay put now. What is your lock stat? Over.'

For some strange reason, the yank chopper pilot keeps referring to us as helicopter 23. I wonder, does he think there is another chopper down here or is he trying to conceal our whereabouts from anyone who may be listening? Whatever his reason is, I'll never know; I'm just so happy we can talk to him, and I know from what he's said that he'll contact base and bring in the cavalry to the rescue.

'This is SAS Patrol 23. Could you please contact the Australian Task Force? I repeat, could you contact the Australian Task Force? Yes, we desperately need your help. I repeat, we need your immediate help. Over.'

'Roger that helicopter 23, I hear you loud and clear old buddy and will notify the Australian Task Force. The cavalry is on the way now so hold on tight, buddy and it'll be there very soon. Out.'

I suddenly hear artillery fire in the distance and the whine of the incoming shells in the proximity of the camp we'd found and the dull thuds of the explosions almost a kilometre away, making me think they're giving us a thankful diversion, which should occupy the attention of the Vietnamese while we get out.

The air is soon filled with an amazing array of aircraft, however, not the ones we want because none of them can reach us. There is no sound made by the enemy who must be doing exactly the same as us – that is, keeping very quiet and holding their cards close to their chest until the last moment. I think it's almost half an hour before the faint throbbing sound of *Iroquois* helicopters can be heard in the distance. This first sound encourages us, and slowly, bit by bit, the pitch gets louder and louder until they finally come zooming over the trees towards our position, following the distinct beeping of our URC-10 signal.

'This is where things will get very nasty, fellas,' I whisper to the patrol. 'Be on the lookout for anything because they'll know we're about to leave. Now get your karabiners ready – it won't be long before the chopper is overhead for the pick-up.'

Everyone readies their karabiners through the rope we now have around our waists and waits impatiently for the signal.

'I'm going to throw blue smoke now,' I say into the URC-10, and I indicate to Clicker to pull the pin on his smoke grenade. 'Get ready; this is where the proverbial shit will hit the fan.'

With rifles at the ready, we watch as the blue smoke soon lifts into the air. Then all hell breaks loose as the Viet Cong in the vicinity begin to engage the planes and helicopters with all sorts of small arms and rocket-propelled grenades. The gunships in close proximity start releasing M79 grenades and rockets at any fire coming from the jungle floor towards them. We watch with anticipation as a helicopter finally comes over and we're relieved as five ropes come streaming out of the chopper and drop through the trees towards us. We haven't seen any sign of Charlies yet, but we know they will be firing at that helicopter and certainly would have seen our blue smoke, so we are ready for them. The ropes have finally reached us through the tree canopy right on top of us, so we quickly hook our karabiners onto them and ready ourselves for our rope extraction.

'*All hooked on and ready to go!*' I yell into the URC-10 as I get thumbs up from them all. 'Now for *Christ's sake* get us out of here fast – there are Charlies in the scrub everywhere around us!'

The ropes instantly go taut as the helicopter rises quickly

into the sky and we're pulled rapidly into the air; suddenly we begin to break through the tree canopies in only a few seconds. All five of us are clear of the trees and are hurtling along above the jungle at a break-neck speed. I look across and see planes and gunships all diving towards the ground, then all of a sudden, I can see green tracers coming up through the thick foliage from the ground towards us, zipping past. We desperately try to crowd together at the ends of our ropes to make ourselves smaller targets for them to hit.

'We're just about out of it, fellas. Everyone okay, nobody hit?' I get thumbs up from all of them and the odd strained smile. 'Good. Hold tight, fellas, bunch together if you can, we'll be out of this shit very soon.'

I look around me and down at the turmoil below, glad to be speeding our way out of here. My heart is pounding with adrenaline. I open my mouth to yell another instruction, when all of a sudden, I feel my rope snap some three to four feet above my head. As if in slow motion, my body starts to fall backwards. Clicker tries vainly to grab hold of me, but I've slipped past him, out of reach. My fall seems gentle at first as I leave my companions and career down towards the trees.

The last thing I remember is hitting the foliage and then nothing, nothing, just blackness …

CHAPTER 5

THE EXPERIMENT

Minh runs through the jungle as fast as he can, for he'd seen the man fall from the helicopter. He can also hear his comrades talking to each other as they run through the trees somewhere behind him, also looking for the man. He is determined to be the first to find the body of the enemy soldier and capture the reward for the *Uc Dai Loi Ma Rung*. He's well aware that the enemy planes and helicopters that are still buzzing above their vicinity, are shooting at anything they see moving on the ground that they perceive to be a target, especially if one of the soldiers is stupid enough to start shooting at these aircraft and give their position away.

Well, those fools are in for a hard time, he thinks from bitter experience as he hears more shooting erupt from somewhere well behind him. *That should hold their attention away from me.* This shooting is followed by a predictable barrage of bombs, rockets and machine-gun fire, which erupt when the pilots see people firing at them and follow tracer rounds back to the source.

Minh quickly skirts any clearing, large or small, hoping to avoid being seen from the air. Fortunately for him and his comrades, some fools further south and some distance from him are stupid enough to still be shooting at the planes and helicopters in the vain hope of hitting one. It's lucky for him, he decides, as this keeps the enemy's attention well away from the place that he's racing towards, because he'd plainly seen where the body had fallen. What a triumph it will be for him to find the body of one of these *Ma Rung* soldiers and collect the princely reward of a thousand *piasters*! It is near here; he is certain of that, so he quickly scans the tops of the trees trying to get a mental comparison of where the helicopter had been when he saw the man fall. *Yes, this has to be close to the place,* he congratulates himself on being the first to find the enemy soldier's body. He stops as he comes to a deep bomb crater made by one of the many American B52 bombs, which were dropped on the area some months before the wet season began.

The water in this hole – that doesn't look right, he thinks and stops to peer at the murky water in the bomb crater. *It should be clear by now but the water in this hole is quite dirty as if something was thrown in.* The crater appears to have been disturbed by something big, bringing up the vulgar-smelling mud from the bottom and contaminating the air around the crater. It almost causes him to vomit when his nose catches the foul stench rising from the water next to him. He quickly removes his rifle and equipment, placing this at the edge of the crater then takes off the primitive webbing from around his waist. Then, without fear, he thinks of the reward if he's right and finds the body. With these thoughts racing through his mind, he jumps into the putrid water and swims out towards the centre of the crater where he finds fresh tree leaves floating on the surface. It's dirty and cold but he ignores this as he takes a large breath of air before gamely diving down into the murky depths below. He can't see anything in this dirty water, so he goes by feel and he blindly swims down towards the bottom. He comes up to the surface and on the second dive, there it is – what feels like a pack floating above a body stuck deep into the soft mud at the bottom.

Another quick gasp of air and he dives directly, ready to retrieve his prize. *Come on you foreign bastard, you are mine*, he thinks as he vigorously pulls on the *Ma Rung's* pack, trying desperately to free the man from the mud below. He tries desperately to lever the body free, but he can't get a firm footing; the man's feet must have been driven deeply into the soft mud by the speed of his descent and now, unfortunately for Minh, he's running out of air again. Reluctantly he heads to the surface, gasping for a breath of air.

I'll have to get help from the others, Minh thinks as he sucks in yet another large lungful of putrid air before he sees his comrades on the lip of the crater. With another deep breath, he yells out excitedly to the others who are now in the process of running past the crater.

'*Throw me a long rope, comrades!*' he yells to them, causing them to abruptly stop and stare at him with a look of amazement as Minh's head appears in the large shell hole. 'The *Uc Dai Loi, Ma Rung* is down here stuck in the mud at the bottom, so I'll need your help to pull him free. Throw me some ropes, comrades, because together we should be able to bring him up to the surface.'

They quickly join a number of toggle ropes together and hurl one end out to Minh, who immediately takes his end firmly in his fist and dives once again down to where the body oddly stands almost upright, still held firmly. He quickly attaches the rope tightly under the arms of the man so it can't come off. With this job done, he swims exhausted to the surface where he signals between gasps to those now waiting at the edge for him to show that the rope has been attached firmly to the *Uc Dai Loi's* body.

'Pull the rope *hard* comrades and we'll get him to the surface,' he gasps triumphantly at the four men who now stand expectantly on the edge of the hole, holding the rope loose and watching him intently, ready to follow his next directions. 'The *Uc Dai Loi* and his equipment are stuck in the mud so pull hard my friends, and we'll get him and his equipment to solid ground.'

The rope tightens and after some heavy work, the body slowly comes free of the mud, then comes quickly to the surface, bobbing like a cork. It's heavy work but, undeterred and smiling profusely, they pull this body with some forty kilograms of pack across the water and finally out of the crater onto solid ground.

'The heavy pack and the ammunition in the webbing are what pulled the *Uc Dai Loi's* body down,' one of his helpers states confidently. 'That's why it lodged him so firmly into that horrible mud.' Then a curious question comes to this small man. 'How did you know it was under the water, Minh?'

'I smelt the stench of the mud, comrade, and then noticed the water had been disturbed.'

'You have done well finding this *Uc Dai Loi Ma Rung* soldier, Minh,' a voice breaks in from behind him; a voice he knows all too well as belonging to his commanding officer, Captain Trung, who leads them in their fight against the Americans and those Vietnamese traitors in their war to liberate the southern part of their country. 'You have earned your reward for such brave work in finding this *Uc Dai Loi Ma Rung* soldier. Well done! If you hadn't been so alert, we would never have found this body.'

'*This man is still alive!*' A surprised shout arises from one of the others as he excitedly feels the pulse on the side of the man's neck. With a little medical experience at one of their training camp hospitals, he is keenly looking over the body, testing the pulse and reflexes. 'His pulse is very weak, but it is still there. I can just feel it, Captain,' he looks around, beaming excitedly at his companions and then across at Minh. 'We will have to revive him quickly and look after him as we've finally caught one of these ferocious soldiers alive.'

'Good work, men. We *must* keep him alive because he's worth a lot more to us than a dead man.' Captain Trung then gives orders to the man bending over to inspect the enemy's body. 'Do what you can to revive him, Corporal; you *must* get him breathing again for as a prisoner he is worth far more to us than dead as he will have tactical information.'

They quickly strip the man's body, removing the pack with its heavy, cumbersome equipment and their medic applies mouth-to-mouth resuscitation. The soldier coughs violently, bringing up a volume of water and vomit so the medic rolls him to one side and cleans the airways, thumping him hard on the back. The *Ma Rung* soldier again violently vomits, bringing up more water but unfortunately to no avail; he remains barely conscious with an extremely weak pulse. Finally, though, the medic manages to stabilise him.

'Keep trying, we have to keep him alive and get him to Major Thong *quickly*. You Minh, you are the hero of the moment so go with haste and find the good doctor; he should be at the staging camp. We will meet you there,' orders the captain, looking at the man and all the heavy equipment and wondering how any individual could carry such a big load through this hot jungle for days on end without resupply. 'Make sure that all his equipment remains with him. I want no one here to remove *any* of his equipment. That's an *order*, do you all hear what I'm saying?'

American planes and helicopters are still zooming back and forth in the skies and any area showing the slightest sign of movement is deluged by machine guns and rocket fire. They swiftly carry the soldier's body away from the battle zone, carefully avoiding open areas.

Another hour passes before they finally pull into the camp complex, dug in at the base of a large hill.

The man, who is barely alive, is moved to one of the numerous caves that over generations their forbears had dug deep into the hill to first hide from the Chinese, the Japanese, the French and now the invading Americans. Within this cave is a small medical area where the soldier now lays, a thick blanket covering his body in an attempt to keep him warm and alive for this strange man coming from the north, Major Thong.

Setting to work immediately, when the *Ma Rung* soldier is brought to him, the attending doctor launches into a close inspection. 'His pulse is now constant but still very weak and fortunately for us the breathing has become more regular.' Doctor Pong then reminds the medic of what type of soldier they have before them. 'However, don't forget he is a *Ma Rung* soldier and if he still remains in a semi-conscious state or his medical condition deteriorates further and if you as the treating medic feel his life could go either way, treat him further.'

'Yes, Doctor. At the moment he is like a newborn baby; laying there as if asleep and is no trouble to us at all.' Turning his attention to the next patient on his list, the doctor strides out of the cave, and the captain stiffly turns to his underlings and with a decided puffing of his chest, he barks his orders. 'Don't become complacent, watch the body, tie him up if he regains consciousness and if there is any major improvement, let me know immediately.' Captain Trung looks down at the well-formed soldier, a worried frown on his face. 'We have to keep the *Uc Dai Loi* alive because when Major Thong arrives later this morning, I'm sure he will want to commence his experiments *immediately*.'

Half an hour later, Major Thong arrives tired yet extremely excited at what waits for him. After hearing the wonderful news, he had barely suppressed a giggle and dismissed the young private who had conveyed the message. He'd hastily thrown some important drugs into a small medical bag and couldn't sit still for the amazing possibilities whizzing around his head. The journey to the facility had seemed to stretch for an eternity and had worn his patience thin.

'Where is the enemy's body?' Major Thong questions sharply as he enters the makeshift medical facility again and notices the soldier isn't there. 'I would like to do a complete examination of the *Uc Dai Loi* soldier *immediately* to see if he meets my requirements – he must be healthy with no wounds or broken bones. Live bodies that are unwounded are very hard to get these days; let me again look at this one so I can check his limbs for broken bones. I was told he fell from a helicopter through tall trees from a great height.'

Without delay, he is taken directly to the soldier by nervous medical personnel, all of whom had also endured a lengthy wait for the important Major Thong to arrive. Having heard of the ground-breaking work he had achieved, and a little about his strange ideas and unpleasant temperament, they gratefully beat a hasty retreat.

The major stares intently at the enemy soldier's sleeping form; his respiratory system has improved remarkably and fortunately he is almost back to normal, but the thing that worries the Major is that he is still only semi-conscious and may have brain injuries from the fall that had been roughly described. With little information, it is crucial to determine the next course of action as quickly as possible.

'I will do a thorough examination immediately so bring some lights to me,' he barks at a soldier who is standing nearby, quite intrigued with the attitude that the major shows towards the *Uc Dai Loi's* body. He adds, 'By the look of this man, he appears to be extremely fit, uninjured and should be suitable for the experiment that I wish to make. Now, are there any wounds or breaks in his body that you've seen that I should know about before I start with my examination?'

'No, Sir; the *Uc Dai Loi* fell from a helicopter into a bomb crater full of water,' replies the Viet Cong soldier, quite puzzled at why the major would want this enemy soldier's body. 'We could not find any wounds on his body but then it's possible the water could have cleaned off any blood. He may have some broken bones from the fall from the helicopter as the aircraft was high above the trees when the *Uc Dai Loi's* rope broke, and he fell. However, when our patrol medic looked at him earlier today, he couldn't find any wounds of any description when we retrieved the body and again when our medic here examined him thoroughly with the same results.'

'Very good; indeed, *excellent*,' replies the major as he looks intently at the body. *This could be exactly what I've been waiting for this past month,* he thinks to himself, *to capture an unmarked enemy body that is alive, with no wounds.* Pleased, he turns his attention to the matter at hand. 'I will do a complete medical examination on this man immediately. I will need your help to move him.'

The *Uc Dai Loi's* body is carefully undressed by the Viet Cong soldiers and Major Thong conducts a very thorough medical examination over the next three hours, checking every aspect of his body. There are no wounds or fractures, a small miracle he feels for a soldier who has fallen from such a great height and to break nothing seems extraordinary.

'This body is exactly what I had hoped for, I can try out my serum on a live, uninjured enemy body!' he announces loudly and almost rubs his hands together in excitement.

He delves into his bag and brings out a box containing his vials of serum.

'I will give him an injection of my serum to slow down his heart rate to the parameters I require and then we can carefully transport him north to my laboratory where I will continue with my experiment.' He grins at the bewildered soldiers around him, who are quite confused. 'I hope to prove my theory of slowing down the respiratory system to be correct. If my theory is correct, who knows what my serum could potentially be used for, especially when all the guns are put away and finally peace comes to our land.'

One of the men carefully lifts the enemy soldier's arm while Major Thong injects a clear liquid from a vial into one of the now-enlarged veins.

'I want all his equipment including his rifle and the contents of his pack scrupulously cleaned and then it can be all moved north with him,' orders the major who now begins to walk around the body, looking down at the still figure with pride, knowing in his heart that this is an important moment in his career; his first live human experiment. 'I want you to treat this man's body as if he is a valuable ancient artefact. I expect you to get the mud off all his equipment as this could cause a water-borne infection. When all his equipment is scrupulously clean, I then want him dressed again to protect him from the multitudes of mosquitoes and other insects that live in this place, so no parasites are able to feed on his body or enter his respiratory system and potentially cause complications.'

'We were lucky, Sir, for his rifle was found just out of the water near the bomb crater,' ventures the soldier who had been assisting the major and had cleaned the equipment. 'It's a strange weapon, Sir; much heavier and quite different to those used by the Americans. It's the first one of its kind that I've seen since being in the Liberation Army. It's much bigger and far heavier than their M16, and you'll be pleased it's in good condition.' Puzzled, he then asks the major, 'Do you want to keep all his equipment as well, Sir?'

'Yes; everything that belonged to this soldier that's in his pack is to stay with him; do you understand?' The major, a little exasperated, explains to the soldiers gathered around him, 'now that I've examined him and given him my serum, I want you soldiers to clean him up thoroughly, paying particular attention to any hair growing on his body as this could harbour a variety of unwanted parasites. We have to remove all that because it could cause me serious problems later on when his condition stabilises. I want him readied immediately for our long trek back to my laboratory in the north where I will do further tests.'

With these orders, the Australian soldier's body is scrupulously cleaned once more this time with warm water and soap and all the hair on his body is carefully clean-shaven from head to toe, much to the glee of these watching soldiers as the bare scalp is now a shiny snow white with all the hair removed. When the major comes back some two hours later, everything is in place for him as now the body is ready to be moved back to his laboratory near Hanoi.

Over the next month, with great care, Major Thong and his party transport the body in a caravan carefully north-west through Vietnam into their safe haven of Cambodia and on to the infamous Ho Chi Minh Trail. During the journey, the major closely checks the body regularly to ensure every aspect of the soldier's respiratory system is functioning as he wants. The soldier's breathing is carefully monitored several times a day and although initially it was irregular, the soldier's breathing improves with each needle and nicely, he continues to stabilise.

The column turns north-east in Cambodia and begins its trek through this rugged but beautiful terrain, following a stream of porters who are hurrying along with their light loads up this odd supply line towards the Laotian border. They are making extremely good time through the jungle and the further north they go, the more complacent the bearers become in the safer territory and the faster they tended to move. The column is spread out well over two hundred metres and the porters talk and laugh amongst themselves. Annoyingly, they are travelling at a pace almost too fast for Major Thong's people who are struggling to keep up with the porters in front.

Boom! Boom! Boom!

A series of sharp explosions erupt suddenly, wreaking havoc on the majority of the column. Claymore mines have erupted, destroying well over half of the column who fall dead in a great black cloud of dust, vegetation and lethal shrapnel that spews across the track. Well before the smoke clears, follow-up concentrated machine guns fire on those trying to claw their way to a standing position. Small arms start to crackle from alongside the trail and the distinctive *pop* of M79 canisters is heard, followed by the deafening roar as they whistle through the air, exploding on impact. Those remaining in the column are caught unawares by the explosions and are shocked to see the shapes of enemy soldiers clad in tiger suits rise up out of the smoke at the edge of the trail; they quickly move forward through the dust, systematically shooting at any movement.

'Quickly, get off the trail you fools before they see us and come after us as well!' orders Major Thong in somewhat of a panic as he sees shadowy forms begin moving through the dust and smoke some twenty metres in front of them. Now, with the strong smell of cordite beginning to waft their way, filling his nostrils with fear, it seems as though hell has suddenly jumped out in front of them. Chills course through his spine as the strong realisation hits home that he won't only lose his precious body but probably his own life as well if they don't get away from the killing zone quickly.

Major Thong shouts, *'Get moving you fools; we cannot afford to lose my subject! Move, damn you, move! Get off this track before we are killed!'*

Frantically, his group charge off the track, pushing their way into the thick jungle to escape the terror. Some realise that they are extremely fortunate that the major insisted that the body be treated carefully, his weight ensuring the smaller party's location at the rear of the column, struggling to keep in contact. Caution is thrown to the wind somewhat as they rush away from the trail a good thirty to forty metres before the major stops them. They stop with the stretcher in the thick foliage of the jungle floor, completely exhausted.

Gasping for breath, many hope the foreign soldiers didn't see them and don't come looking for them and their precious cargo, unarmed except for the rifle that the *Uc Dai Loi* carried and a pistol that the major now brandishes about.

'It's those American Special Forces with those Montagnard mercenaries they've enlisted to help them control our people,' whispers one of the couriers as he crouches down low beside Major Thong in the dense undergrowth. 'They must have been watching the trail. We are very fortunate indeed to have been so far down the back of the column and missed the explosives they had set on the trail. Major, the speed we were going was a blessing in disguise and helped us escape this deadly raid.'

In The Ambush Position

Staff Sergeant Abraham King had waited hours for a suitable target to come along this section of the infamous Ho Chi Minh Trail; a soft target, he had been told by his superiors, so his newly trained men could try out the tactics he had spent hours teaching them back at their base in the mountains. The Montagnards are very good soldiers with no love for the Vietnamese and had eagerly adopted some of the tactics that his Australian friend, Peter Jackson, had told him they'd developed in Vietnam. Photos from spy planes had shown that the Vietnamese were sending many couriers to and from North Vietnam along this section of the trail. He'd hoped to hit a south-bound supply group loaded with food and weapons, but none had come south so this north-bound supply column would have to act as their initial tactical test.

He and his men had landed the night before some two kilometres away to the east and had spent most of the previous day and all of that morning getting into position and setting up their claymore mines. It had been worth the effort when he had seen from his vantage point what was coming along the trail towards them.

'Goddamn it, so many couriers,' he whispers to Jake, another Special Forces Sergeant laying near him. 'We'll wait until the leaders are almost through before we spring the ambush; that should allow most of them to get within the killing ground.'

'Okay, Abe, that sounds good, I'll let them know what you want,' Jake immediately passes the instructions on to the small men who he knows have no love for the Vietnamese and have centuries of scores to settle. They smile at Jake with expressions on their faces that show their eagerness for this assault and settle down behind their weapons, content to wait for the claymores to explode. 'Let the first ones get almost through the killing ground to that point we've marked on the trail before we spring the ambush. Wait until you hear the mines explode before you move forward or open fire with your personal weapons.'

'Easy; easy, a little further,' mutters Abe to himself, oblivious now of the man next to him as the couriers begin to move past just in front of their position. '*Fire!*' he yells, hitting the firing mechanism of his claymores, and his friend does the same. He feels the hot blast of smoke, leaves and debris surge past him and hears the explosions of other claymores going off either side of him, mowing down the men directly in front of their position.

Immediately, as the blast passes over them, he and his men are up and moving forward into the killing zone. The men who had been happily talking and laughing as they walked along this section of trail are now mostly contorted, still forms grotesquely dumped on the trail, dead.

'*Cut-off parties, move out!*' Abraham hears Jake yell to the men in Vietnamese and sees a group of three with an M60 machine gun move quickly down the trail some twenty metres before they go to ground on either side of the track. The gunner aims the machine gun down a straight section of trail just in case others much better armed than these men come streaming up the trail to support the bearers, who are only lightly armed with old weapons they'd captured from past wars.

'Search the bodies and put what you find in packs!' he hears Jake yell out to the men and the stillness is shattered by the crackle of small arms fire as the badly wounded are put out of their misery by these willing men, eager to take out an old score against the Vietnamese for the decades of abuse that their people endured.

'Unfortunately, a few towards the back were out of the killing ground and got away, Abe,' Jake says, pointing down the trail to the thick jungle where some of his men had seen a group of people desperately fleeing off the trail into the depths of the jungle. 'The man who told me said they were carrying what appeared to be a stretcher or something like that. Do you want us to go out and find 'em as it could be someone of importance?'

'Don't bother, Jake; we could lose men to their fire in that thick vegetation and anyway, the choppers will be here very soon as the contact message was sent as soon as the initial claymores were blown,' Abraham says sharply. He starts to find the killing of so many in this manner a little sickening. 'As soon as the bodies have been searched, pull the men together and move them back to that small clearing we passed coming in. This was a good ambush, Jake; no casualties of ours and very successfully conducted by our guys. These men have done well for their first time out.' Then he thinks for a moment. 'It will be interesting what materials we get from them for our intelligence people.'

Once the bodies have been searched, Jake gives an order for

their withdrawal to the small clearing they passed well before they reached the trail. As they approach the clearing, they hear the familiar sound of a number of helicopters moving in their direction from the east towards their extraction position.

'The men did a great job today on their first ambush, Abe,' Jake says, quite pleased at the results as they wait for the choppers to arrive. 'They'll be good soldiers with some more training under their belts. Hell, these men should account for themselves extremely well against the North Vietnamese.'

They are soon loaded onto the helicopters and fly back to their base in Vietnam. Both Abraham and Jake are happy with the outcome of this initial ambush and the performance of these men in their first conflict against the Vietnamese. The overarching objective is that the Montagnard men, fully trained should be excellent soldiers and if used correctly, could tie up a considerable number of North Vietnamese in the area.

At The Ambush Site

Major Thong and his group lie still on the ground some fifty metres from the ambush site, waiting for hours while the enemy soldiers wreaked havoc on the decimated column, searching the bodies, taking their weapons and collecting any papers or articles of value. Finally, the noise of a number of approaching helicopters signals the end of the ambush, causing some to give a sigh of relief, but the over-cautious major waits for the enemy forces to climb aboard the aircraft. He hears the constant beat of the rotors start to diminish into the distance, then drops his head with relief when the noise is gone completely. The jungle is strangely silent, except for the sounds of a troop of monkeys whose curiosity has finally brought them to look at the devastation that's left on the trail.

They wait nervously for almost another hour before finally, Major Thong is willing to venture out onto the track to see what is left of their comrades. There is absolutely nothing they can do to help those who had been caught in this deadly claymore ambush. Dead and twisted bodies lie everywhere about them for the next hundred metres showing the major that this American ambush has been a complete rout on their column. They have been very lucky indeed to be left alive after this furious attack. They move cautiously past these twisted bodies, looking at the still forms of people they had been laughing and joking with hours before.

'I'm taking no chances of stress on the *Uc Dai Loi*, so I've altered the serum slightly to relax his body a little more so that it's completely at ease,' the major tells the orderlies while he fossicks in his medical bag for a syringe and a bottle of his serum. He picks up the limp arm of the patient and feels for the pulse before injecting the serum again; then once more they are on the move towards the north. Next, he selects two tablets, throws these into his mouth and flushes them down with a large gulp of water from his canteen to calm his own shattered nerves as he realises how close to death he had been.

North Vietnam

Two weeks later, a little longer than Major Thong had calculated, this small column of men finally enter North Vietnam and are relieved to meet a number of vehicles waiting for them on the Laotian border. They are speedily trucked to a government research centre just west of Hanoi where the body of the Australian soldier is carefully taken into the laboratory for further research.

'I want you to wash and clean the body thoroughly once again for it's been well over eight weeks since it was cleaned properly the last time. You have to make sure not a scrap of dirt or any other impurities are left on his body or in any crease of the skin because we don't want any infections taking hold,' the major tells his staff, who have been waiting for him to arrive. 'Pay *strict* attention to any hair that may have grown on the body and be sure to clean and trim his finger and toenails and remove any dirt. Also, tell me immediately if you find any insect bites such as mosquitoes or ticks.' Then he looks at a young medical lieutenant who is aiding him. 'I have stressed to the staff from the beginning that I want this body to be surgically clean when your people have finished their jobs.'

He lifts an arm and checks the pulse and is pleased with what he finds; it's good, a very slow, regular pulse with a heartbeat telling him his strict overseeing, which he'd insisted on, has paid off. The attendants start the laborious job of cleaning the body with soap and warm water, which by this time is quite stiff from lack of movement.

At the end of two hours, the extremely long, exacting job is finally finished to the major's satisfaction. He's pleased to find no bites on the body, which passes his stringent inspection.

'I am impressed by the thoroughness of your job and the dedication you've shown to the subject's body.' His comments please his staff who had meticulously done this exacting job; compliments from their superiors are rarely received. 'I'm extremely pleased with the serum I've developed and especially with the results it has achieved with this body; you will note the subject's hair has not grown on the body.'

'My men are pleased to have worked on this mummy, Major,' says the young officer, thinking the body is dead. 'Is this the same system used to preserve our famous Chairman Hoe?'

'No. *Certainly not!* This enemy soldier has been preserved *alive* to show our young people who they are fighting in the south of the country. This body I have treated with my serum will show our young people *exactly* what their enemy looks like,' he stresses. He lifts up one of the body's arms. 'Feel his pulse, Lieutenant, and this will show you what you can expect, you can call this man the "living dead". You'll note the pulse is slow, but blood is still pumping around his body.'

'Yes, I can feel a faint pulse,' the young officer says. 'Will this man ever wake up, Sir?'

'Hardly, he's like I just said, he's the living dead.' With a laugh, he goes on to explain what he intends to do. 'I'm having his uniform washed in an antiseptic solution and when that's done, we'll use the same procedure on his equipment. Once the cleaning is completed, Lieutenant, we'll dress him again in his uniform and place him in one of our special glass containers with all his equipment on and his rifle held in his hands.' The major grins with pride, brimming with confidence at this important achievement. 'Once he's in that container, we'll turn on my gas and monitor the performance of his body over the coming weeks.' He turns, smiling again at the young officer before explaining a little more about what he hopes to achieve. 'I find this experiment very exciting, particularly with the gas, as I've been able to derive much information from my serum trials. We were extremely lucky to have captured such a good unwounded enemy specimen to do my initial ground-breaking work on. My staff have been absolutely wonderful and have done everything I asked of them, down to cleaning this man's teeth.'

Towards evening, the clothes are returned after cleaning, so they start the arduous job of dressing the now quite stiff body into his full combat gear. With this difficult assignment finally done, they arrange the enemy soldier's body so that he stands in the glass case with his rifle firmly in his hands. It looks as if he's just about to get onto a helicopter and go out on a combat patrol.

'Now the only item left for us to do, which is definitely out of place with this soldier's stance, is his eyes,' the major says, making a final inspection of the body. 'You will note at the moment they are closed as if he's sleeping, and it certainly doesn't look right for a man who's about to go into the jungle to fight his enemy to be asleep. The components of my gas have had lubricants added to them which are designed to keep the flesh soft and to stop any deterioration so when we open his eyes they shouldn't be affected by the atmosphere as he's isolated from atmospheric conditions in his case. He will be immersed in my gas to stop his body from drying out because the subject won't be blinking his eyes to lubricate them so this is the next best thing to have.' He pauses, thinking for a moment about anything he may have missed or overlooked. 'I sincerely hope the lubricant we're using will keep them moist so they don't deteriorate with time because if that happens, we'll have to fit him with glass eyes which I'm afraid will detract from what he really is,' he smiles at his understudy. 'The living dead you could call him, Lieutenant, and you wouldn't be wrong by using a strange statement like that.'

With great care not to damage any part of the iris, his staff gently push the eyelids up until the soldier's blue eyes are staring straight ahead as if watching everything they do, alarming some of those nearby as the body now looks almost alive. Major Thong steps back, admiring the figure in front of him as the glass case is finally sealed and the gas is turned on. To the major's initial horror, the gas is cloudy and distorts the visibility of the soldier; however, after a few frustrating moments and a great deal of suspense, to his relief the gas finally settles and clears, giving an excellent view of the *Uc Dai Loi, Ma Rung* soldier dressed in full combat equipment, appearing as if he's ready to jump out of his glass case and immediately go into action.

'It was possibly the lubricant in the gas had to settle so that caused the initial distortion in the case as it's slightly heavier than the gas. Now it has settled and is clinging to the subject's skin.'

It is almost two weeks before Major Thong returns to the museum and this time, he's accompanied by high-ranking Party people and military officers who gather around the glass case and stare at the man inside, some thinking wrongly that the figure inside is a dummy, while others assume it's a corpse that has been brought back from the south.

'What I want to see is firstly how long my gas lasts and secondly, what the effects are on a living body.' Major Thong's first words surprise some people as they gather around the figure of the Australian soldier; some look with disgust at this man and what he stands for. 'This *Uc Dai Loi, Ma Rung* soldier is actually alive but my gas has slowed his respiratory system to over a millionth of what it should be.' He points to a row of gauges set at the bottom back of the glass case. 'These gauges show the pressure of the gas he's immersed in, his body temperature, his heartbeat and a number of other body functions, functions you would expect a living being to produce.

Gentlemen, you could call him the "living dead" if you wish, and by saying that you wouldn't be wrong.' The major chuckles again with some pride at his achievements. 'If my calculations are accurate, and I'm sure they are, in one hundred years' time from now we may have to take him out to wash and shave him so the figure we have here looks presentable.'

'How does it work?' asks a colonel who is known for scoring points and making himself look good with his senior colleagues. 'Surely, after such a long period of time, if this experiment of yours works, he'll start to look quite old, and his condition will have begun to deteriorate to that of a corpse?'

'A good question, Colonel. On the contrary, gentlemen – one year is like a second with this man's ageing process. It is over two weeks since he was shaved last and there is not a hair on his head or a whisker to be seen on his face,' the Major tells them, pointing with pride to the Australian's clean-shaven face. 'He cannot hear a word of what's being said or make any movement whatsoever as his metabolism is as described before, a second is a year; he is like a living statue in a state of limbo you could say, and no feeding is necessary to keep his condition. He is here specifically for our young people to see and to get to know what our enemies look like.' He looks seriously at his audience hoping they understand the importance of what he's saying. 'How many of our young people have actually ever seen an *Uc Dai Loi, Ma Rung* soldier in real life; yet we take them into our army, train them and expect these young people of ours to go south in whatever unit they are in and get them to kill people like this man?'

'A very interesting concept you have here, Major,' replies one of the generals, walking quite enthusiastically around the figure in the glass case and looking at the camouflaged uniform of the combat-equipped Australian, taking note of the forward-pointing firearm grasped in his hands, as if he is about to spring out and attack them. 'This is a very fitting way to treat one of our enemies.' He pauses for an instant as he contemplates the possibilities that the major's invention may have, trying to put this invention together in a combat scenario that they could use. 'Would it be possible to use your gas on their defensive complexes, Major? For example, could we fire a concentrated form of your gas using modified artillery shells to carry it in an attack on places such as the strongly fortified American base, Khe Sanh? If something like that was possible, our attacking troops would only have to walk in after the artillery barrage and take the base over without suffering the huge losses of men as we unfortunately do.'

There is a light ripple of laughter from the crowd of officers gathered around the glass case as they think of the proposition that the general puts forward.

Major Thong's next statement, however, soon puts a damper on the proposal as he explains the fundamentals of how his gas works.

'This unfortunately would be impossible at this stage of my experimentation, General, because at the moment the gas is extremely light and is immediately absorbed by the atmosphere as soon as it's exposed; however, one day I hope to be able to deliver something along the lines of what you ask for. That phase of my experimentation is a long way off, but I will be working on something along these lines in the future. However, in the meantime, I have one of their soldiers here on display and it is showing the effectiveness of my gas and serum that I treated this soldier with.'

'Good work, Major,' says the general, pleased with what he's seen. 'I urge you to carry on with your experiments because if they are as successful as we've seen here today, it won't be too long before we can bombard their forts with your gas. We are losing far too many good young men at the moment and as a small country, we cannot afford to keep having these huge losses. Major, we desperately need a secret weapon of some description to even up things; something along the lines that you are proposing would be excellent and would save many thousands of lives.'

'I'm heading south again shortly, for six months this time,' says Major Thong. He is quite enthusiastic with the response from the officers so he quickly adds, 'This time, hopefully we will get an American soldier to continue on with my experimentation.' He turns to douse a few worried looks among those listening. 'As far as this *Uc Dai Loi* is concerned, there shouldn't be any trouble with me being absent because the procedure is quite simple. It's only a matter of keeping this body immersed in the gas and I have enough gas stored here at the centre to last more than one hundred years.'

Major Thong spends another two months in the north finalising his experiment and checking the results before he readies himself for the arduous, very dangerous trip to the south of Vietnam. Trucks again take him to the drop-off point near the border with Laos. He's happy with the work so far, but he'd love to get another enemy soldier in as good a condition as this Australian.

The column is mostly made up of porters carrying ammunition and food to their beleaguered soldiers in the south. His destination this time is a secure base in the hills of Two Corps area, just to the east of the central highlands; a relatively safe place he's been informed by his superiors, except for the occasional bombing raids by the American planes. This column winds up a sharp incline some ten kilometres from their base. It's been an exhilarating climb for this fit young scientist, but he'll be happy to put his feet up for a few days, study his notes and get another prisoner quickly so he can continue his important experiments. They've reached the top of a large hill and he can now see the track in front of them just starting to wind down into the jungle below. It's a beautiful view of this rich, almost pristine valley that has unfolded itself before them. *I'm going to enjoy working in this wonderful place*, he thinks, looking down into this peaceful setting at a waterfall cascading over a cliff in the distance.

Boom!

The whole track seems to erupt, dropping virtually most of the column. The major's body lies in the middle of some of the porters, their arms and legs crossing each other forming a grotesque pattern of death in the late morning light. Men in camouflage fatigues move in quickly, finishing off any of those that are still alive.

'Another successful ambush, Abe,' says Jake as he looks over the fallen men. 'You're gunna miss this excitement when you go back stateside. You won't know what to do with yourself once you're back in a civilised world again, hey?'

'I've been in the army too long already, Jake,' Abraham replies, looking over what had been a wonderfully placid place until the claymores had exploded. 'I've had enough of killin' to last me ten lifetimes. I'm going back to the States to marry that girl of mine, take some leave and think of what to do.' He is deep in thought for a while and Jake looks at him with interest, for Abraham

King has become quite a legend in the Special Forces. 'I may even write a book about this goddamned war. Yes, that's what I'll do. I'll sit down and write a book so the young folks back home, both black and white, will understand the truth of what happened over here and know how the politicians on both sides of the house have played us for fools and for their own selfish gain.' He looks down into the now-placid valley at the waterfall in the distance, admiring the view. *It's a lovely place except for this goddamn war,* he thinks as he tries to shut the massacre that lies in front of him out of his mind.

*   *   *

North Vietnam

Back at the laboratory just outside Hanoi, life goes on as usual. The years come and go; the people working there have their orders. There is no shortage of people to do the mundane jobs; just a strong back to keep the place clean and change the gas when the pressure drops below the required level. These are the simple jobs where there is no expertise required, all that is needed is someone with the energy to follow orders. One year turns into two, then three.

There are groups of people who occasionally come into the museum, and they file through the exhibitions and look curiously at what the Party has out on display depicting what has come to be known as the 'American war'. Many are startled at the figure of the Australian soldier standing in his glass case with his camouflaged face, his blue eyes staring out over the museum as if he's watching them and is ready to jump out of the glass case to attack them. Small children hide behind their mother's legs, afraid of him while others just stare, making sly comments about his blue eyes and his camouflaged uniform. Some of the girls quietly admire his tall stature and rugged good looks. Under the camouflage cream, it is difficult to recognise him, but some visitors wonder if he is alive like some say or if he is just a life-like statue there to show them what their enemies look like.

Nineteen seventy-five comes and goes. The Americans have gone now, forging a peace treaty with the North and soon the puppet South Vietnamese Government is defeated in a swift and bloody campaign, and they now have, at last, the one country that Ho Chi Minh had promised them so many years before. This is the first time since the French left so long ago that they have one country, but to get this far they'd suffered much. There is much happiness in the whole country now that the fighting is finished. In the capital, Hanoi, people stop looking at the skies in case of American war planes fly over to bomb targets in and around the city.

Uncle Ho has been dead a long time and lies mummified in his shrine for all Vietnamese to see. Now, new people run the country but unfortunately most of its people are poor and desire things; small luxuries that were once out of reach to all except those in power. They had been told that when they won the war of liberation, these things would be theirs, but still they wait. The Americans have placed sanctions on their country, so all sorts of goods are in short supply.

Unfortunately for the Vietnamese, they have troops now fighting in Cambodia after putting up for a number of years with the antics of the hated Pol Pot; leaders had no option but to invade this neighbouring country to oust him to Thailand. Now people endure the Khmer Rouge raids across the border.

Affairs aren't good with China either, one of their old reluctant allies who now threatens their country with reprisals for their unavoidable Cambodian invasion. Chinese intervention is making it appear there may be another war with another major country and many of the young people have been pressed into their army, so their country is ready to defend itself once more if this invasion by their northern neighbour materialises.

After all this fighting, the country is poor and the American sanctions are biting hard, with the new conflicts costing their country a lot of valuable Dong which they haven't got, and the people strive for self-sufficiency. At the Ho Chi Minh laboratory however, everything is almost the same with the exception that now the emphasis is being put on farming and feeding the population and so most of the war-related experiments have been put to one side in an adjoining room in favour of experiments into agricultural sciences, so their country can be better equipped to feed themselves.

CHAPTER 6

BORN AGAIN

Vietnam 2001

Many years have now passed and all the war-related items of long ago have gone into a separate museum at the back of the laboratory and the emphasis is still on agricultural sciences and the production of food. New young people now sweep the floors and clean up the mess that appears after groups of visitors have traipsed through the centre, looking at the latest in agricultural technology and the new innovations the government is looking at to bolster the weight of the next rice crop. Vietnam's large population, now nearing a hundred million people, is still desperately trying to feed itself by incorporating the latest in agricultural technology. The technology needs to be tailored to suit Vietnam's farming techniques as they strive for self-sufficiency in food production.

Noc Nue has been at the centre now for three years and does the menial chores at the laboratory. She had been a smart girl at university with good grades in agricultural science because her father had told her that this was what she should do in order to get ahead in this workers' heaven. Good jobs for women, however, are hard to come by in this communist country, but she applied for a job at the food laboratory as a technician, hoping to eventually get into some of the experimental fields that she's heard the centre deals with.

Three years have passed rapidly since she started work as a junior, but she finds she's only given very minor experimental tasks. However, she is required to clean up the laboratory and adjoining buildings after the other technicians have finished their experiments or have shown any visitors through the centre. She finds this work simple and boring but it pays a meagre salary that many people would take from her if they had the opportunity. Noc has just broken up with her latest boyfriend, one of the new intellectual youths whom she'd met in her last year at university who seems to have a lot of money at his disposal. He has links to the burgeoning middle class that now seems to be appearing everywhere in their society. He's been spoilt by his well-to-do parents and thinks everything belongs to him, including his girlfriend. She had put up with his pathetic attitude for long enough and has just ended their relationship. Now she is looking for another man, a man who is well-off and, unlike the former boyfriend, a man who recognises her abilities in her job and treats her kindly and with respect.

She is sick of doing these simple assignments though and wishes for some tasks that are more pertinent to her studies, rather than doing the sweeping and cleaning. The menial tasks are allotted to her mostly by elderly people who run the laboratory and she is quite sure she could do their job as well as, if not better than, them. She's also certain they know this, and that's why they keep her at arm's length away from all the important work with the new crops. Today they have given her a broom instead of a microscope and she has been told to sweep the exhibition area again. What a drag! There has been only one small group of visitors through that area today so why would it need cleaning? She looks at the floor as soon as she opens the door and notices that it's spotless. With so few people being in the museum part of the centre for years, what would you expect? *Damn, what a waste of time!* she thinks as she walks through to where the foreign soldier is standing in his glass case in the centre of the floor.

She stops for a moment, looking at him, noting again his sparkling blue eyes. Now wouldn't that be something different to talk to Wai about after work? *He's a little older than I am but quite good-looking in a strange Western way,* she muses, again, looking at his camouflaged face with his blue eyes that seem to stare almost unrelenting at her, sure that they follow her every move. Is this just her vivid imagination or are they vacantly looking out across the room towards her? She finds this quite unnerving, almost as if he's aware of her presence and trying to read her thoughts but can't move in the glass case to reach her.

'I'll bet you had plenty of pretty young girls chasing you when you were alive, *Uc Dai Loi,*' Noc says out loud as if talking to the soldier and then looks at him for quite some time, evaluating him. His blue eyes just continue to stare straight ahead across the room as if he's ignoring her. 'I bet you liked to take out girls when you went into town on leave; I bet you took out beautiful girls who would immediately sweep you off your feet. I bet you would love to be treated in such a way now, *Uc Dai Loi,* especially when you're alone in this room with a beautiful woman like me and we're the only ones here?'

After talking to him for quite some time, Noc is about to leave when she happens to look down at the plaque with his particulars stamped in bronze at the bottom of the glass case. She begins to read a little more about him when she sees green mould – lots of it – on the inside of the glass container towards the bottom and it looks as if it's spreading along the glass at the base.

There must be a gas leak or something very wrong with this side of the case. What are they going to do with your body now anyway, Uc Dai Loi? 'What a waste! I have better things to use your body for,' she murmurs dreamily. 'I can understand keeping Uncle Ho well-preserved so people can see him because he was our great leader, but with this handsome foreign soldier, now that the war has been over for so long, he should be sent home so his family can put him in his grave with some dignity.'

She looks intently at the construction of the glass case, trying to work out how it's closed to keep the gas in and decides that there has to be a leak down there somewhere for the mould to be growing so vigorously inside. Noc notices a number of screws from both top and bottom that, when tightened, would clearly pull the glass hard up against the attached sealant. It's quite possible, she thinks, that one or more of the screws has come loose and the sealant has aged and warped and is allowing fresh air to seep into the case causing the mould to establish and grow.

'Hmm, now, if I undo those screws, I'll be able to open your case, *Uc Dai Loi*,' she says. She gives a little laugh as if reprimanding herself for the stupidity of talking to this man's body. 'I'll soon get rid of that filth at your feet, *Uc Dai Loi*. With that gone, I'll tighten the screws up properly; that will make you a brand-new soldier that your people will be proud to see.' Then, with a cheeky laugh and with many more amorous thoughts running through her active mind, she says, 'We'll all have to be on our toes with your case open, young man, particularly if you start to chase us around in such a small room.' Again, she laughs to herself at this silly joke and thinks of the ramifications of this suggestion. 'Yes, this room is far too small and with the door shut you would easily catch me, *Uc Dai Loi*. Heavens above; a big man like you would be far too swift on your feet for a small person like me to evade for too long.'

These latest thoughts cause her to break out in a girlish giggle. She's happy now, going back to the workshop, whistling a pop tune, quite pleased that she's found a good job to do. In no time, she's back at the glass case with an array of tools that include screwdrivers and wrenches to open the front of the case.

'A few minutes of not being surrounded by your gas shouldn't do a big man like you any harm, *Uc Dai Loi*. Don't worry, your home will only be open for a minute or so while I remove the mess, then I'll have the glass back on in place in no time at all and then I'll turn the gas back on, so you won't even know I've been there. No one here will know, except you, that your case has been opened.'

Noc works her nimble fingers on the catches, and it doesn't take long to remove the front of the glass case. She pauses for a moment, sniffing the air, trying to detect the smell of escaping gas, but thankfully she can't. There is no such smell of the gas that's preserving him, so she sprays some cleaner on the mould and starts rubbing vigorously on the bottom of the glass with her rag and in no time at all starts to remove the filth that's accumulated over such a long period of time. It comes off easily with her vigorous efforts and, after ten minutes or so, it has the look of new glass. She's about to replace the panel when she notices more mould right at the back behind him, so she pushes in past his legs to remove that as well. She reaches forward, spraying the glass and as she stretches past his body, she feels his knee move slightly against her shoulder. She laughs nervously, thinking she isn't going to make another glib comment about him being alive and now waking up. She dismisses the movement as nothing more than an overactive imagination, but comments to him, 'That will do, *Uc Dai Loi*. Be a good boy and stay still while I clean the back of your case.'

Then, strangely, she starts to feel pressure pushing on her shoulder, very lightly at first. It then increases as she edges towards the back of the case. Again, she laughs at her imagination and attributes the weight of his legs on her back to him perhaps falling over a little. She makes a mental note to straighten him when she is finished.

'I only want to clean your home, so just behave yourself and be a good boy, *Uc Dai Loi*. Don't be so impatient because I'm not going to bed with you just yet; so please wait until your home is clean and don't be such a naughty boy and try something so silly.' She laughs and fleetingly looks up before continuing with her cleaning chore. She scrubs at a stubborn bit of mould with her cloth, puffing with the effort. 'Be patient.' The sponge makes funny sounds as she scrubs. *Squeak, squeak.* 'Be a patient man please.' *Squeak, squeak.* 'I can have your case nice and clean for when visitors come in here especially to see——'

Suddenly she feels *Uc Dai Loi*'s knee move down as if his leg is bending, and almost immediately, he begins falling over her prone body. So she backs off, quickly grabbing at his waist in an attempt to steady him, but she is not quick enough and feels his full weight come crashing over her, pinning her small body to the floor, surprising her with his weight.

'You're relatively soft for a dead man and don't smell at all,' she purrs to herself as she desperately tries to free her body from under his. She is now pinned uncomfortably to the floor – not a completely unpleasant experience.

'Noc, are you alright?' comes a sudden call from the door. It's Wai, one of her friends, a girl of similar age to her and who'd studied agricultural science at university with her. Wai lives in the same house, sharing the rent, and helps her with the chores at the centre. 'I could hear a lot of noise and heard you talking to the *Uc Dai Loi* from the other room. What are you doing to this man, you naughty girl?' She laughs when she sees her friend's predicament. 'Are you trying to have it off with Uc Dai Loi? If you are, it's my turn next after you finish.' She looks at the sight of the large, uniformed body lying spread-eagle on top of her friend, both of them sprawling half out of the case. 'Don't be greedy, Noc. Heavens, you can't have him *all* to yourself; you should know that.'

'Could you *please* help me, Wai?' Noc tries to wriggle free of the man's heavy body but, with his arms on either side of her small frame and the heavy equipment on his back and the large rifle stretched across her stomach, it is difficult to move; it's more than enough weight to pin her down. 'I'm stuck underneath the *Uc Dai Loi*'s body, Wai; and he's so–so big and so very–heavy. I'm afraid–it's–it's impossible for me to move him off. Could you help me please?'

'You are right; this man is very heavy,' Wai says, laughing as she tries to roll his body off her friend, but the rifle lodged between the two makes this exceedingly difficult for a small person like Wai. 'Do you always do it with Western strangers like this man? He has a very big body, and you are so small, I wonder what he's like. Have you seen if he's very big?'

Still pinned, Noc finally has her right hand free and with

a devious smile at her friend, she dives her hand into the camouflaged uniform and feels the groin area with her fingers and is extremely surprised at finding this part of his body warm and quite soft.

'Get him off me *quickly*, Wai; there is something very wrong with this man, something terribly strange! It's almost as if he's asleep and not just a corpse like we all thought.'

With all her strength and a great deal of effort, Wai finally takes his hand off the rifle and is able to roll the soldier's body over and off her friend, freeing her at last. They both sit there next to his side, panting, looking at each other with silly looks on both their faces and then back at the soldier, laughing at each other's stupidity.

Wai decides to investigate further. 'Let me have a look.' With her deft hands, she undoes the buttons to his fly, exposing all. She stammers, 'Look at it, Noc, it's growing!' She is quite startled and then pokes it. As if it has a mind of its own, it springs to life.

'What is happening to him, Noc?' she says and she quickly withdraws her hand, quite embarrassed at what she has unwittingly just done,. Confused, both women look at each other in shock and back at what stands to attention, looking very much alive. 'He is dead, isn't he? *Good heavens*, Noc! This can't be happening to us! This can't be true; what have we done to this *Uc Dai Loi*? He appears to be reviving from a very deep sleep I think.'

A loud groan vibrates from the body that now lies between the two girls, shocking them both to the core. Next, the man frees his other arm from under the rifle, sending the weapon clattering noisily to the floor, and instantly his arm moves upward towards his face. This distinct movement is followed by more groans from the man.

'*Let me up!*' screeches Noc.

Wai quickly scrambles to her feet. 'I've had enough of this. It's too much; I can't stand this any longer. I'm getting out of here now and getting someone who'll understand what's going on with this *Uc Dai Loi*.' Wai is now quite pale and very frightened and looks once more at the writhing body in front of her on the floor and immediately bolts for the door. 'I'm going to get the curators now, Noc. They'll know what's happening to this *Uc Dai Loi* and they should be able to give us some help with him. You'd better move away immediately from him, or he may hurt you.'

*   *   *

'Where am I? I ask, 'I feel like I've had a bad dream.' I lift a hand up and vigorously rub my eyes, as for some reason they feel sore. It's as if I've had sand or something acidic thrown into my face. I can now see two vague silhouettes moving to either side of me, so I focus on the nearest one. 'Who are you?' My vision starts to get a little better. I blink my eyes a number of times, lubricating them further, and this figure soon comes into my vision. I look up and see this attractive young Vietnamese woman just in front of me, staring at me as I vainly try to sit up, reaching out towards her for support, but unfortunately, I can't reach her and find myself falling back to the floor.

'My name is Noc. Welcome to Vietnam, *Uc Dai Loi*,' she says in broken English, smiling uncertainly at me but putting her arms out to meet me as I try for a second time to get up. Fortunately, this time she's ready for me and our hands meet. Then she grabs my arms and pulls me up to a sitting position, so my face is level with hers. 'You've been asleep for a long, long time, *Uc Dai Loi*. I hope you feel … better now that you are awake?'

'*Shit house!* Where? How? How did I get here? Who are you?' I surprise her as I say this in Vietnamese, and she gently holds me as I sit next to her. She's a very pretty young lady but she has such a strange look on her face – surprise. 'I can't stay like this; I'd better stand up.'

My first attempt to stand is a dismal failure and I come crashing back to my knees with the girl holding on and supporting me.

'Here, let me help you,' says the girl as she grabs me under the arms as if I'm an old man, and this time she slowly helps me remove my pack. It's thirty or so kilos of weight, which has been inhibiting my movements and ruining my balance. With the pack off and with her help, I finally get to my feet. I stagger around, supported by this pretty young woman. 'Be very careful in what you try to do or you could hurt yourself *Uc Dai Loi*. There you go; that is good, you've made it,' she says with a shy smile.

I feel like a drunken sailor who's just lost the bottle. I lean for a moment against some sort of large glass container and find I gain more of my balance each time I move. My head feels as if it's starting to clear so I'm able to think a little better about where I am. My past starts quickly rushing back through my mind.

'The last thing I remember is falling from the helicopter and hitting some trees,' I tell her, much to her surprise as now there are no slurred words. *Thank heavens for that course I did in South Australia just before we came over here*, I think to myself. Gaining more of my confidence each time I say something, I fire a number of questions at her. 'When I hit the trees, everything went blank from there on. Where is the rest of my patrol? Did they make it out okay? Did they come around to see me when I was in the hospital at Vung Tau?'

'I'm sorry, *Uc Dai Loi*, but you are twenty-five kilometres from Hanoi in the Ho Chi Minh exhibition rooms,' she tells me slowly, quite surprised at what I'm saying, and I feel her fiddling with the front of my cam gear, straightening things up. 'Here, let me tidy you up. I do small chores occasionally at the centre but mostly I am a cleaner here.' Then she really floors me: 'Do you realise, *Uc Dai Loi*, that I was just a little girl when I first saw you standing in this glass case?' She reaches around and looks at the date on the bottom of the glass case. 'You have been here long time now, ever since nineteen seventy, which is well before I was born; that is thirty or more years ago. Did you realise you sleep for so long?'

'*What?* What are you telling me?' I say, my memories flooding back but in somewhat of a turmoil. '*Thirty years!* You've got to be joking, girl – a few days perhaps, but heavens above, not thirty bloody years?'

The girl lets me go but stands close by while I stretch my muscles back and forth, trying to get the circulation going throughout my entire body, but for some reason, they seem tired, extremely tired. With each movement I find they are beginning to respond and start to loosen up, as if I've just finished a nine-miler. I soon feel like they are getting much better, much better indeed and very quickly.

Out of instinct, I bend over and pick up the SLR where the big rifle lies on the floor by my feet. It feels good to hold the weapon once again. I check it. It's mine and it's clean so I check the magazine and am pleased to find it's fully loaded with a full thirty-round magazine. I'm surprised; it's almost as if someone has just done the job for me. I look up the barrel and notice the tape is gone from the threaded muzzle which I'd put on before leaving camp. It's there to keep the water out and I know damn well that I'd fired the weapon in our getaway and the rounds should have broken the tape, but the remainder of the tape should be still around the barrel. There's something dramatically wrong here, something very wrong indeed with this entire situation, especially with this pretty young thing that is holding me up.

'Why am I still in my combat fatigues?' I ask, suddenly realising that I'm still fully dressed as if going out on patrol, even with grenades which are still in my webbing, and I'm not wet, as I remember it was raining through the night. I look at the glass container behind me, seeing the reflection of my face, black and green, but not the way I usually do it, making me very pleased I picked up my rifle as I'm so confused. I look at this young woman and nervously ask her, 'What the hell is going on here? You have to tell me. I have to know where I am and why I'm here. Why am I still dressed in my combat fatigues? I would have expected to be in the hospital at Vung Tau after my fall.'

'As I told you before, you are at the Ho Chi Minh centre close to Hanoi, and you been here since nineteen-seventy.' She then points behind me to a brass sign at the foot of the glass case. 'You've been in that glass case, *Uc Dai Loi*, ever since I can remember; you have been an exhibition to the Vietnamese people, so they know who their enemies are and what you look like when dressed for battle.'

Shocked to the core, I'm about to ask more questions when suddenly I hear the loud hammering sound of feet on the floor – many feet all coming my way at a fast pace. I spin around instinctively, cocking my rifle and putting one up the spout. It's the other girl who was here earlier; I vaguely remember her when I woke and saw her shadowy figure as she left me and ran off. She's with three white-coated attendants and, oh shit, they're being followed by two soldiers and the bastards are both carrying AK-47s. The two sweating overweight soldiers see me standing in the middle of the room. They stop, staring at me. If what the girl has said is true, they likely don't believe the situation they've just encountered.

I've got to cover myself if that's the case, I think to myself. They slowly start to swing their weapons off their shoulders down towards me and begin to raise their rifle barrels at me in a very sinister fashion that I don't like at all. Everything seems almost to be in slow motion, but thankfully by the looks of these soldiers they're well overweight. I'm extremely lucky; they're probably base wallowers here doing some cushy job, otherwise I'd most likely be dead by now if they were good, professional soldiers.

'You silly bastards, that's a *big* mistake.' The SLR bucks at my shoulder, filling the room with the loud reports of the short burst of fire, which instantly spews death on the two men in green uniforms. They're slammed backwards by the impact of the big 7.62 mm rounds hitting them square in the chests. I feel a cruel smile cross my face as a large dose of adrenaline surges unrelentingly through my body; I watch the two being thrown back and knocked to the floor.

'Raise your hands, now!' I shout in Vietnamese. It has the desired effect on the other four as their hands quickly shoot up into the air. 'Come here the lot of you; now move, damn you! *Move!'*

They sheepishly walk towards me, their hands high above their heads, staring straight at me but strangely for some reason not in fear, this time it's more so curiosity, which totally surprises me.

'How many more soldiers do they have stationed here at this establishment? How many others are in these buildings that I'll have to round up before it's safe?' I study their reaction to this question because it will tell me if they are lying and if I have to deal with any more of their troops.

'Th—those of us in this r—room are the only ones on duty today,' comes a curious stammer from one of the attendants, but for some reason it sounds more out of excitement than fear at my evident resurrection. 'We finish here tonight then go home, as no one works here in the evenings.' Although still nervous, he explains with a shrug of his shoulders, 'I don't even know why we have soldiers here because they never do anything to help us around the research station.'

'You are alive after all these years,' says another young attendant, lowering his hands and gently reaching towards me more out of sheer curiosity and he touches my arm, feeling the muscle. 'You have been in that case many years, *Uc Dai Loi*. It is incredible. We all thought you were dead and preserved as a mummy like Chairman Ho in your glass case. Some even thought you were a dummy and asked us why you were still here as the war with your country finished almost twenty-five years ago.'

I'm still confused but relent a little. 'Lower your arms but be careful not to touch anything and don't make any sudden moves or do anything stupid like those two men did. If you do as I tell you I promise you won't get hurt,' I say, wondering what in hell's name I'm doing here and, more to the point, what I am going to do with them and how in the blazes I am going to get out of this place if what they are saying is right, particularly if I'm actually in North Vietnam. That is, if they are telling me the truth and I am in the North, where the hell are we?

Boy, I'm now very grateful that I did that Vietnamese language course six months before we came over here on my second tour of duty. It was a bloody joke at the time, but I'd been shown how important it was by Abe at the ox cart when he was able to tell me exactly what they were saying.

'You are now in the Socialist Republic of Vietnam,' one of the older attendants tells me with a large grin that I don't quite understand as he feels my arm, still grinning stupidly at me as if I'm a freak of nature in some sort of show and I'm the main attraction. 'You have been in that glass case over there, *Uc Dai Loi*, since I was a young boy and came here with my father to look at the war exhibitions that were on display at the time. We all thought you were a mummy just like Chairman Ho, particularly when the American war had been over for a large number of years.'

'But I remember I fell from a helicopter,' I tell them, getting irritated at consistently being told it was years ago when to me it feels like yesterday. 'We were doing reconnaissance work in the south of Long Khan Province when we had a contact with your military and were being extracted by rope. How did I get here?'

'We were told you were brought here by an army officer many years ago. He was a very special man, our Major Thong,' he says with a great deal of pride in his voice. 'He did wonders with bodies, but unfortunately, he went missing in the south and it was assumed he was killed during the war of liberation. It was a long time before any of us came to work at this facility and you were already here standing in your glass case for a number of years. We don't know any details of how he got you or how you came here because the war had finished many years before we started to work here. All we knew is that you were an enemy soldier during the war, and you were brought here during the conflict. This was told to me one time when I asked a colonel about you, and he told me that a Major Thong had you on display for our young people to see what our enemy looked like and so they knew who we were fighting when they went south to the conflict.'

I listen to this man in the white coat explain this preposterous story. I quickly glance at the glass case just behind me when he mentions this and immediately back to the group of people staring at me. *Are they telling me the truth about being here thirty-something years?* I keep asking myself, thinking it's got to be a trick to gain something from me. I further confuse them when I tell them what my intentions are because I've got to warn our people what the Vietnamese are doing to me so they can take countermeasures to neutralise whatever this scheme is. Is this some fiendish plot they have concocted to try and win this bloody war? I throw a couple of wild cards into the conversation, confusing things quite a bit.

'Do you people *realise* what your government is doing? What they have done to me, for whatever the reason, is against the Geneva Convention. Do you see that what your government has done to me is a war crime? They have broken international law by keeping me here in that glass case at this facility. Do you understand what you've told me if this war has been over for almost thirty years?'

'What has been done to you, *Uc Dai Loi*, was done when the war was still going in the south. We are all food scientists here and innocent of such things that happened before we began working here – we had nothing to do with what was done during the war. We are here because we are agronomists and are doing agricultural experiments so we can lift the tonnage of the rice crop for our farmers, by growing better cultivars, so our country can become self-sufficient with our food production, not reliant on other countries to help us feed our people like it was when you were alive.' His eyes are large and full of emotion.

'I've got to get out of here and back to my unit as I'll have to warn our authorities what's been going on at this so-called research establishment. I'll have to tie you up, so don't do anything stupid and warn the authorities that I have broken out of here,' I say, pointing to the glass case before looking around the room. I am relieved to see very small windows situated high up the wall that would be almost impossible for these people to get through. 'Better still, I'll lock you in this room so you can't warn the authorities of my escape.'

'Honestly, that is what happened to you, *Uc Dai Loi*, because the American War, as we called the conflict, has been finished for close to twenty-five years; they will do nothing to you,' says another one of the attendants, almost visually pleading with me to put down my rifle and give myself up. 'Many people from your country come here regularly to visit our beautiful land to enjoy our holiday facilities. They look at all the war-related things and learn from us the truth of what happened here with the Americans during our war to liberate the southern part of our country from their cruel oppression of our people.'

He suddenly stops talking, realising he may have said the wrong thing when he thinks of the attitudes of the communists toward their people. These haven't changed at all as long as he can remember.

'Why have I been kept here so long if the conflict is over?' I say, annoyed that my body wasn't sent home when the war finished. 'What are those two people over there doing with automatic rifles in an agricultural centre? Because they are the same rifles they used against me during the war. I'm still at war with your people. I'm still at war with North Vietnam,' I say in a very disgruntled voice, not believing at all what these people are trying to tell me. 'Until someone I know and trust tells me any different, I'm afraid I'm still at war with communist North Vietnam.'

'But, Sir, we are telling you the truth about the war being finished because it finished in nineteen seventy-five with the Americans withdrawal. We won and all your soldiers and the Americans went home many years ago. No one shoots at anyone over here now because we're at peace with the countries around us.'

From where I stand looking at my surroundings, what he's trying to tell me about this being an agricultural research centre makes absolutely no sense at all. 'Again, I ask you, why haven't I been sent home and who were the two people I just killed with the guns? I point directly at Noc. 'I will take this girl there as a hostage and I'll also take those guns your soldiers had with me because if you are at peace with the world as you all are saying, you'll have no use for automatic weapons such as these in this agricultural establishment.'

There is dead silence from them all as it finally dawns on the three men that I mean business and can't be persuaded to do anything else. What an experiment they are letting walk out the door; what a breakthrough this Major Thong must have made all those years ago and now it seems that this experiment of his is just walking away from them, leaving them with nothing but memories.

I carefully check the two dead guards, taking their guns and ammunition with me, pulling a device out and taking the handpiece with me. To give me a head start, I lock the other four in the room with a promise from them that they won't try to escape for at least an hour. Once outside, I look around and make sure no one is coming. I quickly break open one of the AK-47s and fling the internal parts away but keep the other and the ammunition I'd taken from both guards, as I may need this later on if I run into any more of their troops as I try to make my getaway out of this country.

'The staff's cars are over this way,' says Noc, now full of confidence. She grabs me by the arm and steers me over to a carpark that is situated behind the buildings. 'That old one is Dr Phou's. He never shuts it properly; I'm sure you will find the keys in the ignition because he always leaves them there. He's the younger of the three men – a nice man, an agronomist but very careless with such matters as this.'

We are lucky, it's as Noc says. To me the Citroen car looks new and very modern. It's parked just outside the centre with the keys in the ignition and when I start the motor, I find the tank is full of fuel, another added bonus for my getaway but to my surprise my escape is quickly being taken out of my hands by this attractive, rather headstrong young woman who now appears to want to help me get away.

'I will take you to the wharves at Haiphong,' says Noc, who is giving me directions. She pauses and bites her lip. 'What do I call you, *Uc Dai Loi*? Because it's quite a long way to Haiphong and we haven't been properly introduced yet. Come on, you have a name. I can't keep calling you *Uc Dai Loi*.'

'My friends call me Peter,' I tell her. It appears that she wants to help me find a boat to get out of this country. 'My name is Peter Jackson.'

She smiles at me, eyes gleaming, and puts out her hand. 'Now that I know your name, Peter, we'll go to Haiphong and find you a suitable boat for you to make your escape in. There are plenty of big boats there from many countries that come and go from this port. You should be able to find one that will take you away from Vietnam, back to your own country.'

We drive to the wharves in Haiphong. It's a long trip and far from a quiet one, for in between traffic instructions she questions me on every detail about myself from the time I was called up in the army until I was captured. She can't get over the fact that I've been in the laboratory for almost thirty years and I'm seemingly no older than she is. I also have problems with this myself. It's almost like I've had a terrible nightmare and I've just woken up, almost expecting my friends to be waiting around the corner to take the mickey out of me now that I'm awake. These thoughts constantly run through my mind, worrying me. What really concerns me, however, is what if they are telling me the truth? What happens now? It's only a matter of time before I'm going to be fair game to anyone with a rifle and soon all police and soldiers in Vietnam will be out looking for me after killing the two guards at the centre. If what Noc tells me is true, I'm sure when the authorities are told of this escape, I'll be given no quarter, so I have to get out of Vietnam as quickly as I possibly can.

'You realise, Noc, your people will be after me as soon as your friends get out and they won't be interested in the fact that I've been in a laboratory for thirty years; now their only interest in me will be the embarrassment I've caused the communist government and the fact that I've just killed two of their soldiers.'

'I realise that, Peter, that's why I'm showing you the way to Haiphong so you can get away easily before they sound the alarm.' She grabs my arm, startling me with this sudden contact. 'Take heart, Peter, you'll be alright. We will get to the wharves of Haiphong, and I am sure we'll find you a boat so you can leave our country and return to yours and carry on with your life as if nothing has happened.'

I'm amazed at the array of cars we pass, particularly with their streamlined shapes and different colours – totally different to anything I've ever seen before, making me wonder if what they've been telling me is right, but I have enough composure to keep this fact hopefully hidden from this talkative girl who's showing me the way.

When we arrive at the Haiphong wharves, I find there are only very large cargo boats and, judging by the flags, I see none of these would be friendly towards me, a fugitive now from their government. I'm sure that if enquiries are made, government officials would be looking for me by now and I would be turned in very quickly by these people.

'I'm afraid if I was looking for someone who wanted to leave this country without proper papers like I am, Noc, this would be the first place they would look, and the airport would be the next. We'll have to go south somewhere to some small fishing village where there is little or no security. I hope you understand exactly what I mean, Noc. I have to get away from the obvious, and by saying that, I mean here. We'll have to go somewhere where there are boats, lots of boats but much smaller ones than these, boats that I will have no difficulty in controlling by myself with these firearms I have.'

'But the boats – they are here,' says Noc, looking at me a little confused, then immediately back at the boats along the wharf, obviously not knowing the flags these ships are flying. 'Look, Peter, I'm sure any one of them would take you when they realise the problem you have with the authorities. I'm sure they would hide you onboard until they sail away from here.'

'We'll have to go somewhere south, where it's not so crowded like here and no one is looking for me,' I insist stubbornly and point out a number of uniformed government officials who I can see lazing around on the wharf. 'There are far too many government employees hanging around here. Just look, Noc! You can see them *everywhere* along the wharf, just looking for people like me trying to get onboard a ship without the right papers. Hopefully, the further south we go, there may be more people who still have some sympathies for the old South Vietnamese government; although, from what you told me, it's evidently been a long, long time since any of them were in power.'

I look at the baffled expression on her face as we drive quickly back to Hanoi. I still have a huge amount of disbelief at my circumstances, and I am desperately trying to come to grips with what I've been told. Frankly, I find it's totally unbelievable for something like this to happen and, if it has, I don't want this pretty little thing with me being caught up and punished along with me for helping me get out of their clutches.

'You'd better get out here, Noc, otherwise you're going to get shot along with me if we're caught.' She watches me intently as I speak and begins shaking her head vigorously at me, showing her displeasure at what I'm trying to say. 'I'll tell you now, I have no intention of being caught by your government, so I suggest you get out now that we're back in Hanoi before the military catch up with us. By now your friends should be out of the centre and would have sounded the alarm.' I see angry tears forming in her eyes. 'They will be looking for this car and for you, my girl, because you have helped. The communists that I knew from my time will frown on anyone giving a fugitive help and that's what you've done for me.'

'No, no, no. I stay with you,' she says with a great deal of determination and stubbornness in her voice. 'This is my big adventure as well, Peter. Look, we will go south now if you want to. My parents were originally from Da Nang and my father was a very qualified man who came north when I was a small girl, looking for work. He landed a good job in Hanoi and brought the rest of our family up to join him, but that was many years ago now.' She pauses, looking at me as if to say, *I'm with you.* 'We can go south now, Peter, if that's what you want, because there are lots of small fishing villages on both sides of the city of Da Nang where you should be able to catch a small boat. You may find what you are looking for there and maybe, just maybe, get lucky and find a small boat that will take you away from Vietnam and back to your country.'

'It's getting dark now and, like I said, your friends must have broken out of the laboratory by this time and sounded the alarm.' I look across at the slim, lovely figure of this young woman sitting there so calmly in the passenger's seat, and for the first time I fully appreciate her efforts to try and help me get away. Hell's bells – if she hadn't been fooling around at the centre, I'd still be in that glass case slowly getting mouldy. Perhaps they would have incinerated me to destroy any evidence of my body being in the north of the country. 'I think it would be wise if we changed cars and keep ourselves hidden as long as we possibly can.' I certainly don't want to incriminate her for being in my presence and helping me like she has. 'I'm sure that your authorities will be looking for this car by now, so if you can, take me to a suitable place where we can get another vehicle, that way it won't be as noticeable as this one of Dr Phou's. They will have a description of this vehicle circulated to their police and most likely the army. Your comrades would have notified the authorities by now that I've broken out of the Ho

Chi Minh Centre and unfortunately they witnessed me killing those guards.'

'I know just the place and it's on our way,' says Noc, with a large sly smile spreading across her lovely face. 'You just follow my instructions, Peter, and I'll show you the perfect getaway car for us to take. If it's there, and I'm sure it is, then we'll be able to travel to the south in comfort and style.'

So, with Noc's assistance, I'm guided through the streets of Hanoi and eventually to an upper-class suburb on the southern side of the city where we finally come to an area where there appears to be a number of up-market cafes. We park down the street, a number of blocks away from the other cars. Again, Noc gets this odd look on her face and takes me by the arm, leading me down this darkened street to the suitable replacement vehicle. It feels strange with me being dressed in camouflaged combat fatigues, pack on my back with a rifle slung on my shoulder and another tucked under my arm.

We finally reach a section of the street that is full of modern cars that graphically remind me how long I'd been asleep. These modern vehicles are parked outside a heap of these swanky establishments, making me pleased that it's dark, as I feel totally out of place.

'Now you wait here out of the light, Peter, and I will see if my ignorant ex-boyfriend's car is there. Your uniform would be out of place in Vietnam in these days as no Westerners dress in that way over here and certainly don't carry firearms.'

This situation doesn't appear to worry Noc because, full of confidence, she leaves me and strides quite quickly across to a row of extremely modern cars, reaching what turns out to be a Toyota sports coupe that from this distance looks to be almost off the showroom floor. She turns and cheekily smiles in my direction before opening the car door, then with another radiant smile, she beckons me across to her.

'He never locks his car,' she tells me, quite proud of her achievement and very happy that the car is here. 'His spare keys will be under the driver's side mat. I've told this stupid man a number of times that he should lock his car properly so it can't be stolen; so tonight should teach him a very good lesson in security and will serve him right for being such an ignorant man who wouldn't listen to me.'

'Do you know this person, Noc?'

'Yes, I know him,' she says, still with the crooked smile stretching over her pretty face. 'He used to take me out, but he only wanted one thing, so after a while I dropped him. This annoyed him immensely as he's used to getting his own way. He hung around me for quite some time, begging me to come back to him before he finally found another girl. Err,' she says, shaking her head and her body giving a slight quiver, 'a very trashy yum, yum girl who would do everything he wanted. I've been extremely lucky and haven't seen him now for quite a few months and, to be quite honest, Peter,' she says with a quick shake of her head, 'I haven't missed that stupid man either.'

The keys are under the mat just like she told me and thankfully the car's fuel tank is also full. So within a few minutes we're well on the road again and immediately start heading south out of Hanoi towards the thirty-eighth parallel – what used to be the border between the North and the old South Vietnam. This is quickly pointed out by Noc, who appears to be certainly enjoying this dangerous escape of mine.

'This is where the old border used to be according to my father when he took our family down to Da Nang for a few days to show us where we originally came from.'

'I expect it would have been a bit of an eye-opener to know where you came from,' I reply. It gives me a little relief to hear that we were finally getting out of the North. 'I expect it would have given you a bit of a shock going back to where you used to live now that Vietnam is the one country.'

'Yes, it did, Peter; but you have to realise my father was an officer in the liberation army and fought with the North.' This statement gives me a huge jolt to know that her father was a member of the Viet Cong. 'That's why he was able to go north when the war finished to continue his career in the sciences at Hanoi University. It was because of this connection that my brothers and I were able to further our educations but, unfortunately for me, I chose agriculture. I expected to be able to get into the scientific side of plant production because our country desperately needs to lift its food production.'

I drive for a number of hours, listening to her tell me of the dreams she has for agriculture and how this is being held back by her superiors who seem to be restricting her in this field. From what she explains to me, it's because she's a young woman. The fact that her father was a member of the Viet Cong likely causes me to neglect to tell her about my family's involvement in agriculture. Just as I start to feel tired, I notice a side road in a suitable place, so I turn off the highway and park a little away from the main road on a small disused track in some thick trees. Almost a good lay-up point, I subconsciously think, and well south of the old border, hoping we're well clear of any police or army units that are most likely out scouring the country around Hanoi for us by now.

'We'll spend the night here, Noc,' I tell her as we pull up because I can see that she's as tired as I am. 'Make yourself comfortable young lady so we can get some shut-eye, because who knows what we'll have in front of us when dawn comes. We'll have to be as fresh as a daisy and be on our toes, for I'm sure by now both the army and police will be out scouring the country looking for us and may be expanding their search this way when we're not found in or around Hanoi or Haiphong.'

We push the seats back as far as they'll go and lay them part way down, trying to get as comfortable as possible in this small sporty car, which was certainly not built for sleeping in. I'm surprised when Noc lies diagonally across the seats. She places her head firmly in my lap and then looks up into my eyes, not as sleepy as I first thought.

'I hope you don't mind, Peter,' she says, looking up at me with those magical big brown eyes. 'When I'm out, I always need someone to sleep with. I hope you don't mind if I rest my head on you like this.'

'Not at all, Noc, not at all.' For some reason, I begin stroking her hair and I realise she's the first female I've been alone with since I left my Alicia to re-join my unit. In my time it was some eight months ago, but in real-time, how long has it been since I was with a woman alone by myself in a car like this? My head spins.

I lie back on the seat with my hand resting on Noc's head, which is on my knee, and strangely, having a female so close to me gives me a nice feeling of security. I stroke her head and feel the warmth of her and straight away I start thinking of my Alicia and what has become of her since I left. *Is she married? She'd have to be if time has moved on so far as they keep telling me.* I sit musing away to myself with this stranger's head on my lap and suddenly realise it's the first sleep I can remember since falling from the helicopter.

It can't be … the communists are up to something sinister, and I feel I'm part of their devious plot. But how is this woman involved, for surely she can't be part of their plan? She's been such a great help to me getting so far from Hanoi, for that's where they'll be initially looking for me, I'm sure. What is all this cloak-and-dagger nonsense about? What have they got up their sleeve concerning me? What have they got in store for me now?

I think of the shape of this car I'm lying in and others that we had passed. I look at the components on the dash and think of the cars I'd seen on the street in both Hanoi and Haiphong. They are much more streamlined and modern than what I am used to. I start thinking about the newness of my own car, a Morris 1100 that I'd bought brand new after returning from the first tour and had parked at the barracks in the unit's carpark when we left to come on our next commitment here. How old that new car of mine would be, I think, as I do a quick appraisal of both machines, and I shake my head, trying to make something out of my predicament.

I think again of the bizarre events and of what the communists are trying to get out of me, and when I look down and see the lovely curve of her cheek, I wonder in the grand scheme of things, how this girl fits in.

Ho Chi Minh Centre, Hanoi

Back at the laboratory, there is great discussion on what to do about the Australian soldier's dramatic escape. None of the staff has any time for the government and most are not inclined to assist them by sounding the alarm and exiting the building any earlier than they have to.

'We should wait in here until morning,' Quang says, looking

at the other three in his superior manner before suggesting a solution to the situation they find themselves in. 'I say the *Uc Dai Loi* has been asleep in his glass case so long now and he certainly deserves to remain free now that he has woken up. I say he should be allowed to go back to his own country and enjoy his life with his family who would have given him up for dead such a long, long time ago——'

'But he is a murderer! We all saw him kill those two men over there!' one of the attendants, Trung, interrupts, showing very little emotion towards the two dead soldiers who still lie in pools of blood some ten feet from them. 'We *must* report him for their deaths as they would have been shown on the security camera or we will be implicated because we saw what happened and we have done nothing. We cannot leave them there, lying in their own blood on the floor, we *have* to do something.'

'We are out of the camera's vision at the moment so we should think of something that would have prevented us from sounding the alarm, for example, we were tied up and unable to sound the alarm of his escape?'

'That *Uc Dai Loi* was rather nice for a Westerner,' says Wai, thinking of how she had held him an hour ago and what they'd done to him just before he woke up. 'I think we should wait until morning and give them a chance to get away. 'What have we got to lose – he's been asleep for longer than anyone I know. We'll probably end up hurting ourselves if we try to get out of the windows and I don't intend to hurt myself for anyone, particularly the authorities.' She quite emotionally grabs Phou's arm, pleading with her eyes for support. 'I say we stay here and wait until the morning before we sound the alarm. Let's give them a good opportunity to get away because I think we owe it to the *Uc Dai Loi* for holding him here against his will for such a long period of time. Heavens, years being cooped up in that glass case is almost a life sentence in itself, particularly as the American War has been over for so long and no attempt was made to return his body to his people.'

'I agree with Wai; we should wait here until morning,' says Phou, putting his hand on her arm and quite quickly appearing to also have a lot of sympathy for the Australian. 'I didn't like those two soldiers who were stationed here, anyway. They were fat and lazy and would not help with our work around the centre. It was only yesterday that I asked for just a little help lifting trays of plants off the back of a truck and moving them into the laboratory. It was those same two lazy people who just stood there laughing at me as I struggled to move each of the trays into the building; if they'd helped, we would have saved well over half an hour. *Ooh*, they thought they were *so* superior to us, just because they were in the military force and were carrying guns around. I'll bet the only thing they ever shot at were targets.' He looks across at the two bodies on the floor in contempt, shaking his head. Phou feels no sympathy for them at all and laughs to himself as he thinks how easily this Australian soldier had killed them. 'You can see clearly how good they were at their chosen profession in allowing this man who had been asleep to kill them so easily.' He waves his free hand towards the two dead soldiers dismissively and shoots Wai a glance.

'I agree entirely with you, Phou,' says Trung. He'd been thinking about the occasion a week before when he'd asked for help from this pair; they had both refused to help him. He'd angrily decided that he owed them nothing and changed his stance. 'This is something we can tell our families about one day. We can tell them about an *Uc Dai Loi, Ma Rung* soldier who has been asleep for years in a glass case at our laboratory,' he urges.

'I can tell them how Noc opened his case to clean it and how he fell out. Then he picks up his big weapon and shoots two of our soldiers dead in front of us. Comrades, what an unbelievable adventure we are having and in the Ho Chi Minh Centre of all places!' Again, he looks at the others, his eyes burning with pent-up excitement at these bloody events, and how the situation has swept them along so quickly.

Suddenly Trung's face changes, becoming far more serious as he thinks of the ramifications this may have on them when the authorities are finally notified and look at the surveillance camera's footage. 'In the morning we'd better get some rope and do something that looks as if we were tied up or we may be in trouble with the government when we eventually report this man missing. Perhaps it would be prudent if we bruise ourselves a little as well to make it look as if we resisted this *Uc Dai Loi, Ma Rung* soldier before he overpowered us and tied us up.' He then stresses on his companions what their course of action should be to avoid the government's anger. 'We should be very careful and stay this side of the museum out of sight so they can't see us, get some rope from the store, and make it seem as if we were tied up by this *Uc Dai Loi Ma Rung* soldier and only got out in the morning to sound the alarm when one of us eventually was able to get free.'

'That is an excellent idea, Trung,' Wai replies, grateful for his suggestion. 'There is plenty of rope in the storage room we can use. I'll get a coil of rope now.'

Vietnam

I wake up very early the next morning, feeling cramped, and quickly look out of the window. It's still dark; I automatically watch the shapes of trees near the car like I did the previous night as if expecting them to suddenly move and for soldiers to rush forward towards me and overpower us. I'm totally confused as I look into the darkness that surrounds us because I've been dreaming of my beautiful girl in America, the one I haven't seen for months, except now it appears those months have stretched into years.

What does she look like now, and more to the point, is she still alive? Has my girl gotten married? Has she had children? What city does she now live in, that is, if she's still alive? These and other questions keep tumbling through my mind because she's the only one my dreams are centred on.

I'm pulled out of this jumbled trance when I suddenly feel a weight on my knee and quickly look down to see Noc move her head in an attempt to get comfortable. I see this very pretty young woman sound asleep with her head on my lap. She's certainly a lovely young creature, yes, but she's not mine. Instantly the memories of yesterday's violent events come flooding back, causing me to carefully reach down, trying not to startle her, stroking her hair as a prelude to waking her. I gently shake her shoulder, watching her as she stirs, her big almond eyes slowly opening as she turns her head, looking directly up at me. After a warm sleepy gaze, I see an initial look of alarm as she flicks her gaze around the car and back to me, no doubt surprised at the strange circumstances she finds herself in. Strangely, she relaxes again and the surprise in her eyes is replaced by another, warmer look.

'I'm afraid it's time to go, Noc, it's almost light,' I tell her as she slowly rouses herself. She turns her pretty face up towards me, looking at me. I think she wonders who this strange man dressed in a dirty camouflage uniform is. She rolls her head slightly to one side and her beautiful big brown eyes envelop me before she reaches up and gives me a little kiss. When she pulls gently away, this time her eyes gleam as she searches my face. I'm pulled into a whirlpool and struggle to say, 'It's almost dawn and err … we have quite a long way to go before we reach the coast, Noc, so … we'd better get started before they realise we're not in Hanoi and widen the search even further. They'll put up roadblocks to catch us.'

'Oh? You are such a hard man, Peter.' She sits up and rubs her eyes. Then, an almost pleading expression appears on her face, and I feel her hand not too subtly start to caress me. 'Do you realise you are the first *Uc Dai Loi* I have ever slept with, and we didn't even make love last night?' She slowly shakes her head. 'It's so early; do we really have to go so soon? It's not even light yet and what a marvellous opportunity we have to get to know each other properly.'

I draw a breath and steel myself for what I'm about to say. I reluctantly encircle her hand, stopping her delightful touch. 'I'm afraid so, Noc … we have to get to the coast before we're found by the authorities. I don't want anything to happen to you and by now there will be a lot of angry people out there frantically looking for me as I'm quite sure I'll be a huge embarrassment to the communist government if what you've told me about them is right. So, we'd better make tracks as soon as possible and get to the coast as fast as we can so they don't take their anger out on you, my girl, for helping me get so far south from Hanoi.'

For the first time since these events began, I feel the pangs of hunger grabbing my stomach and realise Noc hasn't eaten since yesterday either. I hope to get a quick breakfast somewhere on the way, perhaps at some small, remote fishing village on our way to the south.

'Alright Peter, we will go now,' she says, looking up at me and almost willing me to wait with her until dawn. 'I will show you the way to the coast, but please remember Vietnam is now the one country. There is no north, no south and both peoples are the same, so please be very careful if you speak to anyone because by this time the People's Army will certainly be out in force looking for you – and me,' she corrects herself. 'Just remember they have informers everywhere.' She looks into my eyes, a worried expression crossing her face.

She sits up, clearly with something on her mind. 'Please be *very* careful because you *must* realise you stand out by wearing your strange-looking army clothes; you are completely out of place even for a Westerner in Vietnam and they make you look very different on the street. If we stop somewhere near the coast, you'll have to promise me, Peter, you will *not* leave this car dressed like this, as you are inviting trouble, particularly with the weapons you are carrying. You will have to let me do all the talking and I'll get our food for breakfast when we reach a suitable place.'

I realise that we have no money to buy food and begin to say as much when Noc interrupts and fishes out a few dollars from her pocket saying, 'Look, enough for food!' Her eyes brighten as she excitedly states, 'I'll have a look in the glove compartment and see if I can find some Dong because that *stupid* former boyfriend of mine always leaves his change in the car.'

Noc rummages through the glove compartment for some money. With a large grin on her face, she soon produces a fist full of notes that look totally different to the Dong I remember when going on leave in Vung Tau.

'As I told you before, my former boyfriend has a very wealthy family and a good job that his parents found for him in the

public service. He's always so very careless with his money and treats it as if it grows on trees.' Her eyes sparkle with her luck, and she states, 'I will buy you something good to eat and a drink of coffee with his money.' With a giggle she looks at me closely and places one finger playfully on my cheek. 'Your face still has little bits of green and black all over it. You will have to wash your face because no one uses that type of make-up these days.'

I am relieved that Noc's idiot ex-boyfriend has left a substantial amount of money tucked away. It occurs to me then that perhaps I shouldn't have been that concerned for her and the situation with her ex, and I question my own motives. Confused, I turn my attention back to Noc, thinking that it is likely been drug money he'd stashed and that I'll deal with him later. 'Noc, I'll let you buy what we want when we reach this place; we both need some food.' I surprise her with my next comment. 'You know, Noc, the last thing I remember eating was a dehydrated ration pack of chilli con carne mixed with cold water when hiding from your people that last night.' I laugh, which confuses her further. 'Maybe there are still some of those rations in my pack that we could eat?'

'I don't think I wish to eat something so old, Peter.' Noc shakes her head, thinking I'm joking. 'We will get something on the way that is a little fresher than your army rations. There is definitely weight in your pack but no, let's get something nice that we can both enjoy.'

Under Noc's guidance, we head for the coast and follow the road south. We soon have the sun rising over the beautiful South China Sea to our left, telling me the next day has suddenly arrived. But what will it bring?

'Stop here, Peter.' She gives my leg a gentle squeeze, which gets my attention. 'There's a small store coming up that I know has good food.'

I park well away from the roadside stall and although I've managed to wipe my face a bit, the clothes are still of concern. After she reminds me not to get out of the car, Noc scampers across the road, chooses our meal and then haggles over the price with the owner before she returns quickly to the car with the cooked fish and drinks.

'The fish looked fresh, but it was quite expensive,' she says, giving me a small grimace at the cost. 'The stall owner said it was caught last night so I had little alternative, because she looked at the car and obviously thought I was rich but wouldn't move very much on price, so I had to take the food.' Then with a giggle she continues, 'But then, Peter, you have to remember *we* are not buying this expensive food – my former stupid boyfriend is shouting this wonderful meal for both of us, so enjoy your fish.'

The food is nice and fresh and tastes fine, but even though I'm hungry, I have difficulty eating very much and give almost half of mine to Noc, who looks at me quite surprised before eating what's left of my share. Once we've eaten, I start driving again down the coastal highway with Noc chatting the whole way, filling me in on what's happened here and there as we go through each small village. Finally, we come to a tiny fishing hamlet on what appears to be a tidal river and stop just away from the wharf with a good view of the boats that thankfully are still all sitting at their moorings. We just sit for a moment, talking of the past as Noc gives me the history of this quiet little fishing hamlet, which her mother evidently came from just after the war finished.

I look around, pleased to note the houses are well back from the river as sometimes during the wet season, according to Noc, the river floods. We watch the people on the boats with interest as they prepare their nets, lines and other fishing equipment well before they leave. It's obvious that they're waiting for the tide to rise so they can steam out to sea to their fishing grounds.

'I'll try to get the last boat out of here,' I tell Noc, pointing to a small craft that looks far less prepared to go than the other larger boats. Realising it is rapidly approaching crunch time, I turn to look at her. 'I'll wait and see if that's the last boat and if it is, that'll be the one I take; however, before I go, I'd like to thank you for helping me get so far away from Hanoi. You didn't have to do so much to help me, Noc, I hope you know that.' I pause again for a moment, looking at this young woman who's helped me much more than I'd expected and hope she doesn't slip up with the authorities when they question her when she returns to Hanoi. By now the police and army will be tearing the place apart looking for me. 'I'm afraid I'll still have to come to terms with the fact it's now years later than it feels. It's something I'll have to adjust to, I expect, because even Australia will have changed dramatically from when I was there last.'

I look her straight in the eyes as if giving her a last chance to tell me the truth – that this is some complicated communist conspiracy hatched up by their government and others to get something out of us. I'm confused as to what it could be because I'm just one of the diggers in our army and know nothing of importance that would have a bearing on this war. I keep asking myself these difficult questions over and over again, because I feel like a pawn in some highly sophisticated communist plot. If not, what the *hell* has happened to me? Is it possible that time has moved on so far into the future somehow without me, just like Noc and others are telling me?

'That's alright, Peter; I've had an exciting time as well.' She gazes at me for a moment then suddenly reaches over and kisses me passionately on the lips. When she stops, I'm stunned, and I stare into her eyes, wanting more. Her eyes have a light that draws me to her, and then once again she touches my groin, exciting me with her soft feminine touch and tempting me greatly. 'What will I tell my friends when they ask me about you? We never even made love and I was sleeping with you all night. What do I say to them when they ask, which they will? Peter, what will I tell them?' She sighs and continues, 'Because they certainly will have expected you to take advantage of me …' She giggles again, but this time it is not the giggle of a girl, but that of a woman. 'How can I explain this – there is very little room in this car?'

Although I remain focused, Noc punctuates every few words of mine with little kisses on my cheeks and mouth. 'You are a very inventive young woman, Noc.' I give a little laugh when I think of this car. 'I'm sure you will be able to concoct a very interesting tale of how this *Uc Dai Loi* took advantage–of the situation and made mad passionate love to you in the front seat of–of your former boy friend's car. I'm sure with your imagination, yes, you should be able to concoct an extremely interesting–story of how the–how the–err–gearstick kept getting in the way–and how we were able to over–overcome such an inconvenience by laying the seats well back so we had plenty of room to–carry on.'

Noc lifts her head back and laughs at my joke, before patting me on the leg. 'I will be kind to you, Peter. In your absence you will not be a villain when I tell my story to Wai. She's a friend of mine who I work with, and she saw you just after you got out of your case. She was the girl who panicked and ran next door and told the others that you had woken up.'

The tide is getting up now and we watch closely as most of the boats, one after the other, throw their ropes off and chug out to sea until finally there is only the one small boat left with a crew of three. I note that most of the heavy preparatory work is being done by one young member of the crew. We are sitting closely together; I'm barely managing to keep my cool as she smells so wonderful, and her mini kisses replay in my head.

'Thank you for helping me, Noc. It's been most appreciated; now you take care of yourself please.'

I kiss her on the cheek, but she grabs my head, surprising me by kissing me hard on the mouth again.

'Drive back to Hanoi, safely ditch this car and be very careful with what lies you tell the authorities. Keep whatever you say very simple so you have no difficulty remembering what you tell them because you will be questioned time and time again and they will be desperate to find me. From what I've seen of your police on the wharfs, I don't think their attitude to people like me has changed a lot from my time. Noc, *please* promise to be very careful and I'll tell you again — keep whatever you say very simple so they can't trip you up on anything. They will be very hard on you if they think you are lying; please be *very* careful what you say.' I have another quick scan of the area and make a decision.

Before she can say anything more, I sling my pack onto my back and quickly grab my rifles and sprint to the wharf. To the astonishment of the young man who has just thrown the rope off, I jump onboard, collar him and go straight to the wheelhouse covering them both and another crew member with the gun.

'You just run the boat out to sea, my friend, and no one will get hurt,' I say to the small bald-headed man who grips the wheel of the boat tightly, quite surprised at my sudden and unexpected arrival. 'Just keep this boat moving out to sea and I won't have to pull the trigger on you or any of your crew.'

I see that the man looks at the AK-47 in my hands and the other big rifle slung over my shoulder; he keeps the boat steaming straight for the heads. I turn and quickly wave to Noc, who by now is standing by the car door, watching us go. I turn back and keep my vision on the crew, who just stand there almost dumbstruck, simply staring at me.

The boat chugs on without anything happening, and I'm pleased when we finally clear the headwaters of the small port and the tiny boat continues to steam quite quickly straight out to sea. I take the cumbersome pack off, place it in the wheelhouse and turn my attention to the man at the wheel.

'Who are you?' asks the small balding skipper who finally regains enough of his composure to look defiantly at me and the guns. 'What do you want with us, soldier? We are just simple Vietnamese fishermen and have no money for you to take, so please explain yourself. Why are you here intimidating us with your firearms?'

'I am not interested in money, I am an *Uc Dai Loi* soldier, and I want to go to Singapore now,' I say in my best Vietnamese, watching the three crew members closely. 'Unfortunately for you my friend, your boat was the last in the port so it's going to be you and your crew that take me there.'

The look of annoyance on the old salt's face quickly turns to a broad grin, showing a row of decaying teeth with a splattering of betel nut stains on them. His next words surprise me completely.

'As a young man, *Uc Dai Loi*, I spent ten years in the Rangers during the war and so did my friend Duong over there,' he tells me, pointing at his elderly companion with a big grin now spread over the withered old face. 'The young man over there looking at you so fiercely is my son, Nguyen. He wasn't born early enough to fight before the Americans pulled out and the North won this war, but now he does most of the work for us on this boat.' His face turns to a look of sorrow as he thinks of what he's about to say. 'I spent two very hard years in what the communists called a rehabilitation camp before I was finally released and allowed to go home to my wife.' Almost immediately and without any thought, his stern face lights up to show the change in his emotions and I'm totally surprised by his next comments. 'We will help you get to Singapore my friend, for I have no love for the communists who now run our country. My name is Bui. But who are you, *Uc Dai Loi?* What is your name?' He looks hard at me with a puzzled expression stretching over his weathered old face, obviously wondering where I'd come from. 'But you are far too young, my friend, to have fought against the communist North like your countrymen did, so tell me how is it that you are in our country dressed as you are in your military uniform and carrying those guns? Where did you come from and how did you get to this little port that we fish from?'

'It's a long story, Bui, but I have plenty of time so please make sure you don't fall overboard when you hear my story because I have difficulty believing it myself.' I quickly give him a brief account of what happened to me, where I've come from and how I stole a car and drove down here from Hanoi.

Even though they saw me wave to her, I completely omit any mention of Noc, for she will have enough problems of her own when she gets back to Hanoi. Bui's mouth hangs open in astonishment as I tell him my story from start to finish. I think he wants to believe me, but the story is so bizarre he doesn't know whether to or not. 'So, you see what my problem is, Bui

– the only people who know about me are those at the laboratory and even they will have problems believing this reincarnation, I expect you could call it, that has actually happened in the last two days. I'm still having difficulty believing that I've been asleep for so long, in what you could call "my incarceration".'

We both look at each other for a full two minutes, then he surprises me by grabbing my hand and shaking it vigorously, as does his friend Duong. But I find Nguyen is a little stand-offish towards me.

'Singapore is a long way from here my friend, but we will do it for you. Anything I can do to … let me put it into your words … "shove it up" my communist colleagues, I will do,' he says with a smirk spreading over his rugged old face, and with a laugh he yells to the other two, 'Cut the motors, Duong, and break out our sails, Nguyen, we are bound for Singapore! With the sails set we will get there very quickly, and we will use very little fuel. We can say we had a breakdown at sea and none of my communist comrades will ever know the truth of where we've been.'

We have been under sail now for three hours and the little boat is making good time with a wind favouring us, when we look to the stern and see another boat bearing down on us from the west at great speed, almost as if it is heading for us on a collision course, because if they don't dramatically change tack, they will certainly hit us.

'What is that boat approaching us at speed? If that boat's skipper doesn't pull out soon, they're going to ram us,' I say to Bui, thinking that Noc had been caught going back to Hanoi and under pressure had told them where I was. 'Do you think it's a government boat and they've heard I was onboard?'

'No, it can only be Thai pirates on that boat. You had better lay low and get out of sight, Peter,' Bui hurriedly tells me, trying to push me down. 'Other boats have had trouble with these people in the past but even though the Vietnamese communist government knows about these attacks, they seem to do nothing to protect us. They don't do anything to protect our fishing boats when at sea; we are evidently not important enough to them, and unfortunately, we have to look after ourselves and fish as a group so they will leave us alone. Unfortunately for us, Peter, they will not allow men like me from the south to carry firearms, so we cannot protect our boats from these pirates.'

'Well, if it's protection you want, Bui, I'll give you what protection I can. I have plenty of ammo with me.' Then, with a short dry laugh, I quickly check my weapons. 'I'd better stay out of sight before they see me and wonder why you have a Westerner dressed in camouflage gear aboard your boat.'

Bui quickly straps the wheel and moves away from the wheelhouse so their attention will be away from me and onto the crew. I kneel on the wheelhouse floor, out of sight, and put the AK-47 down next to me and instantly ready my SLR in anticipation of the worst-case scenario. If the other boat does turn out to be Thai pirates, it'll be on, but now that it's closer it certainly doesn't look like any of the government patrol boats that I've seen tied up in Haiphong Harbour.

I crouch out of sight until there is a mighty thud telling me that they have grappled us. This is followed by a lot of yelling coming from the Thai pirates as both boats collide and bounce off each other. I hear the sound of grappling irons towards the bow and many feet as men scramble aboard our boat and the clamour of foreign voices screaming at the crew in a language I don't understand. I instantly look across the deck just in time to see a large knife being wielded above Bui's head. I quickly jump up, lifting the big rifle to my shoulder and tap out a short burst towards this individual. At this short range, the rounds almost cut the man in half. I quickly look to the bow and see two more pirates threatening Nguyen, who is by the mast. They hear my shots and begin turning towards me in the wheelhouse and start drawing a collection of pistols. They're far too slow; two more short bursts from the big rifle and both of these men are kicked back by the force of the large slugs tearing through their bodies. They fall over silently, their bodies twitching on the deck. Two others have just jumped onto the stern and see their comrades dropping like flies, so they make a desperate attempt to jump back aboard their own boat, but again, two short bursts cut them down. The battle with the pirates, if you could call it that, is swiftly over, lasting less than a minute. I walk over with my rifle at the ready, covering the bodies while the others are just getting up off the deck. They excitedly crowd around me, all smiles with the results of our short, sharp defence of their boat. Bui, smiling broadly at me, comes towards the wheelhouse and is the first one to speak.

'Thank you for saving us, Peter. I haven't seen one of those big rifles of yours work so well since one of your training team members was with our battalion for a month on an operation we did near the Mai Tau's in seventy-two.'

'Bui, you have to remember I caused this situation; if I hadn't been here with you, you wouldn't have been so far south from Vietnam and would have been on your fishing grounds with the other boats laying your nets. You would have been safe from these pirates somewhere in calm waters pulling in plenty of fish instead of taking me well out of your way towards Singapore. I'm afraid you have to take that into consideration when you thank me for saving you because you wouldn't be here if it wasn't to help me get away from your country.'

'Let's have a quick look over the pirate boat,' Nguyen says. It is the first time I've seen him smile since I've been onboard. 'There may be equipment onboard that we could possibly use on our boat.'

We all cross to the pirate boat and find it quite narrow, not really suitable for fishing. We open a hatch and look at what type of engines they have. There are two enormous petrol motors, far too big for a fishing boat for they would be too costly to run on a meagre income. It's obvious that this boat wasn't constructed for fishing at all; it was built for speed and had been designed to catch other craft at sea – either boats like Bui's or small cargo vessels that ply these waters. If they had to get away very quickly from a target, with these motors they had the capability to do just that. We check the fuel tanks and find that they are almost full. So these pirates clearly hadn't travelled very far to find us.

'These people come out from the south of their country,' Nguyen tells me, now a bit more friendly, which pleases me. 'As you can see the boat has a low silhouette, so they just cut their motors and drift along, picking up any boats in the area on their radar. Our sails wouldn't have helped and I'm afraid we would've been a dead giveaway when they picked us up. They must have thought we were a luxury yacht of some description and they'd thought they'd found a real prize to capture.'

'It looks like I now have my own boat to get to Singapore, Bui,' I say, laughing a little as I feel the adrenalin still pulsing through my body after this short and bloody clash. 'I would like to thank you, your friend Duong and your boy Nguyen for your trouble and generosity and for taking the risk with a man that you didn't know. I won't forget you; I promise you that. Now my friends, let's search their boat and see what else we can find that you people can use with your fishing as payment for helping me. Surely there must be something onboard that you can use.'

'You sail your boat carefully,' the old man says, seemingly a little peeved perhaps at not needing to take me the rest of the way to Singapore, but happy that he doesn't have the risk of being out at sea too long and having to explain to the authorities why he was so far south. He immediately bursts into a broad grin. 'Don't take too many of those pretty Chinese girls out when you get there. I am told they are very horny.' He laughs at my circumstances and vigorously shakes his head as if wanting to warn me about them. 'But I'm told they are also very expensive so, if you do, I hope you have plenty of money.'

'I'm afraid I have none, Bui, so let's see if there is any onboard the pirate boat; I'll need some when I get there — but not for women,' I stress with a grin.

Firstly, the bodies of the pirates are searched, with watches and rings and any money being taken. Next, they get their just deserts and are thrown overboard as food for the fish. Finally, we do a thorough search of the boat, but unfortunately, there is very little that can be used by the Vietnamese, except, surprisingly, a small strong-box full of US bank notes that we share, and a small radar set I willingly let them have for their kindness. So, in no time they have the radar uncoupled and onboard their boat, and with handshakes all around we say our farewells to each other.

I'm pleased to see the change in Nguyen from the surly young man, who obviously didn't understand my position, at the start of our voyage to a bright courageous youth. He is a very brave young man who I'm sure will look after his father and his father's friend.

'Take care of that father of yours,' I tell him, just before I leave their boat. 'He's a great man so please look after him and he will teach you all you need to know about fishing and life because, from what he told me this morning, the communists gave him a hard time at the end of the war.'

'Thank you, *Uc Dai Loi*, for your kindness and explaining about my father, for he has said nothing to me of the war. I will look after my father. I promise you that,' says the young man in the kind of tone that tells me he really means what he is saying.

CHAPTER 7

A FRENCH CONNECTION

Hanoi

Pierre Bulvarl is a French journalist of no repute, that is, with other men's women. Even with that, he's not doing it very well, for his last little fling had caused him to flee France very quickly or suffer the wrath of a prominent politician over his promiscuous behaviour with this man's only daughter. He'd been extremely lucky and was warned by the girl that her father knew of their blossoming affair because, according to this young lady, her father had hired some villains to take a knife to intimate parts of his body, so he'd quickly grabbed the first flight out of France to the former French colony of Algeria. There, he'd spent a number of months living the full life of a wealthy expatriate, but again, unfortunately for him, his past quickly caught up with him and, lucky again, he got off lightly with just another timely warning. It was an acquaintance who'd heard that the infuriated father had finally found out his whereabouts, so Pierre had to quickly and discreetly disappear once more.

This time he'd chosen another former French colony but, unlike Algeria, the colony was on the other side of the world, well out of reach of the furious father. By using a number of disguises and false passports and hiding his final destination, he quietly reached Vietnamese shores, but unfortunately with only the money he could carry with him, as the girl's father was able to pull strings and have his assets in France frozen. From what this acquaintance had told him, it was evidently through his bank transactions that the girl's father had been able to track him to North Africa. The father could possibly use the same system to follow his movements again.

This small, struggling third-world country had been a backwater since the war with America and seemed to have jumped from one crisis to another and now appeared to finally be getting onto its feet as its peasant economy slowly begins to gain momentum. Pierre's been there now for five years, squandering most of the money he'd been able to bring with him and now has to survive on his wits with whatever story he can concoct and uses a nom de plume to publish the stories he finds. He has been lucky and is being looked after by one of the many bar girls he'd met. She has for some strange reason taken a shine to him, and she supports him when he's short of a dollar. Pierre is a reasonable journalist, when he puts his mind to his work, and writes good stories from time to time. Unfortunately, with the bar maid's support he's become lazy and relies more on easy stories. He's happy, for now it appears he's far enough away from Paris for his past not to catch up with him. The only word from France has been that his former girlfriend has married into the Paris establishment and is gone. Not so her father's unrelenting anger towards her former suitor, and from what a friend has told him, he is turning over every stone desperately trying to find him.

He'd reached Vietnam well after the trouble with the Khmer Rouge in Cambodia and has been in Hanoi ever since, taking advantage of the cheap living and is always looking for an easy story that will pay well and relaunch his journalistic career back in Paris – that is, when he can finally get back. However, he is unwilling to do the hard yards to get the really good stories and he sits relatively quietly watching this small country stagger from one crisis to another in its efforts to lift the living standards of its people. The communist government is striving to improve its image on the international map as a regional power of Southeast Asia. Vietnam is starting to achieve this, despite the American-sponsored sanctions, which initially bit hard into their economy; but with tenacity and hard work, they have finally been able to work the system and become a regional power.

The communists had made many mistakes just after the unification of Vietnam and had squandered, if not destroyed, a lot of the academic talent the south had, resulting in many of these people leaving their shores. Those who had money had flown out, while others had jumped on boats and fled to sympathetic countries in the region to be settled as refugees. The remainder who worked for the South or served in the armed forces or were perceived as a threat, were sent to rehabilitation camps for so-called 're-education'. The death rate in these camps was horrific and as a consequence, much of this valuable talent was wasted. As a kind of political cleansing, anyone who disagreed with the communist regime or had a past with the government of the South, was immediately sent to one of the camps. Most of the re-education camps are now defunct, but the south's huge agricultural potential, which had been ignored in the flurry to establish themselves had ground to a halt under this new regime. Now, albeit painstakingly slowly, this large peasant industry is starting to grow again. Gradually the economy is improving, and once more they are able to feed themselves and not be dependent on handouts from Russia or other sympathetic communist bloc countries, who in the nineties had developed their own style of democracy. But the country is still poor with a very low standard of living.

Pierre thinks about these unfortunate consequences as he sips his drink, looking out the window at the mid-morning rush. It makes him wonder why these people always seem to be in a hurry in this hot, characterless climate.

Now what can I concoct for my next story? He dreams as he tips his drink up once more while watching the people moving quickly past. He thinks of his financial status. He has to have something to pay the bills with, even in this dirt-cheap place, and being European doesn't help his situation if the authorities become involved. 'A human-interest story should do it,' Pierre says aloud. 'Perhaps a story of some American GI who has post-traumatic stress caused by the war and goes berserk years after the war finishes – perhaps in a shopping mall with an automatic rifle and he yells out Vietnamese slogans as he murders these people in front of him. That kind of story should do the trick, especially with the availability of guns in America.'

He looks across towards the door as he tries to organise his thoughts. More people come in off the street and he sees Nong Duc, a Vietnamese he befriended two years previously, a man who has a lot of government contacts and who has supplied a number of very good stories to him in the past. He watches this man as he looks around the restaurant, as if searching for someone. *What does that man want at this hour?* Pierre thinks, as his acquaintance finally sees him and gives him an enthusiastic wave before forcing his way through the milling crowd of customers and finally arrives at his table.

'You are always in here drinking through the day,' he says, pulling up a seat at the table and looking very thirstily at the drink Pierre has in his hand. 'We are lucky today, Pierre, because I have a very big story for you, a very big story indeed, my friend. It's one that will make the headlines in *every* newspaper all over the world and could even re-launch a successful journalistic career.' Then, with a laugh, he gives a strange look that his companion doesn't understand. 'That is, if you can get this story out of this country, because I feel our government will try and quash any mention of this almost science-fictional story. Unfortunately, it will be a massive embarrassment for them when the world finally gets to know about this very strange but true story that I learnt about while listening to some gossip that my colleagues were discussing this morning.'

'Another whisky please bartender and a refill for mine.' Pierre puts his hand up, indicating to the waiter. The stories this man had supplied in the past had kept the wolf from his door. 'What have you got for me today, Nong? I'm afraid I've had a very poor week, hardly enough news to pay the rent so I need something really big this time to tide me over until the next one happens along; so, tell me, what is the story you have for me that you tell me I'll have difficulty getting out of the country?'

'As I told you, this story will fix that for you, my friend, and establish you as one of the top journalists in the world, that is, if you can get this story out to the international press,' Nong says, sucking his drink with gusto before looking up at Pierre. 'How about a killer, an *Uc Dai Loi Ma Rung* killer? A top Special

Forces soldier from one of their elite units, a man who is just in his mid-twenties but has been in Vietnamese custody for almost thirty years; how does a story like that sound to a top world journalist such as yourself? Just tell me, what would your readers think of such an impossible story being spread on the front of tomorrow's papers for all the whole world to read?'

'What do you mean about this Australian man?' Pierre answers, pulling another mouthful of whisky from his drink and looking across at Nong casually, trying to downplay his friend's enthusiasm. 'Some Australian kid comes over here on a holiday, gets drunk and kills some old woman in some remote Vietnamese village. Those sorts of stories will only be news Down Under and then only for a short time and that's as long as the man's a footballer or some sort of sportsman. Nong, I need something really *big* with graphic details to tell and photos of the people involved. I have to have something that will have readers talking to their friends about; it has to have them waiting for their daily newspaper to arrive, so they can read the next exciting segment.'

'No! No, no, it's not a story like that, my friend,' Nong says, a little put off by the Frenchman's blasé attitude to what he is saying. 'This man was one of their elite Special Air Service soldiers who disappeared thirty years ago in the old South Vietnam. What I have heard about it in my department is that he fell from a rope during a helicopter extraction thirty-plus years ago – I believe you can confirm that on the internet, as the *Uc Dai Loi* government has a thirty-year release plan. He was found by Vietnamese soldiers almost immediately and was given special drugs by this brilliant Vietnamese scientist, a Doctor or Major Thong, who unfortunately disappeared after treating this man some three months later back in the South. It is presumed he was killed in action and was unfortunately a great loss to their country. This *Uc Dai Loi, Ma Rung* soldier was taken by Major Thong to a special laboratory – the Ho Chi Minh Centre, not far from Hanoi. They grow and experiment with grains there now but, during the war this was a top-secret establishment where they conducted trials on the production of secret weapons to win the war for us.' He looks at the Frenchman trying to gauge his interest. 'I expect you have heard of it?'

'Yes of course I have,' he replies, wondering what this has to do with a soldier from a war that had finished long ago.

'During the American War, this Dr Thong did experiments for the war effort there, and behind the research area is a small military museum where these war-related items were moved to and stored when the war was over. Evidently, this *Uc Dai Loi Ma Rung* soldier was kept there in a glass case surrounded by a special gas the good doctor had developed as an exhibition for our people to see what our enemies looked like.' He then adds a little bit more as he'd seen this very exhibition as a child with his parents. 'I actually saw this man as a child and thought it was a dummy made to look real, but who would expect this man to wake up thirty years later, kill his guards and escape?'

'It's *impossible* to keep a human alive in that manner, or any animal for that matter, for so long. How did they do it? Did they freeze him?'

'This *Uc Dai Loi* was frozen in time, but not by ice used in conventional refrigeration. The doctor used a top-secret serum that he had invented, and this man was kept in a glass case filled with a gas that kept him alive. Late yesterday afternoon, however, he was somehow accidentally revived and broke out of the glass container they'd stored him in. He was fully armed and shot and killed two of our soldiers who guarded the research centre and imprisoned the rest of the people at the laboratory. He has taken a hostage with him, a young woman who worked as a junior technician-cum-cleaner at the laboratory and they've disappeared somewhere in Hanoi in one of the staff cars.' He looks across at the Frenchman, who by this time is sitting on the edge of his seat, listening intently to every word Nong is speaking. Nong pauses for effect and takes another long sip of his whisky before continuing. 'With the two automatic rifles this soldier has taken from the guards, plus who knows what he has in his backpack, he has enough weapons with him to start another Vietnam War. Are you interested in him *now*, my friend? I feel this could be one of the biggest stories of this century when news of this incident finally breaks out in the public domain.'

'*Hell!* wh—where did you get this from?' stammers Pierre, almost spilling his drink as he clings to every word Nong has just told him. 'We've *got* to find him before the authorities catch him and get his story because if the communist authorities get him first, they'll kill him to save face and avoid the embarrassment of being found out that they were doing experiments on enemy soldiers during the war. Where is he now? Where do we start to look for him to get the complete story of how he was captured, and more importantly — what happened at the Ho Chi Minh Centre where he escaped from?'

South Vietnam

Noc leans against the mudguard of the car, watching the boat, and sees Peter jump onto the deck of the small craft and talk to the people onboard. He lifts his arm and waves to her before he turns and looks towards the sea. She goes to the front of the car, sits on the bonnet, and watches the boat until it's just a speck in the distance before she finally turns back to the car for the long trip back to Hanoi.

I'm such a silly woman; I should have asked that handsome Uc Dai Loi to take me with him to Singapore, she muses as she starts the motor and puts the car into gear, thinking all the time as she goes about the events that have suddenly overcome her. *How did all this happen to me? How am I going to explain this to the authorities when I get back? They just won't believe me if I tell them the truth.*

She begins to think everything through, trying hard to put herself in the place of the innocent hostage. She finally gets just to the outskirts of Hanoi and parks the car on a side street. As she gets out, she sees a large bottle of soft drink, partially full, on the back seat. She picks it up and is about to take it with her but then suddenly remembers whose car it is. Smiling to herself, she undoes the fuel cap and pours the soft drink into the tank.

'That is for trying to take advantage of me, you arsehole,' she says quietly before taking the rest of the money that's in the glove box and carefully wiping the steering wheel, the glovebox, and other parts of the car she may have inadvertently touched during their trip south. Once satisfied with her cleaning job, she leaves the car and walks back down the street, confidently humming a pop tune, and takes a bus into the city where she sees a large park and gets off at the next stop. She quickly walks back to the park, casually finding a secluded spot and just sits in the shade for a while, pondering what to do. She has to formulate a plan, a simple plan that's easy to explain to the authorities when she's questioned. She tosses every aspect of what possibly could have happened backwards and forwards until she's quite satisfied in her own mind with what is the most simple and feasible, and more importantly – easy to remember.

Keep my story simple, Peter told me. Keep it simple. It must be simple so I can't be tripped up by their questions. I have to be seen as the innocent hostage taken while he made his escape from the centre.

Finally, when her mind is made up, she tears her clothes and goes across to a nearby tree, bumping her head on the trunk a number of times, causing a small bruise to appear with specks of blood forming on her forehead. She ruffles her neat hair and rubs some grass and soil on her head then confidently walks slowly to the nearest police station where she turns herself in.

'I work at the Ho Chi Minh Research Centre just west of Hanoi,' she says with tears streaming down her face. 'I was taken by this big foreign man in a strange army uniform to the park where I was knocked out and left for dead. I woke up an hour ago and I didn't know what to do so I came straight here for help. Please, Officer, can you help me? You *have* to catch this man as he's *extremely* dangerous and has a number of army guns and could kill more innocent people if he's not stopped. He's already killed two poor soldiers at the research centre and could kill more if left at large too long.' Noc allows another large tear to roll down her cheek.

'When was this?' asks one of the police officers, quite surprised by her statement. She tells them her story again, surprised they don't know, as she thought the alarm would have been raised well before now. The police officers take in her dirty, torn attire, quite amazed at hearing such a strange, almost unbelievable, story. They do not take their eyes off her face and look at the bruise on her forehead, which has now suitably swollen to quite a size and has started to turn a nasty blue colour, and this along with her red eyes from crying, looks convincing.

'I think it was early this morning, I'm not sure as it was dark,' she tells the startled officers who are listening to this amazing, brutal story. Then she begins sobbing some more. 'He drove around Hanoi for a long time in one of the staff cars, finally going to Haiphong to the wharves, wanting to get out of the country that way. He looked at the boats but saw our security people's presence on the quay, which annoyed him greatly, before coming back here. Officer, I'm afraid I don't know how long we were there but then it became dark, and I became really afraid because he kept swearing about our government and making crude comments about Vietnam and what he would do if he was caught. It was a terrifying experience, spending such a long night alone in that car with him, not knowing what he would do next. Once we came back to Hanoi, he drove around the streets for quite some time before stopping somewhere in the city. I can remember the place distinctly because there were trees to one side. He was horrible, swearing all the time, and made me get out of the car and took me into what turned out to be a park. The next thing I recall was that for some unknown reason he became very agitated, pushing me to the ground – I thought he was going to rape me and then he became extremely violent and hit me hard with something here on my head. I must have been knocked out for quite some time because when I came to, it was light, and I found I was lying in the park. Officer, I didn't know what to do so I came here to you to get help.' She suddenly breaks into more tears and through large sobs finally says to the now half a dozen police officers around her, 'You *have* to catch him, Officer, because he's–he's a very dangerous man and is armed with automatic weapons, and as I've said to you before, has already shot and killed two guards at the Ho Chi Minh Centre before he grabbed me by the arm, locked the other staff in and with me. It was terrifying for me to see those two poor men lying there in their own pools of blood, bleeding all over the floor in what used to be the museum. I'm afraid he could–he could hurt more people if he remains at large because he has a number of rifles with him that he took from those guards yesterday.' Between large sobs, she goes on to explain in detail what happened and how this man killed the two guards at the research centre, locking the others up before taking her with him as a hostage. She is quite surprised however that the police don't know anything about this incident because she was sure the others would have broken out of the Ho Chi Minh Centre's museum well before now and would have certainly sounded the alarm sometime after they left last night.

'I will take you back to the research centre and see how your colleagues are and find out just what's going on,' offers one of the burly policemen, much to her relief. 'You don't have to worry Miss; we'll catch this man and when we do, we'll punish him severely. Unfortunately, these Westerners think they can just come here on holiday and are free to do whatever they want to our people. We will make him pay dearly for what he's done to you; I can assure you of that.'

'He wasn't a tourist, Officer, he was the soldier who used to be kept in a glass case at the Ho Chi Minh Centre and has been there ever since the war. I was cleaning his case when he fell out on top of me and he–he became alive again and when the others came in, he killed both of the soldiers who came with them and took their weapons and me as a hostage. Officer, that's how I came to be here.'

'I saw that soldier when I was a boy,' the policeman says to her, quite startled at what she's just told him. 'Surely he was dead?'

'No. I thought he was dead too, but when I opened the glass

case to clean it, he fell out on top of me and somehow woke up.'

When they reach the research centre, she finds to her surprise that the others are still inside, now being vigorously questioned by the authorities. There are soldiers everywhere and many police are sifting through the establishment looking for evidence. Noc is taken to a room where she is questioned by two men in civilian clothes for well over an hour. Every so often she breaks into tears as she goes over her simple story time after time, explaining again how she was driven around for a long time before going to the wharves in Haiphong and eventually back to Hanoi to the park where she was knocked unconscious. They look at her with her bruised forehead and her red eyes, and she gains much sympathy. Finally, she's relieved when they let her go back to her companions.

'We couldn't get out of here until late this morning,' she is told by the others. 'After seeing him kill the two soldiers, we were not game to try, because he may have been outside and started killing again with that strange big gun he had. I don't know why they left it with him, especially with the ammunition still in the magazine.'

'Oh, look at you, Noc,' says the attendant, staring at the blue bruise on her forehead. 'He is a very brutal man this *Uc Dai Loi*; I hope they leave no stone unturned in finding him because we can't have armed brutes like that running around Hanoi.'

She tells them the same story of how first they went to Haiphong where it annoyed him greatly when he saw the security personnel walking around the wharf watching the ships that were tied up at the docks.

'He was furious and drove back to Hanoi to a park and sat there a long time muttering to himself in his own language' before he roughly pulled me out of the car and the last thing

I remember was him swinging a piece of wood at me.' At this stage, she doesn't trust anyone and thinks it is safer to tell the same story to all. Who knows what they could say when the authorities question them again, she thinks, and surely they will. *They may even ask them what I said after I joined them,* she surmises. 'When I woke up it was light; I didn't know what to do or how late in the morning it was, so I went to the nearest police station, and they brought me back here.'

That night after a torrid, tiring day being questioned time and time again by different people, Noc and Wai are finally allowed to go home together. They have been friends for a long time, ever since university, and they live together in one of the poorer suburbs of Hanoi. Wai had listened to her friend's story but doesn't believe Noc could have been treated the way she said she was and is determined to find out the truth of what really happened in those almost two days her friend was away with this *Uc Dai Loi* soldier.

'Tell me, Noc, did you touch him again?' Asks Wai, obviously knowing full well there is more to her friend's story than what she had told the police. 'When he first woke up, he didn't appear brutal like you said, you know, when we first let him out of his glass case. He was only brutal to the soldiers because they were carrying guns and were lifting them towards him. Come on, Noc, you were away with him for almost two days. You were alone with him; something exciting must have happened between the two of you. What did you talk about? Because he spoke our language extremely well for a foreigner. Come on, Noc, there is much more to your story than you told them. Something else must have happened between the two of you while you were travelling around in Dr Phou's car for all that time. He was a big man and very handsome for a Westerner.'

'You are a friend, Wai; we went to university together and have lived together in the same house for some years now, but you will have to promise me not to tell anyone, otherwise, if you do, I'll be in trouble with the authorities.' After a while, the story unfolds. However, she doesn't tell her friend about changing cars but leaves open anything that may be seen as sexual by her friend, especially sleeping with him in the car last night. 'He left the car and ran to the small fishing boat and the last I saw of him was on that small boat waving to me, bound for Singapore. In some ways I was a fool not going with him to Singapore, because there is not much here for me at the research centre the way those elderly people treat us.'

They are still chatting about their adventures when they reach their house and are surprised to find another European there – a large overweight Frenchman who's been waiting for them for quite some time now.

'Good evening, girls. Would one of you young ladies be called Noc?' he says, looking at one and then the other. 'I would like to ask some questions if one of you is that girl who was taken from the research centre yesterday by the *Uc Dai Loi* soldier … for you were away with him for a day and a half?'

The two girls glance at him and then at each other. They are quite shocked that the story appears to be out, wondering what this man wants to know. Is he anything to do with the police trying to find out where the *Uc Dai Loi* is? Noc thinks she will have to be very careful with this man as he may be a police informer.

'Yes, I am Noc; what can I do for you?' she answers, not liking what she sees of this man and certainly not trusting him at all. 'What do you want?'

'I am a freelance journalist. My name is Pierre Bulvarl and

I write for a number of French newspapers,' he says, looking straight at Noc, now seeing for the time the bruise on her forehead. It is as if he is summing her up. 'I heard a strange story about an *Uc Dai Loi* soldier who had been here a very long time, ever since the war of liberation in fact, and was kept in a glass case full of a secret gas in the back of the research centre museum. This strange formula he was immersed in was invented by a war-time scientist going by the name of Major Thong, and I was told that you were cleaning mould out of his case when he woke up. Another girl – is that you?' he says, turning and looking at Wai, who sheepishly nods her head, not looking at him but at the ground. 'You go and get the other staff, which included two armed soldiers of the People's Liberation army. The *Uc Dai Loi* soldier immediately shoots and kills them with his rifle. He ties the others up and locks all of them in the centre before he takes you away with him in one of the staff's cars – an old model Citroen I believe; is this right? Tell me, is this really what happened at the research centre yesterday?'

'Yes,' Noc says, stunned that this man knows all these vital details and is now quite annoyed with herself for telling her friend Wai the correct details of what actually happened. 'That is correct; who told you?'

'That doesn't matter.' He pauses for a full minute, letting his presence sink in, letting the girls realise that he knows a lot about their story. 'I would like to know what happened to this man.' He watches both girls closely before he says, 'I will pay you for your story.'

The story is out but how does this man know so much about it? One of the staff must have told someone or the interrogators must have leaked what they'd been told by the staff. Is he really a journalist or is he a police informer? All these thoughts run quickly through Noc's active mind. She is in disbelief at this man and what he's just told them. Anyway, she hadn't been told not to tell anyone else, so she goes through her simple concocted story about being in the park with him and desperately hopes that everything she tells him is enough for this horrible man.

'So, that's all that went on?' he says, looking intently at her. He sees the nasty bruise on her forehead but is having difficulty believing the simple story. 'No, more than that happened in over twenty-four hours alone with this man, surely, as you were away for well over a day and a half.'

'I was only with him until late in the night when he did this to me,' she says, pointing to her head. She begins to cry again. 'When I regained my senses in the park, both he and the car were gone. That's when I went to the police and reported his escape from the Ho Chi Minh Centre. I'm afraid that's what happened.' Quite annoyed with this man and his arrogant stance she then points to her head. 'Why would I lie after he did *this* to me?'

'There must have been something else that happened, surely. You drove to Haiphong Harbour with him when he was trying to get out of the country before you came back to the park in Hanoi. Please think very hard as he could have said something quite insignificant that would give me a clue where he was trying to go to from Vietnam.'

'Well, there was one other little bit I almost forgot, as I thought it was almost idle talk,' Noc tells him, hoping this will get rid of the horrible man. 'When we were down at the wharf in Haiphong, he mentioned something about trying to get a ship home or at least as far as Singapore. It might be a good thing if you try to get there but I doubt he would have had the time to get that far from Hanoi, as he left me in the park sometime early this morning, well before sunrise.'

'Why thank you, Noc; that's very interesting,' he says, looking at her in a strange way. 'I'll see what I can turn up. Here is your money. Thank you for your help.'

When they return to the centre in the morning, all those who witnessed the escape of the Australian are told to climb into the back of a truck.

'Where are we being taken?' Dr Phou, a man in his early thirties, asks one of the guards at the back of the truck. 'We have important experiments to carry out on a special strain of rice we received from Thailand two weeks ago.'

'You are to be taken to a special camp where you will be interrogated again so we can find out exactly where the *Uc Dai Loi* has gone.'

CHAPTER 8

SINGAPORE

The seas are good to me on my trip to Singapore, with calm weather all the way allowing the two large petrol motors to get me there in almost record time. It also allows the small pirate ship to slip almost unnoticed into Singapore Harbour, past the many large ships anchored there. However, I get some amused stares from the few sailors onboard one of the anchored ships, probably wondering what a craft of this size is doing trying to compete with the big boys for harbour space. Given the way I'm dressed in my camouflage uniform, maybe they wonder whether I am a pirate with ulterior motives, sussing out potential targets. I'm relieved when I finally find a small jetty just off the main shipping lanes where a number of luxury yachts are tied up. By the look of them, they are the type of craft that wealthy businesspeople would use for pleasure on a weekend getaway, and from the stares I get, they likely pay a king's ransom to tie up here. I throw a line over a vacant spot on the end pylon and tie up quickly, afraid my camouflage fatigues will draw far too many unwanted questions if I hang around this swanky area of the port for too long.

Unfortunately, this very plain little ship has a number of bullet holes in the side from me finishing off the last of the pirates when they were trying to escape. I quickly leave the boat and scoot off amongst the high-rise buildings, now quite worried that my weapons may attract far too much unwanted attention, something I don't want to experience until I get into our embassy, wherever that is in this large city. I do what I used to do on leave in a strange city and look immediately for a taxi, as the driver will certainly know where the embassy is.

The city of Singapore has changed dramatically since a number of us spent a lusty R and R at the Billford Hotel in the sixties. I gaze in awe at the tall buildings that have sprouted up from nowhere. Heavens, they are everywhere, I think. I'm impressed to find how such a large population centre has expanded. It's obviously had good management. Again, I'm fortunate to meet a taxi on one of the not-so-busy streets just off the jetty, some one hundred metres from my tie-up point, so I immediately flag it down.

I'm quite relieved when I'm able to stop him. 'Take me to the Australian Embassy.' He's surprised, and I expect a little nervous, but extremely curious at me being dressed in camouflage combat fatigues, backpack on my back. But it's the rifles I have slung over one shoulder and other equipment dangling around my waist that intrigues him the most. I feel I owe him an explanation as to why I'm dressed this way — something to put him more at ease or I could have him calling the authorities on his two-way. I suspect I'll have enough trouble convincing the people at the embassy who I am and where I've come from. 'Come on; don't look so bloody surprised, my friend. There's been a covert exercise in and around the harbour with the Brits.' I give him a little laugh, trying to remove any tension.

'They had us trying to sink their bloody ships in the harbour like our Z Force did during World War Two against the Japs, but unfortunately for us, your local security boys were far too good – most of our blokes ended up in the slammer and got nowhere near a target worth hitting.' My bit of bullshit is supposed to baffle his brain. 'I was extremely fortunate being the only one of our squadron who got away and I think most of that was just sheer good luck and not any skill on my part.' I can feel his eyes on me and deliberately don't look directly at him.

'Ah, very good; they tell me our security at the harbour is the best in the world. They have to be that way, so our shipping lanes are safe. Our economy relies so much on international trade passing through our port, both from the east and the west ... oh, and of course you people Down Under.' I see him looking at me in the rear vision mirror, summing me up once again and I hope my comments have the desired effect. 'This is wonderful news to hear, Sir. As you know, the sea lanes have been quite unsettled these last few years with pirates from our north taking hold of unsuspecting ships, stealing their cargo and either holding the crews for ransom or murdering them when they get aboard; they throw their bodies to the sharks. It's about time that the major countries of this region such as yours took this threat more seriously. It's pleasing to see them being part of this exercise.' He nods his head in approval and continues. 'There needs to be some concerted action to stop this unwarranted behaviour by these ruthless people. They seem to come out of nowhere and play havoc with unsuspecting ships. The worst thing is, there are people who have too much money and buy a luxury yacht and try to sail their boat around the world with little sense of the dangers they face from pirates and the sudden storms we get cropping up in this area from time to time.'

'Yes, like your people, the Australian Government is evidently quite concerned about pirate actions on our sea lanes.' This seems to position me quite well with him and I am prepared for most questions, just in case I have been noticed. 'It's pleasing that our unit has started these extensive training exercises with your government and the British because I have to say these exercises are extremely important to both of our economies.'

I can see from his expression this story seems to settle him down security-wise, but like all taxi drivers I've ever met, he's as talkative and inquisitive as most, making me happy that he appears to be at ease with me and the weapons I'm carrying. He continues to prattle on about past pirate activities – the more he talks, the less I have to say for I realise I know absolutely nothing about modern-day Australia's economy, if it's almost thirty years into the future as people keep telling me. What I've seen of the large buildings, the way people are dressed and especially the cars on the streets of modern Singapore, I am now in a new world.

'Unfortunately, this is the only currency they gave us because they didn't tell us what country we'd be dropped off in; it could have been Malaya, Indonesia or even the Philippines. You'll have to be a gentleman with me and tell me please what the exchange rate is as this is not your currency or mine.' He's quite surprised when I pull out a large wad of foreign banknotes and pay him with US greenbacks, knowing from my days on leave that this is usable in most Asian countries.

'No problem,' he says with a laugh as he pulls up in front of the Australian Embassy, giving me a crafty grin. 'However, it will cost you more for your ride today. Your government is paying for this exercise you've just completed, so it's not a cost on you but the people who sent you out to blow up these ships. Anyway, my friend, how do they know you've sunk these ships?'

'The charges we plant emit a coloured smoke so if you see a smoking ship someone has been successful.'

He leaves me standing there, looking at the embassy and wondering what my approach should be with the embassy staff, because this place is totally foreign to me. So, with butterflies churning around in my stomach, I make my way into the building, not knowing what to expect from the Australian officials. I have no idea what their reaction to me and the weapons I'm carrying will be. *Bugger them!* I have an overwhelming feeling I am getting closer to home and to safety being here at our embassy. *So bring it on*, I think.

Many heads turn and look hard at me as I briskly move up the steps loaded up with rifles and a backpack. I arrive at what appears to be the reception area where I get worried stares from all those behind the counter. Finally, a young woman hesitantly comes across to see me, eyeing off the weapons hung over my shoulders and the grenades hanging off my webbing as well as the grubby condition of my combat fatigues that now, literally, are starting to show their age.

'Can I help you, please, Sir?' she timidly asks, not taking her eyes off the two guns and the grenades.

'I've been a prisoner of war in Vietnam,' I tell this startled young lady as she seems to cringe and back away from the counter, looking for support from the fast-approaching security guards, again, eyeing off the rifles dangling over my shoulders. 'I want to see the ambassador or someone in authority please. Tell him I am a member of the Australian armed forces and have been a prisoner of war for many years in Vietnam and I want to go home.'

She is a petite little thing and it's quite obvious that she's not used to having a dirty, armed man dressed in fatigues turning up unannounced telling her he was a prisoner of war. Why would she? My appearance has clearly put the embassy staff into turmoil, and I'm quickly ushered into a small adjoining room out of sight of everyone and then relieved of the guns, webbing and pack.

I look across a table at a middle-aged man and a younger woman. They seem to have great difficulty understanding why I'm here. I expect the fact that the war in Vietnam has been over for such a long period of time doesn't help my credibility at all; this alone causes total confusion.

'Could you please fully explain your circumstances, Sir? We find this a highly irregular occurrence, as you would understand – having someone dressed as you are and arriving at our embassy and carrying all those weapons of war,' says the man who is directly across the table from me who has a look of sheer disbelief written over his face. 'We have not been made aware of any Australian tourist being taken prisoner by the Vietnamese authorities in the last twelve months.'

'Tourist? Do I look like I'm a *bloody tourist?*' I yell at him, getting more than a little annoyed at this stupid, irresponsible assumption he makes. 'I'm not a bloody tourist, I'm a member of the Australian Military Forces and I've been held prisoner by the Vietnamese for the last thirty or so years!' I look across the table and tell them everything I can remember of my last patrol, finishing off with the events of the last three days. They are totally aghast each time I tell them of the killings I had to make as I made my way here. Both of these embassy representatives are shocked at my outburst and visibly seem to cringe away from me. They look at each other in absolute disbelief before looking back across the table at me, trying to take hold of what I'm saying.

'Let's get this straight please, Sir. Are you trying to tell us that you've been a prisoner of war in Vietnam since 1970?' the man eventually says, looking hard at me, obviously not game to call me a liar, probably because of the lethal hardware I came in with. 'If what you are saying is correct you would be almost sixty and yet you look as if you're – let me say – just a little over twenty-five or somewhere in that age bracket. Honestly, Sir, how do you expect us to believe you when you say you were born in nineteen forty-five?'

'I've *told* you what happened. I dropped off a rope in a hot extraction by helicopter on the seventh of August nineteen seventy. I've also told you *every* detail of the patrol in which I was leading – *who* was in my patrol and *every* detail of our extraction up until when my rope broke, and I dropped into the trees; that was the last thing I can remember.' I suddenly think of something I hope is important in getting them to believe me. 'Here is one of my dog tags.' I pull the small chain from around my neck and pull the bottom tag off, flicking it across to them. 'You can also have the service number of my SLR rifle checked because we had to sign for our weapons when they were issued to us on arrival in that country. That should corroborate my story.' I reach over the table and grab a piece of paper and a biro and sign my name. 'That is my signature that I used when I signed for that weapon.'

'Yes certainly; we will have that done immediately,' the man tells me, looking at the tag but still with a look of total disbelief spread across his face. 'You have to realise, Sir, this year is 2001 and you haven't aged; how is that?'

'I don't know. Look – until three days ago when I woke up and found myself lying on the floor on top of a Vietnamese girl, I can remember nothing.' The little man in charge almost gasps as I continue. 'I'm as amazed as you are at what has happened and at the actual date it is today. Now what are you going to do about it? I'm sick of prancing around Asia and just want to go *home!*'

Canberra

'Come in, gentlemen. Thank you for your attendance at such short notice. Make yourselves a coffee and take a seat. We have some very strange business to discuss in regard to one of our missing soldiers.'

The men are high-ranking Australian army officers called in by the brigadier general for an urgent meeting to deal with a strange situation that has suddenly arisen in Singapore. Finally, the officers have their drinks and are seated around the table, looking to the brigadier general to explain the reason they've been called together so quickly without any warning and with no agenda for the meeting.

'Thank you for coming in this morning, gentlemen. We have some very important business to deal with concerning, supposedly, one of our missing soldiers from the Vietnam War. I will tell you now gentlemen, please don't think I'm talking about bodies or graves, because I'm not.'

'What is it, Sir?' asks a colonel, a little perplexed. 'Have they found more remains of one of our soldiers? I know from one of the current affairs programs that there is a new group of former soldiers over there at the moment looking for the remains of the missing soldiers. Have they found some more bodies, Sir?'

'Unfortunately, it's not that easy, George. As I said, it's not about bodies or remains because it appears that a young man has turned up in our Singapore embassy claiming to be a soldier who disappeared on operations in the seventies. All the questions asked so far by the embassy staff have been answered by this young man and, surprisingly, they fit with the intelligence reports of his disappearance that we have.' He pauses while an aide hands out reports to the seated men. 'You'll see the patrol report given by the patrol in their debrief after they returned to Nui Dat from this conflict. On the papers are emails from our Singapore embassy with a copy of a dog tag and a signature, which, when checked, we found to be the same as what this missing soldier made when signing for his rifle, which he willingly handed in when he arrived at the embassy yesterday.'

'How old did you say this soldier was?' asks one of the officers, leaning forward on the table. He is intrigued with the story that seems to be unfolding, as it appears to him, like a bad lie that has been conjured up by a crazy lunatic journalist who's probably been on the whoopee weed in Vietnam and is trying to get some notoriety from this action that happened such a long time ago. 'It's not one of these damn wannabes trying to overstep the mark by claiming to be someone he isn't?'

'That's what we initially thought, Harry, but this person has everything down pat as if he was actually there. He is around twenty-five and arrived at the embassy yesterday dressed in the specific type of camouflage uniform the Special Air Service soldiers were issued in Vietnam at the time.' He pauses again, allowing the impact of his words to sink in. 'This soldier carried two loaded rifles over his shoulder and had grenades on his webbing, and in his pack was the correct personal gear that the SAS used to carry. He also carried an issue claymore mine.

Gentlemen, this man says he is Sergeant Peter Jackson of One Squadron and that he dropped off a rope during a hot extraction. I've looked up the records of the patrol report and what he has said is correct. This, to me, is the worrying coincidence of this whole story, as these patrol reports, which will be put out by the war memorial aren't due to be released for another year. Consider the possibility that what this soldier says is correct.'

'I knew this Peter Jackson,' says another officer. 'He was a highly decorated soldier. I can remember when this accident happened. We were extremely lucky we didn't lose other soldiers in this extraction incident. His rope was evidently cut by ground fire, and he fell off into the jungle. His body was unfortunately never recovered; so, you're telling me this man is claiming to be Jackson?'

'Yes.'

'It has to be one of those damn pests that spring up from time to time,' the same officer who spoke earlier says, breaking in again. 'Send the bastard packing because this will only destroy the reputation of genuine soldiers and especially this brave soldier you are talking about. General, we certainly don't want that sort of thing happening to the genuine heroes that Bill is talking about.'

'Unfortunately, it's not that simple, Harry. We have to go through the procedures and treat this man as genuine even though it appears highly unlikely to be the case. The fact that he entered the embassy heavily armed with an SLR, which, by the way, had been converted to fully automatic – the way the SAS used to change theirs – and was also carrying an AK-47 with well over two hundred rounds on his body, *and* he didn't shoot anyone at the embassy, means ... we have to treat his story seriously. Gentlemen, firstly I want to compile a range of questions that we'll send to Singapore for this soldier to answer – questions that only the real Peter Jackson would know the answers to. We'll also send a message to the Vietnamese Government to see what their reaction is to the whole affair. After that, all we can do is wait and see how he responds to our questions. Some of these questions, by the way, would only be known to the Jackson family, as they are about what he did before he was conscripted.'

'He was a Nasho?'

'Yes, he was one of three national servicemen who passed their cadre course held in February nineteen sixty-six, did his para course, a med-aid course then signed up, which the other two also did.'

Singapore

The embassy is good to me. Whether they believe me or not (the more likely option), is another matter. They put me up in embassy accommodation and supply me with another set of clothes. It is good to have a secure room at the embassy and I'm able to sleep properly for the first time since my big awakening, knowing that there is good security here. This time I try to sleep with both eyes almost closed.

The next day I'm awake early, but after breakfast it's more of the same. The embassy has obviously been in contact with SAS command in Australia because they present me with a whole range of questions, some of which I already answered the day before. This time, however, they are mostly about the unit patrols we'd done from Nui Dat, both in my final tour and the tour before when Johnno was wounded and when I was left behind by the helicopter and rescued Abraham from the ox cart. After lunch, the questions continue, but this time they relate more to my two trips to New Guinea and training at Swanbourne and the courses I'd done during training.

I fully understand the red tape I have to go through to establish my identity, and I know how odd this story must sound to army command, because I know that if the boot was on the other foot and if *I* was doing the interviews, I'd have difficulty believing someone could be held in limbo for close to thirty years – something I still struggle with myself.

Am I actually thirty years older or am I just having a bad nightmare, and would I wake up shortly on the jungle floor back in Vietnam? Blood tests and a number of photographs are taken and then it's back to more questions. Thankfully, it's over by mid-afternoon. I've almost had this day mentally by this time; hopefully this is the finish of the questions for me.

Oh, how wrong I am! After a short break of some fifteen minutes, I'm taken back into the interview room and this time I find a stranger sitting there waiting for me with one of the embassy staff.

'Good afternoon, Peter. My name is Pierre Bulvarl. I am a journalist,' he says to me, looking me straight in the eye. There is something suspicious about this man, putting my senses on high alert. 'I've come from Vietnam to find you. You are now a very famous man you know – living thirty years in a glass case and not ageing like the rest of us.'

I look across at the embassy official who is sitting to my right to find out who the hell this strange Frenchman is; only Noc and the three fishermen knew Singapore was my destination.

'We've interviewed Mr Bulvarl,' says one of the embassy staff. 'He appears to confirm your story, so we are allowing him to interview you. Is that alright with you, Mr Jackson? If it isn't then the interview won't go ahead, but I'll remind you that everything you say will be recorded.'

'It'll be fine; I'll do anything I can do to move this damn matter along and clear everything up. All I want to do is get back home to Australia and pick up my life where I left off, if that's at all possible.'

'I have spoken to staff at the institute where you were kept all those years and they have told me how you were kept there but recently escaped – and then Miss Noc explained how you knocked her out and left her lying in the park. But I'd like to know: how did you get here? Incidentally, the Vietnamese Government claims to know nothing of you and completely denies your existence. They say everything about you is a sham and is all to do with American propaganda about prisoners of war. What do *you* have to say about their answers to your escape?'

'The Vietnamese Government that I knew in the nineteen sixties and seventies would have said exactly the same; so, nothing has changed with them in the time I've been asleep. Can you imagine what would happen if this was a Western country doing these things and experimenting on prisoners of war during a conflict?' Then I use the Nazis as an example. 'You have heard of the stories that have come out of concentration camps after World War Two? Well, I'm a living example of what the Vietnamese did.'

'Peter, you will be able to tell Mr Bulvarl all you want. The information about the patrol you served in will shortly be on the internet and open to all who want to view that information,' says the embassy official, obviously trying, along with the journalist, to confirm as much information as possible. 'Just remember we will be recording everything that is said to get a clear picture of what happened over the last few days you spent in Vietnam when you broke out of the Ho Chi Minh Centre.'

'Internet? What's that?' After they explain the strange term to me, again, I tell my story again, from the start of the patrol to when I fell. I go along with Noc's story of the park; however, as I had wondered how she would explain the circumstances to cover her role in my escape on the fishing boat, I make it sound like the fishing boat was from the north and don't mention any names because I am well aware that I am dealing with a communist country and that they would take it out on anyone who antagonised the regime. I finish off my story with a description of the attack by the Thai pirates and how I was able to get here using their boat.

'Unfortunately, the fishing boat I was on was attacked by pirates. I had to kill five Thai pirates who came aboard the fishing vessel on the way here. I searched that pirate boat after the fishing boat left me there and found a box of US dollars,' I say this trying to disguise the fishing boat and not mention the small radar the Vietnamese took, because such an instalment onboard would lead the authorities to them. 'The money from their boat was the only currency I had to get to the embassy. The boat is tied up on the end of a small wharf in the harbour. That's all there is to my story; now all I want to do, gentlemen, is get back to Australia and get on with my life, if that's at all possible.'

'Thank you, Peter,' says Bulvarl in a matter-of-fact way and then he turns to the embassy official. 'Thank you for your time. What Peter has just told me this afternoon fits in with what the people in Vietnam said yesterday. I now have all of this amazing story.'

I hope it's my last night in Singapore and I'm now grateful that this French journalist has turned up out of the blue and confirmed my story. I seem to get tired easily now as it's probably the mental strain – something that used to happen in the bush. My sleep for some reason after this interview is very light; probably the meeting with the Frenchman has done something to my senses, letting me know that the Vietnamese authorities would now know where I am. I do as one of the men in my squadron once said and I sleep with both my eyes open.

I find the bed is incredibly soft, something I expect I'll just have to get used to in a civilised country. I've tried it both nights, but old habits die hard, and I find I sleep better on the rug on the floor. From habit, and probably military training, I mess up the bed to make it look like someone's asleep there. It's just after midnight and for some reason I'm restless and having difficulty sleeping.

All of a sudden, the night air rushes unusually into the room, and I hear the scraping sounds of someone coming through the window. I tense myself, waiting on the floor beside the bed opposite the window, now instantly alert. In the poor light I see a shadowy figure clamber through the open window and approach the bed, standing at the foot. Suddenly, whoever it is raises his left arm out in front of him.

Thump, thump, thump, thump.

A pistol with a silencer attached. I quickly swing up from the floor and grab the pistol arm, feeling more vibrations as the next bullets are fired, but this time into the ceiling. I crack the hand down hard on the end of the bed frame with all the force I can muster. There's a sharp cry of pain and a snap followed by a dull thud as the gun drops harmlessly to the floor. I let the arm go, which is a mistake. He is much smaller than me but has some knowledge of one of the eastern fighting methods and hits me hard in the stomach with his right hand, causing me to double up with pain, the wind knocked out of me. I quickly roll to one side, feeling a stab of pain as a knife digs into the flesh along my ribs.

'No you don't, you *bastard*,' I spit at him, getting angry at being caught like this by this nog. I grab the knife arm as he makes another thrust towards me, pushing it harmlessly into the air but not letting the arm go, and then with all my force I knee him hard in the groin. There is a gasp of agony from the man as it's his turn to double up. I pull him around hard, finally letting him go. There is the sharp sound of breaking glass as his body hits the other window and a sharp scream as he cascades out, taking most of the shattered glass with him. There is a brief silence then I hear a dull thud as his body hits the edge of the concrete drive one storey below.

Lights begin to flick on everywhere as I look down on the still body lying in the drive. Next, I hear the sound of many feet pounding along the passage floor and to my relief the door bursts open, and security guards come charging in as if the embassy is under attack.

'*What the hell's going on in here?*' the startled security officer yells at me. '*What's all the noise about? Who* broke the window?'

'I had a visitor,' I say, calmly turning back to the window. 'You'll find him down there.' I point to the prone figure lying where he fell and judging by the awkward angle, he may have hit the curb that runs along the concrete driveway. 'I hope there are no more like him about because I'm stuffed.' It's now that I feel the pain from the wound in my side and the dampness of blood, so I quickly add, 'I may need someone to look at my ribs because that little *prick* had a knife as well as a gun and could have done more damage than just grazing my side with his bloody weapon.'

By this time, it seems like many guards are in my room,

looking at my bloodied side, then down at the figure sprawled in a grotesque fashion on the concrete pavement below. I stand slightly away from these people near the foot of the bed, not wanting to field any questions, when an older man comes over and asks me to show him my ribs so he can see what damage was done. It is the doctor who'd given me a thorough medical check the afternoon before.

'You've been very lucky, Peter,' he tells me, doing a close inspection of my side. 'The knife has struck your ribs and then shied off, taking some flesh with it and causing some bleeding. We'll patch you up a little but fortunately, it's only a graze. Heavens above, a bloke like you should be used to this sort of thing. It'll be sore for quite some time though by the look of it, but you're tough enough to handle a simple knife graze,' he says with a funny kind of smile on his face. 'After what they've told me about you and what you've been through recently, you should have no trouble surviving a little ordeal like a simple attempted stabbing.'

After this assault in the embassy, they don't muck around with me any longer. The wound on my side is carefully tended to and I'm dressed and then they have me on the first flight out in the morning with an army officer on one side and a plain-clothes fellow on the other. I think that once I am in Australia, I will be free to go, but again I am wrong.

We land at Sydney Airport under tight security and straight away I'm whisked off by ASIO or some other secret mob to be debriefed again. For almost a week, I'm asked all sorts of questions over and over again and find I go through just about all my life as if it were yesterday but not just my military career. They check everything that I did before my call-up, even questions about the school I went to. Finally, they bring in two men in their late fifties who look vaguely familiar except for their age, but they have no problems recognising *me*.

'Shit! It *is* you, Pete,' says the first one. 'How ya' goin' Jacko, you old bastard? I haven't seen you for quite a while. Don't tell me you've been shacked up with some lovely Noggy sheila. Is that why ya' dropped off the rope 'cause you had one lined up?'

'*Clicker* – it's you, you old prick. And Jerry, how great to see you both again. I'd recognise you fellas anywhere.'

We meet in the middle of the floor, hugging and laughing at each other. What a wonderful meeting it is! Afterwards, we sit at the table going over everything dealing with our last patrol, talking about detail after detail and laughing at each of the situations we'd been through together during both tours.

'What about old Johnno?' I finally ask, hoping he got over his wounded leg. 'How is he going after that last wound in his leg?'

'I'm sorry that it's me that has to tell you this, Pete, but he died last year – something to do with his heart,' Clicker tells me, looking down at the ground for a few seconds. 'But he never forgot that it was you that saved his life at the Landing Zone that day and if you hadn't ordered that chopper to put down so we could treat his wound and give him that drip, he would have died well before we got to Vung Tau. It's funny; he used to always talk about that on occasions when we got together like we are now.'

After quite a while of listening and taping our discussion, one of the heavies comes up to the three of us.

'Well, Mr Jackson,' says the spook. 'Judging from what we've heard from your discussion, it appears that you are who you say you are. It's hard to believe that this actually happened but somehow that Vietnamese scientist has had you preserved for thirty years. What are you going to do now?'

'I'd like to go home and see what the situation is there and how things have progressed in my absence. The wheels told me that my family haven't been told that I'm still alive. I want to do it as quietly as I can because I don't want to ruffle any feathers – my family would have written me off years ago. I expect I'm one of the names on the memorial board in the municipal hall. When that's finished, I want to go to America because there are two people in the States I have to find, if they are still alive. One is my fiancée, and the other is her brother who I rescued in Vietnam. When the visits are over, I expect to return to my unit because being a soldier is the only thing I'm trained to do. Soldiering is all I know.'

'If you give us their names and they are still alive, we'll find them for you as soon as we can – we have a good working relationship with the United States and the CIA. We'll contact them and give them the names of the two people you're looking for and see what they come up with.'

'Look, I don't want to go through the same sort of thing with the Americans as I've done with you people,' I tell him, a little worried. 'I'm afraid I've had all the questions I can take from you fellas, so, could you please play down what has happened to me with the Yanks?'

'I can understand your situation,' the spook says with some sympathy in his voice. 'I'll pass that on to our people.'

I give him both Alicia and Abraham's names and the occupations they had when I knew them. I expect that, like my own parents, they could both be dead. I feel a dull thud in my heart for a few seconds, thinking of them, but this is too much so I turn and go back to my reunion with Clicker and Jerry.

The authorities stick to their word and quietly take me back to my hometown in Tasmania. They've already told me both my parents are dead and my brother's son is running the property, which is now three times the size of the place I knew as a young man. My brother, with his wife, has retired to a small fishing town called Bridport and potters back and forth to the farm, that is, if he's not playing bowls. It's with regret that I decide to let sleeping dogs lie and leave things as they are in Ringarooma.

'What have you found out about my two friends in America?' I ask when all the local matters are cleaned up. 'Is there any word about Alicia and Abraham? What are they up to and, more to the point, are they still alive?'

'Your friend Abraham is now a senator for Alabama and a strong voice in the United States on defence and civil rights. He's married to a woman called——'

'Ophelia,' I say, cutting him off. 'Abe said he was going to go into politics when he finished with the army.' I remember what we discussed on our hunting trip and also think of our conversation that last night. I smile as I try desperately to envisage them being married and hope that everything has turned out well for him, as I can't imagine him being a politician and doing all the double talk politicians do.

'How did you know his wife's name?' he says, looking at me, the surprise written over his face.

'He was going out with her when I first went over there,' I tell him. 'Boy! Can she talk! You just can't get a word in edgewise with that woman once she starts. Abe said when I told him I was going to propose to Alicia that he would marry Ophelia, but I didn't realise he was serious.'

The spook doesn't say anything for a while, just notes what I said about my two American friends before he starts again with his report from the CIA. 'His sister, Alicia, on the other hand is a doctor practising in New York, specialising in cancers,' he tells me, looking at his notes before he looks up again. 'She is married to a man called Julian Ashfield whose father came out from Germany after the Second World War. They have two children, a girl in her mid-twenties who is a doctor and a boy in his early twenties who is studying to be one.' He shakes his head. 'The whole family are doctors from what this report says.'

My heart sinks to my boots; this is the very thing I was afraid of, but I gather my thoughts and thank them. 'Thank you for that, I'm glad that they're both still alive and have made a success of their careers.' I'm pleased with the results as ASIO appears to have done a good job finding out this information for me.

The plane I'm on is enormous. My first flight in a 747 had been from Singapore. It was dark when I was hustled onboard by my security detail and didn't have time to look around. However, this time I'm more relaxed and being flown in business class, with the Australian Government picking up the tab. It's luxurious and the hostesses for some reason are fussing over me, spoiling me rotten, much to the surprise of my escorts. The 747 is a monster when compared with the 707 or the DC6, which I'd first travelled on for my leave to Singapore and Hong Kong. The route is similar to that of my first trip across the Pacific to LA and then through to Washington DC when going to receive my award from the President. But on that trip I didn't receive the attention I am now from the air hostesses, who to my surprise seem to be fussing over me as if I'm a dignitary or someone of importance.

I thought it best to approach Abe with caution after such a long time, so again, I have the Australian authorities arrange the meeting with him under the pretence of a semi-diplomatic affair because I don't want to spook him, especially under the strange circumstances of my reappearance, virtually out of nowhere. I'm a little nervous when I walk down the long foreboding corridor and knock hesitantly on his door and feel quite uncomfortable meeting him like this after so many years, but I still give a sigh of relief when the door is swung open by a pretty young staffer who looks up and smiles at me sweetly.

'Welcome to Washington, Mr Jackson,' she says cordially, ushering me and the security man into the quite spacious office. 'I believe you are here on defence issues, Mr Jackson and have a number of points to bring up with the senator, which are of concern for both our countries. Yes, the senator will see you now, Sir, so please follow me through to his office.'

We walk through her office to a spacious room where I find a middle-aged man with neatly cropped hair showing tinges of grey down either side. He is working through reams of papers that are neatly piled up in front of him on his desk. He looks up instantly, not seeing who's here, and quickly rises from his cluttered desk to meet his Australian guests. He hurries around his desk. We are no more than two metres apart when he stops and an astonished look appears on his face as he suddenly recognises me. His mouth is open as if he's about to say something, but nothing comes out.

'Hello, Abe, it's been a long time,' I say, as he just stares at me, mouth open wide, his hand out ready to welcome me, but just looking at me as if he's paralysed. 'I'm pleased to see you're looking both fit and well these days my friend. By the way, how is that lovely wife of yours, Ophelia?'

'Pete … is it you?' The words are very faint, as if he's seen a ghost, then he gives a sharp shake of his head. 'It *can't* be you! No, no, you're dead,' he blusters, trying very hard to control his emotions but having very little success.

'No, Abe, I'm still the one that found you behind that ox cart all those years ago in Vietnam. I'll bet you've never forgotten that either for it's something that would stick in your mind forever!'

'It can't be you. You're dead! You … you haven't aged like the rest of us.' He suddenly begins to gain some more of his composure. 'Can I see your scar? You were shot by a drunk when you were having a beer with Dad in a bar in sixty-nine when you came over the second time to see Alicia.'

'Yes, I was having a drink with your dad and his good friend Eli after working all morning on your father's trash truck,' I tell him gently as I pull my shirt out, showing him my ribs on the left side. 'There were four of them, all half drunk. A bullet did this to me. It was fired by a young punk called Jones who didn't like me drinking with Negroes. I picked up a hunting knife and threw the weapon I'd taken from one of his mates earlier and it went into his right shoulder and that, luckily for me, stopped the fight before anyone else was hurt badly by those racist idiots.'

'But that scar is still new …' Confused, he inspects the wound. 'That all happened years ago, and this wound you're showing me is new, as if–if–this happened a few months ago.'

He is starting to get quite agitated now after seeing the scar on my ribs and I want to quieten him down so we can have a proper talk. I don't want him to be too emotional or things might get out of hand, and I certainly don't want something like that to happen with a man who's been one of my best friends. Abe is confused, quite flustered and probably a little scared at me turning up like this so unexpectedly out of the blue, particularly as I haven't aged. I expect I would be the same if our roles were reversed and I was being confronted by a friend who had disappeared without a trace then suddenly turns up years later and hasn't aged at all in that time. I have to tell him what has happened to me and what has caused me not to age so he can understand.

'Abe, could we please sit down because I need to tell you about what happened all those years ago and you'll need to sit down because it's a long story – a story I've had difficulty coming to grips with myself since I woke up in a museum somewhere near Hanoi.'

He baulks at my words and slides almost uncontrollably back into his chair, and we sit looking at each other for quite some time across his desk. I begin telling him my story and what I remember right up to Singapore. Abe looks at me, not believing it's me, so, to break this impasse, I tell him about the letter I sent him the day before I went out on that last patrol – a letter letting him know my intentions with his sister.

'I wanted to finally gauge your reaction to me marrying her, Abe, and in that letter, I asked you if you'd be my best man. Now, however, according to ASIO – which is our equivalent to your CIA – she lives in New York and is happily married to another doctor, and they have two children that are in their twenties.'

'She cried for a long time, Pete,' Abe tells me, looking very sad and just staring at me now, I'm sure wanting to believe me. 'Lucky for her, she met this other doctor some eighteen months later. They went out together for quite a while and they were married. He's a white man, but a good man, almost my age. His father was a German who came here after the war and ran a small dairy farm in the mid-west somewhere not that far from the Canadian border.' Abe pauses a while, looking intently at me before he continues. 'No, Pete, you shouldn't see her; it'll only reopen a very big wound. I don't think she could handle it now because too much has happened since you disappeared.

Unfortunately, we've all moved on with our lives except you.' He shakes his head sadly. 'Goddamn it, Pete, I'm afraid I'm having trouble myself just talking to you and if Alicia saw you now as you are, she'd be devastated at what you've just told me.'

'If I can just see her,' I tell him, quite upset at the drama I caused her to go through when she thought I was dead. 'If she's happy now with a husband and her two children I'd hate to destroy that. I'm sure you know what I mean; having her distressed is the last thing I'd ever want. If–if I could see her from a distance one last time, that will have to do.'

'What are you going to do now?' he asks, fidgeting badly. I expect I've given him a bad shock as well seeing me like this. 'You are back, but time has moved on and unfortunately, Pete, you haven't. You're still the man I last saw when I dropped you off at the plane.'

'I have a brother, as you know, who's been working on the family farm. He's retired now. He's got a couple of lovely kids who seem keen on running the farm. I wouldn't want to muck them up either so I'm not going back home. They don't even know I'm alive yet. I don't think I'll even tell them I'm alive; it's better if I stay dead and don't go home and disrupt everything. Unfortunately, I don't think they would understand any of it anyway. I expect I'll just stay in the army.' I suddenly think of what I'm saying. 'That is, if they'll have me. Technically, I'm still in the army but would I fit in with such an organisation now after all these years away? I'm afraid I'm a dinosaur and don't relate to anything anywhere at the moment. You know, Abe, then I think of what their reaction would be if I turned up unannounced at Swanbourne. What if the army won't have me back? I'm afraid I don't know what I'm going to do if something like that happens.'

'Pete, I'm afraid I can't help you with this dilemma; honestly,

I don't know either.' Abe thinks for quite a while before finally he gives me an answer. I know he desperately wants to help me but is stumbling over how he can do this. 'I've got to go to New York tomorrow, so I can make an appointment to have lunch with Alicia. I do that from time to time. Would that do for a start? Then, we can think of what else we can do to get over the coming period and introduce you gradually perhaps?'

The following day we travel to New York, talking frankly about the past and the great times we had together as young men, which seem to me like yesterday. However, to Abe it's three decades ago and a heck of a lot of water has passed under the bridge. On reaching New York, I wait outside the restaurant for Alicia to arrive and to my delight I see my wonderful girl get out of a taxi just as bright and happy as I remember, only now she's a beautiful middle-aged woman but still with all the charm and sparkle I can remember from when I took her out. I find it very difficult not to rush up to her and give her a great big hug, but that would ruin everything, so I just watch her enter the cafe to meet Abe.

On the way back to Washington, we are both quiet with very little being spoken, and he can see I'm upset at seeing her. Abe looks across at me, noting my concern before quite seriously he says, 'Do you realise that Alicia saw you as she went into the restaurant? Pete, you should know my sister has eyes like a hawk and misses very little. She came in and just before she sat down said to me, and I quote, "I saw a man outside the restaurant who reminded me so much of Pete, but this man was so young, so full of youth just like he used to be." With those words she quite frankly shocked me. I hope my surprise didn't show because it took quite some time for me to recover.'

I'm staggered by this. I just sit in silence listening to Abe tell me exactly what she'd said when she reached him, and I instantly have to know something about the man she married, and their family.

'Tell me a little bit about her husband, and for that matter, his family, so I can understand them. Tell me about Julian and the sister of his – you know the one you told me had disappeared in Iraq while she was working over there. What happened to her, does anyone know?'

'It's a strange story, you know, Pete. Julian lost his only sister in Iraq,' he tells me, a little surprised at my question and he looks across at me. Then, seeing my interest is genuine, he continues. 'She was working for a small American oil company doing their testing of samples that the geologists brought in. She wasn't able to go into town freely because she was a woman in an Arab country and kicked up about wearing stuff on her head like they expect all women to do. I think she had trouble with the men over there, not in a kinky way mind you but just the way Arabs treat their women. Anyway, she was an engineer and, from what Julian told me, an extremely good one and was involved in building some sort of machine for oil exploration, she told everyone. We all thought she was crazy and then one day she and her machine just disappeared without any trace. The US Government and the oil company both did extensive searches for her, and we went over to Iraq ourselves and looked privately, but no one could find a trace of either the vehicle or the woman. She and her machine had somehow disappeared. I think Alicia and Julian lean on each other quite a bit, having both lost someone who was very close to them.'

We go out to dinner that night, talking over our lives and with me now reminiscing about what I'd lost after seeing

Alicia during the day. The next day, Abe takes me and my ASIO shepherds to the airport for the long return trip back to Australia. We look at each other for quite a while and then hug each other as old friends do and promise to keep in touch.

'Let me know how things go, Pete,' he says to me, very sincerely. 'If there is anything I can do to help you get back on your feet just let me know. I want to see you get on with your life and get some sort of career and see you succeed, because that's important to me as well.' He thinks for a moment before writing some details on a piece of paper. 'Here are my phone number and email details so you can contact me when you get established. So get a good laptop so we can correspond with each other.'

CHAPTER 9

BACK ON THE HORSE

Sydney

I arrive back in Sydney in a total quandary about my future because I've put all my hopes and aspirations now on going back into the army. What if I'm not suitable for this modern-day army? I wonder. What if I'm treated like some curiosity or, worse still, a type of antique and thrust back into a glass case again? Perhaps I'd be pulled out each time a scientist wishes to look me over once more to see if I'm real or if they can work out what the Vietnamese scientist did way back when. However, I'm determined to go back into the army, whatever the ramifications may be, as that's the only thing I know. I could easily lose myself in their ranks and there are plenty of ways to do this if I become desperate.

I'm taken to an army research facility south of Sydney for a full medical. Here I go through every test known to man. I'm cynical now because that's the way it feels after having strangers looking at me and doing tests that I don't understand. I'm relieved when the tests are finally over as it's no fun being pushed and poked by people you don't know, all of them in long white coats and all being called 'Doctor'. The memories of my nightmares linger during the day, causing me to wonder if the tests will stop me from getting back into uniform and doing the only job I've ever been trained to do properly.

'Well, Mr Jackson—er—Sergeant,' says an official-looking man who turns out to be the head doctor at this establishment – a professor. 'You'll be pleased to know that the tests reveal that you are extremely fit and healthy, both mentally and physically. The only blemishes on your body that we can find are the two scars on either side of your ribs. I had a good look at them, and they look relatively new, so please tell me what caused them.'

'One is a bullet wound I received in an argument twelve months ago and the other …' I give a dry laugh about the incident in Singapore. 'I'm afraid with the other one … I had a little altercation with a man who came at me with a knife. I'm glad neither of them was serious.'

'I'm afraid, Sergeant, you'll have to be more careful with whom you associate or the next one might be straight in the middle. Anyway, you should be pleased to know that you're good to go. Your unit should be proud to have you back with them, especially now with terrorists running riot around the world.' I'm quite relieved and extremely pleased when he changes back to my condition. 'Quite frankly, Sergeant Jackson, I'm at a loss to understand why your unit sent you over here for testing in the first place. Do you have any idea why this happened or what this is all about?'

'I'm sorry, Doctor, but I'd be only guessing, and I can't help you. I was just sent here without any explanations whatsoever.

Perhaps they are thinking of some new medical procedures for troops to undergo after training – you know, something to gauge their fitness and their suitability for whatever their unit is required to do.'

'Well, if the members of our armed forces reached the physical and mental standards you have, they'll be well-placed to defend this country if the worst were to happen.'

'Thank you, Doctor.' I wonder what he means and hope my off-the-cuff comments have distracted him somewhat in other directions. 'It will be great to get back to the unit. I've been away far too long, and I don't want to lose touch with any advanced training.'

I put my clothes on as quickly as I can, elated that I've passed the tests and jumped through their hoops. All I want to do now is get back to my squadron and start doing some meaningful training, and if an operation comes up that gives me the chance to get into action again, all the better. There is however, one hurdle to overcome. Now that I've shown these people I'm fit, both mentally and physically, will they take me back into the unit? I keep asking myself over and over again.

I feel a little shaky and hope I won't be put away in base squadron or in some crappy posting that will give me a limited opportunity for active service, because that's the main reason I initially joined the army and the SAS.

Across The City

In another part of Sydney, a number of senior officers sit around a table looking at the piles of paper in front of them.

'We have seen the reports and now the medical papers on this

Sergeant Jackson, which are in front of you. I would like your comments please, gentlemen, about the tests that have been run on this soldier.'

'I see it like this, General,' answers a brigadier, shuffling through his papers before looking up once again, 'he was and still is an exceptional soldier. Really, you only have to look at his record before his disappearance; it exceeded most of his peers. To use his initiative the way he did to get out of Vietnam and make his way to Singapore, by himself, dressed in his combat fatigues *and* openly carrying the weapons as he did, shows the tenacity and the skills this man has. This is something you only read about. I say, Sir, let him go back to his unit and we can monitor his performance from over there. I'm sure we'll soon know how well he performs under pressure.'

'Thank you for those comments, Doug.' The general looks purposefully across the table at the other officers and then he asks another for an opinion. 'What about you, Brian? Do you think he's fit and capable to be a member of today's army?'

'I've heard what Doug has said,' he responds, again looking down at his papers, purposely flicking them over. 'I'm afraid I have reservations about him. It's hard to believe that he's been suspended in time in a glass case for all these years, thirty I believe. *Hell*, this soldier was in Vietnam before me, and this man is not even thirty and yet we are treating him as if he is the same person. I'm afraid I have great difficulty accepting this man because of what he is, but I expect we only have to wait; you'll see, time will prove this man a fraud.'

'We'll take what you say on board, Brian,' says the general, a little annoyed at the comments. Then he looks at the last man at the table – a small, thin-looking man with a well-kept moustache, who is studying his papers with great interest and appears to be reading one of the extracts very carefully. 'What about you, Bill? What do you think about Sergeant Jackson? Do you think he's the real deal or an imposter?'

Bill looks up at the others, carefully weighing up what each of them had to say before he finally speaks.

'I was the troop commander of Peter Jackson on his first tour of Vietnam and was responsible for promoting him from private to corporal at the end of his tour of duty. He was an exceptional soldier then and I found he treated everyone fairly whether they were a private or an officer. We've monitored him since he arrived in Singapore, and what he did to the Vietnamese assassin was typical of what the Peter Jackson I knew would have done. We have done blood tests on him, and checked his dentals, DNA is out too, at least for comparative purposes. I've also compared a group photo we had taken late in nineteen sixty-seven to one taken in Singapore when he turned up at the embassy, and in my opinion gentlemen, they are of the same man. We monitored the meeting with Senator Abraham King, the American sergeant he saved while I was with him in Vietnam and the shock reportedly shown by the senator was evidently one of recognition. I have to say, gentlemen, I was completely shocked myself at first sight when he returned from Singapore. It's the same man, no doubt about that. He's fit and I believe he should go back to the unit where we can monitor his progression and keep an eye on him.'

'Thank you, Bill. I tend to agree with you,' says the general, looking about the table and getting nods of acceptance from the others. 'I believe we give his details *only* to the unit commanding officer and have him monitored for at least the first six to twelve months and see how he performs both mentally and physically and reassess his situation, based entirely on his performance in the unit. This, gentlemen, should give us an extremely good idea of how he fits into the unit in modern times.'

All around the table agree with this assessment; even the brigadier who has reservations, grudgingly nods his head.

'As long as the monitoring is carried out quietly,' says the general. 'We don't want to impair his performance as a soldier by having all his peers staring at him. I want the commanding officer to be the only one in the unit who knows about him and that he's being assessed. The commanding officer, by the way, was in another squadron doing his cadre course when Jackson was a corporal. Who knows, he may know him vaguely. Either way, it will be a very interesting meeting for the two of them.'

'It's a pity we're getting absolutely no cooperation from the Vietnamese regarding his incarceration,' says the brigadier, looking across the table at the reaction of the others. 'They say that such a soldier does not exist, and they have never conducted any experiments on our soldiers during that war. They're *bloody* liars, that's all I can say. Jackson is proof of what they did. Unfortunately, they don't want to lose face by admitting they conducted experiments on our troops. Don't they know that the serum that Jackson was given is a world-first and could be used for who knows what in modern medical science? The Americans also told us of how they monitored strange happenings at one of their research laboratories around the time Jackson broke out, and the French journalist who followed him to Singapore died under strange circumstances after we allowed him to interview Jackson. The story he had been compiling went missing but, unknown to the Vietnamese, however, before we allowed him to interview Jackson, we insisted on a copy of all his work for our records. They certainly make interesting reading when it's a third party's notes with no bias attached that has documented the events as they happened. All I can say about the attitude that the Vietnamese are showing is that they are very short-sighted as far as the gas and serum is concerned and barefaced liars about everything else concerning the laboratory where the tests were obviously carried out. How convenient it is for them to refuse to admit this research ever took place. They, along with the rest of the world, are missing out on this breathtaking invention from one of their own scientists.'

Country NSW

I'm sent to the infantry centre at Singleton for a month to brush up on modern infantry tactics and do a crash course in the new weaponry that the army now uses. I find the advances that have been made in my absence to be very exciting and I readily adapt to them, almost like a duck to water.

It's with a lot of trepidation, when this advanced training is finally finished, that I take the long trip back to Perth. I've been away a long time, but to me it seems little more than a month since I fell from the chopper and blacked out. Seeing an aged Abe and talking to him about events was one thing, but when I saw Alicia meet Abe at that restaurant, I realised fully just how long I've been away …

I keep wondering how I'll be accepted back into the unit after so long. Perhaps it would be wise for me not to mention that I'd been there before, to let them think this is a new assignment for me and say nothing to attract their attention, for I'm now the stranger in the unit. It will be interesting to see their reaction to me suddenly turning up out of the blue without doing a cadre course, especially with three permanent stripes on my arm – I bet there'll be people there that will have their noses out of joint. This time I'll be the newcomer and won't know anyone or the little idiosyncrasies that happen in a small unit. I'm sure a lot of blokes will be more than a little shitty about me coming in still holding my rank – something that never happened in my previous time at the unit.

Perth Airport

'Sergeant Jackson,' says a corporal who looks a few years older than me. 'Welcome to the unit. Here, I'll take that kit bag if you just follow me please. We'll head out to the camp at Swany and then you'll become acquainted with what we have over here. It's quite different to other parts of the army.'

I follow him out to the carpark to a Land Rover and watch as he throws my gear into the back. We head off towards the city of Perth, and boy, has this city changed in the time I've been away! I stay silent as we move through the city and see new highways, freeways and rail lines going everywhere. My sudden silence doesn't go unnoticed by my driver who looks across and starts to give me a full briefing on the city of Perth.

'You'll find it's a nice place, Sarge. You'll soon get to know it and enjoy what we have along the coast, particularly if you like surfing, fishing or diving. Quite a number of the fellas do that at weekends and bring a number of good ones back to the mess.' Next he goes on to point out the good and bad parts of Perth. 'We're just about at camp, Sarge. I've got to drop you off at the commanding officer's room first before I take you to the sergeants' mess and you'll be able to meet some of the other snakes we have. You'll find they have a nice mess out towards the coast so you should settle in very quickly once you get to know this place.'

He drops me off at the administration building and I make my way to the commanding officer's room, which to my relief is in the same place as I remember it when we came home in nineteen sixty-eight after our squadron's first tour of Vietnam. There's no waiting and I'm ushered straight into his office.

'Welcome, Sergeant Jackson,' says a colonel in his mid to late fifties. 'I'm pleased to have you back in the unit. It's been a long time since we met, even though it was only briefly, and I have to say, under extreme circumstances.'

'Yes, Sir, it has been a long time,' I say, sharply saluting the man in front of me. He has aged a lot from the raw second lieutenant I'd met before at Collie while I was on cadre staff. 'I was pleased to have been able to help you in that pub brawl, Sir. They were a pack of drunken bastards who we gave, shall I say, an adequate lesson in manners. Has your left hand recovered okay? Because the last time I saw it, Sir, it was quite swollen and had a bandage on trying to compress the swelling.'

'Well, I'll be damned, it *is* you,' he says, getting to his feet and coming around the desk to me. 'I was called by a colleague of mine and told this unbelievable story about you coming back, almost I must say from the dead.' He shakes his head hard, believing what I've said. 'It's over thirty years since that fight in the pub. When you came in you looked like the man who I stood back-to-back with in that fight at the Collie Pub. How great, Pete, welcome back. It's absolutely wonderful having you here. Welcome back to the unit.'

I have never been hugged by an officer before in my life, but with this man, even though I've only met him the once, we'd fought side by side in a nasty encounter in one of the many hotels at Collie. To me, it was only fifteen months ago, and we'd saved each other's bacon in this pub brawl and won against half a dozen drunken thugs from one of the coal mines who just wanted to bash someone. They'd picked on this man, so I'd stepped in and helped him defend himself. After his welcome, we sit on either side of his desk, allowing me to tell him my story from start to finish.

'I had hoped to get out of the army after the second tour and marry my American fiancée and run the family dairy farm in Tasmania, but unfortunately those times have finished for me and now all I have left is the army.'

'We'll help with that,' he tells me quite confidently, which is a pleasant surprise. 'Things have changed quite dramatically here but unfortunately there have been no major deployments for the unit since Vietnam finished.'

'I'm more than ready for my job, whatever it may be, Sir,' I tell him, knowing now I have a friend who knew me and would help me settle back in the unit. 'I found out at the infantry centre that some of my training is more than antiquated when I was doing my refresher, but I'm a fast learner at most things and I realise I have a lot to pick up, particularly with the weaponry used these days.'

'I noticed from briefs I've received that you've been to a number of places familiarising yourself with weapons and radios we now use,' he tells me, showing a bit of a smirk, which tells me that he's been following my retraining programs closely. 'I'll bet you're more than pleased they don't do CW anymore with their communications, because I remember you complaining about it during Collie that you were tone deaf when it came to CW if it got over ten words a minute. It's good to see that you've done these updates and I notice from these briefs that you passed them all very easily. I'll be able to assist you in any updating of knowledge when you require it here, so please don't hesitate in asking for my assistance or any guidance if there are any difficulties that arise in getting you updated.'

'Thank you, Sir. I appreciate that. It will be great just getting back to the unit. Sir, I just want to get back into the thick of things immediately now that I'm here and get right on top of my trade.'

'Good to hear, Sergeant, good to hear. I'll get you into the thick of things, as you call it, straight away. We are a patrol sergeant down in Three Squadron, so I'm putting you into that slot. They will be going to northern Australia for a two-month work out, so prepare yourself for that exercise with the long version of the Land Rovers we are using these days. They leave Monday. Are there any questions about your new posting?'

'Not at this stage, Sir. It's just nice being back at the coal face where I'll meet my patrol and we'll go on from there.' I salute, turn and leave. My heart is thumping with anticipation at how lucky I am to meet a man I know, as I'm sure he'll make certain that I'm given a go. That's all I want, and I plan to make sure I don't let them down because I'm just happy to be back in the unit and in one of the sabre squadrons, where I belong.

The first morning back at Swanbourne, I get up bright and early and go for a run along the beach. It's a wonderful, stimulating exercise, to be out in the elements, pushing myself along with the salty air from the sea breeze rushing into my lungs. I'm the only early morning jogger on this back beach, the quiet atmosphere giving me the feeling of freedom that I haven't felt for ages. The occasional spray hitting me and the sounds of the sea bashing into the shore makes me feel quite exhilarated. I'm away almost an hour before I'm back at the sergeants' mess. I have a quick shower and change into my camouflage fatigues, before I make my way to the sergeants' mess for breakfast and meet the rest of the sergeants.

'Peter Jackson. I've just come in from Infantry Centre,' I say, introducing myself to the other sergeants. We shake hands before I settle in and quietly listen to their conversations about upcoming and recent events in the unit. All of this is talk of past events and in *their* past, but a decade after the Vietnam War finished – still quite a strange fit for me.

It appears two of them have spent time as privates in Somalia in part of the squadron a few years ago. Except for the two who are now seen by the others as old hands, no one has seen any action at all because the squadrons have spent years laboriously training and waiting in anticipation for some event to happen. Even during the Gulf War in ninety-one there was a commitment for them to participate, but the war was over well before they saw any action.

The remainder of the week is spent getting ready for the squadron exercise in northern Australia, and for the first time I meet the men who will be under my command during this coming exercise.

'My name is Peter Jackson,' I tell them as we gather around our vehicles. 'Off the parade ground and out in the scrub, it's Pete. Now, who are you fellas? I need to know the men I'm working closely with.'

Individually, they introduce themselves, a bit bemused at the introduction given by their new sergeant – a man they know has only just arrived in the camp and has very little if any experience in their unit and the type of work they are expected to do. I have Purse, a private, as my driver, and my gunner is Gil. On the other vehicle the driver is Mick, another private; Johnny, a lance corporal, is the gunner; and the navigator is a corporal called Paddy. They are a motley lot, but I immediately like them. I'm impressed with the six-wheel-drive Land Rovers that evidently members of the unit have designed and developed themselves – a vehicle and mode of transport I'm not familiar with as most of my work was done scrub bashing through on foot in both bush and jungle.

'I have a lot to learn about this type of transport,' I tell my men as we move around the machines, and I'm filled in on all aspects as we ready our vehicles for the coming exercise. I'm proficient with the standard army Rover used in my day but these six-wheel-drive machines are huge and are something quite different to what I'm used to. I find it quite exciting to learn the intricacies of these machines and what these extended monsters are capable of doing.

The exercises that we're about to commence are north-east of Geraldton in northern Western Australia, so the squadron moves up the west coast highway in convoy to the training area, well over a thousand miles from Perth. That's another important thing I have to update and learn about – distances are now all in metric, but this only came in the year I did my first tour of Vietnam. I suddenly remember the dramatic mistake our patrol made on one operation when climbing a small feature towards the Nui Tie Vies – the whole patrol thought the height of this small hill was in feet but soon realised it turned out to be in metres and was over three times the height we first thought.

'The purpose of this exercise is to hone your navigation skills and be able to move to any of the specific checkpoints we have set up over the training area. You're expected to find your position either by day or night,' the officer in charge tells us at our final briefing, probably for my benefit as I'm the only new patrol commander here. 'Initially, there will be no enemy, but your progress will be monitored on your ability to reach your checkpoints without detection within a specific time frame, which you'll be required to work within.'

I may have been green with our new mode of transport but not with a map and compass, which I spread out on the bonnet of the Rover, and we go over our route together with both of my crews. They seem surprised at my familiarity with this situation as I go over this with them, marking in the checkpoints and familiarising them with the map and some of the rough spots the wheels have us going through that can be picked out by the closeness and number of contours shown.

'Are there any questions about the way we'll be heading?' I ask them, wanting to get their reaction to the route we've been given. 'I want you all to be familiar with every aspect of this route we are about to take just in case any unforeseen event happens. For example, if our two vehicles somehow get split up or an accident happens or for some unknown reason you end up by yourself in some isolated spot somewhere out in Woop Woop, then any one of you will be able to know your map and get out and back to civilisation under your own steam. If, for example, it's an accident and the person doing the navigation is severely injured, again you'll be able to get back to civilisation then alert them back at headquarters about what happened and you'll have the capability to bring them back to the site where the accident occurred.'

There are no questions from any of them, making me a little disappointed, however, it's probably because they don't know me very well, but that will change. I also have a feeling that we are all being assessed in our roles in these Land Rovers. Groups of us are sent off separately as all of the allotted routes are different and it's not just a case of following the leader. My two Rovers have some two hundred or so kilometres to travel to get to our next checkpoint across some extremely inhospitable, rough country. For our first trek, the route is designed to test all these navigational skills that each of us is supposed to have.

'We'll act alternately with each Rover leading for approximately fifty kilometres,' I tell them before we start. 'I want each Rover checking the other as we go so as to find any navigational or potential errors we may make getting from point A to B, and I want any one of you who notices a wrong direction to notify the others and me so this fault can be corrected.'

By using this system, we reach the designated spot an hour before dark. The checkpoints are manned, mostly by corps of signals, who handle the communications and when we finish, an officer is assigned to take the times and then he goes on to allot each patrol the next route.

'You buggers made damned good time,' one of the sigs says to Gil, almost giving me the impression they weren't expecting us for a number of hours.

'A piece of cake when you have navigators like us,' Gil retorts to the surprised sig. His next comments make most of us who hear him turn away to control our laughter. 'When do you give us the really hard stuff? You know the type of track I mean, something hard with complicated topography to pass through – one of those difficult tracks that we can really test our mettle on?'

'Don't wish for too much because you'll find the other snake will be gunning for you lot if you do times like this too often.'

Fortunately, it's not long before an officer comes over and gives us our next reference point, this time some three hundred kilometres in a different direction altogether. This route is due north through more broken country with the estimated time of arrival about lunchtime tomorrow.

'This time we're being generous to you boys because you have been given an option on this one,' the officer tells us, then proceeds to point out on a map our destination. 'As you've been behind the wheel most of the day, you can have a sleep here or somewhere on your way. We'll leave that entirely up to you lot on how you want to deal with this situation. Now are there any questions you have with this route you've just been given?'

'Well, you heard the officer,' I said, putting some of the responsibility back on them. 'What do you boys want to do – sleep here for a while or do we have a nap on the way when our concentration starts to wane? It's roughly three hundred clicks to get to our designated position and from studying the map, there are a number of rough spots on the route.'

They look at each other, a bit confused at being part of the decision-making. Obviously, this sort of thing hasn't been done very much with them before, so I make a suggestion to help them.

'In my opinion, we should leave now and see how we go sleep-wise and if we feel tired then stop for some shut-eye. But I want you fellas to let me know how you're feeling on the way. What do you think?'

'I'll go along with you, Sarge,' says Paddy, looking over to the others, a little bit confused at being again involved in the decision making. 'What do you reckon, fellas? Head off tonight and have forty winks when we need it like the sarge says? That's what I think we should do.'

They all agree with Paddy and me, so we brew up while looking over our maps, knowing we'll make any minor decisions on the route. With this out of the way we quickly drink our brews and leave. With the other vehicle following close behind, we move out at high speed on our course for the checkpoint that's some hours away.

Onboard the second Land Rover, Paddy and his two crewmen talk about the day's events and how easily they achieved their target. Then, the topic of their new sergeant comes up – a man they've only known barely for a week.

'What do you think of our new sarge, Pad?' asks Mick as he drives after the other Rover. 'It's hard to put a handle on him, isn't it? He's different to the other snakes back at camp, almost as if he's been in the unit before but I know he hasn't because I asked one of the old fellas who's been here some twenty years and none of 'em knows him.'

'Yeah, he doesn't know a lot about our kind of Land Rover,' replies Paddy, staring towards the front, his goggles stopping the dust that is belting at them from the vehicle in front. 'But boy can he read a compass and plot a course! It was all his effort that got us in so far ahead of time back there; I hope you fellas realise that. What do you think of our new sergeant, Johnny?'

'I know the other snakes had their noses put out of joint when he turned up,' answers the gunner, a man who says what he thinks. 'He has a different way of getting you to do exactly what he wants – easy-like, and when the decision is made you almost feel that you did it yourself, but it's the way he wanted it done anyway. I like his straightforward attitude.'

'Did you see the look on those sig's faces?' laughs Mick without averting his eyes from the vehicle in front. 'I heard that the other snakes were saying we'd be lost for most of the time and then we turned up when we did well before time and well before most of them; took 'em all by surprise.'

'Anyway, we'd better be as good with the compass as he is because the fifty kilometres are almost up and we'll be the lead machine. So you'd better concentrate on the direction we're going; I don't want it to be our vehicle that gets us lost; he'll be just behind us with his compass out checking our route.'

The fifty kilometres are up, and Paddy's machine takes the lead. They've been told that it isn't a race but there is always a large amount of pride in coming in early, so we continue north at a quite rapid speed. I watch Paddy's machine, occasionally checking the compass as a guarantee we are going in the right direction. Another fifty kilometres, it's almost dark and the ground starts to get a little uneven, so again we change positions, and my Rover takes over as the lead vehicle.

'We're a third of the way,' I say, as we come abreast with the other vehicle. 'Do you want to break now or continue? Personally, I'd prefer to go on for at least another fifty-odd clicks. What about you boys?'

'*We're with you, Sarge!*' Paddy yells back. 'We could do the lot if you want; we're all fine and wide awake.'

'Good then, let's do it,' I say, pleased that they are with me. 'We'll take the lead for the rest of the journey. There are about two hundred clicks to the finish. However, from the look of the chart, the ground deteriorates somewhat for the next twenty-odd Ks, so the pace will be a tad slower; make sure you keep a check on me. I don't want to go off over some bank somewhere and have your machine follow us over.' I see the looks on their faces and laugh. 'I don't want that happening because I'll need you lot to pull me out.'

The final two hundred kilometres left are reasonable, with some bad stretches that take more time to navigate, but we're fortunate as a full moon slowly climbs up and illuminates the ground in front, making our job with the night vision goggles so much easier. With Paddy and his group keeping a check on my navigation, we finally creep into the staging point at three in the morning, much to the surprise of some very sleepy sigs. With a shake of their heads, they check us in. We roll our sleeping bags out alongside our vehicles, each of us very pleased with the result of our cross-country navigation. Mick is just about to enter his swag when the sig, who's a friend, pulls him aside with a little timely warning about some of the other sergeants whose noses are a little out of joint with us coming in so early.

'Shit, you blokes made good time, Mick; you're the first vehicles to arrive,' the surprised sig tells him, making me proud of my men. Then he whispers a warning. 'Just be careful on the next stage because there will be enemy vehicles to contend with and the other snakes will be gunning for you lot after showing them up.'

'That's alright, Sam, I'm pretty sure Pete knows this. Look, we'll just be doing whatever job they give us, so we'll play everything by ear.'

The next stage of the exercise is to locate specific roads and observe the traffic without being detected. To complicate things, as the sig told Mick, we'll now be under constant threat by roving enemy patrols with orders to harass and if possible, capture us. To make things worse, we have to be alert to aerial reconnaissance by both civilians and the military and this means there will be no rest for us as everything in the air will be on the lookout. To avoid this, most of our movement will have to be by night to avoid being caught out in the open by one of these aircraft; it's extremely dry and every vehicle will leave a tell-tale dust cloud behind it, plainly visible through the day from the air.

We move out in the evening towards the designated road, which turns out to be a section of the main highway some three hundred kilometres to the east. By midnight, we're in a maze of rough gullies and re-entrants that look positive at first but, when we try them, they turn out to be blind gullies. We stop to thoroughly study our maps and work out a safe route through this labyrinth of gullies and steep ridges. There is none that we could use without running the risk of being detected by one of the many enemy patrols, or worse still – hitting an obvious ambush site. I'm sure these people would relish capturing us just because I'm new.

'According to my calculations, we should be here.' I place my finger on the map, indicating our position, and get nods of agreement from each of my men. 'Now, if we continue along this path, we should exit at this position here. Fellas, this is one of the many logical ways out. Now if I was the enemy commander, I would have read my map and would know this and if I wanted to stop these reconnaissance patrols from getting across to the highway, this is the obvious place I'd have an ambush set to stop a patrol like ours getting through.' I point to the place on the map. 'On this pass here, you'd virtually catch anyone who's stupid enough to try to use this route to reach the Princes Highway; it's so obvious. We should steer well away from that position.'

'You're spot on, Sarge,' Paddy says, studying the map and running his finger along the proposed route. 'But we'll have to go right back to here to get through on the best of the alternate routes.' He pushes his finger on another point some twenty kilometres of rough broken ground to the west of our position. 'Going through that country will take the best part of a day because we'll only be able to travel at night and then there's no guarantee that we won't get hit somewhere over here. Again, it's the only obvious alternative route out of here so we'll be in for a contact either way. The next alternate position is over two days away.'

'You can also bet our comms would have been intercepted as well,' Johnny tells us, pleasing me by throwing this scenario into the ring. 'I heard what Sam told Mick last night. So I bet there's a number of enemies who know exactly where we are tonight and will have good ambushes set on any alternate route we choose, so we have to be aware of that.'

'It's almost as if the wheels want us to be hit to see how we handle a contact,' Purse says, studying the map and then running his finger over each of the proposed ways through, trying to work out another way. 'It's almost as if they've left us two choices, both of which can be covered easily by the enemy vehicles. Do you think the wheels are deliberately sending us into an ambush site?'

'That could be the case, Purse. However, there's another option that I don't think the wheels have considered,' I tell them, I think surprising each of my men. 'I've been looking at the map's grid lines of the obvious route out of this quagmire.' I run my finger along the obvious way they'd think we'd take but stop partway. 'If we can get up here tonight, we should be able to get straight across to the highway by morning but, looking at the contours and the distance between them, I reckon the only way to get up here is by winching the vehicles up. Now by doing that, I'm quite sure we should be able to avoid any ambush that our enemy is proposing to set, and if it works, we will be in place to monitor the traffic on the highway by first light tomorrow morning; the contours are pretty good from here on. Questions please fellas? If there's a problem I want to be cut down.'

They study the proposed route I've given them. I can tell by their attitude that they like the idea but are uneasy about doing such a manoeuvre because the risks are extremely high, especially doing what I propose at night. To everyone's surprise, it's Mick who speaks up, strongly supporting this critical manoeuvre.

'I think it's a good idea. Look fellas, you should know we're all on trial here, even you, Sarge, so really what have we got to lose? It'll take a good day to go back and around to the alternate route and who's to say that we won't be hit in some ambush going that way because, as you've all pointed out, it's the obvious alternate way across to the highway and these bastards are gunning for us. Let's have a go at that incline because if it is too steep and we're unsuccessful, we can always go back and try the alternate route to dodge the obvious ambush sites.' His next words completely sum up the situation we're in, giving me full support for this alternate route that I'm proposing. 'Quite frankly fellas, none of us have anything to lose in trying this route out – nothing to lose and everything to gain, and quite frankly, I like your suggestion, Sarge.'

'It's done then, fellas,' I say, before anyone else can make a negative comment. 'We'll see just how good our winches are. If this manoeuvre works, we'll be in place well before morning and that should confuse our enemy no end and the wheels too for that matter; they're expecting us to go on these easier routes.'

The two Rovers reach the area in about ten minutes, and it takes another ten to secure the end of the winch to a small flattish area that would just take a vehicle the size of our six-wheel-drive Rover.

'Gil, you and Purse go up to where we'll secure the winch,' I tell my offsiders, because I'm not prepared to risk their lives on a venture like this, particularly when it's only a training exercise. 'Be ready with chocks when I get up to you blokes.'

The winching begins. It's slow at first, up quite a steep slope, but finally the Land Rover is in position sitting precariously at the halfway point. I won't be happy, however, until the chocks are well in place and the vehicle is firmly secured.

'I've got all the brakes on. Now, chock the wheels because this may be the hard part getting them to hold,' I tell them, giving a sigh of relief when they indicate that the chocks are finally in behind the wheels and the winch is loosened off just a little to see if the chocks hold the weight of this large machine. I'm relieved when they hold the vehicle beautifully. I watch as my two crew members quickly run out the winch cable once more, and I'm even more relieved when the cable finally reaches the top of the rise and they disappear from my view. I nervously wait to see one of my crew indicate the cable is firmly secured to a large boulder ready for the next stage up to the top of this hill. I talk out loud to give the two at the top, and myself, confidence and to give all my crew enthusiasm in what we're jointly trying to do. 'Okay boys, this is the last leg, so let's make sure everything goes right. Now, easy does it. That's good fellas; we're there.'

We've finally done it; the Rover is on the top of the ridge. I turn the vehicle around so it's facing the bottom of the incline, looking down this steep slope at the other half of my team who stand looking almost in awe straight up this imposing slope at us. We're slaving in the moonlight with our vision helped by our night vision goggles and we begin to get ready for the final phase of this exercise.

'Anchor the back of our Rover with the drag chain to that rock so it's secure and we can't move forward, because it has to take the weight of both machines this time. Right, run out the winch from both vehicles,' I tell them, as they eagerly take the cable down to the halfway point, meeting two of the other crew to join both cables together. 'We'll bring the other vehicle up the whole way and save the stuffing round in the middle section and having to chock the wheels. This manoeuvre will save a lot of time and effort fellas. We'll need all the time we can get with this little exercise because I want to have our O.P. in place ready for the morning sched.'

Both winch cables are now firmly connected, and the second Rover is brought up gradually to the first section using its own winch cable. I breathe in deeply once the cable is fully wound in because we're halfway there. For the last step I will use the winch from my vehicle to bring Mick's machine up to mine. After a period of heart-wrenching tension and stress, finally both these large, formidable machines are sitting together high on the top of the ridge and well away from the edge of the slope. It's good to see the excitement of our achievement etched on each of my crew's faces.

'Well done, fellas, well done! Now I'm sorry to hassle you blokes but we've got a lot to do tonight so let's make tracks for that road,' I tell my crews, who I feel don't think or believe we can do such a feat, especially in the dark. 'Get these vehicles moving men, because this is only the first step in what we have to do tonight. You'll find we've got a hell of a lot of work in front of us once we reach that road – we have to find a suitable place for our O.P. and then camouflage the Rovers before it's light. We have to make both of them invisible to any aircraft that will most certainly be flying up that road looking for us when we radio our position.'

The track we take is reasonable for the outback and runs down a ridge broken with small, blind gullies running off either side of this spur, and these run away into more broken land, according to my map. So, we stick doggedly to our route, hoping the map is accurate and will take us directly to the highway, because until our next comms, our route is secret. It's difficult terrain and it takes most of the night before we finally locate the highway and another hour slowly cruising along before a suitable lay-up point for both vehicles is found. It's a hollow on the other side of the highway, just off the road. It is big enough to comfortably hide two vehicles the size of our six-wheel-drive Land Rovers. The vehicles are carefully camouflaged with bushes placed discreetly in our nets, hopefully making them invisible from the air. I'm sure as soon as headquarters get our comms this morning, people will be scouring the road for us. A small ridge is all that is between us and the highway – a suitable viewing platform, which enables a good view of any vehicles travelling to and from Geraldton. Our position is close enough to the highway to get not only vehicle stats but also their number plates, information that will round off any surveillance we do.

'The Rovers are in place so send in comms to HQ. Tell them that we are now in position and will report all traffic that uses this road,' I tell Johnny, pleased with our progress to be at the highway almost a day ahead of schedule. 'Let them know we'll be taking note of all road usage from this time on. As soon as that's done, get some shut-eye, because I'll take the shift until morning. Well done fellas, it was a marvellous effort by you all getting up that slope in the dark. Thanks very much for your support. I'm proud of what you've all done tonight.'

I sit alone on top of this small ridge taking the first shift in the awakening day. I'm pleased with the efforts of my men – men who'll call a spade a spade. We'll get along fine. Back at the lay-up point, my men are just bedding down, finding the best spots to roll out their swags. They're all dog-tired but full of adrenalin from what we've just been able to achieve.

Head Quarters

'Patrol 23 is now in position and will be monitoring the highway,' says the sig on receiving our message.

'Good God, they were quick,' replies the orderly officer, coming over to the set and staring at the message that's just come in, as if questioning its legitimacy. 'We weren't expecting anyone to be in place for at least another thirty hours. That's strange, where do you think their route was? We were expecting them to run into one of our cut-off groups early this morning.'

'I have no idea, Sir.' They both go over to the large wall map of the area and point to the area of our previously radioed position. 'This is the route we expected them to take as their previous grid reference was here.' He points to the map, now quite confused with the message. 'They would have had to come along this route here and, as you know, Sir, we have that covered with two patrols, one here and the other one across here. Both those patrols were expecting them to arrive sometime before dawn.'

'Do you think they have the right road, James?' He suddenly thinks of whose patrol it is. 'It's that new bloke, that Jackson fella; he's new to this part of Australia – you know the one that got here late last week? I'll bet he has the wrong road, but we'll soon know when he sends in the first vehicle descriptions from his O.P.; it will give me the greatest privilege to tell them.'

'If they do have the right road, they certainly would have had to come through here, Sir,' the sig replies again, moving a pencil over the map indicating the area of operation and the course they expected us to take. 'The last sched they sent was from this position here, Sir. The commander deliberately put them in this area that we've blocked off just to see how Jackson handles the ambush. We were expecting them from late morning to midday from the estimations of their last sched when they would supposedly run into our blocking force we have here.'

'How in the name of *hell* have they been able to get right across to the road and miss the ambush we have set?'

'After seeing the man who is running that patrol, I'll bet they are sending in a bogus position hoping we'll move the ambush. We'll have to wait for their next sched, Sir, which should be half an hour at the most before they hit the blocking force.'

'Yes, I agree with you, I think they could be sending in a bogus position, hoping the cut-off group will intercept that message and move out looking for them,' another sergeant says, coming into their conversation and looking at the large wall map of the designated area of operation. 'If the cut-off group moves to accommodate their new position, then they could slip through and across to the highway unopposed. That's what I would have done, Sir, because blind Harry would have known this is the only way out and, from what I've seen of Sergeant Jackson, he's certainly no fool.'

'Bob could be right about them, Sir, sending in a bogus signal knowing full well it could or would be intercepted by the enemy and expecting us to move the blocking force to accommodate them.'

'No, I don't believe it's a ploy to get the blocking party moved. They must have the wrong road. Leave the cut-off group in place and wait and see what happens tomorrow at their next sched. If it's the same position, we'll send a plane up the highway sometime in the morning and see if they are there, and if they are, how well they've camouflaged their Rovers from aerial surveillance.'

'That's if they have the right highway, Sir, and on the off chance they have, let's see if the plane can spot them,' says the sergeant in charge of the signal post who's just as puzzled as the others at how the two vehicles the size of these Land Rovers could have reached the highway so soon, able to bypass the units that had the access to their route covered. 'In my opinion they must be on the wrong road because look at the topography for God's sake. That's a hell of a distance between their two last transitions. No, it can't be. It's impossible to go any other way than through where we've set the ambush.'

Princes Highway

'We'll take over now, Sarge.' It's Gil and Purse to take the first shift. Gil thrusts a cup of hot brew into my hands. 'Has anything come along this morning that we should know about?'

'All peaceful, Gil. Just the one car, and I'll bet the bastard was speeding,' I say, laughing along with them. 'Better be on your toes, boys, because if my reading of the situation is right, the next thing we'll get is an aircraft or something that will try to find out where we are. This is why I tried to get us as close to the road as possible because normally our boys would have the O.P. back a few hundred metres or so from the road. Anyway, I'll get you relieved in say two hours' time, so keep your eyes open and I'll see you later.'

I thoroughly check out the camouflage on our two units before going in to find the other three who are already cooking breakfast. I am pleased to see they haven't done away with the dehydrated rations, and I note the boys are cooking enough for the four of us. I also notice they've gone over the two machines, making sure our camouflage is covering everything just in case we'd been sloppy early this morning in the dark. I find it pleasing that they take this exercise so seriously.

'Breakfast is ready, Sarge,' Paddy informs me, passing over a dixie of I-don't-know-what, but the smell is good. 'We've already checked everything and put a few branches on the vehicles to make it look a bit better. Is there anything else you'd like us to do, Sarge, before you take a nap?'

'No thanks, Paddy.' I am starting to feel the strain of the last two days, which have been practically non-stop. I'm just about to slide into my bedding when I suddenly think of something that could be important. 'Fellas, when you send your sched in, delay the time of the last vehicle by some ten minutes. By doing that it should give us some sort of buffer against what you could call intercepted communications.' I get a few sniggers from the three of them. 'Come on, fellas, it's just a safety provision – I'm sure there will be quite a few people in the enemy units with their noses well out of joint, and the best way to find us would be to intercept our communications and get our position that way. Once they've done that, they could possibly work out where the signals are being sent from by the positions of the vehicles we're reporting and work out where we are when the vehicle is at a known point further down the road. You can bet they'll try something a little devious like that to find where we are, because if I was in their position, that's exactly what I'd be doing.'

'Roger, Sarge,' he says with a laugh. 'You know that stunt we pulled last night was an absolute pearler; no one in his right mind would have gone up there in daylight but to do it in the dark was unbelievable. We gained well over a day and bypassed any ambush the cut-off groups would have set for us. You're right, Sarge; I'll bet there are a damn lot of noses out of joint in the cut-off groups and I bet they'll be wanting to get any information they can get their hands on from the blokes on the sig sets, because I know they can be bribed with a few beers after these exercises have finished.'

'Time will tell, Paddy, time will tell. I'll get some sleep now and thanks again for all the support you fellas have given me; I really appreciate that.'

The sun beats down mercilessly on our roadside observation post but we're well under cover so it's to no avail. We report all the traffic that moves along the road and come in on each sched. At close to midday, a plane flies low up the road, so it's reported, but our cover must be good enough because it doesn't detect us. On the third day a number of Land Rovers travel back and forth, looking for us. Day five comes and we get the surprise order to return back to a rendezvous point, so we take our camouflage netting down, break cover and move down the highway to the others.

'There has been a breakout of violence in East Timor,' our commanding officer tells his senior non-commissioned officers. 'We have to move back to Perth. It appears we could be sent over with other United Nations troops to calm things down. We'll have to get as much bush time up in the short time we have left and prepare for an immediate departure to Timor. So, this exercise has been terminated.'

Perth

Two days later at Swanbourne, all officers and sergeants of the squadron are brought before the officer in charge and briefed about the situation in Timor and what our roles over there may be, if sent. He then surprises us by announcing that all officers and senior non-commissioned officers will have to undergo a psychiatric assessment.

'These tests should only take maybe an hour at the most,' the officer in charge informs us. 'The army unfortunately is trying to cater to the whims of our political masters. Evidently, after Vietnam, there were a lot of psychological claims that the government couldn't quite agree on, so some sort of test is being put in place for all our officers and senior non-commissioned officers to keep these damn politicians happy. So, while the men are preparing to go to Collie, you lucky people will be visiting a psychiatrist from Western Command so this head shrink can do these psychological assessments and tell you if you are sane enough to control your men.' He sees some uneasiness with some of my colleagues so, with a bit of a laugh, he tries to ease this situation we're about to be put through. 'With these tests it will mean no one here can say they're insane when this deployment we're about to do in East Timor is over.'

This announcement is treated as a joke by most of us. I pack and wait for the call because I'm not worried about it. I've been through this type of bullshit before when I came back from Singapore. Since I returned from Vietnam, I've had doctors of all varieties looking at me from every angle and still finding nothing wrong, so what could they possibly find wrong with me this time?

'Come in, Sergeant Jackson. Take a seat,' the psychiatrist tells me, trying to be friendly. 'First thing in this exercise I'll be asking you a number of questions, and for the next stage of the exercise I'm going to put you under hypnotic analysis. I'll then compare the test results of your conscious answers to your subconscious mind and see if there is any difference. It should be interesting when comparisons of the two are made.' Then with a big smile he goes on, 'You'll find there shouldn't be a great deal of difference between the two.'

'That will be fine,' I answer, hoping the whole thing won't take too long. I don't trust the motivations of these sorts of people.

The questions go on for something like twenty minutes. They are simple and straightforward but when he comes to the possibility of killing another person in armed combat, he pauses to get my reaction.

'What are your thoughts on this, Sergeant, because you people will be the intruders in East Timor and I'm sure there will be many people over there that will resent you being there and could possibly take action against you?'

'I will follow my orders and will not hesitate to kill if I have to.' This, to me, as a soldier, is the logical way to answer such a question. 'It's very simple – I'll do what I'm told and protect my men.'

'Thank you, Sergeant,' he says, showing no reaction whatsoever. I expect he's heard this type of answer before from the others. 'Now, if you could lie down on the couch for me, we'll undergo the next part of the examination. I am going to ask similar, if not the same, questions while you are under my hypnosis. Are you happy with that, Sergeant?'

'Yes, Doctor,' I say, wanting to get away from this and back to my packing as I'm looking forward to getting into the scrub once again. It seems ages since I had jungle around me; I find this comfortable.

I lie down on the couch, close my eyes and listen to him talking, and soon I feel like I'm drifting off to sleep. I immediately start dreaming of Alicia and Abe. Then, all of a sudden, some of the various contacts we had in Vietnam come rushing into my thoughts and I find I'm describing these bloody clashes in detail – where I was left by the helicopters, my flight through the jungle, when I see Abe, a prisoner, traipsing along behind the ox cart.

Next, I find I'm talking of Johnno, how he was shot and how we rushed him by chopper to Vung Tau. Finally, it's me falling, falling from the helicopter and dropping into the jungle. Then I find I'm suddenly talking to Noc in Vietnamese and laughing at her sexual innuendo while moving down to the coast to the fishing village. I dream I'm onboard that little fishing boat, talking to Bui while sailing to Singapore and vividly recall the sharp conflict with the Thai pirates before returning home to Australia. Then I find I'm just walking into the unit, when I wake up.

The shrink is looking at me with an unusual expression on his face – a look of both surprise and horror etched from ear to ear and one that says to me that whatever he has asked me, my reply has knocked the pants off him and he wasn't prepared for the results he's received.

'Er, you've been in the army before, Sergeant Jackson? Quite a number of years in fact, from what you've just told me.'

'Look, Sir, I've been in the army now ever since I was a private.' I pick my words very carefully, not lying but not wanting to give the psychiatrist any free shots or any particulars about my past experiences in the army. 'I've been a sergeant for quite a while now, Sir, and I'm looking forward to going into action, wherever it may be. Now if you are finished with me, I've got to get back to the mess and finish my packing as we have exercises coming up shortly. We have a lot of bush training to do at Collie and I have to get all my equipment ready for that because most of the men have had very little if any jungle experience and may be relying on me.'

He lets me go but I'm sure I haven't heard the last of it. I feel certain that in the next few days, unless I do something about my past, it's going to rear its ugly head. So I make the decision to pre-empt any fallout by seeing the commanding officer, as he already knows about me and may be able to help prevent this from going any further.

'Unfortunately, Sergeant, the commanding officer is over east in Sydney,' the orderly corporal tells me. This doesn't help at all. 'He'll be back tomorrow evening. Do you want me to tell him you need to see him, Sergeant, because he'll be tired after such a long flight?'

'Yes, that would be fine, Corporal. Just tell him that I believe my situation is urgent and I may need his assistance.'

The psychiatrist immediately refers his findings to the officer in charge, stating that one of his sergeants appears to present a psychological abnormality and shows signs he is not who he seems to be at face value, and from questions under hypnosis, it appears he has obviously served in the military before and has seen a lot of combat.

'Sir, I have problems with your Sergeant Jackson,' the psychiatrist tells the officer in charge, obviously quite confused after the examination. 'Major, if what he told me under hypnosis is correct and normally it is, he ought to be almost in his sixties. I find this very hard to believe because he looks fitter and younger than me and, to make things worse, under hypnosis, his subconscious informs us he's been in armed combat before, directly killing sixteen people and possibly more indirectly. I have all this on tape. However, some of what he said was in a foreign language that unfortunately I was unable to understand. Major, in my opinion, we need to do further analysis on this man to find out more about him.'

'Captain, you must be mistaken,' the officer in charge replies, a little indignant that the psych is trying to make a mountain out of a molehill with what Jackson had said. 'Sergeant Jackson hasn't been with us very long, but I've found him to be an excellent patrol commander and extremely good in the field. Let me hear the recording please and I should be able to put your mind at rest.'

The disc is played through and by the time it's finished, the officer in charge is just as confused as the psychiatrist with the content of the recording, especially when he hears of all the killings that happened in the sixties and early seventies. There is a break of thirty years until the present time when more killings happen. Jackson also says something in a foreign tongue that neither of them can understand.

'I'm sorry to have to do this to you, Captain,' the officer in charge tells him. 'I'm afraid I'm going to have to impound this recording until the commanding officer of the unit returns tomorrow. Look Captain, there has to be some simple explanation for this, and the commanding officer is the man who had Sergeant Jackson posted to my squadron – he should know of this man's background much better than me.'

The next day it's a little after three when the commanding officer finally arrives back at camp. He's tired, having spent some five and a half hours on a plane returning from the eastern states. He decides to check in at the orderly room before he goes home, just in case something has come up about the coming deployment to Timor. His orderly corporal is still there and tells him Sergeant Jackson wanted to see him.

'Send for Sergeant Jackson now, Corporal,' he tells him, curious at what the sergeant wants after just coming back from the exercises up north. 'Are there any other pressing developments that I should know about since I've been away? If there is, I'll deal with them now.'

'Nothing, except the squadron, is back early from the exercises up north, Sir,' he tells the commanding officer, and almost forgetting the psychiatrist's experiment on officers and sergeants, he quickly adds, 'We had a psychiatrist from Western Command here doing psychological assessments with all the officers and sergeants of Three Squadron prior to their imminent overseas detachment to Timor.'

On hearing this, the commanding officer's face immediately turns grim in anticipation of hearing the worst news on a subject he'd hoped would die a natural death. He had wanted to keep Sergeant Jackson's predicament to himself, but if this is what he thinks it is, it could complicate the situation of Jackson immensely.

'Send for Sergeant Jackson, Corporal, and also get the officer in charge of Three Squadron over here ASAP,' he tells the startled corporal who is now wondering what has just happened to get such an immediate response. 'I will see Major Jacobson first, as I wish to talk to him privately. After that, if necessary, we'll talk to our Sergeant Jackson and sort out any problems we have.'

Major Jacobson is a little surprised when he's informed the commanding officer is back and wishes to meet him immediately, but he's happy to go and see what it is he wants, thinking it may be something about their coming deployment to Timor. He'll also have the opportunity to bring up the issue of Sergeant Jackson and the strange report from the psychiatrist and try to get this sorted out immediately. Hopefully, there is some terrible mistake in this report somewhere and he will be able sort things out. He doesn't want to lose a man of Peter's capability just before the unit does its first offensive operation since Vietnam.

'Come in, Bill,' the commanding officer says when the major

is shown into his office. 'Take a seat. Get two cups of coffee please, Corporal.' He quickly turns back to the major. 'Did your exercise up north go off well? Were your patrol commanders up to scratch?'

'The exercise went off extremely well, Colonel. Your Sergeant Jackson was magnificent. Both his tactics and his map work were brilliant. He seems to be able to read a map as if it were a newspaper. I'm really pleased you had the foresight to have him sent over to me as the replacement.'

The coffee arrives and they settle down to their discussion, Major Jacobson still wondering why he's been sent for so soon after the colonel arrived back at base. It has to be more than a general chat about their exercise up north, he thinks. Maybe it is about the coming operation in Timor, and he has more information about that.

'Bill, I won't beat about the bush. I believe you had a psychiatrist do sessions on your officers and sergeants yesterday – one of these new-fangled tests that our political masters are insisting on these days and want us to do them on our men, Sergeant Jackson being one of them. Is that correct?'

'That's correct. Sergeant Jackson's report was quite strange,' he tells the colonel. 'In his report, the evidence leads you to believe that Sergeant Jackson has already been in combat. The tapes indicate it was in Vietnam, but not recently though. This is the difficult part of the test, the part that I quite frankly don't understand at all. According to the tape the psychiatrist took, it was almost thirty years ago that he saw action. It was almost as if he wasn't under hypnosis and made the story up as he went along. Why? Why would a soldier who showed so much potential, as he has, do such a strange thing during these tests?'

'You'd better hold on to your seat, Bill, for what I'm going to tell you requires the highest confidentiality and cannot under *any* circumstances leave this room. Only me and the highest officers in the country know of it, and now you as his commanding officer will be privy to what has happened to Peter Jackson.' The officer pauses a few seconds before he begins the story. 'I first met Peter Jackson in nineteen sixty-nine at the Collie Pub. He was probably two years older than me and had just been made up to corporal ...'

The commander then relates the whole story and watches as the man before him goes through various phases of disbelief.

'And then recently, many, many years later, I received a phone call telling me that he would be re-joining the unit. It's a staggering story but I can assure you he is the *same* Sergeant Peter Jackson, with Military Medal and bar, that I knew. I can vouch for that. Bill, you have one of the best soldiers I have ever come across in your squadron. I can also vouch for that. He is one of the best jungle fighters the unit has ever had. If you like, I can have his patrol reports of both his operational tours of Vietnam released to you for you to read. From these you will be able to judge the ability and courage of this man for yourself so you can make up your own mind about his ability.'

'This is hard to believe, Colonel, but you give me no choice,' the officer in charge says while staring at his commander in disbelief at the information he's been given. He has the tapes from the psychiatrist stating almost exactly what he's just been told by his superior. He decides that he'll have to go along with what he's just heard. 'I was amazed when I was told and have listened to the tapes a number of times. It's incredible that such a thing could be done to a human body over such a long period of time.'

'Sergeant Jackson should be outside now. He has an appointment to meet me. I assume he was a little worried about the psychiatrist's tests your squadron underwent yesterday,' the colonel states, looking with some hope at the officer in charge and trying to gauge his reaction. 'I can call him in to personally meet with you if that's what you would like to do.'

'That would be fine, Colonel,' Bill says, starting to come to grips with the situation that's been thrust so bluntly in front of him. 'I would like to congratulate him on such a good observation post he ran in the last exercise. As you know the country is quite open and we tried our hardest for four days to find him but failed miserably.'

He picks up the phone and asks the corporal to send in Sergeant Jackson. They wait patiently for him to move in, the colonel thinking all the time about how he is going to handle this situation between the two. However, this is taken out of his hands by Major Jacobson, who immediately stands and turns to meet him.

'Come in, Sergeant. That observation post you and your men set up on the road was the best I've ever seen. I was just telling the colonel about how you and your men winched the two Rovers up that steep slope to get to the road and bypassed the enemy we had waiting for you.' He pauses a moment before he continues. 'Now, Sergeant, on a different matter altogether, as you are aware, we have the psychiatrist's tests, which you were part of. I expect they were quite confusing to you as well as me when I received the results of yours yesterday.'

'Yes, Sir, if what I dreamt while under hypnosis was an accurate account and came out in the way I believe it did, then you know of my history and events that took place almost thirty years ago.'

'Yes, I do, Sergeant,' he says. 'I have to say I was staggered to find out about your military history from your tests. Then, Colonel Dempster filled me in on the total event. Sergeant, I find it a privilege to have you in my unit, especially considering we will probably be deployed to East Timor within the month. Your expertise in jungle warfare will be of immense value to us and hopefully you'll be able to pass as much of your experience onto the other men as you can in the limited time we have left before our deployment.'

'Thank you for your confidence in me, Sir,' I tell them, a great cloud of doubt clearing from my conscience. 'I promise you, Sir, you'll have all the expertise I've accumulated at your disposal.'

'It will be fantastic to have that sort of expertise in the squadron,' he tells me, before changing the subject to a more difficult item. 'Colonel Dempster also told me you are the recipient of the Military Medal and bar. Do you intend to wear them on official parades and military functions?'

'No, Sir. Colonel Dempster has put a lot of trust in me and allowed me to become a member again of this great unit. If I was to wear them, questions would certainly be asked of Colonel Dempster, you and me that would be very awkward for any of us to answer and, I might say, completely unnecessary. Sir, I do not want to betray that trust both Colonel Dempster and you have shown.'

'That is unfortunate, Sergeant, but I can understand your feelings. I thought it would be good to have such medals on display on our parades but now I understand the consequences of you wearing these medals.'

Colonel Dempster ushers me to a seat and we talk about the exercise and about the growing storm that may shortly erupt in East Timor. I'm pleased to have two extremely good officers on my side and look forward to our coming deployment in East Timor.

'Thank you, Sergeant, for filling us in on events,' the colonel tells me, then dismisses me. 'You have no worries about the psychiatrist's report becoming public. We will personally make sure it dies a natural death.'

I salute both these officers and move out through the door, very relieved that both of these men are on my side. My only worry now is getting my patrol ready for the brief training and our coming deployment in East Timor.

CHAPTER 10

EAST TIMOR

The *Black Hawk* helicopter skims across the water just above the waves towards the dark, foreboding blob on the horizon that is Timor. There is quiet amongst the two patrols that are sitting in the guts of the aircraft, waiting in anticipation of our landing, and I see from the looks on their faces that they are expecting the worst, with this being their first combat mission. I have the same five with me that I've had at my back since I returned to the unit some months before – good blokes all of them, and keen, but unfortunately with absolutely no combat experience at all. We've had barely a month of training in the bush at Collie since our exercise with the Rovers in northern Australia, so I've worked my men hard in this totally different environment to what we'd had up north. We work long hours in this bush, where I try to pass on as much of my experience as I can from my time in Vietnam, and also endeavouring to give these men some inkling of what the conditions could be like when we finally get into the bush in Timor.

I find that working my men this hard has had a definite impact on the other patrols who initially thought it a bit of a joke with what I was getting my men to do but, when they had seen the results of this training, they had soon begun working in a similar fashion. This work has had a snowball effect, with most of the sergeants in the other troops taking up the mantle and I'm pleased to see them trying hard to outdo us.

'Land coming up,' comes over the intercom as the dark blob in front of us gets larger and larger and now there is a huge land mass straight in front, making me forget these thoughts of training.

'Get ready, first patrol. Okay boys, check your equipment. We're almost there.' I know this will be the first offensive action they've been involved in and think back to my first patrol with Johnno and start making comparisons between the two. I pass on some of the titbits he'd passed on to me from his experiences in Borneo. I'm proud of these men who've taken on what I've taught them and have trained hard, and I know they will give me their best when we put our feet on the ground. 'Make sure everything is secure and there's nothing loose to make a noise; we don't want anything rattling on our equipment when we get into the scrub,' I tell them and watch as they quickly do a visual on themselves, doing little jumps up and down, making sure all their personal equipment is fitted properly and is ready for when we get on the ground and into the scrub.

The *Black Hawk* is skimming over trees now, pushing quickly inland south of Aidabasalala. The helicopter slows to a pause in the air. Our ropes are out almost immediately, and we slide down and into the scrub. Then the *Black Hawk* is off again to drop the next patrol into their observation post a number of kilometres north of us. They are to observe some other small rural settlements to see if any pressure is being applied by the militia to influence their population in the coming secession from Indonesia.

We've been given the task of monitoring movement, if any, from the border towards the town of Aidabasalala, which is only a few clicks to the eastern boundary of the Indonesian province of West Timor. Our task is simple – to report any militia activities across the border towards the town and, if requested by headquarters, to stop them.

This is my patrol's third observation post since being over here and the furthest away from Dili. Our first two completed observation posts have been thankfully uneventful, with no signs of the militia activities designed to put pressure on the villagers, coming up to their vote for independence from Indonesia. With this patrol, however, the powers that be want our choppers to fly away from Timor to throw the militia off and come into our position from the south of the country so that pro-Indonesian militia don't report our presence to the Indonesians.

'Mick, we need to get to this high point here by mid-morning,' I tell the scout I'd selected from my group, pointing my finger on the map to show the position I want to reach that could have a good view of this small township. 'We should be about here if the chopper was accurate with their drop-off point. Judging by the map, if you can follow this ridge here, we should reach this hill and set up our observation post hopefully by mid-morning. It will also give us enough daylight to do a thorough recce of the hill so we're familiar with all tracks and any obstacles we may come in contact with.'

He gives me a nod and we move out in patrol order through the gloom of a very early morning towards our potential observation post. The bush isn't very dense here, so everyone is on high alert expecting contact at any time. It's most likely that the noise of the helicopter has been heard by someone with loyalties to the militia who has reported this to their masters for some favour.

It seems like only a couple of months or so since I was doing exactly this type of operation in Vietnam. It's still hard for me to accept the fact that I've been asleep, if you could call it that, for nearly thirty years, because the jungle is much lighter here and I am patrolling with different blokes, but the rationale is exactly the same – you find 'em, you watch 'em and if you have to – kill 'em.

Dili, 40 Days Previously

The situation in East Timor has moved very quickly. It was only forty days ago that we and Ghurkha troops landed on Dili's Comoro airfield to secure it for our infantry, while fully armed Indonesian TNI soldiers watched on. It seemed as if they were grudgingly some sort of umpires for an exercise we were doing, and they were there only as spectators to see that we did everything according to the rule book. We came down out of our *Black Hawks*, expecting the worst from either the TNI or their lackeys – the militia, who were rampaging unchecked through the streets of Dili, obviously not wanting the province to break away. They certainly didn't want us there to monitor the atrocities that were going on. We'd seen the graphic photos of bashings, beatings and killings of innocent people on the local television by this bastard minority who were doing exactly what the Indonesians wanted them to do and, unfortunately now we have them watching us cordoning off the airfield under orders from the United Nations. We had gone over the plans of the airport just before we left Darwin and now have specific areas designated for each patrol to secure as soon as we hit the ground.

'Follow me to those buildings,' I order my group as soon as our feet touch the runway. I'm afraid I feel like a medieval knight dressed in this strange clobber that the soldiers of this era are expected to wear. This body armour is something I'll have to get used to in this modern-day army. 'Extended line, move quickly but don't run. Look for anything that looks suspicious.'

We move across to the buildings on the edge of the airfield, carefully looking for anything out of place and thankfully reaching our objective at the edge of the airfield without incident. We quickly go to ground, taking up defensive positions on the airfield's perimeter, prepared for anything that the militia may throw at us as our position here seems to be extremely vulnerable.

'We are to hold this section,' I tell my men as we get undercover behind what appears to be large concrete posts. They quickly adopt firing positions securing this end of the runway. 'Take note of anything you think is out of the ordinary or shouldn't be there and we'll check it out to see what it is and if it's harmless.'

It's a long night, but thankfully uneventful. We're glad to see the sun – big, red and round like a disc coming slowly over the hills and lighting up the whole area. Finally, the shadows are gone, leaving us with another very hot day.

'Be alert, fellas.' I let them in on my own feelings, as this could be the most vulnerable time. 'If we're going to be hit, it'll be when our air force starts to come in, because these bastards would get maximum casualties if they hit one of our planes trying to land loaded with our troops.'

I breathe a welcome breath of fresh air when our planes finally arrive. I see them as small dots getting bigger as they approach. Boy, it's good to see the Australian *Hercules* aircraft finally approaching the airfield and we watch in awe as one giant after another come zooming in over our heads straight down the runway, making my stomach tight as these ever-reliable planes finally land and begin to disgorge the Second Battalion. These men are quickly deployed around the airport, taking much of the pressure off us and the Ghurkhas. I'm still amazed that there has been no conflict between our men and the Indos as it is quite obvious to us grunts who are now on the ground that they don't want us here. We can see them watching us from the positions they are deployed at around the airfield and feel their weapons pointing in toward us.

The next day, another phase of the operation is worked out with part of Two Battalion going under escort, this time, by the Indonesian TNI troops. They depart the airport, securing the port facilities for Three Battalion who are waiting off-shore to come in on the new troop carrier *Jervis Bay* – a strange-looking fast catamaran that the army is using these days.

By evening, we have two full battalions of men on the ground, spreading out and nullifying the local militias in and around Dili that have created such unnecessary havoc among the innocent population, murdering a lot of good people who wanted independence from Indonesia. Other bands of militia have forced many of these poor wretches to go across the border and live in poverty-stricken conditions in poorly constructed shanties, similar to what the Arabs had done around the borders of Israel. I hope the Indonesians either allow them to build proper homes or send them home to East Timor after the militias have been neutralised and, once this happens, life for the population can eventually get back to normal, allowing them to elect their own government and get on with their lives in peace.

Aidabasalala

Fast track forty days and we finally reach our target – a small hill between the Indonesian border and the little village – and set up a temporary observation post in heavier scrub, enabling us to look down on the town of Aidabasalala, which seems almost deserted at the moment. There are only a few people to be seen so far on its long street and these few individuals quickly scurry from house to house, clearly in fear of the militias who evidently have these poor wretches scared shitless by their presence just across the border. The town of Aidabasalala, according to our map, has one street that stretches like a large crescent to the north-east with houses down either side. Two-thirds of the way up, there is also another street branching off that runs to the west some hundred metres where it meets a small road, also going to the west, just to the north of our position, on a small hill directly towards Indonesian West Timor. This road, which branches off the main street also has houses on either side for a short distance. However, these soon peter out as the road runs into a sharp little valley that goes almost straight through to East Timor's border.

'There appears to be some sort of stockade – or is it stockyards? – down there in that paddock,' Paddy says, looking down from the observation point to the east from where we are. 'What in the name of heck do you think it could be? I can't see any sign of stock of any description around the town. Do you think what stock the villagers may have had has been taken over the border by the militia?'

'They could have been,' answers Mick, a country boy from Victoria who's also staring down at the stockyards, likely trying to see if there is a loading ramp of some description to truck them to market. 'It wouldn't surprise me if the stock was stolen when you read how the militia have treated these poor buggers living in these rural communities.'

We take a look at the structure below our position and agree it has to be some sort of stockyard, but like Paddy and Mick have pointed out, we can't see any live animals below our position anywhere around the village. Not one cow, calf, or even a goat can be seen anywhere below us, even though there are numerous empty paddocks on either side of the town, growing what appears to be rank grass – ideal for feeding stock.

'From what I heard, the militia took most of the stock and drove them through to Indonesia,' Mick continues with what had been reported in the newspapers. 'When you look around this little place, the poor bastards who stayed in the village have absolutely nothing to live off or make a living from.'

'You're right, Mick, when you look around the village, these people have absolutely nothing visible – no stock and no crops at all to make a living from,' Gil observes then begins to sum up everything for all of us. 'You know fellas, the militia need their arses well and truly kicked for what they've done, and later on I hope we can do just that so those pricks can learn the difference between right and wrong.'

'I will leave Paddy and Purse at this temporary observation point to watch the town while I take you three to do a preliminary patrol around the top of this small hill. We can find out how the land lies and the best place to establish our observation post. We'll try to identify strong points that we can easily defend if our present position here becomes known and if this hill is assaulted by the militia, thinking we'll be a pushover and won't do anything to protect ourselves or the villages below.'

'It's a good idea to know every inch of our area thoroughly, Sarge,' Paddy explains, supporting my statements to the men and then he breaks out with a big smile. 'So, if things get nasty and we are attacked by screaming hordes, we can implement quick countermeasures if we have to defend our position or, if the wheels want us out, we can make a strategic withdrawal in another direction.'

'At the moment, Paddy we're an unknown to them so we have to make sure we keep it that way and just watch this town and the border for militia movements and report what we see back to HQ.'

We leave the two and I take the remainder of the patrol slowly north along a disused track that follows the lip of this little ridge some two hundred metres, and we soon find ourselves looking down on the other road that heads towards the Indonesian border. Exactly like the map shows, there are another two rows of houses, again situated on either side of the road for a short distance before petering out into scrub. Once the road leaves the last few houses, it runs west for a few kilometres finally turning south-west towards the border where we can see a couple of cars parked in the shade, probably the Indonesian border security.

'You're right, Pete; this could be the major entry point that the militias could be using to get into Aidabasalala. From here, we would be able to observe any goings-on without being seen,' Gil comments at what he sees below us. 'You'll also note there's a small track which leaves the main road to the border and climbs up to this point we're looking down from. Hell, we'd have to be on the ball if someone comes up here from the border; they'd walk straight into our position either here or further down where the other two are.'

'Do you think we'd be wise to move our observation post to this position?' Mick asks, pointing out the advantages we'd have here over the other observation site. 'If they came up here from the border, they'd be in the other position where Purse and Paddy are well before we realised they're coming?'

'That's a good point, Mick,' I reply, pleased that he's thinking strategically. 'We'll collect the other two when we finish our recce and then move back here and set up our O. P. permanently because from here, we have a beautiful view of both the border and the village and can easily access back to where Paddy and Purse are if we want to watch the bottom end of town. I noticed a disused track coming straight up the hill past the stock yards to where they are watching the town.'

We continue the circumnavigation of our small hill, finding no other tracks and taking note of other important features that we may have to use in the future. After two hours, our recce is complete and we find we're back at the observation post with the other two who are bored stiff, still looking down over the small town, I expect now wishing for some movement from these houses below to keep them awake.

'Did anything exciting happening while we've been away?' I ask Paddy as I look down at the houses; still with very few signs of life or any communal activities that you'd expect to see in a small country town such as this.

'Nothing to report, Sarge,' he replies, with his boredom beginning to show, having just been staring down over bare paddocks and the almost sleeping village for well over an hour waiting for us to return. 'You could fire a shot up the main street and no one would notice. It appears that everyone in the town is too scared to leave their homes except for the occasional person who from time-to-time dashes madly across to a neighbour's house. There they go; you can see what I mean.' He points out an individual rushing from a house to another building. 'There's another one heading off with a sprint as if his pants are on fire.'

'Paddy, we've had a good look around this hill, it would pay for us to move the observation post north so we can watch the road coming in from West Timor because there is also a well-used track coming up here from the border road that can be accessed before they reach the houses. The northern point is the best place for us to defend that track if we have to. If anyone is coming over from the border, they'll continue to use that road until they're challenged or something major happens. The road from the border gives the militia easy access to the houses almost immediately; so, our first priority will be to observe that road and see if it's regularly used by the militia from the border and if it is, by whom and for what. If the wheels ask us to stop any infiltration, that's where we'll do it.' I point to what could be a suitable spot on the map. 'We can set up an ambush down there and stop any infiltration into the village and, from our observations at midday, I noticed that position is just out of sight from both the village and the border.'

With everything dead quiet in the village, the observation post is moved strategically to a position where we can see the last dozen houses of Aidabasalala but also gives us good visibility for over a kilometre of track right to the where the Indonesian border is. More importantly from my perspective, it also provides a good view of the track coming up the hill to this position and good coverage for us if someone has seen us and decides to try and spring a surprise attack on our position up the hill.

'It will be interesting to see how many lights go on tonight,' says Paddy, a little pissed off at having to stay in the observation post for a big part of the afternoon and now probably wishes he'd done the recce with the rest of us and someone else had the job of watching the village. 'We should also be able to use our night scopes if we hear anything on the road. This will give us a big advantage, knowing what they're doing, what arms they have and what numbers we're up against coming from across the border.'

'That's a good idea, Paddy,' I tell him, glad that he's got the patrol's operations well in focus as we'll be in this position for a number of days. 'From this point, we should be able to see them leaving Indonesia on their way to the village because from reports given to us, they scoot over the border, cause a little mayhem with the village and then hurry back into Indonesia and safety.'

From our new observation post, we have a good view right to the border and can actually see the Indonesian border personnel at their post keeping security; that's if you can call a couple of cars they have parked under a tree at the border, security. The day goes slowly by with us taking turns at the observation post with someone checking the bottom part of town regularly through the day to watch the other end of the village. There is still very little movement from the village with only the occasional person sighted and even then, it's a quick dash from one house to the next.

'They are fairly shirty,' says Gil as he watches a couple of women move quickly up the road and disappear into a neighbouring house. 'I'll bet the militias are ruling the villagers with an iron fist which makes me wonder how many of those poor sods they've killed or taken — or should I say forced — over the border with their stock because I'm still to see any animals of any description. From what I saw on the box, those bastards drove most, if not all, their stock across the border so the unfortunate villagers have absolutely nothing to earn a living from. I haven't seen any cultivation or vegetable gardens near the houses that you read about. These poor bastards were forced over the border and they won't let them come back. Hell! They must be living in sheer poverty somewhere in some shanty that the Indos have thrown at them to live in and the ones that didn't go have no stock or gardens to keep the family in food or to earn a living from. You know, I haven't even seen any form of domestic animal at all, you know what I mean — cattle, pigs, chooks or ducks that you usually expect to see in villages like this one.'

What Gil says is right. The militias have driven thousands of East Timorese people over the border with their stock into Indonesia where, if they are lucky, they now live in tents. More likely, the poor wretches are living in some hovel or whatever they could scrounge up and for some unknown reason they're being stopped from coming back to their homes by the Indos so they would be worse off over there than here.

Our first night falls and I run a picket, manning the observation post to what is a complete non-event with no movement at all from the border or the town. The next day is much the same with the exception that two of the patrol go to the previous observation post so they can do a visual check on any movement from the bottom part of the town, but I find nothing has changed.

The third night finally falls on our O.P. and I note a feeling of boredom growing on my patrol, making me smile. I've won the first picket this time as we draw for our positions each night; I watch patiently for the moon to come up as I look down towards the border through our night scope. It's close to ten and I'm about to wake Purse for his shift when I see people; probably a dozen moving up the road from the border towards Aidabasalala and, by the look of them, they're all armed. So, I wake the patrol in case some of these pricks come up the track towards our observation point.

'I'd better send a message through to HQ and see what they want to be done about these bastards,' I tell the others who are now taking turns with the night scope, looking down on the column of the militia as they slowly move up the road towards the village and fortunately for us no one uses the track that approaches our position. I quickly scribble out the information and give it to our sig and give the patrol a little niggle that may stir them up. 'Who knows fellas? We may be lucky and find they want us to stitch the bastards up on their way back to Indonesia, you know something interesting to break the boredom.'

'This is Patrol 23 to Base. Fifteen armed suspects leaving Indonesia for Aidabasalala; waiting for instructions. Over.'

The message is sent and it's obvious the O.C. is up as almost immediately we receive the answer.

'Base to Patrol 23. Do nothing, observe. I repeat; do nothing. Just observe and see what comes of this. Out.'

So, with some annoyance, we just watch as these shadowy figures walk quite confidently up the middle of the road, completely unchallenged into the village. Once there, they split into twos and threes and begin entering the houses as if they're doing a coordinated search for someone. After a brief time in the building, they come out and move to the next house. From one house, three shots are heard before the two militia soldiers exit. Even from this distance through our scopes, we see that these bastards appear to be laughing to themselves at whatever they've done to the occupants. They move on, continuing their search down the street.

'I'll leave four of you here,' I tell my men. 'Mick and I will go to our first O.P. position and see what's happening at the bottom end of the village because, if I'm not mistaken, those pricks are doing a coordinated search and they are obviously looking for someone of importance who's evidently hiding in one of those houses. It's quite clear the militia have been tipped off by someone.'

Mick and I make quick progress back to our original observation point where we can look down now on the bottom end of town with the aid of the moonlight and watch as the militia do their house-to-house search, systematically moving from each house down towards the bottom of the village.

'Mick, the bastards seem to be looking for someone,' I say to my companion as we move quickly into our first position. 'What, or more importantly, who do you think they're after? We've seen no one enter the place since we've been here so whoever it is has been here for quite some time being hidden by the villagers and has only just been dobbed into the militia for some favour.'

'You could be right, Sarge; it's almost as if they are doing a head count of the villagers,' Mick says, screwing his eyes up and looking in his night scope. 'I wonder if they could be looking for someone from elsewhere who they've been hiding in the village and have only now been dobbed in. If that's the case, whoever it is must be someone of importance to justify a full village search of this scale.'

'You're right, Mick; they are certainly looking for someone who must be there at the moment, but who?' I say, as we stare down at this end of the village. Then I point. 'Look down there. See, they've even sent two people down as a cut-off party just on the road going out of the village at the other end so whoever it is can't get out that way. We haven't been told of anyone of importance being way down in this area. Heavens, who the hell could it be to justify the militia doing a search of this scale tonight?'

We keep a close check on the search and watch as the militia go methodically from house to house moving down the street. Occasionally there's a shot fired followed by two more from a different direction; a little like the signal shots that the Viet Cong used to notify others in their vicinity that we'd landed and were in the area. I wonder what this means here because I'm sure none of us has been seen and we certainly wouldn't be hiding out in the village. It's my turn to gaze down the street and, with the aid of my night glasses, I scan the houses to this end of the village. Once again, I carefully scan down the row of houses well in front of them, to those they still have to search because any one of those dwellings could have someone hiding inside who the militia is now looking for. I'm just about to move my gaze on to the next house when I suddenly see two shadowy figures make a frantic dash from the back of a house and run across some paddocks in the direction of the stockyards.

'We've got company,' I tell Mick, lifting my glasses and looking across at him. 'There are two of them a long way off at the moment but heading in our direction. They are almost to the stockyards now. There, do you see them now? They're just near the yards and about to go through them.'

'I've got them,' he says as he focuses his night glasses on the two fugitives who are climbing the rails. 'They are just in the stockyards now and you're right, they're certainly heading our way. They have been there quite some time to know of this disused track that comes up this hill.'

I lift my scan back to the houses just in time to see two more people leaving the same building as if they are in hot pursuit of the first two; unfortunately, these two are both carrying rifles, so they are obviously militia.

'We have two more people following them towards us and this time I'm afraid they're both armed,' I tell Mick who lifts his gaze and homes in on the second pair some two hundred metres behind. 'We'd better locate the first two pronto and get them out of trouble or the two pricks following will certainly catch them. They must have some strategic value to the militia or the Indonesians otherwise these pricks wouldn't be risking a full-scale search like they're doing at the moment.'

'Okay, they appear to be coming straight up the hill towards us,' he responds, dropping his gaze once again to take in the first two. 'Hell; they are making enough noise trying to get away from those other two pricks following them. Shit, they're like a bloody herd of elephants coming up the hill. The two blokes behind them have an easy job following them – they're sure making a racket.'

We leave our position and go down the old, unused track that the two fugitives appear to be following. We'd seen it when we set up the observation post earlier this morning and from the look of the growth, it has been rarely used. It is overgrown. We had decided to discount this track because of the good position for our lookout further along the ridge. Now, thankfully, it is bringing the first two people who are hoping to make their escape right to us. We move down the hill towards them, positioning ourselves on either side of this disused track and waiting so that we can take the two simultaneously. From my dark position, I listen to the noise of the scrub being torn apart as the pair of fugitives who are frantically move up the old track towards our position. I can hear the heavy breathing of a person who's close to being exhausted now as the two people clamber up towards us, breaking the scrub as they come; obviously quite desperate to get away. We wait quietly until the two are finally abreast with us.

'Now,' I quietly tell Mick as we both move forward; catching the two escapees and pulling them quickly to the ground, forcing our hands over their mouths to prevent them from making any sound. 'Lay quietly or you'll get us all killed.' To my surprise, I suddenly realise the person I have is a woman. 'Do you speak English?' I say my hand roughly over her mouth stopping any sound. 'If you do, nod your head.'

A vigorous nodding occurs so I slowly release my hand which is followed by some deep breathing before she starts to speak.

'I'm an American journalist,' she gasps, trying to catch her breath before continuing. 'Help us, please. The militia is after us. They will kill us if you don't help us get away.'

'Get them up to the track,' I whisper to Mick as I let this woman up. 'I'll take care of the two following these women but be quick and be quiet. Wait for me at the top where we were watching from.'

I move down the track a little further before turning back off into the scrub, listening to the noise of the others as they move further up the hill. Blind Harry couldn't help but hear them which to me is an enormous advantage as they will be concentrating on the noise from above and shouldn't be looking to the side. I also have the advantage of my night vision glasses, something I initially thought was a bit of a joke until tonight. I wait and finally see the two who are in hot pursuit, pushing their way through the undergrowth up the old track quite quickly catching up with the first two. The first one is using his rifle like a walking stick with the other right behind him. This second man has his rifle slung and is slouching over watching the ground on the incline, only looking up at the man in front occasionally so he doesn't trip on his feet.

Now you slimy bastards, see how you handle me, I think to myself as I step forward, grabbing him by the head and pulling it back, my hand over his mouth and then pulling the K-bar straight across his throat. He hardly struggles, just gives a faint gurgle so I drop him to the ground. I take two very quick steps forward, grab the other bloke by the back of the shirt roughly pulling him back to me, dropping his rifle as he comes. Then, I thrust the K-bar forward driving it straight through his neck and then ripping it out. They are both small men, so I easily lift each body and put them well off the track in case there are others who follow them up later. With no bodies to find here, I hope they won't be suspicious of our presence. I pick up both their rifles, sling them over my shoulder and then follow the track towards the top of the hill to where Mick and the other two should be waiting for me.

'Everything alright, Sarge?' he whispers as I come up to them, looking at the two extra rifles I have over my shoulder. 'It appears the other two turned up by the looks of those two weapons you have.'

'Yeah, the silly bastards must have got lost on the track back there,' I tell him with a grin. 'We'd better get back to the others or they'll start to worry about us. Is there any more movement in town?'

'Yes, the militia are still searching the houses but further down the street from where these two came from,' he tells me, looking down towards the village. 'They're showing no interest in this old track and they're not moving towards this point so they must think these two girls are further down in the town or have hidden somewhere else away from the village.'

'We'll get back to the others pronto and get on the blower to let the blokes back in Dili know of the house-to-house search that the militia is doing.' I curiously look at the two women who are standing quietly behind Mick. 'We'll also have to find out a little more about our two guests, who they are and if they're important the wheels can safely accommodate them somewhere back in Dili.'

We take longer than we normally would to make the four hundred metres back to the observation post; again, thank heavens for the night vision glasses as they make our job extremely easy. We're soon back with the rest of the patrol.

'There's been no movement on the track since you left, Sarge,' says Gil as he welcomes us into the lay-up point. 'One of us has been looking that way while another has been looking out for you blokes. Who are our new guests?' he says, looking a little intrigued at the two young ladies who have just followed me into our position. 'We weren't expecting you blokes to bring back guests for the evening meal.'

'Ladies, I think it's time you quietly introduce yourselves to the rest of the patrol,' I tell them, showing just as much interest as the others. 'Once we know who you are girls, we can let them know back at base that you're with us and you're safe; then they can work out a quick way of how to get you both out of here without creating a civil war.'

'My name is Tiffany Black. I'm a reporter for Associated Press of America and this is Tiepeco Senarmia, a cousin of the potential President of this country,' she states, looking at her fellow escapee and then back at me. 'We have been in hiding since the decision to vote for independence was carried out and the people here have been keeping us out of sight from both the militia and the Indonesian authorities.'

'People have been hiding you for that long?' I say, listening to her incredible story. 'How did you get all the way down here? We're a long way from Dili and so close to the Indonesian border.'

'People hid us and, at night when things start to catch up to us, they would move us on to another safe house,' she tells us with my patrol listening at this stage, although Mick is still looking along the way we've just come in case others have decided to come up the disused track from the town. 'We have been hidden in Aidabasalala now for well over two weeks and thought we were safe being so close to the Indonesian border. I think most people knew we were here but hid us from the militia. Just after dark tonight, however, we were told to get out quickly as our position had been betrayed and the militia knew of our presence and were coming to get us and unfortunately, we wouldn't be safe in the village anymore. Obviously, someone has probably sold us out to the militia or more likely mentioned us in the wrong circles as these people have been good to us. As soon as we were told that we'd been betrayed, we took off and headed for the jungle and that's when we ran into you two,' she looks across at me gratefully and gives me a big smile. 'Thank you for saving our lives because, if you hadn't been on that trail, those thugs who were following us would have certainly caught us; we were totally exhausted and on our last legs when you stopped us and should I say took care of the two people who were following us.'

'Johnny, would you get on the radio and patch through a message to base? I'll put the message together now so they know who we have with us.'

I quickly draft a message to base and hand it to Johnny.

'Patrol 23 to Base. Have in our care Miss Tiffany Black of Associated Press of America and Miss Tiepeco Senarmia, a Timorese National. Militia active at Aidabasalala tonight and house-to-house search was conducted after dark. Two militia dead. Position not compromised. Waiting for your instructions. Over.'

Almost immediately the message is returned.

'Base to Patrol 23. Well done! Will contact you in the morning. Make your guests comfortable. Out.'

I revamp our roster with the instructions to wake me as soon as the militia start to return to Indonesia. It's on the first shift just after midnight when Purse gently shakes me awake and points down the ridge to a string of lights on the main track moving quite openly back towards the Indonesian border.

'They're cocky bastards, going back with lights on like that,' I tell him as we both watch the procession below us, counting the people we can see as they quite blatantly move along the road back to Indonesia. 'I'd love to put an ambush on them now, a few claymores on that track and we'd have the lot. Those people are pretty bloody cocky alright; I wonder if they are showing those lights knowing the ladies are up here somewhere, in an attempt to scare them into doing something irrational to make it easy to find them tomorrow?'

'You could be right, Sarge; doing something like that would certainly scare someone up here who's hiding from you.' He then confirms my count. 'They are two men short of what they entered the village with so they're all there.'

'That's what I counted, thanks for that Purse. Wait until our battalions boys get down here because this sort of thing that we watched tonight will change quite dramatically. Look, I'll take over now; who's the bloke you have to wake?'

'It's Mick at two.' He stops for a moment in deep thought; looking at me as if something is worrying him. 'Sarge, did you really kill those two militia earlier tonight while you and Mick were getting those girls?'

'Unfortunately, I had to Purse. There was no alternative. They weren't very far behind the girls, and they were both armed – I had no option but to stop them permanently otherwise they would have found us as well.'

'Thanks, Sarge, I had to hear it from you,' he says, looking a little bit relieved and then slips off for his nap.

The sun hasn't come up yet when I awake. I sit there listening in the still light of the early morning; there are no human sounds, just the noise of the jungle, bringing back vivid memories of a few months ago. *This reminds me of the jungles of Phuoc Toi Province, over near the Nui Tie Vies,* I think as I take in this view of the valley in. *Except the soldiers I fought back then weren't quite the slackos that I saw last night.* These things are so clear in my mind but I know now they were years ago, and I'm quickly brought back to reality when I hear someone start to move around, sounding like a herd of proverbial elephants at this hour. It's one of the young ladies getting up to take a leak.

'Just be careful not to startle anyone,' I warn her, 'and don't move away too far from this position.' I whisper, not wanting one of the boys to be startled by any sudden movement. 'They are most likely all awake but just be aware you're not alone here.'

'Thank you for that,' she says, smiling in my direction. It's the American woman, the reporter. 'I'll just go down here a little way. I won't be long; you can look out for me if you would,' she says before moving off just out of sight a little way in front of me. She's away probably five minutes before she returns, stumbling over some branches and waking everyone in the patrol in her haste to get back.

'I'm sorry if I woke you guys up, but I had to go urgently. I may not have eaten much but you can't stop nature, can you?'

'I think most of us are awake anyway. If they weren't you're a good alarm clock for them.'

During breakfast, the American woman fills me in on her activities and how she came to be in East Timor. She's already told me of the circumstances of her being so far south from the capital of Dili but the rest of what she has to say is interesting and gives us some idea of what's been going on and how badly the militia have treated the rest of the population now that an independence vote will be held.

'I came over to East Timor just after the decision was made to try for independence. I'd read about the massacre in the cemetery some time before and saw shots of this on television and this whet my appetite for the adventure that could be here leading up to the vote for independence. I needed a good story to establish myself as a journalist and thought this was the kinda place to find one, so I did stories leading up to the independence vote and became friendly with Tiepeco and her family. However, it was then that the militias came out in large numbers and began slaughtering people who were wanting independence from Indonesia which included most of her family.' She gives a stifled sob as this has obviously upset her quite considerably knowing these people. 'There were Indonesian TNI soldiers standing on the corner across from their home, watching the mayhem and unfortunately, just letting this slaughter happen but doing nothing about stopping it or controlling the militia. One of Tiepeco's family saw the militia coming and led us out the back of their house and fortunately got us to the next village where we hid. We've been on the run ever since then and, like today we've been only just two jumps ahead.'

'We have company, Sarge. I can see militia coming across the border again,' Gil tells us as he looks down the road towards the border crossing and we can plainly see a large group of armed people coming this way. 'There are about a dozen of them that have split off the main bunch and are heading up this track towards us.'

I look down to the west and see close to a dozen men armed with a variety of rifles moving up the spur that leads directly towards us; not what I'd call good soldiers as some have their rifles over their shoulders as if they are on safari. There are another fifteen or so are heading along the track at quite a fast speed towards the village.

'Send a message through to headquarters quickly, tell them that we may be sprung and could need help if we are found,' I tell Johnny, not taking my eyes off the column of men coming up towards us. 'They must be looking for the two ladies after last night's abortive effort to catch them.'

'Patrol 23 to Base. Twenty-five to thirty militia in the vicinity. Twelve approaching our position. May need assistance if sprung. Over.'

Our answer is exactly what I had expected the OC to say.

'Base to Patrol 23. Avoid contact if possible. Your priority however is to protect your guests at all costs. I repeat, protect your guests. Out.'

'It's just what I expected,' I tell the men who are also not surprised at the outcome of the message. 'Form a linear ambush along the track behind this position but only fire if you're seen or if we're compromised in some way. If it's possible, let the silly bastards go straight through, our main objective at this time is to protect these two women.'

We quickly conceal ourselves just off the spur behind our observation point with the little track just in view as I assume the militia will be looking down into the valley when they get to our position. *Let's hope the silly bastards are well bunched up if we have to spring them,* I think as we just lie there waiting for the first one to come into view. I don't have long to wait before I hear their yabbering. *Hell! It's as if it's a Sunday school picnic with these blokes,* I think, as we hear the crunching of many pairs of feet as they approach. They pass by me but stop where we had the observation post and start stare down on the track and watch the others as their companions enter the village, turn to the south and quickly move towards the bottom of the village. There are twelve of them bunched up together, all yabbering as they wait for the others to get further into the village. It's almost as if they know the girls have come up here. *Boy! Could we do some damage if we hit them now, bunched up the way they* are. A distinct sound is heard. *A bloody cough! Who the bloody hell has coughed?* A look of surprise shows on their faces as they hear the sound. They begin turning towards us and their rifles start to come off their shoulders.

'Fire!' I command and all rifles crackle into life, spitting death on those in front of us. They hardly get their rifles off their shoulders before they're hit; all either fall to the ground or are thrown back by the force of the shots hitting them at such a close range. In those few seconds, there is a sharp roar of automatic rifles and then total silence falls as suddenly as it started. I look over the carnage we've just created; twelve lives simply wiped out in a flash. It's over in less than thirty seconds.

'Get ready to move. Johnny, send through that we've been sprung and we'll move to a different location.'

'Patrol 23 to Base. Position compromised. Have had contact with the militia. Twelve enemy KIA. Will move position to different Loc Stat. Over.'

Almost immediately a return message is received, with Johnny passing this up for me to read.

'Base to Patrol 23. Maintain position in the area of Aidabasalala. Are your guests okay? Over.'
'Patrol 23 to Base. Guests okay. Out.'

'We've been ordered to maintain a presence in this area,' I explain to the patrol, bringing my map out so I can quickly suggest another position something I have up my sleeve. 'If we go to this point here, we will have almost as good an observation post as we have now, but it means we have to move across their main access track and across to this river here. The worst thing of all is we'll have to do it now in daylight. Questions?'

'We'll have to move from here, Sarge,' says Gil as he concentrates on the map. 'I think the sooner we get out of here the better. Those other militia would have surely heard the firing.'

'Take the breach blocks or bolts out of all the weapons and bring them with you. You can drop them in the river when we cross and then throw the rifles to the shit house. We'll use the track that the militia used to get to the bottom of the hill quickly. It should be obscured from the border so the Indos shouldn't see us make the move to our new position and will probably think all the shooting was done by these dick heads for some reason. Is there anyone on the track at the moment?'

'No, Sarge,' says Johnny, looking from one end to the other. 'It's all clear as far as I can see right to the border. There's no movement from the Indos at the border either; it's almost as if they didn't hear the shooting, Sarge.'

'Good, let's move out. Mick, take my place, I have a present to leave for the others when they get here so we know when they've come to this area.'

As the patrol moves out, I take a pin out of one of my grenades and carefully place it under one of the bodies of a man with a lovely, studded belt that looks very collectable. With Mick leading, we move off quickly in single file down the track the militia used only a few minutes before. When we reach the foot of the hill there is the main road, if you could call it that, from Aidabasalala to Indonesia, the way the militia had come to get into the village. Fortunately there is no movement from either the border or the town that will prevent us from getting across this road.

'Move across the track in pairs,' I instruct them, watching as the first pair quickly moves to the scrub on the other side of the road and go to ground while the rest of us cover the track both ways in case we have more militia coming either from the border or back from the village. The next two cross. Finally, they're all across, leaving me the only one left. I break a branch off and carefully sweep the road behind me, removing any tell-tale sign that someone has crossed here, a trick I learned from a tracking course at Ingleburge many years ago. We make good progress through the scrub until we reach the river where Mick pauses just in the trees; he turns, signalling me up.

'We can't cross here, Mick,' I tell him looking at the river. 'There's not much water here I know but it's far too open and it's much too wide. Hell! Blind Harry could see us if we crossed here. There's no cover on the other side either, so move further along and we'll see what it's like – we'll stand out like dog's balls if we cross here and try to move up that bank to the jungle. That's it, just follow the river upstream a tad until the scrub thickens and we'll see what it's like up there; we'll be out of sight of our former observation because I'm tipping there will be visitors up there shortly.'

The scrub we're in is heavy so we stick to the cover it provides and slowly move upstream to where, thankfully, there's a corner where the stream narrows; unfortunately, it's deeper and well over our knees. However, there's good overhead cover on both sides which will enable this crossing to take place unobserved. I'm relieved when the last of us is over and into the scrub on the other side.

'Move up that ridge someway and go to ground. We'll have a spell there, which should enable us to see if we've been followed up and I'll do some area beautification at the creek just in case we left a few signs that we've crossed here,' I tell them, looking at the scene in front of us. 'It's a beautiful spot here worthy of a photograph. Looking from here, there's cover right to the top of the hill and, who knows, maybe just maybe we could find the right place up there for the O.P.' I turn to my second in command. 'Purse, could you help me do a sweep job on the riverbank just in case some smart arse walks up here looking for us and finds our tracks?'

It's almost noon when we reach the top of the ridge and look out over Aidabasalala and across towards the knoll that we'd had our O.P. on earlier. It's a good spot with plenty of shade to rest in and to the east and south-east our view is uninhibited for the full length of the village – probably a better position than our previous observation place. I look back to the west and get a good view of the Indonesian border and I can just see the border check point and the cars of the Indonesian border guards have parked in the shade of the trees. It's obvious they haven't connected us to the shooting or they probably think it was the militia annoying the population of Aidabasalala while looking for the girls, making me pleased that we're still an unknown factor to them.

'Send our new location through to Base,' I tell Johnny as we settle into our new observation post. 'Tell them we have a good spot across from our previous position and our visitors are both okay.'

'Patrol 23 to Base. At new location xxx, xxx. Good view of Aidabasalala. Guests are both well. Over.'

Almost immediately, the radio springs into life as if waiting on our call and we have our return message from HQ, likely pleased that we got clear without a scratch.

'Base to Patrol 23. Continue to observe Aidabasalala. Out.'

With comms over, we set the observation post up with Purse taking the first shift. He's able to observe from back in the shade which will obscure him from our previous position and also stop any glare escaping from the binoculars he has trained on the town and our former observation post.

'Make sure you don't expose yourselves to our old O.P., fellas,' I warn them, just in case people come up from the other way. 'I'm afraid I'm expecting the militia to be there shortly. They're nice blokes and I'm sure they'll let us know when they get there. Gil, you organise the first shift; Paddy, you come with me and we'll do a quick recce of this hill and see what we have at this site that we can use to our advantage.'

We are away for almost an hour checking any entry and exit areas, places which people could move up on our position without our knowledge and, more importantly, a good escape route if we require it later on. All of this information is drawn on a map and will be duplicated this information onto each patrol member's map when we get back. Paddy and I have been back ten minutes and are about to transfer the information onto the other patrol members maps when I get a signal from Purse who's at the observation post.

'There are people in the old O.P.,' he tells me, looking across the valley with the binoculars. 'I've just seen movement; there, you can see them now, next to that small tree on the edge of where the O.P. was.'

I raise my glasses and sure enough, there are two militia men in our old position moving about looking out across the valley towards us. *It won't be long now,* I think as I put the glasses down and turn back to my companions. I watch as Paddy instructs the rest of the patrol in the transfer of the different escape routes from his map to theirs and explains the rationale behind our way of thinking when there's a single sharp explosion from our old observation point across the valley.

'How terrible! It appears they must have found that grenade of mine that I somehow misplaced,' I mutter to Paddy. 'Now we'll see what happens. This could be interesting. How many militia did you say there were in the other group, Gil?'

'I counted fifteen, Sarge,' he says with a smug look on his face. 'So, they've come up the other way so they'd catch the two girls in the middle. They will be starting to think the girls are smart little cookies and are now armed so that should slow them down a tad.'

A few minutes later, two of the militia members are seen running onto the main road back to Indonesia. Ten minutes later, a slow procession of eight people move onto the road carrying two others on makeshift stretchers towards the Indonesian border. They are met by more people just across the border who have obviously come to help get the wounded back to their base.

'Eight and two make ten and two on stretchers, twelve,' I mutter to myself as I watch the bedraggled group move out of sight. 'They must think the two girls have a bit of firepower after this. Unfortunately, the next time may not be so easy because they could learn something from this little escapade.'

It's towards night-time when our next communication is sent back to base with the details of the day's events. Not wanting to alarm the wheels back at headquarters, I tell them of this afternoon's happening and the casualties the militia sustained.

'Patrol 23 to Base. Militia returned to Indonesia. Unfortunately,

it appears some injuries have occurred to them. Guests are both okay. Over.'

'Base to Patrol 23. Continue observations of Aidabasalala. Expect relief possibly tomorrow. Suggest you set an ambush on road to the border to stop Militia from interfering when your relief arrives. Out.'

'Well, that is a pleasant surprise,' I say and call the patrol over for some instructions. 'It appears that we are to be relieved sometime in the next couple of days, I expect, a company of one of our battalions and you'll also be pleased that headquarters has asked if we can set an ambush on the outlet road to Indonesia. It's to give them some form of support when the infantry arrives so we can stop the militia from ambushing them. It's assumed by headquarters that they will be warned of the coming troops, and it wouldn't surprise me if the little pricks didn't try something on our boys after what happened to them here today.' Next, I ask them a simple question. 'Does anyone know here what a punji stake is?'

There are some blank looks amongst my men, but I'm surprised when the American reporter, Tiffany, speaks out.

'I read an item once on the Vietnam War where the Viet Cong used to use sharpened sticks to protect their bases from our troops attacking them.' I get a puzzled look from the young woman. 'How can we use something like that here?'

'That's exactly what they are, boys.' I can tell that the men are interested but they know nothing about them. 'Because there are only six of us, not counting the two young ladies and we have no claymores; we'll be out-numbered considerably so we'll cut say, two hundred punji sticks and site them over the road from our ambush site to assist us if there are too many of them in the killing ground for us to handle.' I hold up a punji that I'd whittled earlier. 'Right, I'll want thirty each; this is what I want.'

We spend the next half hour before dark cutting the lethal little weapons that were used so successfully against soldiers in Vietnam. I am quite surprised to see both the girls collecting their share to take down to the track.

'These people killed most of my family,' says Tiepeco sadly, her eyes almost bringing tears. 'They are bad people who do everything the Indonesians tell them and even to the children they are cruel. Anything I can do to help, I will. I know how to use a rifle as my uncle was with Fretelin for nearly twenty years and on his visits home he showed me how to look after myself and fire a rifle.'

With punjis collected and sharpened, then we move down to the creek crossing under the shade of some large trees, just up from where we came over. Once over the creek, we listen for a few minutes before we cover the last leg to the track.

'We'll put the ambush in just before the track junction to our old observation post; that way, it stops any of them going up the hill,' I whisper to the rest of my patrol, hopefully explaining the rationale behind the ambush. With no questions, I lead them down the track until we reach that junction. I choose a straight section of track for the ambush with a good view of either side and just out of sight of the border. 'Carefully place your punjis opposite to your firing position in the manner I showed you back at the O.P. so they produce the maximum result if someone goes that way to get away from our ambush.'

It takes slightly longer than I'd anticipated, but finally we're finished and are able to take up our positions along the track and begin our wait. We pair up with another person and take it in turns sleeping. Tiepeco is with Paddy on the town side while Tiffany is with me at the closest point to Indonesia and from here, I'm able to watch right to the border with the night vision glasses.

'If things go ape shit, I want you to grab your friend and go directly back to the O.P. and wait for our Battalion fellas to turn up this afternoon,' I tell Tiffany, looking sideways at her lying beside me with one of the old rifles she'd taken from the militia yesterday. 'I don't know how many will come but I expect it will be quite a few so make sure you are prepared for the worst when they do.'

'I'll be alright, Pete,' she says, looking down along her rifle like a real pro. 'My father used to go hunting when we were kids; sometimes it was deer, other times we hunted hogs and he allowed my brother and me to go with him and he'd show us both how to fire a rifle. Wow! What a story this will be to the readers back home! Imagine me in an ambush with you Special Forces guys!' She immediately turns her head, looking at me, making me suddenly realise for the first time what a lovely person she is; even in her old clothes, so carefree and almost without a worry in the world. 'Most of the people back home have never heard of East Timor, Pete; or, for that matter, where it is and unfortunately, they don't know anything about what's happening here. It's my job as a reporter to let everyone back home know all the facts about this place and the horrible abuse and suffering these poor people are putting up with from this so-called militia. They've murdered these people in their hundreds just to stop them from achieving their independence from Indonesia.'

Just as I'm about to answer her, I see movement at the border and quickly signal the others to be on alert. We settle down and wait for the militia to arrive. They are coming quite fast; straight up the track towards us. Most have their rifles in their hands this time but still, some of the silly twits have them over their shoulders as if they are going on the proverbial duck-shooting trip. When will they ever learn? I've told Paddy to start shooting when they get to a certain point opposite to him. I've counted twenty passing me. There are another seven to go when he opens fire and a few seconds later everyone opens up. People in front of us start falling. Others, quite bewildered by the shooting, dive for the cover on the other side of the road; their screams tell me they've found the punji sticks. I shoot two of the seven not in the ambush and the other five flee, running down the road and dropping their rifles to make their escape quicker; they run as if it's an Olympic hundred-metres dash.

'*Cease fire!*' I yell at the top of my lungs and there is a stunning silence. 'Mick, Gil, Purse, come forward with me. The rest of you, cover us. Tiffany, you watch the road towards the border in case others come.'

The four of us move forward cautiously, rifles at the ready, looking from body to body. There are fourteen dead and another eight wounded; some seriously from gunshot wounds but most of them lie unceremoniously in the punji sticks with bad lacerations to their legs and bodies, unable to extract themselves from these lethal little sticks.

'They are disarmed now,' I tell the others who are covering. 'Those of you with medical kits bring them forward and we'll treat the wounded. Johnny, get onto HQ and get a chopper down here immediately for the wounded and we'll get them to a hospital. Unfortunately, most are beyond our help.'

'*Patrol 23 to Base. Have sprung ambush. There are eight wounded. Two serious, Guests are okay. Over.*'

'*Patrol 23. This is Base. Well done. We will send chopper for the wounded and your guests. Out.*'

'A helicopter will be on its way shortly; that sounds really good,' I tell Johnny after he gives me the news. I suddenly realise the casualties we have. 'Do they realise how many wounded there are here? I hope they've got the numbers right when they say they're sending a chopper down because if it's a *Black Hawk* they will be pushing to have enough room to fit them all in.'

'I told them how many there are,' Johnny says but he is suddenly interrupted by the American girl.

'I've got the story of a lifetime here,' Tiffany says. She has produced a camera and has started to take shots of the ambush site and the wounded that are being treated. 'Wait 'till people at home see these with the brutes getting it dished back out to them in such a manner.'

'Tiffany, I'd appreciate it if you didn't take any shots of the punji sticks,' I tell her, putting my hand on her camera just in time to stop any photos being taken across the road. 'This is a United Nations operation, and they may not like this type of thing being used. Johnny, Gil, Purse, start to collect the punjis. Our ambush is finished now. I don't think the militia will attack us again today, but we may need the punjis again if we have to set another ambush in another place.'

Lucky for us, they've just finished retrieving the last stakes when I hear the sounds of a number of rotor blades thumping in the distance from the north. Just above the hill, I pick out the welcome shape of a *Chinook* helicopter gradually getting bigger as it comes in towards our position.

'Get onto the radio and let them know that it's safe here for them to land,' I tell Johnny, looking around for a suitable landing site. 'Take Mick and set up a little protection towards the Indon border over there.' It's just in case someone tries to get smart and have a shot at the chopper. Purse, take a marker panel out to the centre of the clearing and then go to ground on the other side of the LZ and keep a watch towards the village, just in case we have more trouble from that direction.'

I heave a red smoke grenade into the open and watch as the big *Chinook* comes in fast, hovers for a few seconds above the ground and then settles in the clearing. Almost immediately, the back door is open and as soon as it settles, six soldiers rush out and secure the area towards Indonesia. From the expressions on their faces, it's quite easy to see this is their first combat assignment. Just behind them, out strolls an officer with a pistol drawn. He walks across towards me and behind him a number of people, who I believe are medics, come scurrying out with stretchers.

'Sergeant Jackson, you have some wounded militia I believe that need immediate transport back to Dili,' he says, looking at me as if I'm some sort of illiterate fool. 'We're here to take them back. Where are they?'

'Over on the edge of the road, Sir. The two most serious are at this end and the two women who we've been protecting are just over there.' I point towards Tiffany who is still taking photos of the scene of the helicopter landing while Tiepeco is chatting with two of my men.

'Very good, Sergeant,' he says, holstering his firearm and looking towards the wounded. 'We'll take the women back as well. You and your men will have to stay until you're relieved sometime this afternoon or maybe tomorrow morning. It will most likely be elements of the Second Battalion who will be relieving you.'

The medics soon load the two badly wounded men onboard and assist the other prisoners onto the aircraft. The officer calls the other soldiers back who are guarding the helicopter and strides arrogantly over to the two girls.

'You ladies are both welcome to come back with us,' he says to the two women, putting on a suave and debonair attitude towards them. 'There is plenty of room in the helicopter for both of you.'

'I will come back with you in the helicopter,' is Tiepeco's answer to him. She then looks at me. 'I am sorry to leave you, Sergeant, but I have friends in Dili who have helped me for a number of months, and I wish to catch up with them and let them know I am now safe and thank them for the shelter they gave Tiffany and me in these last few days of this madness.' Then, she surprises me by reaching up to me and kissing me on the cheek. 'Thank you so much, Sergeant, for protecting us the last few days because, without that wonderful protection you gave us, they would certainly have caught us both and if that had happened, I dread to think of how we would have been treated.'

'I will be staying with these men,' Tiffany states boldly, setting this officer back on his haunches somewhat. 'These men saved our lives yesterday, so I'll be coming in when they do. I have more photos to take of this place while I'm here.' She immediately jumps on her bandwagon as a reporter. 'The world has to know of the plight of East Timor and its people and how they are being so badly treated by these thugs who call themselves Timorese Militia. If these men are coming in tomorrow, then I owe it to them to wait with them and I will come in at the same time.'

A look of sheer disbelief comes on the officer's face, and he stares at Tiffany for a few seconds in total amazement as he slowly takes in what she's just said. 'Very well, Madam, the choice is yours but you'll have to realise we won't take any responsibility if anything happens to you out here. You'll be on your own; do you understand what I'm saying?'

'That's alright, Captain,' she says, looking hard back at him in a very belligerent way. 'We've been up here by ourselves for months; what difference will another day or two make? I want to catch up with a few people in the village and record those events that happened here, both in town and on that hill.' She turns quickly and points to where we were yesterday. 'We were up there, and the militia would have caught us if it hadn't been for these brave men stepping in and protecting us, so I owe it to them to stay here until they go in.'

The enemy rifles are the last thing to go onboard before the helicopter is finally loaded and lifts off, moving slowly at first but gradually gaining height and speed. It gets smaller as it gains more height and is soon just a speck in the northern sky; almost hidden by hills with only the faint sounds of the rotors telling us they'd been here. Finally, even that disappears and once again we're on our own in this extremely volatile place.

'Let's get back to our observation post before we have unwelcome guests calling on us now the hardware is gone,' I tell the men, motioning them to start moving back to our hide in the hills. 'You should have gone back on the chopper, my girl,' I say, turning to Tiffany as we move back to the river. 'It will be quite some time before the battalion boys are here this afternoon. I only hope no one decides to make another attempt at coming over and causing more trouble because they may have been watching this road and might know how many of us are down here. I hope you understand what I'm saying?'

'Certainly, Pete, I wouldn't worry about them now,' she says, still furiously taking photos of what seems to be everything on the road where the ambush had been set. She continues talking as she does her camera work. 'When you lose as many men as the militia have in the last two days, you'll find they tend to be a lot more should I say, conservative with any future actions because some of the people you killed today and yesterday would most likely have been their leaders. If those people are removed, it makes the others far more cautious with any more aggressive actions they may think of taking.'

'Perhaps you're right, Tiffany, but I'm afraid old habits die hard with things like this. I'll still be happy when we're back in our perch on that hill and are looking down on the town and the river. I'm afraid I just feel much safer with trees around me; it makes it quite difficult for people to take pot-shots at you from a distance.'

When we're finally back to the relative safety of the observation post, I tell the men to get a few hours of shut-eye while we wait for the battalion to arrive sometime this afternoon. I sit at the observation post, looking out across the valley to where we'd camped yesterday before looking back towards the Indonesian border where I note there are now quite a few more cars as if they are expecting the next attack to be on them. The big difference however, is at Aidabasalala. I look down to the houses where the street junction is and find everything is so calm and people have started to finally move about on the streets talking to each other as if they know we are in the vicinity protecting them. It isn't a ghost town anymore as they obviously know the militia has been dealt a substantial blow. These good people had their businesses to run, their farms to work and whatever else they do in this small community. It's wonderful to see the transformation of this small border town happen so quickly and once again these people start to live their lives free from the terror they've had to put up with for so long from the militia.

'Do you see anything down there?' a soft voice says from behind; it's Tiffany, her camera still dangling from her neck like a real pro. She comes over and sits down next to me and we look out together at this dramatic change in this small border town below. 'These people are gentle people, Peter; they just want to get on with their lives and be free for the first occasion in such a long period of time and not be told what to do by the Indonesians or some sort of lackey with a gun. This will be a good country once everything settles down and a parliamentary democracy of some description is established so the people who lead them are responsible for their actions.'

We chat about this, looking down at the houses and the roads leading to them and the people who all of a sudden are out in the street going about their business, talking to each other perhaps thumbing their noses at the Indonesians and the militia. There are children playing in the street for the first time since we've been here, like they do in most small country towns that I'm familiar with. It's as if at last this huge veil of uncertainty has been finally lifted off this peaceful little village as they finally realise that the cloche of dictatorship has been lifted and they are now free to get on with their lives once more without any interference from the militia.

It's the middle of the afternoon when I hear the roar of motors and look across to the northern section of town and see the distinctive shapes of M113 armoured personnel carriers as they enter the town. They slow down, their backs grind open and men in camouflage fatigues quickly spring out leaving these reliable machines. They start taking up strategic positions covering the streets while others, in a predetermined fashion, fan out on either side of the road. With the APCs leading, they slowly move through the town, welcomed by the population who are standing in front of their houses, watching these soldiers approach; clapping and laughing and some people throwing flowers at them.

'The chopper will be a little later than first thought,' Johnny quietly tells us, bringing me back to earth with a jolt. 'Unfortunately, they'll be here to pick us up sometime tomorrow morning and hopefully should be here before dinner, Sarge. The message says we're to hold our position on this hill as an observation post for the battalion while they stabilise things in and around Aidabasalala.'

'Good! We'll meet them in that paddock where that old house is not very far from the river,' I tell him, turning to the others who've been sleeping with one eye open but have heard the sig set and are now well awake. 'We will evidently be leaving in the morning, fellas, so it's business as usual tonight and we'll run a piquet on the O.P. Johnny, contact the officer in charge of the battalion and let him know what our position is and that we'll be running this O.P. on the track towards the border for them. Tell him we have a good visual access right to the border because we don't want any of his troops doing a sweep or something equally as stupid this way and bumping into us.' Suddenly, I have an afterthought to involve his troops with the town. 'Let him know there are two dozen bodies that will require a burial on the track to Indonesia and up on the knob where we had our first O.P. there's another dozen or so that will also need burial.'

It's a long night with no movement from the border whatsoever; a good response to our ambush yesterday morning but finally, just before midday, we're given the word from Johnny that we've all been waiting for.

'The helicopter is close to leaving Dili, Sarge.'

'Right, pack your gear, fellas. We're moving out within half an hour,' I tell them with a bit of a laugh. 'There's a chopper just about on its way and I bet none of you wants to miss your ride back to camp.'

'I haven't thanked you for saving our hides, Pete,' says Tiffany as we scramble to get our gear together. 'You'll have to come and have a coffee or something a little stronger with me when we get back to Dili.' With an wicked glint in her eyes she adds, 'I'll put on a spread so I can thank you properly in a much more personal way.'

'That would be nice, Tiffany, I'd enjoy something like that.' I look into her sharp blue eyes and find them shining up at me, making me feel quite eager to accept this very welcome invitation she's offering. 'I'm looking forward to having a few days off, so I'll certainly take you up on this wonderful offer you're making.'

We scuttle down the hill and cross the stream and are soon making our way through the undergrowth to the perspective Landing Zone which is no more than a hundred metres from the stream. The old house is carefully checked out once again as well as the surrounding scrub, just in case there are unwelcome guests who sneaked in and are waiting for us to give us an unwanted farewell. We only have a short time to wait however before the now-familiar sound of the *Black Hawk* comes vibrating down the valley towards us over the town. It gently hovers over the Landing Zone for a few seconds before the wheels touchdown and we quickly rush over and climb aboard. I'm looking down at Aidabasalala as the *Black Hawk* lifts off, watching the battalion fellas as they continue to stabilise security in the village when I'm quite surprised to feel a warm hand grasp mine.

'Pete, I'll give you a call when we get back,' she tells me, holding onto my hand tightly. I look across at Tiffany and again I'm melted by those beautiful big blue eyes of hers. 'It'll probably be tomorrow morning because it'll take me some time to find somewhere to live. From what I assume, there won't be much to worry about finding a place now that your people have troops on the ground.'

'That'd be great. I'd like to have a drink with you when we get back from here; I'm afraid it's been quite a volatile time. I expect I'll have to blame you girls for stirring up the militia the way you did and causing all the excitement because we normally expect to just be watching tracks and doing mundane things like that with no excitement happening around us whatsoever.'

'Come on, you're being far too modest, Pete. If you two hadn't been on that track the other night, those people would have caught us; I'm sure of that. You've got to realise when you and your friend intercepted us, we were totally exhausted and on our last legs. We had nowhere to go or hide and it was only a matter of time before they'd have caught us. Who knows what these bastards would have done with us if we were caught because their reputation with prisoners, especially females, isn't very good from what Tiepeco told me.'

'Tiffany, I'm just glad we were there to help you and Tiepeco avoid being caught. Fate happens to all people you know, so let's have a few drinks and a laugh about this tomorrow and, if you like, we'll get pissed together and celebrate getting out of Aidabasalala in one piece. Deal?'

'Deal,' she says quickly, a lovely smile breaking out. She clasps my hand even tighter, those magical eyes simply sparkling up at me, turning me on. 'You have a date for twenty-four hours' time. I'm really looking forward to having a drink with you. We can go over everything that happened in the last few days so I can get my report done, and all the events that dramatically unfolded when you and your men turned up the other night and intervened so decisively with the militia.'

'Tiffany, that would be very nice, I'll look forward to your hospitality. We'll have a date then as soon as both of us get our reports out of the way then we can relax properly, have that nice meal and a few drinks.'

The helicopter comes in on one side of Dili airport and lands not far from a number of other choppers lined up just off the tarmac. The rotors are turned off and the doors are opened and then, with a bit of relief, we get out and walk towards the buildings to be met by the hierarchy of the unit and a group of other diggers who want to find out firsthand what went on at Aidabasalala.

'We'll do a debrief in half an hour; that will give you time to take a shower and clean up,' the squadron second in command tells us as we meet members of our base support staff who have come to welcome us back. They have obviously having heard of the clashes we've had from the sigs and are wanting to get these details firsthand, the same way we'd waited on the Landing Zone for information of contacts in Vietnam. 'There are a few details we would like your account on. After that, Sergeant, I think your patrol has more than earned a number of days off to recharge your batteries.'

After a quick shower, we meet with the operations officer and the officer in charge and give a detailed account of our five days at Aidabasalala; how we met the two women and our first contact with the militia which was caused by one of the women coughing. They look at each other and frown a little when I tell them we used punji stakes that we placed on the other side of the track to even things up a little in our ambush as this had stopped the militia from going to ground and returning fire.

'After all, Sir, there were only the six of us and we didn't have claymores; we couldn't afford to have them going to ground on the other side of the track and returning fire as we could have sustained casualties. We had to equal up the odds somehow otherwise the battalion blokes may have come in under fire. I'm sure these people would have set up an ambush of some description for them somewhere on the road coming into Aidabasalala.

'I think it's best to say nothing of the punji stakes, Sergeant,' the officer in charge says with a big grin on his face as he is probably thinking of my background. 'Your patrol has done an incredible job and made the infantry's task quite a lot easier in the area of Aidabasalala. I'd like to thank you personally for rescuing the two women, especially Tiepeco who, from what I've been told, is related to the people who may be in government in a few months' time. Well done, Sergeant; a job well done by your patrol!'

I finish the debriefing, relieved that the wheels have accepted what we've done in the patrol as part of the operation. Now, all I want to do is to have a few drinks with the boys and relax with them. They have exceeded what I'd expected of them on their first contact with enemy forces and I intend to buy them a few drinks and show my appreciation. They have all given me unswerving backup.

CHAPTER 11

DILI

I wake the next morning with a slight hangover. We've had our night out and I hope the men's morning is like mine – quite sluggish.

I'm just in my fatigues after my morning jog when there's a sharp knock on the door; it's the orderly corporal with a large smirk on his face.

'Sorry to bother you, Sarge, but there's a young lady in the orderly room asking for you. She's a bit of a looker actually; an American by the sound of the accent and she seems to want to see you quite urgently. Is there something up that we can help you with?' he says, still with this silly grin on his face. 'You fellas must have really made an impression on her on that last patrol you did at Aidabasalala to have her looking you up straight after you get back.'

'Come on, Jimmy, give a bloke a break; she's a reporter damn it. She's probably after an exclusive story about what we do up here, so I'll have to be very careful with what I say; who knows what she's liable to say when she sends off a full report to that paper of hers in New York. Heavens, you know what reporters are like.'

'Hell; you'd better be really careful what you tell her then, Pete because the wheels get a bit iffy if you say too much.' He's finally lost his stupid grin, but I still think he's trying to get a bite from me. 'You'd better be extremely careful what you tell her, Pete because, from what I've been told about your patrol's effort two days ago, they could almost make a movie out of your clashes with the militia and I'm certain you don't want that.'

I go across to the orderly room with Jimmy by my side and to my delight find Tiffany waiting for me. She comes over and kisses me on the cheek, treating me as if I'm a long-lost friend. I'm surprised and quite elated with this reception she gives me as I didn't expect such a welcome like this, which will give Jimmy plenty of ammunition to talk about tonight when he meets the other members of the patrol for a beer and get to know firsthand what happened.

'Peter, I've been able to get a place not far from the old Portuguese Government House,' says Tiffany, quite excited as she looks up at me with those lovely eyes which are now shining enticingly at me. 'So, if you are free today, I'll cook us a nice dinner and we can talk about the past five days we were at Aidabasalala and you can help me with my assignment. You can fill in some of the events that happened while you guys were there that I didn't notice. How does that sound?'

'I'll look forward to it, Tiffany. I've got the day off, so I could help you with the meal but first I'll check with the orderly room to find out when I'm due back at the barracks and we can do our planning from there. Now seeing you are going to cook up a storm, do you want me to bring anything to go with the meal, like a bottle of good wine perhaps or I can scrounge up something to eat from our mess or maybe something more appropriate from town on the way to your place?'

'That would be very nice, although I've already bought some wine and stocked up on food. Look, Pete, we should have plenty; you can shout next time you come.' She has a mischievous look in her eyes. 'Look, I'll wait for you to check things out with your orderly room then if everything is alright we can leave together and have a relaxing day.'

'Unfortunately, I have to be back by 08:00 in the morning,' I say to Tiffany as I walk out of the orderly room, a little disappointed at this and again, I'm quite surprised as she clasps hold of my hand as we walk away, almost like lovers. We walk through the streets of Dili to her small apartment.

'My boss Kerry O'Flaherty had it lined up for another reporter who is supposed to be coming over from the States in a week or so's time. It's only a small continental-type house with a bedside living room, but with beautiful panoramic views extending right over the bay as far as you can see; it would be worth millions of dollars if this was back home in the States in a place like California.'

'It certainly looks nice, Tiffany,' I say, turning away briefly and looking across at the naval ships sitting at anchor in the bay but I'm very quickly dragged into the small bungalow by this lovely young woman.

We've barely entered the room when she suddenly turns quite excitedly towards me, putting both her hands on my shoulders and looking up into my face with her eyes sparkling, showing all of her pent-up emotions at me being here.

'Peter, I've bought a number of good quality wines so that will save you from going out again and I've plenty of food in the kitchen for both of us, so what about we have a lazy day here just by ourselves and you can help me with my report so everything that happened is recorded in the correct order.' Then, she reaches up and vigorously kisses me hard on the lips, quickly pulling back and looking seductively at me. 'On second thoughts, let's have a quiet day just to ourselves and just stay here and later we can go over your stay at Aidabasalala because that will be the culminating part of my report. What do you think, a lazy day here?'

'I'll enjoy that immensely as it will enable me to unwind,' I tell her, bending forward and kissing her wonderfully soft lips. I'd been taken aback by her forward moves a few seconds ago but I'm fully recovered now. Unfortunately for me, Alicia is a memory that I have to get over; I'm afraid that if it keeps imposing itself on my thoughts, it will eventually eat me up. Tiffany is offering me this opportunity to remove Alicia from my mind and I have to take this opportunity.

My arms go gently around this beautiful young woman, pulling her quickly to me. I feel her body come willingly towards me as she responds to my advance, kissing me back before lifting her head back a little, looking up at me for a few seconds, summing this situation up before partially breaking away and steering me with her other hand to the adjoining room and then aggressively pulling me down onto the bed with her. We embrace eagerly as if we have only a few minutes left in this world, rapidly taking each other's clothes off and frantically attacking the other as if every second of this wonderful encounter will be our last.

We lie together as one after seemingly hours of furious lovemaking, both holding the other so tightly as if there will be no tomorrow. Finally I find myself dropping off into a deep sleep, still holding each other as if the world is about to finish. Both of us are showing the strain of the last few violent days at

Aidabasalala. My mind is alive, I find myself gliding through the jungle killing the Viet Cong on the ox cart and there is Abe tied to the back and all my Vietnam experiences come flooding back through my mind as if they are just happening here. This dream, that is if it is a dream, goes on until I finally find myself falling, falling and then I'm desperately trying to get back to the others I can see above as I hang below the helicopter. My body appears to be shaking terribly hard as if something is causing it to vibrate vigorously and away, somewhere in the distance, I hear a strange woman's voice continually calling out my name.

'*Peter, Peter wake up please, wake up for heaven's sake!*' Tiffany tells me, her arms on my shoulders, vigorously shaking me again hard, trying to wake me up. 'Please for *God's sake* wake up, you're having a bad nightmare. You're not in Vietnam now; you're here in Timor with me so please wake up. Look, I will comfort you; there's nothing to be afraid of; you're here in Dili with me!'

My eyes spring open and there she is, her beautiful face just above mine showing all the traces of concern as she looks down at me, frightened and obviously wondering what the hell I'm talking about.

'You're here with me, it's alright, all those things are passed now,' she says with a worried expression etched all over her beautiful face. 'Peter, you've been talking in your sleep of Vietnam for some strange reason, but that war has been finished since before we were born. It's long gone, you're here in Timor with me now, don't worry because things have quietened down since your troops arrived. Please relax and make the most of this break. Let's enjoy ourselves before you go out again.'

'I'm sorry I woke you with such a lot of tripe, but it was a long few days. You're right, we're safe now so let's relax and enjoy ourselves and not think of those bad boys down at Aidabasalala,'

I say, pulling her down to me and kissing her hard on the lips, finding she's returning the kiss. 'Do you want to eat yet, Tiffany? I can cook up a storm like those people on television always brag about. I'm sure what I cook will satisfy you.'

'No, I just want to stay here with you, lunch can wait,' she says, rolling on top of me. She has a concerned look on her beautiful face. 'What have you got left that I can take? I'm hungry for something that you've got and I'm afraid I don't mean food. What are you going to feed me with this time, Sergeant Jackson; some of the same I hope?'

An hour later, draped in just towels, we finally emerge from the bedroom to make ourselves a meal. We eat the food sitting comfortably on an old couch, looking north over this beautiful bay with an excellent cab sav in our hands that Tiffany had scrounged up from a friend of hers the day before.

'Where to after this?' she asks, looking at me a little concerned; a situation I haven't thought about. 'I know your patrol will be going back out very shortly but how long do you think you'll be in Timor?'

'As far as I know, we'll be going out again in the next few days but to where, I have absolutely no idea until our briefing. They will most likely tell us tomorrow so we can prepare our kit for whatever it is. It will probably be somewhere to the west in the border region. It appears they're the main zones my unit will be working in as I suspect that's where the majority of the trouble is coming from at the moment. Villages in the areas that border Indonesia I suspect will be our main objectives and I think our commanding officer's aim is to saturate these areas with patrols and report on any known infiltration routes that the militia may have, so like at Aidabasalala, we'll report whatever the activities are and, if required, stop them like we did down there. I'll let you know when we're supposed to leave so you'll have some idea when we'll be back as most of our surveillance patrols over here are around eight to ten days in duration.' I smile at this beautiful young woman who I met by sheer chance who is now looking up at me quite innocently, a worried frown etched over her pretty face probably thinking of our previous patrol. 'That is unless it's like at Aidabasalala and we have multiple contacts all the time with their damn militia and have to rescue lovely American journalists like we had to do on our last patrol.'

She says nothing and just nestles further under my arm, holding on to me more tightly as if her life depends on me and me alone; a move that gives me a lot of confidence in her. I pick up her small frame, feeling her arms go around my neck and easily carry her back to the bed where I place her down gently. She looks up at me her eyes sparkling, enticing me to join her so I drop my towel and move down to her. Kneeling beside her, I reach over and gently kiss her on the lips before drawing back and slowly sliding down next to her, cuddling up to her soft naked form before kissing her breasts until both nipples are quite hard, nuzzling down her stomach, gently arousing her.

'Oh, Peter just come here and love me,' are the last words that she says to me before we become entangled with each other once again.

At night, again I dream of Vietnam and the contacts we have and fortunately, this time I wake up when I hit the trees. Thank God; this time I've woken up myself, so I assume that the dream is mine and Tiffany is asleep and I haven't also woken her like last time. I carefully look at my watch. Hell! It's late. It's seven thirty and I have just half an hour to get back to the unit. I quietly slip out of bed and dress into my cam gear and turn, moving back to Tiffany who is just starting to stir so I kiss her gently awake.

'Unfortunately, I have to go now, my beautiful girl,' I say, bending over this wonderful sleeping beauty, kissing her again lightly on the lips and then drawing back, looking into her shining blue eyes which are still clouded with sleep. She stares up at me as if trying hard to entice me back to bed with her. 'Thank you for the many wonderful moments we've had together over the last twenty-four hours.'

'Peter, I'm not going anywhere. I'm a journalist and have a job to do here and that's reporting the facts about the transition of East Timor to democracy, remember,' she says, smiling up at me with an almost innocent look on her face. 'I've had a wonderful time with you. Thank you once again for getting both Tiepeco and myself out of the hands of those horrible militia people. Honestly, Peter, if your patrol hadn't come along when you did, who knows what would have happened to both Tiepeco and me with those terrible men so close to catching us? It makes me shudder when I think of what could have happened if you hadn't been there.'

'Tiffany, I came here with you because I like you. I've never seen a woman who was able to look after herself like you did the other day. You handle that old firearm you had as well as any man I've ever met, and I've met a lot in my military career. You take care please and look after yourself and I'll see you when I get back after this next patrol as you mean a lot to me and I don't say that lightly, so until we get back, please just behave yourself and I'll cook the next meal we have together.'

I kiss her once more and quickly turn and move out the door and make my way back to our billets near the airport. I find

I'm on cloud nine having spent such a wonderful time with this beautiful young woman.

As soon as I come to the compound which houses the unit, I push the past out of my mind and immediately switch to now and instantly start to wonder what the wheels have in store for our next patrol and what part of the island we'll be asked to go to this time. More importantly, what will our mission be after the torrid time we spent on the border at Aidabasalala? What will the wheels expect us to do on this coming patrol? I just hope this will be a routine surveillance patrol that will absolutely bore us to death so we can relax for most of the time we're out.

Tiffany lies in bed for another half an hour, thinking of the marvellous Australian whom she'd just met in such an inhospitable place in an isolated region of Timor right next to the Indonesian border. She thinks about the time they've spent together and wow; isn't he an exceptional lover! She lies there remembering how fiercely they'd made love, how he'd been able to gently turn all her buttons on with so little trouble and how he'd made her explode so successfully time and time again. But his dreams, they were another thing; almost out of this world but he seemed to be reliving them! They were extraordinary and, for some strange unknown reason, they were centred not on what they had just been involved with in Timor but strangely on the conflict in Vietnam. That was over well before he or she was born. How could he talk of such things, intimate things that happened so long ago in a different time and in such a different theatre of war? She tries to gather her emotions up a little so she can think rationally. She wonders, did Australia have troops fighting alongside America in that brutal conflict?

'I never knew Australia had troops over there fighting alongside

with our men,' she speaks out loud, quite puzzled at what he'd said and in such graphic detail. He had described each clash as if it was something he'd actually lived through. *'That's stupid, he's not much older than me.'*

Tiffany thinks for a moment before reaching under the bed, grasping hold of the tape recorder. She'd put it there when he went to the bathroom just in case he started talking again in his sleep like he did earlier in the evening. If this happened, she wanted to be prepared so she could capture every minute detail and see if the subject was the same as before; she wanted to get this unusual story he was rambling on about and check it out.

The recorder is a sensor-driven and works on any sound that is emitted and these sounds immediately burn into life on the disc. She listens to their romantic chit chat and the noise of their lovemaking, again marvelling at how he'd pressed all the right buttons and turned her on to heights she'd never reached before. The noise of their lovemaking stops and they're both asleep and the recorder is dormant, sitting there biding its time for any murmur that either of them would make. She hasn't got long to wait when his voice comes through very clearly; again, he's talking about Vietnam. They're on an ambush patrol. He describes the claymore mines going off and he describes this graphically in detail as if he was actually there. Then, it seems that he and other men are almost ready to leave when suddenly they're exchanging shots with the North Vietnamese on the track. The patrol moves away from the ambush point, cutting through the jungle to a what he referred to as a Landing Zone, half a day away. Next, he speaks of a vicious firefight at this Landing Zone as they are leaving; people are shot, the helicopters go and he's on his own. Tiffany listens, awe-struck by the account of this battle. She is intrigued by the details given of this event that went terribly wrong somewhere in Vietnam, especially since he had been sound asleep at the time.

What an extraordinary man I've found! But, just who is he? She thinks for a moment about how to decipher this amazing story he's just told her in his sleep. *'I'll take this recording to my boss at the office. Kerry may be able to shed some light on what this wonderful guy is talking about.'* She wonders what his reaction will be when he hears what Peter said about a war that he's far too young to have been in. Her instincts as a reporter are now well and truly taking over from that of a lover. She feels there is a huge untold story here that she's virtually sitting right on top of. *Who knows what there could be here? There could be some strange story in this that he was somehow involved in, but the time frames are completely wrong for a man of his age. What an exceptional man I've just met and here in Timor of all places!*

Kerry O'Flaherty is sitting behind his desk going through a heap of papers he'd acquired dealing with East Timorese independence when there's a soft knock on the door and Tiffany walks in.

'Morning, Tiffany. I hope you've recovered from your little ordeal in the jungle with Tiepeco and those Australian Special Forces soldiers,' he says, looking over his papers at her shapely form which he finds is dressed to kill. He watches as she immediately plonks herself down in the chair opposite him. 'Let's have a good look at this adventure of yours and you can explain how all this led you to a godforsaken place like Aidabasalala. Goddamn it girl you were away for over two months, we were worried sick about you not hearing a word from you and only getting the occasional hint from the resistance that you were safe?'

'I still have the last four days to write up,' she tells him, wanting to do a good job on her involvement with the Australian Special Forces soldiers. 'The time I spent with the Australians was very, or should I say *extremely*, turbulent and I want to give that my full attention so nothing is left out. There is no doubt that those men saved Tiepeco's and my lives by intervening when they did, and I want to do them justice for all the events that happened from that time on. I have to say they were the most professional soldiers I've ever met and made the militia look like the cowardly, back-stabbing curs they really are. Look, Kerry, please bear with me because I want to do this story properly so these men who rescued us get the full credit for what they actually did to get us both out of the village and how they virtually tore the militia apart and spat their remains out.'

'Okay; would three days be enough?' he asks her, looking up, admiring what he sees across the table from him. 'Because I have a few other tasks I want you to do for me, but they can wait until you finish this article about these Australians. Now, is there anything else you want to discuss about your time with Tiepeco up until you reached Aidabasalala and became involved with those Australian Special Forces?'

'Well, yes, there is but not about Tiepeco and me.' A strange, almost mystical look comes over her face which confuses him somewhat. 'Did the Australians have any forces in Vietnam assisting us during that war?'

'Yes they did; they had eight or ten thousand men over there,' he tells her, a little surprised and wondering what this is leading to. 'They also had advisers in what they called the Training Team, but their main force was in a province south of Saigon called Phuoc Toi where they had a number of large battles with both local and North Vietnamese troops and accounted for themselves extremely well. You have to realise I was only a very young reporter at the time on my first overseas news assignment. I'm pretty sure they withdrew their troops in and around seventy-two or three; anyway, it was about that time, but why, what brings this strange question about a war that finished almost thirty years ago? What are your reasons; why do you ask such a strange question, Tiffany?'

'The leader of the Australian patrol who saved us was a man of about twenty-five called Peter Jackson, a very nice man. We spent yesterday together before he and his patrol were assigned out again sometime this morning. Yesterday, while he was sleeping, he talked about operations he did in Vietnam. He was agitated and throwing himself around so I woke him up. He apologised to me for talking in his sleep but last night, I took the liberty of putting a recorder under the bed just in case the same thing happened again.

'Well, go on. What happened that has you so interested in what he said?' asks Kerry, a little interested now but pissed off because this Australian had obviously slept with Tiffany last night; something he'd like to do himself. 'A young lad talks about time in Vietnam. How is something like that so strange? He probably has a good imagination for unsuspecting young ladies like yourself, Tiffany. Are you quite sure this man was asleep or was he just having you on with this dream of his – you've already told me he's too young to have served over there so what are you on about?'

'Look, Kerry, I know when someone is asleep or not,' she says, starting to get annoyed with him and is now glad he'll hear the sounds of them making love. *The bastard; that should give him something to think about,* she thinks wryly. 'Just listen to the content of what he says when he's asleep and then you can tell me if he's making things up because Kerry, what these men did at Aidabasalala impressed me much more when they almost annihilated that group of militia.'

The recorder is played through with Kerry showing a little mock annoyance during the noisy lovemaking but, when they get onto the patrolling, she notices a distinct change in his attitude. He's almost sitting on the edge of his seat when he hears about Peter rescuing a person called Abraham and blowing up an ox cart. The next segment is in America; a fight in a bar, the presentation of a silver star by the President and meeting some woman called Alicia. Again, he's in America to see this woman and is involved in another fight in a bar which is finished when he throws a knife at the gunman, but he's wounded in the side by a bullet, making Tiffany think of the two fresh scars she saw on both sides of Peter's body and is pleased she didn't ask about them as this could have tipped him off about the recorder.

They're back in Vietnam again with more firefights and eventually it finishes with him falling from a rope below the helicopter.

Tiffany and Kerry look at each other in amazement, each trying to interpret what really happened so long ago in Vietnam and America and how this young man could have all this accurate information. More importantly, they wonder what happened when he fell from the helicopter.

'This is staggering information if it's right in what he's saying,' suggests Kerry, trying to come to grips with what he's just heard on the tape. He attempts to put this into the correct time perspective from the date of the war ended to where they are now. 'How can it be? You said that he's just twenty-five, so this man wouldn't have been born when the Vietnam War was raging and yet what we've just listened to is about times and places that I know are correct. This has completely bamboozled me. Can I play it again please, Tiffany? I have a strange feeling there is something unusual going on here that neither of us fully understands – as you told me before, he's far too young to have fought in the Vietnam War and to accumulate all this accurate information and freely talk about these accounts in his sleep as if he was actually there.'

They listen to the recording once again and he finds more things fall into place and more dates and times that they've overlooked, completely baffling them both even more. The more they listen to this sleeping man talking, the more intrigued they both become with what they hear.

'I'll have the report on our rescue here sometime later this week,' Tiffany tells him now for some reason a little uneasy with what she's just done. 'When you hear what his patrol did, that should add a lot more to our mystery man. I'll find out how long they'll be out and I'll have him around again when they come back and who knows what we may find out this time, there may be more about what he's saying, especially after he fell into those trees because that fall has obviously woken him up.'

'Tiffany, can I keep this tape while you're doing your report? I'll give you another to replace this one so you can use it if he comes around again. Look the first thing I'll do is to check the Australian army records; they have a release time of I believe thirty years for most of their units so I may be able to get them a little earlier through the appropriate channels I have at their War Memorial in Canberra. Who knows, they may even be the same for their Special Forces, so let's see what I can come up with from these sources,' suggests Kerry as he tries to think of other ways he can substantiate records of foreign soldiers who served in Vietnam. 'I'll also do a check through our own military records as I have a number of names I can have looked up and checked out that were mentioned when he was in the States. You go and do that report of yours for last week, Tiffany, and I'll see what I can come up with by say in a couple of days' time while I check a few dates and try to piece a few things together.'

Two days later, Tiffany arrives back with her report on her last few days at Aidabasalala. She looks at the report once again and is shocked and quite overwhelmed at the events that unfolded, especially when she realises she was an intricate part of the course of these events and possibly, if Tiepeco and she hadn't been there, it may have been a straightforward surveillance job. She suddenly thinks about how Peter had quickly dispatched the two men who were following them up the hill and how ruthless the Australians had been each time they dealt with the militia and how, with such a professional approach, they had literally torn the militia apart and virtually spat the remains out. *'What sort of soldiers are these Australians to handle the militia so ruthlessly?'* she mutters to herself as she thinks of Tiepeco and her being involved in all of these contacts the Australians had.

'Come in, Tiffany, take a seat. I've spoken to people in the Australian War Memorial, and they will be emailing all they have on this Peter Jackson tomorrow. I've also spoken to people in Washington, and they'll send me any war citations they have for foreign soldiers in 1968. For some reason which I find strange, they weren't so open as far as American soldiers were concerned, which is a little unfortunate. However, there are many other ways of getting what you want to know out of the system.'

'You've done very well,' she tells him and hands over the documents she had worked on during the day. 'You'll get a bit of a surprise at what Peter's patrol achieved at Aidabasalala when they rescued Tiepeco and me. Do you know they killed over twenty-seven and captured twelve militias in four days at three different times? Kerry, I knew they put the brakes on the militia, but I never stopped to think of how many men they'd killed until I wrote up this report. What sort of soldiers are they?'

'Special Forces are a different kettle of fish when it comes to soldiers, both in our army and obviously theirs.'

Kerry takes her documents that she'd written and quickly reads them while Tiffany sits and looks at him across the desk, watching as he flicks through the pages, making the odd comment.

'What happened to the militia who were following you up the hill when you made your initial escape from the village?'

'I asked the other patrol member who took us to the top of the hill – Mick, I think his name was – and he told me that Peter cut their throats and put their bodies well off the track so they wouldn't be seen if others came up that way later on. They both had night vision glasses on so he could see who was approaching. The man who took us to the top of the hill had them as well. Kerry, when they moved, they made no noise whatsoever; they were almost like ghosts, you just didn't know where they were until you were next to them.'

'So, when you were at the observation post above the trail and the militia came up to your position, do you know who it was that coughed?'

'Yes, it was Tiepeco. She'd had a cold for something like a week. She was next to me when she did it. They just simply hosed the militia with their guns as soon as they heard the cough. The shooting was over in less than half a minute; the lot of them were dead in that instant.'

'The ambush – who initiated that?'

'The end soldier in the patrol; he was a corporal and second in command to Peter. When they reached a specific point, he opened fire. Those who weren't shot in the ambush instinctively jumped into the scrub on the other side of the trail and were immediately impaled on the stakes that he had his men set directly across from the ambush site. There were only a few of the militia who weren't in the ambush that got away. I think there were five. They just dropped their rifles and ran back towards Indonesia. Again, this ambush was over very quickly and virtually wiped out this group of militia.'

'Good God; I wonder if we have soldiers like this. You know the stakes he had set up were widely used by the Vietnamese against American soldiers in that war; they called them punjis.' He suddenly thinks of them using these lethal little sticks. 'Whose idea was it to use punji sticks?'

'Why it was Peter's suggestion; the other members of the patrol didn't know what they were when he mentioned them. I was the only other person there who knew what they were for, because I'd read a number of articles about the Vietnam war and how the Vietnamese used to protect their camps from our troops.'

'We'd better not mention those little weapons,' he finally says to her with a grin, wondering what he will do with this report for, being a United Nations operation, they would probably frown on their use. Now, however, he is more interested in Peter Jackson and where he's come from; he can smell a good story and wants to find out more about this unusual Australian sergeant. 'Thanks for the report, Tiffany; it's a bit of an eye-opener with this type of thing happening here in Timor. What you've written is almost like Vietnam all over again. This story will give our American readers a good insight into what's actually going on in East Timor; it is ideal in portraying exactly what thugs the militia really are and will make the public at home aware of the plight of these unfortunate people. I'll email this through to New York later today so it should be ready for tomorrow's papers. I expect you'll be seeing this Jackson guy again when his patrol comes in – I'd like you to find out as much as you can about him, Tiffany, especially with this Vietnam business that seems to be lurking in the background. You may be sitting on a massive story and you may not realise the enormity of what you've actually got until you have the last piece and find out what happened to him after he hit the trees; that could add another dimension to the Vietnam side of this story.'

'I hope to see him again after this next patrol is finished; it should be over in a few days. He told me it was a surveillance patrol somewhere near the Indonesian border.' She shakes her head as she realises that was exactly what their last patrol was. 'Their last patrol was supposed to be a surveillance job as well. Heavens, I only hope this one isn't as complicated as the one I was involved with and they have no trouble with the militia. I phoned his headquarters this morning but unfortunately, they were very vague about what they were doing and wouldn't give me any details. The only thing I could do was to leave a message saying I wanted to see him and to give me a call when his patrol is finished.'

'Nothing, Tiffany, absolutely nothing; you've done everything you possibly could have. They normally keep their operations very close to their chest and are quite secretive about what they do. You'd probably find if you were his wife, they still wouldn't give you that type of information; the green berets the States have are exactly the same and keep everything they do away from people like us.'

'You know, Kerry, these last few days I've really missed that man,' she says with a strange, glazed look in her eyes. 'I really hope that what I've told you isn't going to hurt him because he's a very nice person and treats me with a lot of respect.'

'We'll be careful, Tiffany. We won't do him any harm; we just want to find out the truth about this Vietnam business he was talking about. It's like I said before, he's a twenty-five-year-old with a vivid imagination and you may not agree with me, but he's probably trying to impress you. Look, as I've already told you, I'll be extremely careful when I talk to my colleagues about what he said in his sleep, but I just want to check times, dates and places and see if I can validate the things he talked about before any decision is made to write anything about what he said. I will assure you now, all I want to do is to find out the truth.'

'Thanks, Kerry. I really appreciate your trying not to compromise him in any way. He and his men are playing an important role in Timor when it comes to pacifying the militia; it's almost criminal not allowing them to make their own minds up to become a nation.'

Kerry sits at his desk after she's gone, pondering over what all this was about. How in the hell could this young Australian soldier dream factual accounts of a war that had finished some twenty-five years ago and, as far as Australia's involvement was concerned, had finished a number of years before he was born? What this man had dreamt about was incredible. How did he get all this information and be so accurate with everything. He plays the disc through again and stumbles on more factual accounts, confusing him even more when the phone rings breaking his concentration. The call is from Washington.

'Jack here,' comes the familiar voice of a colleague crackling through the old telephone. 'I've looked up that Vietnam soldier you asked about. He's a real doozie, a Negro in Special Forces; silver star the first tour and bronze star and bar on the second tour and he's now a United States Senator so we'd better tread very carefully on this one, Kerry. This man is a real American hero and his constituents love him. What this man says he does, and he sticks up for our boys in uniform, and he has a lot of support in that area as well.'

'You've done well, Jack. Now, were there any reports of an Australian being involved with him when he received his first medal, a man called Peter Jackson perhaps? Did he have anything to do with King and his award because from what I've heard over here, he was rescued by Jackson?'

'Yes, there was, Kerry. When Abraham King received his silver star from the President, standing alongside him was an Australian Special Air Service Soldier called Peter Jackson. Jackson had earlier been involved in an ambush the previous day and then they had another contact on the landing zone with North Vietnamese soldiers while covering their exfiltration. It appears that Jackson was left by the choppers who were under extremely heavy enemy fire. From what I read in the report, he moved west by himself towards Highway Fifteen when he ran into the group that had King captive and evidently rescued him; probably saved his life when you read the account of what happened. When you read the whole thing, these awards read a little like a Hollywood movie script and I'm talking about Rambo.'

'Like that is it? So, what I've heard over here is correct.' This further confuses Kerry. 'How the hell could a twenty-five-year-old know these intimate details of accurate times, places and describe these critical events, in his sleep, when he wasn't even born yet? If he's twenty-five now, he was born five years after the guy in Vietnam fell off the rope; things just don't add up Jack,' he says, quite puzzled. 'Goddamn it, Jack! What if this Jackson guy says in his sleep turns out to be correct? There has to be a woman involved somewhere back in sixty-eight; a woman called Alicia that this guy keeps talking about who he met just after he got his silver star. That gives you a good timeframe to work with. It could be a member of the King family or maybe a close friend of these people; I'd be grateful if you could look a bit closer and a little deeper to see if you can find any woman by that name close to or related to the good senator. We could be sitting on a massive story here so please, Jack, just keep on digging and see if you can find this woman.'

'I can't answer that question yet, but I'll have a good look into King's family, Kerry. We'll see what that brings up and if there's nothing, I'll look a little further out to family friends or associates. Anyway, what's all this about? It sounds like you're onto a really good story. Hell, man, if you're in East Timor, it's a long way from there to Vietnam so where the hell are you getting all this information on the fire fights the Australian Special Forces had and all this information about what happened to King? You're talking about late nineteen sixty-seven, sixty-eight.'

'I'm afraid I don't know what I've got yet; I'm just doing a little scratching around at the edges at moment, Jack, but I'm sure we're onto something very strange and really big and, if we can get to the bottom of whatever it is, who knows what we'll uncover. Would you be able to email as much as you can get on this Abraham King guy before he became a senator; and yes, his immediate family as well; I want the lot. I want to see what this guy's really made of and if he's as tough as what he appears to be in the Senate.'

Balibo

I'm given the orders for the patrol to do a straightforward surveillance operation of part of the border near the town of Balibo; a town most Australians my age will remember for the murders of a number of Australian journalists who were covering the story when Indonesia first invaded East Timor in the early seventies – that is, all Australians except me, for my memory stopped a number of years before this tragic event happened. This was just a few years before the Indonesian invasion of East Timor took place and I only know this because Gil was talking about it to Purse after the patrol briefing. After scrutinising the map, I intend to station the patrol on an obscure knob above the town.

A truck drops us off early in the morning a number of kilometres from our target and we creep into position just before dawn, being very careful not to disturb anything or anyone that may be about that has militia sympathies and let them know we're in the vicinity. I'm not surprised to find very little cover on top of this knob, yet this place offers an excellent viewing platform for both the border and the town, so I rotate the patrol in the observation post and send back regular messages of any signs of militia activity. We see very little enemy movement on this part of the border; we only see one group of militia quietly crossing one night close to our observation post. We quickly report this to a company of the battalion who I hope have ambushes set up on tracks coming from the border. The whole patrol was very satisfied to hear the cascading of gunshot reports and see sudden flashes some twenty minutes later, knowing that the battalion boys had made contact with them and, by the looks of the muzzle flashes, have given them exactly what they deserve. As the time draws out, I'm once again looking forward to some time off which I hope to spend again with Tiffany and recharge my batteries and be able to forget about what we're doing here on the border for a couple of days and occupy my mind on our blossoming relationship. I'm pleased when our time draws to a close as we've been in this position for over ten days now and I'm extremely glad when our final day comes along and it's time to discreetly withdraw with no one seeing us leave.

'Pack your gear, fellas,' I'm pleased to tell them when the message comes through from headquarters to pull out of this position. 'You'll be pleased to know that another patrol is going in somewhere close by as we speak.'

We carefully move away from our good observation post to a landing zone some three kilometres away and wait for the helicopter to arrive. It's a pleasant surprise for me when we get back to the headquarters and I find a message from Tiffany asking me to come over when I get back. This will have to wait until our debrief and I have a few beers with my patrol – an important tradition we'd established in Vietnam that enabled the patrol commander to show his appreciation for a job well done. This is an opportunity to sort out any minor disputes between patrol members so that everything is settled well before we go out again.

Two hours later, after a quite a few beers with the boys and copping a huge amount of harmless ribbing about Tiffany since they are all quite familiar with her after the last patrol, I walk up the steps to of her house, armed this time with a couple of good bottles of red. I'm quite surprised when I knock on the door and it's flung open; without any warning she literally jumps into my arms, almost making me drop the wine.

'Oh, Peter, it's so good to have you back here,' she says,

snuggling into my arms, quickly lifting her head and planting the biggest kiss on me. 'I've been so worried about you after the last time. I kept thinking of those damn militia and you being out there with only so few men and I didn't know where you were this time.'

'Look, sweetheart, it was only a boring reconnaissance patrol,' I tell her, kissing her again and grinning to myself but hoping to calm her down a little and reassure her that a lot of our work is just normal routine patrol work or just boring reconnaissance work. 'We just sat at the top of a lovely sunny hill and looked at the border the whole time we were out and didn't see anything the entire patrol. The weather was absolutely brilliant and to make things worse we had such a lovely view of the coast that made your mouth water when you thought of what you could do in the surf or on the coast. I found it quite annoying to look through the binoculars to the reef and see a couple of fishermen hauling in good sized fish, but unfortunately, the coast was too far away to go fishing or even to have a swim but that's all we could think about after the first boring day with absolutely nothing happening.'

'Come on, Peter. You just play down the job you people perform. I know from what your men did at Aidabasalala that it's far more important than what you are letting on. Oh, if only I was with you.'

'I'd much prefer you to be in town where it is safe, and I know nothing will happen to you.'

Still entwined together, we move back into the house. The only sound is Tiffany kicking the door shut and me cautiously putting down the two bottles of wine without dropping them. I carry this wonderful young woman to her bedroom, collapsing on her bed. We passionately kiss each other, drag the clothes off each other until we're completely naked and then aggressively make love as if we are the last two people alive.

We lie together after expending all our energy, holding each other before dropping off into a deep sleep. I soon find I'm back in Vietnam this time falling off the rope from the chopper again, trying to get back to my Alicia who is calling out to me to come home or go to somewhere that is safe. I find Noc is there sitting on top of me in the museum, talking to me in Vietnamese, encouraging me to get up. Finally, with her help, I'm able to stand and it's nice to feel the blood surging through my veins and the stiffness disappearing. I hear people coming; I can hear their footsteps coming down the corridor and from the sound of it there are quite a few people moving toward us. Oh hell, there are guards! I swing the SLR up and start shooting them. Finally, I'm in Singapore being questioned by the French journalist in the Embassy when for some reason I suddenly wake in a sweat, quite confused as these chaotic thoughts keep running through my head.

It's halfway through the night, my body is drained by these dreams. I wonder why they are all of sudden reappearing now. I look over at the beautiful young woman sleeping peacefully next to me. It's as if my association with her is bringing all these vivid memories to the surface constantly flooding my mind, engulfing my sleep, and making it impossible for me to get any rest – something that's never happened to me before. I suddenly wonder if it's my subconscious that's bringing forth this guilt that I have of cheating on Alicia, and this is what's causing my dreams to emerge. I quietly slip out of bed, careful not to wake Tiffany and just look down at this beautiful creature. Should I tell her about myself? Because I can't go on sleeping with her and having these vivid, quite erratic dreams about my past otherwise she'll think I'm queer. I'm quite nervous as I've never had anything like this happen to me before anywhere, but then I've never been with another woman since knowing Alicia. What's wrong with me? Is it her presence that's doing this? What is happening to me? I quietly cross to the window, deeply disturbed and look out towards the sea. Everything is calm and I find the moon is up making the sea look like a silver plate on this peaceful night.

My mind is full of jumbled thoughts. *I've got to have peace of mind if I'm going to remain with this young woman and, I'd like to – I find her company wonderful and calming. I'll tell her in the morning and hopefully that may get rid of the dreams; I've got all tomorrow with her, so I'll pick the right time and moment to tell her.* So, with this squared away in the right part of my mind, I quietly go back to the bed and slip in beside her. I carefully snuggle up beside her and soon find I'm dropping off into a sound sleep that fortunately doesn't include any of dreams this time.

I feel a set of lips close smoothly over my mouth and, through the haze of peaceful sleep, I find Tiffany's face just above mine, so I kiss her back.

'Good morning, darling,' she says, kissing me again. 'You've slept well; I've been watching you for quite some time now and you looked so peaceful just lying there sound asleep. Come, just look at the way the sun is up and shining into the kitchen. I'll tell you now, it's going to be another beautiful Timorese day so let's spend the whole time by ourselves in my flat just doing absolutely nothing that represents work of any kind. We don't even have to get dressed because I like looking at you with nothing on; we can make love the whole day and think *nothing* about our work.'

'That would be wonderful. Have you anything in mind or do you just want to stay here in bed?'

'That's exactly what I mean; we just stay here and catch up with ourselves. Peter, life is far too short to do anything else and I have only two days to catch up with my man when he keeps going off to war and leaving me behind. Peter, I worry about you and the patrols you are required to do all the time. I just want to spend all my time with you. Would you be happy with that my loveable man because I now know what you're good at as well as your soldiering?'

I look up at her seeing this beautiful naked young woman, her face just above mine as she lies on top of me, smiling down at me, seemingly giving me the strength to tell her about my former life. Is this the right time to tell her of my past and get it over with but then will it shock her to be with an old man like me? Yes, this is the ideal time for me to tell her, to let her know of the other me before we get too involved with each other.

'I have something I want to tell you, Tiffany. It's for you and you only, no one else is to know. It's about my past. Have I got your word that it will only go as far as you because if word of this gets out it will finish me as a soldier?'

'Peter, of course you have my word. For heaven's sake, please don't tell me you've robbed a bank or something stupid like that. If that's the case and you've done something serious in your past, I don't want to hear about it if it's going to ruin our relationship. I'm not interested in anything of your past, especially if it's something bad that you've done before you came into the army because I only want you as you are now, not with any of your baggage.'

'Unfortunately, it's nothing as simple as that. I wish it was not so complicated. This happened while I was in the army.' I sit up on the bed holding both her hands carefully in front of me and looking her full in the face, taking a few seconds to think of how I should explain my background to her and do it as simply as I can. 'How old do you think I am now that you know me a little bit better, Tiffany?'

She looks at me quite confused. 'Twenty-five or possibly twenty-six at the most; but what's that got to do with the things you're going to tell me? You're just a little older than me, that's all. Pete, why are you putting so much emphasis on how old I think you are? What I've just told you won't be far off the mark, I'm sure.'

'Tiffany you'd better sit down please.'

She moves back from me, a little unsure at what I'm going to say and sits back on the bed on my ankles, her knees over my legs as if expecting me to run off, looking quite worried at me after my opening comment and more than a little puzzled at why I've asked such a strange, almost mundane question.

'I was born on the first of April 1945 which makes me fifty-six next April.'

Her mouth drops open, she stares at me as if I'm trying to trick her in some way or as if I'm pulling some sort of stupid joke on her to try and put her off. I go on further and tell her my story from start to finish, not leaving anything out.

'So, you see I'm not a bank robber or anything as easy as that, Tiffany; I'm just an older man in the body of a twenty-five-year-old. Now, do you have any questions you want to ask me?' She looks at me for a moment, mouth open so I try and speed her reaction up. 'Come on sweetheart please say something, after all, this should interest you greatly as you are a newspaper reporter.'

'Peter, I know most of the story,' she says, surprising me. Then, she shuffles forward on her knees, throwing her arms around my neck, kissing me lightly and looking across at my worried face. 'You've been talking in your sleep while you've been here.

Remember when I woke you up that first night? You were talking in your sleep about Vietnam. Peter, I set up a recorder so the next time you talked in your sleep it was copied. I did it because I was quite surprised about you talking of Vietnam because it was finished before I was born, and I couldn't work out how you knew so much about a war that was over before you were born. I took the recorder to Kerry to try and get some answers about what you were saying. He's my boss here and had been to Vietnam as a war correspondent, so I thought he'd make some sense out of what you'd said. After hearing it, he said you were a young man trying to impress me and that he'd check the information with a friend in Washington and find out as much as he could about some of the people you were talking about in this dream of yours such as the man you saved on the ox cart, Abe I think you called him and his sister Alicia and their validity.'

'Oh *shit*! Can this man be trusted with this information? Hell; I don't want this to get out, I can't even go home because the friends I had are in their fifties or sixties or they're dead. Even my brother is sixty and he has children who are married and they look even older than what I do. Oh Tiffany, what the hell did you do that for?'

'I'm so sorry, Peter,' she says, with tears pouring down her cheeks. She grabs hold of me in a tight embrace. 'I was so confused, hearing what you said, and I wanted to find out what this was all about. I'm so sorry but I thought Kerry would be the ideal person who could find out about what you were talking about because of him being involved with that war as a young reporter.'

We sit together on the bed, our arms around each other, holding each other tightly, with no answers coming; we say very little to each other. What will this mean and what sort of impact will it have on me and, more importantly, how in hell do I get out of this one?

'I know,' she finally says, looking at me, breaking into a big smile. A crafty look spreads over her pretty tear-stained face. 'I'll tell him that I've found out that it was your father that's still missing in Vietnam, and you've talked to his former patrol members about his last patrol, and you asked what really happened to your dad. You could also say you read his patrol reports as, according to Kerry, they are now on the internet and that you are just following in your father's footsteps being in his old unit. Peter, how does a story like that sound? Is it plausible to have gained access to patrol information in such a way?' She reaches over and kisses me on the cheek, smiling at what she's trying to concoct and, I think, quite pleased with herself for thinking of this clever charade that may just get me off the hook particularly if we can handle it properly. 'To me, that's the obvious answer, Pete, and it's completely feasible. Just look at your age. You're only in your mid-twenties and you could say your unknown father is your hero; a man your mother told you about from the time you were a small boy. I hope members of your Vietnam patrol still survive and you've met them because they would've certainly told you about him in a different way to which a patrol report is compiled. I'm assuming that those reports are very blunt and quote statistics in a very boring public service way. I'm sure they would have described the patrols you shared with them in quite a different living way, with much more detail of what happened in the contacts your patrol had and there would be much more humour in what they wrote, a much different and much more human way than some form of official bureaucratic document that's put out by the army to explain the results of a patrol ambush for example?' Then she uses another good example. 'I bet you had difficulty believing it was you when you saw the report of you saving that American who was tied to the ox cart while you were going to the west, am I right, Peter?'

'Yes, you're right and yes they did; as I met two of them just a few months before I came back to the unit and we talked about the patrols we did together and the risks we took in each of these conflicts and laughed about small incidents that happened when out on these patrols that never got into patrol reports. Why do you ask?'

'You could also say they gave your mother a book that one of them had compiled on the patrols he did so she had some idea of the work your father was doing and furthermore, when you were in your teens, you read this book numerous times which gave you the incentive to join your father's old unit to try to imitate his career path. How does that sound? Does something like that grab you, my beautiful man? Because something like this could have actually happened and certain people you work with would certainly have written them up with much more graphic detail than your 2IC who evidently took your report.'

'You're a genius, Tiffany; that sounds like a wonderful suggestion,' I say, showing some relief at this mad scheme she's proposing to tell her boss and enthusiastically plant a kiss on her lips. 'Do you think he will go for it? I just hope he stops his entire American inquires when you tell him this story because if he speaks to Abe, I know he'll get a blunt reply. However, Alicia as I've said knows nothing of these events. I don't know what they'll say in a situation like this and particularly how she would react if he interviewed her for our relationship was quite close. I know I could speak to Abe and get his assistance to somehow block any inquiries, but to get Alicia to conform to what you say, well that would be something else as she still thinks that I'm missing, presumed dead in Vietnam.'

'Don't worry, I'll talk to him,' she stops as if she's thinking of something else. 'Peter, what if you came along with me and he could see that you aren't old? What do you think if you came with me and met him?'

'Okay, let's see him right now, Tiffany; that should hopefully put my mind at rest and stop these bloody dreams I'm having. After this, if you still like older men, we can come back here and get extremely raunchy as you suggested for the rest of the afternoon,' I tell her giving her a big kiss.

'Why, Mr Jackson, I'd be very flattered; yes very flattered indeed.' She reaches over and returns my kiss very provocatively on the chest then moves up to my lips. 'I don't know if I can wait that long, can you?'

Kerry O'Flaherty is at his desk impatiently flicking through papers dealing with the fast-moving events in East Timor and having in his sight the lead-up to the first Timorese elections, when he's surprised to have Tiffany knock on his door.

'Come in, Tiffany,' he says, getting up and politely coming around the desk to welcome her to his office. 'Good that you're able to get over to the office at such a critical time and you must be ...'

'Peter Jackson,' I reply, reaching out and shaking his hand tightly before sitting down in one of the chairs he offers. 'I've heard a lot about you Mr O'Flaherty and your background in journalism from Tiffany.'

'Call me Kerry, Peter.'

'Thank you, Kerry. As I was about to say, you're just the man I want to see; I hope you can find out a little more about my father who unfortunately went missing in Vietnam during that war.'

'Your father?'

'Yes, he went missing well before I was born; some roping accident from a helicopter ,my mother said; evidently it was in what the military calls a hot extraction when he was in Vietnam.' I am being purposely very vague on times and dates, hoping that this will throw him off even further. 'Fortunately, we haven't had any of those yet. Tiffany was telling me how you have some good contacts in the US that may have some theories on what happened to him on that extraction and how he died because unfortunately they haven't found his remains yet even though they know almost the exact location where he fell from the helicopter.'

'I've done a few half-hearted inquiries but unfortunately, I've have had very little success so far,' he says, physically squirming at these direct questions I'm asking. 'I've had a friend look into the timeframe when he was in America; I think Tiffany said it was nineteen sixty-eight or around about that time.'

'Yes, he was over there to receive an award for valour well before I was born and, according to my mother, it was around that time of 1968 when he was on leave, just before your summer as she said he complained that it was hot wearing his winter uniform. He was awarded the Silver Star for saving an American soldier's life and later that year he was awarded the Military Medal by our own government. I only hope I can be as good a soldier as my father was and carry on his tradition.' I put the pressure right back on him, pushing him to the brink to find out how much more information he's been able to ferret up from these American contacts he told Tiffany he had. 'As I told you earlier, I wasn't born and must have been a twinkle in his eye when he came to Sydney on R and R late on his second tour to see my mother, so if you do find out more about him, please don't hesitate to let me know because my mother lent me a book that his patrol compiled so she knew what type of patrols he'd been involved in on both the tours he did with the Special Air Service. I've also taken his patrol reports off the internet and jotted down as many facts as I can on the patrols he was in. I found that unfortunately they are very clinical, almost vague compared to what his mates had written in their memoirs. I made a point of getting everything I could about him and wrote down all this information for future reference, that is if I ever decide to do our family history or a book about his army life because from what his friend Clicker said when writing about their patrols, some of them were should I say quite volatile compared to ours. Tiffany even suggested it should encompass both of us as we're in the same unit, though the conditions are dramatically different from what I've read of his patrol reports and from what his friends told me they didn't have the state-of-the-art equipment we're issued with these days such as night vision glasses.'

'I'll certainly do that for you, Peter,' he says, appearing to want to steer away from this subject quickly, trying to turn the conversation around to our last patrol. 'You are having an interesting time here in Timor according to what Tiffany has told me. Goddamn it, that patrol you guys did at Aidabasalala when you two first met was quite, should I say, exciting. Do you have any further comments you'd like to add to make a good story out of what your patrol actually achieved in those few days on the border? From what both girls told me it was rather a hairy patrol and you had a number of clashes with the militia.'

'Unfortunately not, Kerry; I'm afraid as serving troops we're covered by the *Official Secrets Act* and this stops me from saying anything for public consumption for quite a considerable time of about twenty years I believe.' *What a clever bastard he is* I think. I'll have to be very careful with this man because he's thinking on his feet trying to get information on our work here. 'Tiffany would be your best bet to get that sort of information about our patrol at Aidabasalala as she's not in our army and is a foreign national. We have no control over what she has to say as she's a civilian and a citizen of another country.' I turn towards Tiffany who's not quite at my side, and look into her beautiful blue eyes. 'As far as I care and I didn't say this so please don't quote me Tiffany; you can give Kerry any details of that patrol after we picked you girls up. I imagine you would have all that well documented by this stage. I'm not saying this but you could give Kerry a good summary of what actually happened at Aidabasalala after you met our patrol.'

'I certainly can. Kerry, I can give you all that information if you like,' she says and it's quite obvious that she's already given this to him. 'I'll write out a full report and give it to you if you would like one. Probably another three days and I'll have the report done in its entirety right to the stage where we left in the helicopter when we flew back to Dili.'

We set about discussing the situation of Timor with Kerry for another half an hour. I listen intently as he directs Tiffany in her news gathering to find out about the situation in East Timor. However, I'm relieved when our meeting with him is finally over and we head back arm in arm to Tiffany's small house.

'There, that should put all your ghosts away forever, Pete. If I didn't know you better and you hadn't told me about your past, I would have thought it was your father the way you put things to Kerry; especially that part you told him about your mother meeting him in Sydney while he was on R and R so that puts your birth well after this fictitious father of yours went missing.'

'I hope so, Tiffany; I feel more relaxed now that I've gone through this charade, as I said this morning, the army is the only thing I have at the moment and if the truth got out to the other ranks about my past, it would wreck my career and at the moment I can't afford for that to happen.'

'You have me now, Peter; I hope I can make you forget these dreams of your past.' Then, she gives an honest answer about the report she has for Kerry. 'You would have noted that I said to Kerry that I'd hand him my report in three days. Well, that was just to try to show him I was on his side because he knows already about the patrol we did together and has a copy of my complete report from the time violence broke out until we met up with you guys on that hill.'

'Thank you, Tiffany, for your help with Kerry, it is very much appreciated and I can understand just why you went to Kerry in the first place with what I was rambling on about in my sleep and how it must have sounded so strange to you.'

My couple of days of relaxation with Tiffany are soon over. She was right; I feel much better and much more relaxed now that my past and my dreams have been successfully put to rest and hopefully Kerry will concentrate on the East Timorese independence and the coming elections to form their first elected government.

I find myself with my patrol back on the border with Indonesia, watching a track for any sign of militia coming across the border to cause trouble in the coming election which is still a number of months away.

After a quick phone call, I find Tiffany is at the beck and call of her boss Kerry and is attempting to firm up stories of the coming election and hoping to do a background series on the leading candidates, all wanting their independence from

Indonesia. She is desperately attempting to suss out what their real ideologies are and if she can find any of these candidates who may have strong communist inclinations. From what I was told that was the main excuse used in the first place for the Indonesian invasion of this former Portuguese colony in the early nineteen-seventies.

'There is to be a rally held by some of the major political parties in this area,' Kerry informs Tiffany at their morning briefing in his small office. 'From what I hear, they intend to form up in front of these buildings and then move down the street to this square where they have a dais set up for prospective politicians of a number of persuasions who will give addresses to the masses. I'll get you to cover the rally with me and get as many photos as you can of the more prominent people who will be there. I want as many individual photographs of the not-so-well-known Timorese hopefuls as you can possibly get to widen our coverage of the rally. This will help us get to know more of the movers and shakers in some of the smaller parties who at this moment are well below our radar. You know the type of person I mean, Tiffany, the ones that could represent specific areas? Then we can do a background check on these individuals and find out what their real alliances are and if possible, who is pulling their political strings from the background that can't be seen by us as yet.'

'That will be fine, Kerry, just fine,' she says, thinking more of her few days with Peter than her job. 'They're not expecting any trouble from the militia are they? The Australians seem to be keeping a firm hand on the situation now they have their troops deployed in and around the country.'

'As far as I know, any troops that will be present will be from other countries such as Brazil who, because of their Portuguese background, will be assisting the United Nations in getting the free elections underway,' he tells her, trying to settle her down. He decides to throw in a red herring to get her mind on her job. 'You'll find it's very interesting when you look at the countries involved here; quite a number of those who have troops policing this city don't have elected governments themselves, so you've got to ask yourself, why are they here? Anyway, Tiffany, that's beside the point; our main objective is straightforward news gathering so we can cover the rally as best we can.'

'Tiffany, today you take your camera so you can act as my photographer at this rally because I want human interest shots of the average Timorese people supporting their candidates whoever they may be and also shots of those people supporting the Timorese independence movement, so the world knows of the injustice these people have had to put up with for so long. You know the type of thing I mean, so our readers get broad coverage of these political events as they happen in front of your camera.'

'I know what you want, Kerry,' she replies, enthusiastically grabbing her camera and following him to the Old Portuguese Plaza down near the docks where they wait for the crowd to arrive with their candidates.

It's not long before a very vocal crowd of people has gathered to hear the speakers put their policies forward and give support to their own political parties, many of whom are now on the dais. She notes this rally has almost taken on a carnival atmosphere created by the political hopefuls with party members draped in the colours of their allegiance and holding flags depicting their philosophies, making it a very picturesque rally, an almost carnival type atmosphere.

'Take plenty of photos of all aspects of this rally,' Kerry diligently stresses again to her, seeing her mind is now firmly on her work and not on Jackson. 'We can use them for human interest stories later on if we have to, so get what name or party they represent too.'

They reach the mass of people jostling for prime positions around the dais in order to see their favourite politicians speaking and to assess their performance against their rivals.

'Heavens, Kerry, there must be a dozen parties here alone, all wanting theirs to be the next government.' She madly takes shots of the jovial crowd as they mingle with the excited people.

'Try to get good shots that show their leading politicians – we can hold these photos back and use them later on in the run-up to their first general election.'

Tiffany is good with the camera and follows his instructions, carefully taking shots of people in the crowd and the speakers who seem to be holding sway with the people gathered. Both she and Kerry move through the crowd, hoping to get a different perspective of each event as it happens.

Kerry abruptly halts Tiffany's movement as they come to a group of people who seem to be watching the rally closely, but their attitudes bear none of the bravado displayed by the majority of the crowd. They stand together almost as a block as if they are waiting for something or someone. Kerry puts his hand on Tiffany's arm, abruptly stopping her from pushing through the crowd; he forces her back, almost pulling her with him, trying to get her out of sight in this section of the large crowd.

'*Stop* Tiffany,' he whispers urgently, forcing her to halt on the edge of part of the crowd. 'Back up a little more and wait. I have a horrible feeling something nasty is about to happen. I think we need to keep well clear of whatever it is. Your camera could make us a prime target if something should break out, so for heaven's sake keep your camera down.'

Tiffany takes heed of Kerry's warning and moves her small frame well back into the crowd of well-wishers, desperately hoping to blend into the crowd. She suddenly wishes the cool, large bulk of her Peter was with her to act as a shield and get her out of trouble like he seemed to do so easily during the rescue at Aidabasalala.

'What's up Kerry?' she whispers. 'Is it that part of the crowd you can see up in front of us? Is that what the problem is?'

'Yes, just look at them. Those people over there could be militia, so just keep easing your way back into the thick of the crowd; as Americans we could find ourselves as targets. Let's put a little distance between them and us and be ready for whatever happens. I've got a bad feeling about this; things could easily get out of hand very quickly and explode.'

They slowly edge their way further back into the crowd, never taking their eyes off those they think are militia and hoping, like the rest of the people, that they will be ignored.

Tiffany doesn't take Kerry's advice though and slyly continues taking photos of the crowd. Suddenly, there is a loud bang as a grenade is thrown towards the dais, exploding with devastating effects on the crowd. Bodies are thrown into the air and people in the vicinity go down screaming in pain and terror as shrapnel hits their bodies. The foreign troops immediately start firing into the air, causing more panic as people around them try to flee this catastrophe. Frightened people scramble over each other, flattening the weak as they try to make their escape, playing right into the militia's hands. Assassins have quickly spread out and begin indiscriminately hacking these people with machetes and large knives, causing complete mayhem in the large crowd.

'*Let's get the hell out of here!*' Kerry shouts, frantically pulling at Tiffany who is now wildly taking shots of the incident. He grabs her roughly by the shoulder and starts to drag her back away from what he perceives as militia. 'For Christ's sake, put that *bloody* camera down; we've got to get out of this crowd fast otherwise we'll be caught up——'

He suddenly feels a sharp pain across his shoulders and his arm goes limp, dropping to his side. He turns and sees the sneering face of a militiaman. He gasps and goes down. Tiffany turns, pressing the camera's button just as she's hit with a single blow across her neck, the large knife dropping her instantly; her small body clumsily falls down onto the camera, next to Kerry's limp form.

The chaos continues as frightened people desperately try to flee the scene of horror which has suddenly sprung out of nowhere and is compounded by the foreign troops who quickly move out into the crowd, firing into the air while others with batons and shields come forward, forcing their way into this mass of frightened people and striking anyone who is too slow in moving out of their way. People are running in all directions, screaming in sheer panic; their only thoughts now are of escaping this carnage.

In the space of five minutes, the square is cleared of people. The violence has ceased and the militia have quickly disappeared with the fleeing crowd leaving bodies littering the whole plaza. The only sounds heard now are of the wounded crying out for assistance, there is no one else as the foreign troops have now cordoned off the entire plaza.

We are finally back in the capital, having just spent another ten boring days watching the border with no movement this time by anyone. We had taken turns manning the observation post and are very glad when the whole thing is finally finished, and we move to a Landing Zone some distance from the observation post where we'll be choppered back to Dili. My only thoughts after this dismal surveillance we'd been given are for Tiffany and the expectation of spending another wonderful three days with her in her flat.

'There's a message from a Kerry O'Flaherty, Sarge,' says the orderly room corporal as I check in to leave my patrol report. 'He's in the hospital after attending a bad riot at a rally that some of the political parties held two days ago. Unfortunately, quite a few people were killed while others were horribly injured when the militia became involved and disrupted the whole affair.'

My heart sinks as I immediately think of Tiffany. Has she been hurt? Is she alright? These are the only thoughts that race through my mind as I hand in my report and grab a Land Rover and quickly drive to the hospital. I think of my other patrols when we finished. *Why haven't I heard from her?*

Kerry, his face morbid, is sitting up in bed with his shoulders and neck heavily bandaged. He's not the cocky man he was when we went to visit him ten days before with Tiffany; he's quite sullen, though his face appears to brighten when he sees it's me who comes in to visit him.

'I'm afraid I have some terrible news for you, Peter,' he tells me when the formalities are over. 'I'm lucky to be alive but unfortunately … Tiffany … she … she's dead. It was a terrible shock for us all,' he says, looking at me for my response. 'We were down at the election rally on the weekend getting news and taking photos of the participants and the people there when the whole thing was deliberately disrupted by the militia. Unfortunately, the troops who were there to guard the rally were from one of the Asian countries and didn't help the situation at all; they just fired their rifles in the air adding to the panic and confusion. Others were quite savage to the people who attended the rally and used batons to quieten the crowd. They were shocking, they just waded into the crowd in an attempt to quell what they obviously thought was a riot. If anything, these methods probably aided the militia's getaway with most of the butchery completed, the perpetrators disappearing from the function.'

I'm speechless and sit listening, dumbfounded by what has happened while we were away this time and how easily the militia have struck and gotten away with butchery so easily.

'Please tell me, what happened to Tiffany?' I finally ask, hoping he will be positive and be able to describe the events as they happened. 'You were with her at the rally, tell me – how did she die Kerry?'

'She was struck down the side of the neck with a machete, almost decapitating her,' he tells me sadly. 'She was taking photos of people at the rally when a grenade was thrown towards the speakers. When this exploded, things went haywire with the militia hauling out all sorts of knives from under their clothes.' He whimpers as he begins to explain these atrocious events as if they are too much for him. 'I saw the man who hit me. If I hadn't gone down when I did and played being dead, I would have been in trouble also. I think this action saved my life.'

'You were very lucky, Kerry,' I tell him, grabbing his arm in a show of friendship, thinking how fortunate he's been to escape such a brutal attack, but immediately turning the conversation back to the young woman who had all my feelings. 'Have you any idea what happened to Tiffany? She was obviously standing next to you when this vicious attack happened, so tell me please, how did she die? Do you have any idea who the bastard was? Who did this cowardly act?'

'Yes, I do Peter,' he says, pulling a package of photos off his sideboard and passing them across to me. 'Have a good look at these; they explain everything. The early ones are of the people at the rally before the grenade was thrown. Now you will see the militia start their abuse of these people who were near them. I saw the man who struck me, and I've seen him around the place before the rally. Now, look at these last photos she took; this is the same man who hit me with the machete. I went down and his next slash with his machete was Tiffany who was beside me. My assumption is that he was her killer.'

I look at these photos she's taken with the last one showing the leering face of a man in front of her with his machete raised, almost on the wayward down stroke. It's a very graphic shot taken by a gallant young lady showing with her last photo the man who killed her.

'Would you be able to find out where this man lives?' I ask Kerry, surprising him and I think, temporarily shocking him. 'I'm not normally a vindictive man; I'm a soldier and, I think a good one, but I'm not going to let scum like this get away with a horrible mutilating murder and this *prick* is still out there somewhere laughing at his success at disrupting this political rally and I don't intend to let him, or his mates get away with what they've done, particularly to my girl.'

'I can certainly find out as much as I can,' he tells me, quickly gaining his composure and now I can see he really wants to have his revenge and sees me as the tool to achieve this. 'I have good contacts in this town; I'll get someone onto this straight away. I have a number of people who I trust and who know their way around Dili and should be able to find where this despicable beast lives because as I said to you earlier, I've seen this man around so he shouldn't be too hard to find.'

'I'll be going back out in the scrub in a few days. See what you can do about finding this despicable man for me, and I'll make damn sure he doesn't kill any more innocent people.'

I leave the hospital with a heavy heart. I had a lot of feelings for Tiffany. Whether it was love or convenience, I don't know. I still have my Alicia there sitting in the back of my mind as beautiful as ever. I suddenly think of what her reactions to this would be. *What would she think of me now, plotting a revenge for another woman's murder?*

The patrol we have this time is in central East Timor. We have two villages to observe just in case pressure is being applied by the militia. One, according to information supplied, is known to have militia feelings so we are positioned between the two to watch the track that joins both villages to see if pressure is being imposed by one or the other. It's a simple task really just to watch the track for ten days and report any militia activity in the area. *I must be getting old,* I think, with my feelings right on the surface. *If this was Vietnam, we'd have our claymores out and would blast the shit out of any bastard who came along and wipe them out and disappear into the folds of the jungle like we used to do.*

The observation post is put in place well back on a hill for the ten days with the only people using the track being the villagers going to and fro one to the other. For the whole ten days, no armed people are sighted. The only people we see are women and children or elderly men and they all seem happy; you can tell by their free actions and the way they meet people from the neighbouring village that there is no pressure being applied to them by anyone with a gun or machete like they did at Aidabasalala. It's a relief on the final day when Johnny receives the call from headquarters telling us that the mission is over, and we are to meet a truck at a designated point some five kilometres away on one of the arterial roads that lead through to Dili.

Raul Despedos is a well-known thug. He enjoys the status the Indonesians have bestowed on him since the popular decision had been taken for independence. He had willingly taken his band of men and without question killed specific targets the Indonesians had given them. They had been directed to these targets by the faceless men trying to prevent this new country from gaining its independence. He and his men had taken a large group of frightened Timorese villagers across the border, forcing them into very primitive refugee camps to try and prove to the world that they wanted to be part of Indonesia, threatening them with mutilation and death if they objected or spoke of their incarceration in these hovels they were given to live in. He is pleased with his work so far and knows he will receive his rewards when Indonesia once more takes over the control of this small struggling country. In his latest vendetta, they had successfully disrupted the election rally that pro separatists had held fifteen days before and he had enjoyed killing the American woman reporter who was taking photos at the event. He is slightly annoyed with himself however for not being able to retrieve the camera the woman had been using and for only wounding the man who was standing next to her. *'If he stays in East Timor, I pledge to you I will kill him!'* Raul had openly brags to his henchmen as he ponders over the events he's been involved in; he looks across the table at his two lieutenants who are busily gorging themselves with food, making him think of how uncouth they are.

'Have you any plans for the coming rally on Friday, Raul?' one of his men asks his leader as he looks up from eating, spluttering food across the table and annoying Raul intensely. 'I hope we can disrupt this one too just like we did before?'

'When Friday comes, we will cause so much trouble this time they will wonder about the viability of secession of this country,' he tells his two colleagues. A nasty sneer spreads all over his pock-marked face as he tries to envisage what actions they will take to disrupt this coming rally. 'When this rally finishes, these foreign troops will wonder what they are doing here and will wish they had never come to our land; we will make them want to leave and *never* return.'

'Who knows? There may be some more American reporters there trying to get stories of our independence,' his henchman says, laughing with his mouth full, again this imbecile begins spluttering food across the table and over his companions. 'These are stupid people with ideas that don't make any sense in this country of ours.'

Just as Raul is about to continue his doctrine of violence, there's a quiet knock on the door surprising all three. He looks blankly at his companions, annoyed at being disturbed when he was about to climb on his soap box. He gets up, sneers at his friends who are both still eating and moves to the door, wondering who it could be calling at this late hour.

'Who is it?' he snarls, opening the door. He is surprised to find a tall man with a bright carnival mask standing there. The look of sheer surprise is replaced with one of sudden fear as he sees the automatic shotgun held firmly in the stranger's hands.

The shotgun explodes instantly, hitting one knee and

dropping him to the floor; he screams in pain, his hands feeling for his almost severed leg. The assailant quickly pushes him back into the building, quickly stepping over his body and lifting the gun to his shoulder. He shoots the closest man at the table in the knee, before swiftly lifting the weapon and killing the third man before nonchalantly turning back to Raul.

'This is for the American journalist you wounded,' I tell him, lifting the gun to his other knee and pulling the trigger. He screams in agony as he desperately tries to pull himself away, his eyes showing how scared he really is. I lift the gun up, level with his nose so he can smell the fumes escaping from the barrel, causing him to bluster incoherently, his eyes wide open in fear now for his life. 'This is for killing the woman reporter you've been bragging about. You're going to hell, my friend.' I pull the trigger, which at such a close range, it virtually lifts the top off his skull.

I walk quickly across the room to the injured man who is cowering on the floor. He's made a feeble attempt to pull himself across the room but the pain in his almost amputated leg has clearly made it very difficult to move. His eyes tell me everything about this coward who must have loved the honour of strutting around behind his boss in all his glory but this has been quickly wiped away with the blast of my shotgun and now he is just a blabbering idiot desperately trying to scramble away.

'I'm going to be generous with you and spare your life so you can tell your friends that there are over one hundred of us spread across your country, each of us with targets; we will pick you bastards off when you don't expect us. We have a list of your names and photos of each of you stupid fools.' I drop a copy of the photo of Raul next to him so he understands exactly what

I mean. 'We've been watching you and your friends, biding our time. Now I'll give you two choices; you either get out of East Timor immediately or if you wish to stay here, you and your friends will become model citizens and leave the political events to take their own course. It will only be then that you people will be left alone; do you understand exactly what I'm saying? Because if you don't you will die like your two friends have just done.'

He vigorously nods his head. 'I understand you,' he whimpers, scared of what might happen to him if he says the wrong thing.

I leave their house by the back door and move away from the building, quickly walking down the street. Ten minutes later, I walk into the unit canteen in my combat fatigues that we wear in camp and buy a beer, but I still have this dull empty feeling in my stomach. *Tiffany has been avenged.*

At the weekend, the next political rally is held with no sign of any of the militia activities whatsoever; masses of people congregate below the forum while their political hopefuls speak of their aspirations for this new country.

We do a number of observation patrols in the next two months, but the sting has gone out of the tour with not having Tiffany to come back to. We're glad when the commanding officer tells us that the tour is over, and we are going home. After only six months, it's a bit of a dream but a very welcome one.

CHAPTER 12

AFGHANISTAN

Perth

Most of the sergeants in the mess have been watching an unthinkable tragedy in the United States and are crowded around the television, unable to take their eyes off one of the smoking twin tower buildings in New York. It is impossible to imagine why a large passenger plane would irresponsibly career into such an iconic building as this. We watch almost captivated as smoke billows out of this large skyscraper, and I ask myself, *What idiot would think of such a gross and cowardly act to commit on those innocent people who are working in that building? For God's sake, why?*

'There's another plane,' says one of my companions as a second plane quickly appears on the edge of the screen heading towards the other tower and suddenly smashes into the side of the building, disappearing from sight with a splash of smoke from the impact; totally engulfed by the building and then more thick black clouds of smoke suddenly appear, billowing out of the hole made by the impact of the aircraft. 'What the hell is going on, who's doing these stupid criminal acts on these innocent people?'

In some ways, this is like watching a science fiction movie that some director in Hollywood has cunningly conceived for his next block buster movie and we're waiting for the trailer to finish before the movie commences. We watch with bated breath much more intensely now than before with both towers pouring out smoke across the clear morning sky. Next, like a gigantic pack of cards, the first building starts to crumple from the crash site down; almost in slow motion – this huge building begins to cascade down on itself. We are holding our breaths watching, not believing what we're witnessing; almost unable to believe our eyes as this atrocity continues to grow. With eyes glued to the screen and very little talk going on between us, we watch this great tragedy unfold, waiting for the worst to happen. A number of minutes go by when the second building starts to crumble in exactly the same manner and begins sliding down on itself, just as if it's by design. Finally, the buildings are two gigantic heaps of smoking rubble.

'It's just as if we've watched this sick B-grade movie,' says another sergeant watching the screen, also spellbound and like each of us, totally unable to believe that we've just witnessed this calamity. 'Bloody hell; what would the casualties in both these enormous buildings be? It must be hundreds, maybe thousands of innocent people killed but for what and by whom? Who the hell is responsible for such a gutless act on completely innocent people?'

'I'll bet the man that masterminded this attack wasn't one of the pilots,' another sergeant comments.

While the sergeants who live in the mess are crowded around the television watching this live drama unfold, I suddenly think of Alicia and her husband, both doctors in New York. As one of the commentators has mentioned, New York Fire and Rescue teams along with medical staff had gone in to try to evacuate people from the aeroplane crashes and they must have been caught inside when the buildings collapsed.

Were they involved? Suddenly, a chill goes up my spine as I think of the ramifications of them being involved in this catastrophe. *Please God, tell me neither of them went into those buildings to treat casualties,'* I think, immediately jumping to the first irrational conclusion that comes into my head; I just hope they weren't some of those people. I have half an hour before the parade, so I go back to my room, quickly pulling out my laptop, intent on sending Abe an email. It will be the quickest way to find out if Alicia and her husband are alright and hopefully not among the casualties.

> *Hi Abe, I have just been watching the attack on the twin towers. I hope your family – by that I mean is Alicia and Julian – are OK. All the best; Pete.*

The computer whirls the email into cyber space. I watch the screen for a while before closing the computer down and quite apprehensively move out with the others for our morning parade.

'You would have all witnessed the attack on the twin towers in New York on this morning's news,' the officer in charge says, addressing the men assembled in front of him. 'Well, the CO has been informed and told me the Australian army has been put on high alert, just in case we're required to take action anywhere, and gentlemen, I mean anywhere. One of our squadrons will as of now begin intensive training to go in hot pursuit of any terrorist group that is known to be involved in the attacks on the twin towers. Every high security building all over this country and all major events will have heightened alerts placed on them. That's it for this morning; so, I'll leave it with you. Carry on, Sergeant Major.'

The Squadron Sergeant Major takes over the parade and the men are allotted specific training tasks under their corporals while we sergeants, along with our officers, are fully briefed by the officer in charge in the sergeants' mess.

'Take your seats, gentlemen,' says the Regimental Sergeant Major as we enter the mess. 'The OC will give you a more in-detail briefing than what he gave to the troops a few minutes ago and he will try and answer any questions you may have.' He turns to Major Jacobson. 'It's over to you now, Sir.'

'Thank you, Sergeant Major. Following on from what I said this morning, Al Qaeda, a terrorist organisation from the Middle East has claimed responsibility for the attacks on the twin towers,' the officer in charge tells us in a much more informal manner than on the parade ground. 'There were four planes that we know of so far; two hit the twin towers that most of you would have witnessed, another crashed into the side of the Pentagon and a fourth crashed into a wooded area just south of Washington DC. Evidently, it's believed but not confirmed that the passengers overpowered the would-be hijackers after they killed the pilots but unfortunately, they couldn't fly the plane; very brave people from what we can gather. Now, questions please gentlemen?'

'Will our army be assigned to assist the Americans?' I ask, thinking that by being given these briefings, a commitment would be on the way. 'It is obvious that the whereabouts of this terrorist group is known. After all, the casualties suffered by the Americans would most likely be far more than they lost in the attack on Pearl Harbor and that brought them into World War Two. This terrorist group called Al Qaeda; where do they come from?'

'The leader is a Saudi Arabian from a family of some significance. They were credited for an attack on an American warship a few months back, but we have heard nothing of them since. However, as to what our commitment will be, Sergeant Jackson, we do not know,' he tells me, looking across in my direction. 'However, the Prime Minister is in the United States on national business. I expect he will be making a statement shortly; it's most likely we'll know very soon once the perpetrators are positively identified. After that, we should know what commitments we'll have.'

'Yes, Lieutenant.' The questions go on. My only thoughts now are for Alicia's safety. It is obvious that we'll be committed, and I don't give a damn where it will be; that is my job as a soldier. But I still worry about Alicia. I still think of her as being my girl. Is she alright? Hopefully, she has not been involved in going into the towers to attend to some of the casualties.

The briefing is finally over, and we begin to file out; I can't wait to get back to my room to check the computer to see if I have an answer from Abe.

'Oh, Sergeant Jackson; could I have a word with you please?'

'Certainly, Sir,' I say, wondering what this is about.

'Congratulations, Sergeant. You've been awarded the Medal of Gallantry for outstanding duty in East Timor.' We shake hands and I'm quite surprised at receiving this award. 'Your performance at Aidabasalala was outstanding. I know it's not the same as a Military Medal, but this has replaced them, so

I hope this will make up for the others that you are unable to wear on parades.'

'Thank you, Sir. I was only doing my duty as were the men with me on that patrol; it was a joint effort by all of us, Sir.'

'But you led them, Sergeant. You gave the orders. I know you have good men as a result of your training, but it was you who gave the order for each of the assaults and, talking to your men and reading the debriefs, it was you and Private Smith who rescued the two women from the militia when they were virtually on their last legs and got them back to your patrol. Congratulations, Sergeant. Well done!'

I leave the officer in charge and go back to the sergeants' mess. It's almost dinner time and I'm eager to see if I have an answer from Abe yet. I can't get the thoughts of Alicia being in either building out of my mind. I open my laptop and look at my emails and yes, there is one from Abe.

Hi Pete, Good to hear from you old buddy. Both Alicia and Julian are fine. I just spoke to them, and they are both working on the many casualties that are coming from the trade centre in one of the nearby hospitals. Cheers Abe.

I'm greatly relieved to get this email. It's as if a large great black cloud of uncertainty has been lifted from me to know that they are both safe and well. I can envisage Alicia treating the casualties from the way she'd treated me with the gunshot wound all those years ago when I'd been with her father that day. I'm daydreaming and quickly snap back to reality and walk to the dining room where the talk is on the twin towers; speculation is rife on what our commitment could be.

New York

Earlier on that fateful day, Alicia and Julian are sitting at the breakfast table chatting about the coming day when the phone rings.

'Charles here, Julian; have you been watching your TV?' the frantic voice of one of Julian's close friends says. 'An aircraft has just hit one of the twin towers; you and Alicia had better get down to the hospital fast because there will be casualties coming in shortly and they'll need every doctor they can get.'

'Aircraft, what sort of aircraft?' Julian replies, initially thinking of some military maverick that has crashed his fighter plane into the building after doing some stupid stunt. 'Alicia, turn the TV on, sweetie; there's something that's just happened in New York that Charles says we should see.'

'No, no it's nothing like that, it was a passenger plane that just flew right into the building,' is the reply. 'It's got to be a terrorist attack on the United States. I don't know yet but both of you should get down to the hospital because they'll need everyone they can get. There will be a lot of casualties coming in very soon because the casualty rate will be enormous.'

While this conversation goes on, Alicia has switches the television on and immediately sees the tower with smoke billowing out of some of the floors towards the top of the building. Julian has just hung up the phone and is moving over to where Alicia is glued to the set, when another plane appears briefly before it crashes into the second tower and instantly disappears into the building. The force of the impact sends another column of smoke wafting into the air; both Julian and Alicia gapes at this horrific scene that has quickly unfolded in front of them.

They are about to turn the TV off and move to the car when

one of the buildings collapses, slowly at first then it gathers speed, almost in what the experts would later call a controlled collapse ending as a great pile of smoking rubble at the base. Too horrible to watch; especially when you consider the building has people throughout the entire structure!

'Oh my God, Julian; we'd better get down to the nearest hospital this minute. They will need as many doctors as they can get,' says Alicia, hurriedly getting out of her chair and turning for the door. 'Who in their right mind would do such a barbaric act to those innocent people?'

'Unfortunately, the world is full of cranks, Alicia, just wanting some form of notoriety,' replies Julian as they leave the house and rush to their car. 'I hope they catch the bastards that masterminded this as it's nothing but cold-blooded murder; that's all you can call something as barbaric as this.'

They speed through the streets towards the city hospital nearest to the towers; a policeman who is controlling traffic steps out in front of them, pulling them up.

'We're both doctors, Officer. Could you get us to the nearest hospital please?' Julian says to the officer just in front of the car. 'From what we saw on television a moment ago they'll want all the help they can get from now on.'

'Okay, buddy, just follow my car,' says the policeman and strides over to a police car that is parked on the side of the road. and talks to the driver and then immediately waves them forward. They follow the squad car with its lights flashing and siren wailing to a nearby hospital. Julian quickly parks their car and they both rush into casualty.

'We're both doctors,' says Julian, as they push their way in. 'We just saw what happened on the television and are here to help in any way we can.'

'You'll find gowns through there,' says an orderly, pointing them in the right direction. They move through, donning their gowns as they go, getting to the casualty area which is now full of patients and with more arriving by the minute.

By evening, they are dead on their feet. The casualties thank God have slowed to a trickle of people but of these, some have serious wounds, having been fortunately found under the surface rubble as the fire service and other organisations started the enormous task of picking through what's left of the structures in a vain attempt to find others caught in the debris. Alicia sits for a while; an orderly has pushed a much-needed coffee into her hands. It's late now but there are still people being brought in. She sits looking down the corridor resting her tired legs. She's been on her feet now for almost nine hours without a break and at one stage was wondering when this tragedy would come to an end.

'Alicia Ashfield, there's a phone call from a Senator King for you at reception,' says a nurse who appears as tired as she is. 'You can take it in here if you'd like to, Doctor; the rush has thankfully petered out. He evidently rang earlier and the staff member who answered said you and your husband were both in surgery, so he said he'd ring back later and talk to you about how this crisis is unfolding.'

'Thanks for that, Nurse.' She takes the phone but feels she has to give this exhausted nurse some explanation for the call. 'He's my big brother. He's probably just ringing to see how I am and how we're faring down here with the casualties; he's that sort of person.' She gives the nurse a tired smile and a short laugh. 'I'm his little sister; he's always checking up on me if something has happened.'

'Hi, Abe,' she says, picking up the phone, too worn out to

say much. 'The worst of this disaster seems to be over now, but Julian and I will stay here until we're relieved sometime this evening.'

'I thought I'd better ring and find out how you and Julian were coping and that you were both okay and if you needed anything at the hospital?'

'We're fine, Abe, thank you for ringing. I'm afraid I'm just a little tired, that's all. There have been people everywhere coming in non-stop through the doors all day. It was what I'd imagine a casualty station in a war zone would be like after a large battle, like you see on MASH. This place was full when Julian and I first arrived here, and they just kept on coming into casualty, filling every piece of space. It eased off two hours ago and it shouldn't be long until we are relieved.'

'I'm glad to hear that you're holding up, Sis. A friend of ours was worried about you so I'll email him and let him know that you and Julian are both okay. He'll be pleased to know. Now, is there anything I can do to help? Anything that you know they're short of because you've only got to ask, and I'll get whatever you want?'

'No, there's nothing that springs to mind, Abe, just a shower and a good sleep, that's all I want,' her tired, inquisitive mind immediately takes over. 'Who wanted to know if we were okay because I can ring them later and thank them for their kind thoughts?'

'Oh, just some old friend,' he says, quite on guard. This reaction surprises her, immediately raising her curiosity as to who it is. Why doesn't he give her a name so she can answer the call? 'When this is over, we'll have to get out for a meal or something and have a few laughs together. We'll all deserve one after this fiasco is over. I've got to go now, Sis, but stay in touch and please call me if you need anything at the hospital.'

'That will be nice, Abe, we'd appreciate that,' but her tired mind is still thinking of his comments about the friend who was interested in her welfare. It puzzles her particularly because he didn't give her the person's name. 'I'll give you a call when all this dies down and we're back to normal.'

Alicia ponders over Abe's comment, trying to figure out their identity. Someone who wanted to know if she was okay, she thought. *Someone wants to know if I'm okay,* she thinks. *It's the sort of thing people ask when they haven't seen someone for a long, long time and a disaster occurs.* She thinks hard, but only knows one person intimately who would ask such a question and who also knew Abe, but it couldn't be him. *He's dead; he's been dead for almost thirty years. It just can't be him.* She shakes her head, trying to snap out of the ridiculous thoughts. *I'm being totally stupid even thinking of Pete at a time like this. Come on girl, wake up, be sensible and for heaven's sake, get your act together!*

Perth

'The Americans have sent a request to the Prime Minister for the Australian armed forces to assist in an invasion force for Afghanistan,' the unit commanding officer tells the officers and sergeants assembled before him in the mess. 'They have identified the terrorist organisation of Al Qaeda as the group responsible for blowing up the twin towers in New York. They've evidently been given a safe haven in Afghanistan by the ruling Taliban Government who unfortunately appear to be thumbing their noses at international law and seem quite happy to allow Al Qaeda and the mastermind – a man called Osama Bin Laden who is their leader and the man responsible for thinking of and organising the attack on the twin towers. When I say "thumbing their noses", The Taliban is allowing him to stay in Afghanistan. The Americans have made the decision to invade Afghanistan in an attempt to capture this perpetrator and the first troops to be sent in will be special forces from a number of countries. The Prime Minister will be making an announcement on our commitment tomorrow. I will now hand you over to your Squadron OC to go through what the squadron is required to do.'

The officer in charge systematically goes through the training schedule set out for us telling us that it will be upgraded and to get our patrols to an extreme state of readiness for the upcoming commitment in Afghanistan.

Afghanistan

I stare through the binoculars towards the cave entrance and watch as people walk in and out. They are dressed like Afghans but there are some that seem to be different; their skin seems much lighter almost as if these people are Europeans. There are six of us perched delicately on one of the many peaks that seem to go on forever, almost to the sky, in this bleak country, but they come to a sudden stop just before the clouds, giving us a panoramic view of our surroundings. Unfortunately, we're not here for these scenic wonders; we are here to find out what the Taliban are doing in these caves, so these magnificent views of this desolate landscape are entirely wasted on us as we have much more important fish to fry.

I'm in a different group with different patrol members as One Squadron was short of a sergeant. I quickly transferred across as this gives me the opportunity for adventure in totally different conditions to what I'm used to and these high, rugged hills fascinate me. It also gives me the opportunity to rid the world of some of these fanatical religious zealots who I have no time for; no matter what religion they belong to, they are causing so much unnecessary grief to innocent people by trying to thrust their stupid beliefs down their throats. This I find totally abhorrent and has nothing to do with any religious beliefs that I know of.

'What do you think of this little gathering the Taliban are holding down there?' I ask Terry, who has carefully wormed his way up to the top of this little peak and comes in next to me. 'They're dressed like Afghans at first glance, but there's something about them that doesn't quite fit the bill. I reckon some of them are definitely Europeans trying to look like Afghanis. You watch them for a while, Terry, and note their mannerisms and tell me what you think. To me, after studying them, they certainly aren't Afghans. It's my reckoning that they're from countries outside this place. Those blokes have got to be Al Qaeda; so, what are the bastards doing here? That's the big question I keep asking myself each time I look down at these brain-washed fools of people.'

I pass the binoculars over to Terry, a Lance Corporal who I'd found to be a good soldier with a great sense of humour. He takes hold of the glasses, rolls the adjustment back slightly before he fits them to his eyes and squints downwards towards the people gathered at the cave entrance. He patiently watches the figures milling around outside the caves, moving his gaze from figure to figure, inspecting each one as they gather around; just as if they are soldiers ready to form up for a parade, clearly waiting for someone to call them to attention and get into line. It's quite obvious that they are waiting for someone or something of importance or of some significance to arrive at any moment in front of this cave.

'Those two across to the left I'd say are definitely European, just from their stance, they're different,' he says, handing me back the binoculars to have another look at these individuals he's picked out. 'Have a real good look at them, Sarge; just their mannerisms for a start are different to the Afghanis I've seen. They are almost like us with their actions and have a hard look at their skin, which is far too fair, almost too light. They've been in the sun, that's obvious as they are brown but have a good look at their complexions – look at their hair; it isn't black like you see with the Afghans we've run into so far. Those two across there are definitely of European origin and you can bet there are more of these people involved that we can't see.'

I carefully scrutinise the two men Terry has mentioned, and I reckon he's right about them, particularly what he said about the hair. They are also standing slightly apart to one side talking as if they are waiting for something to arrive but what? Suddenly there's the distinct sound of motors and immediately the figures below look across to the left to where a rough track comes into the cave complex and soon two very beaten-up trucks, probably of Russian origin, come rattling their way down the track into the open area near two large boulders to the other side just in front of the main cave complex.

'They've got company,' I tell him as the trucks come to a halt in the middle of the group who enthusiastically gather around the rear of the vehicles as if they are to carrying something of importance. 'What the *hell* is in those two trucks? They all seem to have been waiting for them but where did they come from? I would have thought that the Yanks would've had the roads closed around here by now so vehicles of any persuasion couldn't use them?'

'They may not expect the Afghans to be using trucks, Pete.'

We watch as the figures below rush around quickly unloading what appears to be long crates from the rear of the two trucks and carrying them swiftly into one of the caves out of sight. It takes about ten minutes before they've emptied the trucks of their loads before moving the empty vehicles around behind a large rock formation. There's a flurry of activity as we watch camouflage netting being dragged out of the back and arranged quickly over them, so they are virtually invisible from the air.

'It's almost dark, we'll try to attach a tracking device to the trucks so we know where they go when they leave this place,' I tell him, wondering where the trucks could have come from, thinking it will certainly be a bonus if we can find their place of origin because it's most likely some form of primitive transport hub that Al Qaeda or the Taliban are using and who knows what other forms of motorised transport they have stored there? If we can find this base it will have to be a prime target for the Americans to destroy with their planes or for people like us to stick a raid in on their base. 'Get Smithy and the other blokes up here and they can cover us just in case we're seen on the way down to the trucks.'

Terry leaves me on top of the ridge and worms his way back some twenty metres to where the others have set up a small defensive perimeter on the lea side of the ridge in amongst a large group of boulders and are covering our rear.

'Sarge wants you to move up and give us some covering fire if we need it later,' he tells them, giving them a smug look. 'The crafty old bugger has something up his sleeve; he'll tell you about it when we get up to him.'

I move back just over the brow of the hill and meet them as they come slithering up towards me, bringing everything with them, almost enough hardware to start World War Three in these bleak hills.

'Two trucks just came in, fellas, and the Taliban we've been watching have just unloaded large crates. Terry and I are going down to fix tracking devices on those two vehicles they have hidden behind some large boulders just down there. I want to try to find out where they go and more importantly what they've just brought into these caves because it could have some strategic value to this area and may give us some idea of what this group is up to. Hewey, when it's dark, set the big gun up there so you can cover us as we make our way down this ridge to the trucks. Now, the only guard we've been able to locate so far is across the valley in that position over there,' I point out the sentry who can be plainly seen sitting in the shadows of a large group of boulders some good five hundred metres directly across the valley from us, and then point out to the route we intend to take to get to the trucks. 'It'll be dark shortly and the sentry shouldn't be able to see us, so as soon as we can I want to move down the escarpment without being detected and go to where they've parked those trucks and see if we can find out firstly what their cargo was and secondly attach these tracking devices to both vehicles. Both of us will be wearing our night vision glasses so don't fire unless you are fired on first, or worse still, Terry and I get into trouble. It's almost dark enough now so we'll see you fellas in a little while when we get back.'

They set the fire support base up as soon as it's dark with the fifty-calibre sniper rifle the centrepiece of their defence. They watch as we leave going down the leeward side of our hill out of sight of the Taliban lookout to the bottom of the valley. Once down, we move quietly around to the left until we can just see the outlines of the two trucks that are hidden from the air in amongst this large group of huge boulders. The light is now almost gone, so we fit our night vision goggles in place on our helmets and wait until it's fully dark before we attempt to cover the last little open stretch of ground to the trucks, just in case they have another sentry stationed in the mouth of the cave. It's dark enough now, so we cautiously move over this last short open stretch to where the camouflaged vehicles have been parked.

'You cover me while I attach the tracking devices up under the trucks onto the chassis,' I whisper to Terry who's quietly looking towards the entrance of the caves, now fully alert for anyone coming back to the trucks for some reason. 'I'll put them well up under the tray so they shouldn't find them unless they do a complete vehicle search, and they'll only do one of those if we're seen near these vehicles.'

'Right, Sarge; go to it. I'm right behind you. I should have a good view of the cave mouth from this side of the front wheel.'

We stealthily move towards the trucks, knowing the only way we'll find out where they came from is to fix one of these tracking devices to each of these vehicles somewhere high on the sub-frame. Once that's done, we will have a quick look in the trucks to try and establish what their cargo was before getting back to the rest of the patrol without being detected. I reach the first one with Terry five feet behind me. I crouch down, sliding under the vehicle and fix the tracking device high up under the chassis, well out of sight of anyone who is having a random look under the truck. With this done, we move on to the next truck, which is over by another large boulder and the closest to the known position of the enemy sentry and the cave. Again, I slide under the truck. I place my rifle on the ground near the tyre and reach up, trying to fix the tracking device high up on its chassis. I just feel the small magnets clicking into place on the chassis and am about to move the device further along when I hear Terry suddenly whisper out a warning.

'We have company – two people coming from the caves this way, Sarge. Keep still; I'm coming under the truck with you. Here's your rifle.'

He quietly slips under the truck with me, carefully pushing my rifle across so I can grasp hold of the weapon. So, huddling together with our rifles at the ready, we wait for the people Terry had seen approaching our position. Finally, I see two shadowy figures coming towards us from the direction of the cave, casually talking as they continue to approach the truck and finally stop just by the truck's door. They are so close that if Terry put out his hand, he could grab the nearest one's leg. They stand there, both lighting up a cigarette, totally ignorant of our presence when the taller one reaches up and opens the door, sending a bright shaft of light splashing out of the doorway as if he's getting something out of the cab. It's a relief to finally hear the door close and once again find we're in total darkness. We're more relieved when they start talking again to each other while they finish smoking their cigarettes, but what they say staggers me because they are speaking in English.

'What's a Pom like you doing up here with these primitive people?' comes the voice of the smaller of the two, a voice that sends a shiver straight up my spine.

Bloody hell, he's a damn Australian. What's he doing here up here?

'I changed over to Islam some five years ago and have been up here for well over two years now,' says a very plummy English voice, reminding me almost immediately of one of my history teachers at school. 'I've been working as an aide-de-camp for Bin Laden now for almost a year,' he utters with the obnoxious snigger of a confident man, his plummy accent instantly annoying me and telling me that he's had the privilege of a private school education. 'He gives me important little jobs like this to further our cause. These people wanted anti-aircraft rockets to combat the Americans, so he got what they wanted from our dealers. Then he asked me to bring them through to this cave so they can be distributed to our troops throughout this region. I'll go back first thing in the morning as soon as it's light.' He takes a large confident drag out of his cigarette as if emphasising this important role he has.

'Why don't you men travel at night; you'd be less likely to be seen by the Americans?'

'Good question, my friend. We travel mostly during the day because it's not safe to drive at night in these mountains, having to use your lights. The blasted Yanks have planes everywhere and bomb any light they see moving through these hills as they are using drones to photograph damn near every valley in the country. We find daylight hours are much safer as there is much less chance of detection in all these hills unless they have people out watching every road which they don't.'

'Do you think these illiterate blokes that are here will know how to use these rockets? I've been told they are a very sophisticated weapon and to get a good aim, they will obviously need expert training to know how to use them,' says the Australian, lighting up his second fag off the first before throwing the butt down a foot from Terry's arm and screwing it out with his boot. 'Some of their troops, if you could call them that, are quite primitive from what I've seen and leave quite a lot to be desired – especially if you got into any sort of fire fight with something like you brought in today. Now tell me, how are they going to learn the intricacies of how to use more sophisticated weapons such as these anti-aircraft rockets that you brought us this afternoon? I'm afraid they're a little more sophisticated than using a rifle or one of those commo

RPG's, especially if they want to hit a fast-moving aircraft. I'll tell you now, James, there's a lot more to weapons like those than just putting the damn thing on your shoulder and pulling the trigger.'

'Are you a trained soldier, Stewart? You appear to know a lot about these rockets I brought in this afternoon.' the Pom says in his cock-sure voice, the voice of a dandy who at the best of times would have annoyed me immensely. 'These people you tend to denigrate will fight when they have to; you just watch them particularly with these arms because you may learn something from them. When Salaam starts teaching them to fire these rockets, you'll find they'll shoot down many American planes as these weapons have a good range. The Americans will regret ever coming to this place when these rockets start knocking their planes out of the sky in these mountains. These people you call primitive will make sure of that; I can assure you the Americans will lose many planes in these hills to these rockets once we have the Afghanis trained to fire them properly.'

'Look James, I did three years in our infantry, so I know about guns and shooting military hardware. I almost went to Timor, but they downgraded the conflict and decided to send up bloody reservists instead; that's when I pulled the pin and came up here.'

I listen, almost laughing, as this silly prick rambles on. I wonder what his Pommy mate thinks of him, listening to the drivel he is spruiking but with his next statement, I have to really control myself.

'You give me decent arms to use and send me against those bloody Yanks and I'll soon show you what soldiering is all about.'

They discuss this conflict with verbal diarrhoea for another fifteen minutes before they've finally had enough of each other and, still talking, slowly walk back towards the caves.

'I've never heard so much crap in all my life,' Terry mutters, looking across as they disappear into the cave before swinging his gaze back at me. 'I'd like to meet these self-centred pricks one day and sort them out. *Bloody hell*; I'd soon show those bastards what bloody soldiering is all about.'

'You'll get your chance, Terry, because they told us exactly what was in the boxes those two trucks brought in this afternoon but let's get back to the others and call base and let them know before any more of these fanatical pricks come out to the trucks and we have to shoot them before we die laughing.'

There are no more interruptions. Fortunately, this allows us to finish placing the last tracking device properly and get out from under the truck before carefully working our way back up the hill to the others. They have obviously watched the two men talking by the truck and you can bet Hewey had them lined up and is now watching us coming in because we don't hear a peep out of them until we get to their position; another good advantage of the night vision glasses. I pull the men back just over the ridge to our former position, leaving one man on the top of the hill to observe any movement at either the caves or the trucks.

'Break out the radio,' I tell Plonkey as soon as we're down to our resting position. 'We've got important information to send back concerning these caves and those crates we saw the two trucks bring in this afternoon.' I go on to tell them of the conversation we overheard while under the truck. 'They were a load of ground-to-air missiles that the Afghans took into those caves. A lot of our planes and helicopters are going to be easy targets in these steep hills and gullies if those missiles are distributed widely, especially if they teach the Afghans how to use those missiles properly. From what we heard while under the trucks, there is a bloke in those caves somewhere that can do just that.'

'*Patrol B3 to Base, Observing caves at Loc stat xxx xxx. Enemy have just received two truckloads of ground-to-air missiles just before last light; I repeat, two truckloads of ground-to-air missiles. We have inserted tracking devices on the two trucks which brought them in so they can be monitored back to their base. Some Western activists are also involved here with this Taliban group. Over.*'

'*Base to Patrol B3. Roger, Sunray wants you to stay on air while your message is passed on to Uncle Sam. Out.*'

We change the man at the observation post and bunk down in this highly inhospitable place, but I certainly don't get any rest while waiting for an answer. It's an hour later when Plonkey receives another message from Headquarters.

'*Base to Patrol B3. Reinforcements will be arriving at loc stat zzz zzz at 08:00. Could you direct them to your location? Over.*'

'*Shit!* That's in this valley here, only two kilometres away,' I say to Plonkey who's also looking at the map I have spread out on the ground, obviously wondering what we'll do. 'The Afghanis down there will certainly be up and hear the choppers come in from the cave and they'll know there's something dramatically wrong.' By this time, everyone is awake, so I have to make a quick decision. 'Terry, you and Smithy go out now to this loc stat and meet the reinforcements and we'll hold this position until you get back because it's quite bloody obvious that the Afghanis are going to hear the choppers coming in and scoot off with their ordinance before the Yanks get here and we certainly can't allow any of that type of missile to get out and be used against our planes because they'll be easy targets in these bloody hills. We'll get into a good position and hold them down until you fellas get back, so you'd better not be too bloody late and allow the Yanks to have a cup of coffee before they set off.'

'Patrol B3 to Base, Will meet Americans at loc stat zzz zzz at 08:00 hours and guide them into position at these caves. Out.'

'Okay, Sarge. We'll go now,' he says, pulling his pack on and certainly not very pleased with having to head off at this critical time of night and obviously realises that he'll probably miss a lot of the action. He knows though that this is a very important task he is being asked to do. 'You've gotta promise us, Sarge, that you won't hog the lot and leave a few of the Abduls for me and Smithy when we get back.'

I watch Terry and Smithy disappear down the hill into the murky darkness and move quite rapidly away from the caves, taking full advantage of their night glasses. I turn to the others to let them know what my plan of attack will be.

'We'll have to get in closer to the caves and, if I'm right and they come out to do their familiarisation with the rockets before the choppers arrive, we'll have to keep them from getting back to the caves, if it's at all possible. We'll try to pin them down out in the open until the Yanks arrive. This will make it much better for us than having them go back into their caves and could certainly save us from taking casualties if we have to go in after them and hunt them down in their stinking rat holes.'

'When I was up at the O.P., I noticed some ledges just to the left of the big cave,' Plonkey points out. 'If we could get down there, that should give us cover from the floor of the valley. The gun would be able to cover the three main caves that the rag-heads seem to be using most of the time. The rest of you buggers would be able to stitch the others up quite easily if they hear the choppers coming and we should be able to stop anyone from getting back in the caves because I don't fancy going in to get the bastards out of there.'

'Good thinking, Plonkey,' I tell the little man who obviously has been having a really good look around while he was on the observation post. 'I should keep Hewey and the gun at the top but I'm loath to split us again so the remainder of us will stick together. It would be best if we get into position now so we are ready for whatever happens in the morning but please be aware of their sentry as he will be looking straight down on us from his position up on that ridge.'

We carefully move down the inside of the ridge, avoiding the sentry who hopefully is asleep just on the ridge on the other side of the cave. To me, they've been very slack not changing him before last light, so hopefully the poor bastard is worn out. Finally, we're in position and now it's only a matter of time waiting for morning to come.

I run a piquet so we can get a little shut-eye as the night drags on slowly but finally the sun starts creeping over the large hills in all its glory and begins to throw weird, almost medieval shapes over the valley floor; first it's light with no warmth at all. It's at this time when the two truck drivers appear and walk briskly over to their partially camouflaged vehicles, talking as they go. It's pleasing to see they do no testing or checks of any description on these vehicles; they just pull the camouflage netting off and then roughly roll it up and throw the stuff into the back before jumping into their trucks. They are soon driving up the bumpy track away from the caves, slow enough to make minimal dust. Soon they disappear out of our sight along this rough track. With the sun well over the hills now and its warm rays starting to beat unrelentingly down on us and the parched rocks around our hidden patrol, it soon becomes a stinking hot day. It's probably some ten minutes later when the Afghanis start to appear and begin moving around the area just below our position and I notice a relief sentry walk out of the cave and head up the hill to take over this important task from the poor bugger who spent the whole of yesterday and last night in this imposing position high above us. It's at this moment that the Taliban start carrying out a number of the large boxes from the caves and begin stacking them under cover where the trucks had sheltered during the night, making me wonder why they need so many of these sophisticated weapons outside. One of these large crates that came in yesterday is broken open and a tall thin Arab-looking man pulls out one of the sophisticated shoulder-held launchers and starts jabbering away to the others who finally have gathered around him. It's obvious he's the fella the tall man mentioned last night, who knows what the launcher is all about. He begins to explain the fundamentals to those gathered around him.

'When the shit hits the fan,' I whisper to Hewey who has the big Yank fifty-calibre sniper rifle trained on the group, 'make sure you drop that Arab-looking bastard with the launcher first because he's the key to them learning how to fire those weapons properly. From the way he's talking to them, he obviously knows something about those weapons. Now, Hewey, once he's down, your next shot is their guard because he's looking down on us. If we're able to take out their expertise and their eyes; that should slow the pricks down quite a bit until our American friends get here.'

The first indication that others are coming into the valley is the harsh braying of a mule and soon a string of these ever-reliable pack animals are led gingerly into the rock-strewn gully down the same track as the trucks had used. They are taken over and tied to a piquet line well in view of us, which stops the arms instruction with most of the Afghanis discourteously leaving the Arab and gathering around in a group with those who came in with the animals, and they begin jabbering away to the donkey handlers.

'If the Yanks are on time, the choppers should be coming in just about now; so, get ready,' I whisper to the others, looking at my watch. 'This is where the situation gets dicey, fellas, and the shit is going to hit the fan big time. Now remember, Hewey, as soon as they hear the choppers, drop that Arab and the sentry.' I point to the man who's now leaning on a large rock without his weapon, most likely quite pissed off with his pupils and looking a little bored towards the newcomers and their donkeys. 'You can plainly see the sentry up by those rocks well away from any cover without his rifle and also watching the men with the donkeys,' I whisper to the others. 'I don't want to let any of these other bastards get back in those caves or move any of those crates they have out of this valley.' As a good afterthought to slow them down, I tell Plonkey, 'You drop a few of those donkeys as well if you get half a chance. That will definitely slow them down quite a bit and will certainly stop them getting any of those crates out of this valley.'

These words of wisdom are hardly out of my mouth when in the distance the distinct sound of the large *Chinook* helicopters can be plainly heard coming in this direction, causing the Taliban just in front of us to stop what they're doing and start looking into the northern sky for some sign of these aircraft.

'*Now*,' I tell them and immediately Hewey drops the Arab and then the sentry high above us and we hose the rest of the group with our small arms, just as they are about to start moving back towards the cave. 'Keep them away from the caves and the boxes because we're going to be by ourselves for at least fifteen to twenty minutes until the Yanks from those choppers can get up to the rim of this valley. Shit, it would've been just as good to land on the rim of this valley as the Taliban know they're here anyway.'

Two Kilometres Away

Terry has thrown smoke and Smithy is signalling the first chopper in when he suddenly hears the familiar sounds of gunfire echoing through the valley behind him making him aware of our predicament.

'*Shit*! It's started already,' he tells Smithy, as he hears the cascading fire of our rifles and the large distinctive crack of Hewey's large sniper rifle. 'I hope these bastards don't drag their feet getting out of the choppers because we've got to get back to the Sarge and our blokes – they're going to need all the help we can give 'em.'

The American troops stream out of the large *Chinooks* and over towards where they wait. There are two helicopters and about forty men all armed to the teeth. An officer comes over to Terry.

'Are you our guide, soldier?' comes the curt question to Terry. Then he hears the noise of the rifles behind him. 'What's all that goddamn gun rifle fire we can hear just over the lip of the hill, soldier?'

'The Taliban would have heard you coming in, Sir,' Terry tells him, hastily wanting to get him moving. 'We'll have to move fast if we want to get to them in time, Sir, because Pete is holding them down for us. Follow me and we'll show you exactly where to go.'

The Cave Complex

We are now getting return fire from a small cave high up on the hill and the bullets are clattering far too close for comfort.

'You'll have to get that prick in the cave,' I tell Hewey unnecessarily just as the big rifle roars and the shooting stops. 'Well done. You keep an eye on the caves and we'll concentrate on the others below us.'

'Sarge, *I think they're re-grouping over near the remainder of the donkeys,*' Plonkey yells out as the incoming fire almost stops with only the odd round periodically thumping into the rocks close by.

There are probably twenty bodies close to the boxes and three of the seven donkeys are down. The Taliban had broken the dragline and are now holding the others just out of sight as the remainder of the donkeys who have smelt the blood of their companions frantically try to pull free of their leads and bolt to safety.

'If I was them, I'd try and get around behind us, Sarge,' says Murphy, looking back towards the hill that we'd come down last night. 'If some of them got to our old position, they'll be able to shoot straight down on us and, unfortunately, we won't have any cover from that point. *Hell!* I hope those Yanks don't stuff around and brew up or take their time getting here.'

It's been a good thirty minutes now since we heard the choppers and had opened up on the Taliban. We've stopped the movement of the rockets and killed the instructor, but, if they are able to get around behind us, we'll be in dire straits because on this ledge we're firing from, we'll be out in the open from our old position. *Come on Terry and Mr America, we need you here desperately now*, I think to myself, a little frustrated at what I think is getting here far too slowly. The next instant, there is a whooshing sound, and a vapour trail leaves one of the caves and races towards our position. There is a great gust of air above our heads and then a huge explosion well behind us. We're showered with burning metal and rock fragments that start falling around us from the missile when it explodes.

'The bastards are using either RPGs or one of their rocket launchers at us,' Plonkey says, quite excitedly. 'I'll try and pick the *prick* off. I'll bet that was a warm-up and he'll have a second shot real soon. Come on you bastard, show yourself.'

We wait tentatively, quite nervously watching the cave entrance and finally see something that looks like a pipe move slowly around the corner of the cave and start to line us up. You can just see the dark figure of a man with the launcher on his shoulder trying desperately to keep in the shadows as he takes aim toward us.

'*Now,*' I tell Plonkey again unnecessarily as he fires at the figure at the mouth of the cave, and I'm pleased to see a man stagger into view just as he pulls the trigger and the next instant a rocket screams into the air well above us and we watch as the vapour trail surges harmlessly into the sky. The projectile appears to run out of steam and falls over the brow of the hill and we hear the muffled roar of the explosion somewhere behind us. A single shot rings out from behind us, kicking up dust off the rock in front of me. We turn but can't see anything. Next, a fusillade of automatic fire comes from over near where the donkeys are being held, forcing us down diving for cover. The Taliban have finally worked a way out to pick us off. We keep our heads down when a second shot comes in, ricocheting off the rock and missing Hewey by just a few inches.

'*Hewey, try and get a bead on the bastard that's behind us!*' I frantically yell out to our sniper. '*Throw your packs over to Hewey so he'll have some protection and then make yourselves as small as you can but keep an eye on the front.*'

Just as I speak, the morning is shattered by a short burst of automatic fire, and I'm pleased to see a body roll down the hill towards us. Thankfully, at last, the cavalry has finally arrived just in the nick of time. I can see shapes of people taking up firing positions on the ridge and start sending a withering storm of bullets towards the Taliban who are now forced to take refuge where they parked the trucks last night.

'Phew, just in the nick of time,' says Hewey, reading my mind, as he aims his rifle up at what looks like an Arab who decides that discretion is the best part of valour and makes a mad dash for the safety of the caves. The big rifle cracks, jumping in his hands with the recoil, and we see the turbaned figure knocked over; he doesn't move. 'Got you, you bastard. That'll teach these pricks to stuff around with us.'

The Americans, who must be in at least company strength, have already reached the floor of the valley and are using a classical system of fire and movement to get around behind the Taliban. Initially, I think that it might be a hard slog, but I soon notice the enemy putting their hands in the air, surrendering. The American soldiers quickly move through the prisoners, professionally searching them for concealed weapons, making them lie on the ground and binding their hands behind their backs with plastic ties.

'Be careful, there are more in those caves over there,' I tell them pointing to where they came from, not taking my eyes off the cave entrance. 'There were people shooting at us from the caves a few minutes before you got here. There are also more rockets in there somewhere so keep an eye on the caves, for God's sake.'

'I almost missed all the fun,' says Terry, finally coming up to us with Smithy. 'These Yanks were really keen to get in amongst them, particularly when that rocket was lobbed over the hill. Hell! They almost sprinted here the last hundred metres when they heard all the shooting and did they move when that rocket exploded above them!' He looks about him, laughing at the reaction of the Americans. 'Is everyone okay, Sarge?'

'A few close shaves, Terry; but other than that, we're fine. They had just got around the back and took a couple of shots at us. That's when you fellas thankfully arrived with the cavalry and took care of them.'

With all the prisoners searched and bound, the next stage of the attack is to find out what type of ordinance the Taliban have in the caves and here I have to put the brakes on the American major who now is fully intending to go into these caves with lights on and guns blazing.

'You'll lose men doing it that way, Sir. Get someone to call on them to surrender and if that doesn't work, I'll be happy to go in with my men with night vision glasses and get whoever is left in the caves because most of those who aren't here are Europeans who I suspect will be Al Qaeda recruits.'

When he realises we have this sort of sophisticated equipment, he quickly agrees to let us have first chop at an assault on these caves.

'Okay, Sergeant; I'll send a squad of my men around the hill in case there are other entrances to these caves from the rear. You know what I mean, some sort of back door which will allow those assholes in the caves to escape with some of the ordinances they obviously have in there.'

When moving through the Al Qaeda people, I notice that the Australian who was mouthing off last night when we were under the truck is not among the dead or prisoners so he must still be in the cave hiding somewhere; something that doesn't surprise me from the rubbish we heard him telling the Pom last night because, he didn't fill me with enthusiasm or confidence that he was a fighter. However, it annoys me immensely having that Pommy prick get clean away particularly if he's been up here so long with the Al Qaeda because he will have had a lot of valuable information that could be extremely useful for our intelligence; so they could learn more about where their ordnance facilities are that they obviously drew these air-to-ground missiles from.

'There's at least one bastard in there that speaks English,' I tell Major Jessup as he brings up an interpreter. 'But don't let him know that we know he's an Australian. There may be more of them in there because they'd have to be Al Qaeda and, if that one's not here, there could be quite a few more still in the caves.'

'Before you go into the caves, have a look at this first,' the major tells us and gives us an A4-sized diagram of the caves. This was on one of the bodies that one of our guys found when he was searching them a few moments ago.' He puts the sketch on a rock, orientates it and goes over it in fine detail. I gather the boys around, so they know the layout of these caves. 'You go in the main entrance and move down this long passage to here where there appears to be a large chamber off to the right. Across here there is another corridor that seems to lead to smaller alcoves, which most likely could be sleeping quarters. That's probably where you'll find most of the remainder hiding.' He gives me a small smile. 'On studying this map, it appears this is the only way out, but we'll still have a look around the hill just in case there is an escape route that's not marked on this map.'

The interpreter asks through a megaphone both in English and the local language telling them to surrender. We wait for a moment, getting no response to either, so my men move up to the cave entrance with me.

'We'll work in pairs, so choose a partner. It'll be straight out of the training manual, fellas; so, which of you bunnies wants to come with me into this burrow?'

'I'm with you, Sarge. This is going to be similar to us training in the killing house at Swany,' says Terry, quickly coming up to me. 'I missed out this morning, so I'll have to make up for it now. That's fair, isn't it?'

'Right, Terry and I will move in until we're out of the light and the goggles start to work. We won't be able to contact you, so when you can't see us, the next pair move up to where we'll be waiting; just like we do in training fellas. We'll use a leap-frogging system so we can cover each other as we go in. You ready to go, Terry?'

'You bet, Sarge. Let's find that bastard that wanted to go to Timor and we'll soon give him something to think about.'

We move in, keeping close to the wall until we're well into the dark. The night goggles begin taking effect and we can finally see to the end of the tunnel, which is thankfully clear, so we wait for the next two to come up to us. I look back and can see them approaching; I give a thumbs up when they reach us before Terry, and I continue to where the large room runs off to the right. I quickly peek around the entrance and straight in front of me some five metres away are two Afghans sitting behind some crates which have been hastily stacked up in front of them for some protection. They sit close together looking towards us, manning an old Second World War Vickers-type machine gun, which is pointing menacingly straight towards the entrance. They're just waiting for the sounds of people approaching and for someone with a light to show themselves in front of the doorway. Using hand signals to alert Terry, we wait for the other two pairs to catch up. He moves quickly to the other side of the doorway where he waits for a signal from me.

Now, I signal. We both step into the doorway and put short bursts each into the two Afghans, almost cutting these two men in half from this short distance. At the same time we quickly move into the room and immediately go to ground waiting as the other two pairs do the same as us. Finally, the six of us are all in the chamber.

The room is huge; filled with crates. I suppose some are the rockets we saw being delivered yesterday but who knows what's in the others, making me wonder if we've stumbled onto some sort of training area which introduces the different nationalities we've seen yesterday to their religion and to the different types of ordinance they have in here. I signal the others to check around the crates in this cavern for other Taliban or Al Qaeda and to be wary of the types of ordinance they could find. Thankfully there are none; it's probably as the major had said, the others who are not accounted for have hidden themselves in their sleeping quarters or somewhere further inside this huge cave complex when they heard the shooting from outside.

'The sleeping quarters are the next on our agenda to check,' I tell the men using hand signals then indicate to Terry to follow me. Our biggest advantage is that we can see in this dark interior that surrounds us. I suddenly think of what would have happened if the Yanks had come in with lights on and guns blazing and lobbed grenades through the doorway. 'Same procedure, stick to your pairs, then you can back each other up if you have to. Terry and I will go to the first room; you fellas take the next and so on. Anyone holding a weapon, shoot! If there are beds, make sure you check under them. Who knows what you'll find hiding under there next to the piddling pot?'

We move down this narrow corridor in our pairs, slightly apart just in case some enemy soldier hears us and blindly puts a burst of auto fire down towards the entrance in the dark. So, working in our pairs, we start carefully going from room to room with one entering, the other backing him up. Some rooms have old beds while others have a type of mattress on the floor. Terry and I move into a room with a bed. A quick look under this primitive piece of furniture and I'm pleased to find we've got our Australian hiding there like the gutless wonder I summed him up to be after listening to the bullshit that came streaming from his mouth.

'Oh, there you are, Stewart old buddy. You can come out now because the Americans won't eat you, they're civilised people you know even though you watch strange things happen in their movies,' I tell him, hoping he won't do anything stupid. I hold the Steyr ready, almost pushing it down his throat just in case he tries something idiotic. 'Nice and slowly now my friend, put your hands where I can see them and no sharp, erratic moves; then I won't have to shoot you and make a mess of your bedroom. That's it, good boy, Stewart, just keep your hands in front where I can see them, and you can come out from under your bed. Nothing horrible will happen to you and I won't have to pull the trigger and dirty your sleeping quarters and give you a third eye or do anything uncivilised like that.'

He slowly comes out from under the bed and is soon standing in front of us looking both ways trying to see us. Knowing we can see him in this pitch-black environment, I look him directly in his face and can see the fear written all over it.

'Who are you?' he stammers, still unable to see us. 'I know you're an Australian by your voice; I'm an Australian citizen you know,' then, further grasping at straws, he surprises me with his next stupid comment. 'I want to see the Australian consul so he can make sure I'm treated fairly by you people.'

'I'm glad you have all your passport details ready, but unfortunately, that will have to wait, Stuey me boy, now just put your hands together please, Sir so I can attach them to this. Thank you, Sir. That's very nice of you to cooperate with us fully and I have to say so willingly – that's really generous. I'd say you must have had quite a lot of experience doing this sort of thing training at Singleton before you decided to get out of our army.'

Terry quickly wraps a thin plastic twine around his wrists pulling it tight while I quickly frisk him, finding a nine-mill pistol. I push him out the door, leaving him in the corridor, and move on to our next room. By the time we finish our search, we have rounded up thirteen more Taliban; seven of them are Europeans. Some of them are terrified at not being able to see us, knowing full well that we can see them. We collect these people as we move back, making them then put their bound hands on the shoulder of the man in front. Finally, our search is complete so with this conga line, we walk out into the bright sunlight, straight into the welcoming arms of our American friends who are amazed at the speed we achieved in the cave complex and what we've just accomplished with our search.

'Goddamn it, man. When we heard the shooting, we just about came in guns blazing but we didn't know where you guys were, so we kinda held back for a little and waited for you to finish your search.'

'I'm glad you didn't go in, Major. There's enough ammunition in there to just about lift this whole bloody mountain,' I tell him, thinking that if I exaggerate a little, they will treat it more carefully when they go in. 'The big room is chock-a-block with munitions of all descriptions so tread softly in case they've booby-trapped some of the boxes.' I then tell him of the two with the old machine gun waiting for someone with a light to come along. This makes him think for a few seconds because that's exactly what they would have done; lost the first few men at the entrance to the machine gun. When that failed, they would have lobbed a few grenades into the room which would have probably ignited the ammunition and blown everything sky-high in the mountain – including themselves.

All the other caves in the area are thoroughly checked out next but it appears that the only thing they've been used for is sleeping. We find a few more of these primitive sleeping areas but no more men or arms are found in these, except in one, there is quite an amount of documents that should make interesting reading for American intelligence and hopefully shine a light on what's going on in this region and give us some significant knowledge of what this complex was used for.

I' have just had Base on the line, Sarge,' Plonkey tells me, putting his headset down and turning towards me, quite excited. 'We're to come in with the Americans and the prisoners. They seemed quite interested that we'd caught an Australian with the Taliban and want us to bring him in for questioning.'

CHAPTER 13

THE STORY IS OUT

New York

Alicia has had a tiring day at the clinic. Cancer is a horrid disease in adults, she thinks, but to have a child of ten diagnosed with this debilitating, mostly fatal disease, is a travesty that she has difficulty explaining. For the last hour, she had been examining a small girl who could have had a wonderful life but had been sitting in front of her with her hair gone from the chemotherapy and absolutely nothing whatsoever to look forward to.

If only there was a vaccine that children such as this could have, she thinks as the mother and child leave. *What is it that causes this horrible disease to infect people so young? Is it in the production of what we eat or something we use regularly? What are our communities doing wrong that's causing a horrible ailment like this to happen?*

'Sorry to bother you, Doctor but there's a Mr O'Flaherty

here to see you,' says the receptionist, poking her head in the door, bringing Alicia's mind back into focus and away from the plight of this unfortunate patient. 'He's a reporter for the *Daily Globe*; he says it's about a mutual acquaintance you both have.'

'Send him in please, Stella; I've finished my work for the day,' Alicia tells her, causing her to wonder what a reporter would want with her. 'Could it be something to do with September Eleven?' she asks her receptionist, quite puzzled at why he's here. 'Have you any idea what this reporter wants with me because I hope he's not going to bring up Nine-Eleven again because I've already covered that well over two weeks ago.'

'I'm sorry, Doctor, I have no idea what he wants; he just arrived at my desk and asked if he could see you. I've read a number of articles he's written for the paper from East Timor. I think he's some sort of war correspondent; you know, the type of person you see on television. He appears to be one of those people who follow different flash-points around the globe reporting details of the conflicts we're involved in; though we didn't have men in Timor during their vote for independence.'

Kerry O'Flaherty had been home from East Timor for a number of months and had almost fully recovered from his wounds when he was in New York and had witnessed the tragedy of Nine Eleven on television. He later read an article on the husband-and-wife doctors, Julian Ashfield and Alicia King, working in together in a hospital, treating casualties from this disaster. The wife's name was one he immediately linked to the dreams of Peter Jackson of the Australian army; the young sergeant who had befriended Tiffany before she was tragically killed by the militia. He had listened to the tape again to make sure of the name. He knew he'd told Jackson when in the hospital that this was the finish of it, but a story is a story and this one could be exceptional if it goes the way he thinks it could.

He'd gone back to Tiffany's house after he left the hospital to collect her personal effects for her relatives and had also retrieved the recorder that was still under the bed. He'd sat on Tiffany's bed and listened to the final tape; a recording of Jackson's last night there which had started with when he woke up in the Ho Chi Minh Research Centre. Most of the dialogue had been spoken in Vietnamese, which staggered him, for he wouldn't expect a young soldier to learn a language he'd never use.

While he was a reporter over there, he learned how to speak the language so he was now able to understand most of the dialogue. He stood amazed, listening to these conversations Jackson allegedly had with the girl Noc and the fishermen while making his escape to Singapore. What had staggered him the most was that these events were not in the days of the Vietnam War as he'd heard previously but had happened just over twelve months ago. Jackson spoke most of the time in Vietnamese; something that would be impossible for a man to speak if he'd never been in that country before. Hell, what had he stumbled on *this* time? This question started ringing through his active mind; bringing out the excitement of a huge story; one that he had difficulty believing himself. It was impossible for a man Jackson's age to recount from listening to recordings his father's friends had made in journals of that war – covering an event with a span of well over thirty years.

'Come in, Mr O'Flaherty.' Alicia smiles as Kerry walks into her surgery. 'What can I do for you? I hope it's not about Nine-Eleven because I've already told the reporters some weeks ago what happened.'

'Yes, I read about what you and your husband did in one of our papers just after I came back from Timor. It was very commendable the unselfish sacrifice you and your husband gave to those people in that totally unnecessary man-made calamity,' he says, wondering what tack he should take with this woman and, as he soon gathers, she's no fool. He decides to firstly see if she knew this Australian sergeant. He decides to be direct with his questions so there is no misunderstanding by her about who he's referring to. 'Doctor, I won't beat around the bush, I'll be quite blunt with you. Do you know a Sergeant Peter Jackson? He's a member of the Australian Army who I was fortunate to meet in Timor.'

Her face goes a grey colour as she finds it hard to control her emotions after this tiring day. Then this stranger mentions his name out of the blue; a name that is etched firmly in her mind.

He watches her slowly sit down, as though she's extremely tired and quite shocked at the mention of Jackson's name.

'I was engaged to be married to a Peter Jackson almost thirty years ago. He went missing in action in Vietnam. From what I could find out from the Australian military, he dropped off the end of a rope and his body was never found,' she says, her hands trembling a little, wondering where this is leading. 'What do you know of him? It was a long time ago when this happened, and I've fortunately been able to move on with my life and get over this tragedy. Have his remains been found somewhere on the jungle floor, is that what these questions are about?' Tears spring to her eyes, and she shakes her head in confusion. 'You … you said you met him in Timor?'

'May I sit down while you listen to a recording that was taken in East Timor some months ago? I find it extremely confusing myself; so, you may be able to help clear up quite a number of questions this recording brings forward. This was taken by a friend of mine who unfortunately was killed doing a story over there during a bid to gain independence.'

Although upset, Alicia sits patiently, looking across the desk and wondering what she'll hear as O'Flaherty sets the device on the table in front of her. Completely confused, she wonders what she'll hear and can't imagine what a recording of a man that was taken less than twelve months ago has to do with her and her Peter.

'As I told you, this recording was taken by a colleague of mine a number of months ago while this soldier slept.' He tries to reinforce the newness and the authenticity of what she is about to hear, being very careful not to mention the age of the soldier. He will keep that up his sleeve for a little while and if he has to tell her, he'll pick the right moment. That will only be if circumstances force him to do so. 'The voice of this man is quite clear so you should have no difficulty hearing what is being said.'

The voice comes through very clearly. He's talking of Vietnam, they are on an ambush patrol, he goes over it detail by detail, a firefight at a Landing Zone, the helicopters go and he's on his own. The person finds himself moving through the bush, killing the Viet Cong on the ox cart and saving the man who'd been tied to the back. The voice goes on giving detail after detail; this time, in America and again, the man gives intimate detail of how he met this beautiful girl called Alicia.

By this time, Kerry has his eyes riveted on Alicia as she is listening, her mouth open, not moving a muscle, too engrossed to utter a sound. She is spellbound at the sounds coming out of the machine as the voice describes the ring he'd bought to show Abe when they went on a hunting trip.

He notices her subconsciously rubbing the ring on her finger, which is exactly as the voice has described. The man is back in Vietnam and talking about a number of patrols; the last one is where they are plucked out of the jungle under fire. The rope is cut by a bullet, and he finds himself falling, falling but stops talking when he hits the trees.

'Would you like to comment on what you've heard so far?' Kerry says tentatively, stopping the recorder, still without taking his eyes off her. 'Do you recognise the voice of the man speaking and … what's your opinion of what he's said?'

Alicia pauses for a long time, reminiscing about the things she's just heard before she finally answers, not trying to hold back the tears that now run down her cheeks. It has been too long, and she has shed so many tears.

'It sounded like Peter … and there are things, intimate things that only Peter and I knew, but he died when he dropped from that helicopter in late nineteen seventy,' she says, desperately trying to regain some of her composure and looking directly into Kerry's eyes. 'How did you get the recording, Mr O'Flaherty? Is this a joke because I don't understand what you are trying to prove?'

'It's no joke I can assure you, Doctor,' Kerry tells her, surprised that she thinks this is a cruel joke. 'There are no dubbings, the recording has not been doctored and it is a direct recording of the man talking in his sleep. Would you like me to play the rest of what is recorded and then we can have a chat about the outcome? Unfortunately, most of the dialogue is in Vietnamese but I can translate it for you.'

'Yes, I'd like to hear the remainder.' Alicia gathers her strength; she has to know.

There's something beneath me. Heavens; it's a girl. Someone is pulling me over. I feel terrible, my eyes hurt as if I've had sand thrown in them. What are they doing to me? I'll try to get up. There's another girl running out of the room.

The voice is now confusing because some of it is in Vietnamese. 'I don't expect you to understand Vietnamese, Doctor,' he says, pausing the recorder as if waiting for her consent. 'If it's alright with you I'll translate what's being said for you, so you understand exactly what's going on.'

'Thank you, Mr O'Flaherty.'

Kerry clears his throat and begins. 'I've got to get up, she's finally helping me," he says, and he goes over detail upon detail naming the girl. "There are people coming. Oh *shit*! They're soldiers." He describes shooting the two soldiers … and how the girl aids his escape. He is completely rejecting what they keep telling him, that he's been asleep for almost thirty years in a glass case in the … the Ho Chi Minh Centre. He talks at length in Vietnamese to the girl while he drives first to Haiphong and then, then south to a fishing village where he describes taking a fishing boat. They are out of the heads and, with the aid of the Vietnamese fishermen, set a course for Singapore.'

He quickly brushes over the killing of the five Thai pirates, thinking she doesn't need to hear about that in detail.

'Finally, he's speaking in English when he's making his escape to Singapore. That's where the recording finished,' Kerry tells her, taking note of her look of absolute amazement and shock at hearing this recording. 'I was as staggered as you with this story and a week later he came along with Tiffany to my office and told me he was Peter Jackson's son. So, we left it at that. However, he makes reference to events that a son could not know without talking to his father and he obviously never did. He is *some* soldier let me tell you, Doctor. He avenged Tiffany's murder in such a way that I think his actions in Dili finished the militia's stranglehold on East Timor.'

He then goes on to explain to her how he gathered the final recording.

'After I was discharged from hospital, I went around to Tiffany's flat to gather up her belongings to send home and found the final recording, which puts a whole new dimension onto this amazing story.' He again pauses before informing her of the award. 'Peter was awarded the Australian Medal of Gallantry for his services in East Timor – when under his orders his patrol saved the two women's lives. This medal was awarded on his return to Australia by their government.'

'How do you know all this?' Alicia asks, quite dumbfounded by the final part of the recording. 'I've been a doctor of medicine for thirty years, for God's sake, and I'm telling you, *no one* knows how to preserve a living being for so long. Are you trying to tell me that some obscure Vietnamese doctor was able to invent such an amazing drug in the early seventies and that Peter's body had been treated with it?'

'Yes, I believe so,' he answers very openly. He notices her acceptance of the recording, so he decides to tell her Peter Jackson's age. 'Do you know how old this man is, Doctor?' He pauses for a brief moment to let what he's saying sink in. 'This man's probably twenty-six at the most.'

'Would I be able to have a copy of this recording please, Mr O'Flaherty? I would like to keep it and play it to my brother because it's obvious that he knows Peter is alive and in the Australian army.'

'Certainly, but if there is a story, I want sole rights to it; is that understood?' His journalistic brain is taking over. 'I would also like to interview you to complete the story. Would you agree to that?'

'I have no problem with that at all,' she says. 'I'll do everything I can to help you gather more information so we can find out what the hell is going on.'

CHAPTER 14

OPERATION ANACONDA

Southern Afghanistan

The throb of the big helicopter's motors is loud in our ears as it takes us into action once again. My patrol is sitting close together in the guts of the machine as it surges through the night skies towards our drop-off point somewhere in the hills a number of kilometres from the Pakistan border. I look out of the window as we skirt between the hills, which seemingly reach well into the heavens above us. Our mission this time is quite a simple one, that is to observe a strategic pass after this operation the Americans called 'Anaconda' and if necessary, act as a blocking force to prevent members of the Taliban or Al Qaeda forces from escaping the net of the American backed Coalition of the Willing and Afghan forces into the rugged confines of the Pakistani border. The battle has seesawed back and forth and finally after some twelve days of acting as the eyes of the Coalition, the initiative has finally swung in the

Coalition's favour and it's now up to small parties like ours to cut off the retreating Al Qaeda forces that could be heading into this rugged border country to escape into Pakistan.

'First team get ready; we will be reaching your drop-off point in exactly two minutes!' yells out the American loadmaster through the darkened interior of the large *Chinook* helicopter. *'The drop-off will be a quick exit out the back so be on your toes, guys, and get ready to go because I want you all out of the aircraft as soon as the ramp goes down. When I give you guys the word to exit, I want you off my aircraft in less than one minute.'*

'Okay, fellas, listen up. You heard what the man said,' I say to my patrol as they do the last-minute adjustments to their equipment, making sure there are no rattles and everything is securely fastened onto their bodies – we can't afford any foul-ups at this late stage of our infiltration. 'As soon as he gives the word the back goes down and we touch the ground, I want you all out so stick together and go to ground as *soon* as you leave the chopper.'

The men are ready for anything with their large packs holding well over a week's rations, explosives and Claymore mines. The extra ammunition bulging in their webbing and their body armour gives them the awkward appearance of medieval knights readying for a jousting match.

'We're coming in now!' shouts the loadmaster over the roar of the engines that comes as a constant drone through the now-open rear door. I can see the dark shape of the ground coming up fast as the helicopter comes rushing towards the ground, cutting its speed somewhat, slowing down slightly as we approach the hilltop.

'Go!' yells the American slapping us on the pack as we pass him, counting us out as each person quickly runs down the ramp onto the ground, our large packs bouncing uncomfortably on our backs. We're outside in less than a quarter of a minute lying flat on our stomachs while the big helicopter lifts and continues on its way to the next drop-off point some kilometres away in another valley somewhere towards the border.

We're lost from view in the shadowy surrounds of this small, flat area used as the drop-off point. We wait and listen for any human noises; everything is deadly quiet except for the diminishing throb we can hear. The big motors of the large chopper are now some distance away and even this is soon lost in the hills as we're left alone in the dark on this still, quite eerie star-lit night.

'If my calculations are correct, we have nearly a kilometre to go as the crow flies until we're in place,' I tell Terry who has just come up to me. 'We should do that easy enough if we follow this ridge here and move down across this gully to the adjoining ridge. The track we want should be in that next valley that we will easily find when the moon comes up; so, let's get moving, fellas; I want our observation post in place as soon as possible and the rest of us in the ambush site well before daylight.'

'That sounds good to me, Sarge,' he says as he makes a final adjustment to his pack, getting ready to move out. 'With a bit of luck, we should be well in place by sunrise and then I can catch up with my beauty sleep while you buggers watch the track for some stupid pricks to come along.'

With Plonkey in the scouting position, the patrol heads out along our ridge. We're fortunate the moon is now coming up and we find there is just enough light for us to move without having to use our night vision goggles. I'm well aware that if we can see the features, so can the Taliban or Al Qaeda scouts because they may have even noticed the slightly different drone of the chopper that hovered for that brief moment when dropping us off. If they did, they would've been warned and any groups in our vicinity could possibly be looking for intruders being let off in their backyard. We should be aware that their sentries could be on high alert looking for groups like ours.

Because of the darkness, we're closer together than we'd normally be in this type of terrain, moving at quite a speed down this spur to the bottom of the ridge. Plonkey is good at scouting in these bare hills and sets a fast pace down the slope to the next ridge but it's not long before we start scrambling up our second incline with the pace slowing dramatically as the weight of our packs starts to take an immediate toll on our endurance, instantly reminding me of the huge ridges we'd climbed in New Guinea in my other life. Unfortunately, none of my current patrol has experienced carrying large packs up big hills, and this soon begins to tell on the men. I grin to myself as I watch Plonkey start to flounder on the steep incline in front with his massive pack waving about precariously in the dim light of this early morning.

'We'll stop for five,' I tell Plonkey, who I'm sure needs a break. 'You've done well, little fella, but I'll give you a spell at the back and let Smithy have a go in the lead. Hell – we can't have him bludging on you down the back, so we'll change you fellas around.' He gives me an exhausted grin as he drops back, and Smithy takes the lead.

The light is just starting to claw its way over the ridge in front of us when we finally arrive at our position on the crown of this steep, isolated hill. Most of the patrol has taken their turn at the front and they are very pleased that we've finally reached our destination. I look through my binoculars around the chasm below where an insignificant track winds through to the next valley, and I take note of a large knob that sticks out some hundred feet above the track where anyone who is using this route will have to pass directly underneath. *This is just what I need, it's my perfect ambush spot, much better than was shown on the aerial photographs from the drone run*, I think as I pull the exhausted patrol members together so I can put forward my plan for the ambush. I want them to fully understand what I want to achieve and how best to use this rugged topography that lies open in front of us.

'We'll catch our breath here, fellas, so have a quick bite and a brew before the sun gets properly up and while you're eating, I'll explain again quickly what we intend to do. You are well aware that our job is to stop anyone escaping from the Americans, Afghans and Allied forces and, as you can see below, we drew this lovely scenic spot where we can watch the wildlife wander blissfully around below us.' We all stare over the bare windswept valley just beneath our position. 'Now, on the serious side of things, you'll note that large rocky knob just below where the track winds under. Well, it's in front of that where I intend to stop anyone from coming through this pass. Two of you, Hewey and Smithy, will stay up here with the sniper rifle and the sig set and will converse with you from the killing ground by using our small personal transmitters; however, it will be *your* job to pass any information we get on to HQ. We'll set up our Claymores in such a position to stop any human wave attacks and especially if they try to get around behind us. Hewey, you can pick them off with that big gun of yours. The bad boys will be in the open from those rocks there to the top where they should be easy targets. Now, if there are too many of them, as may be the case, we can all move back to this ridge in stages and, as a last resort, blow the knob into the track and block it, forcing the buggers to go out in the open to get around the mess it should create.

This will give us an easy target when they try to come over the top. Questions please, boys? I want to be torn apart if there are better options or if I've got something wrong. Please let me know if there are any better alternatives you can think of. Fellas, once we set this ambush, our objective is quite simple. I don't want anyone, and I mean *anyone* passing our position and getting through to Pakistan or hiding in the hills – we're here to stop them so they don't threaten the general population as they did before.'

'Sounds alright to me, Sarge,' Terry tells me, as he looks over the ambush site with Hewey. 'Are we going to use all the claymores to protect us, or will we use some of them as offensive weapons on the track in the killing ground to really slow down any forces we strike?'

'We'll only use two for our own protection; the other four will be in the ambush site. If there's a large group, we'll have the option of either calling in an air strike or using the claymores we'll set on the track. The wheels have told me that the air force will be available for us to use as a first-strike weapon if we need them. Now, we'll have to register this position with the Yanks, so they don't blow the shit out of us by mistake. So, boys, I intend to register the position on top of the ridge here, even though four of us will be in that area just above that large rock formation. It's quite simple; if we have to use airpower, we have to be back at this point with Hewey and Smithy or we'll be burnt to crisps along with the bad boys.'

With Hewey settling into his position on the top of the ridge, I watch him begin sighting the big gun on specific targets to the extremities of the track well above us so he can give us instant backup while we set up the claymores along the track in the ambush site.

'He should give us plenty of protection to both ends of the valley,' Plonkey says as we move down towards the track. 'How many claymores are we using, Pete?'

'All of them; we'll site two claymores strategically across there to protect our ambush position with the initiators at our fall-back place just above us,' I point out where our fall-back position is. 'Now the remaining four will be used as offensive weapons on the track when Abdul comes along. What we set up should stop any group from getting away into Pakistan. With these set, the final step is to lay the charges on the knob before taking our positions above the claymores. We'll be well away from this large boulder which will give us a clear view of the ambush site.' I point out to them our positions. 'Only as a last resort will we blow this boulder and send it down onto the track below; that will hopefully block this escape route and cause the Taliban to have to come out of the valley and around this feature, leaving them open to rifle fire from Hewey's position; that is, if they are going to use this venue to get through to Pakistan.'

The day becomes hot as the sun soars through the sky, baking everything below it, including us. The only thing alive in sight is some sort of buzzard high above us continually doing large circles around our valley on thermal currents; I expect looking for a reptile or some other form of food. Operation Anaconda had been a success, though it had been touch-and-go for nearly ten days before getting the results the planners wanted. I hope we've been given the right area to guard because there's as much action here as on the main street of Melbourne on a Sunday when all the football teams have a bye. The sun is almost on the way down when the quiet is suddenly broken by Hewey's voice coming through loudly on the small personal radio headsets each of us has.

'You'll be pleased to know the drought is about to break, boys, there's finally a bit of action approaching you, fellas; you have two people who have just entered the valley and heading your way.' I can just imagine a very bored Hewey putting the crosshairs of the scope on them before he asks me the predictable question. 'They are just on half a kilometre away with no place to hide. I have them in my sights now, it's a lay down misère to get both of 'em. Do you want me to just pick 'em off before they get to you fellas, or do I leave them alone for you blokes to have a little bit of excitement when you round them up?'

'No, leave all the excitement to us, Hewey; we'll catch them under the rock,' I tell him, not wanting him to start anything too far away because, who knows, they may be important people or more likely the forward elements of a larger force. 'No shooting for heaven's sake, Hewey; just keep your eyes open because this may be the opening of the floodgates and there could be more of them coming through.'

I turn to Terry who's just near me. 'Right, there are two people at the head of the valley coming this way. Plonkey, you two cover us; I want to take them quietly if I can. Terry, you and I will move down to the lee side of the rock just above the track and surprise them. No shooting unless it's a last resort, okay? Now let's get into a position to take them when they come past.'

'Roger, Pete; I'm pleased we have something at last to break the boredom and keep our minds active. Shit, you know I was just about asleep when Hewey woke me up.'

Terry and I quickly move down the lee side of the large boulder we've been lying behind, make our way to just above the track and wait out of sight behind a cluster of small boulders. They should pass no more than five feet from us. The times like this go slowly and I feel a strange surge of excitement for a few moments as I wonder who we'll get. This quickly passes and the wait seems to drag on for ages but eventually first one person and then the second pass just below our position. We make our move – quickly springing out on the track behind our quarry, our guns levelled on these two people.

'Put your hands up,' I say, sounding exactly like John Wayne in a cowboy movie with my Steyr pointing at the tall man in the front, knowing Terry has the second covered. They both have rifles and stop immediately at the sound of my voice. 'Now raise your hands very slowly and drop those rifles to the ground.' There's a little hesitation but thankfully they both let their rifles clatter to the ground at their feet while their hands grudgingly move above their heads. 'That's good to see; you've obviously done this before. Now, step away from your weapons, nice and slow; well done!'

I cover Terry as he moves forward and quickly searches the first one, removing his web belt and finding an assortment of knives in different locations all over his body.

'You, on the left; put your hands behind you, one at a time and very slowly. That's good; I was obviously right; you've definitely done this before.'

Terry wraps a fine plastic cord around his hands and pulls it tight.

'Now you,' I tell the second man while Terry quickly removes his web belt and searches him, finding more knives. 'Your turn; lower your hands one at a time behind your back.' He grudgingly lowers his hands behind him for Terry to secure them when I suddenly recognise this man as the shadowy figure we'd seen during our operation at the caves complex two months before. 'You can turn around now, James. How nice to see you again and yes, so strange for us to meet an important man such as you again! How is Bin Laden these days? I hope he hasn't gone through to Pakistan yet because the Americans would love to pop a few questions to him.'

This comment startles him, the shock of recognition registering on his face as he turns, staring at me for a number of seconds, sizing up the situation. As we'd seen before, he's a man who's never caught for words.

'Do I know you?' he says in his plummy English accent, eyeing me off, clearly quite puzzled that someone has recognised him in this remote corner of the world. 'Have we met before somewhere; some other place perhaps?' He pauses for a moment, sizing the situation up and grasping at straws. 'But you're an Australian by the sound of your accent and unfortunately, I haven't been over there as yet. Was it in England perhaps, was it in London where we met?'

'No, we haven't officially met yet, James. Now, if you and your friend can move up off the track and follow my colleague up there to those large boulders you see above you, that'll make me very happy because I won't have to pull the trigger and make such a mess of this lovely, scenic spot where we met.'

We follow Terry up the incline and around the boulders to where the other two are waiting for us.

'Get Smithy to patch this through this to Headquarters, Plonkey. Tell them we have two guests that we would like them to pick up. Both are members of Al Qaeda. The first is an Englishman who calls himself James and the other man with him who is certainly a European national, but I don't know his nationality.' I look across at this other man, knowing he understands what I'm saying, hoping to get some response from him. 'Now tell me please, where do you hail from, my friend? By the look of that blonde hair of yours, you could be Nordic, you're certainly not what I'd call one of the local lads that I've seen hanging around this scenic place we have here.'

The man ignores me, giving me a sullen grimace perhaps at being caught, but unfortunately saying nothing, so we have no accent to judge him with. By the look of him, he's certainly European, maybe Scandinavian for he has blue eyes and I'm sure he has blonde hair under the Afghan-style headgear. Smithy wastes no time in getting this message through to Headquarters. When this is done, he turns around to us smiling, giving an enthusiastic wave before his voice comes through on my small headset.

'You've certainly stirred the pussy up, Sarge. They went ape shit when I told them about these two. They're sending a chopper out asap, so we'll have to take them to this point here at grid reference xxx xxx. It will take us about half an hour to get to that point. Shit! It'll be almost dark when we make the pickup position, but it will be good to have these two off our hands just in case we get others coming along during the night.'

'Come on man, be serious; what do you think you'll gain by turning us in?' the Englishman states as he overhears the conversation between the two of us. 'I can make it well worth your while if you and your men just turn your backs and let both of us just walk away.'

'I'm sorry I can't do that, James,' I tell him, quite surprised at his sudden willingness to communicate for he'd been rather stand-offish when he realised we knew his name and I expect he's still wondering how we know him. 'If you want to bribe someone, you'll just have to wait until you get back to wherever they take you. We're here to do a job, my friend and I intend to carry that out to the letter.'

'Look, can I speak to you privately?' James says, struggling to get up with his hands secured by the thin plastic cord. He finally makes it but finds he's restricted by Terry. 'For Christ's sake man, will you let me be and just listen to what I have to say? It should be of interest to you all.'

'Okay, let him come over, Terry, but you come as well so you can hear everything,' I tell my second in command as James moves his six-foot frame fully in front of me, taking in a large breath of air before looking down on me in his annoying, aristocratic way.

'My patrol has no secrets from each other, my friend, so now, what is it you have to say? We're running out of time very quickly to make the RV point for you blokes to meet your chopper. It'll be there shortly and that's something we don't want to miss, isn't it?'

'I'm a dammed British agent, you fool. I've been with the Al Qaeda for almost a year now, and if I go back, people will see me because the Taliban have spies everywhere and you and your men will have blown my cover. It's taken quite some time to establish a presence here and gain Al Qaeda's trust.'

'From what I heard you say previously, it was well over two years, but I'll be lenient. Give me a code or something substantial and I'll have my people check it out while Smithy's got the radio out. Give me something tangible as a recognition of your status with Al Qaeda and we'll get our people to verify it and if it is accurate, you can piss off down the road with your scaly mate – as I told you before, we have a job to do here,' I tell him, much to his surprise. 'The men in security can do that check on you as they've had plenty of experience with people like you. They'll be able to do it much quicker and more thoroughly than I can and I'm quite sure they'll have your profile stored in a file somewhere. It should be just a matter of opening a book and getting your

CV out and, like any efficient office, they'll look at your work credentials and know exactly who you are and what important jobs you've done for Bin Laden in the two years you've been with his group.'

'Look, you damn fool! You'll blow my cover if you do that,' he says with a sudden, irrational outburst of anger. It's the second time he's called me a fool, a word I don't particularly like. 'They don't know I'm here; I've been working in Afghanistan undercover for twelve months and have just got into a position of trust with Al Qaeda. If you talk about me or take me back, my cover will be blown and my work here and my positioning that's taken many months to achieve will immediately go down the drain. Do you understand what I'm trying to tell you? Do you realise the intricate position I'm in with Al Qaeda?'

'Look, fella, the last time I heard you speak you said you'd been here well over two years. As far as I'm concerned, you are an Al Qaeda prisoner and you'll be treated as such. Hell! Being the big man's aide-de-camp, you and your companion may even be able to give your friend Bin Laden's position away to the Americans; that is, if you're as pally with him as you told your other Australian mate, Stewart,' I tell him, still simmering at being called a fool by some Pommy upstart who I wouldn't trust as far as I could kick his aristocratic arse. I won't budge on sending him back. 'If you're sent back, I'm sure the British government will be able to use some highly imaginative ploy to get you out of jail and back into the field. You can shut your face for now and take it up with someone who's higher up the tree than me and my patrol.' I don't take my eyes off this Englishman with his holier-than-thou attitude towards us. 'Terry take this prick away to the pickup point before I forget myself and do something I'll regret. If he won't shut up, gag the bastard. I don't want to listen to this sort of whining crap, especially when he's a security threat to us if a big group of Al Qaeda come along and this man is still yelping out.'

'Come on, Jamesy boy, back to your mate,' Terry tells him, roughly pushing him away towards the other prisoner, still yelling and screaming.

I turn back to Smithy who still has the radio set out.

'Contact Base and let them know that we have this prisoner who claims to be a British secret agent. The name I heard him use up here was James; however, I've also heard him say he is an aide-de-camp to Bin Laden so, if he's sending information back, they would know him.' I suddenly think about the secret agent in the movies that I watched as a kid – James Bond. This firms my resolve to let the high-ranking people make the decisions as to what to do with this whining prick of a man. 'I want the bastard off our hands as soon as possible – with all his grizzling he's a security risk to us if he's here much longer; we have enough to do.'

Smithy immediately sends the message through, letting Base know what our situation is with this prisoner we have on our hands; I'm sure they'll make the correct decision without our help.

'Patrol B3 to Base. Have one English prisoner who claims to be to be a British secret agent. He claims it will compromise his position if he's sent back. The name we know him as is James. Over.'

There is a pause for a few minutes before the reply comes through to Smithy but it's a very easy answer to understand.

'Base to Patrol B3, the Chopper is on the way. Send both prisoners. I repeat, send both prisoners. Out.'

The two prisoners are quickly hustled up the hill just over the lip into the next valley across to their extraction point and we wait for the *Black Hawk* to arrive with the Englishman still protesting that we've compromised his position. He quickly shuts up when he hears the helicopter approaching. He certainly doesn't have the cool head of the secret agent in the movies that I vividly remember as a boy. The helicopter is coming in fast and is with us in barely a minute. It hovers; the wheels only just touch the ground before the doors are opened and both prisoners are handed over to the people onboard.

'Goodbye, James, a good secret agent like you should be back out in the field in no time,' I tell him sarcastically, trying to rub it in. 'Keep up the good work, 007. We'll fill in for you while you're gone, so have you got any tips for tomorrow while you are on R&R?'

He grimaces at me before he's pulled roughly away from the door and it's slammed shut. The chopper lifts off into the night sky and is soon lost from view in the shrouds of darkness.

Washington DC

The phone rings on Senator Abraham King's desk. It's been a busy day as he has reams of important legislation dealing with the war in Afghanistan which has been presented to the Senate for review. He knows it's important for the men in the field and he wants to make sure that this legislation is sound and won't disadvantage any of them because he knows firsthand how soldiers are used as pawns by their political masters and in some cases are classed as expendable, but he's quite determined that these sorts of things will not happen on his watch.

'It's your sister calling, Senator,' comes the soft voice of his receptionist as she passes on the message.

'Put her through please, Mavis,' says Abe, pleased at this welcome break from the tedium that is scattered in front of him on his desk. 'Good morning, Alicia. What a wonderful surprise to have you calling this morning! It's certainly a pleasant change to what I've got in front of me.'

'Hi, Abe, I have to come down for an important seminar this afternoon and thought that we could have a bite to eat this evening and discuss a few personal things. Unfortunately, I have to be back in New York midday tomorrow – are you free this evening for dinner?'

'Yes, certainly; that will be a wonderful break from this bullshit. I've got all this damn legislation we've been presented with dealing with the situation in Afghanistan; unfortunately, it just keeps piling up in front of me. I'd like to get off, but I won't be able to make it until seven. I'll get my secretary to book a table at Alfredo's. I'm sorry but will that time be okay?'

'Sounds wonderful, I'll see you at seven. I'm looking forward to a quiet dinner and a chat about old times. Bye, Abe.'

That evening, Abe takes a taxi to Alfredo's, an up-market restaurant he'd found to be excellent during his time in Washington. It's slightly out of the way and isn't used by other politicians so there is never the problem of having to avoid them and their noisy parties – something he can't stand. Abe has had a close relationship with his sister ever since childhood and enjoys her dropping in from time to time when she occasionally comes to Washington. She gets up when she sees him walk in and they give each other a big, affectionate hug before they both go to their table and sit down, looking at each other for a moment.

'I had this seminar on cancer rehabilitation,' she tells him. 'They had me as one of the guest speakers at the forum. It's very important, what they're trying to do with the cloning of cells, so I accepted the invitation, came down to Washington and spoke on some of our breakthroughs. It's also a good opportunity to catch up with you, brother and find out what's going on in this fictitious world of politics I find you living in these days. So, tell me, what's new in town at the moment?'

'Ah, mostly they're on the war in Afghanistan and trying to track down this Bin Laden character who's supposed to be in the south of that country,' he tells her, trying not to divulge anything that's deemed to be classified; however, he always finds this extremely difficult. 'The military is launching a large push that's going on at the moment. It's called Operation Anaconda, and it's designed to trap the Taliban and any members of Al Qaeda as they try to get out of the trap and escape into Pakistan.'

'That's a very interesting strategy, Abe. Is Peter involved in this Operation Anaconda as well?' she says without flinching, hoping she has caught him off balance. 'I have a tape with me that I'd like you to hear.'

He pales as if he's been hit with a mallet, but the politician in him recovers very quickly. Their eyes meet; both brother and sister are very strong-willed people and are a match for each other even when she's dealt him a sledgehammer blow straight out of the blue.

'Yes, Peter's alive. He's the same man you remember but he's different to what you'd expect. He's the same person you used to know when you were going out with him thirty years ago.'

'What do you mean he's the same person I used to go out with?' she asks, quite surprised at this strange comment. 'He'd be the same as we are now; the same Peter, only older, so what do you mean by such a strange statement?'

'I was staggered when I met him just over twelve months ago. I couldn't believe it was him when he sat me down in my office and told me what happened to him all that time ago, I swear it was as if I was talking to a ghost. He asked me if he should see you and I told him no; not because you didn't want to see him, but because you were happily married and to see him as he was would have upset you. He wanted to see you one more time, so I took him to New York where I met you one evening for a coffee. He waited outside and watched you go into the cafe.' He pauses for a while, letting what he's just said sink in. 'Do you remember what you said to me when you came in? Because you actually saw him and made a comment to me on what you had just seen. You said and I quote: "*I saw a man outside the restaurant who reminded me so much of Pete, but this man was so young, so full of youth just like he used to be.*" I'll never forget what you said that evening because you actually did see him. Do you remember that incident outside the cafe, Alicia?'

The look on Alicia's face is one of absolute astonishment as she remembers clearly. Suddenly the reality of who it was hits her and now she realises the depth of what the reporter, Kerry O'Flaherty, had told her, a fact that she had been too emotionally stressed to take notice of – everything he had said, and the enormity of the information Kerry O'Flaherty had given.

'Abe, I have a recording that I would like you to listen to please,' she tells him, reaching over the table, grabbing his hand and giving it a little squeeze, with most of her aggravation gone. 'The tape was given to me just after Nine Eleven by a reporter who met Peter in East Timor some months before. I wasn't sure what the voice on the tape meant and thought that you were hiding the fact from me that he was alive. Abe, I'm so sorry for thinking badly about you so please, listen to it and tell me what you think because I still have great difficulty believing what I hear.'

She pulls the small listening device from her bag, places it between them on the table and once again listens to Pete's voice and his dream. They both have tears welling in their eyes when the tape finishes and the cold reality of what had happened to him all those years ago becomes quite apparent to her.

'He told me what had happened, but it was nothing as graphic as this,' he says, wiping a tear from his eye. 'When he first walked in on me, I honestly thought I'd seen a ghost. Here is this young man whom I knew so well who hadn't changed in thirty years talking to me about things that happened as if it were yesterday. Alicia, it was quite tragic listening to him, I'm afraid it took me quite some time to get over that meeting. That's why I wanted to shield you from what happened to him.'

'But was it Peter or was it someone else who was after something and was just playing on your emotions?'

'It was Pete alright because I asked to see the scar that he received when he was having the beer with Dad. You remember; you dressed the wound when he reached the hospital? I didn't tell him where it was or what side it was on, but he knew what happened and he knew the name of Dad's friend and he lifted up his shirt and showed me that scar which really proved to me he was legitimate.'

They sit silently, looking at each other across the table when all of a sudden Abe takes her hand and gives her another little squeeze reassuring her that he is serious, letting her know he is on her side and not trying to hide anything.

'I think both you and Julian should meet him, now you know he's still alive,' he tells her, giving her hand a squeeze once more. 'Look, Alicia, I'll make some discreet inquiries and find out where he is at the moment and, if you like, we'll go to Australia and both you and Julian can meet him so you can see what the Vietnamese did to him.'

'Abe, I'm so sorry I thought badly about you; how can I make it up to you? I'm *so* sorry, I'm afraid I just got carried away when that reporter told me that he was still alive, and I heard his voice so clearly on the recorder. I thought you were hiding the fact he was alive from me but had overlooked what the reporter had told me about his age.'

'He still cares about you, Alicia, because as soon as he saw what happened on Nine-Eleven, he emailed me from Australia, asking about your safety because he'd heard that firemen and medical personnel had gone into the towers to treat casualties before the towers collapsed and he thought you and Julian may have been among those people.'

Southern Afghanistan

The helicopter is a decreasing sound in the black night sky as we finally return to our observation post a hundred feet above the track. We re-join the other two members of the patrol who were left behind to keep a close vigil on our ambush site just below our position.

'I hope everything is quiet on the western front?' I ask Plonkey as we move back into position, still thinking about the strange Englishman and why the hell he was here in Afghanistan. Was he really a convert to Islam as he'd told the other Australian James that night or was he simply an adventurer who had picked the wrong side in this horrible conflict? 'We'll set up a roster on the piquet then everyone will get some shut-eye. I'll take the first shift as I'm wide awake; we'll do two hours on and four off. Terry, I'll wake you for the next shift. The two on the gun will have it easy while we're here because they'll be our early warning group and our backup if people come through this valley tomorrow.'

I'm awake well before the last shift is over, lying there looking at the stars and thinking of my strange past and of that peculiar Englishman we'd captured. I wonder why an educated person such as he is in a place like this. I check my watch to find there's a good hour to go before it's light when I hear a faint clinking noise and instantly I become fully alert. I stare through the night-vision goggles and am finally able to see what appears to be a string of donkeys coming into focus at the far end of the track. It's a sizable group and they're moving towards our position at a considerable speed and see each one of these small pack animals they are apparently using loaded to the hilt with equipment and being led by an Afghan with rifle slung over his shoulder. A number of Afghans follow this first donkey and, from the look of them, they are armed to the teeth with some carrying what look like RPG's over their shoulders. The first group are followed by more donkeys with their packs piled high on their backs and more men follow each donkey. I quickly shake the others from their sleep so we're prepared for when these people arrive at the ambush site below us.

'Get onto the blower,' I whisper to Plonkey. 'Wake Hewey and Smithy; tell them we have company approaching; a large group coming towards us. Ask Smithy to try to get an air strike on this valley ASAP while the Afghans are still out in the open, then we can achieve maximum results.'

Plonkey quickly patches through this message and then turns to me a little agitated at what Smithy has been told by base.

'Shit, Sarge. They've told Smithy they'll be at least thirty minutes before they can get here and they tell us we've got to hold up the column of Taliban until the planes get here. Do you think we can do it? From what I can see, there's a hell of a lot of men and equipment coming our way with a lot of RPG's.'

'Unfortunately, they give us no option, Plonkey. We'll have to play this extremely smart until the Yanks arrive. We'll wait until the front of the caravan is almost through the claymores then we'll blow them. Get ready and use your ammunition sparingly because knowing how things work up here, the Yanks' bloody half hour may be an hour or more. We'll also have to play for time until those damn planes get here.'

The Afghan donkeys are small, sturdy and sure-footed animals well-suited to this extreme terrain and appear to be carrying massive loads that the Taliban are perhaps taking through to Pakistan. We watch as they move towards us at a quick pace with the front animal still making the annoying jingling sound from his harness as they nonchalantly approach the claymores; all still quite unaware of us being just above them in our ambush position. They are quite clear now through my night glasses and the thing that staggers me is there is not one man in this large group of people that has a rifle in his hands ready to fire and they are simply slung over their shoulders as if they don't expect any trouble.

'Remember, fellas; don't fire unless you have a target in sight. Now, get ready for the blast of the claymores.'

'We'll wait for you to fire first, Sarge,' Plonky whispers to me, clearly confident with our preparations.

They're right in the ambush position so I press the initiator, opening the doors of hell on to those individuals below us on the track.

Boom!

The four claymores explode as one, covering the track below us with a thick cloud of black smoke and dust as thousands of the small lethal steel pellets are hurled forward onto the group. No one fires and as the smoke begins to slowly clear, we see the devastation our mines have created. Down below me lay the first bodies along with the three donkeys leading the caravan. Occasionally an arm rises in a desperate attempt to get up before it aimlessly flops back, unable move or support the body below. I look down upon this scene in the dull pre-dawn light, my rifle cradled in my hands as I count the dead and dying men that litter the front of the track. The lead donkey riddled with shot lies on its side, shivering occasionally and throwing its leg about, kicking the air in a futile attempt to get up. I watch this death charade before focusing my gaze on the remainder of the caravan who had gone to ground and are now scanning the heights for the aggressors.

'Stay down and don't show yourselves,' I whisper through clenched teeth to the men who are all aiming their rifles at the Taliban troops; some are easy targets where they lie behind precious little cover. 'Wait until they start to move away; wait until I fire. Hopefully, they may think this could have been a roadside bomb that one of their comrades had trodden on. We're going to bide our time until those planes get here; this little exercise could buy us a number of valuable minutes.'

So we lie doggo, looking down at the Taliban who are desperately searching. The half-light is now casting shadows over the hills, making visibility for them extremely difficult.

'If I was them, fellas, I'd let a few shots go in the appropriate places to try and draw our fire,' I whisper to the boys quietly through my clenched teeth, not taking my eyes off the men directly below. 'So, if any shots come our way, ignore them. Things may become quite hairy for the moment and their bullets could be very close. Keep your heads down because I don't want any of you fellas sporting a third eye, okay.'

'Right, Sarge, we'll just wait for you to fire first,' replies Terry, almost grinning but still not taking his eyes off the men below. 'But don't be greedy and shoot too many because we all want some Abduls for our own tally.'

As predicted, a number of Taliban open up, putting well-placed shots at likely places. They continue for a minute or two with their shots echoing loudly around the valley but not one of my men returns their fire, even though some bullets have landed extremely close to a few of them, making me very proud of their discipline in resisting this urge to shoot back.

Finally, there's silence with shooting finished and what I'd been hoping for suddenly happens with some hesitantly standing up and looking around about them at the destruction. Some even put their rifles back on their shoulders and start to wander around the area, picking up weapons of those caught in the mine's blast and begin pocketing other little trinkets of value from those bodies nearby.

'Take some targets each, left take left, right take right,' I tell them, not wanting them to shoot at the same targets.

There are now more than forty Taliban out of their rat holes freely walking around our ambush sight below us as if nothing had happened. We watch as they continue to collect from some of the dead, while others begin to strip the cargoes off the unfortunate dead donkeys and begin strapping this extra load on to the remaining animals. Finally, one man starts to lead one of these laden donkeys forward past his fallen comrades towards the border.

'Fire.'

The selected targets below us begin to fall as we fire. They are initially very slow to respond. There's a sudden frantic rush for cover to escape our unrelenting rifle fire and soon all of our targets have dried up completely with only the laden donkeys standing on the track.

'Only fire when you have targets,' I tell the men when we find our targets have evaporated. 'Pick off the remainder of the donkeys so, if they leave, they'll have to carry everything out of there on their backs.'

The last remaining donkeys are soon picked off and lie like quivering hulks, causing me to feel sorry for them. I wonder how many others have fallen in similar circumstances during this insipid campaign. There is soon a lull in our firing as the Taliban have now found a secure position behind the many boulders on the floor of the valley and we find it's difficult to get targets now to shoot at.

'Be alert, boys! They will know where we are by now so they may try to flank us on the left,' I say, looking down at the rock-strewn area where large boulders give a maze of cover, almost right to our position.

'I hope those planes aren't going to be too much longer,' comments Plonkey, staring at the rocks below. There is a big boom as Hewey picks someone off from the top of the ridge. Silence again as they reassess their positions.

'It looks like they are making their move now,' says Terry, pulling off a shot and we all watch the turban-covered figure collapse, fall back and lie still on the ground. 'They'll soon find a way to reach those rocks and we could find ourselves in trouble from that small ridge to the left.'

The bark of the large sniper's rifle from the ridge above

us reminds us that Hewey is still there, so we start a phased withdrawal back towards him. We make our second defensive line and have taken up our firing positions when our former position is hit by a large barrage of RPG fire, throwing rocks and dust into the air.

'Good timing, Sarge,' says Plonkey, staring at our former position now covered in dust and debris from the exploding shells. 'If we'd have stayed there any longer, we'd be history now. Come on, where are those bloody planes?'

Our old position is now crawling with Taliban who are not happy with the outcome. It had certainly been wise to move when we did.

'Fire the last two claymores and as soon as they go off, move to the ridge as the smoke should cover our withdrawal; Hewey will cover us from up there,' I tell Terry, who quickly fits the firing mechanism and presses it down causing the surrounds to erupt around the unwitting Taliban. 'Let's get the hell out of here and up to the ridge while the dust is in the air, before they regain their composure and come up here looking for us.'

It is close to thirty metres of open ground uphill to reach the ridge. I think we do this in world record time and quickly drop in place alongside Hewey, just as the smoke starts to clear from our last claymore explosions showing just how many Taliban had fallen.

'Get on the blower and find out where the hell those *bloody* planes are, Smithy. Tell them we are under constant fire and will be withdrawing shortly if the air force have decided to take a damn holiday.'

Smithy hardly has time to reach for the set before there is the welcome scream of jet engines just overhead so I grab for the radio.

'This is cut off patrol B3. Welcome to the war, gentlemen. The bandits are near the smoke just above the track. Over.'

'I see them B3. I hope you've left plenty of those Abduls for me. I need some good practice. Over.'

'We are on the ridge above the smoke. I'll have one of the men put out a marker panel to make sure you don't give us any of your goodies. Over.'

'I see you on the ridge B3. We'll keep the entire ordinance for Abdul, happy shooting. Out.'

He does a quick turn and then comes screaming in just above our heads, dropping two large sinister-looking silver canisters off his wings just above our position. I watch almost spellbound as they tumble earthwards dropping just to one side of the smoke and once again opening the doors of hell to those in our old position. Just above the track a flame erupts, covering all with a large sheet of flame. No living being would have the capacity to have survived that fiery furnace.

'There's their birthday present B3. Happy hunting guys; now give us a call if you need any more assistance. Out.'

We watch the area for another hour; there is no shooting, nothing moves. It's like looking over a morgue after a funeral.

'We'll have to do a recce and see if anyone survived. Hewey, you and Smithy stay put up here with the sniper rifle and give us some cover if we need it. The rest of you boys come with me and we'll see if anyone was lucky enough to have survived that napalm attack.'

So, in a rough arrow-head formation covering each other as we go, we carefully work our way back down the slope. The sight is horrible with charred bodies lying everywhere, their clothes burnt off, most lying facing where we had been. Their weapons point towards us, their ammunition having exploded with the intense heat generated.

'Here's one that's alive!' yells out Terry to my left, pointing his gun at a terrified young lad who was probably in his late teens and had luckily managed to wedge himself under an overhanging rock. Most of the napalm had deflected away from him. 'He's only a young bloke, he's burnt down one side and both his hands but he's been lucky, it's miraculous he's still alive.'

'Herb, crack out your first aid kit and see what you can do for him. Smithy, contact Headquarters. Tell them we have a prisoner who's badly burnt and also tell them we'll need assistance to bury these people – we just can't just leave them out in the open like this for the buzzards to eat.'

Herb moves over and starts treating the terrified youth as well as he can while the rest of us finish the recce. The napalm had only engulfed the Taliban who were attacking us, so we are very careful while move down to the track. The pellets from the claymores had carved into them.

'Search the bodies for anything of strategic value,' I tell them, hoping there will be something that the intelligence people can use. 'Take anything that you think could be of intelligence value; put to one side in a pack or bag and we can sort through it later to see if it's worthwhile.'

We start the grizzly task of searching the bodies; a task I'd become accustomed to doing ever since my days in Vietnam when we'd blow the claymores and rush out onto the track and quickly do a body search. Now, some thirty years later, we're still doing the same thing. Finally, the job is over with the weapons collected and in a pile just off the track, inconspicuous to anyone coming by.

Now it's only a matter of waiting for the helicopters to arrive and hopefully being replaced in this sector by another patrol.

The mess around us would most likely compromise our position and worse still – we are out of claymores to use as protection if another large group comes along.

'Party of four and a donkey has just entered the valley,' comes the crackle of Hewey's voice through the radio. 'Do you want me to pick them off, Pete or do we challenge them going through?'

'No, Hewey. Only shoot them if they see this mess and turn around and try to do a runner; we'll see if we can capture them first,' I tell him, a little sickened with what we'd done today and not wanting any more bloodshed if we can avoid it. 'We've got another four on their way, coming towards us so get behind those rocks up there but don't shoot unless we have to because they could be of intelligence value like the first two.'

We scramble to an outcrop of rocks just up from the bodies, hoping that their attention will be on the little smoke that is still oozing from cracks in the rocks above us where the napalm must have collected and was still burning. We wait eagerly for the group to arrive; again like medieval highwaymen hiding behind the rocks, wondering who it was this time. The small group finally appear around the rocks; three men, one who appears to have his hands tied and another who is obviously a woman by her garb with only her eyes showing from under her burka. We allow them to almost pass before springing out weapons at the ready, covering each individual in this group.

'Put your hands in the air and I promise you won't be harmed,' I say, hoping desperately they'll understand English well enough not to do anything stupid. Unfortunately, the rear man is a slow learner and makes a desperate effort to swing the AK47 off his shoulder towards us.

'No you don't, you stupid bastard,' I hear Terry say and

hear his weapon spit death the same time as mine. The man is kicked backwards by the impact of the two short bursts from the Styr's with the AK47 in his hands, cascading a number of harmless shots into soil at his feet and we watch as he slumps to the ground. Thankfully, the other two raise their hands immediately on the sound of the gun fire when they see their comrade cut down.

'*Don't shoot!*' yells out the tall man in almost perfect English at the front of the donkey as if he feels he would be next to feel the bite of our bullets.

'*Don't shoot me, I'm an English newspaper reporter!*' shouts the man behind the donkey, quickly holding up his bound hands to show us he's a prisoner and that he's tied to the animal's harness in front. It's at this moment I suddenly realise what he is. 'Don't shoot, I'm a reporter from the *Daily News*, I'm their captive and they've been trying to get ransom from my paper for my release.'

'Cut him free,' I say, not taking my eyes off the tall man at the front of the donkey or the woman on its back.

Plonkey cradles his rifle under one arm and with the other, reaches down and takes out the large hunting knife from his webbing. We'd frequently ribbed him about the weapon and watch as he quickly slashes the bonds that hold the man's hands tightly together, freeing the Englishman who immediately starts flexing his fingers, trying to get the circulation moving in his hands once again. Then he turns towards Plonkey, smiling profusely at being finally released.

'Thank you for releasing me, I'm certainly glad to see you boys,' he says, still working his hands vigorously to get the blood circulating freely. 'Unfortunately for me, I've been strapped up like this for quite a few days. These people were taking me through to Pakistan where they intended to hold me for ransom,' he looks at Plonkey and then at me. 'From your accents you sound like Australians?'

'Yes, we are,' Plonky tells him, speaking to all of them and then pleasing me with the next order. 'Move up off the track in case there are more of the bastards coming. We don't want to be caught down here in the open.'

'Move up to our first position and we'll grab Hewey on the way,' I tell them, wanting to get the reporter away from the ambush sight. 'He should have finished bandaging the young bloke by now so we'll take them all up together.'

We move quickly up through into the ambush area and I hear a gasp of shock from behind me as the reporter sees the carnage we're moving through.

'Good god! What the hell happened here?' He utters when he sees the bodies in front of him and the dead donkeys strewn over this part of the track. I turn, looking at this man as he simply stares. 'What the hell went on here, soldier, who did this?'

'We're a cut-off patrol for a large operation the Americans are doing in Southern Afghanistan,' I tell him, very aware of the horrid mess left from our claymore ambush and now not wanting him to see too much more. 'We're here to stop the Taliban and Al Qaeda moving out of the operational area. I'm afraid you may see some things that show you the brutalities of modern warfare so please, ignore them and continue on to the top of the hill where you'll find other members of our patrol.'

Plonkey ties together the three bag loads of papers and items we've accumulated from our search of the bodies in the ambush site, swings them on to the back of the donkey and ties them securely to the saddle horn before looking at me.

'Anything else for the donkey to take to the top?' he asks, gazing over at the pile of small arms we'd stacked just off the track. 'There's still room for some of these weapons or do we just render them in operable?'

'Take what you can then we'll do another trip down here and get as many as we can on the next trip.' I wanted to get this reporter as far away from the ambush sight as quickly as possible after my experience with Kerry O'Flaherty in Timor because now unfortunately, I have very little trust for the press. Who knows what type of story this man will concoct if he sees too much and put it into print.

We leave the track and scramble up to our ambush position, still belching clouds of smoke from the napalm. Luckily the effects of this attack aren't visible from the path we're now taking to the top of the ridge. Hewey joins us with a very subdued young prisoner who by now has his burns covered with bandages. Our column pushes up just over the top of the hill so we're out of sight from the track. We move past Hewey who's still looking down the barrel of the large sniper's rifle to where the track enters the valley and will give us ample warning if more people come into our valley.

'Is everything okay, Sarge? A few new faces, I see. What do we have this time, friends or foes?'

'Some of both unfortunately,' I tell him, then quickly turning to Smithy and his radio set. 'Give HQ a bell please, Smithy and let them know we have a number of prisoners and more importantly we've rescued a member of the press as I'm sure his paper will be over the moon with his release.' I turn and look at the newspaperman and apologise to him. 'I'm sorry but I didn't even ask your name. Please forgive me for being so inhospitable but there are quite a few things we have here that are unfortunately occupying my mind at the moment.'

'William Plumber,' he says quite jovially making me wonder

what was coming next. 'But, Sergeant people always call me – ha, ha, ha, ha – Bill the Plummer,' then he finally controls his mirth; I expect very pleased to finally be out of his bondage. 'It's alright. Don't take any notice of me as you've got a lot on your plate. I'm just so pleased to be free and almost out of this mess; thanks to the efforts of you and your men. I work for *United Press* based in London and have been over here since this shindig started trying to get a gist on what's happening with the American and other forces.'

'Did you get that, Smithy, this gentleman is Mr William Plumber of *United Press?*' I turn back to the reporter. 'They'll be pleased to hear that you're okay and have been released because if they're anything like the press at home they will have been frantic with you being missing for so long.'

'As soon as I get back, I'll send them a despatch and let them know I'm still in the land of the living and tell them what has happened to me. I think they'll be quite surprised when they hear where I've been because it's well over a month now with not a word to anyone and to think I was rescued by Australians of all people,' he then gives us another strained laugh. 'Even that is a story in itself.'

We chat for some time while we have a bite to eat, discussing the war and Nine Eleven and wondering where this all this will end. Smithy has been in touch with our HQ and comes over to me smiling.

'They'll be coming in with a relief patrol and a burial party this afternoon and they'll be taking us out with the prisoners. They also want us to collect all the usable firearms we can get. They don't want them getting back into Taliban hands and used against us in any future conflict.'

'I'll take two men back down and collect what weapons we

can find and use the donkey to transport them back to the top. You and Terry finish your brew and we'll go back down to the track. We'll leave in ten minutes.'

With Terry in the lead, we cautiously move back down to the track again knowing that if there is any movement further along we'll have the full support of Hewey and his sniper's rifle.

We find the hot sun has already started to bloat the bodies, making our stay in the vicinity quite difficult as the noxious odours increasingly drift our way. We load the last of the rifles onto the donkey who now isn't showing any of the traits of stubbornness you read about and come to expect from these pack animals; perhaps he's catching the smell of death as well as us and wishes to leave this area as quickly as he possible can. Finally, the small arms are loaded onto this animal's back and we can't get away quickly enough. Eventually, just over an hour later, we reach the others on the top of this ridge.

'We should have just bent the barrels on each of the rifles and left the bloody things where they could find them,' Terry tells Hewey with a chuckle as we finally return to the top with our load of arms. 'I'd love to see Abdul lining us up and shooting the man next to him or have the weapon explode in his face. It'd be poetic justice to have something like that to happen to those back-stabbing pricks.'

It's an hour before dusk when three choppers come in. I almost thought we'd have to spend another night in our observation post but, just when I was about to give orders to deploy as we'd done the night before, a signal comes through telling us to get ready to leave. Not long after, I hear the welcome throbbing sounds of the incoming helicopters. It's been a long day crammed full of adventure but we need a spell to unwind. The big helicopter, the *Chinook*, flies on and lands on the track.

I expect they will be removing the bodies from the ambush site and the poor souls who were incinerated by the napalm. We're told later that another patrol was on the track. I don't know where and quite frankly at this stage, I don't care. I'm just pleased to be getting out of this shit of a place and be able to take a welcome spell for a few days.

Washington D.C.

Abe is at his desk going through reams of papers dealing with this war and he's found it to be a long hard day. The President, a man he puts up with out of respect for the office, has just had his advisers send reams of more legislation to the Senate and he and his staff have been going through the papers. He's had enough for the day and starts to think of his Australian friend Pete and what he's up to. *'He's the lucky one,'* he thinks out aloud. *'He's still got his youth, although by default, and he certainly doesn't have to put up with this mountain of crap that now decorates my desk. I know, I'll ring Alicia; she wants to meet Pete. I'll see if I can arrange a meeting,'*

'Alicia, its Abe. I'm snowed down with all this legislation and just had a thought. Would you and Julian like to go to Australia and meet Pete soon? Look, I need a break badly and perhaps you need to sort things out with Julian about Pete. I'll find out what his movements are and we'll go from there.'

'Abe, that sounds a wonderful idea. When do you intend to go to Australia?' she says, surprised at this coming from Abe who previously seemed quite reluctant to go any further with any type of meeting.

'I'll find out where he is and what he's doing. Just leave it with me and I'll sort things out. I'll ring you when I get the details of his whereabouts. He's still in the Australian Army, and from what I gather the same unit so he shouldn't be too hard to track down although the unit he is in are very protective with the whereabouts of their men.'

'Okay, Abe, I'll leave it in your capable hands to do the organising. Come back to me with the details so we can organise our end and Julian and I will take some leave from our practice.'

'Alicia, just leave your agenda open please. I don't know what his movements are. The last e-mail I have was from Afghanistan. He's over there you know and he doesn't know that I've told you that he's alive. He still cares for you even though he knows it's an impossible situation after what's happened.'

'I've told Julian all about Pete. We had a little session about it the other night. Like me he's having trouble believing what's gone on; but unfortunately he's still hung up on what happened with his sister in Iraq. You know Abe as soon as I told him about Pete, he decided to go through his father's blueprints again but he's gotten nowhere. The machine his father invented evidently just doesn't seem to work or he's looking at it from the wrong way; he's not an engineer like his father.'

'Well, you'll have to prepare him to meet a man whose been there and done that because he's going to see what happens when you lose something. Sis, Pete really loved you but now you've moved on with life and he has as well. He has to meet a woman his own age and do the same thing as you've done. Anyway it's time you both met again and get all this suspense that's affecting your life out of the way.'

'Abe, I know what you're saying but it's different for you; you've already met him. I've still got to do that and Julian has a sister who's disappeared and he has to come to terms with that as well. I loved Pete but he disappeared and I married Julian and now I love him. We've been very happy, however he's got to come to terms with the fact his sister disappeared in Iraq under strange circumstances and, from all accounts, could be dead. Now Pete's not going to have any bearing on Julian's situation at all, but her existence is a conundrum. Do you understand where I'm coming from, Abe?'

'Yes I think I do. Anyway, only time will tell. You just wait on my call and be ready to go Down Under as soon as I find out what Pete's movements are, then we'll coincide ours with his.'

The United Arab Emirates

William Plummer has been back at work now for just over a week and has had a number of weeks in rehabilitation in the gulf which had given him the opportunity to quietly work on the story of his adventure and he has just posted it off to head office in London. He'd been strangely impressed by the almost casual attitude of the small band of Australians who had rescued him from the Taliban but he was, however, deeply concerned at the mass destruction they had inflicted on their enemies just before his captors arrived on the scene. The Australians had obviously saved his life though, there was no doubt about that. He'd read accounts from other westerners who had spent years imprisoned while their captors had patiently waited for their ransoms to be met; mostly by family members who publicly lobbied the government and employers to meet their captors' demands of the ransom. He'd also heard of the public executions of a number of those whose ransom had been denied and felt that may very well have been his fate. He'd been told by the paper before he left England that he was to get his story on British troop movements as they were the main interest at home. They had told him in no uncertain terms to stay with the coalition forces to get his stories and to do all he could to keep out of harm's way for they weren't prepared to back him if he was captured trying to get some unnecessary story from the Taliban's perspective which, unfortunately, he had tried to do.

He casually looks out over the water from the bar in the luxury hotel that the company had generously installed him in for his rehabilitation. He was contemplating whether he should go back to Afghanistan for further stories or should he just look for a quieter, more mundane life in a civilised country and marry some lovely country lady. He looks out the window at the beautiful view of the ocean before he takes another sip of his drink when his train of thought is suddenly broken by an American voice from behind him.

'William Plumber, I've been looking for you,' says this quiet American who has approached him. 'Do you mind if I have a word with you about your adventures in Afghanistan? I read that article you wrote in *United Press* papers dealing with your experiences in Afghanistan; it was posted on the net by your paper. It mentioned how you were finally rescued by a group of Australian Special Forces troops who were part of blocking force after Operation Anaconda.'

'Certainly, Sir, be my guest,' he says, a little surprised at this invasion of privacy and politely gestures to this American journalist to take a seat with him. 'You are another reporter I assume. Can I buy you a drink?'

'Yes, that would be lovely, my name is Kerry O'Flaherty, you probably haven't heard of me. I've been working on a story dealing with a Sergeant Peter Jackson,' he tells him, wondering how much he should say to this Englishman. He decides to play him with a straight bat, not wishing too many people to know. 'From what I read, I believe you were rescued by him and his patrol. Could you tell me a little about the circumstances of your situation and how you came to be rescued by this Sergeant Jackson and his men?'

'He only had a small but important part to play. I had been chasing a story about the Taliban and Al Qaeda and unfortunately ended up their prisoner. I think they were taking me to a safe haven in Pakistan when the Australians ambushed the party,' he stops for a few moments, his interest suddenly being aroused, wondering why this American wanted to know about this Australian Sergeant Peter Jackson in particular. 'You should have seen the bodies. They were everywhere and they had already collected intelligence information which they took with me up to their base on top of a ridge. Now tell me, what's this all about, what story is it that you are following?'

'I have been following his career now since he was in East Timor,' explains Kerry, not really willing to let too much out. He now wanted the story for himself even though he'd promised Jackson he'd do nothing when he had well and truly sorted the militia out. He'd changed his mind when he found the last recording at Tiffany's house as this had put a whole new dimension on everything. 'He was quite deadly in the work he did over there. I think the militia were very happy when the squadron he was serving with had finished its tour of duty and returned to Australia. What did he accomplish to your knowledge on this mission where you met him in Afghanistan?'

'As I told you, I was a prisoner of the Taliban. I was tied behind a donkey for a number of days when we entered this valley. I was with two male Taliban and a female when these Australians came out from behind a large rock. One of Taliban tried to fight and they shot him and took the other two prisoners.

On the way back we went through what looked to be an ambush site. There were bodies strewn everywhere.'

'Sounds like they took you through a claymore ambush site from what you've described. He's good at setting those ambushes up; he did a number of those in East Timor with outstanding success. What else did you see?'

'They loaded up the donkey with intelligence material they had collected from the dead before we moved up the escarpment. It appeared to have been burnt out badly by chemicals of some description. We met another member of their patrol who had been rendering first aid to an Afghan youth who had been badly burnt.'

'Hmm, it sounds very much like that area had been napalmed,' he says, looking at the Englishman in surprise and wondering why napalm would be used. 'I don't suppose you saw any more casualties in the burnt-out area above the track when you were moving through?'

'No, I only saw the bandaged youth. They took us up to the top of the ridge and that's where we left from. A *Black Hawk* helicopter landed in the valley and took us and the Australians back to Kabul. When we arrived back, I was taken away by the Americans for what they called a "debrief", he pauses for a moment, briefly thinking about his rescue and what he'd seen. 'I'd like to meet this Peter Jackson again one day and thank him for saving my life because he sounded like a very courteous person.'

'How old was Peter Jackson?'

'Twenty six to twenty eight at the most; it's hard to tell when they are in camouflage fatigues and hadn't washed or shaved for a number of days. Why?'

'Oh just wondering.'

Afghanistan

Time has gone quickly for patrol B3. Our final assignments after operation Anaconda are long-range surveillance patrols where we are out in the rugged hills for long periods of time, watching tracks and reporting any movement we see. I don't mind this, the terrain is rough and I find the best way to move is carrying the supplies by the ever-reliable donkey. The animals seem to relish the rough conditions and are able to carry extraordinary loads into areas where you would be unable to take a vehicle.

It's on the completion of one of these patrols that a number of officers and sergeants are called in by the Officer in Charge for what we think is a routine briefing and to have further patrols allocated.

'Well, men, our assignment in Afghanistan is over and we'll be going home for a period to recharge the batteries. You've earned a rest. We'll be replaced by another squadron. Tell your men to start and pack their gear. We fly out of here tomorrow for a well-earned break. Well done, gentlemen!'

CHAPTER 15
EVALUATING OURSELVES

'Have you heard about Iraq?' Terry asks me, now a full corporal. 'I know there's a lot of sabre rattling but rumour has it the Yanks are going to invade the country and sort out Saddam Hussein once and for all and stop him producing weapons of mass destruction as he used on the Kurds some twelve months ago in northern Iraq. Word also has it that we'll very possibly be going in with them this time. It's evidently a little different from Desert Storm in ninety-one.' He pauses momentarily as if wanting confirmation from me; no one is giving anything away. 'From what I was told by some of the wheels, the Yanks were very pleased with the Squadron's performance in Afghanistan and want our support in Iraq as well.' He looks hard at me. 'Have you heard anything more reliable than just this digger talk, Sarge? I bet you blokes would have had quite a few briefings on this subject by now?'

'I've heard the rumours also, Terry,' I tell him, but I have great difficulty concentrating on what he's saying, having had some surprise guests two weeks before. 'Until we are told officially, it will only be a rumour; you know how things work around this joint. For the moment, I expect it's going to be a lot of hard training up north with the Rovers and then another trip back to Afghanistan.'

I've been living down the south-west of Perth in a small shack I'd bought when we came back from Timor, somewhere just to get away from camp. I use it, taking my leave, doing some fishing and having the occasional bottle of wine from one of the excellent wineries of the region. I was taking it easy this day, completely relaxed, sitting back on my deck chair, basking in the beautiful weather and looking out to sea with a glass of red wine in my hand, wondering what I am going to do with myself in the long term, for I have no intention of staying in the army forever. I have not quite a year of my enlistment to go, and I am seriously thinking of getting out of the army. It seems I've had a lifetime of killing and pitting myself against all types of enemies and getting myself tangled up in some very strange situations like in East Timor.

I'd like to go back to Tasmania to the farm but there is nothing there for me now as I don't want to cause any unnecessary friction with my brother and his children – they wouldn't believe it was me anyway and I don't want to go through any stupid rigmarole to prove who I am. At least down here, no one knows me; I can just fade away into obscurity, become a beach bum and do the odd job around the place for the local farmers and maybe, just maybe run into some lovely young woman who wants a companion. While watching the ocean and the occasional car that goes past, I think about what I'll catch in today's fishing and the predicament I have found myself in, wondering what I will do about my future.

A car pulls up in front of my unit. I watch the vehicle, not recognising the man in the passenger's front seat who's looking across towards me. I'm quite intrigued at who it could be; I suspect probably some tourist who's lost their way and is looking for directions. To my absolute astonishment, however, it's Abe who gets out of the driver's side and looks across the bonnet to where I'm sitting and gives me a cheery wave before quickly walking around the car and over to me.

'I have a surprise for you, old buddy,' he says, smiling after we give each other an almighty hug. 'I hope you've got plenty of that wine with you, Pete, because I have some guests who want to desperately meet you. I thought I owed you a little surprise after you shocked me to the core when you turned up. We've been waiting for your unit to come back from Afghanistan so we could spring this little surprise on you.'

I turn and look back at the car and see a stranger who I've never met before, get out of the front passenger's side and look intently at me, as if summing me up. Both rear doors open almost simultaneously allowing both Ophelia and Alicia to emerge; they stand next to the car and stare at me. I only have eyes for her; we look at each other for a long time, I'm surprised at this unexpected meeting – is this actually happening or is it just a dream; a figment of my imagination?

'I'm afraid I had to tell her, Pete. Things started to catch up with me big time because unfortunately she heard a whisper and started to get the wrong slant on everything concerning you. I had to tell her the truth; otherwise, she would have had everything wrong. Then, she really wanted to meet you.' He gives me a forlorn look that I hardly notice and then shrugs his shoulders. 'So here we are, Pete, warts and all I'm afraid, my friend.'

We walk towards each other, slowly at first; staring at each other, not quite believing the situation. We hesitate a little and then rush the last few yards and vigorously embrace each other, both of us crying, desperately holding on to one another. Finally, very slowly we pull apart and look at each other, with me immediately thinking of what could have been.

'You haven't changed at all,' she says, finally letting me go and staring up at me, wiping tears from her eyes. 'Oh, Pete, it's just so good to see you after all these years. I knew it was you as soon as I held you but … you're the age of my children. What happened?'

With those words, I suddenly come crashing down to earth with a giant thump and quickly realise things have changed dramatically for both of us and, unfortunately, irreversibly so. I now try desperately to get control of my emotions.

'Alicia, you'd better introduce me to your husband. I know the other woman with you; it's Ophelia.'

'Julian, this is the man I told you so much about. This is my Peter.'

'How are you, Julian?' I say, grasping his hand, looking at him and thinking, *She has a good husband by the looks of him.* 'It's lovely to meet you at last. Welcome to Australia.'

'It's a pleasure to finally meet you also, Peter. Alicia and I have spoken about you a lot over the years,' he says, eyeing me off. 'Peter, please forgive me for staring at you. As you know I'm a doctor of medicine and I find it very difficult to meet a man my age who looks the same age as my son; I'm afraid this will take some time to get used to.'

'That's alright, Julian,' I tell him, thinking about how I can calm him down. 'It took me a long time to adjust to what had happened to me as well. However, certain circumstances probably forced me to accept my predicament very quickly; otherwise, I would have been dead, and I certainly didn't want that.'

We look at each other for a little while longer, before I turn to the other older woman who is now standing quietly just behind him. I go up to her, kiss her on the cheek and give her a big welcoming hug.

'It's lovely to see you after such a long time, Ophelia. You know, you've hardly changed at all in the time since I saw you last. You're still the girl who knows how to keep Abe in his place.'

That seems to break the tension that I feel at this meeting and the next thing I know, I'm caught in another bear hug and drawn to her.

'Pete, I couldn't believe it was you that Abe was talking about,' she says, taking my breath away with her hug. 'You haven't aged at all. You're just as I saw you last, all brawn – you're just exactly the same, but Julian is right, you're the age of my son. Heavens: you'll have to tell us what happened to you back in Vietnam.' With sadness in her eyes, she says, 'Of course you know I lost him a while back, Peter?'

'Yes, Abe told me, Ophelia. I'm so sorry, but you're here with us now. Come inside lovely lady and to be honest mine is a *very* long story, so please, come inside everyone. I have plenty of wine and some beer in the fridge. We have a lot of catching up to do so we'll get a few grogs into us and you can enjoy Australia and, while we're doing that, we can all get to know each other once again after such a long time.'

They follow me inside, looking closely about them at my abode which is just a little hideaway; a little three-roomed shack

I purchased when the squadron came home from East Timor. I wanted to have somewhere private where I could relax and be by myself and reflect on the turmoil that had gripped me – I'm still coming to grips with it myself.

'I just needed a place to go, somewhere quiet and away from camp,' I tell them as they walk into the living area-cum-kitchen. 'Somewhere to do a little fishing and relax and try to get my head around the disasters that I've been involved with over the years. This seemed to be the logical place to do that and it's far enough away from camp for me not to be pestered to do the odd jobs that come up from time to time; somewhere quiet where no one knows me, and I can relax, with plenty of good fishing close by to take my mind off personal things that are happening.'

'This is a lovely place you have here,' comments Alicia as she stops in the living area and looks out across the sea to the west before turning back to me. 'It's a marvellous place; you could come down here to your shack as you call it and relax, knowing you wouldn't be disturbed by anyone. Do you come here often, Pete?'

'Weekends, when I'm not on duty back at camp, I can just disappear down here where no one knows me – which I've found is a huge advantage. Now, let's see if I can get this right. I don't know what you drink, Julian but, Abe you're a beer drinker, a martini for you, Ophelia. Now, do you still drink Bacardi, or have you found something else, Alicia?'

They look at each other for a few seconds until the silence is broken by Julian who grins at the stunned faces around him.

'I'll have a beer thanks, Pete. I haven't seen Alicia drink a Bacardi for a number of years, but I think on an occasion such as this it certainly justifies one. Would you be okay with a Bacardi, sweetie?'

'That will be fine,' she says with a big smile that almost says to me, *You remember what I liked.*

Abe and Ophelia both crack up laughing as if I am a magician or something, but it had the desired effect, and everyone is loosened up and it's nice to see no one holds anything back.

'Alicia and I had a dinner date in Washington, Pete. It was there that she successfully ambushed me. She'd had conversations with a reporter, a man called——'

'Kerry O'Flaherty,' I break in on Abe. 'I met a nice young lady called Tiffany when we were in East Timor just over twelve months ago. She was an American reporter and she worked with this man but unfortunately, she was killed when we were out in the scrub. After the trouble he had over there, I thought I had an agreement with him to shut his mouth about what he knew about my past, but obviously, I was wrong.'

'What do you mean?' Alicia asks, surprised at me breaking into Abe's story. 'Do you know this man?'

'Yes, I know him. He was Tiffany's boss in East Timor. I think he guessed the significance of what I'd said during my sleep in Timor.' I notice the puzzled look on their faces. 'Look, I'll go back to the beginning of what happened in East Timor. As she was confused and curious, Tiffany recorded what I said in a dream the next time and asked her boss about it as he'd been in Vietnam as a young reporter. He'd obviously done a check on my past and decided to pursue the matter. To me, that's why he was talking to Alicia about my past.' I shake my head in annoyance at what I'm just finding out. 'I'm afraid I'm beginning to wonder where it will end with this man.'

'What will we do about him?' says Alicia, getting quite aggravated at her personal privacy becoming public knowledge if O'Flaherty continues his enquiries. 'I thought Abe was hiding something from me, that's why I told him I'd cooperate with what he was trying to uncover. I hadn't listened and thought that Peter was the same age as us and Abe had been hiding the fact that he was alive from me,' she says, starting to cry as she slowly goes through the events of their meeting. 'I had no idea what had happened to Peter after he dropped from the rope, and then he played the recording. He told me the man he'd met was young, but I was so annoyed that I ignored this point; I didn't believe that a human body could be held in limbo like it was for so long without ageing.'

'That's alright, honey,' Julian says, putting his arm around Alicia in a forlorn attempt to stop her crying. 'If we stick together, it will turn out okay because he's only one man and if we say the one thing, he won't be able to do very much. Look, we'll just deny everything he says, just like the Vietnamese Government is doing – no one is questioning them on their stance about Peter's existence.'

'Alicia, would you be able to play the recording he gave you, so we all know what we're up against?' I ask her, a little out of frustration but also trying to get everything in the right perspective. 'It will give everyone here an idea of what we're talking about. I haven't heard them since Tiffany played one of them to me well over a year ago in East Timor and, from what you've said, there's another one I haven't heard concerning when I was released from the glass case in Vietnam where the Vietnamese were holding my body. Once we've heard them, we'll know exactly what he's got and be able to put a good plan in place that will combat whatever this man's story is that he's attempting to put together.'

We sit around the table, listening to the tape as it goes through my life. It's a dreamlike dialogue of past events. Julian and Ophelia are absolutely dumbfounded when they hear me speaking of my past; they sit there eating up every word listening to the drama that is my life unfolding in front of them. Even Abe is sitting on the edge of his chair at his part. During the final tape, it is Abe, the most fluent Vietnamese speaker among us, who translates the conversations of my escape with Noc and the Vietnamese fishermen. When the tape is over, they all stare at me as if they're expecting the next instalment of my life story, so I verbally finish the Australian part, explaining the testing I'd gone through, how I finally re-joined the army at my former rank and how the officer in charge of the unit knew me from when he was doing his cadre as a one-piper.

'Evidently, this Major Thong had invented a serum and from this a gas that has the ability to completely preserve living bodies, which effectively stops any ageing,' I explain to them, trying to give them some idea of how the gas worked. 'It wasn't until the Noc undid the case to clean the mould off the bottom and inadvertently let the gas out, that I woke up; all my recollections and memories start from that point. It's the Vietnamese side of the story that Kerry O'Flaherty hasn't got yet and if what happened to the French journalist Pierre Bulvarl who followed me from Vietnam is any indication, the story will stop. The military authorities allowed this man to interview me in Singapore and knowing how closely they intend to guard their secret, the story of what they did to me for those almost thirty years will finish with him, and we won't have to worry about Mr O'Flaherty ever again.'

We sit, looking at each other in silence for quite some time, trying to absorb the extraordinary events that had dominated my life when all of a sudden, Julian speaks out.

'Hell, this is going to sound bizarre, but oh well, here goes.

My father may have invented a time machine back in nineteen forty-four and I'm quite sure now that's what is responsible for my sister's strange disappearance,' he says, bringing us all back to reality and startling us with these random comments about his father's invention. 'We had a small dairy farm in the mid-west where my parents brought us up. My mother died of cancer when I was in my late teens and the following year, I started university, so I guess I was able to lose myself in my studies to get over my grief.' He turns to Alicia, taking her hand and looking deeply into her eyes. 'That's why I love you so much for the work you're doing with cancer patients now, sweetheart.'

'That's lovely to know, my beautiful man but please go on with your story; you have us all intrigued about your family and what they went through. Please tell us about them and what you believe was your father's time machine, perhaps this could explain your sister's disappearance.'

'Okay, sweetheart, I'll continue.' He looks back at us; I think, getting his confidence back with Alicia who is still holding his hand, giving him mental strength. 'As I said, I was at university in New York studying to be a doctor and Sandra, my younger sister, was just going through college at the time in her final year when Dad was killed by the Nazis who were after his notes — he had a host of notes regarding his experiments and findings. When I think back to the time, I'm quite sure that she only told me half the story.' Again, he turns to Alicia, his eyes watering a little. He squeezes her hand as if to get more confidence before he continues. 'I haven't told you this, Alicia because I was too embarrassed to tell you that … that my father was a top scientist for the German Third Reich and he and Mother came to America to get away from the Nazis towards the end of the war. That's why we were raised on the farm in the back blocks of America so they wouldn't find him. Unfortunately, however, after some thirty-odd years, they did. I was at university when my sister came home from college one day and found them all dead at the kitchen table. There had evidently been a shoot-out in the kitchen and Papa had obviously killed them all, but unfortunately in the process, they had killed him as well. We still own the farm at Clareville because I … I kept it for sentimental reasons and for somewhere to go to get away from New York.

'One wet day, years later, when we were at the farm and I had nothing to do, I began looking through my father's office just to see what he had there from his youth, trying to find a little about their side of our family because we knew virtually nothing about him or my mother or anything that would throw a little light on them and what had caused him to be killed. My sister had told me a little about them just before the funeral, but I wanted to see what I could find out for myself.' He then stands and says, 'I'll be back in a moment.' Turning to Abe, Julian asks for the car keys, which Abe gives him then he walks outside, leaving us looking at each other in puzzlement. We don't have long to wait though as he comes back inside a minute later carrying a large leather bag, which he places on the floor and from it, withdraws a small and very old briefcase.

Gingerly, he opens the briefcase and takes out a collection of papers. As he does so, the light shines on the faint but unmistakable Nazi eagle emblem on the front. 'This is one of the things that I found in his office that absolutely floored me and possibly could answer some of the questions I have about the strange disappearance of my sister in Iraq.'

I notice that Alicia is just as surprised as the rest of us, and she is listening intently.

He fossicks through the briefcase before bringing out other reams of paper. He puts them on the table. Then we proceed to go through the papers page by page. Everything is written in German and is done in such a precise way. I have difficulty understanding anything other than the diagrams, so it's up to Julian who has studied German to explain what he can of the material he's laid out in front of us.

'Evidentially Papa brought his entire work from Germany so, to be to able read it, I had to study German at university as well as medicine – I certainly didn't want someone else translating this for me because after they done so, they would've known exactly what I had,' he continues, a source of pride in his voice. We seem to have hit a roadblock with the papers. 'My sister, Sandra, was the practical one of us when it came to designing and building things when growing up. For example, as children when we were always building playhouses and things like that, she could always build them bigger and better than I could. I think she used to do that just to show me up because I was the male child in the family. She thought it strange when I chose to do medicine at university and become a doctor. I think she assumed I would follow in Papa's footsteps and complete what he'd started, although I didn't know about the time machine that he'd developed for the Third Reich at the time. I didn't know about that until she disappeared and I began looking through his personal things and found this briefcase holding these papers. I know all this sounds a bit far-fetched but bear with me.'

'How did you know about this story, Julian?' I ask, quite intrigued. 'Did your sister tell you about his work or did you find out about what your father was doing when you found these papers of his?'

'I'll get to that in a moment, Pete. First, I need to fill you in on the events as they progressed, so you get the whole picture of what happened to our family.' He goes back to explain his mother's death. 'As I said, Mamma died of cancer some two years before Papa. Her accent was quite different to his but as children we didn't pay much attention to this. She was our Mamma and was kind to my sister and me; having a loving mother was all that mattered to us. It wasn't until I came home for Papa's funeral that my sister told me about the events that led to his death. I was a little worked up at the time because of the nature of Papa's death; the way he'd been murdered. She told me Papa had worked for the Nazis on some secret project and let slip the name of one of the men, a man called Eric Kessering who killed my grandfather and destroyed the laboratory they worked at to hide the existence from the invading forces, so they didn't know what they were working on. She surprised me again when she mentioned that he worked with our Grand Papa on this same project, and she told me a little about his background before he was brought to Germany, instead of going to the camps because of his engineering skills. She also told me how he found Mamma hiding in my Grand Papa's room under the bed when he was about to leave. He had to get out of Berlin before the Russians took the city and had gone back for the papers he knew our Grand Papa kept under his bed and there she was, hiding from the Nazis. So, he pulled her out and took her with him.'

'More drinks, everyone?' I ask, wanting to keep everyone comfortable. I want to learn as much as I can about Alicia's in-laws, especially the part about time travel as, strangely, it appears I may not be the only one to have been held in time. I am pleased that he's brought this up because it is a good way to stop talking about the turmoil of my own life. I quickly get them more drinks and sit quietly, listening as Julian continues with his story.

'The Nazis had a laboratory set up in the western suburbs of Berlin and Papa was the head scientist who had been ordered by the Reich to build a time machine. They evidently knew they were losing the war and wanted to travel into the future and gather secret plans for advanced weapons to take back to Germany, build them early in the war and take over the world. A simple plan really, but would it have worked? Thankfully, this idea didn't come to fruition and fortunately for the world they never finished the project; otherwise, what would the world look like now with the Nazis in control?'

'Why did your father pick America to come to, Julian?' Abe asks, confused at why a top German scientist would come to an enemy country towards the end of the war to live. 'Wouldn't it have been easier to just lie low in Germany or go to South America where many went into hiding until things in Europe cooled down and it was safe to continue his work? He could have started his work up immediately when he got over there, and no one would have worried him; some of the countries like Brazil are huge, some four million square miles and it would have been virtually impossible to find him or for that matter even know he was there.'

'This is where it's difficult. You are family, I've wanted to get this off my chest for a long, long time,' he says, looking around at each of us, apparently wanting someone to say, *Tell me what happened.* This was the situation I'd been in with Tiffany, and I have to say I felt a lot better when I told her the truth about myself, and this stopped me from having those vivid dreams of my past.

'Firstly, my father was German; his name was Von Crease. I've spent a lot of time researching on the internet and looking through archives for things about him and it appears almost every country that fought in the war was looking for him; not as a war criminal mind you, but for his knowledge of time travel. Secondly, my mother was a Polish Jew, so they changed their name to Ashfield in an attempt to hide. That's why they went west and started the dairy farm out there. I expect Papa's theory was solid and that he was right with his thinking – who in their right mind would look at a dairy farmer somewhere in the back blocks of America when you are looking for a top German scientist?'

'No one,' breaks in Ophelia, who has been uncharacteristically quiet. 'No one in their right mind would look at a dairy farmer and say, hmm, now that's a top German scientist, would they? They would have to be stark raving mad to think of that, totally mad and you'd have to be mad to believe them.'

'So, you are half Jewish!' exclaims Alicia, looking with quite a lot of surprise at Julian who immediately takes her hand softly in his and I notice he gives her hand a little reassuring squeeze. 'So that means our children are part Jewish, part German and part Polish from your side of our family. How wonderful! What an exciting mixture of nationalities we have in our family tree! We'll have to document this and tell them someday, sweetheart. How do you think they will react to being told something as unique as this?'

'I have no idea, darling. It's something I had to come to grips with myself when Sandra told me just before Papa's funeral. Initially, I was quite shocked when she first told me but, after thinking about what she'd said, I kinda liked the idea, although as far as religion is concerned, as you all know I'm fairly neutral.'

'So, a number of allied countries were looking for your father?' I ask, very interested in what he is saying and wanting to keep them off religion and on the subject of Julian's father and how he made the escape out of Europe towards the end of the Second World War. It is more *how* he got out that I am interested in rather than *why*. If a scientist as well-regarded as he had evidently been, could get away so easily from the allies, how many other Nazi officials had escaped to neutral or non-aligned countries and gone to ground like this Kessering character that Julian has already mentioned? 'How did he get out if every country that was involved in the war was looking for him? Surely if their intelligence services were worth their salt, they should have been able to track him down?'

'You have to realise it was quite chaotic in Europe towards the end of the war and the number of displaced people wandering around was staggering but, from what Sandra told me when she picked me up before the funeral, it appears that my mother was a contributing factor to their escape. You also must realise that there were refugees everywhere and the intelligence organisations were looking for an individual, not a couple and my Dad was the only one who knew of Mamma's existence, and he had been murdered when they destroyed the research centre.' He stops for a moment, deep in thought. 'I think the fact they left Europe just before the war was over and changed their name to an English one, may have helped them remain obscure from the intelligence agencies, who by this time were scanning every country for him. Evidently, many bureaucrats knew of the project and gave details of the laboratory and the aim of the project to the allies. It certainly helped that the Nazi Kessering killed the rest of the staff and burned the laboratory to the ground. This meant that a lot of the avenues available to them to follow up on any leads were closed permanently and all working records in the building were destroyed. There was a huge manhunt for my Papa when hostilities finished because he was the only one left who knew about time travel and of the experiments they were carrying out in the laboratory. It took the Nazis almost twenty-five years to find him and Kessering had more details than any of the others and knew him by sight. Sandra showed me a newspaper cutting of Papa and Kessering that she took from Kessering's pocket when she found the bodies showing both Papa and Kessering standing together in Nazi uniforms.'

'Your sister actually searched the bodies when she found them?' Abe appears to be quite surprised at Julian's intriguing revelation. 'Heavens above, she must have been a brave girl to find the body of her father and all the other bodies in the room to then be able to search those who killed him.'

'Yes, she did. Evidently, Papa had told her who had killed our Grand Papa, so she disregarded the two young men and only searched the older man and found he was this man Papa had spoken to her about; it was Kessering who ordered the research establishment to be burnt and the other scientists shot.'

'That was a brave thing to do, sweetheart,' Alicia says, putting her hand on his in a comforting manner, perhaps gaining a different perspective of what she had thought was her wayward sister-in-law. 'I hope we can find your sister one day as it would take a lot of intestinal fortitude to go into a room full of bodies and search even one of those people, particularly when one of the bodies was your father.'

'Yes, it would, sweetheart, but I'd better finish telling you the reasons why the others would have given up.' He stops for a moment, looks about us and sees that we all want to hear more.

'I expect a lot of the others gave up over the years when more pressing things came up; for example, the Cold War with the communists and the Space Race would have been important priorities at that stage. That's another reason why I kept the name my father used in America because I'm sure there are still people out there looking for these.' He retrieves another few pages from the briefcase, causing everyone to take more interest in them than ever before. 'It was about a month before Sandra disappeared in Iraq and unfortunately, I still hadn't made any sort of connection to it and her disappearance.'

'I can remember that distinctly,' says Abe. 'I had just gotten into the Senate, and we spent a lot of time in Iraq looking for her. She was evidently running around with some strange-looking four-wheel-drive vehicle that she'd built up from virtually nothing. The people she worked for informed us of this; they told us of this strange custom-designed Land Rover she was working on but, from what she'd told them, it was a research vehicle specially designed for oil exploration and that she used this vehicle for exploration to assist the company and speed up her work of evaluating of the samples the geologist brought to her.'

Julian nodded his head in agreement. 'When you read Papa's notes, you'll find the rear end was exactly what the Germans would have built on their time machine to house the time capsule and other components. From there, they would take the power from the motor and compact this energy into something called a time warp which, according to his notes, will cause the vehicle to virtually vaporise to travel through time. Unbelievable, I know, but there it is. What the Germans had problems with, however, were the components to transfer the power across to the time module that was built in just behind the driver's seat. From all reports I've pored over, they were made out of inferior quality material and were breaking down when put under extreme stress. This pursuit of excellence put their production of the time machine back months, if not years, and Papa insisted that everything they built into their machine had to meet specific standards of quality in production. He was worried that they would go on a trip and the parts would break down or malfunction and they would be stranded somewhere in time and wouldn't be able to get back from their mission. I don't expect it would have been a worry for them going into the future because the parts required should be readily available or could be made specifically for the machine. Imagine going back in time to well before the Industrial Revolution when the type of component you wanted wasn't available, couldn't be produced or hadn't even been thought of yet. It would have been an absolute disaster for the people in the time capsule because they would have no chance whatsoever of getting back to their own time. Unfortunately, they would be stuck in the past, probably for good.'

'So, everything points to your sister building a time machine while she was working in Iraq,' I say, more than a little interested in this project now that Julian has explained most of it to us. 'Why would she do this herself and not get help from someone; for example, one of the people she was working with could have helped? To me, getting help would have been the logical thing to do in a situation like that.'

'Evidently, a group went into town to have a few drinks and to look around but because a female was with them having a drink, the locals didn't like it. They objected to the group strongly, so she left and from that time she devoted her spare time, as she called it in her letters, to her project. Initially she explained to us in great detail about stripping down and doing up the old Land Rover's motor but after a while there was little word about the vehicle and more on the testing of samples that she was doing in the laboratory. The only time she went into town was to get spare parts for her project from a dealer who carried parts for these old Land Rovers.' He gives each of us an exasperated look, now quite worried about his sister's strange, unknown disappearance. 'She didn't even bother coming home for Christmas but preferred instead to go traipsing around Europe, I expect looking for some of our long-lost relations and seeing the sights like most tourists do nowadays but that wasn't the thing that worried us, it wa——'

'She could, however, have been getting parts unavailable in Iraq for the machine she was building,' I interject, thinking of different possibilities. 'They would certainly have everything she wanted in Europe and of the high quality she would have needed. It would be only a matter of transporting them back to their base where she was building her machine.'

'That's right, Pete; the last letter we received from her was to say she was going to take the Land Rover out on a test run.' You can see Julian is likely thinking of what I'd just said as it fits in with his theory of her disappearance. 'We didn't pay much attention to what it could mean, did we, Alicia?'

'Julian and I had just started going out, so you could say that his mind was on other things,' Alicia says a little coyly. The strain of embarrassment shows on her face with her thinking of the disappearance of her sister-in-law. 'The testing of an old English four-wheel-drive had no interest to us at all.'

'Did Sandra have a boyfriend or someone she was dating?' I ask, quite intrigued with this girl and her vehicle now that it appears I may not be the only one who was lost in time. 'Perhaps he may know where she is and what she's been doing or perhaps even what happened to her when she disappeared.'

'She did have a boyfriend at university whose uncle was the one who got them their jobs with the oil company, but the boyfriend was sent to the Caribbean while she went to Iraq. They evidently corresponded for a little while from what she wrote in her letters, but it didn't last. I have no idea where he is now.'

'What makes you think she turned the old Land Rover into a time machine?' I ask Julian, thinking there may not be any connection. 'Julian, I'm playing devil's advocate here, so let's look at all the possibilities we have in front of us. For example, was it something she inadvertently said about time travel or are you putting two and two together and getting five now that you've compared it to the information in your father's papers?'

'Pete, with your type of investigative mind, I'd like you on my team when I'm doing surgery,' he says, light-heartedly. 'You look at everything and then analyse it thoroughly before you move on to the next step.'

'I was a patrol medic on my first tour of Vietnam,' I tell him. 'I tried to help Alicia with homework from the hospital one night. She was in her third year. I lasted about five minutes and ended up watching a late-night western after Silvo and Andrew had gone off to bed. I found there is a lot of difference between a doctor and a patrol medic, Julian.'

Julian continues on with his story and what his sister may have evidently built. 'There were some things her workmates had told us when we went over to Iraq that we could not put a label on until I re-read Papa's notes. They said the only thing that looked like a Land Rover when she finished with the machine was the grill. The vehicle had this large, balloon-shaped construction on the back.' He pauses for a moment, grabs a biro and draws this odd shape over a vehicle. 'This is exactly like the drawing that one of the employees did for me when we went over there looking for her. I've been thinking long and hard about it – it's a structure that's totally unnecessary on any vehicle, especially in the desert. Now look at this.' He flicks through his father's notes and brings out a similar diagram. 'Pete, I believe my sister has created the world's first time machine and unfortunately, she's out there somewhere with this machine, but … how will we ever find her?'

'Julian, I'm afraid I don't know either. What happened to me was a medical procedure using drugs. The drugs used are beyond belief and had something to do with slowing the respiratory system down where, while on these drugs, a second equals something like a year, Noc was telling me. I didn't even need a shave when I woke up thirty years later. But in the time it took me to get to Singapore, my facial hair had grown, my head looked like I had a close crewcut, and I needed a shave badly. Just thinking about what has happened to your sister, from what you've described, it is more of a mechanical procedure where the machine evidently takes the space in, say, a capsule to and from the future or the past. Sorry to say, but, unfortunately no one knows if she went forward or backward in time. I'm sorry, but I just don't know the answer to how to find her.' Then, thinking of what the Germans proposed with their machine, I ask, 'Do you know how far in the future the Nazis proposed to go?'

'Some thirty years in time, Pete, why?'

'From what you told me, that would be close to this year from all accounts if she follows their procedures to the letter.'

We talk for a long period before we finally head off to bed, having consumed a reasonable quantity of alcohol. Being the only single person aside from Abe and Ophelia, I end up on the couch on the veranda. I lie there thinking about what we'd said and about this girl that's somewhere out there in time. *What has become of her? Did she go forward or back in time, but the big question is — where is she now? If she'd gone back in time, she could have contacted her brother by leaving something for him such as a letter or note to let him know of her whereabouts. No, she must have gone forward in time.* I keep asking myself questions over and over again before I finally drop off to sleep.

In the spare room a similar situation is occurring. Julian and Alicia lie together looking at the ceiling, thinking of what was talked about during the evening, and also having trouble sleeping.

'That is definitely Peter, you know,' says Alicia, looking up into the dark. 'What he said tonight about me doing my homework, him trying to help and then going in to watch television with Mum and Dad and watching an old western movie was just as it happened. I remember watching the last little bit with him. Julian, not even Abe knows about that. Heavens, he's so young; how in the world did that Vietnamese doctor do what he did to keep him so young?'

'I looked at you when he said it,' Julian says quietly, looking across at her in the dark. 'There was a look of utter shock on your face; something I haven't seen before. It's like you saw a ghost. Are you alright now?'

'Yes, darling, I'm over it now. I have you and the children to thank for that. He's such a young man so I hope he can settle down because he's been through a lot. The man I knew and loved will overcome that and I'm sure he'll eventually find someone.'

'It sounded like he almost did in East Timor. What a disappointing life he's had so far! She was the second girl he's lost — how tragic!'

'I'll have a talk to him tomorrow and give this back to him,' she says, feeling his ring on her finger. 'Perhaps it will help to find him another girl because, sweetheart, it's been extremely lucky for me.'

I'm back from a long run along the beach and find all four sitting on the veranda talking. When they see me, Alicia gives me a wave.

'We've been waiting for you before having breakfast,' says Abe, I think a little worse for wear after consuming more than his share of wine. 'I'm not as young as I used to be, and you just kept filling up my wine glass.'

'It helped with the conversation, Abe. You were all relaxed and didn't hold anything back. That made for a good, interesting evening and I learnt about Julian and Julian's sister, and you learnt about me and what I've gone through.'

After a typical army breakfast for recovery – a good round of bacon and eggs and toast done to an old army recipe – we're back on the veranda relaxing in the sun, looking out to sea when Alicia grabs me by the arm, pulling me up.

'Show me your beach. I'd like to walk with you a little and we can talk about the past. Is anyone else coming?'

It is obvious that this is all pre-arranged as each of them uses some lame excuse – Ophelia is happy to sit and enjoy the view; Abe is a little seedy and Julian is going through the papers again, before putting them away. This leaves Alicia and me alone to walk along the beach toward the breakwater.

'Peter, I know it's you. I found it very difficult to believe the story that the journalist told me about you, and I thought we were dealing with an impostor posing as you. When I fronted Abe a couple of months ago and he told me about meeting you, I still found it hard to believe him. I was looking at you last night and it was the person I used to go out with, but it wasn't until you mentioned my homework and that western movie that I fully believed it was you. You and I are the only people who knew about that night at Mum and Dad's. I'm so sorry things didn't work out for us.'

'So am I. Abe took me to a meeting that you had with him in New York and I watched you walk into the restaurant to meet him. I knew then that you were gone out of my grasp. It staggered me when Abe told me you saw me; it was then I knew I had to move on. I'm sorry but that's the way it is. You have a wonderful husband who cares for you, so look after him and your children.'

'What about you, what are you going to do now; are you going to stay in the army or have you other plans?'

'I could but I'm tired of the killing and the conflicts I've been involved with; two tours of Vietnam, East Timor and Afghanistan and the next will be Iraq. That will be enough for me. Hopefully, I'll find a nice woman and settle down; it'll probably be like Julian's father did – I'll switch off and milk cows for the rest of my life.'

'Oh, Peter, I just hope things work out for you,' she says, a tear in her eye. 'I just keep thinking of what could have been.'

'Don't. You have a lovely husband who dotes on you. Just look after him. If he starts stuffing around trying to build that time machine of his father's, give me a call.'

They leave about midday travelling back to Perth; another chapter in my life is finally closing. I remember my mother's words that she once told me, '*With every opportunity closed another door always seems to open.*' I hope she's right …

CHAPTER 16

IRAQ

Perth, Australia

The rumour mill is running overtime as the debate about whether we are to be going to Iraq gains momentum after each newsflash on television most nights describes the gassings and other atrocities carried out in the north against the Kurds. The perception that is being given is that Scud missiles have been used to carry this gas to the targets. One commentator even infers that they have super Scud missiles, which have the capability of nuclear warheads, but this is soon denied by some professor so-and-so as being impossible with the resources that Iraq has. Officers and sergeants are being briefed about our coming deployment, but we have to remain tight-lipped with the other ranks about where and when our next deployment will be made. The meeting with Abe, Alicia and their families south of Perth is all but a distant memory now, even though it has only been two weeks since I hosted them. I've promised to write to them and keep in touch – a promise I intend to honour, for true friends are very hard to come by in this volatile time and I don't want to lose touch with them again now that they know what the Vietnamese did to me in the early seventies.

I was however very interested to learn about the disappearance of Alicia's sister-in-law, Sandra, almost thirty years ago and I wonder if it is possible that she's built the time machine her father had invented. If the time she intended to travel was forward some thirty years as the Nazis envisaged, then that would put it at this year, so that could be interesting to see if something turns up.

We have spent a week up north practising with our six-wheel-drive Land Rovers, honing our skills with these large, very versatile machines that we will rely on entirely for our survival in the coming conflict. I have Terry as my gunner – he's a corporal now – and Mick, who's very savvy with these large vehicles, having done an extensive automotive mechanic course after our stint in East Timor. He's now back as my driver with the rank of Lance Corporal so it's good to have two fellas who I've already been overseas with, because we almost know how each other thinks and, in an emergency, that type of knowledge will be just like winning the lotto when we do our next deployment.

The exercise has been a gruelling week of navigation, finding checkpoints and plotting our course across huge stretches of this bare, somewhat desolate land with our wheels thinking of areas as close to the topography as we'll be working in. Naturally, we are having to avoid the numerous enemy patrols that the regiment has placed in strategic places to test our navigational skills and our ability to evade them. They've scattered these groups at random around the area to make it difficult for us to reach our objectives on time and it's my impression that these enemy units have been told by the wheels to do everything they possibly can to catch us. So far, with skill, initiative and a lot of good luck, we've been able to avoid all of them and have made good time. It's the last night so we carefully move towards the finish line that is still some ten kilometres away, knowing there will be enemy vehicles in the vicinity trying to capture us.

On the last night of this tiring training exercise, it seems that the enemy patrols are gunning for us; we're the tall poppies they want to knock off our perch. We now have less than a day to go to finish this exhausting exercise before packing up and moving back to Perth where our commanding officer will announce our next deployment to all the squadron which will be to Iraq, as allies of the Americans.

In the past few days, we've travelled some four hundred kilometres with most of this travelling being at night, so we aren't picked up by the many aircraft in this area, both civilian or military, who have been told to keep an eye open and report any vehicles moving in the open. I look down at my watch and find it's almost midnight; it's about time to stop for a break. Each of us needs a short rest to recoup our sensitivities as these have begun to wane dramatically as we begin to tire. It gives us the opportunity to relax a little and regain our concentration for this final push through to the base camp.

'Light ahead, front left,' Terry whispers down to us and Mick quickly brings the Rover to a halt, cutting off the motor as we scan our front. We notice the small light flickering off and on well to our front left. It's an erratic exercise pinpointing someone's position as if this person has dropped something on the vehicle's floor and is looking for whatever it is with the small pencil torch that most patrols carry onboard to highlight maps or look for objects that have been mislaid in the dark. 'That's got to be an enemy vehicle to be as slack as this. That operator should've have had the light hidden much better than this.'

'Well done,' I whisper back to Terry, pleased that he still has his faculties switched on. 'You've probably saved our bacon – they are a good few kilometres away from us and we were moving directly towards them and could have passed very close by, so they would've heard our motor. The bloke on duty in that vehicle would have definitely heard our engine; if we'd kept on this course, we'd bloody near run into them.' I turn across to my companions with a dry smile on my face, trying to hide what I intend to do. 'It's our last day so let's have some fun at their expense, something they won't forget in a hurry; if these were real circumstances with what we're about to do, they'd all be dead. We'll park right here, boys and do a close recce of them on foot and find out just who the hell they are and if they are, as I suspect, some of the groups playing enemy, then we'll have a little game with them and stamp their vehicles to show them they shouldn't be so bloody careless. If we'd been a real enemy, that light could have easily cost them all their lives. That my friends shouldn't be ignored, and we shouldn't let them get away with it.'

'What do you mean when you say, stamp their vehicles, Sarge?' Terry says, a little confused.

'We'll do exactly what Stirling did in the Western Desert in World War Two, when they first started this unit up.' I explain what I'd read in the book called *The Phantom Major*, it fits the scam I have in mind. 'The wheels of the day who were in charge of the Pom army at the time, didn't think much of this specialised unit he was putting together so I expect, to prove their worth to this group of officers and men, they would make dummy attacks on air and naval bases and other installations throughout Egypt, embarrassing the establishment with so much success that the security at these front-line bases was drastically tightened up. They would write out a note with the grid reference and something like – *You are now blown up you slack pricks, if we were Jerry, you'd all be dead by now.*' I look at my watch. 'So, *23:30 hours, Wednesday,* hide this note on the vehicle somewhere so that it will be found later and people will know they have been attacked and their vehicles, planes or ships have been destroyed. Stuff having a spell, boys; I'm afraid this has stirred me up. I only wish we had some Time Pencils to put on our smoke grenades and hide them onboard their vehicles. Unfortunately, this time, fellas, a note will have to do or if either of you have a texta you can write something sweet over the back of their vehicles to show them they shouldn't be so careless in war games. Technically, they'd lose two Rovers and both their crews would be dead.'

'I have one,' Mick says, smiling across at me. 'We'll soon make whoever it is pay for being so careless – you're right, Pete if we were Iraqis they would all be dead, it's as simple as that.'

'We also have tubes of Cam cream that we can paste over the rear of their vehicles with that,' Terry suggests, with a broad grin. He's lost all his sleepiness and is rearing to go. 'We can use that when we stamp them. This should make a mess that everyone will see and will be very hard to clean up way out here.'

'That should do the trick. Look, we'll park here and creep over to them and blow the bastards up before we continue on to the finishing line,' Mick excitedly says. 'Damn I wish we had some Time Pencils too, they would do an excellent job and show them right up, especially if we let them hear us and we have one of those tied to the grill and it goes off just when they start chasing us.'

'We could still hide some onboard,' Terry says, getting into the swing of what we are about to do. 'There are plenty of places where we could place these grenades with the pins out and they would vibrate free as they move along.'

Terry's and Mick's eyes are lit up with the prospect of a little fun on our final night; this will give them something they can lord over the other fellows acting as the enemy. The thing they don't realise however, is that in this so-called game, they will gain stealth from this little exercise if we are successful – a vital component and something they will probably need later on in their military careers. It'll be vital training for this coming campaign I know we have lined up in front of us in the next month or so.

'What are we waiting for, Sarge? Let's get their damn vehicles stamped and show those bastards up as being such slack pricks,' is Mick's impatient taunt to Terry and me. 'We'll send those bastards a message they'll never forget because those pricks have had the damn easy part of this exercise, or so they think. We'll change that right now.'

It takes a good half an hour to get in close to our enemy's machines. There are two Land Rovers parked slightly apart, their guns trained either way as the manual states, while leaving a clear space in between them for the crews to sleep. We can see the five bodies on the ground, sleeping between the vehicles but where is the sixth man? This person is obviously awake and on guard because it was he who had the light on that gave away their position, so using my fingers I warn my companions that one of the crew is missing and to pick this individual up before we move in.

'There are only five,' I whisper to the boys, hoping to stem their enthusiasm a little and stop them from going headlong into the Rovers to write their messages. 'There's another one on piquet somewhere. We have to find him first before we move in and plant our letters, so beware and find that bloke on guard first.'

We carefully search the area with our eyes, not making any sudden moves towards the vehicles before finally Mick spots him.

'He's sitting in the passenger's seat in the left-hand Rover behind the 30 Cal, so we certainly don't want to let them know we're here,' he whispers to me, pointing to the closest vehicle. 'You can just make him out against the skyline when he moves. Watch the left-hand one and you should see him.' We wait patiently, watching the closest vehicle and trying to pick out the sentry. 'There, you can just see him now fidgeting as he tries to get comfortable in the seat of their Rover.'

'Right, I'll cover you both while you hide your messages. Mick, you take the one with the piquet as you picked him out and Terry you fix the other one. Also, take their vehicle numbers so we have a positive identification. It's too dark to identify who they are but once we have their numbers, they're ours.'

'I've got a Philips-head screwdriver with me,' Mick tells us with a crafty look in his eye. 'Why don't we remove one of their number plates and take them with us then it won't matter if they clean their Rovers up, we'll have them cold?'

With me covering them and the piquet in sight, the two quietly move around their respective vehicles and plant their messages. Then, they make a mess of the back of one and the front of the other Rover with their Cam cream and texta. They are away for probably ten minutes before finally I see first one then the other approaching me through the gloom. Again, the night vision goggles have been wonderful for picking out every detail of our targets and allowing Mick to remove the front number plate from one vehicle and the rear plate from the other.

'Well done, fellas. Now let's make tracks out of here. We have a long way to go to get to the final checkpoint and there may be others just like these fellas in our way. If there are and we see them first, we'll have fun with them as well.'

The trip is slow as we're well aware there may be more biding their time with someone on piquet listening for us heading for the finish line. It's a little before five in the morning with the sun struggling to push its way up over the ridge to the east when we finally move into the last checkpoint, much to the surprise of a sig who wakes up with the sound of our approaching Rover. He ticks us off as being in and then makes some derogatory comments about sleeping at the wheel which we ignore, too tired to back chat him and we pull over to one side for some well-earned rest. I'm proud of my two companions as they've performed their jobs extremely well on this last exercise and have worked tirelessly at every obstacle we've encountered and accomplished every facet of the course; jointly responsible for what we've been able to achieve during these little night excursions. The final thing they do is screw the number plates Mick took to a pole outside the sig centre.

With our exercise over, the squadron moves in a convoy back to our base in Perth where, the next day, we are told by the commanding officer to pack our gear because we will be going to assist the Americans in the invasion of Iraq. A hush goes over the assembled diggers who now know they are destined for Iraq and won't be doing another tour of Afghanistan just yet. I suddenly think of the difference between this announcement and Australia's commitment to Vietnam when the then Prime

Minister Harold Holt made this proclamation by radio in nineteen sixty-six; all the diggers in both east and west blocks went berserk when this commitment to send a Special Air Service Squadron to Vietnam was made public.

Kuwait

No time is lost; a week later, the squadron and accessories are in Kuwait, 'the gateway to Iraq' as we've been told by the officer in charge. This small country is hot and flat and there is sand everywhere. I think the only reason anyone would live in a place like this is that there is oil underneath the sand that's helping to drive our western economies and, who knows, this invasion probably has more to do with that oil than the so-called weapons of mass destruction the press keep talking about which they found in the last invasion ten years before. The story is that these people have, according to experts, super Scud missiles now, which contain large, unknown quantities of explosives and lethal gasses like they used on the Kurds in the northern part of the country. And whatever else these weapons could be carrying that the Iraqis are supposed to have. Who cares about things like that? We're professional soldiers here to do whatever job our government gives us because this is why we joined the army in the first place.

'The OC wants to have a word with you, Pete,' the orderly room clerk says, coming across to our vehicle and watching our preparations. 'I have no idea what it's about, he just said "Get me Sergeant Jackson, I want a quick word with him", said I'd find you over there near his tent.'

I walk to his temporary HQ, quite puzzled as to why I've been singled out for his attention so early in the piece. He's new to the unit but has already served time with one of the battalions in Timor and, from what I've been told, his company performed extremely well against the militia up there. So, a little puzzled by his early summons, I walk over to his tent which is doubling as his office.

'Ah! Come in, Sergeant,' he says, looking up briefly as I enter. 'That little stunt you pulled on the exercise back in Australia has finally caught up with you.' He looks me straight in the eye, smiling at me before he asks me to take a seat. 'Operation Falconer is the code name for the invasion of Iraq that is due to start shortly; however, we're led to believe by American intelligence that there are mobile Scud missiles sited in this region.' He flicks his finger over an area of the map well to the north of Baghdad, towards the area occupied by the Kurds. 'The Americans are worried that the Iraqis could initiate a pre-emptive strike just before Operation Falconer starts and who knows what these missiles will be armed with? The American intelligence also believes that they may have a larger rocket hidden somewhere and that they will employ these like they did last time at Israel and other vulnerable targets in the area including here because they still claim Kuwait as theirs. Now, if they are more lethal than they used before, as we're led to believe, and Israel does come into the war, the worry is that other Arab countries such as Syria and possibly even Egypt may enter the battle in support of Iraq and that could be what Saddam Hussein wants. However, at the moment they are on their own with the other countries that neighbour them only paying lip-service in supporting them. This, however, could change quickly if Israel enters the fray and becomes a combatant. Now, Sergeant, because we need someone to slip over the border early to find these rockets before things get nasty and we're bogged down, I'm directing you and your crew to locate them so they can be knocked out of the equation well before the shooting starts.'

'Yes, Sir, I believe we can find them. I have two very good men with me and, given a little bit of luck, we should be able to locate those rockets and destroy them. Has the American intelligence told us how many missiles the Iraqis are supposed to have in that proximity, Sir?'

'Intelligence reports tell us there could be anything up to eight in the area here and these will be on trucks that are commonly called mobile firing platforms which give them the ability to move around very quickly and fire from different locations. They are of Russian origin and could drop as much as a ton of explosives on specific targets inside Israel, Saudi Arabia and probably even here if they want to stir the Americans right up. From what we're told from intelligence, they have evidently improved the payload and the accuracy of their missiles quite substantially in the last ten years since the first Gulf War. Sergeant, some experts here are even saying they may be armed with nuclear warheads by now and if that's the case, they would wipe Israel or any other specific targets such as here, off the map. If they are able to launch any such missiles as those when this war starts, the casualty rates on our side could be enormous.'

'What about air strikes, Sir; could the Americans knock them out with these because that would be a very quick solution?'

'The Americans feel, and I tend to agree with their way of thinking, that they would be unable to knock all of them out with coordinated air assaults. They have reverted to a ground attack before they're launched and that is where we come in, Sergeant. They feel their aircraft would get most of them but couldn't stop them all from being shot at specific targets. They can't afford anything like that to happen to our so-called allies in the Middle East. Pete, if these experts are correct and there are some nuclear weapons amongst these Scuds, it would only take one of those missiles to be launched and it would wipe out a complete country and millions of people would die.'

'When do we leave, Sir? My men and I have our Rover ready to start and, as you realise, Terry has already done well with the advanced missile training we did a month before the last exercise. Would it be possible, Sir, to take some extra missiles with us just in case we need to destroy a large target from a distance? In this sort of situation, we could very easily need them.'

'Yes, by all means; you can take four but for Christ's sake don't lose any; otherwise, you and I will both be in the poor house for the rest of our lives. They're worth sixty thousand dollars each.'

'We won't, Sir. They won't be wasted, Sir, because Terry is good at his job, and he'll make sure if we have to use them that you'll get your big bang.'

'How's the Arabic? I heard you all did the course before you came over. You may need to be able to communicate with the local population at some time while you're over the border; or do we put on an extra person with you who speaks the language fluently, would something like that help?'

'Mine is just fair, Sir. I'd probably be able to get food in a supermarket with a little bit of a hassle but that's all. Mick's language however is excellent – you'd think he's a very light-skinned Arab the way he prattles away. Unfortunately, I think Terry's is on a par with mine; able to communicate but not to any large degree.'

'One good linguist should be fine; just as long as one of you is fluent and the other two passable. Ready yourselves for over the border tonight. Bring your patrol back, say in two hours and you'll get your maps and a final briefing from the American intelligence people who will be coming over shortly to advise us what they expect you to achieve by going over early. Sorry about the rush, Pete but the countdown has already started. If you think there are more questions, hopefully the intelligence people should be able to answer these for you when you come back, so get your Rover ready for across the border tonight and we'll see you in two hours for a final briefing.'

I walk out of his tent and back to our lines full of confidence, and feeling proud of being chosen for such a daring mission well in front of the onset of the war. Terry and Mick are still putting the last few things back after stripping and checking everything to make sure we only have to jump into the vehicle and we're off. They were a little disgruntled at me getting them to do this so soon as some of their mates were lazing around and gave them quite a bit of lip when we started but they soon knuckled down to the job when they realised that I would be helping them, and I wasn't going down to the mess with the other sergeants for a beer while they slaved away in the hot sun. We were halfway through with these checks when I got the call to see the officer in charge.

'How's the rearranging going, boys?' I ask them as I get near to the machine. 'Is there much more to do? I'm here to help.'

'Nearly finished, Sarge; just this rear section and we're done,' Terry says, jumping down to me. 'Are we having a beer when we finish? Because I reckon we've earned a couple of cold ones after being in this bloody hot sun all afternoon.'

'I'm afraid not, fellas. We're heading over the border tonight so get a couple of bottles of rum and two weeks' rations from the Q-store. Oh, and we'll take four missiles with us Terry;

for Christ's sake, pack them in carefully, we don't want any of them falling off. When we're finished, come with me for a final briefing with the OC and he'll supply us with whatever maps we need for the job but please not a word to anyone as this is for our ears only.'

'*Shit*, Sarge! You're serious, aren't you?' he splutters out, almost unable to control his enthusiasm at a chance like this to go over the border early. 'Did you hear what Pete just said, Mick? We're going over the border later tonight.'

'Yep, heard it all. We'll take the Rover to the Q-store and load it up with the extra rockets and rations and then bring it back here.'

We drive the few hundred metres to the Q-store where we find Taffy who has obviously been warned to expect us because he's waiting with a pile of rations, our missiles and I also notice a bottle of rum each, along with our thermals.

'It gets bloody cold out there of a night when the sun goes down, fellas,' the sombre little Welshman tells us, eyeing off the bottles of rum as they're passed over. 'It may be hot as Hades now, boys, with the sun up but you wait 'til night falls and you'll think you're all in bloody Antarctica and you'll need more than this rum to get ya through.'

'Thanks, Taffy. We'll remember that, won't we, boys? Afghanistan was a little the same; stinking hot during the day and cold at night, especially when Anaconda was on and we were well above the snowline doing that long O.P.. Come on, fellas, shake a leg. We have a tight schedule to keep; let's load all this gear onboard and we'll get over to the operations tent so the OC can give us our final briefing, then we'll know exactly what's what.'

The officer in charge is in the company of two Americans and our operations officer; they stop whatever they are discussing when we come into the tent.

'Come in, Sergeant. Bring your men because we're just discussing your best route and the mission we have set up for you.'

'Thanks, Sir. We'll be interested to know what's in store for us. These are my two men, Terry and Mike, who will be supporting me in this operation across the border. What do you have in store for us?'

There are no introductions to the two Americans who are there to brief us. We just sit down and wait for the briefing to begin, and the two Yanks open up in front with what they expect us to achieve on this mission.

'Guys, we have quite a few mobile Scud missile launching pads in this area that our planes and drones have picked up over the last two weeks. They are on the backs of trucks and can be moved to any location very quickly. As far as we know from the last photos sent to us this morning, they've been in this area here now for the last four days, so I assume that's their permanent position.' He puts a small stick onto the map and points to a spot two-thirds the way up Iraq. 'This is the area where our drones have photographed their launch sites. What we're worried about is, if the invasion starts, they will be fired indiscriminately at any neighbouring country such as Israel. The Iraqis know they haven't the forces to stop us, so we suspect that these rockets will be fired into adjoining countries with what you would say catastrophic results; especially if they are nuclear as some so-called experts are saying.' The look on this intelligence man's face is as if he's speaking to a group of complete morons. 'If this is the case, Sergeant, we firmly believe these people could have the capabilities to virtually wipe out the entire country if any one of these missiles just happens to be nuclear; particularly if the country is relatively small like Israel or here in Kuwait. If that happens and if the missile is nuclear and it is launched prior to the invasion starting, there will only be patches of sand left and unfortunately, we'll all be history.'

'Firstly, Sir, how long have we got to get into place to destroy them?' I ask, looking at the map's grid squares and trying to judge the distance the missiles are from this point. 'And how many are there in this district that we have to find before this operation gets started? For example, will we have any maps depicting the sites the drones have established missiles to be stationed in?'

'It's quite possible the operation will start in say maybe five days' time so, as you can see, time is running out fast for you guys to reach your targets.' He is not giving any specific times, I expect in case we're caught. The one speaking looks intently at me as if to say, *Why the stupid questions? Just do the job for God's sake.* 'From our intelligence and from the most recent aerial photos we know there are at least six of them in this area here. Now, if you haven't blown them by the time of the invasion is due to start, we'll send in planes and attempt to get them all before they are fired. Now, if this scenario happens, Sergeant, we just hope they are slow in firing them so there are no unfortunate complications with neighbouring countries we're allied to, such as Israel or this one which unfortunately Saddam Hussein still claims as part of Iraq.'

We leave the intelligence people and the briefing and move back to our vehicle. We now have our maps and coordinates of the area we have to search and the route they expect us to take, but the thing that puzzles me is why they would display their hardware as blatantly as we've just seen from the aerial photographs. Why wouldn't they hide them in anticipation of the American attack, so no one knows of their position or, for that matter, that they even exist?

I spread the map out over the bonnet with the route the OC suggested while the two others gather around and look at other options we may need. We probably have half an hour before it gets dark, so I want to be sure what our route is, get over the border quickly and get into a position as soon as possible to do a detailed reconnaissance so we can carry out our mission as soon as the OC gives us the thumbs up.

'It will be far too slow doing the route that the OC and Americans want, hell it would take us five days to get there and by that time the war will have started. I recommend we go through here and then swing around onto this section of road, well behind where we know there are checkpoints and go straight north, using our night vision goggles and then, if we are able to drive all night, we'll be very close if not there at the target by morning. Now, fellas, questions please; have I overlooked anything?'

They both study the map, going over what I propose for some period of time before Terry finally makes some comments. 'Your route looks good, Sarge, because theirs would take at least two and a half days at least to get into position. If we can get most of the way tonight, we should be able to have a good look around tomorrow and establish what the hell the Iraqis are playing at, moving the Scuds around in full view of everyone. It's almost as if they want the Yanks to find them.' With his next comment, he hits the nail right on the head, making me pleased with the way he's thinking because they are my thoughts to a tee. 'If I had missiles with the capacity of taking out my enemies, I'd have them well-hidden, right away from the dummies, hoping the enemy is too engrossed in watching those in plain view to look for the real ones that are hidden somewhere completely different.'

'Or I'd show them the location of my dud missiles early,' Mick cuts in, making another very good point. 'And at the last moment, move the dummies away so all eyes follow them to a completely different area so far away that they'd have no difficulty firing the real ones when the Yanks start the war.'

'So would I fellas, so would I. That's what worries me about the briefing we've just been to. I'm afraid it just looks too clear-cut to me. There's something fishy going on with this whole Scud missile deal. Oh, and by the way, fellas, before I forget, that tagging of the vehicles we did back over in the west on that last exercise is what got us this job; did you realise that?' I laugh at the looks of surprise shown on their faces. 'I certainly hope we don't live to regret that little escapade.'

Iraq

The sun is well down when we cross the border, driving into the desert for half an hour before swinging around to the right and eventually striking the main road. To our south some kilometres away, we can easily see the Iraqi checkpoints towards the border lit up like Christmas trees, instantly drawing all the attention that way.

'Put the pedal down, Mick, and let's put some distance between us and the border. We have something like three hundred kilometres to do before the sun comes up and I want to have the Rover well and truly hidden by that time.'

'Right, Sarge. We should be able to maintain eighty to

a hundred easily on this road but what do we do if there are roadblocks further inland?'

'If they're lit up like the one back there, we'll see them in plenty of time and we can take evasive action if we strike one. The Yanks didn't have any marked on the maps because the drones would have certainly seen them so go straight up the road as fast as you can and we'll decide what to do if we strike any roadblocks. We're going to do exactly what the Yanks and the Boss told us not to do and that is belt up this road because, in my opinion, that's the last thing anyone will expect their enemy to do before the shooting starts. Hopefully the further north we are the more complacent the Iraqis will be to us being there.'

We have spent three hours doing just over ninety kilometres an hour going straight north when, in the distance, we pick out rows of lights coming our way as if a convoy is making its way south towards the border.

'Get off the road,' I tell Mick, wanting to get as much information as I can before the invasion starts. 'They wouldn't have seen us yet, so we can get a count of what's coming our way. Mick, you take troop carriers. Terry, the weapons carriers and I'll do the overall numbers. That way, we'll have a pretty good picture of what the Iraqis have coming towards us and what's in that convoy.'

We're lucky; the terrain is relatively rough so we're able to park near a shaggy knob. It's one of the best features in the area we could have hoped for, to hide us, and it is close enough to the road to identify the types of transports which will soon be moving in front of us. The first two vehicles in the convoy are a type of jeep with what appears to be fifty-calibre machine guns mounted onto stands in the back; these big weapons being the convoy's forward protection. The gunners are standing behind their weapons, but their barrels point to the sky as if they are pissed off with being in the front position of the convoy and are expecting an American aircraft to come swooping down at any moment. There are over one hundred and sixty vehicles in the convoy, a lot of large semi-trailers with a tubular configuration that can only be rockets of some persuasion. They have finally passed, going south towards the border but I assume that's not their final objective. I want to positively identify the area to which they are heading and that can only be done by inserting a tag on the last vehicle, or by us following the convoy to wherever they're going which is out of the question as we have other rockets to find and nullify.

'Put a fire in the motor, Mick. I want to catch that last truck and put a tracking device on the loader itself and a bomb somewhere on the rocket or whatever it is it's carrying. They're only going slowly so we should have no trouble getting up close behind that last truck and putting a tag on the chassis.'

'How the *hell* are you going to do that?' says Terry, quite mystified at what I mean and how I intend to get onboard without being noticed. 'They're not going to bloody well pull over just so you can climb on the back of the truck, you know? How do you expect to get aboard that truck; what harebrained scheme do you propose, Sarge?'

'The Yanks do it in the movies, so why can't we do it here for real?' I tell the confused pair. 'You'll have to get up really close to the back of him, Mick, without touching the truck and I'll go across from the bonnet and leave the tracking device on the chassis and plant the bomb on the rocket with an electronic timer so it can be blown at any time later.' I smile at the confused looks from both of these men. 'Come on, fellas; let's hope we have better luck than we did when we set those devices on the trucks in Afghanistan, Terry. Our boss over the border has to know where this lot of hardware is going and if they are real rockets that the Iraqis are moving or just a large heap of decoys sent south to confuse the Yanks when their invasion starts.'

'Do you really want to do this, Sarge?' Terry says, very worried at the stunt I am proposing. 'God! You be careful. You aren't one of those bloody Hollywood stuntmen you know. There will be no re-runs if you fuck this up the first time. You'll have no one standing in for you; this one is the real deal you know. Don't bloody well fall or do something stupid.'

'I have full faith in both of you to pick up the scraps, so pass me a charge as I've got one of the tracking devices in my webbing.'

The Rover is coming up fast behind the convoy with Mick keeping to the centre of the back of the truck, hoping the driver is switched off. Being at the end of this long line of vehicles and concentrating on the truck in front of him, he doesn't notice us coming up behind. Terry passes me the timed charge, so I carefully move onto the bonnet of the Land Rover while Mick manoeuvres just behind this last truck, hoping that it's dark enough for the truck driver not to notice us in the rear-vision mirror. It's a large semi-trailer with what looks like a Scud missile lying down on the tray on its side. Mick's driving is brilliant; he brings the Rover up quickly behind the truck, so the bumpers are almost touching. I step off the bonnet just to one side of this large missile. Fortunately for me, the truck is only going at about thirty-odd kilometres an hour, so I make the move quite easily to the back of the tray. I place the tracking device in a good position under its sub-frame and the next step is to plant the bomb under a panel somewhere on the rocket. I move halfway up the missile and carefully remove what appears to be an observation plate, fitting the explosive charge inside and feeling the magnets clicking onto something metal behind the panel. I also note that the missile is one that has a core and isn't just a hollow pipe that you'd expect from a fake. Once the cover is replaced, I move quickly back to the rear of the truck so I can easily get back on our Rover. Mick sees me coming back and again moves the Rover up close to the rear of the truck. I brace myself, quickly leaping onto the bonnet, grabbing the windscreen as I land to steady my fall. As soon as I land on the bonnet, Mick brakes and instantly draws back away from the rear of the truck.

'Drop the speed off and let's lose 'em,' I tell Mick as he slows the Rover down using the hand brake so no lights are shown, almost to a stop, allowing me to resume my seat and then in one swift motion he turns us about and begins to head north once again. 'Thanks, fellas; well done, Mick! You both supported me beautifully.' Then with a laugh at their serious faces, I add, 'Mick, I'll put your name forward for a place in Hollywood's hall of fame when this is over. They desperately need drivers like you. Oh, and by the way, that could have actually been a missile, fellas, because it had working parts under the panel where I put the charge in. It wasn't just a large hollow pipe that's been made to look like a Scud to fool the Yanks. That weapon could have been the real deal. Anyway, they will know if it's real when they activate the charge.'

'You're a fucking maniac, Sarge, doing that,' says Mick, now concentrating on the road as we head north almost flat out trying to regain the time we've lost. 'No one back at camp would believe it if I told them what you've just damn well done. Hell that was a damn good move to put a charge on that missile; even if it's a dud we'll know where they are setting their rockets up.'

'You had better contact Headquarters, Terry. Send this information through with our position. This should give the Yanks something solid to think about.'

'Patrol B3 to Base. Position xxx xxx. Just passed a convey of 160+ vehicles. Seventy troop carriers. Sixty-five trucks with heavy weapons. Twenty-seven possible rocket launchers. The remainder is security. The last truck has a tracking device planted on board and the rocket appears to be genuine. I repeat, the rocket appears to be genuine and has a bomb planted in its mechanism with an electronic timer. Over.'

'That should give them something to think about when they read this,' he says, smiling as the message goes through to Headquarters. 'It's a pity we couldn't have hit one as they went past with one of our rockets. It would have made one hell of a mess of one of those semis. That way, we'd certainly know for sure if the rocket is the real deal or not.'

'There's a message coming through from H.Q., Sarge.'

'Base to Patrol B3, Well done! Continue on to recommended position to find and observe hardware at that loc stat. Out.'

'*Shit* Pete! We should have done what you said and hit one of those rocket carriers with one of our missiles. That would have got things moving with a big bang and we'd know for sure if it was a genuine rocket or not.'

'That would have started the bloody war, Terry, and I'd prefer it if the Yanks did that. It's not our job to press those sorts of buttons; we're just here to quietly observe and find out where the rockets are and report back our findings to the OC and they can make a few bangs at the appropriate time.'

We drive up the road with quite a bit of quibbling from Terry who still wants to stick a rocket into one of the semis. It would have been great, but we'd have well and truly blown our cover, so we continue the last fifty or so kilometres to our designated area, just hoping that the rockets seen by the drones we are looking for are still there. It's late now, getting towards sun-up and we're fortunate to find an eroded gully that we can slip the Rover into so we're out of sight. It's a neat fit with not quite a metre on either side free and I'm pleased to see Mick do this difficult manoeuvre in one quick, efficient motion. We get out, securing our machine just as the sun starts to come up and finally slip the camouflaged netting over the vehicle before looking at each other and asking ourselves what to do next.

'Take a couple of hours and get some sleep,' I tell the other two. 'I think you're going to need every bit you can get. I'll have a look around our immediate area, so don't shoot me if you hear a noise coming back into the re-entrant.'

This response only gets a laugh from the other two who spread themselves out on the ground under the vehicle, leaving me by myself. I climb to the top of this gully with my binoculars and systematically search the area for the rockets that had been reported by the drone. Across roughly a kilometre and a half of bare, inhospitable plain is a collection of what looks like run-down mud or earth huts and virtually nothing else to be seen. There is obviously no one living in them as parts of the roofs are down and there are certainly no Scud missiles anywhere in the vicinity because it's too flat and there's absolutely nowhere to hide them for miles; nothing is here. I go back to the Rover and check our grid references to the map and then cross reference these to the GPS with the distance we've come from the border and again check these to those on the map. There's got to be a mistake as it's quite obvious to us that someone back in Kuwait has stuffed up big time somewhere along the line and I don't want it to be us carrying the can for someone else's massive stuff-up.

'Everything okay up top, Sarge?' comes Mick's muffled voice from somewhere below the Rover.

'There is nothing out here to hide a bloody piss ant under let alone a Scud missile on a fucking great semi. The whole area is as flat as a frigging aircraft's runway. Those intelligence people, if you can call them that, are way out.' I pause, letting what I say sink in. 'They must have made a mistake with the rocket's positioning. Turn the GPS on so Headquarters can find our position and then contact Base and we'll sort this out ASAP. I reckon the Yanks have made a bloody big mistake with their positioning or given us the wrong coordinates. It's just far too flat and far too open all the way across to the hills to hide any bloody Scud missiles that are on the backs of semis. I could see for miles right over to those hills on the left and there was absolutely nothing visible anywhere around here.'

'Patrol B3 to Base. Position we've been given is flat with no, I repeat, no cover. Check the grid references please to see if a mistake has been made. Over.'

'Base to Patrol B3. We have your grid position. References are ooo xxx. Which is the correct position we were given? Over.'

'Patrol B3 to Base. As you can see we are at the given reference of ooo xxx according to our GPS and the map. Will maintain our O.P. but the area is flat and a waste of time, please check with the Yanks what grid they've given us. Over.'

'Base to Patrol B3. Maintain O.P.. We will check the given grid references with the Americans for you. Out.'

'This is a bloody waste of time fellas; you can see there's nothing here anywhere. You can see for miles. It's like I said, it's as flat as a bloody billiard table without any billiards balls to get in the way.'

Kuwait

'Tell them to stay in the pre-arranged area where the Americans say the Scud missiles are sited,' the officer in charge tells the sig when he comes in with the message. 'Contact the Americans and tell them I have an urgent message from our unit that's infiltrated into Iraq and switch on that tracking detector, and we'll see where the Scud missile they tagged is.' He looks at the corporal sig with a strange, mystified look on his face. 'How the *hell* did they get so far up north so quickly?'

The two American intelligence men arrive just after sun-up, curious to know what the fuss is about and thinking the Australians are a little uneasy at one of their teams being sent out three days before Operation Falconer is due to start.

'Good morning, gentlemen. It appears that we picked the right crew for the job you gave us. Last night our men followed a convoy of 160-odd trucks that were heading south to a position unknown. Evidently Sergeant Jackson boarded one of these trucks and installed a tracking device on the last vehicle and a bomb with an electronic timer on the rocket so we can blow it up at any time you wish. All we have to do is initiate it electronically. Here is the message that was sent through last night; it may be of some interest to you.'

The spook takes the message and reads it, then hands it on to his companion who appears to read it a number of times before he, too, looks up.

'Patrol B3. Position xxx xxx. Convoy of 160+ just passed seventy troop carriers. Sixty-five heavy weapons. Twenty-seven possible rocket launchers. The remainder is security. The last truck has a tracking device and rocket has a bomb with electronic timer. Over.'

'Again, you gentlemen can have the pleasure of igniting it at the appropriate time.'

'We had no idea they were this close. How reliable is this man you sent out to do this assignment?'

'He's one hundred per cent. If he says he's tagged the truck, then it's tagged. The position of the tagged truck is here.' He points to the wall map to a position west of the north-south highway. 'They came down the highway and turned off here. He says there are twenty-seven trucks in the convoy capable of launching the rockets and well over two hundred troops that are obviously guarding the hardware. That's quite a formidable force we have here gentlemen, particularly as there are so many rockets close to Kuwait.'

'Goddamn it! They could virtually obliterate Kuwait with all that firepower at their disposal,' the second man says, seemingly getting quite agitated at getting this type of information back so soon after the patrol's infiltration across the border. 'I'd better get onto high command about this turn of events. There are plenty of informers in this place to let them know what their movements are. Hell, man, if they hit this place with half those rockets, there would only be sand left in Kuwait.'

'Where is your man now?' the other stooge asks. 'Would he be in a position to do something for us?'

'That's the other point; he's in position over three hundred kilometres away, near where you said the rockets were installed,' the officer in charge says, getting a little chuffed at the high-handed attitude of these two so-called American experts. 'If there are any rockets in the vicinity, they will find them. Now, are you certain that the grid reference you gave us when you were here last night is the correct one? Because our men say the place is flat and there are no rockets in sight, unlike the photos you showed us before the patrol left. He's in the correct position you gave us yesterday as you can see quite clearly from the beep we are getting from his GPS.'

'I'll check them again if you like,' he says, fumbling in a briefcase, quite nervous now at being questioned about their accuracy. They are both a little put off by being told they are wrong. He finally pulls out some papers and hands them across to the officer in charge. 'Here they are, Major; you can check them yourself. These are the correct coordinates of the position given to us by the drones.'

The officer in charge takes the papers and looks at the grid reference that they've just given him, checking it against the ones they had given him yesterday and also on the position they are getting from the GPS.

'Oh *shit*! They're different. You gave me the wrong grid references yesterday. They are a hundred and fifty kilometres out – no wonder they have nothing to see. Get them on the blower this instant and give them the right coordinates immediately, Corporal. Sergeant Jackson is right – there's nothing there!'

'Base to Patrol B3. The grid references for you are yyy. xxx, I

repeat, your grid references are yyy xxx. Over.'

'Patrol B3 to Base. I have the new grid references of yyy xxx. I will correct our position immediately. Out.'

Iraq

'We have been given the wrong *bloody* reference numbers and are almost a hundred and fifty kilometres out of position,' I tell the other two who have just stuck their heads out from under the Rover. 'That means we're just wasting our time here, fellas, and unfortunately we only have a couple of days to do our recce of the missile sites. What do you think of driving the last little bit in daylight?'

'If we put Bedouin-type headdresses on and put this on the aerial,' Terry says, holding up an Iraqi flag that he evidently bought at a stall in Kuwait as a souvenir, 'we should have maybe half a chance and just about make it. What do you reckon, Sarge; give it a go? Who dares wins?'

'I think Terry's right, Sarge,' Mick says, looking at the flag and then at his companion. 'They haven't seen our cam gear yet which is totally different to what Yanks and the Poms who fought in the last gulf war used; I reckon we could get away with it. It's only a couple of hours if we drive flat out. We should be able to bite our nails for that long, surely.'

We replace our helmets and goggles with an array of headgear we've seen the locals use in Kuwait until we finally start to look a little like Arabs. Terry is determined to use the Iraqi flag and slips the one he'd bought for a souvenir over one of our aerials to finish off our disguise.

I study the map and find some rougher country just to the

west of the reported sightings so we head straight up the highway to the area we've been designated as fast as our Rover will go.

We're almost there when we come over a rise and there, some five hundred or so metres away to my dismay, we see what looks like a small convoy of vehicles approaching us from the other way.

'Oh *shit*, fellas, they would have seen us by now,' I tell the others who are immediately on full alert. 'Just go past and wave but whatever you do just keep on going. If they turn a gun towards us or look like shooting first, we return fire but nothing unless something like that happens. Do you understand, Terry? We're out numbered at least ten to one with what's coming towards us in that small convoy.'

'Right, Sarge,' Terry replies, a little apprehensive about my no-fire order. 'I won't fire unless those bastards are going for their guns, so they had better have their hands in sight and have their barrels pointing in the other direction.'

The convoy is made up of a number of jeep-type four-wheel-drive vehicles and four trucks; one with no canvas which is full of soldiers whose backs are toward us. The others are covered, probably carrying ordinance of some description down to the border. We're all scruffy, not having had a shave now for three days. Terry, with his darker complexion and sitting above us and to their side, could possibly at a pinch pass as an Arab. He sits there behind his fifty-cal and nonchalantly waves as we pass the first vehicle. I breathe a large sigh of relief as we pass this vehicle without incident. We look at each other and smile, noting the gun on the back, with its barrel pointing to the sky. It looks like a Browning 50 cal, similar to ours that Terry has in his grasp. He returns the wave and looks at us as if he wishes to be here with us and not going towards the border. I'm pleased with our deception as the rest of the Iraqi soldiers pay little or no attention to us as we rush past, with some soldiers hardly turning our way and just continuing on heading quickly towards the border.

'*Shit!* That was a heart-stopper,' Terry says, taking a deep breath, immediately blowing out his cheeks and then looking down towards me as the last truck passes. 'Pete, you gotta remind me to take out a lottery ticket when we get home because I think we just bloody well-earned it on this one.'

We continue on up the road for another ten minutes before the terrain begins to change quite dramatically and becomes more undulating with a few small hills and more of the same adobe-type houses we saw at the other place, nestling at the bottom of the hill. I quickly check the map and find these eroded gullies stretch for miles on the other side causing small hillocks to rise between them. But standing out between all these gullies is one hill larger than the rest looking almost as if it's been put there by some god.

'We'll find somewhere to hide the Rover. Once that's done, we'll have a good look around and see if we can come up with some missiles. If those rockets we're looking for are hidden around here, it's most likely that technicians or guards will probably be watching out for people just like us, so we'll drive past that hill and come around the back. Keep your eyes open, fellas, for off-road tracks that have plenty of use from this highway and anything slightly different that stands out that the Iraqis could be using as an observation post. Something up high like the top of that hill we just passed.'

'There's one on your left now, Sarge,' says Terry, looking at just what I've been talking about. 'It leads straight to the back of that strange-looking knob we just went past. Do you think they have a base or something back there hidden away from this highway? From the tracks we've just seen it could be behind that hill; there's been a hell of a lot of traffic going that way recently.'

'They could have, Terry. Look, we'll secure the Rover in one of these gullies up front.' I do a quick check, getting a more accurate distance from Mick. 'How far do you think we've come down the main road from those tracks?'

'We're now one and a half kilometres from where they turned off,' Mick says, looking down at the speedo and breaking into the conversation. 'Sarge, do you want to hide the vehicle at the first opportunity and then do our recce on foot?'

'Yes, as soon as we can but make sure we can't be seen from that big knob because that's the obvious place to have an observation post if there's a base nearby where all that traffic appears to be heading. We'll hide the Rover in some gully within range, have a brew and a bite to eat while we have a good look at our map and later, we can work our way back on foot and see just what we can find behind that hill because that's where all the tracks we passed should lead to.'

We're out of sight of our target and turn overland for probably another kilometre before we find just what we're looking for; a deep re-entrant just big enough where we can comfortably hide the Land Rover from the prying eyes of someone travelling past. Mick backs down the slope out of sight while I remove the tell-tale tyre marks back probably some two to three hundred metres. By the time I'm back, the boys have the camouflage net over the vehicle so there's hardly a trace of us being here. I spread the map out on the ground and we gather around closely, looking down at our position and comparing that with the new grid reference of the locations sent up to us by our OC this morning.

'We are here,' I tell them, pointing at the position I've marked on the map. 'The Yanks indicated the Iraqis had missiles here, here and here. Now, this one we should have seen almost from the road but again unfortunately, I saw nothing at this point that looked anything like a Scud missile. What about you fellas? Did you see anything that looked like a Scud on a firing platform?'

'I saw nothing, Sarge, not even a camel,' says Terry, shaking his head, looking up from the map as if we are wasting our time once again and then he points to a small hill clearly marked on the map. 'I was looking across there and you could see right to this small hill. We should have seen at least two of the missiles, the size they are and the truck that carts them, particularly if they were in the launch position as the photos we saw indicated. There was nothing there whatsoever, not even tyre tracks to say the trucks had been there to service the missiles in the last few days. The only tyre tracks we saw were those going around that funny-looking hill coming this way. I'm sorry to say this, Sarge, but I reckon those bloody Yanks have given us another bum steer because a missile the size we passed last night would stick out like dog's balls particularly if they had them set up to fire in the positions they indicated at that briefing. Do you think the ones we passed last night were the ones that were supposed to be here?'

'They could have been, Terry. Look – we'll have a quick brew and a bite to eat and then we'll see just what we can find near that hill. Come to think of it, it's not even marked on this map and a feature that size should be here. The Yanks surely wouldn't miss something as large as that when their planes or satellites were doing their survey work for them. Surely they would have marked a hill as big as this one when they flew over doing the mapping and used it as a reference point for the missiles that are supposed to be here. Even the old maps the Poms made before the Second World War should have had a thing the size of this damn hill marked on it. Heavens, you'd think no surveyor worth his salt would have missed a hill as big as that.'

'Yes, they may have just copied old maps that the Poms made between the First and Second World Wars when they had control of this place,' Mick says, looking at me almost in disbelief after studying the map. 'Quite frankly, Sarge, like you just said, I can't see how any surveyor worth his salt would have missed a feature as big as that. They've got real photographs of this area that should have picked that up as they did with the missile sites we saw at that last briefing we had.'

We sit in the sun just near the Rover, brewing up, looking around us and chatting while we wait for the dehydrated rations to cool. We go over the map in detail a second time, just in case we've missed something that could make a difference to our assumptions because these assumptions will have a big bearing on what our next move in this place will be.

'There is an array of small ridges and gullies that wind their way in the direction of that strange hill,' I say, looking hard at our map, trying to find the best way to do a good reconnaissance of the area and not be seen from any observation position on any of the high points in the area. 'We've seen those wheel marks that appeared to wind around behind that feature as we came in, so we should make sure we have ground cover right to where we want to go because, if I was in charge here, I'd have my observation point on a hill such as the one we passed. Now if we follow this gully, for example, along here, it passes right to the bottom of where that hill is supposed to be. So, we should get a good look around if we go to the top of that feature. It should give us a panoramic view of the whole area and that way, with a bit of luck, we'll soon find out where the frigging Scud missiles are stationed.'

'You're right,' Mick says looking around at me. 'We would certainly get a magnificent view of everything from the top of that hill across to where the Yanks had those missiles marked.'

'Even if there's nothing along the re-entrant, we should still get a good look around the area right up to that strange hill,' Terry says as he opens his ration and checks to see if it's cool enough, taking a spoon full and blowing on it before he puts it into his mouth. 'Bloody good stuff this,' he continues with his conversation, with a mouthful of food. 'You're right, we should be able to see the other missile sites if they are here like the Yanks say.' He points his spoon towards the hill. 'The whole area should be pretty flat once we get up to that point and we should be able to see where the traffic is going once we get to the top of that feature and see if there are missiles in this vicinity.' He then shakes his head. 'From up there, they should stick out like a sore thumb, that is if they are in their firing positions.'

'Yeah, we should also be able to see where those tracks that were coming this way lead to from the crest of that hill,' Mick interjects, pointing once more towards the hill. 'If the rag-heads have a base somewhere to the back of us, we should be able to see it without taking the risk of driving out in the open like we've just done getting down here.'

'That's a good idea, fellas. As soon as we finish eating, we'll go over towards that hill and have a good look around. Who knows what we may see from up there but be aware they may also have an O.P. up there themselves that would most likely be facing towards the highway. I didn't see it, but the top of that hill is the most logical place to have their observation post because you'd be able to see everything for miles either way from up there.'

'We'll take a few charges just in case we find something worthwhile blowing up,' I suggest. 'There's got to be something going on across that way to be taking all that traffic from the highway because those vehicle marks were new, so keep your wits about you and your eyes open for anything unusual.'

We finish our food and find we're much too keyed up to feel the effects of no sleep last night. We use what the re-entrant offers as cover and check our position regularly, with one of us occasionally going to the top of the gully to look out across the plain and to check our bearings. By using this system to check where we're going, we slowly move along almost to the base of the small hill. We're not in a hurry and have been travelling carefully for almost two hours in this dry heat that seems to hang around us, sapping our energy when moving too fast and now making us wish for wind or a small breeze of some description that would make life much more tenable. We've moved a good five kilometres with Mick who this time is leading the push along the re-entrant. All of a sudden, he cocks his head to one side and stops, putting his hand up and listening intently to the distant sounds of engines. This increasing noise of these motors continues to grow louder and appears to be coming straight towards us.

'We've got company, fellas; it sounds like there are vehicles closing in on us fast,' he says from the front, making Terry and me hurriedly move to the top of the crest to join him. We look across the plain at a cloud of rapidly approaching dust and we wonder if it's the hill they're going toward. 'It looks like it's a couple of trucks. No there are three. Whatever they are, they're bigger than the four-wheel-drives the Iraqis normally use for reconnaissance.'

Through the clouds of thick dust, we realise the three vehicles we can see approaching are definitely trucks with tarps covering whatever load they're carrying in the back.

'*Shit*, Pete! I hope we haven't activated an alarm of some description and they know we're here; we only have our rifles to defend ourselves,' Terry mutters, looking at the approaching vehicles. 'If they are after us, there could be thirty to forty men onboard trucks of that size. What are we going to do?'

'Just sit tight, Terry, and keep your fingers crossed that we haven't activated any alarms and we'll see what happens. Get ready for the worst-case scenario, boys.'

'But then why would they have an alarm set in this gully?' Mick asks. 'We passed nothing worth looking at.'

We watch as the three trucks come thundering straight towards us. We crouch down with hardly anything visible above the lip of the gully, holding our rifles at the ready; expecting the worst of this situation that's suddenly arisen. They are within a hundred metres of us now and closing in fast, causing me to have the feeling they have somehow found where we are and are racing ahead to try to cut us off and overwhelm us with their numbers. At the last moment I'm relieved when the leading truck suddenly veers off towards the strange hill and races past covering us with a cloud of dust. I drop my head to the ground, thinking how foolish we've been when I suddenly realise the track behind the hill is nearby and visible now a few metres in front of our position. We'd been too occupied with the trucks coming towards us to notice the track some twenty paces out on the plain. The trucks continue to speed on, going along quite close to the edge of the gully, then altering their course straight towards the hill and for the first time I see the two large steel doors that had been obscured between a couple of huge boulders. These large steel doors start to slowly grind open, allowing the trucks that have now slowed down to a crawl to finally enter through this large steel door into the hill to whatever the Iraqis have hidden deep inside, before the doors start to close again behind them.

'Bingo,' I say, turning to the other two now with a broad smile etched over my face and a feeling of sheer relief twisting around in my gut at not having to fight our way out of our perceived situation. 'It looks like we could have hit the jackpot, boys! Did you see those large doors open for the trucks to enter the hill? What do you think these smart pricks have hidden inside this bloody base in that hill? I bet it's not a bloody Scud missile base they have in there.'

'If it's one of those rockets we saw them moving last night, it has to be something really special,' says Terry, turning toward me. His look of relief is replaced by one of curiosity. He breaks out into a broad smile as he thinks of what could be inside. 'They either aren't taking the risk with it on a truck or it's far too big to mount on one. Either way, Pete, it would be worth our time to have a closer look at what Saddam's men are doing over there in that hill; I bet it isn't a Scud missile site they have hidden over there. I reckon it's something much bigger than what the Yanks are expecting.'

'I think you're right, Terry,' Mick cuts in, just as curious, but still coming to grips with the strange event we've just witnessed here this morning. 'There's got to be something totally different inside that bloody hill, something they don't want anyone to know about, Sarge. You can bank on that, and you can bet it isn't a Scud missile like they were moving on those trucks last night. *Hell!* Last night could've been one large diversion to make the Yanks follow the missiles to the wrong place because you'd think one of their satellites or surely their planes or drones would quickly pick up the ordinance we saw on the road last night well before we reported that convoy's movements back to base?'

'You're right, Mick, there's got to be something really special in that hill for them to hide whatever it is. They obviously don't want anyone to know about it; so, let's continue along this gully and get as close as we can to that base. Who knows, we may even be lucky enough to be able to get inside. Then, if we can, we'll be able to see exactly what these pricks are up to and let the brass back in Kuwait know what we've found because I can almost guarantee that this isn't going to be a Scud missile site they've built into that hill.'

With Mick in the lead, we slowly continue to move along our gully wondering what we've stumbled on, stopping every ten minutes to gauge our progress towards the hill and finding with each stop that we are closer. With the afternoon shadows now starting to cast strange shapes over this re-entrant we're moving in, we bunch up a little closer so we can support each other if we have to. We know we're running out of light and haven't had any sleep now for well over thirty-six hours, but we can't afford to be careless now that we're so close to whatever this object may be. After the last scare, we're also looking for any listening devices the Iraqis may have put in this gully to warn them of people snooping around. Mick suddenly stops once again and beckons me forward to his position.

'There seem to be very large pipes of some description up ahead of us,' Mick quietly whispers as I reach his position and find we're standing in front of three massive pipes that enter the gully from the direction of the hill. The pipes are steel; they stand some five metres or so apart and are at least a good two hundred centimetres in height. 'What the *hell* do you think these would be used for?'

'I don't know, Mick, but don't touch anything until we check them out thoroughly for trip devices or alarms of some description. We don't want anyone accidentally sounding off an alarm, or worse still, electrocuting themselves because those pipes are steel,' I tell them, well aware now that a place such as this could be much more sophisticated than we first realised, evident by the grill installed, probably to stop roving Arabs or animals from entering. 'Just be careful please at what you touch until we check out the grill thoroughly because they could have some form of sophisticated surveillance or defensive device attached. Search for any sort of device that looks out of place or any wiring that you think shouldn't be there. Now if you find anything out of the ordinary, let me know immediately so we can work out how to deactivate it.'

'This grate seems quite primitive, Pete. It almost looks like a stormwater grate that shire councils use and it appears to have been built in hurry ... looks to be held on by only four large butterfly bolts,' he says as he does a detailed inspection of the grate. 'There's nothing sophisticated about this at all. Hell! It's quite primitive really, just the two butterfly bolts top and bottom and thank heavens there is no wiring on any of them that I can see so far. If it was electrified, the metal pipes coming through the ground would just short out any charge. Pete from what I can see, this is very primitive, there is no surveillance equipment here at all, just these primitive grates to stop any animals getting in.'

After a close inspection, we quickly removed the bolts without any trouble but, before we enter, I turn to them both and issue a quiet warning.

'No talking once we're inside this pipe, fellas, because pipes like this carry sounds and vibrations extremely well so tread lightly and we'll only use hand signals to communicate. Now it's getting dark, so set your night vision goggles up now because we'll use them in the pipe. I'll lead us in, so be alert and look for anything that could give us away; now you both know what to do if I need backup.'

I move into the pipe, hesitantly at first, as quietly as I can. I hear the other two following suit at five-pace intervals. I'm soon in the dark and have the goggles down over my eyes and cautiously follow the pipe some four hundred metres straight into the hill to a right-hand bend. I carefully go around this bend, expecting the worst but am relieved to find it immediately starts to become light once more and I'm soon able to lift my night vision goggles and see what I'm moving into. I move slowly into the light, still looking for anything that could alert the people inside to our presence but come to an abrupt halt at a junction of pipes all of a similar size to the one we're in that go off in different directions. I look up from where I stand to where the light is coming from and I am amazed to find I'm looking straight up into the exhaust system of a very large rocket.

Shit! If that thing were to be fired now, we'd all be cooked alive and blown out of this pipe! Dramatic thoughts instantly rush through my mind as I look up in horror straight into the exhaust system of this huge rocket that's some ten metres directly above my head. I instantly think of the heat generated by such rockets I'd seen on television of American space rockets that launch satellites with rockets into space. *Hells bells; what have we stumbled onto in this place – this would have to be at least twice the size of any of those Scud missile they had on those trucks we passed last night.*

I look around and count seven other pipes all of a similar size to the one we came through, all meeting in this one spot directly under the tail of this massive rocket, all going in different directions as if dispersing the heat well away from the launch plate. It's quite obvious to me now; we're under an exhaust system of a rocket launching platform and these pipes we're in are designed to take away the heat generated by the huge thrust these large missiles create when fired.

'Make sure you mark the pipe we came in so we know which one to take when we go,' I whisper nervously to Terry as he comes quietly up to me. 'When Mick gets here, we're going up to take a look around upstairs and just see what the Iraqis have set up here. I'd hate to take the wrong pipe out – we'd be well and truly cooked if that thing above us was fired while we're still in this damn pipe.'

To one side of the pipe is an iron ladder going up directly under this first rocket, so I indicate to the other two that I'm going up to have a look. I stealthily move to the top and cautiously peer over the lip of this enormous pipe we're in. I'm shocked and totally amazed at where I am and suddenly find myself under what the Iraqis have built. The whole centre of the hill has been hollowed out into a huge antechamber and is lit by massive lights similar to those you expect to see on football grounds that have to light the entire centre of this hill. The rocket is sitting on a railway line that transports it sideways onto this single launch pad which we're directly under. Further down this rail line there are other rockets ready to take the place of this one and they can be rolled into position very quickly once this one has been fired. Up to the right is what the Yanks call an observation deck which I suspect is for the flight controllers. They have shuttered windows in the front to shield those people watching the launch and they are protected from the heat these rockets would create with the blast. I look along the railway line again and count five other missiles ready to move into the launch position. Each of the others is shielded by gigantic, moveable, heat-repellent screens.

The clever bastards! I think as I look at their launching pad and indicate to Terry and Mick to come up. They join me and both gape when they reach me and see the type of superstructure and weaponry that's sitting right on top of us.

'We'll have to disable this firing line, so fix scissor charges to the rails with your explosives so that the complete sections of line under this launch platform drop down this large exhaust pipe. I want them to go off in one hour. That will give us ample time to get out of here and back to the Rover. If we're lucky, it should dump that bloody rocket down this hole where we came up and that should take them a few days to clean the place up and by that time, hopefully the Americans have got their act together and will have started their invasion of Iraq. Any questions, fellas?'

'No, Sarge,' they whisper in unison.

We quickly go about the job of setting the charges on the line. Mick is acting as a lookout, well aware that from time to time we could possibly be seen from those in the observation deck as we frequently see the shadowy forms of people moving about behind the shuttered windows. Terry and I go about setting the charges on the rails, so we gain the maximum effect from our explosives, completely cutting the line from under this first rocket and hopefully dropping this large missile down the exhaust tube.

'People coming,' whispers Mick, looking across to the left to a group of people moving rapidly our way. '*Shit!* These people are using slave labour,' he whispers to us when he sees four people approaching in light blue boiler suits who are flanked on either side by men in military uniforms. Both guards are carrying short-barrelled firearms slung over their shoulders, obviously guarding the four in the boiler suits. Unfortunately for us, these men are coming directly towards our position under this first rocket.

The guards are cradling their submachine guns casually under their arms and thankfully seem to be totally switched off, talking to each other as they approach our position. They continue to chat as they near the rocket and, unfortunately for us, one of the guards happens to look down just as they go past the exhaust system and immediately sees Terry who's crouching on the ladder just below the lip of the exhaust pipe. His mouth begins to open in shock as the thought starts to register. Terry acts quickly; he reaches up, grabs the startled soldier's weapon by the barrel and pulls it sharply towards him, bringing the guard who has the sling around his neck with the weapon. A sharp, muffled, scream comes from his lips, then there is a crunch as he hits the bottom of the pipe. Terry immediately follows him down, jumping onto him. There's hardly a scuffle as the stunned man is quickly finished off with his knife. The other guard turns towards the muffled sounds, looking away from where I'm standing behind one of the rocket's fins. I step forward and drive the K-bar deep into his throat, then push him into the exhaust pipe.

'Another one coming down,' I say down the tube to Terry, who nimbly steps to one side, out of the way of the falling body. I turn towards the cowering prisoners who are in total shock, K-bar in my hand, motioning them toward the ladder where the guards had just disappeared.

'Don't hurt us, please. We are Kurdish prisoners working on this project,' one man quickly says in broken English after hearing me talking to Terry. 'You are not Americans or English. Who are you people?'

'We're Australians. Now move down into the pipe and you

won't be hurt.' I look down the pipe and see Terry gazing up, rifle pointing towards the top. 'Four more people coming down, Terry. Don't harm them; they're Iraqi prisoners.' I quickly turn back to Mick who like me had also hidden behind one of the rocket fins and now stands glaring across at the Kurds with his rifle pointing directly at them. 'You'll have to finish off setting Terry's charges up. Have you got the goods to do it?'

'Yes, Sarge; he'd almost finished when they came,' he says, crouching over the charge and taping the explosives firmly to the rail. 'I won't be long; there are just a few things left, little things like this to finish off and I'll be with you.'

We quickly finish setting our charges on the track, putting a timer on a fuse that leads to the exhaust tube. I set this timer for fifteen minutes in case we've been seen from the observation deck, although there are no rapid movements, warning lights flashing or alarms, so we may have been extremely lucky and not been seen.

'Mick, go down to the others and get them out of the pipe. I'll give you a good five minutes to clear the pipe before I start the timer, which should give you ample time to get the Kurds out.'

I watch him scurry down the ladder to the bottom of the pipe to where Terry and the four Kurds wait.

'We'll have fifteen minutes from the time Pete sets the fuse so get these people out of the pipe fast and head for the Rover. He'll catch up to us after he's set the fuse; it will give us just enough time to get back if we run,' Mick tells them as he reaches them. 'We'll take these people with us so grab the guards' guns and any ammo those two have and get moving so we are well clear of the pipe. These other four can explain what goes on here when we reach the Rover and clear the area; I'm sure our friends back in Kuwait will be dying to hear what these rockets are going to be used for because these people should know everything about them and what they are capable of doing.'

'The missile that is on the launch pad is a nuclear weapon,' the prisoner who spoke to me under the missile tells Mick, startling him with this announcement. 'They have forced us to work on this site for well over a year; there are other Kurds in cells to the back of the complex and they have been used along with us in the construction of this firing platform.' He looks at Mick and Terry, a worried frown on his face. 'I hope your charges won't cause the rocket to explode.'

'No. The charges we set will only destroy the track and drop the missile down here,' Mick tells him, more for his own confidence than theirs as they move rapidly along the pipe. 'It shouldn't detonate the warhead, but we'd better get out of here fast. Just hold onto us, my friend, and move as quickly as you possibly can. We have to warn Headquarters about what we've stumbled on.'

With the aid of the night vision goggles, caution is thrown to the wind and thankfully they're soon out of the pipe and running down the re-entrant in the moonlight with the four Kurds hot on their heels.

We've been lucky as there is still no movement from above; only the sounds of the others running down the pipe. I give them a good five minutes from the time the noise of their departure finishes before I start the timer for the charge and hastily slide down the ladder and, with the aid of my night vision glasses, I clear the pipe in record time. The fifteen minutes seem to have dragged out as I sprint along the gully. I hastily glance at my watch and I realise that the ignition time is almost up, so I'm pleased when I finally catch the others just before the Rover. I also realise that time doesn't stand still, and we've missed our afternoon sched; so it's important now to get the news out about this sophisticated establishment back to base so they know what sort of rockets we've stumbled on.

'Get HQ on the blower immediately, Mick,' I tell him, and I can see he knows the urgency of the message. 'They have to know about this place and put it out of action permanently so those rockets can't be fired; otherwise, if they get those rockets flying, we're all going to be in trouble; the Iraqis won't hesitate to use weapons such as these when their backs are against the wall.'

Mick is just breaking out the set when our explosives go off, shattering the peaceful night air and I think we all give a great sigh of relief when there's no big secondary bang and no mushroom-shaped cloud accompanying the blast.

'Patrol B3 to Base. We have just disabled a rocket firing platform at loc stat yyy xxx. Over.'

'Base to Patrol B3. What type of rockets? Over.'

'Patrol B3 to Base. We have released four Kurdish prisoners who say that these missiles are nuclear. I repeat, the missiles are nuclear. There are seven missiles at the site. I repeat, seven missiles. Over.'

'Base to Patrol 23. We wish you to question the Kurds. Stay in general location and be ready for backup. Out.'

'We'll have to move somewhere away from here,' I tell them, not wanting to alarm our guests. 'The soldiers from the rocket base will, I'm quite sure, come looking for these four and this gully we followed from the site comes straight back here.'

'You're right, Sarge,' breaks in Terry. 'They may, with a bit of luck, think it was these fellows that set the explosives and I'll bet they'll want to take a few heads for killing their mates and blowing up the launching gear.'

'Your man is right, Sergeant.' We turn to one of the Kurds who has come over to us. 'We were taken from our homes in Kirkuk about a year ago by Saddam's men and brought down here to work on the missile base. Evidently, they were having trouble with their rockets in getting the guidance system working correctly. They will want us back for I'm sure they will blame us for this explosion and the death of their men. We should go now for they will surely be looking for the four of us and come the way we just came as that is the obvious way to get clear of the base quickly.'

We pack the camouflage net and with the four Kurds clinging on wherever they can, we move out of our position, travelling north and eventually finding our way back onto the highway. We quickly move some five kilometres up the road before following the map to a number of rough gullies where we find another ideal spot to hide the Land Rover. The four Kurds are quite intrigued at how we are able to navigate so well at night with our lights out in this rough country.

'Turn on the GPS then get on the blower again Mick and tell HQ we've had to move camp and let them know what our new Loc Stat is.'

'Patrol B3 to Base. Have moved our position for security reasons to grid reference zzz xxx. Over.'

'Base to Patrol B3. Please question the Kurds and see what you can learn from them. They may be able to add valuable information about the rocket base. Out.'

Kuwait

The American intelligence has been called back again after the first communication with the Patrol B3 and the two agents arrive just after the officer in charge has finished the second call. They are a little put out by having to make another trip to the Australian Headquarters at such short notice, but they realise they are important allies even though their commitment to this war is very small and they have men over the border that could have important information.

'What is the problem this time, Major?' the first operative says as he walks into the very small communication centre as if his time is being wasted by this energetic young officer. 'I hope your men have stayed out of trouble because we'll be unable to send a force in after them as it may give away our timings for this attack. You said their last message that you received was very important.'

'On the contrary, I would say it's *extremely* important. I've just had another message from them telling me their new position. Gentlemen, they have just told me they have disabled a nuclear facility and are at this very moment questioning some Kurdish employees who they were fortunate enough to get away with them from the site.'

'They've just disabled a *what?*'

'A nuclear s——' the major says but is cut off by the American.

'*I heard you.* How do they know it's nuclear? The Iraqis don't have nuclear facilities; if they did, we'd know about them.'

'Isn't this war about weapons of mass destruction, gentlemen? If it isn't that, what are we doing here?'

'Of course, it is about weapons of mass destruction, but we were thinking more of germ warfare the Iraqis have already used on the Kurds,' the American quickly says, suddenly changing the subject. 'Where is the patrol now? Are they still in contact with the Iraqis? Will they get out of this nuclear facility?'

'They are evidently hidden in a different location and are

questioning four Kurdish employees as we speak. These men who were forcibly working for the Iraqis at the rocket facility are being debriefed at this very moment. They evidently took custody of them when they disabled the rocket launching platform. After that, they moved their location some five kilometres north to hopefully a safe position where they won't be found.'

'Message coming through from Patrol B3,' says the sig, listening intently to the set as the message comes out.

'Patrol B3 to Base. Have questioned the Kurds at length. The weapons are all nuclear. Were aimed at adjoining countries. Israel, Kuwait, Saudi Arabia, Egypt and Jordan. Are unsure what else were targets. Over.'

'Base to Patrol B3. Well done! Stay close for further orders. Out.'

'There you have the situation with our patrol,' he says, handing the message out for the Americans to read. 'They are close enough to monitor any further developments at the base and are hopefully safe from searching groups of Iraqi infantry who I assume might be now out looking for them.'

'We'll have to get this information back to our people immediately,' says the sleuth to the man with him who hasn't said a word. 'Nuclear weapons aimed at adjoining countries are something we hadn't reckoned on and this creates a whole new ball game with what we intend to do. We'd better get this war started; otherwise, we may lose a hell of a lot of troops. Goddamn it, man, if one of those rockets lands here, we're all gone.'

Iraq

'We are to sit tight and apparently now wait for the war to happen,' I tell the others who are sitting next to the vehicle in a circle. Our Arabic language course is now being tested to the limits with broad grins coming from the Kurds as Terry's and my language skills leave a lot to be desired. Mick, on the other hand, is having very little difficulty talking to them and soon finds out what towns they're from, their occupations before they were brought to this base, and a little about their families who they haven't seen for well over twelve months. This worries them greatly as they suspect their loved ones would most likely think they are dead after being carted away by the Iraqi special police with no reasons given for their internment.

'I was a teacher of engineering,' says the older man who had first spoken to us back at the nuclear facility in his broken English. 'I haven't seen my family now for almost fifteen months,' he tells us slowly and this time it's us who have to concentrate as he tells us about the loved ones he left behind. 'My eldest boy was very bright and was following in my footsteps to become an engineer; he is almost twenty-three and was studying at the local university when I was taken away by Saddam's police with no explanation given to my family. The first thing I knew, there was a knock on the door one evening by his special branch. When I complained, they dragged me from my home and threatened my family with death if I didn't assist them. I'm afraid I don't know what has happened to my son or, for that matter, the rest of my family. Since the time I was taken, I haven't been able to communicate with them, so I don't know how they've been treated.' He has a sad look on his face as he thinks of his family. 'He may even be dead now because that's what they threatened me with if we didn't cooperate with them and make their rockets fly accurately to specific cities in the neighbouring countries.'

'Are there any other children in your family?' I ask, trying to forge a bond between them and us that could be an advantage later on. 'Have you any other family members, for example, does your eldest boy have any other brothers and sisters younger than him?'

'I have four children altogether; a girl, twenty-one, another at nineteen and another son aged——'

'Sorry to cut in but there's a message coming through from HQ,' Mick says. 'The Americans are sending a company of airborne soldiers and want us to meet them at this grid reference. Pete, it's just a little further north than where we had the Rover earlier on tonight. The American airborne is going to take the hill before morning and they want us with them as guides. So, when the invasion of Iraq happens, we have already taken this hill where they have their rockets. They obviously deem them as a great threat, so things are starting to hot up big time.'

'We can assist you in your attack,' says the teacher, keen to help us and his friends back at the rocket complex. 'As we told you, my friends and I know the base very well. There are a number of entry points that the Americans can use to overcome the guards, but these doors are all locked from the inside.'

'Go on, my friend, tell us what you know and I'll just jot down the layout of the base and mark anything you think is of significance,' I say to him, pleased that he is willing to help and knowing that he's thinking of his friends who are still in Iraqi hands at the missile site.

'There are only forty guards, and the rest are scientists and staff who keep the base running and do the technical work to launch the rockets. There are only six guards on duty each night while the rest are in their sleeping quarters which are here. There are four rooms that house the officers, they are here.' He points to the rough sketch I'm quickly drawing, showing me firstly the barracks that hold the men and next where the officers are housed and then, with a short laugh, he continues. 'It's very rare for the officers to do guard duty and they only do this when dignitaries or people of importance are coming to look over the base. This door here leads directly to the launching bay and, as I said, all these entrances are bolted each night from the inside.' Next, he points to a position away from the entrances. 'There is a staircase here which leads to the observation post up here at the top of the hill which gives them a good view over the highway and the large area to the east where they had their dummy missiles stationed earlier to fool the Americans.

'*Hell*, Pete, I'm glad we didn't follow the tracks that we saw because they would have seen us on the highway and could have reported us to the guards if we'd come around the same road as those trucks.'

'You certainly would have been intercepted if you'd have followed the same route as the trucks,' another Kurd cuts in before going on to tell us about the dud missiles that the Iraqis had installed some kilometres away. 'From what I was told by one of the guards, the Iraqis had a number of false missiles on trucks that they intended to move away from this site a number of days before the expected American assault so their attention would be diverted. This would then enable them to fire their rockets unhindered at their targets in adjoining countries. From what I overheard from one officer who was talking to a technician, the rockets could be fired at about five-minute intervals all at adjoining countries that have some affiliation or leaning towards the west or other areas where they knew there was a concentration of American forces.'

'The crafty bastards,' I say, thinking of the ramifications on places like Kuwait and Israel. 'They would have fired at least three before our people realised what was happening and before any of them reached their targets.' Next, I turn my attention to the man who was describing the location of the guards in this complex. 'Please my friend, continue on with your description of the complex particularly where we'll find their guards and what else they have inside for people like us to nullify.'

'This is the observation place where the six men who draw guard duties each day are stationed,' continues the Kurd, pleased to get on with what he's describing. 'Two of them are expected to do a circuit of the entire base every two hours. This entails a physical sweep of the ground floor area to check that everything is in order and that none of the workforce has broken out. Lastly, the doors into the actual rocket site that are used to bring in supplies and equipment are here. It's a large cargo door that you may have seen open when the three trucks entered late this afternoon. They are made out of steel and are extremely big so that the rocket parts can enter partially constructed. This saves the workforce a great deal of time at the site only having to do the final assembly,' the look he gives us shows the importance of acting sooner rather than later. 'The equipment that came in today was for the last rocket on the firing track and to get that operational. The seven rockets are designed to be dispatched at ten-minute intervals so theoretically they all could be launched in just over an hour.'

I have been furiously taking the details while he describes to me the layout of the entire rocket site the Iraqis have built under this hill they've created to hide the rockets. When he's finished his description, I have a very detailed map of the whole complex. He has designated the area where the personnel's sleeping quarters are where forty-odd soldiers should be asleep. There are the rooms that the officers use and where some of the scientists sleep, and the lock-down section where the Kurdish forced labour are held when they're not at work. The next important piece of information is to go over again how to get to the lookout where we should find six soldiers there on duty who, in case the complex comes under direct attack from outside forces, have the ability to raise the alarm to an outside barracks located some ten kilometres to the south.

'It's critical that these people in the observation post are silenced first so they can't warn the Revolutionary Guards that this base is under attack,' the older man tells me, quite worried that we may be entering into a major battle if this happens. 'If this lookout post is not pacified silently, they will send a message to their camp. It's from here they have up to one thousand Revolutionary Guards who will come across to support this base and protect it from outside forces while the firings are taking place. They are heavily armed with both tanks and artillery and are there specifically for that reason.'

'Thank you for the warning, Akram; we'll make sure the guards are nullified quietly first. Is there any electronic surveillance at the base that we have to dismantle to get in the way we did earlier?'

'No, from what I've seen and heard this type of security system is to be fitted by the staff but fortunately they've been too busy getting the rockets operational as the Iraqis know that an American attack is imminent and as yet the electronic security system hasn't been fitted to the exhaust tubes where you entered today.'

Finally, I show him the diagram I've drawn to see how credible my interpretations of the layout of the base are and if I have the sleeping quarters of the personnel in the correct positions.

'Yes, it is very close. Would I and the other three be able to come back with you and release the other Kurdish prisoners who are interned inside the rocket base?' He then gives me almost a pleading look. 'Sergeant, I feel it is our duty to do this as we have made good friends amongst them, and they will know we haven't deserted them.'

'I have no problems with that except it will be up to the American officer who is in charge of the attacking troops, but I could make that suggestion to him that you people guide the Americans who come in with us and show them where the doors are locked from inside as you know the facilities much better than us.'

We drive to the rendezvous point and wait for the helicopters and the American airborne soldiers to arrive. Well away from the hill, we sit at this point, listening intently for any noise of the searching Iraqi troops and hoping they will leave any large-scale search until the morning. We also hope they don't hear the noise of the approaching aircraft bringing in the American assault force in. Fifteen minutes later, a dull drone from the large helicopters comes from the south towards our position, so I activate the modern version of the URC-10 ground-to-air beacon that will draw them to us. The drone becomes a crescendo as the big helicopters come in, hardly touching the ground, putting down both Hum-vees and then the men with their assault equipment. Each helicopter spends only a few minutes disgorging its cargo before quickly lifting off and disappearing into the night sky. I walk over to what appears to be the young officer in charge of these troops.

'Good evening, Sir. Welcome to Iraq. Sergeant Jackson, I believe we are to lead you and your men to your target.'

Major Campbell,' he says, staring at me. 'So, you are the men that found the missiles. Is it that hill over there?'

'Yes Major, I have a plan of the layout of the facilities to show you where everything is. One of our Kurdish friends explained to me a short time ago where their sleeping quarters and their guard stations are and finally, where those not on duty are sleeping. This is the layout of their complex, Sir; according to what the Kurds told us'

I show him my sketch while he calls his other officers over to us and quickly runs through the plan I've drawn up of the interior of the hill so they have no misconceptions of what lies in front of them with their assault.

'My men and I will lead some of your people into the complex through the exhaust pipe they have at the rocket launch platform. According to Imran – one of the Kurds we released – there should be six guards on duty, two of which do a sweep of the area every two hours. Imran and his men are willing to lead you to where the guards sleep; there are forty of them. However, the problem will be the six men on duty at the lookout point here at the top of the facility. These men have the ability to draw on outside assistance if they are not put out of action quickly and quietly. Two of these could be anywhere in the complex when we arrive. That will be a job for my men – to find and put them out of action without them raising the alarm as we're told there is a large force of something like a thousand Republican Guards some ten kilometres from this base. These soldiers will come to their aid if there is an attack on this facility and, from what the Kurds have told us, these men are well armed with both artillery and tanks so it's critical for those six on duty to be outed.'

'That's good; you've got the situation worked out for us, Sergeant. Some of my men will go with you just in case you need backup and help you open this joint up silently from the inside, otherwise unfortunately we'll have to blow the doors and if that happens as you've told us we'll have a fight on our hands.'

The major deploys his men at each of the entrances while we, with six others and a young Kurd, enter the exhaust pipes and quietly move along in the dark to where we find the tail section of the rocket crumpled in an obscure way on top of the two guard's bodies. Again, the night goggles are of huge advantage and help the three of us navigate the pipe to the rocket. I'm extremely pleased to find most of the lights have been turned down in the launch area but it is light enough to lift the night vision goggle up, looking suspiciously around the interior. Finally, I see no one and we cautiously climb our way into the chamber housing the rockets. It's all quiet and for some reason I still feel alert as I've been looking for this entrance to be guarded but I'm certainly relieved when I find that it's not.

'Show us the way to the Observation Deck,' I ask him in my broken Arabic, almost causing the young man to laugh. 'We'll take care of the guard while you and the Americans open the doors to the outside; then, I'm sure you'll be able to release your friends once the Americans have control of this site.'

'The first door to the outside is over there.' He points to a door across from the standing rockets to one of the Americans. 'Now follow me and I'll show you where to go to get the guards.' He leads us to a staircase that winds its way up to almost the top of the hill past the observation deck.

'It's at the top of these stairs where you'll find them,' he whispers, drawing back and allowing us in front. 'It's in a small room at the very top of these stairs. Allah be with you and your men.'

As quietly as we can, we scale the staircase, hoping that the American troops are slow to get to the sleeping quarters. We are relying on stealth as, once the noise starts down below, we'll have to have these guards out of action before they can activate any alarm. I reach a door just as all hell breaks loose down below with a lot of yelling and the sound of shooting. I quickly kick the door in and charge through the opening, finding two startled men sitting at an observation window that looks down towards the highway. I'm pleased to see both are well away from their radio set and have just been staring out towards the highway.

'*Hands in the air!*' I yell in Arabic, startling the two, knowing that Terry and Mick are right behind. '*Hands in the air!*' I hear the splutter of a Steyr behind me and in that instant the man at the window dives across and tries to swing an AK-47 towards me. I have no option but to squeeze the trigger. I feel the sharp vibration of my weapon and see his body flip sideways, slumping to the floor and lying still. The other guards, who are on their beds away from their weapons and their radio, have seen what happened to their friends, and thankfully have the common sense to raise their hands quickly.

'All accounted for,' I hear Terry say behind me. 'We have four live ones here and two dead; that's the lot.'

'You speak to them, Mick, while we cover you.'

'Right you lot. Hands up and move forward,' Mick barks and moves towards them, pulling their weapons from where they hang on the ends of their beds and throwing them into the centre of the floor. He then searches each man for any hidden weapons and removes their web belts that also hang on the ends of their beds, throwing these into the middle of the floor with their weapons.

'All clear, they're clean.'

With hands on their heads, we move the four downstairs to where the Americans have herded the rest of the Iraqi troops and staff. When the American troops broke into the barracks, some of the guards desperately tried to get their weapons but were quickly cut down in a barrage of fire. All the officers had been dragged out of their rooms with little resistance and were herded together with their men. The Kurdish forced labourers were initially shocked at the appearance of foreign troops in the facility, not knowing what to expect from these invaders. However, when they see their fellow prisoners with the foreigners, they soon lose their fear and rejoice at being set free and we watch this emotional reunion as they jumped up and down with their friends, finally able to celebrate their freedom.

'Thank you for your cooperation,' the American major says, coming over to us as we escort the four guards from upstairs to the centre of the dome where they join the other Iraqi prisoners who are all sitting with their hands on their heads. 'It went off very smoothly; almost you could say like a training run. They didn't know what hit 'em. Your map was right on key, and everything was exactly where it was supposed to be.'

'I'm glad it went off smoothly, Sir. I was a bit worried that they would have set a guard on the exhaust tube where we came in. I'm glad they didn't, otherwise, we would've had a fight on our hands getting to the doors.'

'It would have been very messy having to break them down, but we were prepared to do just that if we had to,' he says with a smile, looking around the interior of the site. 'Goddamn it, they have a lot of hardware in this base. I wouldn't like to be in Kuwait if one of these babies happened to hit the joint, particularly if they are nuclear as you say they are. There'd be nothing left of our forces in that little country.' He hesitantly looks around at the small rail system, counting the number of rockets that could have been launched so quickly when the invasion occurred. 'Seven of the mother fuckers; all ready to go. We wouldn't have any troops left in the Middle East if they'd begun firing these babies at our border positions.' He shakes his head again. 'Hell, man, we wouldn't have much of an army left.'

I watch as a couple of men in military uniform who don't look like soldiers take testing equipment across to the rocket that we've blown off the rails. He runs his equipment up and down the rocket for several minutes before walking across to Major Campbell with a serious look on his face.

'There are radioactive readings coming from that rocket on the launch pad, Major,' he tells us in a very matter-of-fact way. 'They appear to be very primitive nuclear weapons from the look of them. From the testing I've done so far, these appear to be very dirty atomic bombs and would have contaminated a large area where they hit if they had been fired. If your men can question some of their technicians, we'll know exactly what their targets were, and we'll be able to analyse what their destructive capacity would have been and what they would have achieved.'

'*Shit!* So they were nukes. We have been very lucky to have stopped them in time.' He turns back to me and takes my hand and to my surprise shakes it vigorously. 'Thanks a lot, Sergeant, for what you and your men just have done. Your decision of making the firing platform inoperable would have saved the lives of our men in Kuwait, including mine.'

I'm overwhelmed by this outburst of emotion by Major Campbell and I'm quite embarrassed by his actions. 'Major, we

are all only soldiers doing the job we were sent out here to do;
just as you and your men are. I think there's a long way to go yet
before this war is over; don't you agree?'

'I reckon I do, Sergeant, but you and your men must be
congratulated for how you've handled this whole situation.'
Thankfully, he moves off with the technician as they begin to
do further tests on the other rockets. I turn and gather Terry
and Mick. 'We'd better establish communications with our base.
They must be wondering where we are and boy, do I need a
drink and I don't mean bloody coffee.'

'That's alright, Sarge,' Terry says with a grin and we start
to go back towards the Rover. 'You'll be pleased to know I
packed an extra bottle of rum in the Rover; I'll get it while
Mick establishes comms.'

We walk out the door, past the American guard, and go the
short distance to where our Rover is parked. Mick breaks out
the radio and Terry the rum, pouring a good cupful each. It's
been a long day and now I feel totally exhausted as the two days
without sleep finally catch up with us.

*'Patrol B3 to Base. We've met up with Americans and the target
has been pacified. All seven rockets were nuclear. No casualties.
Over.'*

*'Base to Patrol B3. Well done men, well done! Wait with
Americans until further notice. Out.'*

We sit down next to the Land Rover, sipping our rum and
rolling out our swags, contemplating where our next move will
be once the war starts.

'What now, Sarge?' asks Terry, pouring me another shot of
rum.

'I think we get some well-earned shut-eye and just wait for the war to start, Terry, then I'm sure the OC will have other jobs for us to do.'

Kuwait

The two American generals are looking over a large map of Iraq. It's early in the morning and only a few hours to go before their army charges across the Iraqi border to initiate Operation Falconer, when they are disturbed by an orderly who rushes into their operation room, very excited.

'Major Campbell and his company have landed in the location designated and met up with the Australian Special Forces,' he says, handing a signal to the general. 'They will be going in almost immediately.'

'Good, keep me posted,' says the general who then turns to the officer next to him. 'The Australian Special Air Service, I think they call them, found some sort of base that they think has nuclear weapons of some description inside. They're evidently some simple type of single-stage rocket in a base cut into a hill; so, we've sent in a company of airborne troops in just in case the information the Australians gave us is reliable. Those guys should soon sort things out. They're under a good officer a Major Campbell, I'm told. They're 101's airborne boys; damn good men. They should soon stitch things up at this secret base they've found, and neutralise those rockets very quickly.'

'Is there any truth in what the Australians are saying, General? Their reputation in Afghanistan is very good I believe.'

'That's the reason we're going in early, James. Their reputation for getting things done over there has been extremely good so

I'm not taking any chances on this one just in case what they say they've found is correct.'

They go back to studying the map on the table for the invasion that will happen in just over three hours' time.

It's not quite an hour later when the same orderly bursts into the room again; this time he's accompanied by another two high-ranking officers who are following him in.

'The objective has been taken, General. It was swift and without any loss of life to us,' he says, almost out of breath. 'They captured seven nuclear bombs on rockets targeting cities and staging points all over this vicinity, Sir.' He pauses for a few seconds before he continues. 'The rocket that the Australians knocked off the rails when they destroyed the launch pad was aimed at this city in Kuwait.'

Their faces go white as they look at each other and silently take in the ramifications of what they've just been told.

CHAPTER 17
THE BATTLE BEGINS

Iraq

Operation Falconer begins, as like any modern-day war, with jet planes in droves screaming across the Iraqi border taking out strategic communication and valuable targets. Scud missiles, either real or decoys, have been identified all over the country and well before H-Hour. Planes and missiles are directed at those targets, dropping smart bombs with pinpoint precision before moving on to the next target with devastating results. Wave after wave of coalition troops leave staging points to rapidly cross the border and race toward their specific objectives with scant resistance from Iraqi ground forces. Special Forces troops – American, British and Australian – have been allotted specific targets along with timetables for their destruction, put in place by the war planners. Most go in to take them out almost immediately once war is declared, while others like us have been observing their targets from hiding places well across the border and strike as soon as war is declared, immediately neutralising these important targets such as communication centres, which are desperately needed by the Iraqi forces.

We are not immune from this and unfortunately, we haven't a long time, only three hours to relax and grab some well-earned shut-eye while the American airborne forces busily fortify the rocket base. A message comes through from our boss instructing us to head for another specific target, north towards the city of Kirkuk.

'Base to Patrol B3. Move north to grid xyz zyx. Monitor enemy activity on main arterial road to Kirkuk. Over.'
'Patrol B3 to Base. Roger. Out.'

Our patrol says its goodbyes to Major Campbell and some of the other Americans who are busy putting up their fortifications around this small but very important hill, just in case the Iraqis attempt to retake this rocket base. They now realise how strategic the launching pad is to the outcome of the war and are probably wondering why the rockets have remained silent. I hear later that a pre-emptive strike by a fighter bomber was carried out on their base camp the moment war was declared, so the Republican Guards should have their hands full, and they won't initially be concerned about the rocket base; by then, too late to mount an effective counterattack.

'I'm sorry to see you guys go; I doubt if any of our troops in Kuwait will ever know what a close call they had; goddamn man,' Major Campbell says as he realises we're about to leave. 'If you guys hadn't got into this complex and blown up their firing track, there wouldn't be much of our army left in the Middle

East; I'm sure no one realised they had this type of ordinance virtually ready to be fired.'

'Things always work out for the best,' I tell him, shaking his hand and then, to my surprise, he grabs me in a big bear hug.

'Just look after yourself, Buddy and we'll have a beer when this conflict is over,' he tells me when he finally lets me go.

We soon find ourselves pushing north again into the coming dawn with the knowledge that coalition planes are already bombing strategic Iraqi targets all over the country. We have changed the Iraqi flag on our radio aerial for the Australian one again, realising just how vulnerable we will be on our way to the north.

'Terry, load one of those rockets into its tube, just as a form of insurance so we're ready in case we meet some heavies.'

'Good idea, Sarge. I'd hate to be caught with our pants down. You know I've always wanted to cost the Australian taxpayer something and this is the first opportunity for me to do anything like this. *Shit!* If I fire one of these rockets, I'll feel like royalty with a price like these damn things have.'

My gunner is good at his job and soon has the rocket fixed in the firing tube and ready to be used at a moment's notice. This is put to one side, and he pulls up the fifty-calibre machine gun into the firing position, making it ready. The sun is well up in the clear morning sky and we are making fast progress towards our allotted position. Way in the distance, we can see small dots like angry wasps diving steeply towards the ground, lifting quickly up once they've released their ordinance on their targets. This is followed by the shudder of the distant explosions as if the clear sky is about to let loose with some heavy downpour. Then far to our north plumes of dark, black smoke start to spiral into the sky, making me hope I'm never on the receiving end of anything as catastrophic as an air-to-ground attack with very little firepower to be able to ward off those attacking planes.

'There's dust coming our way, Sarge,' Mick suddenly says, bringing my mind quickly back into focus and causing me to look straight up the road in the direction we're going. This immediately puts me on full alert as the contours of the road had hidden their approach and now it is too late. 'They've got to be Iraqi vehicles. It seems to be a small convoy coming this way. The poor bastards are probably trying to get away from the air attacks up north. Do you want me to leave the road and head overland? Those pricks are closing in fast and would have seen us by now.'

'There's nowhere to hide out there,' says Terry as the Iraqi vehicles quickly close the gap between us. 'What are we going to do, Sarge? Do we make a dash for it – they would have seen our dust before we got over that last rise?'

'No. Just keep going straight at them, Mick as if we're one of theirs. Terry, are you ready with the 50-cal? The distance will be too short by now to use your rocket. Don't fire until you see the whites of their eyes. Surprise is still ours because they probably think we're one of theirs being so far north. Fire when they recognise we're the enemy; they won't be expecting any coalition forces to be this far north so early in the war and most certainly not a small vehicle like ours.'

'Do you want their flag up again?'

'No, it's too late for that sort of guise now; just put the pedal down Mick and get in as close and as quick as you can.'

My driver does what I say and plants his foot so the distance between us continues to decrease at a rapid rate until we're almost level. The Iraqi soldiers in the first jeep see we're not one of theirs and soon start to frantically scramble to bring their guns onto us.

'Fire; take the first two, Terry, and I'll handle three and four!' I yell as I hear the slow throb of the big 50-calibre machine gun behind me start thumping at the nearest vehicle only some fifteen metres away, coming straight at us as Terry does his job on them. His gun's big bullets tear into the jeep with devastating results; the driver is almost cut in half and is knocked across from the wheel into his companion who is also slumped over. Their vehicle turns sharply with a roar thankfully away from us, and flips over, almost hitting the side of our Rover before cartwheeling for a short distance and finally coming to a halt on its side. I'm concentrating on the third and fourth vehicles who, to my pleasure, have swung across in front of us and are coming down the other side, making it easy for me to hone my thirty-calibre machine gun onto them. I begin firing short bursts at the first one, making them lose control, then quickly start hammering on the other, knowing that Terry will by now be on the second with his heavy machine gun. The driver has slumped on the steering wheel and his vehicle starts to veer dramatically away from us as I switch my fire from the fourth to the fifth Jeep, whose occupants are desperately trying to get to their weapons and turn them on us. It's an almost futile effort to stop the accurate fire I'm pouring on them. The sixth, seeing the damage done to the others in front, has broken to the right, away from the column and is now heading flat strap away from us, across extremely rough terrain with Terry giving them a final burst as they flee from our guns. Their gunner has been hit and I watch as he slumps forward over his machine gun, but the driver keeps going flat out, bouncing

away from us over this very uneven terrain, soon making his escape over a small ridge and dropping out of sight.

'Just keep driving flat out,' I tell Mick. We pass the last vehicle as it veers out of control straight towards us, all occupants now just contorted bodies slumped haphazardly over their seats. 'We're past them now, Mick, so plant the foot and let's get the hell out of here before someone else comes along – or even worse still, one of the American planes sees us and shoots first and doesn't realise who we are. Find a good place up in those hills to the left well away from the highway; somewhere nice and quiet to hole up so we can observe this main road.' Then with a sarcastic laugh, I add, 'However, more importantly, we should catch up with our beauty sleep so we're on the ball and ready for anything that may come along.'

'Good idea, Pete, a bloody good suggestion,' Terry says, starting to show the strain of the last few days. 'I'm afraid I'm about stuffed with all these constant contacts we seem to get since crossing that damn border.'

The area we drive into becomes broken with small hills and sharp gullies that will give us ample protection and plenty of cover for the Rover; hopefully we can find a good place to allow us an elevated vision of the main road. Finally, we find just what we need – a small gully high up on the ridge with quite a lot of stunted bushes on the crest that should be just what we want for our observation post, and these will give us plenty of scope to camouflage the Rover just over the top and out of sight from the road. The thing I like most about this spot is that we're well back, a good thousand or so metres away from the road so no one should randomly happen to stumble upon us way up here.

'Find a good spot somewhere up here that will also hide us from the road as well as the air as I don't want to be strafed by any of our planes,' I tell Mick as I look around this broken landscape. 'Somewhere we should be able to see the road from the top of this ridge and report any enemy movement from up there and hopefully get some good information back from Base as to what's going on with this war.'

'*Shit!* We had a close call with those frigging jeeps,' Terry says, checking his gun before jumping down and joining us to put the camouflage net over the Rover. 'If we'd have broken early and tried to outrun them across this country, those bastards would have had a turkey shoot with their fifties. Hell, we'd have been in all sorts of trouble trying to get away from six of them. It was a smart move just going straight along the road at them, Sarge. Like you said, I think they thought we were part of their bloody army until we were right on them. Once we were in close, we had the advantage, and it was far too late for them to do anything but keep coming along the road towards us.'

'We'll brew up now, fellas, while I contact Base and let them know that we're in our designated position.'

'*Patrol B3 to Base. We are in position at loc xyz yxz. Have had contact with enemy, six vehicles on road at xyz yyz. No friendly casualties, Over.*'

'*Base to Patrol B3. Observe the highway for the next twenty-four hours. Will send you new objectives on termination. Out.*'

We sit in our high position, taking it easy for the next twenty-four hours but, more importantly, catching up on the overdue sleep that we desperately need and reporting any Iraqi troop movement on the road. It's Terry's shift, just after midnight when a large convoy of some twenty-odd trucks, some quite big with strange looking loads that could possibly be heavy weapons are seen moving north in quite a hurry. Terry quickly picks up the mic from the sig set and sends this information through to our Base.

'Patrol B3 to Base. Large enemy convoy of twenty-three trucks moving slowly north in front of us at position xyz yxz. Over.'
'Base to Patrol B3. Roger. Will notify Puff the Magic Dragon. He's in your area and should enjoy a little interlude like this. Out.'

Terry has woken us, so we only have a few minutes to wait before we're startled to see a bright red line drop from the sky directly onto the vehicle at the front of the convoy. The sound that reaches us is like a long burp and quickly moves on to the next two trucks. It momentarily stops, leaving the first three trucks burning profusely with the sound of small secondary explosions breaking the silence as whatever is flammable immediately bursts into flames and explodes. The fourth truck, unable to stop, crashes into the one in front and instantly erupts in a sheet of flame as presumably its fuel catches fire and instantly explodes. The red line drops again from the sky and begins slicing into another three or four trucks and, methodically using long bursts, working its way along the road with devastating results. Through our night glasses, we see the people frantically run from the wrecked trucks. Other trucks in the rear of the convoy break away in a vain attempt to get away from the road. Unfortunately for them however, the ground is far too rough for this type of road vehicle, and I see one hit another and tip over. Other vehicles are soon struck by this dominant red line which seemingly appears from nowhere high above them and literally devours them like some mystical dragon. In a matter of a few minutes, there is nothing left on the road but the hulks of burning wreckage.

'Puff is certainly an awesome weapon,' Terry says, watching the burning wreckage some distance below us and shaking his head. 'Those poor bastards didn't know what hit them. I'm glad the Yanks are on our side because how do you combat something like that when you don't even know where it is?'

'Hell, the first thing you know is that you're on fire, burning,' Mick comments as he views the scene of absolute devastation below on the arterial road. 'Those poor bastards. What would you do to avoid such an attack? Hell, you don't even know it's there until that red line spits out of the heavens at you, blowing up everything in sight.'

'If our enemy had such weapons, we wouldn't have the ability to travel at night as we do without the use of lights,' Terry tells him. 'Any light you use is a dead giveaway to Puff or anyone else like us that's watching the roads.'

My memory suddenly flashes back thirty-odd years and I think of myself as a young man standing in our bunker on the top of Nui Dat on my first tour of Vietnam. The whole patrol had just stood there, totally fascinated like we are now watching, quite awestruck as an old *Dakota* they'd made into a very primitive Puff the Magic Dragon quickly broke up an ill-fated attack on the plantation fortress of Binh Ba. It makes me shudder just thinking of the poor bastards trying to get through the wire with a weapon as daunting as Puff, spitting death down out of the dark from somewhere high above them.

'We'll have to be careful if we venture down on that road tomorrow because there's going to be a lot of troops coming out of hiding,' I say, looking down below and seeing figures trying to hide among the rocks along the road, moving everywhere over the attacked area. 'I just hope they don't venture too far this way, otherwise this position we have will be compromised and we'll have to move.'

The night goes on slowly with whoever is on piquet constantly watching the road. To have some of the survivors wandering into our camp and us having to fight our way out is something we don't want. I'm relieved when morning finally arrives and we're able to look down on what remains of the convoy. There is one, no two trucks, that somehow have survived the night's onslaught. We watch them finally pull one that tipped over last night back on its wheels and join those who are congregating back on the road. These three remaining trucks busily pick up survivors; we're pleased when the evacuation is complete, and they finally move quickly up the road to the north. They are packed into every available spot on these remaining three trucks.

I report their departure to our sigs. The remainder of the day goes slowly with only light vehicles such as jeeps or pick-ups scurrying back and forth along the road. They're moving quickly and seem to speed up when they pass the wreckage of the night before as if they're scared of it. I wonder do they think that if they stop to bury those poor wretches, they may become a part of it/ I'm relieved that it's a good quiet day that allows us to catch up on the sleep we missed out on. We run a piquet of one hour on, then two off, reporting all traffic from our high vantage point, but as far as we know no aggressive action is taken. It's not until just before evening that the message we're waiting for finally comes crackling through the radio directing us to another destination further north.

'Base to Patrol B3. Meet Patrol A4 at enemy airfield grid xyz xyz at 12:00 hours tomorrow. Over.'
'Patrol B3 to Base. Roger. Out.'

Kuwait City

The bar is awash with American servicemen relaxing after a long day watching screens showing their troops advancing to their specific targets, while others have kept their supplies rolling out. This bar is one of the few places where alcohol is served in this highly religious city. Most of these soldiers have left their screens to another shift who take over the handling of communications, so they can finally relax. Most are from supporting ranks in the city but there are a few who have been serving in forward units. These are easy to pick out from the base wallowers for they have a certain look on their faces that tells anyone who knows soldiers that they have been through the mill already. It's a group of these men that interests Kerry O'Flaherty, so he moves up to one such group to see what they've had to manage so early in the war.

'Can I buy you gentlemen a drink because by the look of you guys, you've earned it?' he asks them as he looks down at their posture, sitting at their table with their backs hunched over, cupping their drinks. 'My name is Kerry O'Flaherty; I'm from the press and I'm doing stories on this war and how soldiers like yourselves are faring. By looking at you guys, I can tell by your faces you've been out in action already; I expect it's a little rough on the firing line in a mobile war such as this.'

'Sure, take a seat, my man, we'll be going out again tomorrow,' one of the soldiers says to him, offering him a chair. 'Tell me, what can we do for you?'

'I'm doing a story on other forces in this war and how they interact with our American boys. I don't expect you guys have had any experience with any of these foreign soldiers that are over here assisting us?'

They look at each other for a few seconds, contemplating whether to answer this man or if they will be breaching their security before one of them finally breaks his silence and gives him a detailed reply.

'We are an elite airborne unit but yes, we have worked with one such group two days ago. They were Australian Special Forces who had been over the border for quite a period of time and had evidently found a missile site some three to four hundred clicks up north from here and we went in to take the place out. There were only three of these guys and they'd had already been into this enemy base and blown up a small rail line putting it out of action, so it was our job to take the base out – to neutralise it properly and stop the Iraqis from getting the firing platform working again. We were relieved this morning and only got back to Kuwait two hours ago.'

'That's very interesting what you say. Would you be able to tell me what went on in this base? I'm doing an article on an Australian sergeant who saved my life in East Timor a couple of years ago. He's over here at the moment but any story you tell me that I can use to boost the prestige of US forces, I'd gladly write it for you.'

'There were only the three of them that we met when we got there, and it was their job to lead us in. They looked like real tough guys, those SAS types.' He looks across at Kerry before continuing his story, contemplating if he is doing the right thing. 'As I said, they had already been in and neutralised the rocket firing platform and immobilised the first rocket by destroying the track. These guys led a group of our boys back in with them to open up this base and, while our boys took out the troops in the base, these Special Forces guys went up the stairs and took out the guards, killing two of them and capturing four more.'

'Like Stan was saying, they'd already been inside earlier that night, going up ventilation pipes to make the rockets unserviceable,' says another soldier, who wants to get in on the article. 'When they first went in, they rescued some Kurdish prisoners and, according to one of the Kurds who I spoke to after we neutralised the base, these guys appeared from nowhere and got rid of the guards quickly, just using knives. He said the Iraqis didn't know what hit 'em. The leader of the Australians was a sergeant; I think his name was Jackson. Yes, that was the name – Peter Jackson. I don't think I'll ever forget him; not quite six foot, but all muscle. They looked really strange in their funny camouflage gear.'

The American soldiers loosen up a little after a few beers that Kerry buys for them; giving him a full briefing of their incursion into the rocket base while others watch the reporter as he excitedly scribbles, rapidly capturing the soldiers' perspectives of the operation. After they've finished describing the action, he buys them all another round of beers before he bids them farewell and quickly leaves with his story.

Somewhere in Northern Iraq

We quickly pack everything away and refuel the Rover from one of our jerry cans before once again moving down to the road. The scene in the moonlight is horrific with bodies, bloated badly from lying all day in the hot sun where they fell near their burnt-out machines. None of the Iraqi troops who passed through during the day bothered to bury the corpses of their comrades. It's sad, but we also have to ignore them and keep moving on our way to our next RV point further north. It's just after four in the morning when we finally reach our destination and, with eyes straining for any sign of our enemy, we drive slowly up one side of an airfield where we hide the Rover in a secluded place behind an outcrop of rocks, which gives us a good view of the airfield buildings where I assume most of the staff could still be situated.

'Get some good shut-eye, fellas. I had a good sleep last night,' I tell the other two, especially Mick who has done all the driving to get us up here. 'I'd say it will be at least two hours or probably more before the others finally show up and it's been a long, tiring day for you blokes so take a spell; you've both really earned it. I'll give you a yell when the other boys show up.'

Mick and Terry crawl in next to the Rover while I take the piquet. I sit in the dark, looking down over the quietness of the airfield, wondering what tomorrow will bring and musing about my strange past, thinking of the opportunities lost to me by the Vietnamese holding my body for so long. I'd probably still be there if it hadn't been for Noc wanting to clean my glass case on the inside. I think about the lovely young women I've been friends with and the chances I've had with them – Alicia, then Tiffany, even Noc who'd thrown out so many not-too-subtle suggestions. I wonder how she is faring and if the Vietnamese authorities have taken out their vengeance on her for allowing me to get away. I think about how these strange events have taken over my life and about all the opportunities I've had and lost. I feel sick of the army and the killings that have occurred in the last two and a half years and wonder how much more conflict will unfold in front of me in the coming months in Iraq before we finally finish this campaign. I just want to meet a nice young lady and settle down in some mundane job and kill no more; unfortunately, I can't see myself getting this by being in the army. I sit in the gloom with the distracting thoughts of real romance running through my mind, wondering what I would do if I found the right woman to partner with and have a family. I'd probably do some gardening or something tame like Mr Average in suburbia and then grow old gracefully with my kids running around me, hoping this would be the worst experience I'd be subjected to while growing old. Will I ever get this opportunity? Will this ever happen to me? I keep asking myself these questions over and over again; it's something I just can't answer at the moment, but then, will I ever have an answer?

Dawn finally creeps slowly over the airfield with no human movement visible; it's a strange sight. Finally, the sky slowly begins to lighten, and I can see the occasional man quickly scramble from one building to another but still, no aircraft is in sight on the runways; not even any damaged ones from US strafing runs. The sun slowly lifts over the airfield and the surrounding date palms. The absence of planes makes me wonder what they've done with the aircraft that should be standing on this airfield ready for action or stored out of sight in one of these large hangers, which from where I sit, are laying wide open for all to see that the hangers are completely empty with no planes in sight.

'Wake up, fellas,' I say, getting to my feet and putting my head under the Rover, grinning to myself as I see them jerk awake at the sound of my voice. 'It's past seven; the other blokes will be here soon so we'll need to have eaten before they get here, otherwise, they'll probably clean us out of tucker, particularly knowing some of Tex's eating habits and the way that man can put his food away.'

'How many of the others are coming up here?' asks Mick, rolling out from under the Rover and shaking himself as he gets up. 'I know Tex's mob is coming up from the message they sent yesterday but are there any more of the boys coming along with them to give us a hand?'

'I have no idea who's coming but hopefully they will be here within a few hours then we'll find out what's in store for us with this airfield – I haven't seen nor heard anything that even looks like a plane yet. The rag-heads have either flown them off well before war was declared or they've hidden them extremely well, somewhere probably in the vicinity of this airfield because they certainly aren't around this place. Just take a look for yourselves and you'll see that the hangers are wide open and completely devoid of anything that will fly. There's absolutely nothing in those buildings that looks anything like a plane and there is no evidence of choppers being here either.'

Just as I speak, a light flashes on the handset indicating a voice message. Mick hurries across to the Rover and picks up the handpiece, looking at both of us as he speaks.

'This is Patrol B3. Over.'

'This is Patrol A4, we're towards the southern end of the runway, fellas,' the strong Scottish accent of Tex's sig booms through to us, making us excited to hear the familiar voice of Shorty, which gives us all a big lift after being alone in Iraq for so long. *'Where the hell are you buggers holed up because we thought we'd be with you by now having breakfast?'*

'There's a small rise about a kay up the airfield on your left-hand side. You'll find us on top of that rise and, like I said, if you skirt the left-hand side of the field, you should find us.' I'm just happy to have people I know coming to meet us after being by ourselves for such a long time, so I give him a warning. *'Everything has been quiet here since we arrived some four hours ago but be aware, fellas,*

there are people in the buildings because we've seen them moving about the airfield, so it's occupied by Iraqi ground staff.'

'Thanks for that, Pete. We've got Patrol A1 with us so there'll be a fair bit of firepower when we get there, so keep your eyes open for our Rovers.' I'm pleased that he hasn't given away our strength. *'Over.'*

'Roger A4. Out.'

'Keep an eye on the buildings and tell me if you see anything poke its head up that looks dangerous,' I tell the other two as I fix my gaze through the binoculars onto the bottom of the airfield. I soon see the shape of first one and then the second of the two Rovers as they skirt the end of the airstrip and start to make their way up the left side towards the place where we've parked. It's not long and they are soon pulling in next to us, giving our Rover protection for the first time since we've been out.

'There's supposed to be twenty-odd planes on this airfield,' Tex tells me when finally, we sit down to discuss our mission. 'We've got to find out where they are. The Yanks were expecting to have some good dogfights with the Iraqi planes but so far, they haven't found any and we've started to wonder where they are or if they exist at all.'

'They haven't sent them to Iran like they did last time,' says Bill, Tex's troop commander and the officer in command of Patrol A1's vehicle; he's only new to the unit and on his first posting. 'Radar reports have definitely ruled that out. I think the Yanks had planes set aside to intercept them if they tried that again. They've got to be hidden around here somewhere because according to the experts they haven't taken to the air.'

'We've been here quite some time,' I tell them, coming into the conversation. 'We haven't seen or heard a plane on this airstrip since we've been here; they either moved them out very early in the piece or they're still here somewhere hidden, but we can't see them. They're certainly not on this airfield, you can have a look for yourself; you can see the hangars are straight across to the right and they're wide open – you can see straight into them. There are however, still people at the airfield as we've seen them quickly moving from building to building as if they know we're here watching them. You'd almost think they are here waiting to turn themselves in or something simple like that. It may be worth our while questioning some of them later on, once we've had a good look around this airfield to make sure we're not going to be ambushed.'

'With the three of us, we'll move off in an arrowhead formation; that way we'll have all-round protection,' Bill says, pulling his strategy straight out of the textbook, much to our surprise and quite frankly giving me the horrors because I'd much prefer to slink around the outside first and not be shot at by someone who has cover and pushes out an RPG in our direction.

'Wouldn't it be better to quietly poke around the outside first and thoroughly check the perimeter first to see if there are any hidden nasties? We can look around the buildings and the airfield from a distance. After all, we've only got to do a perimeter search to see if it's clear of troops or armour,' I say quickly, not wanting to get off on the wrong foot with this new officer. 'By doing that, Sir, we don't give anyone a free target out in the open; we only have to find their planes and that can be done by stealth with less chance of any of us taking unnecessary casualties.'

'Pete's right, Boss,' Tex intervenes, not wanting to be out in the open giving someone hidden a free shot either, which tells anyone with a radio what our strength is and what arms we have on our Land Rovers. 'It would only take one RPG round and we'd lose a Rover and take serious casualties and we certainly can't afford something like that out here at this early stage of the campaign.' He imparts a little uncertainty to this young officer, giving me a wink. 'They probably know our tactics and will take out the lead vehicle first, just like cutting the head off a snake you kill him pretty quick.'

With Tex's not-so-diplomatic help, he finally agrees to a more covert search but with much less risk involved. So, using the same principle as the infantry do – using fire and movement – we push around the outside of the airfield and soon establish that all the planes are gone and there are no tracked vehicles hidden close by to complicate our stay. With the hangar doors wide open we can see they are completely empty. The planes have obviously been moved out and hidden well before the invasion but how or where have they been taken?

'There are people in those buildings just below where we met you, fellas,' I tell them. 'We've seen them down there just before you blokes arrived. I suggest it's time we pay them a visit and ask some pertinent questions.' I smile at the nervousness of the other two patrol commanders. 'Who knows, fellas, fate may be on our side, and we may even get lucky and find those planes all intact.'

We quickly move our Rovers into a position surrounding the building and, with machine guns aimed at almost every window, we leave it up to Mick who speaks the language best, to encourage them to come out. He does this in a very interesting, diplomatic way which I think surprises the new troop commander.

'We have you surrounded; you have one minute to leave the

buildings unarmed,' Mick says in perfect Arabic so there's no mistake with what he means. 'If you don't come out, we'll blow the *shit* out of these buildings with you in them.'

There's a sudden rush of people coming out with their hands high in the air. They are immediately searched and separated, with some going to each of the Rovers to be questioned. Unfortunately for us, each person has the same story – the planes were towed away the day before hostilities broke out with the Americans and unfortunately their whereabouts is a mystery to those who were left behind.

'They took the planes away late one night,' says one individual we're questioning. He's quite scared and is pointing to the north. 'They towed them that way up the road in the middle of the night. I don't know where they went because they didn't tell us. The only thing we were told by the officer in charge of this airfield was to stay here and keep the base going until they came back. So, we stayed here as ordered and did our jobs as we were instructed and have been waiting for them to bring the planes back ever since. Without the planes, I'm afraid there's not a great deal for us to do on the airfield except basic maintenance on the buildings.' He points towards the hangers. 'As you can see, we have done most of our maintenance and even quite a lot of paintwork on the buildings.'

'All these people we've questioned are saying the same thing, no matter who you ask,' Tex says, looking at the bedraggled lot collected in front of us. 'It seems the planes were dragged away five days ago and the pilots, ground crew and engineers all left here by bus the same night. The aircraft were towed away somewhere to the north and hidden but how far away they were taken is the big question. Who knows, perhaps they may have even built storage facilities in some isolated place after the pummelling they got last time? So they decided this was the best way of preserving the lives of the pilots and their aircraft for they lost a lot in the last Gulf War. That's the easiest way for them to keep their runway and buildings intact and to stop any collateral damage.'

'We'll radio Headquarters with what we've found out,' says Bill, a little perplexed at not finding anything at the airfield, but he makes an obvious statement. 'I expect we'll just have to go out and look for the damn planes when the Americans come and the situation around this airfield stabilises a little more. Heavens above, a fighter plane wouldn't travel very well on these roads, especially if it is being towed by a tractor or a truck at night.'

'Could they have used a straight piece of highway to get them airborne and out of sight?' Tex asks, trying to find a simple solution to the missing planes. 'From what I've read, that's what the Germans did towards the end of World War Two; they just used their roads as runways as some of their roads, particularly the autobahns, had long straight stretches that made an ideal place to take off from. These people could have done the same thing – I've seen some sections of sealed road that could easily be used as runways.' He pauses, thinking for a moment. 'Maybe the people on the radar would think they are coalition aircraft they haven't got flight details of yet?'

'They probably could but the Americans would still have picked them up on their installations; I think they were waiting for them to get airborne. So, why wouldn't they have just taken off from here instead of using one of the highways somewhere else; after all their fuel, spare parts and facilities are here in the hangar. What would they do when they needed to refuel?'

We wait, thinking of the fate of these planes while Bill radios through to Headquarters that we are in control of the airfield but haven't found any planes. I find it's quite an anticlimax to all of us but hopefully, by searching the immediate area, we could possibly find these missing planes close by.

'Patrol A1 to Base. Search of airfield for planes was unfortunately negative. I repeat, we have found no planes at this airfield. Over.'
'Base to Patrol A1. Roger that. Have your forces secure the base for an imminent US landing. Over.'
'Patrol A1 to Base. We will make sure this airfield is secure for the coming US landing. Over.'
'Base to Patrol A1. US landing will be within one hour. I repeat, the US landing will be within one hour. Out.'

'We have to secure this base for an American landing in one hour,' Bill informs Tex and me as soon as the message is through. 'We'll secure the buildings and have a presence in the middle. If you can take the southern end of the airstrip, Tex and you take the north, Pete, we only have to wait until the planes come in as the Americans have their own airport security. Later we can look a little further out for those missing fighter planes once the Americans take over the airport security. They shouldn't be that far away, surely. Planes, like they had here, would be quite cumbersome if they were being pulled up the highway by a tractor or a truck, especially out on some of these unsealed roads.'

'When you drive to the bottom of the airfield, Tex,' I quickly tell him just in case there have been explosives laid, 'check the tarmac just in case it's been tampered with, and we'll do the same going north.'

The hour is just over. We've checked each of the buildings for unwelcome surprises and locked the Iraqi ground staff in one of the large hangars towards the end of the airfield. Tex takes the southern end of the airfield while we take the north checking the runway as we go just in case mines have been planted in the expectation of the coalition using the airfield; we finally settle down in the shade of some date palms to wait for the imminent American arrival. The first indication that planes are coming is the screech of a jet fighter doing a dummy run over the airfield before we hear the distant throb of the heavy motors of large transports planes coming our way. We see the black dots on the horizon of these large planes, which start coming in very quickly towards us, and finally watch as one after the other lands. There are C1 and *Hercules* transport planes; they immediately disgorge their heavily armed troops as soon as they're on the ground. The troops rapidly deploy and spread out in a prearranged holding patterns around the airfield, securing it against any possible Iraqi attack. The young officer's voice comes through our radio making me wonder what he wants.

'This is Patrol A1 to B3. Over.'
'Patrol B3 to A1, I hear you loud and clear, send. Over.'
'The American commander wants the area cleared. Could you do a recce of the northern area please, Pete, and I'll get Tex to do a similar sweep of the southern approaches, so could you take your two blokes and head north and see what you can find in that direction? Over.'
'Roger A1. Will do a sweep to the north. Out.'

I am a little annoyed at the complete lack of security in this message which tells anyone who may be tuned in to our frequency and has been listening to these orders, that there are only three of us doing this surveillance sweep to the north.

'Bloody officers; they will never learn about security,' I say to Terry and Mick, a little peeved at coming so far north and finding nothing. 'Every frigging Iraqi with a radio who is tuned in out there listening to our frequency will know who's in this damn vehicle and will probably be calling us by our first names when we go north. To overcome this, I'm going to do a large sweep further out, well to the west, coming around here.' I point to the map I've laid out on the bonnet of the Rover to what appears to be a large wadi due north of the airfield. 'Once we clear the wadi we can move to the east and swing around here coming in where we were waiting for Tex. Are you fellas happy with this nice little scenic trip our officer is requiring us to take? Questions?'

'We're with you, Sarge,' comes the reply from both, who appear to be just as annoyed as I am at this inexcusable breach of security.

We speed out towards the west of the airfield across this large bare plain which is punctuated by a few rocky outcrops making good time with this diversionary sweep and finding that the area is clear with no Iraqis in sight. So, with nothing in front of us, we move the Rover north and then swing in towards where I'd noticed the wadi marked on the map and eventually, we see the outlines of the date palms coming up in the distance to our right. We're coming in from the western side away from where any eavesdropper would've expected us to come; so, if there are any unfriendly eyes scanning for us, it's quite on the cards they should be focused on the eastern and southern sides of the date palms towards the airfield and towards the highway that goes directly to the airfield.

'Slow down a tad, Mick, so we don't leave any tell-tale trail of dust,' I tell him as we get to within a kilometre of the wadi.

I lift the binoculars to my eyes, scanning the whole area for movement, expecting to find an Iraqi soldier behind each date palm. 'Take us in nice and slowly so our dust is kept to a minimum; that will allow us to sneak into the wadi from this side which hopefully they aren't watching and see what's around under those date palms. Hell, those date palms are so darned thick you'd easily be able to hide a battalion of men in there so be alert, boys because I don't want any unexpected surprises to spring out and bite us on the bum.'

We move in carefully, scanning the whole area, clutching our weapons tightly, but the only thing I can is the date palms rising slowly in front of us, their fronds moving in the slight breeze. They appear to stretch out close to a mile either way, offering welcome shade to any traveller in this inhospitable area of land and I keep thinking of what could be lurking under their shade that's hidden from our view, waiting to overwhelm us. If there are troops let's hope they are at the southern end looking towards the airfield. I feel my gut tighten with these thoughts spinning through my mind as I continue looking for any movement behind this myriad of palms. The Rover is down to a very slow crawl now with Terry and I levelling our weapons on the wadi as we slowly approach, inching our way forward to the first few date palms and the welcoming shelter from the sun they offer us. We sit in the cool shade of these date palms, nerves tight, carefully scanning our surroundings for any provocative movement, our weapons moving with our eyes before Mick pushes further into the wadi; quite alert and looking for any tell-tale signs of life – life that could suddenly rise up extremely quickly and threaten us.

'To the left there appears to be something large in the shade of those palms,' Terry suddenly exclaims, swinging the big gun towards what looks like camouflaged netting covering something quite big. 'Do you want me to give it a short burst with the fifty just in case it's some form of armed vehicle?'

'No, Terry, if it was an offensive weapon, we'd be dead by now and gunfire would immediately warn anyone further in the wadi that we're here. Let's get in closer to whatever it is first and then we may be able to see what it is without giving our position away.'

We sit there quietly scrutinising the object for probably five minutes before I finally give Mick the order to move slowly forward towards it. As we get nearer, it becomes quite apparent what the object is.

'It's one of their bloody fighter planes,' Mick says in surprise through clenched teeth as we look at the now obvious shape concealed under the netting. 'They must have moved it up here from the airfield and hidden it under these date palms. Hell! Who in their right mind would look for fighter planes under bloody date palms for Christ's sake; particularly when there's no runway for them to take off?'

'There's another one up further to the north,' says Terry excitedly, looking at another object just to the left, obviously another plane from its shape. 'They've even blocked off the air intake to stop sand and grit from getting into the engine. Pete, you would never see these from the air if you flew over this wadi a dozen or so times. Who, for heaven's sake, would look for fighter planes out here under frigging date palms of all places and with no runway for them to get into the air? Hell! You could understand them if these were frigging jump jets but they're not. There's nothing for these aircraft to take to the air on. They'd either have to be taken to a straight piece of highway like Tex suggested this morning or back to the airfield which is now occupied by the Yanks.'

Over the next hour, we do a careful circuit of the entire wadi, finding no one. It appears the planes, a variety of Russian *Migs*, have been stored here. We count seventeen all told, sitting carefully camouflaged under these large date palms.

'We'd better let Bill know what we've found out here so they can cart them back to the airfield and get them out of the elements,' I tell the other two as we look at the millions of dollars' worth of hardware we've just stumbled on. 'Get him on the blower please, Terry and let them know what we've just found here.'

'Patrol B3 to Patrol A1. Do you receive me? Over.'
'Patrol A1 to Patrol B3. Receive you loud and clear, send. Over.'
'Patrol B3 to Patrol A1.We've just found the merchandise we were looking for. They are well camouflaged and at grid reference yzx zxy. Over.'
'Patrol B3 hold your position I'll get sunray. Over.'

There is a long pause. Evidently, the sig or someone nearby is rushing away to get Bill to the sig set.

'Patrol A1 to Patrol B3. This is sunray, stay in place until reinforcements get to your loc stat. Out.'

'It sounds like we've stirred the pussy up a bit again, Sarge,' Terry says with a grin as he puts the receiver down. 'I can see them now falling over themselves trying to get onto a truck to get out here to have a look.'

'Park right over near that plane, Mick; it's in a lovely shady spot and from there we can watch the track coming in from the highway.' With the Rover hidden on one side of the plane and a good view of the eastern approaches, we settle down to wait for the others to come into the wadi. 'We may as well brew up, fellas, and have a bite to eat while we wait for the cavalry to arrive; it's close to dinner time anyway.'

We haven't long to wait before we see a large cloud of dust as Bill and his Rover turn up, followed by a couple of Yank Humvees hot on their heels. They get out of their vehicles as if they've just come ashore at Normandy in landing barges; expecting the worst I think but finally they see us sitting in the shade having our brew and begin to wander around the area. Looking like awe-struck tourists, they photograph everything concealed here.

'We'll get this one sent back to Australia,' I tell Bill when he finally comes over to us. 'It's finders keepers in this game you know and I'm sure they'd like one of these in their exhibition at the war memorial in Canberra.'

'Well done, Sergeant. Heavens, who would think of looking in a grove of date palms for the missing fighter planes?' he says, before immediately turning to an American major who has come up next to him. 'It looks like we've found those missing planes I was telling you about when you arrived here, George.' He vigorously shakes his head. 'For some reason, the Iraqis have hidden them in here of all places.'

'I'll be goddamned. You're right; who in their right mind …' The Yank major trails off, walking around the plane; like Bill, a little awe-struck. 'You haven't come across any of the pilots or technicians or any other people that maintain or fly these machines I suppose, Sergeant?'

'No, Sir, we were doing a sweep north of the airfield and found these just sitting here under these date palms. We'll move off now, Sir. We have yet to finish our survey of the northern part of the airfield and who knows what we could find when we look a little bit further out to the east?'

'Very well, Sergeant. Carry on and let me know if you find anything else of interest or if the Major and I can be of any further assistance in securing this airfield before the Americans move their own planes in.'

CHAPTER 18
THE AIRFIELD IS CLEAR

The members of my patrol finish their drinks before it's back into the Rover once more and out into the hot sun and away to the east. Unfortunately, it is to a much more barren landscape with large rocky outcrops that dominate the area, making our travelling very slow and somewhat dangerous as the Rover is throwing up quite a bit of dust. With many large peaks around us giving anyone with a set of binoculars a good view of us coming their way, it makes me feel more than a little naked being out here alone with just one vehicle and the three of us making up the crew in this vast, bare wilderness.

'I'm sorry to have pulled you away so soon but I'm afraid I couldn't stand the crap that was going on back there any longer, fellas,' I tell my crew, who I feel are wondering why we are heading out again so soon. 'Anyway, we have an important job to finish; we need to make sure this section to the north of the airstrip is clear of any Iraqi troops who could possibly give those back at the airfield a headache. We don't want to lose any planes although there is a lot of airport security there now.'

'We understand, Sarge,' says Terry, I think, grinning to himself at seeing me in this sort of situation for the first time. 'Mick and I couldn't stand all that bullshit either, Sarge, and boy, there's going to be plenty of it going on back there between our Lewy and that American major.'

'It will be interesting though to see who claims to have found those planes, Sarge,' Mick says with a laugh. 'Which one do you recommend we put our money on that will claim the credit of finding those aircraft?'

We have a laugh at the prospect, with me putting ten bucks on the American major as he has the highest rank while Mick chooses Bill our superior as we are under his control and Terry surprises us both by putting his money on the two of them.

'It's just the order of rank; our Lewy is the senior Australian officer there and gave the order for the surveillance and the Yank major outranks him. There will be a general somewhere telling everyone how we found those missing planes. Hell, you blokes are slow; it just goes by rank, haven't you two woken up to that yet?'

We've been travelling for a number of hours when we finally come to the north-south highway – the main artery that connects the major towns to the north with Baghdad. We sit on a small hill, watching this now vacant thoroughfare; nothing is moving in front of us. We find that the land starts to deteriorate even further into deep gullies that look promising, but we find they are blind and have to back out. We're finally out of this tangled nightmare of gullies so I get Mick to stop in the shade of one of the small steep hills while Terry sends comms back to the airport. We sit around, talking of the day's events back at the wadi while getting a feed ready, as darkness is now less than an hour away.

'We have absolutely no hope of getting back to the airfield tonight, fellas. We can harbour up here and finish the job properly in the morning; I don't like doing a job and leaving whatever is left of our area half done so I expect our return to the airfield could probably be about midday with a bit of luck tomorrow,' I tell them, looking around at our position. 'While you get comms out of the way, Terry, I'll go to the top of that feature over there and have a good look around and see just how the lay of the land goes and, with a bit of luck, find an easy way out of this mire of bloody hills I've got us into. Mick, if you could check our tracks in and cover them if it's necessary, then we can bunk down here for the night and finish our clearing patrol in the morning and like I said hopefully be back at the airstrip by just after noon tomorrow. With a bit of luck, timed for just about lunchtime; it would be nice to have some real food.'

'Sounds like a good idea, Sarge. Do you think we could get a shower in the morning when we get back? It's been a week now and I'm a little itchy.'

'Unfortunately, Mick, we'll just have to wait and see what the Yanks have been able to set up while we've been away.'

We each get on with our separate tasks, so I climb the small hill and finally sit on the summit and try to map out a good way through this maze of hills and gullies. I'm pleased I came when I did as night is now creeping over us quite quickly. I look back down the way I'd come up and can hardly see the Rover in the little gully off this main re-entrant, now that the boys have the netting out over the machine. I do some simple comparisons with the map and soon establish a possible track through these gullies to what appears to be a high plain that stretches away to our east. I'm able to plot a course through this quagmire of small hills and gullies. I'm just about finished and about ready to go back to the boys when I hear a faint noise from further along the same re-entrant we're using.

It sounds almost like laughter and looking further to the north, I can see what looks to be a wisp of smoke and a slight glow down in the gully that can only be made from a small fire. The sudden realisation that we're not alone in this inhospitable place shakes me to the core. I watch and listen for a few moments, a little excited but also pissed off that we're not by ourselves. I wonder who it could be, when I hear the faint sounds of laughter again and then someone talks in a loud voice. It's Arabic, making me scurry back to the Rover and the others who are just in the process of breaking out their stoves and selecting what rations to have for dinner.

'We've got company, fellas. I'm afraid there's a fire smoking probably a kilometre away to the north in this same gully. I could see their smoke and hear them talking so have the Rover ready to move if we have to make a quick exit. Whoever it is, they're making a hell of a lot of noise and seem quite confident at being out here by themselves. They could be Iraqi soldiers because they are certainly not American troops as, to my knowledge, we're the only coalition soldiers this side of the airfield.'

'Are we going over to see who it is?' Mick asks, looking inquisitively at me. 'They may be preparing some form of attack on the airfield; that has to be the nearest coalition forces to this place and the Iraqi forces would know by now that the airfield is in American hands with all the air traffic they've had this afternoon. They could be sending a force over there to destroy any Yank planes while they're on the ground.'

'We'll have a quick bite first, fellas. By that time, it should be completely dark and then we can use our night glasses to get in closer and see who the hell they are and whether they are friends or foes. If we can get in close enough, we should learn who they are and what they're up to and if they are preparing an attack on the airfield.'

We eat dry biscuits as we're worried that the cooking of the dehydrated packs could send out a tell-tale scent to those further up this gully; so, the stoves are packed away. We sit, waiting for darkness, going over the map and then applying cam cream to break up the outlines of our faces. It's another half an hour before it's completely dark and we're able to move without detection.

'Time to go, fellas; Terry, it's your turn to take the lead. We've about a kilometre to go but be aware – whoever they are, there may be sentries out to warn them of people like us being in the vicinity.'

The night goggles give off a strange greenish-yellow aura to our eyes but enable us to walk comfortably along the bottom of these deep gullies, seeing everything as if it was day and making it possible to pick out every feature in front of us. The goggles give us the ability to see the odd little animal that's out stalking its prey well before it sees us; once this happens however, these small creatures scuttle quickly out of our way. We've carefully zigzagged our way through these gullies for half an hour when Terry suddenly stops and puts his hand up with his thumb down, signalling that he sees an enemy and indicating for me to come forward to his position.

'There's a sentry up on that point to our front left,' he whispers, indicating a high knob to our front. 'He's looking down to where their fire is as if there's something going on down there. Pete, they're not Iraqi troops because it looks as if the sentry is carrying an old World War Two 303 rifle, so who the hell are they? There, you can just see the weapon just behind him, leaning against the side of that rock he's sitting on.'

'Cover me while I check him out,' I whisper back, slinging my rifle and signalling Mick to come up just as an ear-shattering scream breaks the still night air, followed by a number of men laughing. 'I'll get the guard. As soon as he's down, come and join me at his O.P.. We should be able to see what the hell's going on from up there.'

I quietly move forward until I'm within two metres of the man and I can see down to a group of men gathered around a fire and probably another six people who appear to be pegged out on the ground. I stop just behind the guard as a man pulls something like a poker out of the fire, lifting it up as if checking the heat and then grinning before he pushes it deep into the chest of the man pegged out nearest to him, causing him to emit another horrible gut-wrenching scream. This obscene act is followed by more laughter from those around the fire and I see the sickly smirk on his face and hear the distinct cackle from the guard as if he's enjoying this sick pantomime that's being carried just out below. I step forward, grab his head and pull it back to me, my hand firmly across his mouth, and quickly run the K-Bar across his throat. There's a gurgling sound; his arms reach up towards me, followed by some thrashing about with his legs and then nothing. I let him go limp on the ground and quickly turn and signal both Terry and Mick to come up and join me.

'What's going on?' Mick whispers as he reaches me. I don't have to answer this as another scream is emitted from below. '*Shit!* They're torturing those people.'

'You take the left, Mick, centre, Terry, I'll take the right. Now don't miss those bastards; they're not getting away with this.'

Our shots ring out in unison and the first six are down before the others realise something is up and they're being shot at. The remainder starts to scatter, trying desperately to scramble clear but there is nowhere to go in this chasm and before long, the last one of these bastards pitches over.

'Mick and I will go down. Terry, cover us! If any of those bastards even looks like moving, shoot them.'

With Terry backing us up, Mick and I gingerly move down the bank towards the camp where a dozen or so bodies now lie. Our rifles are trained on the bodies in front of us just in case one of them is lying doggo. We systematically kick any weapon away from these prone bodies before finally moving towards the people these Arab tribesmen have strapped to the ground.

'Don't hurt us please! We are Danish backpackers,' one of the young people shouts out in English and you can see the terrified look on his face as we slowly come up. 'We have done nothing to these people; we were just looking at the ruins and doing a little digging to see what artefacts we could find.'

'Take it easy, fellas, take it easy,' Mick tells them, not wanting to scare them any further. He lifts the goggles onto his helmet, hoping they'll see he's human for they appear to be terrified at what's happening around them. 'We'll let you go in a sec, my friend. We are just making sure these other arseholes are dead; once that's done, we'll let you all go so please be patient, okay?'

'They're all cactus,' I say to Mick, then signal Terry to come down from the ridge and quickly cut the bonds that hold these young people, before looking at the two on one side nearest the fire. 'I'm afraid these two young fellas don't look too good. I think we are too late; they may be dead.'

I cut the bonds that hold the two and their hands just drop

loosely to the ground. I feel for their pulses, but unfortunately there are none.

'How are they?' Terry asks as he comes up to us and shakes his head, lifting his goggles as he looks at the crumpled form of the nearest one. 'Unfortunately, Sarge, it looks like we were too late to help them.'

'Yes, I'm afraid so, Terry. Both these two young fellas are dead.' I look over to the other four who are hastily rearranging their clothes and shakily getting to their feet after Mick has cut their bonds. 'The others look alright; just scared to death that's all. Hell, we just got here in time.'

Two of the young ladies rush over to the bodies, crying. One almost flings herself at the body in front of her, moaning bitterly before looking up at us with our blackened faces and camouflaged clothing.

'We did nothing wrong to justify what these people did to our friends; we just went to the ruins like I expect most tourists do. *Why? Why* did they … do this to us as we did nothing wrong?' she splutters out in desperation with tears running down her face.

'I have no idea, sweetheart.' I see the shock in her eyes and then ask them a very pertinent question. 'Do you people realise that at the moment there is a war going on in this country?'

'No,' she stammers, quite shocked at what I've just said. 'We've seen a number of planes go across the sky while we have been looking around these archaeological sites out here for well over two weeks now.' The attractive young woman then stares at us blankly; hardly believing what I'm saying. 'Who are you people? Where do you come from?'

'We're Australian soldiers doing a clearing patrol for an airfield some kilometres south of here,' Terry tells them. 'We were just about to make camp when we saw the smoke from the fire. Unfortunately, we got here a little late to help your two friends. I'm sorry, Miss, that we were too late getting here to help them.'

'We had better get back to the Rover, fellas. Others may be close and could have heard the shooting and might come here to see what it was.' I turn back to the four people to find out how they came to this remote area, given we are miles from any town. 'How did you people get here? Have you a vehicle of some description close by that you've been travelling in because this place is very remote?'

'The old ruins we were looking at for the last week are further along this valley that way,' says an attractive girl who tells us her name is Gina. She points the opposite way to which we'd come. 'We had been camping at the ruins now for five days doing simple excavations and seeing what artefacts we could find when, late this afternoon, these horrible people came to the site. That—that man there,' she points to the body of a swarthy, evil-looking man and breaks out with a sob. 'That man told us about more—more ruins over this way that sounded very interesting, so we followed them, and when we got to this point, they pulled guns and knives on us, asking us for our money, credit cards and passports.'

'Did they all come this way with you?'

'Yes,' says the man whose name turns out to be Karl who is quickly doing a body count. 'They tied their horses up to a long rope and all of them came with us to this place. When Jonas asked how far the ruins were, they just laughed at him and immediately pulled their weapons out, threatening us. First, they told us to hand over our money and credit cards because according to him we were desecrating a sacred site. When Jonas spoke back to them, they hit him over the head with a rifle butt and when Nigel tried to help, they hit him hard over the head as well. They were both tied up here and then they grabbed the rest of us and tied us up as well. That was an hour ago when they lit this fire and started to heat water and cook food before putting that strange-looking knife into the heat.' He points to a type of large knife almost the size of a machete but with a strange, curved blade. By this time, the distressed lad is almost crying and in a quivering tone he explains what these Arabs did to them. 'They ate their food while they waited for that knife to get red hot and then burnt down either side of their bodies, laughing at the agony they were being put through, making them scream before heating the knife again and a little later–' Then with a large sob and some difficulty, he continues with the events. 'They pushed that hot knife, deep into their chests causing them great pain–' This statement is followed by more sobs as he tries desperately to control his emotions. 'These men are nothing but butchers and would have most likely killed us all in the same manner if you people hadn't come along when you did.'

'I'm sorry we didn't get to your aid quicker,' I tell this distressed young man. 'Unfortunately, we didn't know what forces we were up against and had to wait until dark so we could get in close and not be noticed. We thought we could have been up against some Iraqi main force units and as you can see there are only the three of us.'

'Would you be able to drive your vehicle through to this point?' Mick asks them, thankfully breaking their train of conversation. I expect he's wanting to bring them along with us as there are far too many unpredictable forces around us to take too many risks, particularly if we run into Iraqi armed forces. 'They could come back to the airfield with us, Pete. There, they'll be safe and I'm sure the American commander will get them out of this mess and home pretty quickly.'

'Go with Mick and Terry,' I say to Karl. 'They will get your van for you, and I'll wait with these young ladies just in case other not-nice people come this way. No lights please, fellas, as Puff the Magic Dragon may be in the air looking for a target and we don't want to run afoul of him.'

'What's Puff the Magic Dragon?' a girl asks, quite confused by what I'm saying.

'It's an American gunship that's heavily armed and moves around at night, catching enemy movement and has an exceptional array of weapons onboard.'

While the boys are away getting their transport, I quickly kick the fire out so there is no sign of us from the air. I'm thoroughly questioned by these three young women who seem completely unaware of the conflict that's going on in this country at the moment. Their ignorance completely surprises me, but then if they've been away from civilisation for so long, they wouldn't have known about the invasion of Iraq by our armed forces.

'Australia is so far from the Middle East, so what is going on? Why do you have troops here fighting with the Americans?'

'We are here as allies of the American and English to stop Iraq from producing chemical weapons of mass destruction such as they used on the Kurdish people last year.' I say nothing of the nuclear rockets we found almost a week ago now. 'Our patrol is doing a clearance sweep to the north for an airbase to the south-east, which the Americans will start using for their own planes to pacify this regime from Iraqi troops. They hope to put a more moderate government in place compared to the one that's here at the moment.'

'We have heard nothing of this or of such weapons you are

describing,' Gina tells me, a little surprised and quite shocked at hearing about this war they are evidently right in the middle of. 'We took advantage of the cheap airfares to come over here to Iraq and to have a look around this country's archaeological sites as they go back thousands of years, much older than those in Europe. We bought an old Kombi van when we arrived in Baghdad and have been travelling around these remote areas for two months looking at these old historical sites; they pre-date most things we have in Europe by many hundreds if not thousands of years.'

Our conversation is broken by the arrival of the boys taking not quite ten minutes to get to the Kombi van and bring it back to us from their dig, surprising the Danes by driving without lights.

'We let their horses go otherwise they would have died being tied up back at their dig site,' Mick tells me with a little smirk. 'Some Bedouin will find himself a nice steed.'

We pick up the two bodies of their friends; wrap them in their sleeping bags and put them in the back of the Kombi van. With their scant belongings onboard, Mick drives back through the gullies to where we left our Rover.

'We'll stay here tonight so get some shut-eye and you can follow us out in the morning,' I tell them, again thinking of Puff the Magic Dragon and how lethal its arsenal of weapons is on unexplained lights that can be seen on the ground. 'I'm afraid there are too many loose cannons out there at the moment to be showing lights in the dark and unfortunately, it's hard for the flyboys to know whose side you're on, so we'll get out in daylight just to be on the safe side. We'll get you back to the airbase tomorrow around midday at the latest, so we'll bunk down here and wait for morning.'

I run a piquet shared between the three of us, as the Danes are totally exhausted after the tragic ordeal they've suffered. Unfortunately, I get very little sleep; a bit like the old fellas once said in the Vietnam days – '*Sleeping with your eyes open.*'

Morning comes upon us quickly; the light slowly lifts over the hills, leaving weird almost ghost-like shadows in the deep gullies making me feel insecure after last night's unfortunate episode with those Arabs. We wake the Danes and share our breakfast with them, eating the dehydrated rations while Terry sends comms back to the airfield.

'Patrol B3 to Patrol A1. Over.'
'Patrol A1. Send. Over.'
'Patrol B3. Have had contact. We have with us four Danish nationals. Will make our way back. ETA approximately 12:00 hours. Over.'
'Patrol A1, Roger. Out.'

'We'll make our way through these gullies here,' I explain to the others with the map spread out over the bonnet of the Rover. The Danes stand back, a little curious now, listening to what I tell Terry and Mick. 'If the track is no worse than this, we should make this large plain in an hour. By the looks of the contours on the map, once we reach our objective, say by about 11:00 hours, it appears relatively easy to go the rest of the way to the airfield. Any questions about the route I intend to take?'

There are none so we move off with the Danes following in their old Kombi van. We concentrate on the job at hand, but in places we find our speed slows to a crawl and on a number of occasions we have to attach a chain to the following vehicle to pull them through some of the rough sections as the Danes' van has great difficulty getting through. Unfortunately, we make very slow progress through the maze of small hills and gullies but thankfully, by midmorning, we are finally just coming out of the last one to what appears to be the large open plain when we hear the sound of quite a number of motor vehicles being driven at high speed across the front of us.

'*Iraqi troops to the front left!*' Mick yells to me. '*Must be close to a dozen or so four-wheel drives and they're packed with troops all heading towards the airfield.*' The next instant, they suddenly change direction and come heading straight for us. '*Shit! They've seen us. What'll we do, Sarge?*'

'We have no option but to fight, boys.'

They've certainly started to come at us at full speed, spreading out as they come and giving themselves maximum firepower towards our position. Terry has the big 50-calibre machine gun working flat out now as do I with my thirty. Two of the leading vehicles start belching smoke and most of the combatants leap off the stricken jeeps, are swiftly picked up by one of the others and taken to safety, out of the effective range of our big machine gun. The others realise now they're outgunned by our big fifty and decide to keep their distance, just sitting back and pouring fire towards us but they are fortunately too far away to be very accurate. We're slightly over the ridge with just the top of the Rover showing, extremely lucky that the big 50-calibre machine gun keeps them back well out of their effective range.

We can't go back into the gully because of the Danes, Kombi van is in the way and even if we did, our speed would be far too slow, and they would be able to pick us off from the tops of the small hills. So, we sit here, not quite in the open, with bullets ricocheting over our heads, trading shots with them. Unfortunately, we're at a stalemate.

'*Use the missile!*' I yell at Terry, who quickly leaves the big machine gun and immediately grabs the tube. 'You'll be a celebrity one day, my friend, you'll be able to tell your kids that you fired sixty grand's worth of firecrackers at these rag-heads, that should impress them.'

He lines up the jeep furthest from us and carefully pulls the trigger. There's a rushing sound across the top of the Rover and we watch in awe as the vapour trail streaks across the open ground past the other jeeps to its target. I'm glad he picked that one for it shows them the range we have and the efficiency of this weapon we are using.

Boom!

There is a massive explosion as the jeep goes up on impact, throwing its occupants and pieces of their vehicle high into the air. The others stop firing and gaze in trepidation at the disintegrating jeep, putting their hands up to protect their faces as bits of jeep finally start to come down amongst them.

'*Reload!*' I yell, passing Terry another missile. He slides this into the tube, locks this in place and quickly takes aim once more.

'That's one hundred and twenty thousand dollars and still counting, Pete.'

Again, he points his weapon at the furthest vehicle from our position, carefully takes aim and fires. We watch once more as the vapour trail from the missile streaks out across the space, almost a kilometre away from us. Once again, the missile causes the Iraqis' four-wheel-drive to stop firing and watch the vapour trail as it streaks past the majority of them to its target.

Boom!

Another of their jeeps right at the rear is unceremoniously thrown into the air and its debris scatters amongst the remainder.

The Iraqis have not shot a round at us since the first missile took off, destroying its target.

'*Reload!*' I yell again, passing Terry another missile but this time I notice hands going up in the air. Thankfully, they've had enough and have decided to surrender, too scared to make a run for it, making me pleased that Terry picked the ones at the rear.

'It's your turn now, Mick. Tell them to keep their hands in the air and walk away from their vehicles and weapons and look into the sun.'

'Walk away from your vehicles immediately and leave your weapons on the ground. We will shoot anyone who's carrying a weapon,' Mick commands them in Arabic and we watch as they walk away swiftly from their four-wheel-drives and their weapons. 'Now face into the sun, hands high above your heads.' It's a pleasant relief when they turn away from us and look directly into the midday sun their hands in the air, completely capitulating to our demands.

The Rover is driven onto the plain towards them at a very slow speed. Terry has replaced the missile with his big machine gun, so we have two rapid fire weapons aimed at our prisoners. I go forward to assist Mick with searching them. There are fifty-five men that are capable of standing so we leave them and search the wounded first, just in case someone tries to be a hero and is willing to die for Allah. There are a number of dead from the jeeps that exploded, with seven who have arm and leg wounds and two we deem as critical who need our immediate attention.

'Do you have any medics amongst you people?' Mick asks and we're relieved that there are two who turn around. 'Move over here.' We search them thoroughly and give them our medical kit. 'Drop your hands and do what you can for them as they are your comrades, make them comfortable and attend to their wounds otherwise they may die.'

Mick carefully searches the remainder of the unwounded while I help the medics administer what first aid they can. The two helping seem surprised at the attention we give them and the wounded men.

'All clear, Sarge. I've checked them out. They're clean, they have no weapons on them but don't let them near their four-wheel-drives.'

Just then, two of the Danish girls appear, surprising me by quickly walking over to us and offering to help.

'We saw what you are doing and we both have medical experience,' Gina tells me and moves towards the injured. 'I am a nurse and so is Helga. We will help you attend to these wounded men.'

'That's nice of you. Thanks, we need all the help we can get.' I suddenly have second thoughts, so I turn to Mick. 'Give that Lewy of ours a ring and let them know we've had another contact and that we'll need assistance with the prisoners and the wounded. That should stir them up a tad into some sort of action and get them out here fast.'

'Patrol A1 this is Patrol B3. Over.'

'Patrol B3 this is Patrol A1 receiving you loud and clear. Is everything alright with you boys? Over.'

'Patrol A1 we're at grid reference xyz xyz. We've had another contact and there are a number of Iraqi wounded. We will need assistance with prisoners, I say fifty-five, and nine wounded, two critical. Over.'

'This is Patrol A1. Roger. We will let the Americans know and will send you the assistance you need. Out.'

'The cavalry is on its way,' says Mick, turning towards us and giving the two girls a big grin. 'They shouldn't be very long, Pete; I told them we have enemy wounded enemies that need treatment badly so hopefully they'll bring some medics along with them; that'll take quite a bit of pressure off us.'

'Give us a hand with these wounded blokes. Some of them are in a bad state and need urgent medical attention. Keep one eye on the other Iraqis. I wouldn't trust them as far as I could kick their sorry arses. They may be over the shock of being blown up and might have noticed there are only three of us that carry arms.'

'There are five of you now,' states Karl as he picks up one of their AK-47s, checks the load, changes the magazine over and puts on a set of webbing. 'I am familiar with guns as I finished my National Service last year.' Then with a cheeky grin, he informs us, 'All male Danes do their National Service; no one in our country is excluded, including our Crown Prince Frederik who has also done military service.'

The fit Iraqis are still facing the sun with their hands held high; Terry has his 50-calibre machine gun covering them and Karl and the other girl both have AK-47s trained on them. Their two medics, along with Gina and Helga, help Mick and I do all we can for the wounded, cleaning them and making them comfortable, stopping their bleeding, covering their wounds, strapping them up and making them as stable as we possibly can, with the girls administrating some drips once the bleeding has been stopped. The two serious cases, with their drips now strapped to the side of a vehicle, rest comfortably out of the sun on some blankets we've pulled out of the Kombi van which has now ventured out of the gully.

Then, one of the Iraqi medics startles me when he asks,

'Why do you people do this?' He speaks in fairly good English. 'Why are you people fixing up our wounded men? We are your enemies and were trying to kill you just a moment ago and now you are saving these men's lives. Why?'

'They are human beings who are badly hurt. The shooting is over now, and they need our assistance and it's our job to look after them and make them comfortable until proper medical help arrives and that shouldn't be very long now.'

'What nationality are you? When we saw you come out of the gully, we thought you were Americans, but you talk English quite differently to what they speak in their movies, and I've never seen a vehicle like you men were driving when you came out of that gully.'

'We're Australian,' I tell him. Then I suddenly think I'm giving out too much information and quickly turn his attention back to the wounded. 'Just go easy on that drip; be careful it doesn't come out because he's lost a lot of blood; that will tide him over until he gets a proper transfusion.'

It's just on an hour when we see a large cloud of dust coming from the south and know that the cavalry, as Mick likes to call them, are almost here. The wounded are comfortable, thanks to the assistance from the two Danish girls and the Iraqi medics who, when they see the effort we are giving their wounded, do what they can to help. The dust cloud turns out to be a Humvee, two trucks with troops in the back and what looks a little like an armoured personnel carrier with a large gun turret that I later find out is a *Bradley* fighting vehicle. All this hardware is a welcome sight and certainly takes the pressure right off us. These vehicles stop and immediately expel the heavily armed troops who quickly surround our captives. A young Lieutenant strides towards me almost as if he's entering World War Three.

'Sergeant Jackson. I'm Lieutenant Willis. We are here to assist you and your men with your prisoners. Goddamn it man, you look as if you've had quite a battle on your hands,' he says, looking around at the prisoners and the four burnt-out jeeps, then across to our six-wheeled Land Rover with Terry sitting behind the 50-cal. 'Those strange-looking jeeps of yours are quite lethal fighting machines when you get into close quarters with 'em like you evidently did here.'

'We're glad to see you fellas finally have come. I'm afraid there are a few too many for us and we have these civilians we ran into late last night to protect although they were very handy for us.' I point to the Kombi van and the Danes. 'I don't think they realised that there were only the three of us here with guns when they surrendered. We haven't checked their vehicles for arms yet, so don't let any of the prisoners near them until they've been searched properly for weapons.'

'We'll take the prisoners back on the trucks. How are the wounded coping? They told us that there were some here that you deemed to be critical?'

'There are two men who we seem to have been stabilised, but they need to get good medical treatment quickly, otherwise, I'm afraid they could die without the appropriate care.' I think it's best that he sees for himself what I mean so we walk over to where the wounded are and he looks down at the two with the drips. 'Luckily for us, two of these Danish girls we came upon were nurses and have assisted a great deal in administering good medical help. As you can see, what we've done is only temporary and they'll certainly need better help and medicine than we can give them out here.'

'That's okay. I see what you mean; look, we'll soon get them back to the camp hospital. We have a doctor there who can do any emergencies that will spring up from time to time.'

'We also had a contact last night at dusk,' I tell him. He turns away from the victims, gaping at me and, from the look I get, he has difficulty believing what I say, so I quickly explain what happened the previous night. 'That's where the Danes come from Lieutenant. They are evidently amateur archaeologists and were doing some excavation work in some ruins when they were set upon by some very unsavoury types of people who began torturing them, so we had to step in and help them. The Danish men's bodies are in the back of the Kombi van. The Bedouins who tortured them to death were left where we shot them; we aren't going to bury the bastards for what they were doing to the Danes. Their dozen or so bodies are back in one of those gullies a few miles to the north from here.'

'You guys certainly don't muck around, do ya? I'll let them know back at the airfield and get them to send out a burial party, we have our hands full here setting the airfield up for our own planes.'

The wounded and the other prisoners are loaded onto the trucks but before they leave, we get a peck on the cheek from the Danish girls. This small show of appreciation has a predictable effect on my companions as it's the first female attention we've had since being over here, making them want to get back to the airport as quickly as we can.

'Thank you for everything, Peter; we all owe you our lives,' Gina says, looking up at me with big, eatable blue eyes. 'Those horrible Arabs would have killed us all eventually if you and your men hadn't come along when you did and who knows what those animals would have done to us.'

'I'm glad we were close by and could help you, so please take care in this place, won't you?' This immediately gets me another big kiss from the girl, stirring me up somewhat looking into her beautiful eyes. Gina quickly turns and follows her companions back to their old Kombi van, leaving the three of us standing alone watching them assemble this convoy with the prisoners going under guard to the trucks and with the Americans driving their jeeps.

'Do we have to finish this bloody tear-arse patrol, Pete?' asks Terry, his voice strained by his reaction to the Danish girls. 'Couldn't we call it a day and go back to the airfield with these Yanks?'

'I'm sorry, fellas, but we have an important job to finish with our clearing patrol. Who knows what else we could run into because Saddam Hussein's harem still could still be out there, and I've got some good vibes they are moving them somewhere north and could possibly be just waiting for us to come along and release them.'

With the Americans driving the Iraqi four-wheel-drives, we watch this small convoy head off back towards the airfield, leaving us to finish our clearing patrol which thankfully turns out to be completely uneventful. It is just routine after the two firefights we've been involved in last night and early today but it's pleasing when we finally arrive back at the airfield towards evening with no more action. If my companions feel as I do, a good sleep certainly won't go astray.

We find the airfield is at the height of activity as more troops have been flown in and have taken up defensive positions around the airfield's perimeter. It's quite obvious to me now, with these new defensive positions in place, that the Americans intend to use the facilities of the airfield to position some of their own fighters and this intent soon becomes a reality as the first flight of F16s pass noisily over our heads. Each aircraft does a tight circle before coming into the breeze with its flaps down to do an almost textbook landing.

'I still can't work out why the Iraqis would have left this airfield completely intact,' Terry says, as he watches another flight of planes come in low overhead and like the others, they turn into the wind to land. 'If I'd been them, I would have either used the airfield myself and taken on the Yanks or moved the planes somewhere safe and mined the air strip so no one could use these facilities without having to clear the airstrip first. It just doesn't make any sense to me leaving stuff here as good as this, completely intact for your enemy to come in later and use it against you. They've just given the Americans a good airfield to use more than halfway up their country.'

'I know what you mean, Terry, it doesn't make any sense when you think about it,' I say to him. I've been wondering about this myself. 'Why would you leave all these good facilities for your enemy to use against you later in the war? The people we ran into earlier this afternoon may have had something to do with that. Perhaps they realised their planes would be shot down like last time and were going to mount an attack of some description when the Yanks landed their planes and try to destroy them on the ground. When you think about it, that could have easily been on the cards. Get in close to your enemy with your vehicles, watch what they are doing and then wait for a vulnerable time when the maximum number of aircraft are on the ground before you mount an attack and destroy their planes where they sit. You'd kill all the American field staff and wreck whatever infrastructure they have moved to the field. There were plenty of people to do just that when the first opportunity came up.'

'That sounds more to the point,' says Mick, wanting to get his ten cents' worth in. 'Get in close to your target, watch what they are doing and wait for the Yanks to become complacent. Then, at the optimum time, attack the airfield, blow up the planes that are on the runway and replace them with yours that you've hidden just up the road. If that plan fails, you wreck the airstrip and kill as many Americans as you can. Who knows, they probably have terrorists ready to die for Allah. You wouldn't know what the stupid bastards would have done because those blokes we ran into this morning were certainly heading in the direction of this airfield; they would have had some form of plan to work through.'

'They didn't seem to be the extremists you read about though. As soon as I launched those missiles, those bastards gave it away pretty quick. They didn't act like they were on jihad or something stupid like that,' Terry says, obviously thinking of the last clash we had. 'They just acted like normal soldiers to me; when the big weapons came out, they knew they were finished and gave up straight away. I'm glad they didn't realise there were only the three of us and I only had two shots left; we could have been in real trouble when you think it.'

'Who knows, they may have thought we were the head of a column of troops?' Mick quickly suggests. 'All armed with rockets similar to what Terry had fired at them.'

'What staggers me though, is why would you take your planes and leave them close by in that wadi of all places?' I say. 'Perhaps they thought they could re-take the airfield and, once that was done, they'd bring their own planes back and then bring the pilots back and fly them out of there. Unless you did something like that, you couldn't even fly them from the wadi and someone would've wandered in there looking for dates and they'd be eventually be found by people like us doing a clearing patrol if they were done properly.'

'Do you think they will serve beer here, Sarge?' says Terry, getting onto a subject more to his liking. 'Or do we have to rely on the O.P. rum that Taffy gave us to steady the old nerves? Hell! The Yanks must have something better than just frigging water because I know their boys like a beer or two just as much as we do.'

'I have no idea what the drinking arrangements will be here; it'll be completely up to their commanding officer who will be in charge of the airfield. Let's go and see what the Yanks have got set up because you're right, all the ones I've met seem to like a drink as much as we do when they knock off and put their feet up to relax.'

Unfortunately for us, however, the American military is very apologetic when we ask about buying a couple of drinks because the camp is dry with their logistics still desperately trying to catch up. So, for us it's back to the Land Rovers and some of Taffy's over-proof rum to lighten our nerves with the other two Australian patrols. We are to one side of the airfield with our Rovers drawn up in a small defensive circle a little like old Western wagon trains used to do in the movies preparing to ward off the Indians; only the Indians in this case are a little more sophisticated than those of the Western era.

'When the war opened up, we crossed the border and came up hell for leather this way to catch up to you blokes,' Tex tells us. Tex, by the way, is not American as his name indicates. He's just an Aussie who loves the sound of good country music and back home he wears Western-style boots around camp; I think just to make a statement about his likes and probably something to piss the officers off who see him in them. 'The OC told us to get the hell up here as fast as we can to help you fellas secure this airfield for the Yanks, so here we are. I don't think we saw an Iraqi until we got here and then it was only the ones at the airfield; even those buggers have now been taken away. Yet you pricks, you can't even look sideways before you have a fight on your hands. How the hell do you do it? It's just not fair you blokes getting all the action and here we are just sitting on our bums now, not even guarding the bloody airfield.' With a big chuckle, he says, 'Although that's certainly something I don't particularly want to have to do because that would just be like going through inf-centre except the blokes trying to get in at the Yank planes are for real.'

'How do you find Bill?' I ask, wanting to get away from this subject and get to know a little more about this new officer he has with him. 'I hear he's straight from Duntroon and our unit is his first posting, is that right?'

'Don't worry about him, Pete, he's got a lot to learn but I think he'll get there. His only problem is he likes hobnobbing with other officers. I reckon he's away with the Yanks hobnobbing now, but he'll soon learn – probably the hard way but when he does, it will be to our advantage. In the meantime, we'll just have to put up with him and coach him along a little like we did when we first got up here.' A frown crosses his face as he thinks of the circumstances we have. '*Shit*, Pete; it's only his first tour and we haven't been here a month yet. I've already done Afghanistan and you're on your bloody third tour, one after the other. Hell, he's got a lot of catching up to do to learn the ropes like the rest of us have – the hard way.'

We huddle in the centre of our little circle, quietly sipping our rum, discussing this war and casually filling in our patrol reports with Tex's people eagerly listening to what happened north of the airfield. Then we see four figures approaching in American combat fatigues with what looks like bottles of water in each of their hands. I'm surprised, it's the Danes.

'The Americans told us you people were over here, Sergeant,' Karl says. 'We will be flown out tomorrow morning on our way home, so we thought we would bring what surplus supplies we had in the van over with us and thank you people properly for saving our lives last night.'

They each hold up two bottles of clear fluid that at first glance looks like water but from the smiles they give us we know it's something else.

'We were told it gets very cold at night, so we used to have a sip each night to keep the chill away,' Gina tells us, passing an open bottle across to me. 'Have you men tried schnapps before? You will find it warms you up and helps you take your mind off complicated things such as you men may have here with civilians like us getting in your way last night.'

They sit down, talking about their adventures and we all share in the seven and a half bottles of clear liquid that tastes something like a cross between metho and vodka. This taste doesn't stop us from pushing out our mugs to try a drop and learn a little about our European guests.

'Now, let us try the drink in the traditional manner,' Gina tells me, smiling and putting up her mug to mine again. Her blue eyes are just above her mug, level with mine, making me melt. She looks across at the rest of our merry men. '*Skol!*' She lifts her mug up like a professional and without any effort quickly throws her drink down and automatically the rest of us all do the same.

'Not too much of that,' Terry says, pulling a face, shaking his head and obviously feeling the effects of the drink which rushes down his throat. 'Our Lewy will probably come over here tomorrow morning and will want us to go out again and do something dangerous. I don't want to do that if I'm still half pissed; you understand what I'm saying. Now, how about another one? I'm just getting the taste of this wonderful medicine of yours.'

The evening settles down with everyone talking of the events of the last two days with Terry telling the others about the planes we found at the wadi just to the north of the airfield and wanting to know who's claiming to have found them.

'Both the Yank Major and our Lewy are telling everyone,' Tex says, smiling at us before breaking into a laugh at the antics of these officers, 'and I quote, *"About the planes we found in the wadi yesterday,"* and unfortunately if you didn't ask any further questions of either of them, you'd swear it was them.'

'I *told* you what would happen, *I told you!*' Terry shouts out, pleased at hearing this. 'Pass your money over, boys.'

We have a good laugh and explain to the Danes about the planes we found hidden in the date palms a little to our north. Gina, who is sitting next to me, has a gulp of her schnapps before she begins to explain their plight and how the Bedouins asked them to follow them to the new archaeological dig site they said that had just been found, and the tragedy that unfortunately followed this with the killing of their two friends.

'We were lying out on our backs, completely bound up like animals to these stakes, fearing we would be tortured the way our friends had been when we heard shots ring out and the Arabs started falling all around us. It was terrifying not knowing what was happening but the next thing, out of nowhere, you people turned up.'

'I heard Jonas scream out in terrible pain,' Helga tells us, weeping as she explains the events that had quickly engulfed them. 'They were ... cutting them open with hot knives, laughing as the poor things screamed out in excruciating pain. I was horrified as I thought we were to be given the same treatment but all of a sudden, this shooting suddenly erupts from up on the hill where their lookout was, and the Arabs started falling over dead all around us. When the last Arab fell, there was complete silence for quite some time before we saw any movement and out of the dark came these men with strange glasses on their eyes like Olympic swimmers walking towards us with rifles pointing at the Arabs and they began to kick the knives and guns away from the dead bodies. Finally, I felt relief when someone was cutting me free.'

'Now tell me, Peter, is this your first time in action?' Gina quietly asks, grabbing my hand tightly and looking up at me with her big blue eyes that are a little misty now from the volume of schnapps she's consumed. 'In Denmark, as Karl told you earlier today, we have National Service for all young men. No one is exempted, no matter who it is.' Then, she gives the same example that Karl gave us earlier today. 'Even our Crown Prince Frederik had to do this military training because our government wants all men to be trained in case of war as our country has been invaded twice in the last century.'

'No, Gina, I served in Afghanistan just before coming over here, and East Timor before that, when they were seeking independence from Indonesia.' I don't want to complicate things by telling her about the two tours I've done of Vietnam. I think the effect of the schnapps is taking its toll on me too. 'Terry and I both served in Afghanistan for one tour of six months. Mick and I served in East Timor last year to calm the militia down so that the country could hold their free elections. You'll find most of the others have done similar tours of duty to these exciting scenic places I'm describing to you; so you see, Gina, there is a hell of a lot of combat experience spread amongst all these men here.'

'I haven't thanked you personally for saving me last night, Peter. If you three men hadn't come along when you did, we'd probably be dead now.' I'm surprised when she quickly reaches over and kisses me gently on the lips and I feel the softness and get a whiff of her sweet-perfumed scent. I find I'm returning this kiss and when I open my eyes, I see hers shining like gems looking straight into mine. 'You'll have to come over to Denmark and visit us when your tour of duty here is over; you can look at another country without carrying a rifle. I'd enjoy the opportunity to show you our country and get to know you a little better.'

'I would enjoy that immensely, Gina. I have never been to Europe and with my enlistment finishing soon, I intend to get out of the army and have a good look around. So, your invitation sounds very tempting indeed.'

'You will certainly have to come over to Denmark and see where we live and learn a little of our culture.' Her reply is anxious and I feel she is giving me a come-on. She pauses before she goes on to describe her country. 'It's a very old country and steeped with the history of Vikings who were our ancestors who settled a big part of Sweden, Norway, Estonia and the other countries around the Baltic Sea. Believe it or not, quite a large area of the British Isles was also colonised by the Vikings just before the Normans came in ten sixty-six.'

The talk goes on with the Danes explaining why they're here and asking us about Afghanistan and East Timor and we listen to Karl explain what he'd done while training in their National Service and find it's quite different to what we did, which was a block of two years, whereas theirs was in segments spread over a longer period of time and not interfering so much with the person's career.

'They will not believe me when I tell them we were rescued by Australian Special Forces soldiers,' Helga tells everyone, pointing us out. 'These men here just seemed to appear out of nowhere with goggles over their eyes, just like the Olympic swimmers wear, and came down the hill firing at the Arabs to rescue us.'

It's late when we finally turn in, the Danes staying with us for the night in our little semi-circle and I feel Gina grab hold of me and begin snuggling up next to me. I put my arm around her, pulling her into my body and probably giving her a feeling of security. The knowledge that we have a lot of Americans around us gives us a more security than we've had for a long, long time. It's a pleasant change to the vicious little circle that we are now becoming used to with just us and the Land Rover and sleeping like the old fellas in the unit used to say, with our eyes open.

In the morning, a billy of water is boiled for a much-needed cup of strong black coffee or the tea that Tex prefers to drink. I have Gina staying close to me, thoughtfully sipping her drink before putting her hand on mine and giving it a hard squeeze as if reminding me what she had said last night.

'Just remember me, Peter; here is my address. Write to me when you get the chance so I know when you're out of the army and come over to Denmark because I will be expecting you when your tour of duty has been completed in Iraq.'

'I will write when we are out of this conflict because I will enjoy meeting you in a much more civilised situation.'

We say our goodbyes to these lovely people who kiss each of us at sunrise when they finish their coffees. We watch as the four of them leave, not so nimble on their feet this time, heading for their billets which are somewhere across the base. I look at the piece of paper and the address Gina gave me.

Who knows, when this tour is finished, I might just take Gina up on her invitation to come over and have a good look at Denmark.

* * *

www.ingramcontent.com/pod-product-compliance
Lightning Source LLC
Chambersburg PA
CBHW060721190726

48285CB00001B/15